THE WELSH LINNET

War Without An Enemy

BOOK ONE

A.J. LYNDON

TretowerPublishing

This novel is a work of fiction. All characters portrayed – other than the obvious historical figures – are fictitious. Any resemblance to actual persons, living or dead, is entirely coincidental.

First published in Australia in 2017 by Tretower Publishing
PO box 349, Caulfield South, Victoria 3162
www.tretowerpublishing.com.au

A cataloguing–in–publication entry is available from the National Library of Australia: http://catalogue.nla.gov.au

ISBN: 978-0-9876261-0-3

Cover layout and design by adamhaystudio.com
Cover photography by David Muscroft / Shutterstock
Sparks image by da-kuk / istockphoto
Printed and bound in Australia by Griffin Press
Typeset by Euan Monaghan

Disclaimer: Tretower Publishing has no connection with either Cadw or the Welsh Government.

"That great God who is the searcher of my heart knows with what a sad sense I go upon this service, and with what a perfect hatred I detest this war without an enemy; but I look upon it as sent from God … God in his good time send us the blessing of peace and in the meantime assist us to receive it! We are both upon the stage and must act such parts as are assigned us in this tragedy, let us do it in a way of honour and without personal animosities."

Letter from Sir William Waller to his friend, now
an enemy general, Sir Ralph Hopton

16 June 1643

1

Chadshunt Hall, Warwickshire, July 1642

THE DUST COVERED rider sat back in the saddle and slowed his horse as he approached the gatehouse, but did not rein in. The gatekeeper, recognising the blue and grey livery of his master's younger brother Hugh Lucie, nodded and stood back. The messenger trotted through the open gates and spurred his tired mount once more into a gallop towards the chimneys of Chadshunt Hall.

Clattering to a halt in the cobbled courtyard of the L shaped Tudor mansion, the messenger swung his leg stiffly over the saddle and threw the reins to a groom. The grey gelding's flanks were heaving and dark with sweat. The messenger had no time to waste. He pounded up the short flight of steps to the stone portico with its panelled double doors.

"For Sir Henry. I am to return with his answer without delay, Thomas."

The grey haired manservant took the letter and pursed his lips.

"Go to the kitchen, Jon, while the master reads this. You know the way."

Rolling his stiff shoulders, the messenger tugged off his woollen hat, untied his cloak and trudged towards the kitchens. One of Hugh Lucie's grooms, he was not past his twentieth year, but the long journey from London, with only a few hours snatched sleep, had wearied him. It was a great distance, more than eighty miles, and he had covered it in two days. Behind him he caught a glimpse of the Baronet's tall, dark haired daughter sidling through the doors. She was breathless and barefoot. The messenger grinned. No doubt Mistress Elisabeth had seen him arrive. Perhaps she was hoping for a letter from a lover, if so she would be disheartened.

The messenger's brief flirtation with a kitchen maid was interrupted by Thomas before he could do more than drink thirstily from a mug of ale, his plate of cold meat still untouched.

"My master wishes for you to go to his study so that he may deliver the reply to you himself."

Thomas's tones were disapproving, as he eyed the messenger's tangled flaxen curls, dusty coat and breeches and mud spattered boots. Astonished, the messenger hastily wiped his mouth with the back of his hand and followed the man servant into Sir Henry's study. He made a hasty observation of well-ordered but comfortable surroundings, richly embroidered curtains swaying gently in the faint breeze from the open casement.

The baronet was standing gazing out of the window at the flower gardens basking in the sunlight. It was a warm day and his pale blue silk doublet was partially unbuttoned, showing the fine linen shirt beneath. His head was bare and his dark hair, threaded with no more than a few grey hairs, hung loosely over his rigid shoulders. As Sir Henry swung round, the messenger saw his aristocratic face was set in a mask of fury, his mouth a thin line.

"Have you brought the bag, Thomas?"

"Yes, Master." He handed a small linen bag to Sir Henry.

"Your name, fellow?"

Jon, Master, er Sir Henry," the messenger stuttered.

"And you are one of my brother's servants?"

"A groom, Sir." The messenger twisted his hat nervously between his hands.

"Very well, you will return to my brother and say this is the message I send to him."

He was holding the linen bag in one hand and the messenger recognised the letter he had brought in the other. There was no sign of a reply. Sir Henry took the sheet of paper, adorned with the broken seal from his brother, and tore it deliberately down the middle. He quartered it and tore it several times more until nothing remained but shreds. Then he opened the linen bag, rammed the handful of fragments inside and pulled the neck tight. He thrust the small piece of linen at the hapless groom.

"Thus my answer. Go now."

Clutching the bag, the stunned messenger withdrew rapidly, keen to escape the furious gaze of his master's brother. As he passed through the hall, there was a flash of bright blue like a kingfisher from the stairs above him. He thought it might be young Mistress Elisabeth, but he had neither the time nor the inclination to linger.

ග

Not a letter from Rafe then. I had heard nothing from him in more than two months but every messenger filled me with hope. The clatter of galloping hooves startled me. I was dozing on a neatly trimmed strip of turf between the beds in the flower garden.

Safely out of sight from the house and reprimands from my mother, I was indulging in hoydenish behaviour, kicking off my slippers and stockings and enjoying the agreeable feeling of the grass tickling my bare toes. The day was humid. The distant clash of swords was my brothers practicing fencing with their rapiers on the lawn. The air was full of the scent of roses. Stray bees from our hives wove busily around the blooms humming as they collected nectar. Our little corner of Warwickshire seemed very quiet and far away from the war of paper, furious speeches and increasingly physical hostilities between King Charles and Parliament.

I skidded around the corner of the house to see the messenger was wearing the livery of Uncle Hugh's servants. While I was disappointed, a messenger in a hurry signified important news and I was determined to find out what I could. I waylaid Thomas as he left Father's study a few minutes later.

"Thomas, why was that messenger in such haste to see my father?" Thomas glanced at my bare toes peeping from beneath my petticoats and averted his eyes, his countenance wooden.

"You will have to ask my master, Mistress Elisabeth," he answered cautiously. "It's not for me to say."

The landing half way up the stairs provided an excellent vantage point for observing, unseen, the comings and goings in the entrance hall. I lingered there behind a large urn, usually filled with flowers or teasels until I saw the messenger leave, clutching a small white bag in his hand, his face grave. I sent my maid Peggy to find out what she could in the kitchen and then hastened back to the gardens to find my slippers before Mother detected my bare feet.

Peggy was waiting in my chamber when I returned. Her round face was solemn, but her black eyes were sparkling with information. "The messenger carried an urgent suit from your uncle, Mistress. Parliament has settled on raising an army to fight against His Majesty. Master Lucie bids your father join him in raising men."

"Fight against the King?" I stared at her in horror. "My father would never do such a thing. How could my uncle entertain it?"

"The master tore the letter in pieces and commanded your uncle's servant to return with them as his answer."

I hurried to find my brothers. They were leaving the lawn, panting and laughing after their fencing bout, doublets slung over their shoulders and patches of sweat on their white linen shirts. Eighteen year old Harry whistled when he saw me.

"Bess, I see from the grass stains on your skirts you have been ignoring Mother's strictures, once more about proper behaviour for a lady in her seventeenth year. If you continue so," he grinned, "It may harm your reputation."

I flapped my hand crossly, in no mood this once for Harry's humour. My eldest brother Will was more discerning.

"What ails you, Bess? You look as if you have seen a ghost."

"He could perhaps have given a gentler answer," was Will's quiet rejoinder to my explanation.

Harry's face glowed with excitement. "But what will it mean for our family? If Uncle Hugh raises men for Parliament, will not Father do so for the King? Will, let us go to him and ask his intentions."

"Be patient, Harry. Allow Father some time to consider. He will let us know his plans soon enough. I fear that Uncle Hugh has not only forgotten the loyalty due to his sovereign but the respect he owes to Father as head of the family. You must be aware, too, that the raising of troops is an expensive matter. It may be beyond Father's means."

Will refused to discuss the matter further. Harry and I followed close behind him, Harry chattering like a magpie while he swung his rapier distractedly, beheading roses as he went. The clouds were darkening. There was a rumble of thunder in the distance.

"There's a storm coming, Will."

"Yes, Bess, I fear there is."

My tall brother turned back and hugged me tightly. Huddling against Will's shoulder, I drew comfort from his closeness, his strength and the familiar scent of sweat, horse and clean linen. I looked up into his taut face, the blue eyes staring over my shoulder at some distant unseen vista, recognising he had given my words a different sense. Was there to be war? And was it to divide my own family? Despite the sultry afternoon, I shivered.

Will looked down at me keenly. "Take this." He swung his discarded green silk doublet, warmed by the sun, around my shoulders.

"Thank you, Will." I could hear my voice was trembling. His lips brushed the top of my head.

"Have courage, Bess. Chadshunt Hall has been here a long while, and the Lucie family longer. We will stand together and all will be well."

ଓଃ

Chadshunt Hall, Warwickshire, December 1641 (eight months earlier)

"Do you know why Uncle Hugh is visiting, Peggy? It is not his custom to visit Chadshunt at Christmastide."

My uncle visited my father two or three times a year. He was generally accompanied by my aunt and cousins. Married to the daughter of a wealthy City merchant, who had brought him a fine estate as her dowry, Uncle Hugh was now Member of Parliament for Horsham, dividing his time between London and his estate in Sussex. Travel during the winter months, even in the comfort of a luxurious private carriage, was not for the faint hearted. Thieves, the possibility of a broken axle or becoming stuck fast in a quagmire, damp beds in roadside inns, all these evils were enumerated by Mother as reasons why it was best to venture no further than Warwick or Banbury between Michaelmas and Easter.

"I couldn't say, Mistress Bess." Dissatisfied with this reply, I tried again.

"What of Will's friends? Have you heard aught of them?"

Will and Harry were returning from Oxford, where Harry was a scholar at Jesus College, to spend the Christmas season at Chadshunt. They would be accompanied by a party of Will's old university friends. It was the first time Will had brought a group to stay at Chadshunt and I was curious to know of them.

"I believe they are all gentlemen of good family, Mistress. They studied with Master Will."

"Or hunted, drank and played cards if you believe Harry."

"Master Harry would do well to mind his tongue. It will cause mischief for him if he remains so free with it."

Uncle Hugh and his family arrived in their carriage, accompanied by two servants, and their coachman, several days before Christmas. I was delighted to see my cousin Celia in particular. We soon found an excuse to disappear to my bedchamber. A year older than me she was betrothed to a wealthy gentleman, Sir John Ridgeley, the owner of a large estate near London. I was disappointed and frankly annoyed at her newly assumed air of superiority. If she had acted so a few years earlier I would have pulled her hair.

"Celia," I probed, "Is there a special reason for this visit?"

"Well, I believe my father has a business proposal he wishes to discuss with yours. I also heard my father telling my mother he wanted to discuss the events since Strafford's execution."

I looked suitably solemn. The Earl of Strafford's arrest for treason and his execution earlier in the year had deeply shocked my father. He had exclaimed that if a man as important as Strafford could be executed at the will of the Parliament then no man was safe.

"And is that all?" I protested.

"Not quite," she replied with a sly grin. "My baby cousin, though you are but sixteen, they are talking of finding a suitable match for you so that you may wed next year."

I threw a cushion at her. She threw it back and decorum went out of the window. Our game of tag around my chamber, shrieking and giggling, was interrupted by Peggy.

"Excuse me, Mistress Bess," she said, magnificently ignoring our panting and dishevelled appearances. "Mistress Cecilia's father is asking for her."

Peggy had been with our family since I was a baby and she a maid no more than 14 years old. She had long ago developed the skill of being blind and deaf to the more boisterous goings on of my brothers and I.

ᔕ

23 December 1641

It was mid-morning, and the frost had melted, promising a pleasant December day, when I heard the clatter of hooves and knew it to be my brothers. I dashed to the door to see six horses coming to a halt in the courtyard. For a few minutes all was confusion as servants came and went, showing the men to the west wing where their horses would be stabled. Packs were removed from horses while the group, happy to have ended their journey, called boisterously to each other and jested. I ran to Harry, who I had not seen for more than two months, and embraced him. Will was shepherding his friends towards the house.

"Bess, let me present my friends to you. This is Edward, this Robert, this Walter."

There was one more man behind them, with his back turned, talking to the groom.

"Finally, my friend Rafe, who pays us no attention."

The tall, fair haired man turned and grinned, bowing deeply and sweeping his feathered hat off his long curls.

I spoke little to Will's friends before the evening, but Rafe winked at me when he caught me glancing his way. I thought this impertinent and was determined not to look at him again. After supper, we had some music in the Great Hall, with my mother insisting I played and sang. I disliked feeling like a performing bear, but obliged the company with a song or two at the harpsichord while they watched politely from chairs and benches. The men then were turning to cards and backgammon, the ladies taking up their candlesticks and preparing to withdraw. I hesitated, uncertain whether to follow. Rafe was deep in a game of backgammon with Will. I took myself off to bed.

Passing by Father's study, I heard voices and stopped. My father and uncle were talking. I lingered, hoping to hear some mention of their plans for me.

"For Bess," Uncle Hugh was saying, "But I fear the times are not propitious for arranging a match. She is but young, and she may be wed at 18 or even 19 as well as she may at 17. I grieve that your plans to build an east wing have also had to be delayed. It was long a dream of our own father."

I peered through a crack in the door. Uncle Hugh was standing with his back to the fire, the glow of the flames making his gold laced sleeves shimmer like a halo. I could not see Father but his favourite chair creaked as he shifted in it.

"It seems this house must endure a little longer in its present guise. But to more serious matters. You believe the uprising by the papists in Ireland is likely to endanger England, Hugh?"

Uncle Hugh sipped thoughtfully at a glass of wine.

"I concur with Mr Pym, Henry, that the Irish uprising is the result of a popish conspiracy, and King Charles is implicated in it. That is why we in the Parliament have voted to send troops to Ireland without consulting His Majesty. We are no longer sure that we can put our trust in him. Indeed, Parliament has now passed the Militia Bill. Once adopted as law, the commanders of the armed forces will be appointed by the Parliament, not by the King."

Father snorted. "You and the other members are dreaming, Hugh, if you think His Majesty will assent to such a bill. It will never be law. Take care of what company you keep, brother. Dangerous nonsense to talk of His Majesty being implicated in popish plots. To give ear to such notions smacks of treason. Beware you do not run your neck into a noose."

"Henry, you are removed from the affairs of the capital, and I fear you fail to understand what is at stake. For some months I have been discussing the sad state of this country with the other gentlemen who train with the Society of the Artillery Garden in London. We are all agreed that the time is fast approaching when our peacetime drills and our arms with which we train will be put to a sterner purpose." Father laughed shortly.

"Hugh, the Society of the Artillery Garden are naught but conceited coxcombs, who spend their days idle while their servants polish their costly armour. I doubt one of them has approached nearer to a battle than inspecting an engraving of the Armada."

Not waiting to hear Uncle Hugh's reply, I tiptoed away. It was evident that Father and Uncle Hugh were embarked upon a discussion of affairs of State and I was not likely to hear anything further of interest. I did not know that the new year of 1642 would bring the final gathering of the storm clouds which had hung over the country for some years.

I knew little and cared less of the brief war between the King's English army and the Scottish army of Covenanters the previous year. Newcastle in the north of England was a long way from Warwickshire. The news of the recent uprising in Ireland by Irish papists had alarmed Mother, but Ireland was also a long way away, and I had no interest in the doings of papists. I knew only that my father spent increasingly long periods of time shut up with his steward. It was much later that I understood. He had seen the way the wind was blowing.

ᔕ

Christmas Eve 1641

After dinner, the servants cleared the Great Hall for dancing, pushing the tables against the walls. The walls were decorated with greenery and bright red holly. My mother had engaged musicians for the evening. All the tenants from the estate were to be there, besides a few gentlemen whose estates lay close at hand. By late afternoon the musicians were busy tuning their lutes and viols in the minstrels' gallery.

Celia and I dressed for the evening with care. My rose silk gown was a source of both pride and grief. It was in the latest fashion from London and underlined the acknowledgement that at the age of 16 I was now a woman. The grief was because in my mother's anxiety to ensure I did not grow out of it, she had insisted on allowing extra length in the skirts. Silk gowns were costly, even for a family such as ours. The length caused me to trip at the most inopportune times. Standing at 5' 6", I had only recently showed signs of stopping my headlong growth, causing my mother much concern.

"You are such a giant, Bess, how are we ever to find you a husband? Men like a woman who can really look up to them, in every sense."

Celia produced a matching rose coloured ribbon. She twisted it into my hair. Long, dark and silky it was completely straight, refusing to curl properly even after Peggy had spent quite some time with the tongs. She had arranged most of it on top of my head quite successfully, but the remainder hung down to my shoulders in gentle waves, rather than the tight curls Celia's was arranged in.

Celia herself was in pale blue silk, her blonde curls threaded with a blue ribbon which matched her eyes. Her rounded child-like face, combined with her modest stature, made her appear younger than me. I envied her curves. I would have to hope that my pale skin, large grey eyes and full lipped mouth compensated for my unfeminine height and boyish frame. We admired ourselves in the looking glass. I curtseyed solemnly to our reflections. Celia giggled and we descended the stairs arm in arm, hoping to make an impressive entrance.

We timed it badly. A fanfare from the musicians heralded the arrival of the massive yule log, dragged by boys from the estate. The hundred guests shuffled towards the Great Hall. Decked with ribbons and greenery, the yule log made its way through the throng until it reached the hearth. Father was waiting, holding aloft a flaming torch. As always I found myself admiring his proud carriage and straight back. His crimson velvet doublet and breeches were adorned with white silk ribbons and his broad brimmed hat bore a feather of a matching hue.

"May this yule log which brings us light and warmth this night, burn for ever."

He poured wine over it and lit it with the torch, to loud applause. I observed that one of the crowd was not cheering. Standing conspicuously near the fire, Uncle Hugh had turned on his heel, presenting his back to the approaching yule log. Father glanced quickly at him, but Uncle Hugh's gesture, if gesture it was, remained unnoticed by the lighthearted assembly, their eyes now on a gambolling group of mummers. Shaking bells and waving wooden swords the men enacted the story of St George, who fought and killed the Turkish knight. In my enjoyment of the play I forgot about making an impression as a grownup lady, cheering St George with the rest of the company, while Celia's younger brothers Hugh and Luke clamoured to play with the wooden swords of the mummers.

In the absence of an admiring circle of men, I decided I was hungry. The tables were spread with a generous supper of geese and other fowl, pies and custards, with roast suckling pig as a centrepiece. Flagons of ale and jugs of hot spiced wine stood ready to refresh the thirsty dancers. I was half way through a generous helping of pigeon pie, ignoring what my mother would say when she saw me eating with unladylike appetite, when I heard a teasing voice at my elbow.

"My Lady, I fear you are faint through lack of food. Please allow me to offer you some sustenance." I snatched up a napkin, wiped my mouth and turned to glare at Rafe, standing with a mocking grin on his face.

"I don't believe I need your assistance, Sir in my own home. And you should know that you need not address the daughter of a baronet as My Lady."

Sadly, I spoke only to his departing back. My mother, unfortunately, was close at hand. Her diminutive stature, dainty carriage and still beautiful blue eyes led the unwary to think her docile and sweet. Much as I loved her, she was a force to be reckoned with within the household. As the youngest of her children and an unwed daughter, I was expected to be submissive and compliant. She fixed me with a clear gaze.

"Bess, that was not a very suitable way to address a guest. Even if Master Beauchamp has done something to offend you, I suggest you make him an apology."

She looked up at me coolly. I could see from the rigid set of her shoulders and the way she was tapping her toe that I had displeased her greatly.

"Yes, Madam," I mumbled and reluctantly searched for the annoying man. I found him rather too easily.

"You may fetch me a glass of wine if you wish, Sir,"

I hissed at him, tight lipped. I looked towards my mother and saw she was watching us. Hastily I attempted a charming smile and swept him a deep curtsey. He returned the favour with a wide grin and a bow. Moments later, he pressed a goblet of warm spiced wine into my hand. He took a bite of the mince pie he was holding and gave me a long look under his lashes. I mumbled a thankyou. He seemed content to stand beside me in silence, grinning and munching his pie. I was wondering if I had now shown sufficient politeness to satisfy my mother when the musicians struck up a country dance tune.

"Would you do me the honour of dancing with me, Mistress Elisabeth?" he said. I hesitated, looking up to see if he was still teasing me, but the blue eyes were fixed on me solemnly. I hesitated, but the country dance was not one I cared to miss.

"Thank you, Sir."

I hastily finished my last bite of pie, put down the goblet, and allowed him to lead me to the dance. The tune was Horse's Brawle, a favourite of mine. Rafe took my hand in a firm grasp as we joined the circle. I found I was enjoying myself. He was light on his feet and regarded me approvingly every time I spun round. The rose silk swayed becomingly about my feet.

After we had promenaded and leapt our way through a further two pavans and two galliards, I felt myself relaxing. Rafe said nothing further to provoke me and was a good dancing partner. He knew all the figures, was light on his feet, and effortlessly kept time both with the music and me. I was accustomed to dancing with my brothers and cousins and found this a novel experience. Will knew all the steps but was not a very enthusiastic dancer, while Harry tended to leap around exuberantly, especially in the galliard, and land on my toes. Dancing with Rafe was a delight. At the end of the second galliard I paused slightly breathless to find my father beside me smiling at us both.

"Bess, my dear, you look fatigued. Master Beauchamp, I am delighted to see you enjoying yourself. I believe my son may wish to spend some time with you."

Rafe bowed to my father, lifted my hand to his lips and turned away. I wondered why Father had put a stop to our dancing.

Panting, and feeling overheated, I decided to leave the hall. Stepping gratefully outside into the frosty air, I heard voices and recognised the mellow tones of our friend and neighbour Giles Blake, talking to Uncle Hugh.

"A pleasant evening, Hugh, spent thus in the company of friends."

"An idle evening, Giles, to speak truth. For those who follow the path of the Lord, it is folly to equate his birth with gluttony and frivolity."

"Are you become a Puritan, Hugh? Have the ways of Parliament changed your views? It was not so when we were boys."

I inhaled a gust of tobacco as Giles pulled fiercely on a clay pipe.

"I seek only to follow righteousness, Giles. I would my brother Henry shared my views. There are those of us in Parliament who seek to steer England on a more Godly course before it sinks once more beneath the papist tide. Our Grand Remonstrance to the King is to be printed and circulated in the hope that the citizens will understand the wrongs of the people and how we beg the King to address them."

"And were you one of those in the Parliament who voted for it, Hugh?"

Giles sounded surprised, but Uncle Hugh pressed on.

"I was, Giles. I cling to the hope that men of good will like you and my brother will support the forces of right against those who would lead His Majesty into evil ways."

"Strafford is dead, Hugh and Archbishop Laud in the Tower. Who else is in danger from the gentlemen of the Parliament? Through their deeds, the King has already lost his most able adviser and is like to lose his Archbishop. I daresay Mr Pym and his friends will resort once more to a Bill of Attainder if they may not accomplish their ends by other means."

Giles's tone was mild, but I detected a note of caution.

"It is more like to be the gentlemen of Parliament who are in danger from the King's advisers, I fear." Uncle Hugh's tone was sharp.

"But perhaps I have said enough. I only sought to sound you out, to hear something of your views and where your sympathies lie."

"Then you may hear them, Hugh, with pleasure." Giles spoke firmly, "My sympathies are with those who uphold the law of the land. I conceive that to be indivisible from remaining loyal to His Majesty."

I sneezed. There was an exclamation and a hand grabbed me by the shoulder. It was Uncle Hugh. I was horrified to see he was hastily concealing a dagger.

"Bess!" he sounded relieved. "You will catch an ague, child in that thin dress." He propelled me back towards the doors.

∽

Peggy was brushing my hair in preparation for the Christmas Day service at our parish church when Celia strolled into my chamber. I coughed at Peggy to do something elsewhere.

"Well?" I crowed as soon as Celia and I were alone. "What do you think of him?"

I was contemplating blue eyes, and athletic legs twisting and leaping in the dance.

"He's not nearly so annoying once you become acquainted with him."

"Annoying?" she said puzzled, "Who?"

"Rafe Beauchamp, who else? Did you not see us together, Celia? We danced and talked most of the evening."

"Bess," Celia said cautiously, "What does my uncle think of you spending time with him? Has he said aught of arranging a match between you and Master Beauchamp?"

I felt discouraged. "Nothing yet, but I feel he will before many more days have passed."

These twelve days of Christmas, spent in Rafe's company, were the most exciting I could remember. Father said nothing of a possible match between Rafe and me, but I reasoned that such matters were not speedily arranged. I continued to hope. Uncle Hugh's family departed after Christmas, followed by Will's friends some days later. By Twelfth Night the house was quiet again.

Left alone with my family, I had leisure to dreamily reflect on every dance, every conversation, every touch of the hand, I had received from Rafe. My joy in these reflections was tempered by memories of Uncle Hugh. My uncle's behaviour puzzled and alarmed me. I had understood little of the conversations I had overheard between him and Father, still less of his converse with Giles and why he had been "sounding him out". No, it was the drawn dagger, hastily concealed, which told me that Uncle Hugh was embarked on some dangerous path. I kept my own counsel, however. Father would be angered at my eavesdropping, Will too most like, while Harry would only laugh.

That Uncle Hugh was increasingly emulating habits of the Puritans was plain for all to see, however. Although his attire was as rich as ever, he had been wearing sober hues in recent years, and no longer danced. The old traditions of Christmastide, the feasting and the singing of Christmas carols, all were condemned by him as popery. As Giles Blake had observed, Uncle Hugh was a changed man. His grave demeanour, the greying and thinning of his black hair, made him seem more advanced in years than Father, the elder by two years. Even his eyes, grey in hue like those of Father, were now at variance with what he had been. Perpetually narrowed in suspicion or wariness, they seemed the eyes of another man.

14 January 1642

My uncle returned unexpectedly in January. This time he was accompanied only by a servant. We were sitting down to dine and my father immediately made room beside him for his brother. Uncle Hugh was looking grim.

"Speak, Hugh," said my father. "What has happened to cause your return?"

"There has been a terrible development, Henry. I warned you that the King is not to be trusted. He has become increasingly suspicious of Parliament. We seek only to safeguard England as a Protestant land, yet evil advisers have persuaded him we conspire to turn the London mob against him. No doubt his papist queen, too, whispers falsehoods in his ears.

A few days ago, the King took a body of soldiers and went to the Parliament when it was in session. He sought to arrest John Pym and four others of my fellow Members for treason. I was there and beheld it all. The King came himself into the Commons, where he had no right to venture and sat in the Speaker's Chair. He respects not Parliament and is seeking to destroy the ancient rights of the people."

"It cannot be. Were those men taken to the Tower?" gasped my father.

"They would have been without doubt, but forewarned they were absent. The King was furious. The following day he made a demand for the five men to be handed over, but his coach was surrounded by jeering crowds. It is the King who is now a fugitive. He has fled with the royal family from London to Hampton Court while the five members are returned in triumph. Parliament controls the city.

Henry, pray listen to me. I am come not merely as your brother. I am come as representative both of Parliament and of the growing number of people across the country who are banding together to support us and to suppress Popery once and for all. All men must decide who and what they stand for. For me the choice is clear." Father interrupted sharply.

"Hugh, be careful how you speak." My mother had turned pale and wide eyed, while Harry was bouncing in his chair with excitement. My father checked himself.

"My dear," he said to my mother, "We are not doing justice to this excellent haunch of venison. These weighty matters should not spoil the appetite. Enough time for them later. Hugh, we will talk further."

He looked pointedly at his brother and turned his attention to his food. Clearly the matter was closed for the moment. That night as I passed through the hallway however on my way to bed I heard Father and Uncle Hugh arguing fiercely. I had rarely heard my father so angry.

"Whatever he has said and done, Hugh, he is still the rightful king! If we rebel against him we rebel against God. It would be sacrilege as well as treason."

"He behaves like a tyrant," my uncle was saying, "We do but seek to bring him to reason. If this be treason, then God help England."

"Hugh," my father's voice was rising, angry and desperate. "You talk of a call to arms as if you would go to fight the Turk, or the papists in Ireland. But this is England and it is other Englishmen, your own countrymen, who you would fight and kill. If you take up arms it will not be so easy to lay them down again. You will be fighting your neighbours, perhaps your own kin." His voice dropped. "We are truly lost if brother turns against brother."

Approaching a little too closely to the door in my efforts to hear their dispute, I trod on a loose floorboard. It gave a loud creak and the door flew open. Father stood there glaring at me.

"Bess, these matters are not for the ears of maids. Go to your room. I will deal with you on the morrow."

The following morning, I rose nervously. I saw nothing of Father or Uncle Hugh, however, and when I enquired of Will, he told me that Uncle Hugh had returned to London. Father was ridden out on an urgent matter. From that time we had little communication with my uncle. I had expected us to be bidden to my cousin's wedding but heard nothing, and wondered at it. The week after Easter, we received a formal note written by my aunt, advising us that Celia had wedded her betrothed, Sir John Ridgeley. She enclosed a letter from Celia to me. In the privacy of my bedchamber I opened it eagerly.

"My dearest Bess, well the deed is done. I am wed. I could wish Sir John were handsome or amusing, but he is a wealthy man and as long as he treats me with kindness I will strive to be content. I must make the best of my life to come, rejoicing in the groves, the dovecotes and the newly built orangery in my new home. Sir John had the orangery constructed to please me, and has bid me make what changes I wish to the appointments of the house and its grounds. He strives to please me in any way he may. I will sit for my portrait soon and altogether will set my mind to the sober duties of a wife and lady.

I regret my dear cousin that you and your family were not at my wedding. There is something of coldness now between your Father and Mine. And besides, with the trouble arising in the realm, my Father and my Husband, how strange that sounds, felt it best to make haste and see me settled before anything untoward should happen. Sir John and I leave for his estates on the morrow, and I truly hope that you may find the opportunity of visiting me at Ridgeley Place before many months have passed. Your loving cousin, Celia Ridgeley."

I read the letter with mixed feelings. I was glad Celia was adopting a philosophical approach to her new marriage. I hoped that she would develop a fondness for the middle aged Sir John, which would sustain her once the novelty of her new position and the orangery had worn themselves out. Although he had appeared to me on the single occasion I had met him to be a man of sober tastes and retiring habits suited to a man of five and thirty, he clearly had an affection for his young bride. For myself, I was determined that I would only marry for love.

2

Chadshunt Hall, May 1642

AT THE START of May, Will returned from a visit to the north of England. He was accompanied by Rafe, his tame falcon on his wrist. I received a brief hug from Will and a deep bow from Rafe before the two men strode rapidly away, Will calling for our falconer. I was not invited to accompany them. I sighed. I had not seen Rafe since his stay at Christmas.

After spending the entire afternoon with Will, Rafe appeared for supper, and I hoped that we might have some converse. Instead, all the talk was led by my father and Will. My brother had brought us news of the most recent episode of the descent into hostilities. As Governor of Hull, under a pretended authority from Parliament, Sir John Hotham had barred the city gates of Hull to prevent King Charles entering Hull. The King had promptly declared him a traitor.

"Why is Hull so important to His Majesty?" I decided that the only way to be heard was to express interest in political matters. Mother frowned at my interruption, but Will smiled encouragingly.

"I am glad you begin to think on such matters, Bess. Hull holds the main arsenal for the north of England. The King wished to take possession of it but the Governor prefers to take his instructions from the Parliament. Those gentlemen wish to remove the contents for safekeeping to the Tower of London. In reality it is for their own use. The Governor of Hull disobeyed a direct order from the King. He is therefore declared a traitor and rightly so."

My father swirled the wine around his glass, gnawing his lower lip.

"I fear the Parliament no longer considers it needs to accede to the wishes of His Majesty. My brother has accused the King of being high handed. Yet now the Parliament encourages disobedience and flouts the King openly. You know, Will that when the King refused to assent to the Militia Bill, the Parliament simply passed an illegal ordinance granting themselves the power to appoint the commanders of the militia."

"Sir Henry, do you expect Parliament to declare war on its own king?"

Rafe was speaking at last but the eagerness in his voice showed that his attention was all on my father. Disheartened, I abandoned the attempt to gain Rafe's attention and concentrated my attention on my plate.

On the morrow, I renewed my attempts to encounter Rafe, lingering by turns in entrance hall, gallery and stables.

"What are you doing, Bess?" My mother arched an eyebrow as she spotted me wandering apparently aimlessly. A little later I caught sight of Rafe and Will heading for the lawn, carrying their rapiers. Will looked surprised as I sidled up to where the two men were shedding their doublets and shoes. Normally, I had little interest in being a spectator at my brothers' practice sessions. Rafe bowed to me with a flourish.

"Your champion will defend you, My Lady."

I had almost forgotten his habit of calling me "My Lady". I rolled my eyes and dipped in an exaggerated curtsey, secretly happy that our relaxed relationship had re-established itself. Now stripped to their shirts and breeches, Will and Rafe began to fence. As light footed as when dancing, Rafe leapt from side to side, trying to get his blade under Will's guard. Both tall and slim, the two men were fairly evenly matched, although Will was already showing early signs of matching our father's heavier build in middle age. This gave Will some advantage in strength to wield the weapon, but first he had to catch the laughing Rafe off guard.

I lolled on the grass, giggling as the two men played to their gallery of appreciative audience, me.

"Have at you, Sir, for a rogue and vagabond!"

Rafe dived forward into a lunge, his arm fully extended. Will laughed and leapt high in the air, twisting sideways and throwing himself on the ground.

"I die, I die."

Panting, Will sprang back onto his feet and the match intensified. Finally, as Will seemed to be pressing his advantage, Rafe sent his rapier spinning with a lightning flick of his wrist. I fluttered my handkerchief in the best tradition of courtiers, and applauded. Rafe came over and bowed deeply.

"I have defended your honour, My Lady. May I have your token?" He reached for the handkerchief, my favourite, edged with lace and with my initials EL. I snatched it back.

"I think not, Sir, you are impertinent," I giggled. Hanging his head dramatically, Rafe shuffled away. A moment later, he and Will were strolling towards the Hall, arms around each others' shoulders. I followed, eyes demurely lowered.

"Bess, come and see my new horse. I found him at the fair in Warwick yesterday. Did Will not tell you of him?"

It was two days later, and I was setting out for a walk in the gardens. Rafe was looking particularly handsome in a pale green silk doublet with silver lace under a coat of emerald green, his blonde curls cascading from beneath a large hat set at a jaunty angle on his head and his deep blue eyes sparkling with excitement. He dragged me into the stables. I found myself looking at a fine, if somewhat ill-tempered roan stallion. He was rolling his eyes and baring his teeth.

"Look Bess," he crowed "Is he not magnificent? Let me show you his paces."

The horse, whose name, appropriately it appeared, was Mercury snorted, ears back, while the groom held tightly to his bridle. Once Rafe was in the saddle, the horse decided to show who was master. He bucked twice and then took off. Under the archway, through the courtyard and across the park, horse and rider disappeared at a gallop. Rafe had lost his hat and a stirrup but was still clinging on when he was lost to my sight. He reappeared a little while later smiling, although with mud on his coat. Mercury came to a halt quite docilely in the yard and only tried to bite Rafe once as he slid off his back. I took this as a good sign of improved behaviour by the horse. I was about to go for a ride myself the next morning when Rafe came whistling into the stable.

"Mistress Bess, I know you are a lady of spirit. May I invite you to take part in a feat of daring?"

Carrying an apple and a bridle, he slowly unbolted Mercury's stable door. Mercury twitched an ear and rolled an eye. A few minutes later the stallion was tossing his head, butting Rafe in the side and generally looking suitably alarming. Rafe had an exaggerated air of relaxation.

"My Lady, would you care to join me?" My mother had told me she had faith in both my intelligence and my common sense. Both promptly deserted me. I opened my mouth, convinced that I was going to accuse him of insanity at such a suggestion. Instead, I found myself instructing Joe, our head groom, to fetch one of the padded cushions used by ladies riding pillion. Joe hesitated and I glared at him. The next moment I was putting my foot in Joe's hand, seating myself behind Rafe on the sidling, snorting stallion.

"Wait!" I cried as Rafe prepared to give the horse his head. I hastily jammed my hat as far down over my coif as it would go, not wishing to lose it, and then clutched his coat tightly. This was no time for maidenly reluctance. Rafe chuckled. It was the last sound I heard for some minutes.

The drumming of hooves was in my ears, branches ripped at my clothes as we flew past, and I was hardly able to draw breath, so fast were we going. Clods of earth flew out from under the horse's hooves as he thundered across the park. We descended a slope. At the bottom lay the stream which fed the fish ponds. Mercury barely checked, merely gathering his powerful hind quarters to leap the obstacle with feet to spare. Finally, as we came to a part of the park where the ground rose fairly steeply, Mercury slowed.

"Stop!" I screamed. Laughing, Rafe pulled the horse to a stop. Knees shaking, I slid to the ground.

"I think, Master Beauchamp," I said between my teeth, "I will be walking back." He looked surprised as I staggered off down the slope.

"Bess wait!" I turned around. "I'm sorry," he said meekly. "Will you forgive me?" I regarded him carefully but he seemed to be genuinely contrite. I allowed him to lift me onto Mercury's back again and we proceeded toward the distant chimneys of the hall at a more decorous pace. Will was waiting for us at the stables. He scowled at Rafe and gave me a little push towards the house.

"I suggest you go inside, Bess, before it comes to Father's ears where you have been." I hesitated, unwilling to be summarily dismissed.

"What were you thinking of, Rafe? Putting my sister in danger with your wildness. Have you no care for either her safety or her reputation?"

"Her reputation, what of it?" Rafe replied incredulously.

"I suggest you treat my sister's virtue with due regard, Master Beauchamp," Will continued icily. "It is as dear to me as my life, or hers."

I crept gloomily away. My brother was at his most tiresome. I intended a retreat to my bedchamber, but I had gone no further than the bottom of the main staircase when I heard Will behind me.

"A word with you, Bess." He marched me into the family dining room and slammed the door. "Sit." I opened my mouth to object that I was not a dog but the expression on Will's face made me shut it again. I subsided grumpily onto a chair. Will leaned against the door, arms folded.

"Bess, it appears that you are not to be trusted to conduct yourself in a manner suited to a virtuous maid and a daughter of this house. You were seen with Master Beauchamp riding pillion, in wild flight around the grounds leaping brooks. I may add that riding pillion on a stallion of Mercury's temperament defies common sense."

"I do not see why it is your concern, Will. I ride as well as you or Harry." I chose to ignore the first half of Will's argument.

"Bess this is not about your horsemanship. What I am concerned about, is ensuring that you do not expose yourself again to loose tongues, as you have today. You know very well that as your eldest brother I share in the responsibility for your welfare. If you were betrothed to Master Beauchamp then I might wink at such a level of intimacy, but you are not."

"Not yet," I mumbled under my breath. Will's hearing was keen and he looked at me sharply. Then he pulled a chair towards me and sitting down facing me, took both my hands in his.

"Bess, I fear you are under some grave misapprehension as to plans for your future."

His voice was gentle.

"Last autumn, Father began to talk of arranging a suitable match for you. You are seventeen now and old enough to be wed. He took counsel of Uncle Hugh at Christmas. Uncle Hugh had promised to give the matter thought, as Father had not identified any suitable gentlemen in this or the neighbouring county. Unhappily, the breach in our family occurred soon after. Since then, Father has been uneasy about the state of affairs in the country, and has resolved to proceed no further with a suitable match for you until things are more settled."

"But Rafe," I began with some uncertainty.

"Master Beauchamp comes hither as my friend Bess, nothing more. His spirits are high, as we have seen again today, and if this has led him to mislead you through his reckless behaviour then I must put matters right. What plans Rafe's family may have for his future I know not. No doubt he enjoys your sweet company, my sister, but you should not confuse that with some notion that either his father or our own pursues an alliance between our families. I can answer for ours that there is no such intent."

He rose to his feet and held the door open for me. Clearly there was no value in my continuing the argument. I went to sit on my bed and think. I was deeply disappointed that Will did not see a betrothal between Rafe and me as likely. At the same time I thought he was ignoring the very real possibility of a love match, a match that I for one was convinced had already taken place. Will would be proved wrong and soon.

For the rest of that day I was moody. Rafe tiptoed around, his normally laughing countenance fixed in an expression of contriteness. Will treated him with a stilted formality. I was surprised that my parents made no comment on the frosty atmosphere. Harry was away at Oxford, and for once I was reluctant to confide in Peggy. It was Rafe who was the recipient of my eventual outburst. He came upon me staring furiously at Will's receding back after supper.

"Are you still angry with me?"

he whispered. I turned, encountered the deep blue eyes and went weak at the knees.

"It's Will," I wailed, "He thinks being the eldest son and heir gives him rights over everyone including me. I wish he would stop treating me like a child." Rafe lifted my hand to his lips, regarding me seriously.

"Believe me, Bess, to me you are a woman."

There was a long pause. To my disappointment, he said nothing more, but gave me a slight bow and marched briskly away. The next day he was gone before breakfast.

ᔓ

July 1642

Two days after Father had sent the messenger back to Uncle Hugh with the torn scraps of paper, another letter arrived. During those two days the household buzzed with talk of the letter's contents and of the split in the Lucie family. This time the letter was from Spencer Compton, the Earl of Northampton. When the messenger left, Father paced the grounds for an hour or more, a solitary figure, head bent in thought. He was not to be approached at such times. I watched him enter the house and go straight to Mother's chamber.

"Father has been asked to raise a troop of horse to fight for the King." Harry's eyes were shining.

"That is not yet decided, Harry," cautioned Will with a frown. Harry looked crestfallen.

"The Earl is charged with raising troops in Warwickshire for the King, Bess. He is approaching those leading families who are expected to support the King."

People in the towns were beginning to proclaim their allegiance. The town of Banbury was for Parliament, as was Banbury Castle. Like our family, Warwickshire was divided. At Chadshunt, the work of harvesting continued. I was leaning dreamily on a gate watching the rhythmic swinging of the scythes when Harry came hurtling to find me.

"Bess, another messenger has come from the Earl of Northampton."

I was unable to see why this was exciting news. "Well, Harry, I suppose the Earl wishes to discover whether Father has decided to raise a troop?"

"No, Bess. The Lord Brooke, the Lord Lieutenant of the county, is bringing ordnance from London to help fortify Warwick Castle for Parliament. It is nearing Banbury."

"What has that to do with Father?"

"The Earl of Northampton has called out the Warwickshire Trained Bands to intercept Lord Brooke's men and prevent them reaching Warwick with the guns. We are to meet them at Banbury today."

"We? What do you mean, Harry?"

Will's voice broke in. "As officers of the Trained Bands, Father and I are about to ride to Banbury. It is 12 miles, and if we make haste we can be there in little more than an hour without overtaxing the horses. The weather is fine and the roads will be dry."

Neither Harry nor I had noticed the clink of spurs as Will approached. He was dressed for riding and was carrying his coat. His sword belt was strapped across his shoulder, his rapier in the scabbard.

"No Will, why should you go? You have had very little training," I exclaimed.

"What mean you by Father and I? I too am a man and ready to fight." Harry was indignant, but Will was already striding rapidly towards the stables, pulling his large hat firmly down over his long fair hair. Harry ran after him, protesting volubly, leaving me trailing behind. Seeing Will was in no mood to stop or listen, I hastened into the house. In the library, I found a similar argument in progress between my parents.

"Anne, you know full well that Will and I are officers of the regular county militia. It's task is a long standing one, to defend Warwickshire. I will leave Harry here. He has not yet attended any musters of the Trained Bands and I grant it would be unwise to take him, even though at the age of eighteen he is more than old enough. But I must have Will. Spencer Compton requires our urgent attendance. We must prevent Lord Brooke fortifying Warwick Castle for the rebels. There is no time to waste if we are to intercept his ordnance on the road."

"But Henry, the Warwickshire Trained Bands meet no more than a few times a year. It is one thing for a gentleman to attend the occasional muster as the law requires, and quite another to lead men unused to following you. The Earl cannot expect you to be at his command at a moment's notice. You have not yet agreed to raise a troop." Mother's voice was querulous.

"Well, matters have moved too swiftly for Spencer Compton I daresay as they have for England. My dear, I have no more time for discourse. Have courage, I do not believe it will come to a fight today. Bess," he continued, "Please withdraw with your mother to her chamber and bid her rest. Call Mary to attend her. Will and I leave at once for Banbury."

Father was also dressed for riding and wearing his sword. I nodded reluctantly.

"Come, Mother, let us retire." I plucked gently at her sleeve and led her through the Great Hall and towards the stairs. I caught sight of Harry, standing mute and white faced with fury in the entrance hall.

"Harry, attend me please." Father was holding out a key.

"While we are away, I pray you open our private store of arms. Take one of the servants with you and commence making a list of what arms we have and in what condition."

"At once, Sir." Harry's eyes brightened and he marched away.

By the time Mother reached her chamber she was complaining of the headache as she sometimes did, particularly when crossed. Her maid Mary loosened her stays and drew the bed curtains. I crept furtively away, hoping she would sleep.

3

Banbury Road, 30 July 1642

I SLIPPED THROUGH the door from the main house into the west wing and the stables. As I had expected, Father and Will were already gone. Our grooms were not to be seen and I quickly saddled my chestnut mare Fairy and trotted under the arch out of the stables before any of the servants spotted me and carried tales to Harry or Peggy. I had a mind to see what was happening on the Banbury Road.

When I reached the end of the lane I turned Fairy's head in the direction of Banbury. Chadshunt village was quiet. Reaching the Banbury Road, I pushed her into a canter, but I had gone no more than a mile when I came upon a score or so of men, marching purposefully in ranks of three towards Banbury. Attired in their workaday garments, some wore old fashioned helmets and all were armed either with pikes, heavy, steel tipped 16 foot long ash poles, which they trailed behind them, muskets or in a few cases only cudgels. I slowed to a trot and passed them cautiously. A few minutes later I heard galloping horses behind me. I pulled Fairy hastily into the hedgerow as five men, gentlemen by their dress, passed me in a cloud of dust without slackening their pace. I had only time to note that all wore swords and some wore helmets when one of them drew rein and turned back towards me. With a sinking heart, I recognised the familiar hooked nose and black curly hair of Giles Blake. He stopped beside me and swept off his hat.

"Mistress Lucie, what do you on this road?" he asked directly, looking hard at me.

I hesitated to admit that I had come forth in the hope of seeing armed men heading into a fight.

"My mare needs exercise and it is a fine day," I mumbled with down cast eyes. He was silent for a moment.

"It is not wise, Mistress, to pass this way today. I suppose your father has departed for Banbury and you seek to follow him. I believe I may safely say he would not wish you abroad at this time. Pray turn back. Would you have me escort you home?" His words were kindly spoken. I shook my head, my cheeks glowing.

"I will return home, Sir without delay. I thank you for your kindness." I turned Fairy's head and rode slowly homewards without further incident. Harry emerged several hours later from his task in the attics, covered in cobwebs and considerably more cheerful. We sat down to a late supper where he regaled me with details of what arms and armour he had made inventory of. I said nothing of my ride. Mother kept her room.

The long summer hours of daylight were over and I was lying sleepless in my bed when I heard the sound of horses' hooves on the cobbles. I leapt up and ran downstairs, pulling on a bedgown as I went. I was in time to see Father and Will walk wearily through the door.

"Bess what do you here? You should be abed," Father frowned. Will grinned at me.

"Well, Bess, we have had famous sport. We met the Lord Brooke's men with their train of guns upon the road the other side of Banbury. We blocked the way and vowed we would ride them down before they could load a single one of their pieces. The Earl of Northampton arrived by and by and called the Lord Brooke traitor. I thought they would fall to brawling, but at last some of the gentlemen with them urged them to retire into Banbury Castle and talk. It grew dark and we had much ado to stop all the men of the trained bands leaving to refresh themselves at the Reindeer Inn." He laughed.

"And then?" I prompted impatiently.

"Why, in conclusion they came forth from the castle, and it was agreed that the guns would be kept there. Neither side is to move them without notice to the other. And so the trained bands were stood down and we rode home. But I am for my bed."

He yawned hugely. Relieved, I returned to my chamber and slept. I thought that would be the end of it but I was wrong.

A week later, the Royalist Earl of Northampton broke the terms of the agreement, launching an unsuccessful attack from the river on Warwick Castle in Lord Brooke's absence. After that failure he laid siege to the castle and the guns were now bombarding it from the top of St Mary's Church. Sir Edward Peyton, Lord Brooke's deputy, responded by hanging a bible and a winding sheet from one of the castle towers, declaring the garrison's readiness to die in the cause of God and Parliament.

"Dramatic balderdash," Father fumed. "A fine gesture while they shelter behind walls of stone ten feet thick. We will see how brave they are when they face a King's army in the field."

He might have said more, but Mother's face had blanched at his reference to a field army, and he turned the subject. Neither did he mention to her that he had obtained a limited store of ammunition from the magazine at Banbury before the siege. It was as well he had done so. The county magazine in Coventry had been seized by Lord Brooke, leaving the Royalists struggling to find powder, bullets and match.

The Earl did not call upon our family to support him in the siege, but Mother's relief was to be of short duration. On 22 August, there was a bloody clash between the forces of the Earl of Northampton and Lord Brooke's forces at Southam, not many miles from our home. Men on both sides died. Within days, Giles Blake brought the news that the King had raised his standard at Nottingham. The time of speeches, petitions and remonstrances was over. The news that we were at war was received by Father in silence, by my brothers with excitement, by Mother with fear. I spotted Father walking in the gardens later and went out to him, trusting my unbidden attendance at such a time would not vex him. The summer's evening was falling and the scent of honeysuckle was heavy on the air. I plucked a blossom and played with it.

"Well Bess?"

"Father what does this mean for us? Are we truly at war?"

Father pulled my arm through his and steered me into the arbour. We sat down on a bench and I leaned my head against his doublet, comforted by his strong presence.

"England is at war Bess with herself, and there can be no good end from that. But for the Lucies we are committed. In truth we were committed the day Will and I rode in company to stop the Lord Brooke reach Warwick. Our allegiance was never in doubt. Yet I had hoped it would not come to this, to open war. How we have slipped from paper combat to raising forces I do not know. His Majesty is a good man, but he has made many errors of judgement and now too many of his people neither love nor trust him. I am a Justice of the Peace Bess. I must uphold the law. For the honour of our family I have decided to raise a company of horse for the King. I do not see any other way clear."

"Will you take the men of the Trained Bands as your company, Father?"

"The Trained Bands are being disarmed, Bess. The Earl of Northampton will attempt to seize their arms. They do not fight outside the county. The King needs men who will follow him to the north or the West Country, or to London."

I digested this information. The question that was closest to my heart forced its way past my lips "And my brothers Father? Are they to accompany you?" My voice shook.

"They are. It is Will's right and Harry's too. They are grown men both and neither would choose to remain here in safety while I fight."

Many of the tenants and the servants too, volunteered to fight once the harvest was gathered in. The younger men were full of enthusiasm, but my father was wary, both of taking away the youngest and strongest from the estate and of the need to balance youthful enthusiasm with the caution which comes with age. Will told me Father felt his hand had been forced.

"Father did not make the decision lightly, Bess. However much we support the King in private, we are now committed as a family to his cause. Our lives and our fortune are all to be hazarded in his service."

"Would you prefer then to remain at home?"

"No, Bess. I must confess my heart beat fast on the day when we blocked Lord Brooke's way. A life of action will suit me well, but part of me fears for our home and way of life. For Harry too I fear. He is young and rash."

Our family took no part in any fighting during this tense time. The local blacksmith was put to work sharpening and repairing swords for the men, some long disused and retrieved from presses and attics. The saddler stitched and repaired broken straps and stirrup leathers whilst our servants rode back and forth to Banbury and Kineton, replenishing essential items. Two of the tenants were taking their wives, on the understanding they would cook and wash for the troopers. One of our servants would attend on Father and my brothers.

Harry's inclusion in the troop remained a bone of contention between my parents. I was puzzled. While three years younger than Will, Harry was eighteen, no longer a boy. I knew of men on our farms who were married and fathers at 18.

Several times I heard Mother's voice raised in passionate plea.

"Please, Henry, do not take him with you. I know only too well how he wishes it. But all young men believe their bodies are as immortal as their souls. I wish that you too might remain safe at home, but I know you see it as your duty."

"Anne, it is not only my duty but that of our sons." Father's voice was rising in irritation. "Harry is a man as much as Will and has made his own decision. There will be younger lads than he who fight. I pray that God will protect them both. If they should fall, we must be consoled that they will have done so in the cause of right."

After a short silence, the door to the library opened abruptly. Mother swept past me, her eyes for once unseeing. It was plain to me at least that Father had made his decision. Will was to be Lieutenant, Harry the Cornet, the standard bearer. Mother's vain pleas ceased, but I caught her longing looks at both my brothers and one day I found her sobbing quietly over a miniature of Will.

ও

Chadshunt Hall, September 1642

Once he made a decision, Father was not one to shirk it or pursue the task half heartedly. Having decided to raise a troop, he went about it energetically, and shortly had recruited some 56 men. It was a goodly number Will said, and all without having to beat a drum in Banbury or Kineton as some gentlemen were doing. The house became a hive of industry. The female servants ran around with armfuls of gloves, hats, shirts, breeches and woollen stockings. Father was frequently to be found in his library poring over a book entitled "Military Instructions for the Cavalry".

One of the tenants, Oliver White, was drill master. White had spent years as a professional soldier in the European wars in the Low Countries. Much of the recruits' training was necessarily on horseback. At first they drilled in our park, but a steady downpour of rain for a day or two led to the horses' hooves churning up the turf. Fortunately there were now some fields of stubble where the harvesting was complete and the troop moved to the fields for their daily practice.

As Mother had said, the trained bands met but rarely beyond the annual muster of able bodied men. I did not recall Father and Will training more than a few times a year. They usually returned from these occasions having spent an hour or so in drill followed by considerably longer in a nearby inn. Constant practice in the use of a sword was largely confined to gentlemen, who invariably used the light, thin rapier, and professional soldiers. For those who were neither gentlemen nor former soldiers, some had limited knowledge of how to use a sword, some of how to use a pike or firearm. Only the gamekeepers were truly experienced with the latter. All those who joined Father were experienced horsemen, but, as I discovered, there was a difference between managing your own horse and manoeuvring with other horses in company.

"I do not see what amuses you, Bess," Harry grumbled. I was standing shaking with laughter holding the bridle of his horse. Harry was limping towards me, mud on his coat, having fallen off yet again. I bit my lip, trying to keep a straight face.

"You should perhaps hold back a little, Harry when the command is given to charge. If you continually gallop off ahead of the troop, you will surely expose yourself to unnecessary danger. And may end in the hedge again when your horse cannot stop."

"You would do well to listen to Bess." Will's voice was dry. "She may not be a soldier but she is an excellent horsewoman. I suggest you look over Father's stable for a calmer mount. Merrylegs is a little too skittish in my opinion."

Harry snorted, but I noticed that the next day he was mounted on a different horse.

ഗ

"What is it, Robin?"

The manservant was standing respectfully in the study doorway.

"White wishes to see you, Master."

"Again?"

Sir Henry shook his head impatiently.

"Oh very well, send him in. We will continue later, John."

The steward bowed his head and gathered up the papers.

"Well, Oliver, what now?"

White entered hesitantly, pulling his hat off his head.

"Sir Henry, there is the matter of arming those servants who remain behind at the Hall."

"I have considered this Oliver, but I do not think it needful. Do you fear Chadshunt will be beset by thieves and brigands in my absence?"

White shifted uncomfortably from one foot to another.

"Sir Henry, what I saw as a soldier in Germany. When towns and villages were overrun – the women."

"What you saw in Germany can be of little import in England. The rebels are Englishmen as much as we. Their leaders are gentlemen and will no doubt respect our womenfolk."

White remained silent. Sir Henry snorted.

"What arms do you propose the menservants take from our ample stores?"

White ignored the sarcasm.

"We have a handful of muskets, Sir, matchlocks. They were no use to our troop of cavalry."

"Yes, yes, I am conversant with the reasons why harquebusiers do not carry long arms and burning match on horseback. Proceed. But stay a moment!"

"Yes, Sir Henry?"

The baronet cleared his throat and smiled ruefully,

"Do not let your fears come to the ears of Lady Lucie, or our troop will be permitted to venture no further than our gatehouse."

ᔕ

Sitting by the window of the drawing room, my eye was caught by the solemn procession across the courtyard. First came Father's manservant, Thomas. Grey haired, well advanced in years, he was marching stiffly, followed by seven or eight other servants. Bringing up the rear was the diminutive figure of Father's page, twelve year old Jack.

I climbed onto the window seat and pressed my nose against the glass as Oliver White appeared, hefting a musket and its heavy wooden rest. He made a survey of the assembled servants and then pointed sternly towards the house. I could not hear what he said, but Jack was protesting. Oliver put a hand on his shoulder and smiled. Dragging his feet, the page retired sulkily.

"Training the servants now, Bess. White fears for your safety." Harry's tone was light.

I chuckled at White's caution. I had caught something of Harry's infectious enthusiasm for the call to arms and my dreams of life with Rafe occasionally mingled with pictures of Bess Lucie attiring herself as a man and riding beside him into battle, a sword at my hip. I was delighted when the rising tide of war unexpectedly washed Rafe my way again. Now I would learn if he cared for me. I had heard nothing from him since May, but Peggy had assured me that it would be most improper for an unwed man and woman to engage in private correspondence. She reminded me that as heir to his father's estate, Rafe too had many duties, including his family's own preparations for what must lay ahead. The whole country was starting to be in turmoil and I reluctantly accepted Will had probably been correct that any marriage plans were likely to be delayed until matters in the country became more settled.

"Will," I enquired breathlessly, discovering him in the library, where he was poring over Father's book of cavalry drill, repeating commands under his breath.

"For what purpose is Rafe arrived? Is he to make a long stay?" Will frowned.

"Rafe has volunteered to fight with a neighbouring troop which Sir Lucius Lane is raising. Sir Lucius is a friend of Rafe's family. Father has agreed that Rafe can remain with us and bear us company while he drills. That is all."

Despite Will's words, I remained hopeful. Those few weeks were very happy. I often found an hour or so to ride out with one or both of my brothers. Rafe usually accompanied us. If he rode beside me I would strive to match his light hearted conversation in kind. If he rode with Will I would watch admiringly as he controlled the temperamental stallion with whip and spur. Sometimes we took our falcons, and would watch them soaring high in the air, then hovering almost motionless until spotting their prey when they would dive in for the kill. With the speed of an arrow they would seize a hapless pigeon or blackbird mid-flight, pinning the struggling bird with their claws and landing with it where the victim, on its back beneath the remorseless claws would succumb to the sharp beak. By the time we arrived at the scene there would often be little left of the kill but piles of feathers. I loved to watch the birds in flight, but would shudder a little at their ruthlessness when I came upon them still subduing their prey.

I was eager to hear more of Rafe's life and family.

"Tell me of your home in Sussex," I said one day as we trotted along decorously, followed by Harry and Will.

"It lies in a fold of the South Downs not far from the sea. It was one of the monasteries closed in the time of King Henry and was given to one of my ancestors. He remodelled it into a modern gentleman's country house, Beauchamp Hall." His voice dropped to a whisper.

"It boasts a ghostly grey monk. He likes to creep up on you – like this," he mouthed, making a fearsome face. I squeaked in mock horror.

"Maybe you will see it one day," he smiled before clicking to Mercury and speeding up into a canter in pursuit of our birds. I followed slowly and thoughtfully. For Rafe to talk of me visiting his home, surely that was a hopeful sign. But then why had he only talked of it as a possibility, not a certainty?

❧

"Well, Oliver, what think you?"

White was watching another dashing but uncontrolled charge of the hopeful troop across the fields. Sir Henry braced himself for more complaints as White pushed his rather battered black hat back from his head and scratched his shiny, bald pate.

"Of the men, Sir? As to the loading and firing of pistols and carbines I have taught them all I know. I have schooled them in caring for their arms and armour and their kit in wet weather as well as dry, especially if the weather is foul. Powder must be kept dry, Sir."

"And what of their prowess in the saddle?"

White's face grew longer.

"If I may speak freely, Sir, I think they believe they train for a day's hunting. There will be no stopping them once they make their charge."

Sir Henry frowned at this plain speaking.

"Do you say too much spirit is as dangerous as too little?"

"Aye, Sir Henry. But I will devise a training ring and we will strive to tame both horse and man."

"Well do so." Sir Henry smiled and turned away.

"A moment further I pray, Sir?"

"Well, Oliver?"

"The arms with which they train."

"I have scoured the county. We have drained the cup dry at present."

White hesitated, pursing his lips.

"There is more?" Sir Henry was beginning to show signs of impatience.

"The powder, Sir. 'Tis old, black powder which has lain in the Banbury magazine I believe these four or more years. I cannot answer for it."

"Nor will you, White," Sir Henry snapped, now thoroughly out of patience.

"Now, pray no more. I trust to your skill and God's providence. Good day to you."

The baronet marched away, the stiffness of his carriage a sure sign of displeasure.

White tugged uncertainly at his moustache. The next day he set up his training ring for the horses where the men could practise wheeling them tightly in different directions, at first singly and then in ranks. He fervently hoped the troop would not be forced into an engagement before the men were ready.

ꕥ

"Rafe, have you considered that a spirited stallion may not be the best choice of mount? You may lose control of him in the heat of battle." Will's brow was furrowed.

"Nonsense, Will, what an old mother hen you are at times," Rafe panted as he braced himself, clutching at Mercury's bridle. The horse had reared up onto its hind legs yet again after a drum had been beaten near him. Observing Rafe's struggles, I reflected that the friendship between my disciplined and cautious brother, and the reckless Rafe, was an unlikely one.

Watching the men trying on their armour and uniform for the first time was a disappointment. I had imagined every man encased in gleaming armour and fully equipped. The reality was somewhat different.

Harry was holding two pieces of tarnished armour with blackened and cracked leather ties attached. At his feet were a metal helmet with flaps at the back and ears, a single pistol and an unfamiliar sword, which was wider than Harry's rapier.

"Harry, what in the world are you holding?"

"A breast plate and a back plate, Bess. I was lucky to get them. Father's own stock of weapons was too small for our troop. He has had men scouring the country for arms and armour. The Earl of Northampton has given what assistance he can. I should have two pistols and a carbine, but these will suffice for the present."

I watched Harry try to strap on the armour plates but one of the ties promptly broke. White came towards us looking irritated.

"These all require the attentions of an armourer, Master Harry. Since we do not have one, we will have to take everything into Kineton for the leather to be replaced. Thank the Lord Sir Henry has managed to come by sufficient lobster tail helmets for all. At least our heads will be protected."

The armour was not very popular. "Bess, I feel like a goose trussed for the oven."

Rafe flapped his arms as he struggled with the ageing, stiffened leather ties on his breastplate.

"I believe I will ride without it." He hissed like a goose, making me giggle. Will, struggling with the ties on his own armour, shook his head at him.

I was more impressed by the men's new leather buff coats. I watched admiringly as Rafe slipped his strong arms into his heavy, long sleeved, thigh length coat and fastened the metal hooks down the front. Made of thick hide, the coat had a high collar and was lined with silk. Its sleeves were finely embroidered with gold thread. The coat had transformed him at a stroke from a handsome gentleman into an officer and a warrior.

"Bess, pray assist me with these hooks."

I turned away from Rafe to note that Harry had undergone a similar transformation. None of the servants were close by, so I helped him with the new and unfamiliar fastenings. I gazed admiringly at my brother's broad shoulders, their breadth emphasised by the thick leather. Father was in the right. Harry was a man now. I gave him an impulsive hug, a lump in my throat.

"What is it, Bess?" His grey eyes smiled down into mine, which were become a little misty.

"It is nothing, Harry, I was thinking you will be a gallant officer. I am so proud of you all."

I watched as the remainder of the troop donned their own buff coats, lacing them up the front with thongs. I could see the leather was thinner and they were unlined, but nonetheless they made a brave showing. My mother was making a slow circuit of my father, looking critically at his coat as he adjusted it with the help of his page.

"Well enough, my love?"

"Indeed yes, Henry, you look very fine, our sons too. I was reflecting on how much these coats have cost. Two pounds and five shillings for each of the men. I fear we will be beggars."

"Anne, we cannot expect our men to fight unprotected. They are all our family, tenants and servants and our responsibility. The coats will offer protection from sword thrusts and against bad weather. But I fear my own coat cost nearer ten pounds, as did those for Will and Harry."

"Oh, Henry," she whispered, "God forbid I should begrudge a penny of anything which keeps you and our sons safe."

I frequently got in the way watching the men fight and admiring Rafe's graceful swordsmanship. My mother came to find me on more than one occasion and strongly suggested that I could be more useful assisting in the house. She put me to work hemming new fine linen shirts for Father, Will and Harry in place of the embroidery which more usually occupied spare moments indoors. Later we made red sashes, my father having ascertained that in the absence of proper uniforms, the King's cavalry would wear red sashes to distinguish them from the fellow countrymen, friends, neighbours and cousins who were now the enemy.

I was watching the men at weapons drill, my eyes shining, lips parted with excitement at the clash of arms, the swift movements of the men's bodies as they practiced loading what I now understood to be the snaphance carbines carried by the light cavalry known as harquebusiers. My eyes rested most often on the tall, slim form of Rafe Beauchamp. His occasional glances in my direction showed that he was aware of my presence and was a little distracted by it.

"Master Beauchamp," called White as Rafe glanced yet again over his shoulder at me. "You'll blow your toes off if you don't pay more attention than that."

White took the carbine carefully from Rafe and raised his voice.

"Observe, gentlemen. When loading or carrying your piece, it must be in the half cock position with the dog catch engaged or the weapon may fire. In action, you will be carrying this ready loaded on a charging horse."

White engaged the safety clasp and glared at Rafe. He dropped his voice.

"I am well aware you are a keen swordsman, but unless you can be certain you will be fighting the enemy hand to hand you need to master how to safely give fire." Cheeks crimson, Rafe bent his head, blonde curls screening him from sight as he belatedly concentrated his attention on the gun. A moment later, I heard a quiet voice behind me. My father had come to watch the progress of the men and had noticed me watching with rapt attention, twisting the ends of my collar in my excitement.

"Bess," I turned to him enquiringly, "You do understand for what these men train, and the price they may pay don't you?"

I nodded in some confusion.

"It's not a game, Bess. War is never a game and when brother fights brother we risk all that we hold dear, and that is more than our lives upon this earth. There is no worse conflict than that between brothers. You would do well to remember that. As would your brothers," he finished quietly. Will was holding his sides laughing after another spectacularly bad attempt at loading and firing his carbine had led to the ball falling back out of the muzzle onto the ground.

ര

October 1642

"The Master requires your attendance in his study, Master Harry. Master Blake is with him and wishes to have speech with you."

"Thank you, Thomas."

My curiosity piqued, I strolled casually after him. Father's study door was closed but a few minutes later Harry emerged, his eyes shining.

"What is it Harry?"

He brushed past me impatiently and bounded upstairs two at a time. I found him in the long gallery with Will, who was clapping him on the back, his eyes wistful. I glared at them both.

"I suppose as a maid I am not permitted to enquire after the affairs of my menfolk?" Will laughed.

"For some men, advancement is speedy. Without having so much as drawn his sword, Harry is promoted from Cornet to Lieutenant."

"Harry, I swear I will box your ears if you do not explain at once." Harry grinned.

"Well, Bess, Giles Blake is also raising a troop of horse. Henceforth our troop and his will train together. His son is but twelve years old so he seeks a Lieutenant. He came today to ask Father if I might serve with him."

"But Harry," I protested, "if you are with a different troop you may become separated from Father and Will". Harry grinned light heartedly,

"Never fear, little sister. Our two troops will be part of the Prince of Wales Regiment of horse. I will still lie close enough to Will to hear his snoring at night."

"Henry, you vowed to protect Harry when you said you would take him. Now he is to fight with another company. For Giles Blake, it will not be a first concern to protect Harry's safety." Mother's eyes were stark with fear when Father told her the news.

"My dear Anne," Father snapped. "It is time you trust my judgement. As Lieutenant, Harry will be as safe or safer as he would have been with me."

"How so?"

"The Lieutenant's station is at the back of the troop in battle. He is placed there partly for his safety so that if the Captain falls he may take his place. The cornet on the other hand rides into battle nearer the front so that he may inspire the troops with the standard." He paused so that his words could sink in. At last she nodded somewhat tremulously.

"And you say Master Blake's troop will be close at hand to yours?"

"I have no doubt of it," he said more gently.

"Well then, I suppose," she broke off, "Bess, have you nothing useful to do? I never turn round but you are listening to matters of no concern to you."

"Yes, Madam," I murmured. I retreated to my chamber, where I would have to suffer neither Harry's gloating nor Mother's querulousness.

4

Chadshunt Hall, October 1642

My time was divided between helping Mother with preparations and spending the precious and dwindling hours with those who were readying to depart. I had little time for riding out on Fairy, but I would sometimes visit her in the stables. I would brush her mane and talk to her about my feelings for Rafe. She would listen and blow gently at me, showering me with wisps of hay from the manger.

Visiting her one sunny afternoon with an apple, I lingered, combing the tangles from her long mane. The afternoon was growing cool and I leant against her warm flank. I heard hooves and turning my head saw Rafe leading his horse into a nearby stall. He was looking thoughtful, but when he caught sight of me he gave one of his lighthearted grins and bowed. "My Lady." I curtseyed and giggled. It had been an unusually warm day for October and he was in shirt and breeches, his doublet slung over his shoulder. His shirt was open at the neck. I looked at his tall body, his chest deeply tanned, admiringly. His face, neck and arms were streaked in places with sweat and dust from riding. I noticed the fair curls on the left side of his head had clumps of dried mud and tufts of grass caught in them.

"Has Mercury thrown you again?" He looked puzzled. Greatly daring, I reached up and plucked a tuft of grass and some dried mud from Rafe's hair. He laughed. I uncurled my fingers, showing him my finds and he brushed his fingers lightly across my palm. We had not been alone together since that wild gallop on Mercury, and I felt intensely self-conscious. He grasped both my hands and pulled me towards him.

"There is a penalty for such familiarity," he said with a dazzling smile, "and I mean to exact it." He wrapped both his strong arms around me, clamping my arms to my sides. The intensity in the blue gaze deepened. He fastened his lips on mine. Strange warmth was spreading through my body as he held me tightly against him. An endless moment later, he released me and stepped back. I edged forward eagerly towards him, lifting my face for another kiss and parting my lips, but he shook his head, grinning.

"No more, Mistress Lucie. I do not intend to fight your brother. He will flay me alive if he catches me trifling with you."

With a long and searching look, in which I detected some regret, he strode out of the stable. I leaned against Fairy until I could catch my breath and my heart stopped thundering.

At supper in the Great Hall I cast sidelong glances at Rafe. He was talking to Will, apparently unaware of me. I felt my spirits sink. A moment later, Rafe flashed me a quick meaningful look, followed by a grin. I finished the meal with a lighter heart. That night of course I was far too excited to sleep. My heart was pounding loudly with the memory of Rafe's kisses and the feel of his arms around me. He must love me as I did him.

The next day, at the same hour, I again visited the stables, my heart already thumping. Would he be there? The stables were quiet once more. I waited next to Fairy's stall until I heard approaching footsteps. I spun round, his name on my lips. It was Joe's brother, Ben.

"Did you want me to saddle Fairy for you, Mistress Bess?"

"No thank you, Ben." The groom nodded at me. Grabbing a pitchfork, he began mucking out an empty stall. I left, disappointed.

The next day and the next I returned to the stables at the same time, but Rafe visited them no more. When we met at dinner or supper he was charming as ever, but somehow we were never alone together. I knew not what to think. A few days later I saw him ride out and Will told me he would now be remaining with his own troop.

I could not bear the idea of being parted from the man I loved. I was also despondent at the idea of being parted from Father and my brothers. Mother was in the midst of conning another long list of items to be made, bought or otherwise procured before the men could leave. I posed to her my urgently worded request that, just as the tenants' wives were accompanying their men when they joined the army, I should be permitted to go along too.

"Forgive me, Bess," she responded drily, "I fear my ears are dulled by the constant ringing in them of swords. I thought I heard you say something concerning yourself leaving with the army. Clearly I misheard." This was not promising but I pressed on regardless.

"Mother please, I could make sure Father, Will and Harry have a hot meal each day. I could mend their clothes if they tear them." She interrupted me again.

"My love, I think you must be suffering from a fever of the brain if you serious contemplate Mistress Elisabeth, daughter of Sir Henry Lucie, riding along with the ragtag of the army, sleeping in a hedgerow and wrapped in your cloak I daresay. Think of the danger to your person and the damage to your reputation which would follow. As to caring for Father and your brothers, one of our servants is accompanying them for that purpose."

I alternately wheedled and sulked, pleading with Mother, but to no avail. I lacked the courage to make the same request to Father without an intermediary. In desperation I turned to Will, always my champion in time of trouble.

"Would you not speak to Father for me, Will?" He rolled his eyes,

"Bess, do you remember the times we have seen executed criminals hanging in chains on the gibbet?"

"Yes," I said, puzzled by his dredging up such gruesome memories.

"Well, that is how Father will serve me, if I propose you accompany us."

I flounced from the room and took out my feelings by playing the harpsichord loudly for half an hour. I could do no more. I looked out of the window. Autumn leaves were beginning to fall. A breeze blew a flurry of leaves against the window with a sharp rattle. Fate had cheated me by casting my lot as a woman.

12 October 1642

It was a wet afternoon, with a chill wind blowing from the north. The men would be leaving within days to join the Prince of Wales Regiment of Horse and the King's army. Oliver White decided there should be one last drill for the two troops, the wet conditions providing a realistic foretaste of what was to come in the field. By now I had watched enough drills for the prospect of a final one to be less than enticing. Besides, Rafe was no longer there for me to watch, and the weather was foul. I settled myself beside a warm fire in the family sitting room and stitched industriously at the fringes for my brothers' crimson silk sashes. Their armour might be old but I was determined they would be easily identifiable as officers and would look the part.

My work was done, and I was sitting with the finished sashes on my knee, gazing into the glow of the fire, when I heard cries of alarm. Dropping the sashes, I raced towards the source of the commotion, which seemed to be coming from the kitchens. I dashed down the service passage, past the doors to buttery and pantry. Will and one of the tenants in the troop were in the act of lowering a man onto a bench against the wall in the kitchen. Behind Will stood Oliver White, his kindly face a mask of anguish. The prone man's head was covered by a bloody scarf. His arms flopped over the edge of the bench. He was very still and I realised with horror he was dead. Several servants were milling around, the women all weeping, while Thomas tried to restore order. Janie the cook was on her knees beside the bench, still clutching a wooden spoon. A haunch of mutton was burning, unheeded over the great fire, while untended pots hissed and spluttered.

Will caught sight of me and beckoned. He was looking shocked, grave.

"Bess, fetch Mother. Tell her poor Nicholas has been shot and killed."

"Nicholas?" he had been my playmate when he was a kitchen lad and I a troublesome child. A tear rolled down my face. Will gave me a little push.

"Bess, go."

I brushed away the useless tears and fled to find Mother. She came hastily to the sad scene. Skirts rustling, she knelt on the rush mat, disregarding the pool of blood which had trickled to the ground.

"Bess," she whispered, "This is not a sight for you."

She gently lifted the scarf from Nicholas's face. I tried to tear my eyes away before she did so but could not. My old playmate was no longer known to me. Half his face was gone, nose and jaw smashed, the left eye missing and nothing left but a pulpy mass of flesh. It might have been a rabbit when a falcon had been tearing at it.

"There is nothing to be done for him, but we must carry the news to his family without delay."

"I will go at once, My Lady," White said hopelessly.

"Thank you Oliver, but no." Mother's tone was gentle but firm. "Nicholas was a servant of the Lucie family. He was our responsibility in life, so too in death. Our servants will ready his body for burial and he will lie in the family chapel overnight. It is only fitting."

Mother realised I had not moved from the spot.

"Bess, please withdraw. If you wish to be of use, you may find Mary and ask her to find clean linen for a winding sheet. Then send a message by Ben to tell the vicar he will need to bury Nicholas on the morrow. Oh, and ask him to ring the bells to mark his passing."

"Yes, Mother."

"And Will? Please ride to the Oddingtons' cottage without delay."

My brother nodded reluctantly. As the eldest son he could not refuse the task of taking the news to a family that their only son was dead. I was truly grateful it was not I who had to find the courage to face the grief of Nicholas's mother. The messy business of dealing with the tragic and sudden death was the lot of the men, and of Mother. Will was gone no more than an hour or so, but when he returned there was bleakness in his countenance I had never seen before. The stiff, proud set of his shoulders was belied by the unmistakeable tracks of tears on his cheeks.

"Will?" he passed me by unseeing, his steps dragging. The door of Father's study closed behind him quietly. Prayers that evening were read by Father with increased fervour. Instead of gathering in the Great Hall, we filed silently into our small family chapel in the west wing. We had rarely used it since the death of our much loved family chaplain years before. Now it gave greater solemnity to the occasion. We prayed for the King, for peace in the realm and for Nicholas, lying wrapped in a shroud, sprinkled with rue. All the female servants were in tears, as was I. When prayers were over, we left candles burning at Nicholas's head and feet. I followed Harry up to his chamber and tapped timidly at the door. I had not the heart to approach the silent Will.

"Well, Bess?" Harry was sitting on his bed looking tired and haggard.

"Harry, please tell me what happened," I begged. He hesitated for a moment but then nodded.

"We were practicing loading and firing our pistols. Our last drill, and our last attempt using live ammunition. It was raining as you know, and Nicholas's powder may have been damp. But I have heard White say the powder was too long in store and that may have worsened matters. When Nicholas tried to give fire, there was a flash in the pan and then nothing. He tilted it up to see what was wrong and then the ball fired. I was standing next to him and saw it happen. White feels himself very much to blame, but in truth he had done all he could with instruction. There were too many of us for him to watch each man at every step. I am not a superstitious man, Bess as you know, but I fear this death by violence may bring a curse upon our family."

In the morning, the whole household, the troop and most of the people from the estate, flocked to our parish church, All Saints, to see Nicholas buried. I was somewhat comforted when Mother told me we would provide a coffin for Nicholas in addition to the usual shroud. Instead of a brief tenancy of the parish coffin, Nicholas would be buried in his own coffin, hastily constructed by Chadshunt's carpenter. The sound of hammering had gone on late into the night. Mother's linen chest had produced not only materials for the shroud, but a little stock of black ribbon, kept ready for such occasions. The ribbon was adorning our hats while sprigs of rosemary were pinned to our sleeves. As the kindly Reverend Hunter, his face ashen, intoned the words, "I am the resurrection and the life", Nicholas's mother sobbed uncontrollably. Her husband stood mute and grim faced. Their daughter Jeny, a maid of maybe ten years and their only surviving child, stood with her head buried in her mother's shoulder, dry eyed.

When the grave was filled and the mourners about to depart, Father held up his hand.

"By your favour, vicar, I would say a word." Reverend Hunter nodded.

Father cleared his throat. In a firm but sombre voice he spoke.

"As head of the Lucie family, I express my personal sorrow at the untimely death of Nicholas Oddington. Nicholas was a loyal servant to our family. He spent the whole of his short life at Chadshunt Hall. The proof of his loyalty is that he volunteered unhesitatingly to join the Chadshunt troop to fight for the King. In doing so he pledged his own life, a life which has been tragically cut short. I honour his sacrifice, which is the same as if he had made it on the field of battle. He is the first of our troop to die for the King. I pray that he will be the last, but if he is not, then others who follow him to a soldier's grave will not surpass his death in honour. I have resolved to have a footstone placed at the grave. Though Nicholas's life was humble, I feel it is fitting that in the circumstances of his death, he has a memorial, not an unmarked grave."

We filed silently from the graveside. I saw Father turn to Nicholas's father, attempting to speak to him. The grief stricken man shook Father's hand from his shoulder and turned his back, gently leading his sobbing wife. Father looked indignant at this rejection. I saw Mother whisper to him.

"Yes, yes very well, I suppose so. I thought he would take comfort from the notion of a stone memorial." Father snapped and taking Mother's arm in his, he swept towards the Hall.

The following day, I accompanied Mother to the tumbledown cottage Nicholas's family lived in on one of our tenant's farms. She carried a carefully chosen basket of food, while I had a parcel under my arm containing a faded cloak of dark blue wool which I had intended for one of our servants. Now it was for Nicholas's mother. To our surprise, there was no answer to our cautious knock at the door. A noise above my head caught my attention. I glanced up to see a loose shutter banging in the wind. There were usually one or two hens scratching around, but today there were no signs of life. Mother lifted the latch. Slowly, we entered the dark interior, its walls blackened by the soot and smoke of fires over many years. It was deserted. Looking more closely, in the dim light I saw that while the small table and two stools were still there, the shelves had been emptied. Candlesticks, plates and cups were all gone. Scattered grains of wheat lay on the floor but there were no other victuals, and the iron pot which usually hung from a hook over the fire was missing.

I peered around outside while Mother finished her survey of the two room cottage. It did not take long. The Oddingtons were gone. Mother's face was creased with concern and I saw a tear come to her eye.

"Where will they go, Bess? I had thought to ask Marjorie if she would like us to give a place at the Hall to young Jeny now Nicholas is gone. Janie can make use of another pair of hands in the kitchens. I will send to Goodman Lamb, the tenant of the farm, for news. Perhaps he will know where they are gone to."

Lamb was unaware that his farm labourer and family had disappeared. Where the little family had fled to in their sorrow remained a mystery.

ꟹ

16 October 1642

The eve of the troop's departure will always remain vivid in my memory. Now that the two armies had gathered in strength, we all expected a major engagement to take place shortly. Father believed one good battle might settle matters. He had heard that the King was planning to march on London.

Father made no speeches that day; and there were no events of note. Yet the whole house hummed with tension and anticipation. In truth, it was nought but a day of waiting, the final waiting. It was also the last day of innocence. Despite the death of Nicholas, my brothers and I continued to think of war as an exciting adventure. It is that I believe which makes me remember it so clearly. Small things linger in my memory, the excited hug Harry gave me when I handed him the red sash with tassels I had made, Will frowning as he slid his gleaming sword out of the scabbard before replacing it with a satisfied nod, Father strolling slowly around the gardens, now strewn with autumn leaves, his arm around Mother.

The months of uncertainty, the weeks of preparation, were over. Minor skirmishes around the country had been followed by a more significant engagement at Powick Bridge outside Worcester. More than a thousand troops of the rebel commander, the Earl of Essex had been routed by the cavalry of the King's nephew, Prince Rupert. We had received word that the King's army had gathered at Shrewsbury and was on the march south towards London. My father's troop, with Captain Blake's troop and other Royalists from our corner of Warwickshire, was to set off along the Fosseway in search of the main army, which we had been informed was approaching Coventry. My brothers, in high spirits and too excited to settle to any proper occupation, laughed and joked, disappearing to check and recheck their already gleaming weapons, armour and saddlery.

Rafe's troop of horse was quartered not far away in Butlers Marston. He rode over to spend the last afternoon and night with us. I hurried to meet him as I saw him dismount, taking a small and wriggling bundle from his servant who was riding behind him with the packhorse.

"Rafe," I called, "How wonderful, is that puppy for me?"

Rafe smiled brilliantly, "In truth he may grow a little large for a lady's lap dog. He is a French breed of hunting dog. Will may wish to take him out with him."

My voice trembled, "Was he for Will then?"

Rafe's eyes softened.

"Indeed not, Bess. I hope he will be your daily companion while your brothers and I are away with the army."

His words were hurried, but they were the words I wanted to hear. The next minute the small excited orange and white bundle was running around my ankles. I promptly tripped over it and came down on the cobbles with a bump. Laughing blue eyes met mine as Rafe helped me to my feet.

"Hector," he said to the puppy with a small bow, "Meet Mistress Elisabeth Lucie. I daresay she will allow you to call her Bess."

He kissed my hand lightly and then stepped back. He looked as if he was about to say something else. I waited expectantly.

"I know Hector is in good hands with you." I had hoped for more.

"Take this," I thrust into his hand my pale green linen handkerchief, trimmed with lace and my initials EL. He would carry his lady's token as a talisman into battle.

"You will always be my champion." I curtseyed dramatically.

"My Lady," he grinned. Casually, he tucked the small piece of pale green linen trimmed with lace and the initials EL into a pocket of his breeches. I was disappointed. I had hoped he would keep it next to his heart. Well no matter, he had my handkerchief.

The next morning, I rose early to watch the Chadshunt troop ride away. Harry and Rafe were to join their own companies in nearby Kineton. The horses were caught up in the excitement.

"Wretched beast, stand still!" Harry was trying to tighten the girth on his saddle while his mount pranced around him in circles. I hurried towards him.

"Harry, let me tie your sash properly." Sighing, Harry obediently stood motionless, or as motionless as his excited horse would permit, while I unwrapped the red silk sash I had made for him from about his waist and began again. Harry fumed and fretted, but at last I had tied the scarf to my satisfaction, a large bow in the middle of his back. I turned my attention to Will.

"Bess, no more I pray you, I will do very well." Will twitched at his own red sash and set his chin stubbornly. My brothers were both anxious to be off, as if embarking on a hunting or hawking expedition, Mother flitting nervously between them. Rafe was laughing carelessly and bantering with the other men. I hovered, waiting for a farewell from him, a public acknowledgement of our relationship. The older men were silent, grim faced, apart from quietly offering advice and assistance to the younger ones. One or two of them, like Oliver White, had fought in the European wars.

Now the men were mounting their horses and Will, as Lieutenant, was marshalling them into a column for the march, under the eagle eye of Oliver White. The two sturdy mules were hitched to the baggage cart, our servant Archie seated himself on the driving seat and the two women clambered up beside him, one of them sniffing and dabbing at her eyes with her apron.

Father appeared from the house. I had seen him earlier, walking alone in the gardens, head bowed in contemplation or prayer, both hands behind his back. Now he was in earnest conversation with our steward. In dress and bearing he resembled a true soldier. He wore a smart coat of deep russet lined with white silk and matching breeches over a doublet of a deeper red. He was carrying the new buff coat and the smart red sash which proclaimed his status as an officer, a Captain of Horse, and his allegiance to the King. I watched proudly as he donned the coat, his page Jack hooking him into it and then tying the sash over it in a large and graceful knot at his back. Father was not wearing his helmet at present but a broad brimmed hat. His rapier hung at his side. Although he was in his forty sixth year he was straight backed and vigorous. His hair remained dark for the most part and if his grey eyes did not see as far as when he was a young man, they made up for it in keenness of insight. He embraced my mother. She kissed him and clung to him. After a moment, she released her hold with obvious effort. and stepped back.

"Henry, my love, be wary. Have a care for yourself and our sons. I rely on your wisdom as well as on your courage."

"And as I rely on your fortitude, Anne. I know I leave Bess and the estate in safety with you." He came across and put a hand on my head. "You must help your mother, Bess and do her bidding now. God willing, we will all return in health and with His Majesty secure, before many weeks have passed."

Father mounted, walked his horse to the head of the troop and signalled. James the trumpeter blew the command for the march. Followed by the baggage cart, the troop trotted sedately out of the courtyard and down the lane. Rafe was near the back of the column. I longed to call out to him. Was he really leaving without bidding me farewell? The next moment, he broke ranks and trotted back towards me. He dismounted and bowed low over my hand. Then he leapt back into the saddle, cried,

"Until we meet again," and cantered off to join the rest, waving his hat. I clutched the puppy so tightly he squealed in protest. I watched until the troop was out of sight and their hoof beats were no longer audible. A little later, it began to pour with rain. I saw Mother glance anxiously at the sky. The roads would turn to mud. I hoped the troop would not be obliged to camp in the open that night.

I spoke and ate little during dinner, slipping pieces of meat off my plate under the table to Hector so that it would appear I was eating. He was more interested in chewing my shoe, settling contentedly gnawing on the buckle. My mother too was quieter than usual, although she tried to keep up a somewhat forced flow of conversation. Finally she gave up the effort to interest me in talking about the weather, the garden or even how I could train my new puppy.

"Try not to fret about Will and Harry too much," she murmured. I started, realising that in my dreams about a future with Rafe, I had given no thought to the wellbeing of my own family. I flushed with shame. We were sitting alone in the family dining room. She rose from her seat and walked around the table to me. We hugged each other, finding support in our shared fears.

ଓ

Sunday 23 October 1642

On Sunday morning my mother and I, along with all those remaining on our estate, attended our usual service at All Saints parish church. Our men had been gone nearly a week. Were they many miles away now on the road to London with the King's army? We had no way of knowing. The Reverend Hunter's voice quavered as he read from Ecclesiastes "To everything there is a season" when he reached the words, "A time for war and a time for peace". We took communion and returned home to a subdued dinner of soup, beef and fowl, a simpler meal than usual. With our men away and possibly fighting, it did not seem right to dine in our usual Sabbath style. I thought of the previous week when we had all gathered in the Great Hall for Sunday dinner. Father had carved a saddle of venison. There had been capons, tarts and jellies. The room had been noisy with conversation and my brothers' laughter.

Around two o'clock, we were startled by the sound of distant booms.

"Thunder?" suggested Mother nervously.

"I don't know, Mother. It is from the direction of Kineton." We listened. The distant crashes continued. A few minutes later, the steward entered.

"My Lady, do you hear those explosions?"

"Yes John, thank you," Mother replied with a brittle smile.

"I believe a battle is taking place, My Lady."

John stood for a tense moment regarding my mother.

"Thank you, John." He bowed and left the room. Mother picked up her embroidery needle again. Her hands shook and I watched as she pricked her finger instead of the linen cloth with its intricate design of flowers and birds. A drop of blood fell on the cloth staining crimson the flower she was working. She pressed her lips together.

"I believe I will rest a little in my chamber, Bess. I have a slight headache."

I went over to my harpsichord, but for once the cool feel of the keys did not calm me, and I broke off midway through a piece.

ઌ

Edgehill, early morning Sunday 23 October 1642

From his position high on Edgehill, Rafe watched the breaking dawn. In the growing light, Rafe could see empty fields stretching before him, far down below. At first all was quiet except for the Royalists' horses, blowing and snorting, the quiet talk of their riders. Rafe's stomach lurched with excitement with thoughts of the coming battle. News had arrived the night before that the Earl of Essex's army was unexpectedly close by. The quartermasters of the opposing armies had blundered into each other whilst seeking billets for their men. Rafe had slept in a barn, tumbled in the straw with his troop. Now the Royalist cavalry were already drawn up on the high ground, while the infantry were being marched in from their billets in the surrounding villages.

"Here, Lieutenant, come and break your fast."

A grinning trooper approached him, pulling loaves of bread from a bag dusty with flour, and throwing them to his fellows. Rafe grabbed a loaf and started eating the warm bread hungrily.

"By all that's holy, Jennings, where did you come by this?"

The stout trooper smiled wolfishly. "Radway, Sir, fresh from the ovens of the village baker. I reminded him of his loyalty to the King and he was content." He fingered the hilt of his sword meaningfully.

Chewing on a second loaf, Rafe loosened Mercury's girth. He checked for the third time that both his pistols were loaded and were in the holsters on his saddle. Mercury was impatient. Rafe led him up and down, finding the repetitive action calmed his own pounding heart. Gradually, the sound of marching feet became audible. Companies of foot began to appear behind him. Sergeants were snapping orders as they martialled the men into their divisions.

"Sir, where are the enemy?" Rafe pointed to the empty fields below as his captain approached.

"Still abed, Lieutenant for all I know. We must wait for them to honour us with their presence."

The morning wore on. Rafe grew hungry once more. His servant was at the rear with the baggage train, so he could not summon him. He found an apple in his pockets with a stale loaf and devoured them, giving Mercury the apple core as a tidbit. There was a buzz of excitement. Looking ahead, Rafe discerned the far-off glint of weapons and armour. So distant they could have been pieces on a chessboard, Rafe saw the forces of the enemy streaming onto the fields below the ridge. As he watched, the antlike columns assumed the shapes of men and horses. Regiments were taking their places, the patterns changing as they moved from marching order into battle formation. The enemy had come in force and were ready to fight. The rattle of drums, blaring of trumpets, the rumble of wagons and the pungent odours of thousands of men and horses drifted faintly towards him.

Rafe picked some wisps of straw off his travel stained coat. Drawing his sword he practiced a few strokes, swinging it at an imaginary foe.

"Lieutenant Beauchamp," came his captain's dry voice from behind him, "You might be better employed checking your men are ready. We do not require a further display of your swordsmanship."

Rafe opened his mouth to reply but then saw one of the senior officers come storming angrily out of the commanders' tent.

"Captain, who is that?"

"Lord Lindsey, our field commander. He has been meeting with His Majesty and the commanders. That does not auger well."

The captain hurried away in search of news. Within minutes rumours were circulating that Lord Lindsey had quarrelled bitterly with the King's nephew Prince Rupert. The Earl had resigned as Lord-General and would now lead only his own regiment that day. For the first time it occurred to Rafe that the battle could end in defeat instead of victory. Yet, as he gazed along the high ridge, regiment after regiment of horse, he felt heartened.

How could a rebel army of butchers' boys, commanded by renegade Members of Parliament and traitorous Lords, succeed against the flower of the aristocracy of England and their loyal men? The regiment's chaplain arrived to lead the troops in prayer. Kneeling with the other men, head uncovered, Rafe joined in the prayers more fervently than he was wont to do. The chaplain ended by reminding them that God was on their side. Cries of "God save the King" filled the air.

&

Rafe trotted along with the troop. They were finally on the march. The creak of leather and the jingle of the horses' bits and their riders' spurs was a constant accompaniment to his thoughts.

His mind raced back and forth between the coming battle and the events of recent months. Bess's face flitted across his swirling thoughts. He remembered the afternoon in the stable when he had impulsively kissed her. Had she been a maid servant, he would assuredly have done more. She was ripe for tumbling, and he envied the man who would be the first to bed her. As for him, he did not wish to lose Will's friendship by seducing his sister. He chuckled to himself. Will was a fine one to begrudge a gentleman taking his pleasure. Rafe remembered their first year at Oxford University. He and Will had been sharing rooms and he had surprised Will more than once with that sweet little wench with the full mouth and the long dark eyelashes. She had disappeared suddenly from the kitchens the following spring. Rafe was quite sure she had been carrying Will's bastard under her apron by that time. But he supposed it was natural for Will to feel differently about his sister, who was a lady…

A sharp command ahead to halt brought him abruptly back to the present. There was a flurry of men dismounting and emptying their bladders. The man in front of Rafe turned his head and vomited noisily on the ground. A few minutes later, Rafe's captain received the command to proceed. The cavalry were to advance down the steep hill and provide a screen for the infantry to descend behind them. The rebel army was awaiting them.

Rafe was disappointed. His regiment, Sir John Byron's Regiment of Horse, were to be in the second line, held in reserve. Mercury was excited and Rafe longed to give him his head. With difficulty, he remained in position at the back of the troop. Ahead he saw a great wave of Royalist horse charge. They were the front line regiments under Prince Rupert's command. In the distance, the waiting rebel horse turned and fled as Rupert's brigade advanced on them at a gallop. The impatient Mercury reared and

Rafe struggled to bring him under control. How much longer? He heard the sound he had been longing for. The trumpeter of his own troop was sounding the advance. The ranks of cavalry walked forward, then broke into a trot. Trembling with excitement, Rafe drew his sword. His eyes were on his captain, holding his sword high above his head. "For God and King Charles!" The captain's sword flashed down. The trumpeter sounded the charge.

5

Edgehill, Sunday 23 October 1642

THE PARLIAMENTARY HORSE were scattering into small groups as they fled the battlefield. Most of the Royalist horse was in hot pursuit, fanning out to overtake and cut them off. Rafe was yelling in his exhilaration as he galloped along. His last headlong charge had carried him away from the rest of his troop. He lowered his sword. The blade was smeared with blood from tip to hilt. His buff coat and breeches too were daubed with dark brown stains. He had little memory of those he had fought.

Rafe pulled the sweating Mercury to a stop and looked around. He was by himself, but the flow of battle had passed on for the moment and there was nothing beside him but a saker. The piece of ordnance had been abandoned by its gun crew. He felt surprisingly hot in his buff coat. Beneath his helmet, his hair was plastered to his head with sweat. He pulled out Bess's handkerchief and wiped his sword blade clean as best he could with the small piece of lace and linen. Then he sheathed the sword and raised his arms to remove his helmet. There was a flash and a sharp crack from beneath the gun…

Holding his discharged musket, the weathered, middle aged dragoon crawled out from underneath the saker in time to see the enemy officer slowly topple sideways off his horse, still clutching a small kerchief in his hand. He had taken refuge beneath the gun after a fierce cavalry charge had scattered his comrades. Hidden from sight he had seized this opportunity, aiming and firing directly up under the officer's left arm as he left himself vulnerable. He caught the bridle of the startled horse and looped the reins over the gun. The horse was a handsome stallion, far surpassing the cheap horse he had as a dragoon. The holsters on the ornate saddle held a fine pair of pistols, embossed with silver. The dragoon drew one from its holster and whistled softly. Kneeling by the fallen officer, he searched him briefly, removing his sword, better quality than his own army issued tuck, and the expensive leather purse. He smiled at it's weight, full of coin. He glanced at the kerchief. It was a delicate one, but already blood stained, and he decided not to take it. He carefully reloaded his musket before mounting and trotting slowly away in search of the remnants of his troop. He hummed a little tune as he rode.

Rafe lay where he had fallen, the blood from the deep wound soaking through his buff coat and into the trampled earth. The wind strengthened, blowing swirling russet leaves into his hair, but he did not feel them.

ᔓ

Late in the afternoon, Harry's Major sighted three field guns lying abandoned by the Parliament troops in their haste to withdraw. "Captain Blake, take command of those pieces and find a means of retrieving them."

"Yes, Sir." Giles Blake peered through eyes reddened from the smoke and wiped his grimy face. His eyes fell on Harry.

"Lieutenant Lucie, go swiftly. We need men, horses and ropes to move those guns. Five horses for each gun. Find out your father's troop and see if they can assist us."

"Yes, Captain," Harry wheeled his weary horse and urged it into a canter past the abandoned ordnance. His was one of only a few troops of horse which had not galloped off to Kineton pursuing the rebel horse. He pressed on in the direction where he had last seen Will. The centre of the field was now filled with heaving groups of infantry wielding pikes, engaged in a desperate struggle. Musket fire had become sporadic as musketeers, having discharged their weapons, used the butt ends of their muskets as clubs. Nevertheless, Harry was wary of stray bullets and feared to approach them too closely. The yells of the pikemen filled his ears, while the ground was strewn with wounded and dying soldiers and horses, adding their cries to the cacophony.

Harry's horse snorted and shied at the sight of another horse struggling to rise from the ground. It was screaming. One of its back legs had been blown off. Harry turned his eyes from the sight and tried to close his ears to the groans and pleas of wounded men. A soldier staggered across his path, blood streaming from his face, an ear dangling by a thread of flesh. Harry swallowed hard and turned his horse sharply aside. After a few minutes he was uncertain as to where he was. Dense black smoke from gunfire drifting towards him made it difficult to see more than a few paces. There were no longer muddy and trampled ploughed furrows under his horse's hooves, so he was nearing an edge of the battlefield, but which edge? If only the smoke would clear. He breathed in a lungful of sulphurous grit and coughed. He could hear the steady beat of drums close by as more infantry advanced. He slowed, uncertain, hearing voices. "Essex hasn't lost the battle yet, boys," he caught. He had blundered into the midst of Parliament's forces. Could he withdraw without being seen? He pulled his horse up short and tried to turn away quietly, hoping that in the drifting smoke, noise and confusion he would be unnoticed.

At that moment, a gust of wind rent the curtain of smoke. Harry found himself staring down at a musketeer, an orange ribbon in his hat, only a few paces away. The man gaped at him, but then marked the red sash and raised his musket to his shoulder. Harry's pistols were empty, as was his carbine. He raised his sword. Could he fight his way out? There were enemy musketeers all around him. It was already too late. The musket was pointing at his heart and he heard a click. His mouth was dry.

"Quarter," he gasped, his voice cracking. He threw the empty pistols on the ground.

"Papist lover's come to us, lads. Let's 'ave a bit of fun before we shoot 'im.'

Two musketeers dragged Harry from his horse. The one who had spoken, a squat man with a scarred and blackened face and dirty straw coloured hair, grinned and casually reversed his musket. The butt end of the heavy weapon hit Harry between the shoulder blades. Crying out, he fell to his knees. His sword was tied to his right wrist and it banged against his thigh as he fell. One of the soldiers tugged at it unsuccessfully.

"Cut 'is 'and off," the man who had hit him howled.

"Give him quarter, Corporal. Then you may treat him gently, as you are wont to do.'

The familiar aristocratic voice had a hint of laughter in it. With a shock, Harry raised his eyes to see the haughty face and grey hair of Archibald Chatterton, a friend of his uncle's, towering over him as he knelt in the mud.

"Your sword, Master Lucie.'

Fumbling, Harry unknotted his sword from his wrist and handed it over.

"I am your prisoner, Sir," he muttered.

"What do you want done with 'im, Major?'

"He is probably carrying some intelligence. Find it. He can join the other prisoners when you are finished with him. Easy pickings for you, Corporal." His voice hardened. "Master Lucie, as an officer, you have some value to us, but try to run and you will be shot. I do not make idle threats.'

And without a further glance, Major Chatterton, who had known him since he was a child, turned on his heel.

The musketeers set upon Harry greedily, tearing off his gold embroidered leather baldric, his carbine belt, armour and buff coat, taking his purse, his gloves, his gold ring. They left him only his riding cloak. Harry remained on his knees while they rifled through his pockets and checked the lining of his doublet and breeches for anything concealed. When they were done with searching him, the corporal pushed Harry face down in the mud and placed a knee in his back while he bound his hands behind him. He hauled Harry to his feet.

"Where's the message then?'

Harry stared at him. The man slapped his face.

"I said where's the message, whoreson?'

"No m message," Harry stammered. This time the man punched him in the belly.

"Enough time wasted on this man, Wilks,' snapped another officer. "You heard the Major, place him with the other prisoners.'

Harry was relieved to join a group of captive Royalist officers, all of whom were strangers to him. Guarded by a few watchful musketeers, they were sitting or standing quietly, clustered together, their hands bound. One of the Royalists, an officer no older than Harry, was sitting on the ground, blood dripping from a scarf around his arm. His face was white beneath the coating of grime, sweat glistening on his brow. The other men appeared unharmed, but all were bareheaded. Their helmets had been stripped along with their armour. Only their torn and muddied clothing and bruised faces hinted at their own struggles as they were captured.

The wind grew stronger and the temperature fell. Harry shivered. His belly and his back ached from the blows. He realised he desperately needed to relieve himself. He edged his way to the side of the group.

"Stand and go no further."

A musketeer levelled his weapon at him, the lighted match glowing in his hand.

"I need to piss. Would you untie me?'

Grinning, the man lowered his musket.

"Do you take me for a simpleton? Piss in your breeches. You will not be the first." He wrinkled his nose.

Darkness was falling and it had grown even colder. An officer of dragoons strode towards the prisoners, looking harassed.

"You are being taken to Warwick Castle. See to it none of them try to run, Sergeant." He jerked his head at a stout man of middle age. Driven forward by the soldiers, the prisoners shuffled towards the picket lines of horses.

"Get on," a trooper grunted. He assisted Harry as he awkwardly mounted the horse, unbalanced by his bound hands. Then he gathered the reins in his left hand and swung himself into the saddle behind his prisoner. Surrounded by a small escort of dragoons, the little cavalcade with its double loaded horses moved off at a trot towards Warwick.

Harry was too numb with shock to consider escaping. In the circumstances, it would have been well nigh impossible. Might they encounter an outlying party of Rupert's cavalry? But the dark road stretched empty ahead of them. Once or twice they passed fresh companies of Parliamentary infantry marching steadily towards the battle field. Of the Royalist cavalry, and possible rescue, he saw nothing.

Warwick lay silent under the looming presence of its castle. Harry had no notion of the time, but thought it must be late at night. Riding across a drawbridge and under the portcullis of the barbican, over yet another drawbridge to the gatehouse and under a second portcullis, they arrived in an extensive courtyard. The Royalists were helped to dismount and had their hands untied. Purple-coated soldiers herded them towards one of the towers, through a door, down a short flight of stairs and into what appeared by the light of the soldiers' flickering torches to be a large dungeon. The door was locked behind them, leaving them in darkness. Too tired to attempt any conversation with the other prisoners, Harry rubbed at his chafed wrists, rolled himself in his cloak, lay down on the scant covering of rushes and tried to sleep. His mind however refused to let him rest. He relived the events of the day, the bungled foray which had led to his capture. An ignominious end to his hopes for distinguishing himself in the field and bringing honour to his family. What must his father be thinking by now? Would he know how and why Harry had disappeared? Would he realise he was a prisoner or would he be searching the battlefield among the dead? Furthermore, Harry had no idea what would happen to him now. Would he be released? Rescued? Unlikely in the middle of the Parliamentary garrison. Ransomed by his family? He knew his father would do anything to get him back safely. There were no answers to his questions and by degrees he drifted off to sleep, in spite of the cold seeping through the rushes from the stone floor, and occasional groans from the officer with the wounded arm.

∽

Chadshunt Hall, Sunday 23 October 1642

It was growing dark, and the candles were already lit, when we heard two horses come slowly up the lane. Thomas opened the door. David Tucker, one of our tenant farmers, assisted another man, a stranger to us, up the steps. Still wearing the red sash marking them as the King's soldiers, both were dusty and hatless, and there was blood staining the sash of the other soldier a deeper crimson.

White-faced, my mother pressed her lips together. She clapped her hands for warm water and herself wiped the blood from the soldier's face as he lay on a settle in the family sitting room. Mary hastily brought a supply of cloths from the kitchen. We stared at each other. Mother's own face mirrored my shocking realisation that this was real, that after months of politics, angry words and posturing between the King and Parliament, we were now at war. Were we prepared? No – in spite of seeing my family and my lover riding off with weapons and armour to join the King's army, as I had watched them go I had only felt the excitement of the men and regret at being left behind. Now I truly felt the fear which is the lot of women everywhere when their men leave for war.

As the light finally faded from the western sky, we awaited further news. There had been a great battle at the bottom of Edgehill, between Radway and Kineton. The King himself had addressed the troops before the battle and had been loudly cheered.

"My lady, surely our army must have triumphed, God being on our side."

The farmer's pleasant face was blackened with soot, his eyes reddened. Glancing at me, his voice dropped.

"I fear there were a great many men killed or wounded, My Lady." Mother turned pale.

"Sir Henry?" She pleaded. "Have you any news of him? And my sons?"

"Don't you fear, My Lady," he said bracingly. "I saw Sir Henry leading a charge late in the afternoon, with Master Will close by. They were both unharmed."

My mother's composure returned a little at this hopeful information, although the man had left the field with his wounded companion while cavalry skirmishes were still in progress. That night I slept badly. I had curled my hair again against Rafe's return. Might I see him next morning? Would he be tired, grimy, smelling of sweat, his blonde hair tangled? There had been a great battle. Surely our men must return to rest and tell us of their adventures? Although nervous, I was excited too. I could not wholly share my mother's fears and instead was occupied with imagining how my family and Rafe might have distinguished themselves. I dreamed of Rafe performing some feat of valour, perhaps saving the life of one of the royal princes and being knighted by the King on the field.

ഗ

Warwick Castle, Monday 24 October 1642

The door to the dungeon swung open. The prisoners, huddled together for warmth like beasts, blinked in the light. A guard stood there, silhouetted against the grey light of day filtering down the stairs.

"On your feet and follow me."

Shivering with cold, the dreary and bedraggled procession stumbled after him up the stone steps. They were marched outside into an immense courtyard. It was early morning. Around the sides, a company of purple coated soldiers were drawn up, armed with pikes and muskets. On the ramparts above, more soldiers stood watch. Other prisoners were already in the courtyard, huddled in a small group. One man, sitting alone on the ground, was clutching his ankle in pain. A soberly dressed clerk moved between the prisoners, approaching each of them in turn. "Name and rank?" he asked Harry. "H Henry L Lucie – L lieutenant," gasped Harry flushing. His stammer, slight when he was relaxed or at home, always worsened at times of tension. The clerk recorded Harry's name and moved on. Shortly they were joined by an orange-sashed officer who introduced himself as Major John Bridges, Governor of the castle.

"You are prisoners of the Parliament and will be held at its pleasure until your fate is determined.'

"You are traitors all," one of the officers shouted.

"Please restrain yourself, Lord Lindsey. I imagine your father would prefer you survived him by more than a few hours. Guards, take him back to Caesar's Tower.

Be silent.'

The ripple of shock among the prisoners had led to a buzz of conversation. The King's former Lord General was dead and his son captured.

"If any of you wish to forswear your mistaken allegiance and fight for Parliament instead, you will be released to join our forces. Step forward if you wish to do so." Nobody moved.

"You have fought gallantly," continued the Governor, "is there no man who wishes to accept my offer?"

The officer sitting on the ground struggled unsuccessfully to rise to his feet. Seeing him move, the Governor nodded curtly at two of the guards who went to assist. The Governor looked hopefully at the officer, now standing shakily between the two men. The back of his cloak was covered in mud and his breeches ripped as if he had been dragged along the ground.

"And you, Sir?"

"I'll hang first." There was a pronounced Welsh lilt to his voice.

"You may yet receive that opportunity," snapped the disappointed Governor. The effort of standing had drained the Welshman's face of colour and he dropped to his knees to the amusement of the two soldiers holding his arms. They backed away, laughing.

The Governor turned once more to the assembled prisoners.

"Gentlemen, you were all given mercy yesterday by the Parliament. Conform to the rules and you will be well treated in accordance with your station. Your families will be allowed to furnish you with comforts. But if you act foolishly, or try to escape, this is what you must expect."

He made a signal. A few moments later, two soldiers emerged from one of the towers, dragging a prisoner. Clad only in torn shirt and muddied breeches, he was shivering with cold or fright. He looked to Harry to be no more than 16 or 17. He was tall and lanky, his youthful face speckled with pimples beneath the dirt. The soldiers bound his hands and stood him against a stretch of blank wall. Six musketeers formed a rank in front of him. As their purpose became clear, the other prisoners murmured angrily and surged forward. Major Bridges gave a sharp command and the purple coated soldiers around the walls raised their muskets.

"Stand back, gentlemen, or every one of you will die here and now." He nodded at the officer in charge of the firing squad.

"Make ready."

The six musketeers blew on their lighted match and touched it to the priming pans.

"Present." The muskets were raised.

"Give fire."

Six muskets exploded. The front of the officer's shirt bloomed with blood and he slumped to the ground, blank eyes staring at the grey sky.

"Take them away."

The soldiers began herding the stunned prisoners past the dead officer and towards two of the towers. Harry was horrified. He had not considered the possibility of execution. While he had faced possible death on the battlefield with equanimity, the thought of being hanged or shot in cold blood filled him with dread.

ᔕ

Chadshunt Hall, Monday 24 October 1642

I rose from my bed before Peggy was awake. I knelt on the deep window seat, breathed on the glass and drew a heart with an intertwined R and E. What should I wear for Rafe's return, should I wear the gown I had been wearing the day he arrived? Would he be carrying the handkerchief I had given him? I imagined it, warm from contact with his body, maybe tucked under his shirt against his heart.

After helping me dress, Peggy paused, seeing the heart on the window.

"What is it, Peggy?" I prompted.

"Nothing, Miss Bess," she left the room. I went downstairs where I was soon joined by my mother. We tried to break our fast, but the bread, although still warm from our bakehouse and accompanied by fresh cheese from our dairy, stuck in my throat. I ate little in my nervous excitement. I started at every sound, thinking it was returning horses.

The wounded man had passed a restless night and was feverish. My mother had some experience of treating injuries from farming and riding accidents, but dealing with a wound caused by a sword was unfamiliar. She had cleaned the wound and dressed it as best she could, giving the servants instructions on how to care for him during the night. He was lying on a cot now. The sight of him prompted my mother into action.

"Bess," she said, "Instruct Peggy and Mary to go through the linen closet. Find some of the older linen and sheets which we can use for dressing wounds. God knows if we will have more poor men like this and we should be prepared."

The need for activity gave me something else to think about. Peggy, Mary and I were soon engaged in tearing linen into strips for bandages, while my mother scoured her still room and the pantry for herbs which might be of most use as pain killers and to treat fever.

So successful a distraction was this that in the end I did not hear the more regular beat of the hooves from a larger number of horses until they were at the door. It was some time in the afternoon. As Thomas opened the front doors, my normally dignified father burst past him without a word. Will was close on his heels. Their grimy faces were weary, their boots mud splattered, the gold braid on their coats ripped, the leather liberally splattered with what I feared was blood. Will's fair hair was blackened with soot, but they were both unhurt.

"Thank God," my mother breathed as, summoned by my cries, she came hastily from the pantry at the back of the house.

"My love, what is the matter? Are you well?"

Father was turning his head anxiously in all directions.

"Is Harry here?" My mother shook her head dumbly.

"What has happened?" she gasped. My father had entered the Great Hall and was pacing its length, at one moment collapsing onto a bench as if exhausted, the next springing impatiently to his feet again. His lips framed the single word "missing", but he seemed unable to speak further. Mother sank wordlessly onto a chair, wringing her hands mechanically.

To Will, then, fell the unhappy office of telling what little he remembered. Of the ebb and flow of the great and terrible battle, he had only confused impressions. It had been a series of separate engagements like the waves of the sea. As to who was the victor, he knew not. He could only answer for those incidents clear in his memory. The all-important sightings of Harry were too few, although Will ran both hands repeatedly through his hair as if by that action he might unleash some recollection hitherto overlooked.

"Captain Blake's company was close by at first. I glimpsed Harry at the moment the trumpeters blew the advance. He grinned and saluted me with his sword. Our two companies charged the rebels side by side. In the melee I lost sight of Harry, my care being for the men I commanded. Our troop suffered few casualties, but towards the end, James our huntsman was mortally wounded. I carried him myself from the field, but nothing could be done for him. I remained with him in a nearby cottage until he died. Mourning James, it was some time before we missed Harry, the troops having become somewhat dispersed. I assumed he was with his troop, as did Father. Then, as evening wore on, Captain Blake found me out. He had seen nothing of Harry for some hours and was concerned. He had sent him to seek our troop for aid in hauling abandoned cannon during the battle and Harry had not returned. I told him that Harry had never arrived. We searched immediately among the wounded. They were being cared for in nearby cottages. Harry was not there.

It was too dark by then for us to search among the dead on the field. We must have hope, for no man saw him fall. We resumed our search this morning, but in vain."

"Then he must live?" my voice trembled. "There cannot be so many dead soldiers but you would have found him?"

I realised I was tugging at Will's sleeve. He grasped my desperate hand.

"I pray he does Bess, but truly there were a great many dead from the two armies, and divers had already been interred this morning. Well, no more of that. We must trust in God's mercy."

Father continued pacing the hall. He had paid little attention to Will's account.

"I fear he has been captured. That is the most likely possibility. I will ride to Warwick Castle and ask to see the Governor of the garrison. It is the obvious place for the rebels to have taken their prisoners."

"Father," Will interrupted, "I will visit James's wife Tess. I will give her what comfort I may."

Father looked at Will, his face sad.

"Yes Will, go at once. I am so distracted with thoughts of my son I forget the family who have lost a husband and father. The rest of the Chadshunt troop?"

"Father, those few men who returned with us have already been stood down. They are returning to their homes. Most of our men have joined Giles Blake's troop and remained with the army."

Father nodded bleakly.

"I do not know if we will see them again at Chadshunt."

It was approaching suppertime, although we had little appetite. My mother with some difficulty persuaded my father to rest and resume his search the next day. Tired and drawn he consented after some argument, but I suspect he slept little. The next day I heard him ride out at dawn, accompanied only by two of his men. None but James had died. I tried to take comfort in that.

∽

Chadshunt Hall, 26 October 1642

Mother and I were sitting, she sewing mechanically and I trying to gather comfort from my prayer book, when we heard the clatter of hooves in the courtyard. We ran outside, Will not far behind us. It was Father and his two men. My mother's hand went to her mouth, Harry was not with them. "What news of Harry?" I cried speeding ahead of her to my father's stirrup.

"Harry lives, but we must be brave. He is a prisoner in Warwick Castle and I have not yet been able to obtain his release or even to see him."

"God be praised," breathed my mother, sinking to her knees on the cobbles. Father dismounted heavily and raised her. She started to cry, whether with relief that Harry was alive, or with grief that he could not yet return, I could not say. We three went slowly into the house. My father sat in his favourite padded chair and relaxed a little in his familiar surroundings while his page pulled off his boots. He had seen the Governor of the castle, who had consulted his list of prisoners and confirmed that Harry was in his keeping. Stern faced, business like, he had ascertained for my father that his son was unharmed.

"But where does he sleep? What victuals do they give him?" were Mother's next anxious questions.

"They do not keep Harry in a dungeon and feed him upon bread and water my dear," Father said with grim humour. Mother's eyes widened further.

"He is lodged in the castle with other officers of the King's army who were taken with him," Father continued hastily. "He has meat and drink and no doubt a bed to sleep in. For all of which we are obliged to pay. I left a fat purse with the Governor to ensure Harry's comfort.

When I asked about arranging Harry's release, unfortunately the Governor told me he was not prepared to discuss the matter, having had no orders yet as to the disposal of prisoners. It appears Harry is in no immediate danger, and for that we must thank God."

My mother's initial relief that Harry was alive was succeeded by unreasonable anger with my father that he had not done more. She felt that had he been more persuasive with the Governor he would have prevailed. That he had shown both decision and courage in entering the headquarters of the enemy army weighed less and less as the afternoon wore on.

Will and I both urged her to be reasonable, but to little effect. Finally my father's patience with her wore thin.

"There is little more I can do, Anne," he snapped. "At present we are in the hands of Parliament."

Will took him aside.

"Father," he said hesitantly, "Is it possible Uncle Hugh might be able to intervene?" My father's face darkened at the mention of his brother. He left the room. It was growing dark and rain was beating against the windows, but I knew he would walk around the grounds, as was his habit when he needed quiet to think.

When he returned from his walk he was in a calmer frame of mind.

"You are in the right, my son,"

he said to Will, smiling regretfully.

"I must not let my pride and ire stand in the way of possibly freeing Harry. I will attempt to find and speak with Hugh. He may be able to do something. Whatever anger he may feel with me, God willing he will not extend that to his young nephew. Harry is no more than eighteen," he said with a catch in his voice.

The next day my father set off, this time in search of Essex's army, although he was unsure as to whether his brother was with them, or if he had returned to his estate in Sussex. Before he left he pressed my mother's hand.

"I will do everything I can to bring him back to you, my love. I swear to you. He is my son as well as yours and as dear to me."

I watched him ride wearily down the lane towards the gatehouse. I fancied the grey in his dark hair and the stoop in his shoulders had not been there before the battle and Harry's disappearance.

In all this time I had been wondering how Rafe did. Already in great fear for Harry, I tried to push to the back of my mind the thought that Rafe, too, might have been captured, wounded or killed. With no public knowledge of our relationship, I could not even express my hopes and fears. I murmured them into Hector's floppy ears. To Father, Mother and Will I said nothing. Only Peggy looked at me as if she would say something.

ജ

Chadshunt Hall, November 1642

The Royalist Army had taken Banbury Castle and was now marching on Oxford. Despite the disbanding of the Chadshunt troop, Will was anxious to rejoin the Prince of Wales Regiment of Horse, but Father had bade him look after my mother and me until he returned. Father had returned briefly from a fruitless search for my uncle with the forces of Parliament in Warwick, and was now on his way to London. We waited.

On a grey and chilly day in early November, I took Hector for a romp in the park. He rolled in the fallen leaves, and chased the few still drifting from the trees, barking. As the light faded and the wind strengthened, I tugged my cloak tighter around me and quickened my pace towards the house, tucking the tiring puppy under my arm.

Will had journeyed to Banbury to visit comrades in the castle's new Royalist garrison, composed of troops from his own regiment. After the brief excitement of being with the army he was chafing at the enforced inaction. Passing through the court yard, I saw two horses being led towards the stables. One I recognised as Will's, but the other, a bay mare, was unfamiliar. I was pleased my brother was returned, while his unknown companion might provide some added diversion for our quiet family evening.

I found Will in Father's study. Still wearing his riding cloak, he was warming his hands before the hearth while talking to a man in the buff coat, red sash and high riding boots of a cavalry officer. I smiled,

"You must be chilled from your journey, Will. Would you have me send for mulled wine to warm you?"

I waited for Will to introduce me to the visitor, a man of modest height with windswept hair and large brown eyes which were regarding me sombrely.

"Bess," started Will, "It is as well you are come. This is Cornet Robert Parker from Sir John Byron's regiment. He has some intelligence which touches you. Please sit down."

He guided me gently into a chair. "I'm so sorry". He held out a crumpled kerchief which I knew only too well – it was lace trimmed and embroidered with the letters EL. The pale green was liberally streaked and splattered with brown, with bloody stains. I started to reach for it.

6

Chadshunt Hall, November 1642

I RECOVERED MY senses shortly after in my bedchamber. Mother and Peggy were bending over me, Peggy waving smelling salts under my nose.

My mother was murmuring,

"Had no notion Bess had a fondness for Master Beauchamp. Do you think it was of long standing? He was Will's friend, I never thought of him in any other light."

Not wishing to hear more of her speculation I sat up abruptly.

"Where is he? I want to talk to him!" I cried.

"Who, my darling?" asked my mother anxiously.

"The officer who came with Will," I said impatiently.

"Are you sure you are feeling well enough?" she cautioned, but I was already swinging my feet to the floor.

A few minutes later I was lying on a daybed downstairs in the family sitting room. At Mother's insistence, I was sipping a glass of wine. Cornet Parker followed Will hesitantly into the room and perched on the edge of a stool next to me. I smiled at him weakly.

"Please," I begged, "Tell me about Rafe. I need to hear how he died."

Parker let out a deep breath. Briefly he told me how he had ridden with Rafe and the rest of Byron's cavalry in their fierce charge behind Prince Rupert's horse. He described the exhilaration of chasing the fleeing enemy.

"Rafe was laughing and waving his sword. We were galloping side by side. We engaged with a few troopers who had stood their ground. We scattered them too and then I fell behind the rest of our troop. When I lost sight of him, Rafe was still chasing the enemy. He had no fear at all. I discovered our troop in Kineton. Rafe was not with them. We reformed our ranks to return to the field but our mounts were blown, and we were proceeding no faster than a trot. There was a saker, abandoned by its gun crew. As I passed it I spied him, half hidden by the gun. Rafe was stretched upon the ground, lying on his side, Mistress. His horse was gone and his helmet lying beside him as though he had dropped it. At first I saw no wound. I began to turn him over and then I saw the blood. He had been shot under his arm. He was clutching this handkerchief. I kept it until I could find who it belonged to. I could see it had been a keepsake from a lady."

"How did he look?" I whispered. What I meant by that I know not, but Parker did his best to answer with tact.

"Very pale, Mistress, but otherwise as if in life. And yet a little like a statue resembles the living person. I touched his hand to remove the ker-chief. It was still warm. We covered him with a cloak."

"I am sure he was removed from the field with all due honour. Is that not so, Robert?" Will said firmly.

Parker stared at him.

"Due honour, yes," he agreed hurriedly. "He was interred the next day with many others slain in the battle."

"And prayers were said," Will prompted.

"As you say. Indeed yes, we all prayed."

"Bess", Will's voice was gentle, "Rafe is buried with other officers in Radway's churchyard. He lies in hallowed ground."

Parker nodded. "Do not fear, Mistress. Rafe did not go into the mass grave on the battlefield."

"Mass grave?" my voice was faint.

"And fully attired," Parker added. "We had no winding sheet, but I would not let them strip him."

Will cleared his throat. "Thank you, Robert. You are in need of rest and refreshment. My sister has the handkerchief." Hand on shoulder he steered the cornet rapidly through the door, leaving me alone.

I hardly understood what I had heard, so shocked and numbed with grief as I was. Yet somehow I retained the words Parker had spoken. Later, I grasped at them for comfort. I pictured Rafe's body borne off the field, carried shoulder high by his weeping comrades. And I had seen the golden metal effigy of Rafe's distant kinsman Richard Beauchamp, Earl of War-wick, in St Mary's Church in Warwick. I imagined Rafe like that, straight and still, frozen for ever in his golden youth, his parted hands reaching upwards towards Heaven.

The succeeding days were a blur. I think Mother would have been less worried had I wept and been visibly distraught. But it seemed I had no tears to shed. In their place I became listless. The whole world seemed blanketed in a soft grey cover which choked my emotions. It cut out the light and, through stifling feeling, stopped the hurting. I stared at the trays of food brought by Peggy or, lifting the spoon or knife mechanically, would drop it again, forgetting what I held. In desperation my frightened mother bade Peggy feed me, and so she did. Like a baby bird I opened my mouth mechanically and swallowed. It kept my body alive.

Peggy brought Hector to my room and threw a ball for him to divert me with his antics. But Hector just reminded me of Rafe, as if I needed further promptings, and finally she took him away, leaving me to my silent thoughts.

I preferred to be left alone, then I could close my eyes and relive those precious kisses in the stable. I saw him again as he waved his hat, calling "Until we meet again". I tormented myself by picturing the future we would never have, the house, his house, never beheld, but which I had hoped would be my future home. Once or twice, falling into an uneasy doze, I fancied I rode pillion behind Rafe into a courtyard on a golden afternoon. In the dream, the courtyard was that of his father's house, and a group of blurred figures stood waiting to greet us.

One night, I found myself upon the battlefield. Rafe was stretched out at my feet. I thought he slept but then, like Cornet Parker, I gently rolled him over. Blood was trickling from under his arm. At first it was a stream, but as I watched it welled like a fountain and then gushed down his side, pooling around my feet and soaking my skirts. Now I was standing by, as Will and Robert and other faceless men lifted Rafe on their shoulders. I made ready to follow them. As I gazed at Rafe, he opened sightless blue eyes and reached out his hand to me. I woke screaming and Mother, now my nightly bed fellow, hushed me and smoothed my hair.

My father continued away from home in his attempts to secure Harry's release, but we received little news. I am ashamed to say that I only thought occasionally of Harry. When I did it was with bitter tears, not only for his enforced absence and how he might be suffering, but for my selfishness in not having him more constantly in my thoughts.

ᔓ

About a week after I heard of Rafe's death, Peggy marched into my room one morning, looking determined.

"Mistress Bess, I can't bear to see you making yourself ill over young Master Rafe. It's time you came downstairs and took the air. A ride would do you the world of good."

"It will make no difference, Peggy, what I do. What does illness matter now? I'll never love anyone else like I loved him." I turned my back to her.

Thus far, I had ventured no further than the family chapel, where, clutching my prayer book like a rope thrown to a drowning man, it had become my daily custom to spend time on my knees, praying for Rafe Beauchamp.

Peggy set her jaw obstinately.

"It's not right, Mistress," she snapped, "I could tell you things, things you won't want to hear."

Her voice trailed off at the look on my face, but realising she had gone too far for silence and could not prevent full disclosure, she began afresh.

"I know young Master Rafe was important to you. Maybe he isn't worth you mourning him so deeply. Heard things in Kineton."

"Peggy, I shall box your ears if you repeat wicked gossip."

Peggy's expression of pity was worse than a blow. Would nothing stop the flow of speech I had no wish to hear?

"Mistress Bess, I don't believe he thought of you as anything but Master Will's sister. It was the saddler's daughter who he spent his time with, in Kineton. Joe saw him at the saddler's too."

"Well of course he frequented the saddler's. They were making him a new saddle for Mercury. They made slow progress and he had to make many visits before he was satisfied. Will jibed that he cared more for his horse than many a man for his mistress."

I came to a stop, realising what I had just said.

"Thing is, Miss Bess" she continued relentlessly, "It's not just going to the shop. Joe was in Kineton betimes. He saw Master Rafe climbing out the window as it was getting light. He was in shirt and breeches, carrying his coat and boots."

I felt the blood drain from my face.

"You're lying," I whispered hopelessly. I knew she spoke the truth.

Peggy eased the door shut behind her. My handful of precious memories, all I had left. Dancing with Rafe, watching him fence, holding him tightly as Mercury tore through the park, and that all important day in the stable when he had kissed me. No more. If I had been heart-broken before, now I felt truly desolate. No, there was one more thing I still had. The handkerchief was carefully put away in a special drawer. I grabbed it, intending to rip it or throw it on the fire. But the sight of the blood stains made me freeze again with love and loss. Whatever Rafe might have been to another, he was still the man I had loved, and I could not destroy the last keepsake he had died clutching in his hand. Finally the tears came, stinging my eyes. I folded it carefully, returned it to its place and went downstairs to try and find a reason for the rest of my existence.

∽

Warwick Castle, November 1642

After the initial tense days in captivity, it became clear to Harry that there was no immediate threat to his life. While this relieved his anxiety, he chafed at the lack of any prospects for early release. By mid November, the days were passing more and more slowly. He shared a room in Guy's Tower with five other officers. Three were from regiments of foot, the others were cavalry officers from Lord Grandison's regiment. They suffered from boredom and low spirits. Tempers were fraying.

One afternoon, Harry was reading, sitting on his bed. The prisoners had been allowed access both to books and music. Harry suspected this made the life of the garrison easier as it provided some limited occupation for the pent up energies of the officers in their charge.

Lieutenant Walter Brett was sitting on his own bed, strumming a lute, when one of the cavalry officers, Lieutenant John Palmer, looked up from his letter in annoyance. He had been frowning and tapping the quill against his teeth for some minutes.

"Lieutenant Brett," Palmer spoke with exaggerated politeness, "I would take it as a kindness if you postponed your musical endeavours until I have finished writing to my father. If I wish to hear music I prefer to listen to Lieutenant Vaughan, who knows when a lute is out of tune."

Brett scowled. "I suppose a request from a cavalry officer must take precedence over my own desires as a mere officer of foot."

Palmer stiffened. "I do not take your meaning, Sir."

"Merely that you gentlemen of horse consider us of little import. If you considered us of greater value you might have spent more time at Edgehill on the battlefield supporting us, instead of leaving us to the rebels and their guns."

Both men were on their feet now, facing each other tensely.

"Gentlemen," Harry attempted desperately.

"I am not interested in your own views, Lieutenant Lucie," snarled Brett. "Of course you will side with an officer from Grandison's."

As Palmer advanced on Brett with raised fists, Harry turned towards the door. Should he send for the guards to stop them injuring each other? He was relieved to see the Welshman Vaughan standing in the doorway, now leaning on a stick to support his broken ankle.

"I think that will be enough, Gentlemen." His voice carried quiet authority and the two men paused, fists still raised. "This is foolishness. What our cavalry may have done at Edgehill is not for us to judge. It must be obvious that those of us captured on the battlefield had not galloped away. If we had abandoned our fellows we would not be confined here."

He paused for the effect of his words to sink in.

"It is galling for us all to be imprisoned. But we still have our honour. We should unite against those who disarmed us and hold us against our will. They confine our bodies. Let us not allow them to also break our spirits."

Palmer and Brett were now regarding each other with some embarrassment.

"If you and your lute will attend me, Lieutenant Brett", Vaughan smiled, "I will see if I can tune it for you." Brett laughed and reached again for the lute.

ᔕ

Chadshunt Hall, November 1642

The King had marched on London and won a battle at Brentford, to the west of the city, followed by a confrontation between the two armies at Turnham Green on the very edge of the capital. Outnumbered by the city's armed citizens, the King turned back to Oxford, Father riding once more with the army. In his search for Uncle Hugh, Father had narrowly escaped being trapped between the two forces.

At Chadshunt Hall, the grey November days dragged for both Will and me. Inaction made my brother short tempered. He made the rounds of the tenants conscientiously once a week, noting any problems with their farms, or other matters which they would normally have referred to my father. Minor matters he was usually able to resolve with the assistance of John Dale, who often accompanied him on these visits.

It was a quiet time of year on the estate, a time of repairs to fences, barns and other buildings which needed thatching or tiling completed before the winter set in. It was as well, for the estate remained short-handed, most of those who had joined the army having remained with Giles Blake when Father returned to Chadshunt.

The days faded one into other, for none brought Harry back from captivity and none would ever return Rafe from whence he had gone. My mother regained her equanimity once my father set out to attempt what he could to free Harry. There was nothing to be gained from being querulous, and she did her best to rally my spirits as well as her own.

With Mother's encouragement, I tried to pretend an interest in matters around me. She bid me accompany her when she made her own visits to cottages on the estate. She took herbal remedies to those who ailed, or ointment and flannel to the elderly suffering from cold and rheumatism.

The tenant farmers and their labourers welcomed these visits. In the larger farms I was entertained by the fire, and plied with food and drink, while the farmer's wife enquired solicitously if there was any news of Master Harry and when he might be released.

In the cottages, I ducked my head to enter a dark and crowded space, with chickens or ducks waddling in and out. The chimney smoked and I was urged to take a seat on a stool by the fire while two or three small children peered shyly at me from behind their mother's skirts.

One morning I made ready for a round of visiting. Will had ridden again into Banbury, to spend a few days with the Royalist garrison. Mother did not appear for breakfast and sent her maid Mary to say she had the headache. I went to her chamber to see how she did. She was resting comfortably against her pillows and smiled at me.

"Just one of my silly headaches, Bess. Pray make your visits without me. Be sure to visit Mercy Smith and her new baby. The infant is a little sickly, I fear. And ask Janie to explain my receipt for calves' foot jelly. Mistress Brampton requested it last week. Oh, and take a few jars of honey. There are so many children complaining of the sore throat. I believe our honey is the best remedy."

By the time Mother had finished her instructions, she was looking tired. She promised to rest and said she would be up and about by dinner time. I left on foot, carrying a large basket with the honey, some herbal brews my mother also recommended for the treatment of winter colds, and a few apple pies our cook had given me, made with apples from our orchard.

I stopped first at the home farm, to explain Mother's receipt for calves' foot jelly. Mistress Brampton was always happy to see me. She had come to the farm on her marriage, when I was only a baby. She enquired as usual about Harry. For the first time I had a little to report. As yet, my father had failed to find Uncle Hugh. Instead, he had discovered the names of several other Royalist officers who had family members held prisoner at Warwick and was now at Oxford exploring a joint approach to the release of our men, possibly through exchanging them for some of the enemy prisoners. Nothing was certain yet, but we thought it a hopeful first step to seeing Harry home again.

I walked on to my next destination, Mercy Smith and her new baby. They lived in one of the cottages on the next farm. I was pleased to see that the mother was well and the baby now thriving. Babies born in winter faced more hurdles than those born in the warmer months. I knew Mother had been anxious that Mercy's new baby, as yet unnamed, would be joining a brother and sister or two in the church yard.

By noon, the sun was struggling from behind the clouds. I lingered at the summit of a hill, leaning my arms on a fence and fanning my face with my hat. My basket was nearly empty. I had only one more visit to make. I gazed into the distance and saw a horse galloping across the fields towards me. I sighed. I felt anew Mercury's powerful hind quarters eating up the acres beneath Rafe and me. My arms were about Rafe's waist and my cheek against his doublet, the rush of air as we swept by, the sun beating down on our heads. The oaks and beeches which had been decked with leaves were now almost bare.

The speeding horse was closer now and I recognised its rider as our head groom, Joe. He was waving his hat at me. Puzzled, I broke into a run down the slope.

"What is it, Joe?" I panted.

"Peggy sent me to fetch you home, Mistress Bess. The Mistress is worse, she has a fever."

He lifted me and the basket onto the horse behind him and sped towards the Hall. I dropped to the ground as Joe reined up in the courtyard. Peggy met me outside Mother's door.

"The mistress does poorly, I fear. She still has the headache but now shivers as with an ague. She has a fever. Should we not send for our physician?"

I tiptoed into Mother's room. Her eyes were closed, but when I entered she opened them. They were overbright and she had two spots of crimson on her cheeks which I did not like.

"Why, Mother, I believe you promised to be well in time for dinner," I said with forced cheerfulness. "It is a beautiful sunny day now, but I fear you need rest. On the morrow, no doubt, some air may do you good. Do you wish Mary or Peggy to bring you a tray?"

Mother smiled weakly.

"I fear I have little appetite, Bess, but it is very cold in here. Some broth perhaps might warm me." I felt her hot head but only nodded in reply. I sent Mary for some broth. It arrived hot and steaming, smelling of marrow bones and onions. Mother tasted it but then closed her eyes again.

"I think I may sleep for a while, Bess. It will refresh me. I will be well soon."

Much as she worried and would show signs of agitation at the slightest sign of anything amiss with her children or Father, Mother never accepted she could sicken herself. I kissed her cheek and left the room, closing the door gently.

Mary saw my anxious face. "I will sit with her and sew, Mistress Bess," she reassured me." I will send Peggy if she needs you."

"I thank you, Mary. Have a hot brick placed at her feet to warm them. I will bathe her head with lavender water when she wakes."

I plodded downstairs to the family dining room. I looked around sadly. I was to dine in solitary splendour today, Mother sick, Will away, Harry a captive and Father seeking his release. For once, my healthy appetite abandoned me. I sat staring at the steaming dish of mutton stew with leeks and the platter of roast duck until they cooled. The voice of Thomas interrupted my dejected thoughts.

"Would you care for another dish, Mistress Bess? I could speak to Janie. You have eaten nothing."

"No thank you, Thomas," I forced myself to pick up my spoon. "This will suffice. It smells delicious."

Thomas looked at me in concern as he poured the wine. If I could not eat I could at least drink. I took a sip of wine and then another. It might ease my fears. I forced myself to eat a few morsels and then went out into the gardens, accompanied by Hector. It was a month since Rafe had handed me the small, wriggling bundle, and my French puppy was somewhat grown. He ran beside me, making short forays after birds, squirrels and interesting aromas. I went no further than the deserted rose garden. The bare bushes and scent of damp earth added to my melancholy. I frequently turned my eyes to the window of Mother's room and listened for Mary, Peggy or any of the other servants calling my name. By mid-afternoon, I was slipping quietly back into Mother's room. She was asleep but her breathing was loud and I did not like her looks. Mary sat beside her quietly. She followed me out.

"The Mistress has been sleeping since you left, Mistress Bess. I think she may be well by the morrow."

I shook my head pessimistically.

"We will pray that she is, Mary."

That evening I called the servants together and we recited our usual evening prayers, I reading aloud from the prayer book self-consciously. I said a heart-felt prayer that Mother would be well soon and Harry free. Before going to bed, I crept into Mother's room again. She was asleep and I thought her breathing was maybe a little quieter. The fire crackled softly, throwing a healthier glow over her face.

"Go to bed, Mary," I said to the vigilant maid. "If Mother needs you she can ring her hand bell."

Despite my worries, I slept until it was day. I hastened to Mother's chamber. I was met this time by Peggy.

"Mistress Bess, I think maybe we should send for the physician." I did not stay for further words but ran past her through the door. Mother was lying in bed but was not asleep.

"Is that you, Bess?" she said a little weakly. She was shivering uncontrollably and her head felt even hotter to my inexperienced hand.

"Dear Mother, you are still ailing. I believe we should consult our physician."

"Nonsense, Bess," Mother forced parched cracked lips into a smile, although her voice broke. "Master Blackthorne does not want to come all the way from Banbury for a little cold. I will be well tomorrow."

ᔕ

The physician left Mother's room, closing the door quietly.

"She has a high fever, Mistress," he said to me. "I have bled her and she is resting. I hope she will do well now. She should have wine and a little broth when she wakes." He paused at the top of the stairs, tapping his fingers against the rail.

"Does Sir Henry return soon?"

When I explained that Father's absence was of unknown duration, his brow furrowed. "And Master Will?"

"Will is in Banbury at the castle. Did you wish to converse with him, Master Blackthorne?"

"No matter, Mistress. I will call again on the morrow to see how Lady Lucie does." He bowed and made his stately way down the stairs.

I gnawed at a finger nail. In obedience to Mother's wishes I had delayed a further day before calling the physician. It was only on the fourth day when she had said to me,

"Bess, your father is out hunting and it grows cold. Make sure he has some warm posset when he returns," that I decided I had waited overlong.

Peggy and I encouraged Mother to try the prescribed wine and broth, but she would take nothing but cold water. By mid-afternoon, she continued feverish and weak. With a heavy heart, I sent Joe to Banbury to fetch my brother. It was growing dark by the time the two men returned. I heard Will bounding up the stairs two at a time, although he checked on the landing. I quietly left the room and threw my arms around him.

"Oh Will, I'm glad you're home. I'm afraid." He stroked my hair and hushed me.

"Try not to worry, Bess. Everyone takes the fever from time to time. Within a day or two, all may be well." His words were hopeful, but he would not meet my eyes.

"Shall I see her now?" I hesitated. I knew Mother would be glad to see Will home but she was sleeping. Reluctantly, Will agreed to leaving her asleep. We ate supper and read the evening prayers, while Peggy attended her.

When Will and I returned, Mother was still sleeping, but her face was flushed and her forehead felt very hot to the touch. Will spoke to her gently.

"Mother, it's Will." She opened her eyes and moaned.

"Henry, you're back at last my love. Is Harry with you?" We looked at each other uneasily.

"Mother," I whispered, "it's Will who is returned, not Father. But I'm sure Father will be home soon," I lied, eager to reassure her. She stared at me blankly and closed her eyes again.

When Master Blackthorne arrived the next morning, he looked at Mother and showed a little surprise, mixed with resignation. It was, I thought, the look of a man who had weighed the chances of the different outcomes, and recognised that on this occasion, sadly he had been wrong. Will being present, he deferred to him.

"Sir, I do not feel the situation is hopeless, but it may be best to prepare yourselves for the worst. I can leave a draught for Lady Lucie if she will take it. I recommend bleeding her again."

Will put his hand on the physician's arm to prevent him saying more. "I thank you, Sir, but no. Pray leave the draught. We will summon you again if necessary."

The physician gave a stiff bow, his expression haughty. He handed a bottle to Peggy with some instructions and, with another bow, left the room. I regarded Will desperately.

"Will, she is going to recover?"

"I don't know, Bess," he said simply. We collapsed onto the cushioned window seat, our arms around each other's waists, and sat staring at the restless form of our mother, tossing feverishly. When Mother woke a little later, she seemed pleased to see Will.

"You are returned then, my son? I hope you will stay awhile." She appeared to have forgotten seeing him the previous day. Will smiled at her,

"I am here, dear Mother, I will remain at your side, have no fear."

Will and I slept little that night, each taking turns with Mary to sit with Mother. She said nothing further, although she moaned and muttered. The fever showed no signs of abating and at dawn I could bear it no longer. I crept into Will's room. He was in an uneasy doze, lying back fully dressed in a chair, his handsome face lined with strain even in sleep and his hair all rumpled up.

"Will," I whispered, "I think we had better send Joe for Master Blackthorne again." Will was on his feet before he was barely awake.

7

IN THE SILENCE of the early morning I heard galloping hooves, as Joe set off once more. Will crept back into Mother's room. I regarded his tired eyes. "Go and rest again, Will. I will call you if there is any change." He nodded resignedly and went out again.

Some time later, I was roused by a sound from the bed. I bent over Mother and she opened her eyes. "Bess," she said and smiled. She turned her eyes away from me. They rested on the blank surface of the closed oak door, its polished wood shining softly in the firelight. She smiled again with great sweetness.

"Oh, Harry," she said, "My darling, you've come home at last." She sighed and closed her eyes, exhaling deeply. Her beautiful, much loved face was in repose. Harry had returned to her at the end. I waited but she did not speak again.

ᔕ

My father buried his wife of twenty two years on a cold, grey day with sleet in the air. We had sent a messenger to Oxford bidding him return. His face on his arrival was ravaged with grief. In some strange way, he also seemed angry. In the wish not to alarm him we had, alas, ended up presenting him with the worst of terrible news. Dismounting from his horse, he said little, but looked at me almost coldly and went straight way to kiss my mother for a last time. He commanded that henceforth Mother's room was to remain untouched. We followed her coffin forlornly to the church, weeping. We had not even had the means of taking the terrible news to Harry. Whether that were a curse or a blessing, that he did not yet know his mother was dead, we could not determine.

After the funeral, Father informed us he had obtained apparently good intelligence that Uncle Hugh was now with the Earl of Essex 's army. Plans at Oxford for winning the release of prisoners made but slow progress. He would renew the search for his brother. Within a week of Father's departure,

Will and I heard hooves as the hoped-for messenger came trotting up the lane. Will broke Father's seal and unfolded it impatiently. The length of the letter, for there were several sheets, I hoped presaged good news. But Will's face darkened as he perused it, and having come to the end, he crumpled it angrily in his hand.

"Will?" I said pleadingly. He looked at me, sighed and thrust it at me.

"There is no good news, my sister. But take it, and welcome." Eagerly I sat down in a chair with the letter and began to read, while Will stood moodily by the fire. "My dear son..."

ᔕ

Holly Bush Inn, Marlow, December 1642

My informant had been correct. I made my way to the Holly Bush Inn, where the earl was in conference with senior officers. I enquired for Colonel Hugh Lucie, announcing myself as his brother, Sir Henry Lucie. Hoping to avoid arrest by the rebels, I wore civilian dress. A captain appeared, who looked at me keenly. "You are not with our forces I think, Sir?"

"I am with His Majesty's forces," I replied honestly. The man frowned.

"Put him under guard," he snapped to a musketeer.

"You will remain here, Sir Henry. I will enquire if Colonel Lucie wishes to see his malignant brother. If he does not, you may expect to be confined."

For some minutes, I was obliged to stand between two insolent sentries. Their remarks ceased when I saw Hugh stalking towards me. A wide silk sash of tawny orange about his waist contrasted sharply with his black velvet coat and breeches. The sash was a stark reminder of where his loyalties lay, and I took a sharp breath, words of greeting still born on my lips.

"Release him."

He gestured me to follow him and led the way to a private room where we could talk undisturbed. A clerk was seated at a small table strewn with papers. Seeing Hugh, he hastily bundled up the papers and bowed, scuttling out. Hugh did not offer me any refreshment, but waved me to a seat opposite him at the table. Glaring, he folded his arms.

"It was most unwise of you to present yourself here, Henry. Did you not realise you were likely to be taken prisoner? You had better explain what circumstance has led to your visit. Have you come to your senses and wish to join our forces?"

I bit back an angry retort. I was relying on his good graces and should not demand the respect I was entitled to as his elder brother and head of the family.

"That is not the reason, Hugh." I maintained a level voice. "Firstly, I must apprise you that Anne is no more. She died of a fever some days past." Now I could not prevent my voice from shaking.

"I am saddened to hear of my good-sister's death," replied my brother coldly. "She was a virtuous lady of good repute. She is gone to her just reward, thankfully leaving you living pledges of her love."

I closed my eyes for a few moments, praying that I might find the words to soften my younger brother's ice cold calm.

"There is more to tell?" Hugh drummed his fingers on the table.

"Hugh, I am come here to divulge to you that Harry was captured at Edgehill. He is a prisoner in Warwick Castle and my attempts to win his freedom have so far borne no fruit. You are apparently a gentleman of influence with the Earl. As your brother, I beg you to use that influence, and have Harry released. He is your own nephew."

Hugh was silent and thoughtful. For a few moments, I dared to hope he was relenting. He stood up and took a few turns around the room, hands behind his back, chin sunk on his chest.

"Henry, I have reflected on this matter, but you may not like what I have to say. I grieve to hear that my nephew suffers imprisonment. However, it has been brought upon his own head by the obstinate views which you hold. It appears that you have infected both your sons with Popish notions. Had you brought them up as godly men, they would not have followed you in this folly of fighting against the people and the Parliament. Can you justify to me in any way why I should exert myself on his behalf? Did he join the malignant army out of filial duty, or was it of his own free will?"

I fought back my wrath.

"Harry enlisted in His Majesty's army voluntarily, in spirited defence of his cause, as did Will. I am proud of both my sons."

"Then there is no more to say." Hugh replied coldly. "I do not imagine Harry is in immediate danger. Our officers are men of virtue and principle, and while guarding him they will, I am sure, see to his welfare. But he was taken in battle fighting for an unjust cause. Ultimately he must pay whatever penalty the people decide. I wish you good night, Brother, and will pray that you and yours come to a right understanding of this conflict."

"Will you not at least find the means of conveying a letter to my poor son? He has had no word from us at all, and sadly we should break the news of his poor mother's death. He is still unaware," I pleaded.

"If you send a letter to my direction, I will see that it finds him."

And with that he turned his back, and I was hustled out. I wrote a letter for Harry hoping that Hugh is as good as his word in this, and the letter would find Harry. As I wrote, I abandoned further expectations from Hugh. In the space of a few weeks, I had lost my wife, my youngest son and now my brother. I would have to prevail with other means to free Harry.

ꚙ

Rest assured, my son, I will not give up.

Kiss your sister for me. I remain, your loving Father."

When I finished reading Father's letter, I sat with it on my knee and began crying weakly. I wept for Harry, for my mother, for my poor Rafe and for my country which had been torn apart.

ꚙ

Chadshunt Hall, December 1642

Christmas was not far away. The King was in winter quarters at Oxford. My father was spending much of his time there assisting the King with the work of his Council of War. He was also meeting families of other prisoners, hoping to arrange an exchange of Harry and the others with rebel prisoners.

Will and I sat side by side on a high backed settle, close to a blazing fire in the Great Hall, one cold evening. "Will, please explain to me why Harry's release is so slow," I said to him in frustration, "Why does it await the release of others? What have rebel prisoners got to do with it? Why can Parliament not just set him free?"

Will's brow puckered. "Bess, such matters are for men to understand. But I will try to explain. There are certain accepted ways of treating prisoners taken in battle. Sometimes they are put to the sword."

"Will, no!"

"I talk about in the heat of battle. Harry is safe from that now. Common soldiers are more like to be freed immediately or persuaded to turn their coats. Officers are considered more valuable. They may be freed by their family paying a ransom in some cases. However, this has not been suggested by Harry's captors. A number of Royalist officers are held at Warwick Castle. It has been deemed best to attempt to exchange them for a similar number of rebel officers who we hold captive in Oxford Castle. Some men are considered more valuable than others, depending on their rank in the army or their position in society. Lord Lindsey is one of those held at Warwick. He is of such high standing that there may be a dispute as to whether he is included in the negotiations. If the exchange can be agreed, it has the advantage that our officers may remain part of the King's army."

"Why should they not?"

"If they are released in other ways, they may be required to take an oath not to take up arms again against Parliament. Any breaking parole who are recaptured would be executed. I believe Harry would regard the taking of such a vow as too high a price to pay for his freedom. And so we wait, and pray, and try to remain patient."

It was easy for Will to talk of patience. Weary of the lack of progress, I resolved to concoct a plan of my own. Besides Rafe, I had received admiring glances from other gentlemen and realised that I might be able to use my apparent charms to effect. Father had described the castle Governor as stern but fair. If I beguiled him, he might feel the unreasonableness of keeping a man from his family at Christmas time.

I plotted carefully if hurriedly. Will was setting off for another night or two with the Banbury garrison. I watched him depart.

"Peggy, why not visit your sister today? You might leave after dinner, spend the night with her and return tomorrow before supper. You look tired and deserve a holiday."

"Well thank you, Miss Bess, I believe I will, that's kind of you. But what will you do while I am away?" She had known me for many years and regarded me with slight suspicion. I returned her gaze innocently.

"Oh, I have some letters to write. And I am fatigued, I will rest."

She nodded, apparently satisfied. It was true that I was fatigued and she could see the weariness in my face. With my mother gone, overseeing the household fell on my unaccustomed seventeen year old shoulders. It was something of a burden.

Once Peggy had left that afternoon, I made my preparations. I found our head groom Joe and briskly informed him he would be accompanying me to Warwick Castle the next day.

Joe was walking from one stall to the next, a sack of oats in his hand. He stooped to pour a generous portion of oats into the next bucket, saying nothing.

"Patience, lad."

He was talking to the horses, not acknowledging me.

"Joe!"

He turned his head. I saw doubt and reluctance in his eyes.

"Mistress Bess, the young master will have my hide if I do such a thing, Sir Henry, too. Do you wish to lose me my position?"

I lifted my chin haughtily.

"Joe, I am your mistress, not you my master. With or without you I will ride to Warwick Castle on the morrow. I will take responsibility. If you are unwilling to be my escort, I will take Ben."

Joe's alarm was heightened by this threat, as I knew it would. His younger brother Ben was no more than Harry's age, and Joe's protective instincts leaped to my aid.

"I will escort you, Mistress."

Scowling, he shuffled towards the next bucket with his sack.

I rose early next day, dressing in one of my smartest gowns, but with my fur lined cloak covering it, fur lined gloves, a large hat over my coif, and my thickest boots. It was winter and with a combined journey of more than twenty miles, I needed to consider comfort. However, if I was to try my feminine charms on the castle Governor, it would not do to appear too dowdy. I fiddled with the laces on the bodice and the falling band until they were arranged to give what I hoped was a tantalising but sufficiently modest glimpse of bosom. I looked myself over critically in the looking glass. Too tall for most men's tastes, my mother had claimed. But my figure was generally considered good, although my skirts would sit a little better if only my hips were wider. My large grey eyes were fringed with long lashes and in spite of recent troubles there was a hint of rose in my cheeks and my full lipped mouth. There was nothing to be done about the small bags under my eyes caused by sleeplessness. I crept downstairs. Hector was sleeping in his basket. I left a note for Peggy to find on her return.

Feeling like a child bent on mischief, I stole down the back stairs at the corner of the west wing and unbolted the back door quietly. Joe was waiting with the horses inside the stables. I had ordered him to saddle the grey pony Bella for me. Fairy was rather too well known in these parts and might draw attention to me. My mare whickered softly when she saw me.

"I'm sorry, I can't take you today," I said. As we mounted and rode under the archway into the courtyard, she whinnied plaintively. The horses' hooves sounded unnaturally loud on the cobbles in the frosty air as we made our way towards the lane.

Joe was essential to my venture. For a gentlewoman such as myself, riding such a distance unescorted was unthinkable, even in time of peace. If my mission was successful, I was hopeful that we could return before nightfall, bringing Harry with us. I had considered taking a horse for him, but decided that would attract possible questions, and might signal our intentions in advance.

I trotted along cheerfully, picturing Harry's fond embrace when I greeted him, the unknown Governor smiling benevolently and pronouncing the words of freedom upon him, lastly the amazement and joy on the faces of Will and the servants when I returned in triumph with my brother.

Travelling steadily, we paused only once to rest the horses and water them at a stream. Despite my thick boots, my toes were frozen, and I stamped my feet to warm them. Joe produced some apples to break our fast, but I was too excited to eat, and Bella crunched happily on the treat. The frosty dawn had given place to a sunny day and my spirits rose as I rode, feeling it was a good omen.

We arrived in Warwick by mid-morning, passing by the cottages of Bridge End and crossing the arched bridge over the River Avon, which lapped the sides of our goal, the cliff top fortress of the castle. As we entered the town, I started to see Parliamentarian soldiers in uniform. Some were marching in files from place to place, others were scattered in twos and threes outside shops and inns. The sight of the enemy soldiers in such numbers suddenly made me fearful. Was I endangering Joe and myself? Warwick had become enemy territory. Joe, riding alongside, saw me slow and reined in.

"Is there something wrong, Mistress Bess? Do you wish to turn back?"

Having it put so baldly to me stiffened my resolve.

"Not at all," I replied firmly, although the sight of the imposing castle high above the river with its many towers and ramparts had sent a shiver down my back bone. The distant ramparts were higher, the towers surely increased in number, since I had beheld them on visits in earlier years. It seemed too short a time before finding ourselves climbing the slope towards the castle. Warwick Castle was a forbidding place. It had been recently repaired and strengthened as hostilities approached. Work was still in progress. The sounds of hammering came from a barricade. Freshly constructed bulwarks topped with cannon rose above our road. As we approached them, I saw they were guarded by soldiers armed with muskets. My thumping heart increased its speed.

"Halt. State your business."

"Mistress Elisabeth Lucie of Chadshunt Hall wishes to see the castle Governor on an urgent personal matter," was Joe's response. We waited quite some time.

"Dismount and follow me."

Leading the horses, we followed one of the soldiers until we reached the stables.

"The Major will spare you a few minutes, Mistress. You are to remain here," he said to Joe. I parted from Joe and the horses reluctantly. The soldier marched beside me towards the barbican and gatehouse, still some distance away. I was puzzled to see what appeared to be large wool sacks hanging from the face of the barbican. We crossed the drawbridge over the moat, also showing signs of new wooden planks, under the portcullis, over a further drawbridge and into the gatehouse.

At the bottom of the gatehouse stairs, a man in the clerical garb of a secretary was standing, evidently awaiting me. We ascended spiral stairs until we reached the top of the gatehouse. The secretary rapped once on the door. "Enter." The voice within sounded strangely familiar.

Pushing the door open, I found myself in a warm and spacious room, clearly the Governor's living quarters. The roof was lofty and the room well lit by large, curtained windows at either end. The stone walls were whitewashed, unadorned other than by two racks for clothing. On the one nearer the door dangled a sword in an ornate scabbard, a lobster pot helmet and buff coat hanging next to it. The further rack held a cloak or two. Below one of the two windows a round table, covered in papers, and several stools, were placed to take best advantage of the light on the short winter's day. An oak chest stood against the wall beside a neatly made bed, the coverlet richly embroidered in hues of crimson and green. Seated in a comfortable high backed chair before a blazing fire, regarding me quizzically, was the tall, broad shouldered figure of Archibald Chatterton, a friend of Uncle Hugh. Taken aback, I blurted,

"Oh," and then flushed. Belatedly remembering my manners, I curtseyed and said,

"Thank you for seeing me, Sir."

He rose to his feet, but made no other move to welcome me. I saw that his clothing, always sober, was now tending towards the Puritan mode of dress, plain collar and dark coat making something of a contrast with his grey hair and with his skin, darkened even in winter from months of campaigning in the open. He wore the tawny orange sash of Essex's army around his waist. As I stared back, he pressed his thin lips together and a frown creased his brow. My carefully prepared words, intended for a stranger, now seemed inappropriate. Clearly, Major Chatterton knew who I was, and who Harry was. Surely that should be in my favour? My starting point, at least, was still clear to me.

"My brother Harry, Sir, is he in good health and spirits?"

Major Chatterton pursed his lips.

"Thankfully, I am not obliged to review the welfare of individual prisoners on a daily basis. The last time I saw Lieutenant Lucie he appeared well enough. I cannot comment on his state of mind."

I paused. What should I say next? The last response was spoken coolly and without any indication of kinder feelings within him.

"Sir," I pleaded, "My mother is very recently dead of a fever. My poor father, whilst grieving for her, is obliged to spend his time in ceaseless anguish and activity trying to obtain my poor brother's release. Will and I are now all that he has left to him. It would ease Father's heart if Harry could be returned to the family. Our two families have known each other these many years, Sir. I have always known you for an upright man, a man of principle. Consider, Sir, if it were your own son John who now lay a captive, how you would feel. Would you not hope for mercy from his captors, remembering such kindness in your prayers thereafter?"

Major Chatterton said nothing, but rang a bell. I waited hopefully. A maid servant appeared.

"Bring wine for the lady and myself."

He turned away from me towards a writing desk and hummed a tune, apparently absorbed in some papers while he waited for the servant to return. I tried not to fidget but caught myself nervously twisting my collar. When the maid returned with the wine, the Colonel poured two goblets and handed me one, smirking. I smiled back uncertainly.

"Pray take a seat, Mistress Lucie," he said in honeyed tones. He seated himself once more in his high backed chair and indicated that I should sit upon the bed.

"This is a soldier's quarters. I fear I have little accommodation suitable for ladies," he said apologetically. I removed my hat and perched on the edge of the high bed, sipping nervously at my wine.

"How is your father Sir Henry? I trust he is well?"

"I believe so, Colonel, but I have not seen him these several weeks since he is from home. As I said, he works for Harry's release."

"Just so, and this of course takes him away from the family. Most unfortunate. I am distressed to hear of your mother's death, Mistress Lucie. Lady Lucie was always a charming hostess and I am sure a most devoted wife and mother to you and your brothers. And Master Will, how does he? Well I trust, or is he also away from home? I had heard he too was fighting for the King, but perhaps he now resides at home caring for you in your Father's absence?"

I was somewhat reassured. These seemingly friendly questions about my family were spoken in his usual low and cultured tones, with no trace of hostility or harshness.

"Indeed you are correct, Sir. My brother Will was fighting for the King. He is presently visiting the garrison at Banbury."

"Ah," he said slowly, "And so you are come here unaccompanied." I realised belatedly that this was not information it was wise to give, but could think of no reply other than the truth. I mustered what indignation I could,

"Indeed not, Sir, my groom waits for me at the castle stables."

He smiled, "Ah your groom, well that of course makes all the difference."

I was puzzled at the change in his manner, which now appeared mocking. He had risen again from his chair by the fire.

"You mentioned gratitude if I released your brother," he smiled.

"I did, Sir," I agreed. He drained his goblet and placed it on the mantle shelf above the fire. Then he gently removed my own half empty goblet from my hand and placed it with his. I stared up at him in some confusion as he returned to my side.

"Perhaps you would like to demonstrate this gratitude to me. It might assist me in reaching a decision."

I was unprepared when he grabbed my shoulders and pushed me hard against the pillows, knocking my linen coif askew. Strands of hair promptly cascaded onto my shoulders. He fastened his lips on mine, thrusting his tongue into my mouth. Then he plunged his right hand into my bosom, tugging hard on the laces to expose my breasts. I floundered wildly, trying to free a leg from beneath my petticoats and finally succeeding in kicking out with my foot. It made contact with his knee and he swore. His left hand had been pressing my shoulder to the bed but now he swung it hard, striking me on the cheek. I screamed. The door burst open and I caught a glimpse of the secretary's frightened face as Will shoved him aside and erupted into the room. He snatched Major Chatterton's sword from its hook and drew it from its scabbard in one fluid motion.

"Leave my sister alone!"

Major Chatterton smoothly removed his hand from my bosom and rose unhurriedly to his feet. He regarded Will steadily.

"Master Lucie," he said calmly, "If you do not wish to join your brother as a prisoner, I suggest you lay down that sword."

"Immediately," he snapped, as Will made no move to obey.

I looked at my brother with a mixture of relief and fear.

"Will, please do nothing foolish. I am unharmed." I indicated the bed, undisturbed apart from a dent in the pillows.

Will hesitated, and then dropped the sword on the table with an angry clatter.

"Now raise your hands."

Crossing the room swiftly, the Governor retrieved his sword. He eyed it thoughtfully, then turned his eyes to my brother, standing with empty hands raised high.

"A gallant attempt, Master Lucie, gallant if somewhat desperate, to think you could confront me unarmed in the midst of my garrison and prevail. I had thought disarming visitors at the gate was an adequate precaution. Clearly I was in error."

Will gritted his teeth, his face white with anger. The sound of pounding footsteps came from the stairs. Two soldiers burst in, drawn swords in their hands.

Major Chatterton nodded at the soldiers and held up his hand to indicate he was not in danger. Holding his sword before him, he strolled towards Will until the blade was touching his chest. Will backed away until his shoulders were against the wall. I watched in horror, fearing any move on my part might worsen matters.

"If I run you through," Major Chatterton said conversationally, "My men will testify you attacked me. Yes, I think that might do very well, should any question my actions."

With infinite slowness, the Governor eased the tip of the blade between the buttons of Will's dark red cassack. The razor sharp edge caught one of the buttons and it spun to the floor with a tiny clink. My brother was standing rigid, beads of sweat standing out on his brow, his eyes on the gleaming steel.

"Or perchance," the Governor continued, "It might be amusing to confine you with your brother, since you place yourself so willingly at my disposal."

Time seemed to stand still, then Chatterton backed away towards me, laughing. In a lightning move, his blade flicked sideways, and a trailing lock of my dark hair fell. He caught it neatly.

"A small keepsake, Mistress. I regret Lieutenant Lucie has other engagements which he is compelled to keep. Sadly, they prevent him seeing you today. I will, of course, pass on your compliments to him." With a mocking bow, he handed me my hat.

"Master Lucie, should you return uninvited to this castle, you will not leave again so easily. Now, both of you, get out before I regret my liberality." He gestured to the soldiers with his sword.

"Escort our visitors as far as the stables. Have a care they do not tarry within the castle precincts."

The soldiers marched Will at sword point down the winding stairs and back to the stables. I hurried apprehensively at their heels.

Safely outside the castle, Will reined in after we had ridden not many paces. He was mounted on Fairy.

"Bess, I rejoice that you are unharmed, but what were you thinking of? Joe, please ride on, we will meet you at the Bush Inn on the road out."

I opened my mouth to reply.

"Hold your tongue," Will exploded. He signalled brusquely to me to follow him. I obeyed, my heart still beating fast from our encounter with Major Chatterton. How to explain my actions? He said nothing until we were outside the town, then he pulled aside from the road and slid to the ground. I did likewise. Will, my older brother, my brother who had rescued me from all my childhood scrapes, now looked at me steadily.

"Well, Bess?"

I cleared my throat, trying and failing to meet his eyes.

"I was trying to rescue Harry," I said with a catch in my voice. "Father's efforts are taking too long. I thought if I used my sweetest smiles on the Governor he might relent."

"And a fine notion that was," Will retorted. "Were you planning to play the whore, sister? For that was how it appeared when I found you with him." He looked pointedly at my bosom. The carefully arranged enticing glimpse of the early morning was now looking decidedly like provocation, as the laces had become loosened in the struggle.

"Oh Will, I'm so sorry. I thought he was going to kill you."

The tears came to my eyes and I dashed them away. I twitched angrily at my bodice and, giving up, pulled my cloak close to cover me more completely. Will looked down ruefully at the small, neat slash in the breast of his cassack.

"Bess, have you been taught nothing at all in your seventeen years? This is not the first time I have had to rescue you from your folly. I will not do it again. Do you understand that?"

I was humiliated. Instead of coming home in triumph with one brother I had ended up endangering the other one needlessly.

"Please forgive me, Will," I mumbled. "There will not be another time, I promise." He hugged me, sighing as he did so.

"Just think, Bess," he said earnestly. "We have lost our beloved mother and our poor brother is being held prisoner. Father could not bear for anything to happen to you or me." He bent and kissed my brow gently. We mounted and rode homewards, wrapped in our thoughts but glad to still have each other.

It was a day or so before I dared enquire of Will by what means he had come to my rescue in the nick of time. Will shook his head at me, still exasperated.

"Well, Bess, you made so many carefully casual enquiries of Peggy and me as to the exact period of our absence that we both had our suspicions and returned early. Thank God for our foresight and Fairy's speed."

My brother was not angry with Joe, recognising he had only agreed to the journey to prevent me travelling alone.

"I have given Joe clear instructions, Bess. In future, he is to bring any such requests from you to me or Father."

Those were Will's closing words on the incident.

Guy's Tower, Warwick Castle, December 1642

Harry sighed, stretched his long legs and tapped the quill thoughtfully against his teeth. He was writing again to his parents, in the hope that he would either be given leave to send the letter, or would find the means to have it smuggled out of the castle. Major John Bridges, the Governor of the castle, had assured the captured Royalists their families would be told they were alive.

But that was nearly two months ago now, and Major Bridges had been replaced by Major Chatterton, the man who had personally captured Harry at Edgehill. Harry had heard nothing from his family. He had the uncomfortable feeling that Major Chatterton was enjoying holding the group of Royalists prisoner, and that he was particularly pleased to be depriving Harry of his liberty. When he addressed the prisoners, his manner seemed intended to humiliate them further. On the coldest and wettest of days, they were made to form up in the courtyard trying not to shiver. Then he would keep them waiting for half an hour or more before he would saunter out, wrapped warmly in a cloak, to make some general remarks about discipline, or to announce some loss of privilege for often imaginary incidents of bad behaviour.

Harry put the letter down and stretched again, glancing around the room with its vaulted ceiling and arched windows. It was one of several tower rooms shared by Royalist officers and although a sizable chamber it was a little cramped for the number of men living in it. Harry guessed that the rooms in Guy's Tower had originally been intended as chambers for the well to do. Each room had a small servant's chamber attached and a garde robe. Now every room in the tower but the guardroom had been pressed into service to accommodate the captive officers and was crammed with an assortment of furniture. In addition to straw palliasses to sleep on, there was a small table, stools, a few chairs, and even rugs on the floor for their comfort. The fire place was tended by a silent maid servant who also brought food and candles. The prisoners were allowed to move around freely during the day. They were permitted to leave the tower and take exercise in the large courtyard. They soon discovered, however, that they were not permitted to climb the mound, where there was a new timber gun emplacement. Nor were they allowed to the top of Guy's Tower, where there was a further gun platform. If they attempted to approach the gatehouse, they found their way barred by purple coated soldiers from Lord Brooke's Regiment of foot. At night, the heavy wooden doors to the tower rooms were bolted. Harry knew that escape was not an option. He was losing track of the days. One was very much alike another in the confines of the castle, but he was fairly sure that it was either the day of, or the day before, his nineteenth birthday. If war had not come, he would have been spending the day with his friends at the university, perhaps spending the evening in a private room, with supper and cards in celebration of the event. As it was, he would probably spend much of the day chipping away at the stone, where he was slowly carving his name with the aid of the small knife he was allowed for eating.

He sighed, resuming his letter, when the door opened. Two of the soldiers on guard duty were outside.

"Lucie, come with us. The Governor wishes to see you immediately." Harry stared at them, wondering at the summons. Impatiently they hustled him from the room. Arriving at the Governor's quarters at the top of the gatehouse, the guard knocked and let him in. The Governor was standing before a blazing fire, an arm resting casually on the mantle shelf. He turned to face Harry, who was standing with his arms folded, regarding the Governor warily.

"Lieutenant Lucie," he rapped, "Arms behind your back or by your sides when being addressed by a superior officer."

Harry was inclined to dispute the respect due to an enemy superior, but reluctantly unfolded his arms. The two men were much of a height and Harry stared the tall Governor in the eye. Smirking, Major Chatterton regarded him.

"I thought I would personally acquaint you of a visit which I have just received from a charming young lady in the person of your sister." Harry stared at him.

"B bess?" he stammered. "Where is she? C can I see her?"

"That won't be possible sadly," smiled Major Chatterton, "She has already left the castle. She seemed to believe she might cozen me into releasing you."

He moved away from the fireplace and towards a bed, which was in a considerable state of disarray, sheets tumbled and pillows on the floor. Chatterton bent over and retrieved a rumpled pillow from the floor. He gestured towards the bed.

"She went to very great lengths indeed, although of course she was not successful. But I took this as a keepsake of an enjoyable hour in her company."

He put his hand into the pocket of his coat and pulled out a lock of dark hair which he placed carefully on the table. Harry stared in disbelief at the rumpled bed linens and the lock of hair. With a howl of rage he leapt towards Chatterton. He found himself staring at a pistol pointing at his heart.

"You will be sorry for this d day Sir, I will kill you," he gasped.

Major Chatterton pursed his thin lips, "I think not. Guards!" he called.

The door opened immediately.

"Lieutenant Lucie has been forgetting himself. His opinions are a little heated, we should cool him down." Chatterton turned back to Harry, "Let us hope a night in one of the underground storerooms improves your manners. Have a care on the stairs won't you," he said silkily, "They can be slippery."

Harry was marched away between two guards, one carrying a flaring torch, the other a drawn sword. Leaving the gatehouse, they crossed the courtyard towards an area of the castle Harry had not been in before. Opening a door, one of the men shoved him in the back. Clutching hopelessly at thin air, Harry fell headlong down a flight of spiral stairs. Shaken and hurt, he lay trying to catch his breath at the bottom while the guards laughed. They pulled him roughly to his feet, placed the torch in a metal sconce and unlocked a door. By the flickering light of the torch, Harry saw a small room, empty but for a few discarded sacks. The air was dank and musty.

"Strip to your breeches, Lucie. You heard what the Governor said. You need cooling down." Numbly Harry obeyed, removing coat, doublet and finally, at a nod from the soldier, his shirt. He shivered. The guards made no move to gather his discarded clothes but remained standing inside the door. One was still holding a drawn sword. The other, Harry realised, was now holding a short length of rope.

"If you feel cold, you may warm yourself with thoughts of your sister's moans as she was ploughed by the Governor."

Without pause for thought, Harry drove his fist into the man's belly. The man gasped, taken by surprise and dropped the rope. The other man grabbed Harry from behind, pressing the flat of his sword blade against Harry's back.

"I think further movement would be unwise. Hands behind your back, Lu Lu Lu Lucie," he laughed. Flushing angrily Harry complied. The man bound his hands tightly and then turned him to look him in the eye.

"What think you, Tom?" The soldier named Tom, grimacing from Harry's blow, slowly pulled himself upright, rubbing his belly. "Is it time to teach Lieutenant Lucie better manners?"

"I'd say so," grunted Tom. "Hold him." For some seconds the only sounds were those of blows, pants from the soldier as he battered his victim with his fists, and gasps of pain from Harry. Finally the man holding Harry relinquished his grip and struck him once, hard in the back. Harry reeled and fell, striking his head. He lay still.

"Time to go."

Tom shook his head and kicked the now insensible Harry viciously in the ribs. He swung his leg back again, but this time the other soldier put a restraining hand on his arm.

"Hold Tom, no more. Our orders were to give him a beating, not kill him."

"That was before the whoreson attacked me."

"I said hold. If he ends up floating in the moat, we may find ourselves on a charge."

Sulkily, Tom lowered his foot to the ground.

"Shame about those slippery stairs, Lieutenant. You should have been more careful." They went out, locking the door and leaving the unconscious Harry in darkness.

Harry awoke from the blow to the head some hours later. His head and body ached abominably and he was shivering with cold. He struggled desperately, but was unable to loosen his hands. He realised belatedly that the soldiers had been deliberately provoking him on the orders of Major Chatterton. The beating had been preordained. The Governor seemed to have developed a particular dislike for him. And he had fallen into the trap very neatly.

His thoughts raced. It could not possibly be true. Bess would never have given herself to this man, even to win his release. It had to be a lie. She would never dishonour the family so by bedding with a man before she wed. Least of all with an officer from the rebel army. She was a virtuous maid. But the lock of hair looked so much like Bess's hair. If the hair belonged to another woman, why would Major Chatterton pretend it belonged to Bess? Try as he would, all Harry's imaginings could not conjure an innocent explanation for that lock of hair. He lay, numb in body and spirit, and unable to think of anything but that his sister had played the whore. He would far rather have died than that she should do this for him.

8

THE NEXT MORNING, Harry woke from an uncomfortable doze, determined to keep his temper when he was released from the storeroom. The day wore on and he remained alone. The guards did not come near him. He spent the day shivering, without food or drink, tormented with thoughts of his sister. He had managed to struggle painfully to his feet, but the room was too dark for him to see anything and his attempts to loosen the rope binding his wrists behind his back only succeeded in increasing the chafing. His fingers had long since ceased to have any feeling in them. His body ached from the blows. The pain in his head from the beating and the fall was worsened by increasing thirst. By the end of that day he began to wonder if they were going to leave him to die. Awkwardly he went down on his knees and began to pray, trying to ignore the scratching noises from nearby rats.

Harry woke, parched with thirst, to the start of a further day in the storeroom. Distant sounds told him that the garrison had started another day. He made his way slowly and cautiously towards what he thought might be the door. He felt wood rather than stone and knew he was correct. He began to kick at the solid door, trying to attract attention. After a few minutes he heard steps approaching. A key turned in the lock. To his disappointment it was the same two men who had confined him there. They looked at him and laughed. His face was stiff and sore, one of his eyes swollen almost shut.

"Bit of a stink in here. Pissed your breeches have you, Lieutenant? Time we took you back to your companions," said Tom, grinning. "Follow us."

They let Harry stumble his way up the winding stairs, across the courtyard and into Guy's Tower, hands still bound. Outside the door to Harry's chamber Tom grinned unpleasantly. "Better mind your manners in future, Lieutenant." He opened the door and then tripped Harry so that he crashed to the floor in the midst of a circle of startled Royalist officers. His clothes were hurled after him. Laughter receded in the distance.

ᏅᏅ

Chadshunt Hall, Christmas 1642

Christmas at Chadshunt Hall that year was far from the joyous occasion it had been the year before. My father returned for the festival from Oxford with the cheering news that lists of names on both sides of the conflict were being drawn up, with the aim of exchanging prisoners of equivalent ranks. In an effort to hearten our dwindling family, my Aunt Mary, her husband Edmund and my small cousin Meg made the long journey from their Devon home to spend some time with us over the Christmas period. Under Aunt Mary's vigilant eye, the kitchens baked mince pies, roasted geese and mulled large bowls of claret. It was hard at first seeing Aunt Mary. Mother's younger sister, her petite stature, proud carriage and colouring so strongly mirrored my mother's that when I caught a glimpse of her entering a room, at first my heart would give a bump.

My father was doubly devoted to the season that year. In spite of, or because of, all our sufferings he was determined to make the best of it. Many more extreme English Protestants now viewed Christmas festivities as the trappings of popery. The eating of mince pies and plum pudding, holly and ivy about the house and the giving of money to servants or apprentices, the sending of presents to friends during the twelve days of Christmas, were all frowned on by the Puritans. That year some Puritans were already disputing the date of Christ's birth, and were calling for fasting rather than feasting. Men and women were to labour as on any other day of the year.

In defiance of the Puritans the yule log was pulled into the Great Hall on Christmas Eve and set ablaze. Our celebrations were modest. Will played his fiddle and I, my harpsichord. I refused to dance. How could I, when everything from the spiced wine which I sipped to the leaping dancers of John Dowland's frogge galliard reminded me of that earlier Christmas? Now Mother and Rafe were no more; and as I attempted to force a mince pie down my throat I wondered what misery Harry was enduring, subject as he was to the cruel whims of Major Chatterton.

Peggy was one of the few who understood the full extent of my loneliness. As she helped me into my night gown, I turned to the window where, long months ago, I had drawn the heart with the entwined R and E. Winter frosted the outside of the glass, the inside misted from the warmth in my chamber. A heart with the letters R and E took shape once more, tracing itself before my eyes. The edges stood out sharp and clear, flickering in the firelight. I stared hard at it for a few moments, rubbing my eyes. When I looked again it had vanished. I breathed a prayer of forgiveness and longing to my lost love. I went to the drawer where the blood stained kerchief lay, carefully wrapped now in a piece of linen. That night I fell asleep with it tucked against my heart.

Christmas Day was bright and frosty. We went to All Saints Church and joined in the singing with the choir to the accompaniment of the organ. Our parish church still clung to the old style, our Vicar standing firm in his view that the new communion tables were for Puritans and had no part in the ritual of Communion which the King cherished. I loved the beauty in the words of the Book of Common Prayer, England's own prayer book. As a child, too young to comprehend prayers or sermon, I immersed myself in the pictured scenes adorning the walls and the ancient images in the stained glass windows around us. Lengthy tirades threatening hell fire had no place at our church in the gentle exhortations of the Reverend Hunter. Today, Reverend Hunter and the organist seemed nervous. When I followed their gaze towards the back of the church I was uncomfortably aware of a knot of men dressed like Puritans. Strangers to the parish, they neither joined in the singing nor took communion but stood throughout.

Wishing to add a few more private prayers for Harry's release, I lingered behind as Will, my aunt and her family filed out of our family pew at the front of the church. "Pray walk on, and I will join you shortly," I smiled tremulously. My father stood by quietly, waiting for me to finish my prayers. As we left, Father bade the vicar a hearty Merry Christmas. Reverend Hunter replied with some distraction. I looked back to see him locking the church doors and leaving in some haste. I thought locking the doors odd, particularly on Christmas Day, but then I noticed that the knot of Puritan gentlemen was standing at a corner of the churchyard, closely observing those who left the church. As we passed by, my father nodded to them pleasantly, but he might have earned a better response from one of the gargoyles adorning the church roof. We returned home to dine on roast beef and plum pudding. I soon forgot the small incident.

ᔕ

Warwick Castle, Christmas Day 1642

For Harry, Christmas inside the fortress of Warwick Castle was not as bad as he had feared. It appeared that the unpleasant Major Chatterton had been called away on other business, at least for a few days. Knowing him absent, Harry was able to relax a little for the first time in weeks. On Christmas Day, the captive officers in Guy's Tower were marched across the courtyard to the castle chapel. As usual they stood in ranks at the back of the large chapel.

The Presbyterian chaplain led garrison and prisoners in a lengthy and rather gloomy service, dwelling on the need for repentance. Harry reflected it was more suited to Lent than Christmas. Once psalms and sermon were at an end, the Royalists returned to Guy's Tower with some relief and began their celebrations of the day. Boisterous and old established songs such as "Bring us in good ale" and "The boar's head in hand bear I" were favourites, with one of the men rampaging around the room impersonating a boar in a boar hunt. The King's health was toasted in the ale and a good, if plain, dinner was provided.

After dinner, a few of the officers improvised a mumming for each other, which caused much hilarity. When all were weary, Lieutenant Vaughan sang plaintive love songs in his beautiful voice. The other officers sat quietly. Many looked thoughtfully at their hands or into the distance, far beyond the castle walls where their families were waiting for them. Harry longed for news of his family. Were they all well? The effects of the beating he had received at the hands of the guards were wearing off after a week or two, leaving only painful bruises. It was time to forget this ill usage as he was, in any case, in no position to even the score. Neither was he in a position to do anything about what Bess might have done. Today was a time for hope, and he enjoyed the day as much as any of the men who were forced to spend it confined in Warwick Castle. He fell asleep thinking of home and family, trusting that he would see them again before long.

The next day, St Stephen's Day, Harry was sitting alone in one of the tower rooms reading. A deep feeling of gloom had fallen anew once the celebrations of the day before were over. He had refused to join the other officers as they paced the courtyard below under the watchful eye of their guards. He heard the door open and looked up. One of the senior officers from Lord Brooke's Regiment of foot stood there holding an open letter. He looked at Harry with something of compassion.

"Lieutenant Lucie, I have a letter to you from your father. It was brought by a messenger from Lord Essex. I believe one of his commanders, Colonel Hugh Lucie, is your uncle. I am obliged to open all letters to prisoners lest they contain any plot or other malicious intent." He handed it to Harry with a nod and left the room.

Finally, a letter from his father, confirmed by the seal which had been already broken. Harry looked at the letter in disbelief. Eagerly, he began to read. Dated some weeks earlier it began:

"My son, it grieves me very much to have to tell you the worst possible news. Your poor mother fell sick during November some weeks after your capture. She had a fever which your sister and brother did everything possible to cure, with careful attendance, treatment from our physician and prayers for her recovery. Had I been there, I could have done no more for my beloved wife. Alas, all was in vain. Within days of her sickening, your brother was forced to send me news that she was no more. Her passing was so sudden I was not able to bid her farewell.

Until now, I have not even found the means to impart to you this news, which may be possibly construed as a blessing. I take no pleasure in adding further to what you may suffer in your imprisonment. It took me much time to discover my brother and to prevail upon him to be of any assistance. I had hoped to persuade him to win your release. But he is obdurate in his refusal to reverse the consequences of what he is pleased to see as your folly, and mine. Finally he consented to bring you this news and I hope it will reach you. At least you will know that we think of you and strive for your release.

Your mother is buried below the floor of the nave of All Saints Church. We followed her to her final resting place. I fear the white marble stone above her head may already be scratched or stained by months of passing feet by the time you behold it. But I trust and believe that time will come. Your brother, sister and I, thank God, are all well.

Pray for the end of this conflict, as we do for you and your safe return on a daily basis.

Your father, Henry Lucie"

Harry sat motionless, clutching his letter, for many minutes. He could scarcely believe that his mother, his dear mother, was no longer in this world. He felt that he should have sensed it, that on the day she died he should have felt her spirit passing. Had she thought of him as she lay fevered and dying? Why had God chosen to take her at this time? And he had a further source of grief of which his father was perhaps happily unaware. Bess had been distracted with grief for their mother. While their father had been away from home seeking Harry's release she had made her disastrous visit to the castle, sacrificing her virtue in a futile attempt to help her brother.

Harry scrambled to his feet. Lifting a stool, he hurled it savagely against the stone wall, snapping one of its legs. He drove his fist into the wall until he cried out with the pain and pulled away, leaving a bloody smear on the whitewashed stone. He paced the room feverishly. He must find the means of being with his bereaved family, he must visit his mother's grave without delay. His eyes fell on his cloak, lying across his bed. He stooped and snatched it up. He would make a dash for the gatehouse, he would take the guards unawares, he would make a bid for freedom.

"My son." He paused in the act of donning his cloak. The voice was in his head, but it was his mother's.

"Do not throw your life away, I beg you. It will not restore mine. Live, Harry, we will be together again some day, but do not seek to anticipate that time. Farewell."

His eyes fell on his prayer book. Cradling his bleeding hand, he fell to his knees and prayed for the end of the conflict which had already claimed too many lives.

☙

Chadshunt Hall, February 1643

The whole country and all of nature seemed to be waiting, for spring, for the next steps in what was now a civil war. There was a light covering of snow on the ground, frosting the snowdrops and crocuses which were just starting to show themselves above the ground. My aunt and her family had returned home, leaving Will and I once more in charge of the house. It was Ash Wednesday. We had attended church in the morning, to prepare our souls by prayer for the Lenten fast. In the afternoon, I decided Hector and I deserved a little enjoyment. I wrapped myself in a fur lined cloak and pulled the hood over my head then set off on foot. Some delicate flakes of snow were still falling, swirling a little as they drifted to the slushy ground. The half grown Hector chased them growling, wet flakes melting on his nose.

In the stables, Joe and Ben were making ready to lead the horses up and down the lane for some light exercise. It was too cold for the horses to spend time out in the fields, but the snow balled in their hooves, making it dangerous to ride them too fast. Fairy was pleased to see me, flicking her ears forward in anticipation of an apple. She nuzzled Hector gently. He was sniffing around her as usual, wagging his stubby tail. I heard a horse trotting up the lane and went outside. The rider dismounted, threw the reins to one of the grooms and ran up the steps. I gathered up my skirts and slithered hastily across the wet cobbles towards the entrance doors. Will was already tearing open the letter. The messenger stood, melting snow dripping from his hat and cloak, in front of the fire in the Great Hall.

Will looked up, "It's from Father, Bess. Good news at last. Harry is to be released." I sank into a chair and started to weep. Will explained that he was summoned to meet Harry at Warwick Castle. The terms of the prisoner exchange were agreed. Harry and a number of Royalist officers were being released from Warwick on the same day that a similar number of rebel officers would be released from Oxford. There was scanty time for preparation.

The prisoners on both sides were to be released at dawn in two days' time. It had been deemed safest that the released captives would make the first leg of their journey to freedom together, and so we were to expect that Harry and Will would be accompanied by other released Royalist officers.

I understood little of what Will said. Only the news that Harry was coming home penetrated the mists of my emotions. I sat trembling, only rousing myself to return Will's hug when he jumped to his feet,

"Bess there is much to be done to prepare for this joyous event. Will you instruct the servants and put things in train for their reception?"

I nodded dumbly, standing like a statue until Will said gently

"Bess? Whence have you gone my sister?" I shook myself, nodded and turned towards the kitchens.

ꟹ

There was a hint of approaching spring in the air. The longed-for cavalcade arrived in the late morning. I heard the clatter of hooves and flattened my nose against a window in the Great Hall to catch an early glimpse of Harry. Fourteen horses were trotting up the lane, a fresh breeze ruffling the horses' manes and tugging at the hats and cloaks of their riders. Will was at the head, Harry close behind him. Joe and the other grooms were standing in the courtyard, ready to stable the horses in the west wing.

I flew down the steps. Will was sitting very upright in the saddle, glowing with satisfaction. Harry looked somewhat older than his nineteen years, tired and haggard. His beard was neatly trimmed and he was freshly shaved, but his hair was longer than I had ever known it.

"Bess", Harry threw himself off his horse and hugged me. "Bess," he repeated, his voice breaking, "Mother."

"We will visit her grave this very day, if you so wish."

Harry nodded mutely. There were tears in his eyes and he turned away from me, dashing them fiercely away. I put a hand on his shoulder, but this time he shook it off.

"Bess," said Will gently. "Harry's home now, safe at last. But I think he may be in need of rest."

I watched Will lead Harry away into the entrance hall and up the stairs towards his bed chamber, an arm draped around his shoulders. I had a thousand questions for Harry, but I realized they would have to wait.

It was not the joyous homecoming I had dreamt of for so many months. Forcing myself to remember my duties as hostess, I turned my attention towards the remaining twelve officers, now all dismounted. Some were whispering to each other, others were staring vacantly at the cobbled courtyard or the entrance of the house. None had made a move thus far.

I dipped respectfully in a curtsey. "Gentlemen, I am Elisabeth Lucie. In my father's absence, I bid you welcome to Chadshunt Hall. Pray, follow me."

The men clustered together in a tight knot as they ascended the steps behind me. It was a larger group than Will or I had anticipated, but Chadshunt Hall, was sufficiently extensive to accommodate them. The Lucies had built it in the time of King Henry VIII using the stones from the ruined Woberley Abbey, demolished at the King's command. It had been enlarged by my Grandfather the first Baronet, as the family had prospered under the reign of King James. In addition to the bedchambers adjoining the long gallery on the upper floor of the west wing, there were several smaller rooms on the ground floor of the main house which could be used for accommodating visitors.

One of the men stumbled as he entered the house, and I noticed he was limping. He looked to be a few years older than Will, at least 25 years old if not more.

"Are you hurt?" I enquired. He turned. Two slanted, startlingly green eyes studied my face. He paused and brushed thick dark hair from his brow.

"No hurt, I thank you, Mistress," he replied in a soft Welsh lilt. "Merely a small token from Edgehill." He straightened his back as if to compensate, drawing himself up to his full height. He was no more than three or four inches taller than me.

What did he mean by a token? I had no time for riddles. The limp must wait until I had leisure to attend to it. I had been unsettled by the casual reference to Edgehill. Had he known Rafe?

The green eyes were regarding me enquiringly. When I said nothing, the officer gave a slight bow and continued into the hall.

For the next hour Peggy, the other servants and I darted up and down the service passage from the hall to kitchens, pantry and bake house. From the kitchens came a babble of conversation as Janie the cook, Polly and Margret the kitchen maids and Joan the scullery maid basted, chopped and stirred. Nicholas's successor Peter was in charge of basting the meat on the spit. I peeped into the kitchen yet again in time to see Janie, face reddened by heat from the fire, smacking him on the head with her wooden spoon.

"Baste it I said, and keep that jack wound up as turns the spit, not turn your back and filch pieces of pastry." I slunk out quietly. With so many to care for I was glad my mother had brought me up to thoroughly understand the management of a household such as ours. We had made more careful provision than usual this autumn. Our brew house supplied us with a constant supply of beer. Store rooms still held plenty of grain, wheels of cheese from our dairy, smoked meats, salted and dried vegetables, jams and honey. At midday I rang the bell for dinner with relief and we all gathered to eat in the Great Hall. I had found the family dining room, recently added by my father, convenient with my family away. For the present enlarged company however, only the Great Hall would accommodate our numbers. Will called for our attention.

"My friends, let us thank the Lord, not only for the food and drink before us, but for your safe return. Imprisoned for fighting for our rightful king, you are all now free. May you rejoice and enjoy that freedom with your families. And may God bless the King and bring peace to this land."

A chorus of "Amens" followed. Will seated himself at the head of the high table, Harry in the place of honour beside him. For a while there was little sound but the clatter of knives and spoons on plates. It was a more subdued gathering than I had expected. The men spoke little. There was none of the laughter and banter I was accustomed to when my brothers' friends made a stay at Chadshunt. Will was making strenuous attempts to engage those sitting nearest to him in conversation. He caught my eye and I realised I should do likewise.

I seated myself at the foot of the table, where I found myself next to the Welshman. "Which regiment are you in?" I asked politely.

"Sir John Byron's," he replied. It was Rafe's regiment.

"Were you acquainted with Lieutenant Rafe Beauchamp?" I asked hesitantly. "He was in your regiment. He was killed in the battle."

"Ah." He drank deeply from his glass of wine, lost in thought. "Was he a kinsman?"

I shook my head dumbly, staring at my plate to avoid his sympathetic eyes.

"Not a kinsman, Sir. He was a friend of Will's," I mumbled, colouring at the half truth.

"I knew him, Mistress. A fine man, courageous, very high spirits."

"Yes, that was Rafe," I said eagerly. "Did you know him well?"

"Not well," he replied, to my disappointment, "His troop was one of the last to join the regiment. I met him the night before the battle. He entertained the men with absurd stories of his falcon and how he would have flown it against the rebel army if he had been allowed to bring it on campaign. It brought to mind Prince Rupert's dog, Boye. The prince takes it everywhere."

"And during the battle?" I prompted.

"Byron's were the second line of horse, supposedly held in reserve. But when the rebels broke and fled, we joined the pursuit. I recall a small band galloping ahead of me. Lieutenant Beauchamp was a part of it, cheering and waving his sword. I lost sight of them and I saw him no more. We chased the enemy as far as Kineton. We should never have left the field."

A shadow came over his face. I realized in my thoughts of Rafe I had brushed aside the sufferings of others.

"What of you?" I asked belatedly. His brow furrowed.

"I managed to rein up, and Sir John himself sent me to encourage our horse to regroup and return. It was hopeless, too late, our men were scattered far and wide. Returning to him alone, I encountered enemy dragoons. I glimpsed a tawny sash in a hedgerow and spurred away, but I was too slow. There were shots."

"They shot you?"

"Not me. It was my horse that fell, screaming in agony. Nant y Glo. His dam was my father's favourite brood mare. "

He shrugged apologetically.

"I rolled clear but when I tried to stand, pain shot up my leg and I collapsed on the ground. I had broke my ankle in the fall. The enemy soldiers were obliged to drag me since I could not walk." He paused. "Lieutenant Beauchamp was one of many good men who fell that day."

I felt embarrassed. In my anxiety to hear Rafe's story, I had ended in reviving bad memories for another man. It was beginning to sound as if Rafe's final actions had been misguided, undisciplined. Would he still be alive, he and others who had fallen in that headlong chase, had they followed their orders with greater restraint and clearer heads?

Harry's voice broke in upon my thoughts.

"Sing for us, Gabriel. The Welsh linnet, we call him. Will you give us a song, Gabriel?"

Harry was bellowing. He must be drunk. Will laid a restraining hand on his shoulder. Harry shook his hand off and reached for his glass, knocking it over. A crimson stream of wine cascaded over the fine linen table cloth.

The Welshman scrambled to his feet and moved with surprising speed to Harry's side. He bent his head and spoke quietly to him. Harry shook his head from side to side like a terrier shaking a rat.

"Fatigued? Indeed, I am not, Gabriel. Well if we are not to have music, let us eat and make merry. A fine repast, and finally a knife sharp enough to be of use."

He raised his knife and before my horrified eyes, slashed deep into his left palm. I screamed. Gabriel tore the knife from Harry's grasp and Will grabbed a napkin, winding it around Harry's bleeding hand. Servants came running and Harry was whisked away to his chamber, Gabriel close beside him.

"Summon our physician, Bess," Will muttered to me as he left the hall.

As one, the other men rose to their feet and tramped wearily from the hall, bowing to me as they went. I surveyed the congealing remains of the feast and the wine stained cloth, now splashed with Harry's blood. Tears ran down my cheeks. My brother was home, but we were still at war, and that war had only just begun.

9

WHAT WAS AMISS with Harry? Master Blackthorne had given him a calming draught. Harry emerged from his chamber late the next morning, his hand wrapped in a bandage. By common consent, we said nothing of the previous day. Hoping it might bring comfort, I offered to go with him to the church to visit Mother's grave.

"Maybe later," he mumbled.

Yet when I made my own visit to the church that afternoon, I found Harry was there before me. He knelt beside the tablet in the nave, his head bent in prayer or sorrow. He stretched out his hand and I saw he was smoothing the inscription carved into the marble. I tiptoed away. We should be united in our grief. I did not understand why he kept himself alone.

As the days went on, Harry continued to spend his time with the other officers, Gabriel in particular. With Will he was friendly, but with me he was distant. He seemed to be shunning my company.

I was becoming increasingly concerned. While Harry had exhibited no further wild behaviour, I could not understand how grief for Mother could create a barrier between him and me. I took Will to one side.

"Will, I do not understand Harry. Did something happen to him at Warwick Castle of which we are unaware? He is not the same person who left to fight. His face is drawn. Somehow he has aged in the months since we last saw him."

"The other officers were equally subdued on their arrival. Perhaps freedom has been in some manner a shock, as was captivity."

"Yet now they talk and laugh, Will. Harry does not."

"I will speak to Harry, Bess, and see what I can discover."

The other men were becoming individuals to me. They were junior officers from several different regiments, both horse and foot. Most were in their late teens or early twenties. All were gentlemen. Walter and Richard were brothers from Sussex. John and Charles were from Hampshire. The rest were from Oxfordshire, apart from Gabriel who was from South Wales.

Their spirits were recovering and by the third day after their arrival I entered the Great Hall to hear laughter.

I was in search of Matthew Stanley. His delicate, fine boned features and his thick mop of blonde curls and blue eyes reminded me uncomfortably of Rafe. He was still in pain from a wounded arm. It had mended badly. Like Harry, he too was withdrawn, lost in bad memories.

"Master Stanley, here is the liniment I promised you." Stanley blushed and ducked his head. "I wonder the surgeon at the castle did not offer you better care."

"The surgeon at the castle did not attend injured prisoners."

I turned, recognizing the voice of Gabriel Vaughan.

"He might have treated Matthew's arm, my ankle too, had there been time. Sadly, there were too many wounded soldiers from the garrison after Edgehill, and all his care was for them."

"Sadly?" I was indignant. "They are rebels, the men you fought".

He shrugged his shoulders matter of factly.

"You are in the right of it, Mistress, but still they are men."

ග

That evening, when I retired to my room for the night, Will followed me.

"Some private conversation with you sister?" I nodded at Peggy to leave me. Will turned away, leaning over the fire and kicking thoughtfully at a log.

"Bess, you will recall your ill advised visit to Warwick Castle, which happily we have been able to keep from our father's ears."

"I wish I could forget the whole episode."

There was a long pause. Will's blue eyes were sympathetic.

"Once we were gone from the castle that day, Major Chatterton had Harry brought to him. He showed Harry your hair. He displayed the bed, sheets tumbled, all awry, and told Harry he had lain with you. Harry believed you sacrificed your honour to try to save him. He is racked with guilt and between your loss of virtue and Mother's death has been driven almost mad."

I sank upon a chair.

"But Will," I gasped," You know that was a lie, did you not explain to Harry?"

Will nodded, "I have, and it was some comfort to him. I was obliged nonetheless to explain how Major Chatterton did obtain this evidence, your situation when I came upon you. The tale so very nearly came true. His mind is easier now, but he remains distressed at what did occur and what might have been. You may find he is still not easy in your company, unjust though that may be."

Indignantly I opened my mouth but Will held up his hand.

"There is more. Harry threatened Major Chatterton. In response, he was taken away and –punished." Seeing my anguished look, Will hastened to calm me. "He has recovered from his injuries." He regarded me seriously.

"Do not fear, little sister. I feel sure Major Chatterton and I will cross paths again. And when we do, I will kill him."

He stooped and kissed my cheek, followed it up with a formal nod, and left my chamber. I sat for many minutes staring into the fire and seeing pictures I had no wish to see. I saw my own foolish behaviour. I pictured Harry's desperate bravery as he defended my honour against the man who was his captor. And I imagined in horrible detail what my brother might have suffered in reprisal.

ᔕ

The liniment was of some use to Lieutenant Stanley. I proffered a second jar to Gabriel Vaughan, hoping it might help his injured ankle.

"That's an unusual ring," I pointed to the ring finger of his right hand as he accepted the jar from me.

"My wife Catherine gave it to me." He rubbed it absently. "It is the lion of the Talbot family, she was a Talbot."

"Oh you're married then?" I said politely.

"I was once," he said softly. "She's gone now." I hesitated, not wanting to intrude. "She died a year ago, of smallpox. We had a year old son Michael. They both caught the pox, somehow I didn't." He stared into the distance. "Many people recover from it, but they died within a day of each other," he said bitterly. "Well, there it is." He straightened his shoulders.

"But you Mistress, you are as yet unwed? Your brother talked of you and your family when we were together at the castle."

"I am unwed," I agreed. "There was someone, but he was killed at Edgehill."

"And was that perhaps Lieutenant Beauchamp, your brother's friend?" I nodded tiredly.

"He was so impetuous, so full of life," I finished desolately. I rose slowly to my feet. He made to rise too. "No, stay there," I sighed, "I have a number of other matters to attend to. I must visit the laundry and the brew house. I need to be busy, it helps me to forget."

ᔕ

I decided that the Sunday should be one of holiday spirit. I hoped it might cheer Harry. Good food was acceptable on the Sabbath even during the season of Lent. I asked our cook to prepare beef, mutton and capons with fruit tarts, nuts and jellies. In the morning we strolled across the fields to church, where we gave thanks for the release of Harry and the other officers. I had been looking forward to hearing Gabriel's voice raised in song to see if he truly sounded like the song bird. However, to my surprise he was not there. On my return to the house I saw him emerging from the stables. He started on seeing me, but quickly recovered himself and enquired if he could be of any use to me.

"By making music for us tonight, Master Vaughan," I replied, "I had hoped to hear your voice this morning at church."

"Then tonight you shall hear me, Mistress" he replied. "But I fear your brother has overstated my talents." He gave me a slight bow and I smiled, letting the matter of his unexplained morning absence drop.

That evening we all, servants included, joined in the music in the Great Hall. I played a number of well known English pieces suitable for performance on the harpsichord such as "The Woods So Wild" and "The King's Hunt". As I finished, I looked around for Will and Gabriel. Both were missing. I heard Will's laugh and a note struck on a lute. Glancing upwards, I saw that Will and Gabriel had made their way silently into the wood paneled minstrels' gallery above us. They laughed and bowed. Will began to sing, accompanying himself on his lute. Finally Gabriel took the lute. In a sweet tenor he began to sing "Let no man steal your thyme". I had rarely heard such a beautiful voice. He followed it with "Seven Months Married". This song about an arranged marriage began,

"Seven months she's been married and all to her grief
Seven months she's been married but found no relief
Seven months she's been married but still she's a maid
Oh she's ruined, she's ruined, she's ruined."

There was much laughter at the words.

"And so," Gabriel concluded as the song came to an end, "You may decide it is better to marry for love than to oblige your families."

He grinned and there was more laughter from his audience in the hall below.

"Now I see my choice of songs is making Mistress Lucie blush. I will sing some more suitable love songs – in Welsh. So you will have to believe my assurances they are more suitable."

This brought more laughter. After these he descended from the minstrels' gallery and sang two madrigals with Harry and Christopher, which he admitted to having taught them during their time in Warwick Castle. They were composed by William Lawes, one of the King's court musicians. Finally he paused to wipe his face and drink some ale. Cries for more were met with a regretful shake of the head.

"Oh, how I wish you had taught Harry a few more madrigals," I sighed.

"Well, Mistress," he said solemnly, "Unfortunately we had no more time left as the garrison insisted on setting us free." He smiled shyly at me and chuckled.

"You have an odd sense of humour!" I blurted with my usual lack of tact.

"That is a fine minstrels' gallery, Mistress. The notes carry well. Has your family entertained many important personages? Royalty, perhaps?"

I pondered.

"Well, King James stayed here once. We have a portrait of him hanging in the picture gallery. He presented it to my Grandfather as a gift. And there are tales of the old Queen, Queen Elizabeth I mean, when she came to stay."

Gabriel nodded at me to continue. He wiped his face again and unbuttoned the bottoms of the sleeves to his russet hued velvet doublet, to loosen it.

"I believe having Queen Elizabeth to stay was as much a burden as an honour, though no doubt it would have been treason to remark it." I smiled at him mischievously.

"How so?"

"She travelled with a large retinue. Before she arrived for her second and final visit she sent instructions that the house was to be clean, and that our family was to move out of all the principal rooms. I have heard that the final insult for my family was that Her Majesty demanded the whole lane, from gatehouse to courtyard be filled with straw to deaden the jolting of her carriage wheels."

He laughed.

"And your own family?"

"No visits from royal personages," he replied briefly, "I wish you goodnight, Mistress Lucie." He raised my hand to his lips.

ᔕ

The next morning I found Gabriel and hesitantly requested some private conversation. A little surprised he agreed. The snow had melted and the weather was fine, although a chilly breeze was blowing. I directed our steps towards the herb garden, which had the advantage of being sheltered and enclosed without giving our conversation an overly clandestine air.

Spreading the tail of my thick cloak beneath me, I sat on a stone bench by the wall in the herb garden and hesitantly began. I explained my lingering concerns about Harry and with great embarrassment enquired if Harry had apprised him of my ill-fated visit to the castle. Gabriel stood by, regarding me intently as I described that day. I told him of the Major's assault on me with as few particulars as possible. He looked shocked. Had I forfeited his good opinion too? A moment later he gripped both my hands firmly and looked his reassurance.

"But wait, there's more," I said miserably. Since Gabriel had clearly been unaware of my visit to the castle, he could be unaware of its aftermath. Taking a deep breath, I told him of how the Major had used my lock of hair to taunt Harry.

"Did Harry mention nothing?" I half feared the answer.

Gabriel's brow furrowed in thought. After a few moments it cleared, and he nodded as if he had found an answer to something puzzling him.

ꟹ

Gabriel enters Harry's quarters in Guy's Tower. Seeing his bed not slept in, he pauses and pushes his thick dark hair back.

"Is Harry Lucie not yet returned?" Two men playing dice are using the silver buttons from their doublets as stakes. Lieutenant Palmer pushes the dice aside and looks up.

"He is not, Gabriel. Something may be amiss, but there is little we can do." He spreads his hands in a gesture of helplessness.

Gabriel frowns, "He has not been seen since yesterday, John. Precious little doubt remains that there is something amiss. The guards cannot or will not say aught of his whereabouts."

"Do you think he was released?" Ensign Black enquires optimistically.

Gabriel props his stick against the table, bends and rubs his ankle. "I think not, William. Harry's cloak still hangs there on its hook. It is more likely he is detained for some reason best known to the Governor."

"Matthew may have more intelligence of him. He mumbled something when the guards bolted our door at nightfall, but his prattling oft makes little sense and I confess I paid him little heed. "Palmer colours in embarrassment. Matthew Stanley is staring vacantly at a book.

"Matthew," Stanley raises his eyes to Gabriel.

"Have you seen Harry Lucie since yesterday?"

"With the guards". He retreats again into his private world.

"Matthew, Harry Lucie may be in danger. Did you see where the guards were taking him? Were they restraining him?"

"Out of the gatehouse," Stanley mutters. "They were marching Harry across the courtyard. One held him by an arm. He carried a torch. The other carried a sword."

Gabriel and the other men exchange uneasy looks. "He has done nothing to merit mistreatment" Black protests.

"That may be no guarantee of his safety, William. If Harry does not return tonight we must act tomorrow."

When the doors are unbolted the next morning Harry Lucie is still not returned. The prisoners in Guy's Tower gather. "We must take action without further delay," Gabriel is saying.

"Could Lord Lindsey maybe intercede?" Lieutenant Brett asks.

"It is as difficult to gain access to him as it is to the Governor. You know, they keep him close confined. There is always a guard before the door of his room in Caesar's Tower. No, Walter, we must take action ourselves. I will approach one of the guards and beg him to take me to the Governor."

"What if we cannot find a guard willing to aid you?" Palmer asks.

"Then we must bribe one, gentlemen".

"The rebels took all we had when they captured us" protests Brett.

Gabriel looks at him steadily and begins tugging off the silver buttons on his own doublet. Then he looks at his right hand and, sighing, pulls a ring from his finger. The little collection in front of Gabriel grows. One or two men still have their signet rings and they add them to the pile. Brett reddens and gets to his feet. He pushes past Gabriel and goes to the window, turning his back on the other men and kicking a booted foot against the stone wall.

"Walter?" one of the men says to him tentatively. Brett turns, a sneer on his thin face.

"I do not believe we should be in such haste to part with the few things of value we have left to us. And solely on the word of a half-witted fool." He glares at Matthew Stanley.

Gabriel says nothing but his face darkens. As he sweeps the pile of gold and silver into his hand, there is the tramp of boots on the stairs. The door to the room flies open. The men have a brief glimpse of two guards standing in the doorway, Harry Lucie between them. Then they push him and one hooks a boot around Harry's ankle. He lands heavily on the floor and the two guards depart laughing.

Gabriel's relief is tempered immediately as he runs his eyes over the bruised face, the battered, half naked body, the urine soaked breeches. It is clear to the silent officers that Harry has been beaten and tortured. The tightly knotted rope has bitten deeply into his wrists. Black is already struggling to release him, but he is hampered as the prisoners are allowed only small blunt knives for eating.

Harry's parched lips form the single word, "Thirsty," with difficulty. Hurriedly, one of the men reaches for a half full jug of ale and holds it to his lips. Harry sips, then gulps and chokes as the liquid courses down his throat.

It is some days before Gabriel attempts to talk to Harry about his ordeal. By this time the livid bruises are beginning to fade. Harry is lying on his bed staring at the vaulted ceiling when Gabriel limps through the door.

"Are you feeling a little recovered?"

Harry nods, continuing to stare at the ceiling.

"You were badly mistreated. Was it by the Governor's command?"

"It was," Harry's tone is hard.

"Why did he order this?"

Gabriel waits, but Harry says nothing. Gabriel sees a tear roll down the younger man's cheek as he hastily turns his face to the wall.

"I will not speak of it."

ထ

"From that time on," Gabriel said sadly, "Harry was not himself. At first of course he was in pain. But as his hurts healed he became even quieter. He was easily vexed and even our attempts at music sometimes failed to rouse his interest. If he was handed a lute he would push it away.

After Christmas Harry received the sad news about your mother. Strangely this seemed to lift him out of his own concerns. He showed great dignity in his loss and prayed a good deal. Now I understand why he would not speak of his suffering. He wished to protect your honour."

"Thank you," I said sadly, "I needed to fully comprehend what my brother endured. I was the cause of all this."

I stared at the frost hardened ground at my feet, covering the first hopeful shoots of chives and garlic. The next moment I felt a hand resting on my head as if in blessing. I lifted my eyes slowly to see Gabriel smiling at me with a look of sadness in his green eyes. He dropped his hand.

"Do not blame yourself, Mistress Lucie. You meant well and for that surely your brother will forgive you in time. Be patient with him, some scars are slower to heal than others, and they are often the ones which cannot be seen."

It was the last proper conversation I had with Gabriel. The men were ready to leave, continuing their onward journeys. Most were intending to visit their families before rejoining their regiments in time for the spring campaign. I regretted their departure. Gabriel had an air of quiet authority which had a reassuring effect on Harry and also I realised on me. I badly needed to feel that matters were under control and the world was not turned upside down.

ᘓ

"A small thank you Harry, and to you Mistress, for your warm hospitality. I will return, if I may, to hear the results."

Gabriel handed Harry a small roll of parchment with a bow, smiling. I had seen him scribbling thoughtfully.

Puzzled, I took the scroll from Harry and opened it. Gabriel had composed a new madrigal for two voices, 'When maids go a wooing'. I was delighted. The scroll had a tiny drawing at its foot. I looked closely and saw it was a linnet. I laughed.

"Thankyou, Master Vaughan and I think the time has come for you to call me Bess."

"Well Bess, if you will return the favour."

"I will, Gabriel," I smiled.

Harry and I accompanied Gabriel down the steps into the courtyard.

"Did you observe the inscription over these doors?" Harry asked.

Gabriel shook his head and Harry pointed. I saw Gabriel rapidly reading the Latin.

"I am shut to envy, but always open to a friend," he translated.

"And so always open to you, Gabriel." Harry and Gabriel embraced warmly. I gave Gabriel my hand. He kissed it lightly. I watched him walk towards the stables. As Gabriel trotted out of the courtyard, turning to wave, I put my arm round Harry's waist. He did not pull away.

"I am so glad you are home safe, Harry. We will be together now, you and I and Will and Father. We will make this a happy home again. I am determined it will be so. And we will have music."

I brandished Gabriel's new song. Harry looked down at me then with a smile. It was a little strained, but still a smile. Slowly, we sauntered into the house together.

ᘓ

March 1643

In early March, Father returned home. He looked weary, but his face lit up at the sight of Harry.

"My son," Father said fondly as Harry knelt formally for his blessing, "God has restored you to us." Lifting Harry to his feet he looked at him critically, "Thinner in the face and a little careworn perchance, but whole and sound in body. We can ask for no more."

Will, Harry and I had by this time decided between us it were best to say as little as possible of Harry's sufferings at Warwick Castle. Will and Harry both were equally determined to kill Major Chatterton. It did not need the addition of a vengeful father.

Father was assisting Sir Edward Walker, Secretary to the Council of War. He was given leave to return home for some time to be reunited with Harry. Parliament had presented terms for a treaty to the King. Hostilities continued in some areas of the country while the King considered its terms. The Royalist garrison at Lichfield was under siege and surrender to the forces of Parliament was imminent.

It was impossible to determine from this conflicting news which way the wind was blowing. But for the moment we rejoiced that Father was home and that our remaining family was reunited.

ᔕ

After some argument, it was settled that when Father and Will returned to the army, Harry would remain behind to guard the estate and me. I protested that I was well able to look after myself, but Will silenced me with a meaningful look. Father was to continue his work for the Council of War while treaty negotiations continued. As the Chadshunt troop was no longer in being, Will's intention was to seek a new commission as Lieutenant with the Oxford Army. Father cautioned him that if the negotiations were successful, there might be no further cavalry engagements. Will's face, when he heard this, was so crestfallen that I turned away, suppressing a laugh. I knew he feared that a premature peace would doom him to a life of inaction.

Harry protested that he was ready to return to the fray. Father dismissed his pleas.

"My son, the King is grateful to you and all others who have already lost life or liberty fighting in his cause. He will not now begrudge you quiet repose at home, enjoying the blessings of personal freedom. Rest, Harry. Regain your health and spirits. If things go badly with His Majesty you may yet be called upon again."

As Will cheerfully made ready to rejoin a cavalry regiment, it was clear that Harry was envying him his liberty to risk his life anew. By this time I had become more circumspect with my own views of adventure. The loss of Rafe, and Harry's own trials, had made me realise that as my father had warned, war was truly not a game.

ᔕ

23 March 1643

A wet spring day. A galloping messenger was no longer of quite so much interest. Since Father had not yet left Chadshunt, army messengers bearing dispatches from Oxford arrived every day or so. I was curious nevertheless.

"For whom was the message, Thomas?"

"For Master Will, Mistress, from Banbury Castle."

I promptly went in search of Will. He was seated with Father in the library before a blazing fire, an open letter in his hand and a look of horror on his face.

"Not fit to live!" Father was finishing some explosive remarks.

"Will, what is the matter?"

My brother's face was white with shock.

"William Compton has written to say his father, the Earl of Northampton is dead, Bess. The earl was killed in battle, and James Compton wounded, at a place called Hopton Heath in Staffordshire. The earl was killed when he was unhorsed and refused quarter."

"How sad, Will. I am so sorry to hear of his death."

I scarcely knew Spencer Compton or his eldest son James, but Will's frequent sojourns in recent times at Banbury Castle had built a friendship with the youngest son William, left in command of Banbury's garrison at the age of 18.

"There is worse, Bess, though it will shock you."

"Worse than the Earl's death?"

"The Roundhead commander, Sir John Gell, took possession of the Earl's body. The Earl had captured eight pieces of ordnance before he fell. Gell demanded its return. In short, he informed James Compton, that if he wished to bring his father's body home for burial he would return the guns." Will broke off, choked with emotion.

Father muttered something under his breath.

Will sprang to his feet and smashed his fist into the carved oak paneling.

"Father, I will ride at once to Banbury Castle and give William what comfort I may."

He pushed open the doors of the library, clearly about to leave.

"But Will, what happened?"

"I cannot imagine what it must have cost James to refuse, Bess, but refuse he did. He would not be held to ransom by such a wicked, unchristian demand. When Gell received his answer he made good on his threat. Instead of returning the Earl's body to his family, he paraded it through the streets of Derby.

ᔓᔕ

Within days of the news about the Earl's death and its shocking aftermath, Father and Will departed. Left at home, Harry fretted like a schoolboy denied a holiday.

"Harry, Father will be furious if you neglect the estate. He relies on you to take his place," I admonished him.

Harry was supposedly looking over and familiarizing himself with the account books in Father's study. Instead, I found him staring out of the window. A heavy ledger was open on his knee, but I saw he had been making small drawings in the margins of horses and cannon. There was even a tiny drawing of what appeared to be a linnet. Harry started and looked at me. The longing in his eyes saddened me.

"Truly, Bess, I try to apply myself, but this is a dry study when I might be fighting. Five months I was constrained within the walls of Warwick Castle. Now I feel I have but exchanged one prison for another. I should have risked Father's displeasure by pressing my suit to accompany Will."

"Harry, you risk more than displeasure if he hears you are lax in discharging your obligations."

I might have spared my breath.

"Is it not yet time to dine?"

Listlessly he closed the ledger. In the afternoon I saw Harry galloping hard up the wooded slopes as if trying to outpace some invisible opponent. That evening, Harry came into my chamber. He entered after a brief knock, leaving me no time to conceal the handkerchief with its fading brown bloodstains. I retrieved it from its hiding place when I was missing Rafe more than usual. He stopped short, seeing the stricken look on my face, and his eyes fell to the handkerchief.

"Is that blood on your handkerchief?" I nodded dumbly. "Is it Rafe's blood?" My small sob answered him. "Then keep it well, dear Bess," he said tenderly, "It is a monument to Rafe's constancy, both to you and to the cause he died for. As for me, I have thought too much on my own concerns."

ᔓᔕ

April 1643

For the remainder of March we heard nothing from my father or from Will. Just before Easter, Father returned one day without warning. He greeted us loudly.

"Harry, Bess, I am returned so that we may be together to celebrate Easter."

Within an hour however, he had called Harry urgently into his study. I lingered in my normal manner, hoping to catch snippets of conversation. When my father had heard my steps passing casually by three times within a quarter of an hour, he flung the door open.

"Very well, Bess you may join us." I hurried to accept the invitation, but there was no warmth in his eyes.

"There are weighty matters to discuss which, sadly, affect the whole family." I attended eagerly to what he might say. He began again.

"Parliament has set up a Committee for Sequestration to confiscate the estates of all who give assistance to the King. Clearly this is illegal and no doubt treasonous. Nevertheless, they have done so, and are reliant on the good graces of the county authorities to enforce this by what means they may. Sadly, Warwick, the seat of our own county government, is in the hands of Parliament. They are aware that we support His Majesty and I believe there is a grave risk that our family estates are in danger of seizure."

I gasped in shock. Harry was tight lipped.

"What can we do?" I whispered.

"Nothing in undue haste. We must take steps, and soon, but these machinations will take Parliament's agents a little while to enforce, please God. They will not take this place without the use of force."

10

April 1643

On Easter Day, my mother's beautiful cloth with its delicate tracery of flowers had been chosen to adorn the altar. Remembering her skill in needlework, my heart swelled with pride and then the tears overflowed. Sad and tender thoughts of my mother were, I realized, detracting from the prayers and hymns celebrating the risen Lord. As I joined my voice with Harry's in the final hymn, I heard movement at the back of the church. The doors, closed against the sharp April breeze, opened abruptly, sending a blast which made the candles flicker and gutter.

"What popish rites profane the day of the Lord?"

thundered a voice. Startled, the congregation turned in our pews as one to gape at the intruders. Two small children began to cry, agitated at the tone.

"Gentlemen, what means this intrusion into the House of God?" exclaimed the Vicar bravely, although his voice trembled.

"Sir," interjected my father, "It is you who profane the day of the Lord by thus intruding in His house."

Harry had turned pale with wrath. He instinctively clapped his hand to his side, but he was not wearing his sword. The speaker with the thunderous voice strode down the aisle towards the altar. A Puritan, he wore white shirt, black coat and breeches. Glossy hair flowed beneath his hat. He was followed by a small band of equally surly looking men, similarly attired and all wearing hats. When he reached our family pew at the front of the church, he paused and glared at my father.

"And which malignant family is this?" he sneered turning to the vicar.

"Sir," answered the vicar, wringing his hands "This is Sir Henry Lucie of Chadshunt Hall, the oldest family hereabouts. Well respected by all."

his voice tailed off. My father had drawn himself up to his not inconsiderable height.

"I will thank you, Sir to leave this parish. Neither your views nor your person are welcome here."

The Puritan stared back at him boldly. "I do not call this building, replete with these baubles and fripperies, the house of the Lord."

He pushed his way past up to the altar, hurled the candles to the ground and wrenched the cloth from the altar, deliberately treading it under his heels. Seeing the delicate cloth my mother had made trampled to the ground, I cried out,

"Leave that be," and ran out of the pew to rescue it. Looking surprised but unconcerned, he caught me by the shoulder and held me at arm's length.

"Well, well what do we have here? Unseemly behaviour for a maid? Maybe she does not deserve that name?"

There was a blur of movement. Taking the man off guard, Harry knocked him flat and stood over him with his fists clenched, waiting.

"Harry, no," I cried desperately, clinging to his arm. To my relief, the man got to his feet and picked up his hat. He smoothed his hair and jammed the hat firmly down. I found myself staring up at a large boil on the end of his thin, bony nose.

"Sir Henry Lucie of Chadshunt Hall. That is very well, and your son, also Henry. I shall remember. I believe you will be hearing from the county's Committee for Sequestration before many weeks have passed."

Followed by his silent companions, he stalked out of the church leaving the congregation and vicar white faced and shaking. The two children, frightened into silence, began to cry again. We returned home in glum silence. Carrying the damaged altar cloth, I clung to Harry's arm.

During dinner my father was largely silent. My heart was in my boots and I made only faint attempts to eat. The Puritan's words had shaken me more than I cared to admit. He had openly threatened Father and Harry. I was terrified that my beloved and courageous brother, so recently restored to me, would be snatched away again by force. In a vain attempt to distract myself, I began to babble of other matters, of Will, of the spring lambing. Harry shook his head at me. He was eating the traditional boiled eggs in green sauce with single mindedness while watching Father intently, waiting for him to speak. Finally Father laid down his knife, the slice of pigeon pie on his plate barely touched. Tugging distractedly at his beard, he addressed himself to Harry.

"My son, you see how the world is going. I never thought that this family would be forced to leave our home, at least not in my life time or yours. We will need to make our plans now in some haste, Harry as events are moving too fast for me. We will need to remove or hide our valuables such as your mother's jewels and some of our more valuable paintings. I will speak to John Dale to ask him to see what stock we can dispose of quickly and without arousing suspicion. We have to be aware that some of our neighbours side with Parliament. Our silver plate is needed by His Majesty and we will need to find a way to deliver that to him.

Despite the insolent threats of that fellow, I do not believe our personal safety is necessarily threatened, at least for the present. But we must not expose Bess to the insults of such men and such behaviour as we have seen today. I believe it might be best to send her for safety to Aunt Mary in Devon."

"I won't leave you and Harry, Father. I am not so much of a coward."

"Bess, it is not a question of cowardice. You are a gentle maid and you are my daughter. I must and will protect you as I see fit. You will obey my orders. Leave us now. I need to take further counsel with your brother."

His tone was pure steel. I stared at the handsome, implacable countenance. There were lines of strain around his eyes, and the furrows in his brow seemed to deepen by the week. I wondered where my father had gone. The father who had frequented the nursery, swung me to his shoulders and bellowed with laughter at my four year old attempts to curtsey, had vanished in the smoke of cannon fire. Glumly I left the room, wandering restlessly until I found myself in the stables, Hector ambling at my heels. I hugged my darling Fairy around her beautiful chestnut neck and promised her that, come what may, I would not be parted from either her or Hector.

ɞ

I slept but poorly that night and succeeding nights. My familiar bedchamber, with its hangings, a place of peace and comfort even in times of grief, seemed suddenly less solid, a less sure and permanent haven. I dreamed of the Puritan mocking me. His face faded into that of Major Chatterton, smiling as he sliced off my lock of hair.

The next night, I dreamed of the effigies in our parish church. One of them had Rafe's face and I wept over it. Then I saw that the stone figure beside it was that of Harry, his hands crossed in death. I woke screaming, "No". I sat up in bed. My night gown was damp and sticking to me. I could hear excited voices below my window. I thrust my head out of the casement. All was dark, but at some distance across the fields I thought I perceived a dim glow. I called loudly for Peggy.

"What ails you, Mistress Bess?" she cried, coming in at a run in her bed gown. Silently I pointed through the window.

"I've no notion of what goes on. Lord save us," she muttered.

"I'll go and find out, Mistress."

Wide awake, I climbed back into bed and sat hugging my knees. Hector looked at me from his basket and I let him climb on the bed. I cuddled him for comfort, stroking his silky ears. Distant cries continued. Peggy returned, looking solemn.

"It's the church, Mistress. There is something on fire outside it. We''ll find out more on the morrow."

I spent the remainder of the night sitting up in bed, Hector beside me. In the morning, I saddled Fairy and rode towards the church. I tethered Fairy to a fence. The remains of the fire were still smoking, watched by a dejected group of villagers. With a shock, I realized that the pile of still smoldering wood was what remained of the altar rails and the organ. I looked more closely and saw pieces of picture frame. Our beautiful paintings had all been destroyed. Torn scraps of embroidered fabric told me that vestments and altar cloths had met the same fate. Tears in my eyes, I turned away from the fire to look at the church building itself. The carved oak doors had been broken in. "No popery" had been scrawled on the outside walls with whitewash. Every single stained glass window had been smashed. My father came striding angrily out of the church, Harry at his heels. Father greeted me distractedly and swept past.

"Harry, what has happened?"

"The work of rebel soldiers. A villager saw them arrive after dark, pikemen, but he was too f frightened to try to stop them. What could have one man have done?"

I reflected that if that one man had been Harry, he would have intervened. And been beaten or killed with a pike, common sense interjected.

"Reverend Hunter has disappeared, Bess. No one seems to know whether he has f fled or been removed."

Father had been speaking to the church wardens. He turned to us and shook his head, "It is sacrilege, Bess, and madness too. Every man knows there are no papists, or friends to papists, here. Those men who were here on Easter Day must be behind this. It is they who sent the soldiers."

The smell of the smoke was unsettling Fairy. She was snorting and rolling her eyes. With sadness, I mounted and rode home.

∽

From planning for how the estate might survive a long period of conflict, our focus now turned urgently on what might be saved if the estate was seized by Parliament. Most of our wealth was in land and buildings. None of these could be either transported or easily disposed of. Nevertheless my father made what hasty plans he could for what could be saved or hidden should the worst occur. In the meantime he urged us all, family and servants, to go about our normal business.

The following Sunday, we set forth as usual to church. The broken windows had been covered over to keep out the weather. Unbroken panes were still visible above the rough wooden patchwork. A mast and part of a sail showed where the apostles' boat had sailed across the Sea of Galilee, while the haloed head of St Peter and the top of an imposing key which he grasped, peeped from the adjoining window. The interior of the church now had little covering the walls, which had been whitewashed. Deprived of the light from the windows, the church was dim and gloomy.

"Bess, look." Harry pointed towards the north wall of the Nave. I gasped. The Doom painting, hundreds of years old, depicting the Last Judgement, could be seen no more. Of Christ and His angels, the castle at the top depicting the righteous being welcomed to Heaven, while the Devil drove the wicked into Hell down below, nothing remained. All had been consumed in the drab covering of whitewash. A rough wooden communion table was standing in the place where the altar rails had been. It barely resembled the place I had been accustomed to all my life. I had spent many hours that week carefully repairing the altar cloth. It would be out of place now and unwelcome. I decided to take it home again for safe keeping. Our vicar did not appear. In his place was a severe man, dressed in black with no vestments. He began by introducing himself as Richard Slade and informing us that he was to be known as the minister. We were enjoined to sing psalms, many of which were unfamiliar, being presumably those psalms most popular with the Puritans. I missed the sweet sound of the organ, now nothing but a blackened pile in the church yard. We sat through a sermon of interminable length, dealing with the evils of popery. Altars, candle sticks, statues, paintings, the sign of the cross, even the Anglican Book of Common Prayer, were all condemned as papist.

When we finally reached the communion, Harry led the way from our family pew at the front of the church, dropping automatically to his knees by the communion table.

"What popery is this?" demanded the new minister. "Stand, Sir, immediately. Good Protestants do not kneel."

Harry opened his mouth to protest, but Father grabbed his arm, hauling him to his feet. "Harry," he murmured, "We need no martyrs in our family." After the service, my father told Harry and me to walk home and he would follow. I saw a mutinous look come into Harry's eye and he opened his mouth to argue. A look from Father stopped him. After a few minutes Father caught us up, frowning.

"I have nothing to report. Master Slade would not say what has become of our vicar, but I cannot think he left of his own free will."

"But, Father," I protested, "Why must we be obliged to attend services there when they are now so strange? I feel quite uncomfortable as if I am praying to a different God. I would rather stay at home with my Prayer Book and pray alone in our family chapel."

Father clutched my shoulders and spun me round to look at him.

"Bess, you are being as foolish as Harry. You know we must attend our parish church every Sunday by law. Would you be marked down as a recusant, a papist or a dissenter? Let me hear no more of this. We have greater matters to worry about than if we like the colour of the sermons in our church."

ᔕ

Harry and I moped around the house. Harry attempted to relieve his feelings by practicing his fencing with Father, or anyone else who he could prevail upon to spend half an hour with honing his skills. I attempted to find solace in my music. When that failed, I stared out of the window at the blossom and green buds of spring. After a few days I decided to start doing something practical. I began making lists and sorting through our possessions. I was sitting on the floor, going through a large chest of clothing in the midst of disorder, when the floorboards creaked. Two warm hands covered my eyes and I breathed in a familiar male fragrance composed in equal parts of sweat and horse. I tore the hands away to see Will's laughing face.

"William," I scolded, "We hear nothing of you for weeks. We do not even know with which regiment you fight, and you do not have the grace to announce your arrival in proper form like a gentleman."

"My apologies, Bess," he grinned. "Well then, like a gentleman may I introduce myself as a Lieutenant in Lord Digby's Regiment, and may I present its newly made Captain of Horse, Gabriel Vaughan."

"Gabriel!" I bounced to my feet, hastily shaking my skirts into some semblance of order and tucking away a strand of my hair under my coif.

"You are most welcome too," I assured him. "And so you are become a Captain, and in Will's regiment. How important you are become," I finished inanely. Gabriel answered me with a wry smile.

"Not really, Bess. It's just that I am a year or two older than some of these hotheads." He clapped Will affectionately on the shoulder. "I think they hoped my sober manner would rub off on them a little and prevent some of their more headlong and undisciplined charges. Whether that is so, we shall see. At least when they try my patience too far, I can use Welsh oaths and they are none the wiser."

Will laughed at this and announced he was off in search of Harry. Gabriel smiled again. I glimpsed the more light hearted man who I had only seen before when he sang. As he followed Will out of the door, I gazed after him. I could not help wishing I had known him when he was young. Although only a few years older than Will, his life experiences had given him the bearing and demeanor of an older man.

Prince Rupert had successfully taken Birmingham and retaken Lichfield. Rupert's forces were now on their way back south, having been recalled urgently to Reading, under siege from the Earl of Essex. Will and Gabriel were riding ahead of the army. Will needed to consult with Father and Harry concerning the dangers of sequestration. He spent most of his brief stay at home closeted in Father's study with John Dale, Father and Harry.

It fell to me to entertain Gabriel. I was keen to hear how the war progressed. I knew the Welsh were a race of poets and story tellers, as well as musicians.

"Gabriel, pray describe for me those stirring scenes you have been part of in recent weeks." I smiled encouragingly, turning my attention again to the disordered heap of baby linen, worn stockings and other garments of doubtful value in our present circumstances. A few moments of silence ensued. I looked up to see Gabriel staring out of the window. When he turned to me, his back was to the light. I could not see the expression in the green eyes.

"We set off from Oxford for the midlands at the end of March. Retaking Lichfield was our immediate aim. Birmingham was on our direct road and held by the rebels. The craftsmen of the town made sword blades for Parliament. Prince Rupert decided to stop the flow of weapons and teach them a lesson to boot. Birmingham is a small town, unwalled. The prince was not expecting to have to fight to take it, but the townspeople had other ideas. They erected some earthworks. Not very high, but enough to provide them with useful cover."

He picked up his goblet of wine from the table and took a gulp.

"They were a small force. Our horse and foot outnumbered them greatly. Even so, they drove us back twice. I suggested that we might take some cavalry and ride through the fields, taking them in the rear. The Prince agreed, so we caught them unawares. We forded the river and advanced right into the town. Still they fought on, firing at us from the houses. We had to fight our way street by street."

A strange look had come over his face. Normally transparent and open it had become fixed like a mask.

"We fired some houses to flush them out." He spoke jerkily. "Their foot eventually ran away. Birmingham was ours, but at a heavy price. Lord Denbigh was mortally wounded in the fighting. A senior commander, killed in a short, messy little skirmish. Prince Rupert was furious. He ordered more looting and burning. That is war."

His voice hardened and he paced back to the window, clutching the cup hard.

"Gabriel," I said hesitantly, "Did you and Will set houses afire?" He avoided my gaze.

"The fruits of rebellion. If the town had not resisted, it would have been unharmed." The green eyes clouded. "And now we ride to Reading. It is under siege from the Earl of Essex. I will leave you to your labours, Bess," he finished abruptly.

During dinner, Will described how the Royalists had successfully laid siege to Lichfield. After a week of fruitless bombardment of the fortified Cathedral close with cannonballs, they had tunneled under the foundations of the northwest tower, and blown a breach in the walls with gunpowder. The Royalists had stormed the close. The defenders surrendered shortly after. During Will's account, Gabriel remained silent.

က

After dinner, my father and brothers once again shut themselves away. A weak sun was shining. I invited Gabriel to join me for a ramble in the park before the short spring day began to grow chilly. We visited the mews first. I knew that like most men, Gabriel kept a falcon or two at home. He admired my own falcon, who was feeling neglected by me. Gabriel chuckled. He caught my enquiring look.

"I was remembering my wife's aversion to visiting my father's mews. She could never bear to think of these birds catching and eating other living creatures," he smiled. "She was a gentle soul."

"How long were you married?"

"She was 17, Bess when we met. And I was but 21, young to wed, or so my father said. But we were in love and a bit impatient." He chuckled, a little sadly.

"It seems such a long time ago now. We lived in my father's house, but Catherine never felt comfortable there. My mother was mistress of the house and Catherine felt Mother treated her like a child. And no sign of our own child starting. About two years after we wed, my father suggested we move into a small manor he owned which was standing empty, the tenant having died. We set up our own establishment for the first time, with our own servants and Catherine being the mistress for the first time too. We were happy there. And when she told me there was a child on the way, I was overjoyed. Fearful too. Plenty of men lose their wives in child bed. I believe I worried more about it than she did. "All will be well, Gabriel,"

she said and it was – then. Our son was born two years ago last Michaelmas. He was a fine lad, strong, healthy, the apple of my father's eye. Then a year ago, with things as they were between the King and Parliament, I was away for a time, helping my father with affairs on the estate. One of my servants came galloping up the lane to tell me they both had the smallpox. A travelling tinker may have brought it with him. The physician came and went, bled them, recommended purges. Catherine warned me to keep away from them, but I couldn't. I haunted their rooms, but never sickened myself."

I suggested we walked on into the park and he agreed, still deep in thought.

I wished I could distract him from lingering sad thoughts.

"Tell me about your home," I said. He looked faintly surprised but began obediently.

"My family's home is in Crickhowell, in Wales near the border with England. It lies in a valley near a river and the foot of the Black Mountains. It's very beautiful. Wet but still beautiful," he smiled. "They say if you grow up round there you must have webbed feet like a duck."

He looked solemnly at his feet, encased in his somewhat dusty leather riding boots. "It's very green because of all the rain, more so I think than your corner of Warwickshire," he said pointing at the windswept park, now looking a little grey as the sun disappeared behind the clouds. An April shower abruptly made its presence felt. Misled by the sun, I had neither coat nor cloak. I made a dash across the park towards the house. Gabriel overtook me.

"Wait Bess, take this," and I felt him fold his cloak around my shoulders. He set off rapidly. I picked up my skirts and ran after him. I returned the cloak to him inside the house, suddenly a little shy and becoming aware of the faint odours of horse, grass and masculine sweat which clung to the cloak. He looked at me thoughtfully.

"Thank you, Bess."

"Why?"

"For listening. The memories of my wife and son grow fainter with time. I rarely speak of them, but keeping grief locked away does my soul no good. Wounds need air to heal, and so do those of the spirit. You too may find that."

He pressed my hand and walked away, his limp a little more pronounced after the dash across the park. The subject of looting returned to haunt me in the evening. I revived the subject with Gabriel,

"I was thinking on the looting after Edgehill. When Prince Rupert's horse chased the Parliamentary horse and overran their baggage train. And when Rafe…?"

I fell silent, twisting my hands in my lap. A hand fell gently on mine and I looked up, startled.

"Bess," he said, "It does neither your friend's memory nor your present peace of mind any good to dwell on the mistakes of that day. I do believe indiscipline led to many deaths including maybe that of Master Beauchamp. But do you know where or how he met his death?"

"He was found on the battlefield next to an abandoned cannon," I said sadly.

"Well then, if it brings you any comfort, I believe you may acquit him of having been part of that group who were seeking the spoils of war. If he was found lying on the battlefield, it is probable he was guilty of nothing worse than misplaced courage."

When Gabriel's kind words fell on my ear, I realised that there had been tightness in my breast which I had not even been aware of. A part of me had long feared that Rafe had not only died uselessly, but perhaps in quest of money, trinkets, other prizes. I started to cry. Gabriel regarded me with compassion, raised my hand to his lips and left me to recover my composure.

Will and Gabriel were to leave early the next morning to rejoin the army, but we made believe that night that all was well, that the men were not about to leave again to fight, that we were not in danger of losing our house and everything we held dear. We conversed and made music. Harry and I performed Gabriel's "When maids go a wooing". Will, who also possessed a fine voice, sang one or two songs composed by the Royalist army which had my father shaking his head as not fit for a maiden's ears, and me convulsing with laughter. Finally Gabriel took up a lute and played a haunting melody which sent shivers down my spine. He then sang the popular song "Gather Ye Rosebuds" by the court musician William Lawes. As usual, it made me cry.

"Come, Master Vaughan," protested my father, "Too sad a song for tonight. Pray play something cheerful before my daughter washes herself away."

Gabriel bowed and obliged by beginning to play one of Dowland's galliards. I clapped my hands.

"Will, a galliard, let us dance!" Peggy was called upon. My brothers, Peggy and I danced galliards until Gabriel complained we had exhausted both his repertoire and his fingers.

With Will and Gabriel gone, I had time for reflection. I realised how little I could remember of Rafe. I still missed him, I assured myself. Yet the sound of his laugh, the shape of his face, were becoming indistinct. When I strove to recall his laughing blue eyes, they were occasionally replaced by a memory of quizzical green ones, and I felt ashamed. I wished I had taken Rafe's likeness when I was at my drawing. I had thought there would be time.

ঌ

A few days later, a letter arrived from Will.

"My dear Father, I regret to say that our efforts to succor the garrison of Reading were too late. By the time we arrived, the town had been surrendered to the Earl of Essex. His Majesty was so furious with Colonel Fielding, the Governor of Reading, that he has been placed under arrest. He is to face a court martial here in Oxford. I remain here with Prince Rupert for the present. I enclose some music for Bess. Your obedient son, Will".

Barely glancing at the half sheet of music, Father passed it to me and then turned his attention to other letters which the messenger had brought. The music was from Gabriel. Inscribed at the bottom were the words,

"I fear I may be in need of some assistance in completing the composition of this song and hope you and your brother will do so when the opportunity arises. May that time come soon."

He had signed it once more with a tiny drawing of a linnet. I smiled and tucked the music away safely in my pocket book. For some reason that I could not have explained even to myself, I did not show it to Harry.

ঌ

I pounced on a furtive looking Harry coming out of the herb garden. "Harry, I swear you are hiding something. Is there some secret in the garden?"

He regarded me crossly. "Bess you are the most tiresome maid. Who knows what trouble your desire for confidences will lead to! No one must know of this."

I folded my arms and drew myself up to my full 5' 6".

"Oh very well, come with me but we must make sure no one observes us."

He peered around carefully and then led me into the herb garden. Mystified, I followed him behind a large rosemary bush in a corner near the wall. He moved aside a row of small pots and the outline of a small trapdoor came into view. He opened it by pulling a wooden ring and I saw the top rungs of a dangling ladder. In the midst of an adjoining bush of thyme, a small clay cylinder protruded from the earth.

"We are concealing plate and other valuables below the ground. John Dale and Jacob constructed this at Father's direction. They have been digging secretly by night." He pointed at the clay cylinder.

"That chimney is for air, should there be a need to conceal a person here. I suppose it is as well you are aware of the measures we have taken." He furrowed his brow sternly in the same manner as did Father. I was shaken but relieved by Harry's disclosure –shaken that Father was considering the situation so desperate, and relieved that he had found at least a part solution for the problem of where to hide valuables. As to hiding a family member or other man, I supposed it was a sensible precaution. We were not papists, so had no priest's hole in which to hide a fugitive. The modest subterranean refuge might prove more difficult to find than a secret room in the house.

ᔓ

May 1643

Urgent knocking at the door of the Hall. I had not heard a horse. I leapt up from my seat in the family sitting room and arrived in the entrance hall. Thomas was comforting a muddy, breathless man. He was wearing the livery of Giles Blake's servants.

"I will send for Sir Henry. You may wait in the Great Hall."

I retreated to my favourite position half way up the stairs. Father strode into the Great Hall, followed by Harry. No more than a few minutes later, the man emerged, heading for the kitchens.

I pushed the doors open into the Great Hall. Father barely glanced in my direction.

"I will send one of the servants to Shenington House to see how matters stand."

"Let me go, Father."

"Too dangerous, Harry. Even if you were not recognized, they would detain a gentleman for questioning. Have Thomas send me one of the gamekeepers. They are accustomed to move with stealth."

I hurried to keep up with Harry's long stride.

"Harry, what is it?" I panted as Harry finished delivering his message to Thomas.

"The enemy have stormed Shenington House while Giles Blake is away with the King. They demanded Mistress Blake surrender the house to them. She refused and closed the gates. They had a hundred men or more and made short work of Shenington's handful of armed retainers. Mistress Blake sent Tom to warn us. He ran all the way. Three of the servants were killed. The family have been ordered to remain in their own apartments. They are little more than prisoners."

"What can we do, Harry?"

"For the Blakes, nothing but to send the news to Giles. I fear Chadshunt may meet a similar fate in the coming weeks. If Parliament attempt to sequester our estates, they may dress it up in the guise of law, but they will only take possession by violence.

Will and I begged Father to fortify Chadshunt, but he is adamant it cannot be done. This is no more than a gentleman's house, surrounded by a low wall. We have no moat, no curtain wall, no drawbridge to pull up. If the enemy come, we are sitting ducks."

Our gamekeeper Matthew returned with the news that Shenington was surrounded by guards. He had been unable to gain entry but could see the encampment in the park. Cattle were being driven off and trees in the orchard chopped down for firewood. Some of the outhouses were in flames.

At supper that night, Father's face was grim. We had included the dead and wounded of Shenington House in our evening prayers. Father pushed his plate away, food untouched.

"When White warned me of the dangers of civil war to our property and our women folk, I believed him to be wrong. I expected this war would be fought between armies in the field. I was in error, I confess it. The whole country of Warwickshire is become a battle ground. I wish White was still here instead of with the Oxford Army. He might provide useful counsel.

I must approach His Majesty, Harry. I will send a messenger, requesting he place a modest garrison at Chadshunt. There were nigh on fifty of our men who remained with Blake's troop after Edgehill. We are in sore need of them now. If he consents, it might be sufficient to deter a small force. I will write the letter now."

Father swept out of the room. I turned to Harry, who was looking thoughtful.

"What should we do, Harry? Will we dig ditches?"

Harry shook his head.

"It would take more than a ditch to keep out a determined force. We must pray that Chadshunt does not fall prey to Parliament before the King can place a garrison here."

ও

The next morning, leaving the dairy, I heard the sounds of a carriage. As visitors were not expected, I hastily inspected my skirts for milk splashes, checked that my hair was tucked neatly under my coif and wiped my hands. I had spent many hours of the night listening for the sounds of an armed force approaching, and I knew there were shadows beneath my tired eyes.

I rounded the corner of the main house as the steps to the unfamiliar carriage were let down. I was amazed to see my cousin Celia alight, followed by her maid. I ran to greet her,

"Celia, what a wonderful surprise. Is Sir John following on horseback?"

"He is in London," she said with a shrug, "Or with my father and his friends from Parliament and the army. I grew weary of being alone on the estate except for his mother and the servants. So I sent a messenger to him to say I would come and make you a visit," she said with a dimple. "A long visit maybe." She added with a little uncertainty, "At least if my uncle has no objection."

Dressed expensively and elegantly, Celia had pearls at her throat, and a large hat with a feather sweeping becomingly down the side. She looked very much the fashionable married lady. And then she suddenly looked again like a child as she peered anxiously at me from under the wide brim of her hat.

"My uncle, is he at home?"

"He is," I hesitated, "And will be pleased of course to receive you."

It was a half truth at best. Fearing we might be overrun by rebel troops any day, Father was unlikely to be pleased by the arrival of another female relative whom he was obliged to protect.

She looked relieved.

"And how did your husband receive your proposal to visit us?" I enquired delicately. " I collect he gave his consent?"

"I do not know. I did not stay for the messenger to return with an answer but left immediately."

A mischievous look flashed across her face. I led the way into the house and left Celia in one of the family living rooms. I found Harry and Father quickly. Harry whistled as I acquainted them with the circumstances of Celia's arrival. Father looked grave.

"The timing is extremely ill," he said. "She is a foolish child to make such a long and dangerous journey with no protection but a coachman. Truly, this is reckless and irresponsible behaviour. Does she not realise her father supports the side of Parliament while we are openly in arms for the King? This is likely to further deepen the gulf between her father and me. Neither will it endear us to her husband's family, who may think we have been conspiring with her." He sighed deeply. "I will speak with my niece."

I was not party to the short conference between my father and my cousin, but when he emerged from the room, she was looking forlorn.

"My uncle has explained why in the circumstances I was unwise to come. He will not return me to my husband, as he feels the roads are not safe for a lady traveling alone. He has told me that I was most fortunate not to be waylaid by the King's troops from Oxford or Worcester. But he is writing letters in haste to Sir John and my father now, which he will send back with our coachman. He said he would make it clear that I am welcome to the hospitality of Chadshunt Hall at any time, although he feels it would be better if my husband makes the journey to collect me when convenient to him. Oh cousin, I am so sorry. I only sought some relief in your company and a holiday from tedium."

Her cheeks were already streaked with tears and now fresh tears clouded the beautiful blue eyes like dew on a bluebell. She looked so woebegone and childlike that I could do nothing but embrace her.

"Wait here," I said firmly. I determined to speak to Father myself. I found him in his study and closed the door behind me. He looked up from the letter he was penning with a frown.

"What now, Bess? You see I am engaged."

He ran his fingers absent mindedly over the edge of his lace cuff. I noticed the edge was frayed and in need of repair. If Mother had still been alive it would have been noticed and mended. I sighed and turned to the matter in hand.

"Father, I would speak to you about Celia."

He interrupted abruptly,

"No more about that willful girl I pray. I was minded to give her a whipping, but that office belongs to her husband, not her uncle."

"Father please, she meant no harm."

"Whether or no she meant to cause harm matters not. She endangered herself by traveling without a proper escort. Had she encountered one of our cavalry patrols they might have detained her as both wife and daughter of rebels. We must thank God she arrived without mishap."

"Then will a letter from you not put matters to rights?" I pleaded.

"Bess, I do not believe you understand. It is not only her own person which Celia has endangered. We do not wish to draw further attention to Chadshunt. Like our country, our own family is deeply divided. At Edgehill my brother and I fought in opposing armies. You already know that Hugh refused to help me win Harry's release. He is no longer the brother I grew up with. He may suspect we have turned Celia against him. Worse, he may fear that having her in our power, we now hold her hostage. We must get word to her father and husband with all speed that we treat her with kindness as our kin. I fear that before the week is out we may receive a visit from an armed troop claiming to be rescuing her."

11

I PROTESTED FEEBLY, but Father was no longer listening. With an impatient gesture he bade me leave him. At least I understood now why he was so intent on his writing. Slowly and thoughtfully, I returned to my cousin. She was looking about her.

"Well," she said, "Tell me of how you have fared since we last met. I have heard so little of you. What became of the gentleman you were enamored of?" she said archly. It was evident her spirits were rapidly recovering.

It was a long and painful task to make Celia familiar with the events of the last many months. She sat wide eyed, and reddened with anger at her father's refusal to help win Harry's release.

"And I," she said slowly, "Have sat at home in safety and have known nothing of these matters. I am so sorry, Bess," she said, "Sir John tells me little about what goes on in the world and my father when I see him even less. I was aware that my father and yours did not see eye to eye on the matters between King and Parliament, but little more. I was not aware that your father and brothers had been in battle. Thank God Harry was finally returned to you. I did hear of my poor aunt's sudden death and was so sad. You must miss her very much."

She squeezed my hand hard, "And you loved Rafe?" she said softly. I nodded silently. "My poor, poor cousin," she said, "But you will love again in time. "

I shrugged. "Until matters are more settled in England, I have other more pressing cares. Are you aware that our estate may be sequestered by Parliament?"

She stared at me, shocked. I realised that my father had said nothing of this to her. My own understanding of the new law was limited, but I knew enough to make her understand the seriousness of our family's situation. I told her of the fate of Shenington House.

"I should try to do something to help," she said thoughtfully, "My husband and father are both close to the Earl of Essex I believe. He has dined at our house from time to time. Maybe if I speak to Sir John on my return home? He might be able to intercede?"

"I thank you cousin," I said "But I implore you to do nothing without my father's agreement. Do not press me to tell you the details, but I made an ill advised attempt to arrange Harry's freedom. It only did further damage and brought me shame."

I turned the subject.

"Pray cousin, tell me of your new home and husband." For the next hour, Celia talked of her gardens, now being redesigned, her orangery, her park, all very good, and then of her servants, some of whom she had become fond of, including her personal maid Joan, who accompanied her.

"And your husband, Sir John?" I prompted finally when we had exhausted her orchards, her mare Sorrel and her own pet dog which she had been obliged to leave at home as he was often sick when he travelled by carriage. "He is well enough, a kind man," she said and abruptly proposed a walk in the gardens, the day being fine.

As always, Celia proved a welcome and amusing addition to our family party and to our evenings of music. Somehow, a gap had been left by Gabriel and Will's departure. Celia's husband, Sir John, wrote to say that he was much engaged in London and would not be able to travel to Chadshunt for some weeks. Until then, Celia had leave to remain.

On Sunday, we made our weekly visit to our parish church in its strange new guise. At the conclusion of the service the minister, Richard Slade, announced that in future, prayers and exhortations, together with psalm singing, were to form the regular order. A communion service would be held only once a month. Beside me I felt my father go rigid and Harry start to rise in his seat.

"Be seated, my son,"

I heard my father murmur in his ear and a firm arm clamped Harry to the pew. We had only the final psalm to get through before we were released into the spring sunlight. We plodded home, Harry openly fuming, my father taciturn and thoughtful. Celia alone seemed composed. I wondered briefly if the services in her church were the same. When I asked her tentatively what she had thought of the service she merely grinned mischievously,

"Master Slade has an overlarge nose and his ears stick out."

The King had refused Father's request for a Chadshunt garrison, saying he could not spare the men to protect every country house, but Father was hoping he might relent. Happily, there had been no more sightings of rebel troops in the days since Shenington had fallen. Our grooms now took turns in riding daily a wide circle around the nearby villages in the hope they might thus provide warning of approaching soldiers.

Father continued to divide his time between Chadshunt and his work in Oxford with the Council of War. At home, he was tightlipped and more uncommunicative than was his wont, closeting himself constantly with Harry and John Dale. Outwardly tranquil, Celia and I roamed the estate on horseback, Hector loping at our heels. I visited the tenants, paying a wordless farewell to the people and the places I feared I would soon be forced to quit. It was a melancholy time.

ᔕ

May 1643

I had risen soon after dawn, a consequence of another disturbed night. It was nearly two weeks since Shenington House had fallen, and Celia's arrival. The mist was evaporating under the influence of what promised to be a beautiful day. Celia had departed the day before to spend a night with friends on a nearby estate. Father was at home and had insisted on sending two armed servants with her. I was enjoying a solitary ramble in the small wood in our park. I wandered dreamily among the trees, soothed by the serenity of the early morning sun streaking through the pale green leaves, dappling the trunks of oak and beech. The wood was carpeted with bluebells and I picked an armful to take home.

My shortest way back took me through the stables in the west wing. I heard the clatter of hooves and the jingle of harness of a number of horses. It was with considerable shock that I saw the head of the column. There were 40 mounted cavalry, orange sashed. Stumbling along beside the man at the tail of the column, hands bound, blood streaming from a gash on his head, was our porter and gatekeeper, Jacob Partridge. The trooper was walking beside his horse. The reins were looped easily over his left arm, but in his right he held a pistol.

Still clutching my bluebells, I retreated out of sight behind the high archway to the coach house, close enough to see and hear what happened. The troops reined in at a sign from their leader. Jacob was pushed to his knees on the cobbles. The officer leading the troop dismounted and strode up the steps to the main door, hammering on it with his fist.

"Open up in the name of Parliament."

There was a short pause and then Thomas opened the door, staring in horror at the belligerent man before him.

"Sir?" he said hesitantly.

"I am Captain Asher Miller of Sir James Ramsey's Regiment of horse. I am here to place the malignants Sir Henry Lucie, William Lucie and Henry Lucie under arrest."

"I am Sir Henry Lucie. But I am no malignant, Sir. My sons are both from home."

Father caught sight of Jacob kneeling on the cobbles.

"Release my servant this instant," he bellowed.

The captain's mouth tightened.

"You are in no position to make demands, Sir. Be silent. Understand that any man offering resistance will be punished."

He turned to the trooper holding Jacob.

"Shoot the porter, Corporal."

"Hold! Do not murder my servant for being loyal, I pray you," Father pleaded. "I will undertake that neither he nor any other will offer further resistance."

"Will you so? A wise decision, Sir."

I gulped. Jacob, I hoped, was reprieved, but Harry must be hidden without delay. I made my way quietly round the corner of the stables and entered the house by a back door. I dropped the bluebells on a table and ran like the wind up the back stairs, bursting into Harry's room without knocking

His chamber overlooked the courtyard, so I was not astonished to discover him in the act of pulling on his riding boots, his sword beside him.

"Harry, quickly, you must hide," I squeaked, my voice cracking with urgency as I tried to muffle it.

"Bess, calm yourself," he replied, "And do not burst in like that, I could have run you through were you a few moments later." I hopped anxiously from one foot to the other, peering through the window at the enemy cavalry below.

Harry reached for his baldric and started buckling it on. A look of desperation was on his face.

"I'll not llet them ttake me alive again." He turned towards the door.

"Farewell, Bess. I love you." I realised with horror that my pig headed brother was intending to fight his way out through 40 enemy soldiers or, the most likely outcome, die in the attempt.

I grabbed his arm.

"Harry, stop! Think! We need to gain you entry to the herb garden and conceal you. Remember that is why you made that hiding place!" He paused briefly, listening I hoped. "The soldiers are congregated in front of the main house. I will check that the back stairs remain unobserved."

He nodded curtly. I flew down the back stairs, nearly colliding with

Peggy as I reached the bottom. Panting, I quickly explained I needed to assist Harry and told her of the herb garden's hidden room. She nodded.

"See Master Harry safe, Mistress. I will hold them up somehow."

I peered cautiously out of the door. To my relief there was no sign of any soldiers between the house and the walled herb garden. We would take the chance.

As I tiptoed back to Harry's room, I heard distant wailing. Edging towards the head of the main stairs, I saw Peggy on her knees in the entrance hall in front of the Roundhead leader, weeping.

"Oh Sir, that I should have lived to see such a day. And the poor mistress not cold in her grave these six months."

She was raising a fine distraction. There was a shout from the courtyard. One of the troopers appeared, dragging the small pageboy Jack up the steps.

"Well, Corporal Clifford?"

"Young scrap crept up on us, Captain, tried to stab me with this." He brandished a dagger. "What shall I do with him?" The captain pushed back his visor and regarded Jack wearily.

"Find a dark closet or cellar, Clifford. Lock him in until nightfall. That will serve."

"And what of the porter?"

"Sir Henry Lucie undertakes no further resistance. Leave the porter kneeling on the cobbles until the morrow. Keep him under guard and see that he does not stir. He will spend an uncomfortable night and that should act as a reminder to his fellows."

"How dare you treat my servants so?"

The commotion was increasing admirably, but I could hear that Father's ire was rising in earnest.

I dared delay no longer. I knocked quietly at Harry's door. When he opened it, I beckoned. Sword drawn, he followed me quietly down the back stairs. My heart in my mouth, I darted ahead of him, scouting for any sight of soldiers. We passed through the rose garden and safely reached the gate into the walled herb garden. I exhaled with relief as Harry pulled up the trap door and slid down the ladder into the darkness below.

"Are you content to remain here?" I whispered.

"I must attempt an escape tonight. Bess, see what you can do to aid me. I will need a mount if possible, and some food."

I nodded and hastily pushed the trapdoor and covering pots back in place. Safely back in the house, I went looking for Peggy to tell her Harry was safe. Entering the Great Hall I saw Father. He was facing the Roundhead officer, his hands in the air while one of the troopers searched through his pockets and a second man pointed a pistol at him. I heard a faint protest issuing from my lips as I took two trembling steps towards him. I was overcome by a wave of shock and crumpled at the feet of the, no doubt startled, Roundhead officer.

ↀ

Sir Henry Lucie watched in dismay as his servants bore his unconscious daughter up the stairs towards her bed chamber. He grasped the banister.

"I think not, Sir." His way was barred by the roundhead officer. "You will remain with me. You are under arrest and I have questions for you." His voice was quiet but firm.

"You prevent me attending my daughter?"

"She has excellent attendance, Sir. Now lead me to your study."

Sir Henry remained stationary, his eyes trailing the small procession as it reached the head of the stairs.

"I am loathe to physically restrain a gentleman such as yourself, Sir Henry, but if forced to it, I will do so." Captain Miller was losing patience. He nodded to his two men, who grabbed Sir Henry by the arms.

"Oh, very well."

With the two troopers following, Sir Henry strode to his study, the officer beside him.

"Well Sir, behold my study. On what grounds do you commit this outrage?"

The roundhead officer removed his helmet and gloves, smoothed his fair, wispy hair and examined the room. Although his hair was thinning, he had not yet reached his thirtieth year. His pale blue eyes were intelligent, his hands strong and capable. Sir Henry surmised the man had sufficient experience as an officer to be wily and intransigent.

"You may take a seat, Sir Henry." Anger surged through the baronet.

"I prefer to stand."

"As you wish. Two days ago, we intercepted a messenger bearing dispatches for you. Once decoded, it was apparent you are a person of some note to the Council of War, and are in possession of the plans for the King's summer campaign. You will deliver these plans to me."

"And if I do not?"

"Then harsher measures may be effected and you will no doubt be taken elsewhere for interrogation.

For the present, my orders are to take possession of the plans by whatever means necessary. Parliament has determined that this is a malignant house.

I am commanded to seize Chadshunt Hall and to detain you and your sons William and Henry at Parliament's pleasure.

We will make good search for the plans. If they are concealed, be assured that we will find them. If you do not cooperate by delivering the plans, and we discover your sons in the course of our search, we will question them in your stead."

"I have already told you, Captain Miller, that my sons are absent. They are with His Majesty's forces."

"Then if that is so, we will search for them in vain. The campaign plans however, are doubtless within this house, and I mean to find them."

Sir Henry closed his eyes briefly and prayed.

"I have nothing further to say to you, Captain. You will search as you please."

"Then you may remain here and observe the consequences of your refusal to help,"

Captain Miller snapped. He nodded to the two soldiers. One began pulling books and papers from their places. The other took a dagger from his belt and slashed into the cushioned window seat, searching for papers. The tapestry cushion destroyed, and nothing found, he turned his attention to Sir Henry's locked desk.

The plans, Sir Henry knew, were well hidden. He thought with anguish of the damage that might be wrought to the house, to the books in his treasured library, the terror that would be caused to Bess and to his household servants. And what of Harry? Had he been released from captivity only to be imprisoned again? Sir Henry watched helplessly as the rebels began their work of destruction.

ᔕ

When I recovered my senses, I was in my bedchamber, Peggy bathing my temples with lavender water. I gritted my teeth, mortified that I was developing a habit of swooning at times of crisis. A reviving draught of spring air was wafting through the open casement. The contrast of the enticing scents of spring mixed with the desperation of the current situation overwhelmed me and my eyes filled with tears. For all the careful preparations of Oliver White the previous autumn, and his arming of the servants, we had been taken unawares. Chadshunt Hall had fallen without a shot being fired. I struggled up onto my elbows, but the effort made the blood drain anew from my face.

"There, Miss Bess," soothed Peggy. "Lie still and you will recover presently. What of Master Harry?"

"Harry is safe in the herb garden, but what have they done to my father?" I whimpered. In my frantic efforts to conceal my brother and stop him getting himself put to the sword, I had almost forgotten Father's plight until I came upon him in the Great Hall.

Peggy patted me reassuringly on the hand.

"Have no fear for the Master, Miss Bess," she said. "He has suffered no harm. He is still within the Hall. The soldiers seek your brothers. They will be searching this chamber presently."

I lay there listening to the regular clatter of booted feet upon the stairs and making their way down the passage through the main house. Forewarned, I was fully dressed and sitting on a chair sipping a cup of restorative wine with a vigilant Peggy at my side when a heavy knock sounded on my door. Hector stood up and growled as two troopers about my own age entered. I grabbed him tightly, fearful of what the soldiers might do if he attacked them.

"Madam," one of them said to me, "We have orders to search the house for the malignants William and Henry Lucie."

Peggy answered for me.

"Well, make haste," she snapped, "Please make no unseemly commotion. My poor mistress is taken ill from the shock of your arrival."

They appeared uncomfortable at the task of searching a lady's bed chamber. They searched quickly behind my bed curtains, inside the big chest and knocked hopefully on the paneling around the walls.

"You'll find no priest holes in this house," snarled Peggy, "This is a Protestant family back to the time of Good Queen Bess, and you might want to remind that officer of yours of that."

Avoiding Peggy's fierce gaze, the two soldiers nodded to me and left the room. The regular tramp of boots going from room to room continued. I was more nervous as to what instructions they had received as to searching the grounds. It was not practical to observe their progress outside the house and so Peggy and I waited uneasily. About an hour after the soldiers left my chamber, I thought I heard distant shouts through my open window. I stared at Peggy in terror.

"Stay here, Miss Bess," she said, "I will go and see. Pray God they have not found Master Harry." I took her at her word and engaged in earnest prayer until I heard her steps returning. She came into the room giggling.

"Lord, Miss Bess, who should they try to arrest but poor Joe, just returned with a horse from the farrier?" I laughed with relief.

"Poor Joe, but how could they think he was one of my brothers? For surely he is wearing the dress of a groom, not a gentleman?"

"They suspected he might be disguised. They dragged him into the house and demanded Sir Henry identify him. Well of course, the Master said Joe was a servant, but one of the soldiers, still hoping he had succeeded in capturing one of your brothers, said to the officer that Sir Henry might be lying to protect his son."

Despite the gravity of the situation, I was amused.

"And my father, did he convince them?"

"With ease," laughed Peggy. "He bade the officer follow him into the family dining room. Shown the portrait of you and your brothers they were no longer in doubt, and had to release Joe to return to his duties."

Painted two years earlier, the portrait was a good, if romanticized, rendering of our family group. It showed Will, tall and handsome with long straight corn coloured hair like that of our mother, blue eyes under well marked brows and chiseled cheekbones. He was formally posed, a sword at his side and a falcon on his arm. Harry was also shown with a sword at his side and, in his case, his right hand resting on the head of a boar hound. Though a little shorter than Will, he was tall and straight, darker complexioned with my own dusky hair and grey eyes. The resemblance between Harry and I had always been commented on as a strong one. The fair skinned Will had inherited the more solid frame of our father and our mother's complexion. I, smiling winsomely in a way that was entirely the imagination of the artist, completed the picture, a songbird on the back of my hand. No more than a few years older than Will, our trusted and much loved head groom Joe was short and wiry. Light enough to ride the ponies we had ridden as children, but strong, he was the ideal build for a groom. He was also considerably shorter than either of my brothers with red hair and a round face. He certainly did not resemble either Will or Harry.

I continued to giggle, slightly hysterically until Peggy suggested I might benefit from going downstairs for dinner, followed by some fresh air.

"What of the soldiers?" I asked, trembling.

"I will find out." She returned in a few minutes, frowning.

"The soldiers will eat their dinner in the Great Hall and be grateful if they know what's good for them." Despite her words of defiance, I sensed Peggy was only telling me a part of the truth.

I had no desire to eat, but in obedience to Peggy's wishes I descended to the family dining room. The doors of the Great Hall were open. I caught a glimpse of soldiers sitting at table. One had his muddy boots propped carelessly on a tapestry cushioned chair from the time of Queen Elizabeth. The hidden door, leading to the library, hung open on its hinges, the delicately carved wooden scrollwork smashed in with an axe. There had been no need for this. There was another way to the library. The concealed passage was for Father's readier access to his most cherished possessions. On the floor lay the smashed marble bust of a Roman poet. A favourite piece of Father's, he had brought it from Italy as a young man. Now it was in fragments.

I bit back a sob and passed quickly on to the family dining room. Only two places were set at the table. Thomas had remembered not to arouse suspicions by setting a place for Harry. Did the second place mean that Father was free to join me? Automatically, I seated myself and washed my hands as Robin held the towel. I stared at the saddle of lamb with vegetables. Despite the disorder and ferment of the morning, the servants had evidently been permitted to continue with at least a part of their duties. My jangled nerves were rattled further by the sprinkling of rosemary on the lamb, for it was under the rosemary bush that Harry was hiding.

"Thomas, where have they taken my Father?" I muttered.

"The officer is questioning the Master in his study, Mistress." Thomas regarded me lugubriously. "I fear he will not be joining you."

Our whispered conference was interrupted by the flinging open of the door. To my relief it was Father. I caught sight of a trooper standing aside as the door closed behind him.

"Leave us," Father snapped at the servants. I leapt to my feet and embraced him.

"You are unhurt?"

"I am. I am glad to see you recovered. Bess, we have little time to spare. I made my concern for you my sole reason for entreating this half hour with you. I fear it will not be repeated and it may be our only opportunity to take counsel. Now, what of Harry?" Father's voice was low, his tone urgent.

"In the herb garden, Father. I stopped him as he was about to hurl himself at the soldiers, sword in hand." I broke off, choked with emotion.

"Then you saved him from capture and probable death. His courage is high but he sometimes lacks the ability to think, which I am pleased to say, you possess." He smiled at me warmly, while I coloured in amazement at this rare compliment from Father.

"What of poor Jacob? And Jack?"

"Jack will be freed later, Bess. He is a brave lad and will not mind a cobweb or two in the cellars. As for loyal Jacob, he tried to prevent their entry. It is fortunate the officer, Captain Miller, agreed to spare his life. Jacob will be freed on the morrow. I pray he will suffer nothing further than sore head and knees."

"But Father, what brought these men here?"

"I had thought at first it was the doing of the Committee for Sequestration, Bess, but I was wrong. The Committee's interest is in our family estates, our lands, our rents, not in our persons. Captain Miller knows of my work for the Council of War. That is why they have arrested me.

He thought to obtain details of His Majesty's summer campaign from me, but he was disappointed. He searched my study while I was forced to stand by, but found nothing of use to him, although he and his men half destroyed it."

His grey eyes were hard as granite.

I reflected on Father's orderly study, the oak paneled walls, dating from Queen Elizabeth's reign, its rows of ledgers and neatly rolled parchment, the polished wooden desk engraved with the family coat of arms and the high backed chair with the tapestry cushion Mother had worked.

"If he found nothing useful, will he will take no further action, Father?"

"I wish that were so. Captain Miller has promised he will find the plans wherever I have concealed them. He offered me no violence when I would not break faith, but Parliament is unlikely to let matters rest. They have me in their power and will take the necessary steps to elicit the details of the summer campaign from me. I fear that I will be taken elsewhere for questioning, Harry too, if they discover him.

Searches will continue, for the plans and for your brothers so that they too may be arrested and questioned. We must be thankful that thus far Captain Miller has shown no disposition to loot the Hall's treasures and his men appear too well disciplined to do so without his command."

"But Father, they are tearing Chadshunt apart in their search. Can we do nothing to prevent it?"

"Nothing but delivering them the plans, Bess, and that I will not do. They are worth more than this house, and more than my life. Yet I have not given my parole, so am not bound by honour to remain here if an opportunity to escape presents itself. I will preserve my life and freedom if possible.

Now, to other matters. I think we may need to confide in Celia. Do you believe we can trust her?"

In the events of the morning I had completely forgotten Celia.

"When does she return from her visit?"

"Before nightfall. Father, I know Celia can appear flighty. She knows little and cares less of the current struggle. But I believe she is sincerely attached to us and would never knowingly do anything to hurt our family."

Seating himself he spoke in an undertone.

"Harry cannot remain long in his hiding place. He may be tempted into rash action from discomfort or impatience. Too, Captain Miller may decide to make a more thorough search of the grounds than he did today. His men abandoned the search in some confusion after the mistake with Joe. Once they have recovered from their error they may decide to resume the search, the more anxious to prove themselves."

"Harry wishes to leave tonight, Father. He has asked for a horse."

He paced the room, deep in thought, before outlining his plan. The herb garden was secluded and, providing the guards were not watching every entrance to the house, it should be possible after dark to make one more foray to Harry. The more difficult matter was that of providing the horse. It would be a remarkably lax guard who would not set a watch on the stables at night, and Captain Miller had already imposed a night time curfew on the household. Any person wishing to leave the estate between sunset and sunrise would need a pass countersigned by him. Father hoped that a horseman leaving in the course of the afternoon might arouse less suspicion. If that horseman was Joe, already detained and cleared, it was possible he might leave unchallenged. He must wait at a predetermined spot at the far edge of the estate, hidden in woodland, until Harry joined him. Joe would remain there until well into the following morning when he would walk back through the park as if returning from some duties elsewhere on the estate. It was by no means a fool proof plan, but it was the best that could be managed at short notice.

"I rely on you then, Bess to…"

The door swung open. "Sir Henry, you have had ample time to assure yourself of your daughter's wellbeing. You will come with me."

I hoped Captain Miller had not overheard our conversation. Father was marched away once more, while I hastened to find Peggy and give her instructions for Joe.

The afternoon wore on. The thud of axes and the sounds of splintering paneling resounded, as the search intensified. Sadly, Captain Miller's control over his men was not as absolute as Father had hoped. I was approaching my bed chamber when the door to my mother's chamber opened. Two laughing soldiers emerged. One had a bundle of Mother's gowns gathered in his arms, while the other carried the tapestry depicting the bible story of the meeting of King David and Abigail.

Mother's maid Mary emerged from the next chamber.

"What are you doing?"

She hurled herself at the nearer soldier, a tall, thin man with skin pitted from the pox. Crowing, he grabbed her around the waist and lifted her off her feet.

"A fair wench, I would know you better." He dropped the heavy roll of tapestry and tugged at her coif so that her hair came unpinned. She scratched at his face and he threw her against the wall, kissing her roughly. I found my voice.

"Stop that. Peggy! Thomas!" I yelled. The sound of pounding footsteps caused the soldier to pause. Thomas dashed up, his fists raised and his usual stately demeanour abandoned. Pushing Mary aside, the soldier drew his sword.

"What is this commotion? Potts, put up your sword immediately. And what are these goods you carry? There will be no looting without my authority."

I would not have thought to be happy to see the Roundhead officer but now I exhaled with relief.

"But, Sir," the other man protested, clutching Mother's gowns tighter in his meaty arms, "This is a malignant house."

"Potts and Lambton, you disgrace the Godly cause for which we fight. We are here to search and make arrests. Corporal," he raised his voice. One of his men appeared from round a corner. "You will march these men to the garrison at Compton. I will deal with them later." He nodded to me.

"Mistress, I apologise for the disturbance. I trust your maid servant is unharmed. It will not happen again."

As bright sunlight turned to gold in late afternoon, I heard the clatter of Celia's carriage. Closely followed by Peggy, I darted out to meet her as the step was let down.

"Cousin," I greeted her, "How pleased I am to see you return in safety. You must be tired."

Alighting from the carriage, Celia caught sight of Jacob kneeling on the cobblestones, an orange-sashed soldier on guard beside him, naked sword in hand. Two more soldiers stood either side of the entrance doors, while others were stationed at various points around the outside of the house. Celia turned to me, aghast.

I looped my arm in hers, turning her towards the entrance. Peggy was assisting Celia's maid somewhat carelessly with the baggage. A hat box fell to the ground with a crash, making one of the carriage horses back, entangling the traces. The other horse shied and caught its leg. A carriage lamp became wedged against the archway to the coach house and smashed. The coachman was trying to steady the horses while Celia's maid berated Peggy for her clumsiness. Noone paid much attention as the red haired groom rode from the stables and trotted down the lane. Once within earshot of the two guards either side of the entrance doors, I slowed my pace. In a low but clear voice I began,

"Such terrible events of today, cousin. Your father's comrades from the Parliament have arrested my father. They did not believe him when he told them both Will and Harry were away from home. Their searches are causing wanton damage."

We paused at the top of the steps. "How foolish," she replied, "My cousins have been from home these several weeks."

We entered the house slowly. Once we were within earshot of another trooper, I paused again.

"Celia, you must send a message to your husband, Sir John Ridgeley. Is he not a friend of the Earl of Essex?"

"Indeed yes, Bess. I will do so without delay." We walked on.

In the privacy of my bedchamber, I recounted the events of the day and, taking a deep breath, told her our plans for the night. By this stage I was almost sure that we could trust her, but I watched the expression on her face closely as I explained where Harry was hidden. I was relieved to see that she showed nothing but concern and an unaccustomed thoughtfulness. She pressed my hand and promised to help in any way she could.

"For this foolish quarrel between King and Parliament is beyond my understanding. Dear cousin, I would see no further harm come to your family or to this house. While I remain here," she said, her pretty, somewhat childish face looking determined and suddenly more mature, "I trust I can be of assistance."

Celia was not long in proving her worth. Before many minutes had passed, Captain Miller was requesting speech with Lady Ridgeley. Celia swept down to meet him, adopting as haughty an expression as one so young and pretty could assume. On her return, she reported that he understood her husband's position and sympathies. She had been unable to reverse the orders either for my father's arrest, or for the night time curfew, but she had won several concessions. The soldiers would confine their night time patrols to outside the house. Continuing searches would be carried out with as little damage as possible and there would be no looting. Most importantly, Captain Miller gave a personal undertaking that he would not use violent means to extract the information he sought from my father. We would even be permitted a brief daily visit to him. I was grateful to my cousin for her efforts.

When the soldiers had left the house for the night, I entered Harry's chamber and selected some of his more serviceable clothes from those strewn carelessly around in the soldiers' search. I crammed them into a cloak bag. Joe had left with a bag of provisions tied to his saddle. I changed into my darkest gown, soft slippers and a drab green cloak. I crept from the house.

Peggy had volunteered for this duty, but I insisted. I did not know how long it might be before I saw Harry again and was determined to bid him farewell. Peggy had reported that two guards were stationed outside the stables, while two others patrolled the perimeter of the main house. I waited until the guard had passed, then slipped quietly through the servants' entrance at the back of the hall. Fortunately the night was inky black and cloudy. Feeling my way without a lamp, I moved cautiously. Once I trod on a small branch. There was a crack and I froze. No sounds ensued and within a few minutes I was inside the herb garden, groping towards the dense outline of the rosemary bush. Slowly and carefully I moved away the pots and raised the trapdoor. "Harry, it's Bess," I whispered.

"That's well," he replied drily. A creak announced that he was now climbing the ladder, a small chinking sound that he had filled his purse. As he reached the top of the ladder he paused, and I saw he was clutching his dagger. All remained quiet and we replaced the trapdoor and its coverings without making a disturbance. Quickly, I passed him the bag and explained where Joe would be waiting with the horse in the woods to the south side of the estate.

"Do not go near the west wing," I cautioned. "There is a curfew and the stables are watched. The soldiers sleep in the barn nearest the house. You were best go out through the orchard." He nodded. There was no time for more words. With a lump in my throat I hugged him, "God go with you, Harry. My love to Will. Send us word if you may do so safely. I hope we will be together again soon."

"My brave sister," he said with a smile in his voice, "With women like you on the King's side, how can his cause fail?" He swept me into a firm embrace. Then he moved stealthily out of the garden.

12

I WATCHED HARRY go with a heavy heart. The next morning I started at every sound until around mid morning I saw Joe stroll towards the stables unchallenged. I breathed a sigh of relief then, for I knew my brother had truly escaped. That day, the soldiers continued to search both house and grounds. When I was admitted to see him in the afternoon, Father listened carefully to my account of the soldiers' hunt.

"Will they find what they seek, Father?"

He closed his eyes momentarily. "I pray not, Bess."

"Cousin, a charming day to be outdoors." Celia had not joined me for dinner, but now her bright voice broke in upon my thoughts as I moodily strummed my harpsichord. Arm in arm, we strolled towards the rose garden, where a few early blooms were in bud. We seated ourselves in the arbour.

"Uncle Henry is in danger."

My eyes widened.

"In danger, Celia? What do you mean? Is he not already in danger?"

"I dined with Captain Miller, Bess. I think I have convinced him my sympathies lie with Parliament. He confided in me that he has abandoned the hunt for your brothers. Half of his men return today to the garrison at Compton as they achieve nothing here."

"That is two pieces of excellent news, Celia. What is the danger to my father?"

"Parliament has urgent need of the campaign plans that Uncle Henry conceals. Captain Miller hopes I may persuade my uncle to give them up. If the plans are not unearthed within the next day or two, Uncle Henry will be taken elsewhere for interrogation."

"Then he must break out from here without delay," I murmured.

ও

"Easy to say I must break out, Bess." Father stroked his chin thoughtfully.

"I must have a horse, or I will be easily overtaken, and I cannot expect

Joe to use the same ruse twice. I must apply to Will for assistance."

"But Father, that will surely take some days to get word to Will? Celia believes you may be removed within a day or two. Besides, how will you accomplish an escape from a locked chamber?"

Another day had already elapsed before I had been able to deliver the warning to Father. Time was short. Escape from the upstairs chamber, difficult though it might be, was not insurmountable. Within hours, Mary had smuggled a long coil of rope into Father's chamber concealed in a basket of clean linen. On the appointed night, he would climb down the rope from his chamber window. How to purchase sufficient time to enlist Will's assistance was less clear. It was the Warwickshire Committee for Sequestration which unexpectedly came to our aid the following day. Four soberly clad gentlemen arrived unannounced. To Captain Miller's unconcealed annoyance, they commandeered the library and proceeded to question Father and John Dale at length about the estate and its revenues. They demanded the ledgers. Some had been damaged beyond repair in the search for the campaign plans.

"God willing, this gives me the time I need, Bess," Father whispered. On the pretext of assisting with the papers, I had insinuated myself briefly into the library. "I believe it will take them an entire week at the very least to gather the information they seek. Captain Miller is furious."

ꟹ

My spirits rose even higher when, in addition to this unlooked for delay, a traveling peddler called at the servants' entrance two days later. Peggy handed me a letter sealed with Harry's signet ring. I tore it open.

"My dear Bess, I have arrived safely. I travelled mainly at night, being as cautious as I know my dear sister would wish me to be. I have seen Will, who is quartered at Abingdon with most of the cavalry. Gabriel is in Oxford. He has rejoined Sir John Byron's regiment as a Captain, now they are returned here. I gladly accepted his offer of a commission as Lieutenant. The troop is tasked with supporting the Oxford garrison. Oxford is crowded with the King's court, courtiers and a multitude of tradesmen and craftsmen who support the resident garrison. It's a motley crowd but it makes for a lively atmosphere, even though I confess sometimes I must pull the pillow about my ears if I am to get a wink of sleep. I do not know when we will be able to meet. Pray tell Father that I am well. I know he will be circumspect in any plans he may form. Take care, my sister and do nothing without Father's blessing. It would deeply grieve Will and I if you should come to harm. Forgive me for not remaining at your dear side.

Your affectionate brother, Harry

Post script

I enclose another musical masterpiece."

I then noticed the smaller sheet of parchment enclosed. It had a half sheet of music, and the words,

"Dear Bess, I am delighted to be once more in the company of your brother, Harry. This is the second half of the song you received from me earlier. It is written, as you know, for two voices and I await the opportunity when I may try its notes out with the second singer. In the meantime, I hope it may entertain you a little in your current circumstances. I wish I could do more."

It was signed with a linnet. I sighed and smiled, tucking Gabriel's music away. For some reason, Peggy's comments the previous year about the impropriety of a secret correspondence with a man had completely slipped my memory.

ග

The gentlemen from the Committee had commenced calling the tenants in to give evidence as to the income of our estates. Sir Henry had not yet heard from Will, but remained optimistic that impediments would continue for as long as was necessary to make the arrangements for his escape. On the following day, however, Captain Miller had him brought to the study, now barely useable after the intensive search. Neatly attired in his usual clean linen, orange sash and dark brown suit, sword at his hip, the officer was seated behind Sir Henry's desk. The once fine piece of furniture was splintered, its carved mouldings torn open in the search for a secret drawer.

"Sir Henry, I command you this one last time to disclose to me what you know of the King's summer campaign and the planned dispositions for his armies."

He stared the officer stonily in the eye.

"Sir, I believe you must recognise by now that your commands are to no avail."

"Then you leave me no option. I have convinced the gentlemen from the committee of the necessity for you to be interrogated without further delay."

Captain Miller was regarding him with compassion.

"I give you this one day to put your affairs in order and bid your daughter farewell. Tomorrow you will be taken under guard to London, to the Tower."

"I will be waiting with horses at one of the clock. You will find me by the tall oak that was struck by lightning."

That last morning, Father had been permitted to work on his papers in the study. I passed him Will's note and he scanned it quickly.

"Then Bess, tonight I take my leave. It were best that you go to your aunt in Devon when I have gone. I have already written to her to ask that she should give you shelter until I may care for you again. You will travel to her with Celia's assistance when her husband collects her."

"Father, might I not go with you? I won't be a trouble, I promise."

"Bess, don't be absurd," he snapped. "It will be a difficult and dangerous venture to successfully flee this place without discovery. I will be carrying the campaign plans with me. To attempt to do so encumbered by a woman would be madness. You will do as I command."

ဟ

Whether it was a servant making a careless remark, or Sir Henry himself overheard talking to Bess, Captain Miller became wary. Sir Henry was peering at the sky from his bed chamber window, gauging the probability of a cloudy night, when the key turned in his door. He was taken aback to see Captain Miller himself standing in the doorway, two troopers behind him.

"My apologies for the intrusion, Sir Henry." The officer sounded apologetic.

"This being your last day here, it may be you hope to escape. My men are to search your chamber afresh to ensure you do not have the means. I must ask you to stand aside while they do so."

There was little purpose in protesting. Sir Henry stood gloomily by as the troopers swiftly discovered firstly a small dagger he had concealed and then the rope, coiled beneath blankets at the bottom of a chest.

Captain Miller regarded the rope, gnawing at his lip.

"I perceive this was a wise precaution, Sir. A guard will be stationed below your window until you leave here to ensure you make no foolish attempts to abscond."

With a slight bow, he left. The key turned in the lock. Sir Henry clenched his fists, impotently. With no means of escaping from the house, Will would wait in vain with the horses. The following morning would see Sir Henry on his way to the Tower and imprisonment. Parliament's spymasters would not hesitate in using torture to extract the information he withheld.

If only he could see his dear wife once more, or even pay a final visit to her chamber. Adjoining his, it remained as she had left it. With his own door shut fast, he could no more visit Anne's unlocked chamber than he could fly the house. It had been his mother's room, his grandmother's too. Dreamily, he recollected his own father's tales of how his grandfather would move between the two chambers through the interconnecting door. He was brought up short by the half remembered tales. Might the door still exist? Why had he not thought of it earlier? Urgently, he ran his eye over the wall between the two rooms. In the centre of the wall was a large closet, extending from floor to ceiling. Behind its doors were shelves of linen, spare bolsters for the bed, bed hangings for an earlier bed. Some had lain untouched since his father's day until the soldiers had searched through the contents, rumpling the layers and disturbing the dust. Sir Henry had rarely opened the closet, his own attire being kept in chests within his chamber. With trembling hands, he kindled a spark and lit a candle. Wary of alerting the guard outside his door by making too much noise, he opened the doors to the closet and examined its dark recesses, running his hands over the back. After a minute or so of frantic search, he felt two vertical creases some two feet apart, stretching behind the shelving from top to bottom.

ও

Captain Miller permitted Father to spend that evening with Celia and me, although a guard was posted outside the door. I felt so tense I thought I would snap like an over tuned lute string. Celia, who only knew that Father was to be taken away to London the next day, regarded me sympathetically as I made a false note on the harpsichord or fell silent half way through a piece. We had kept her in ignorance. The fewer people in the secret, the easier it was to maintain some semblance of normality. At ten o'clock, Captain Miller entered.

"Sir Henry, it is time to make your farewells. We ride at first light."

Father nodded sadly and rose to his feet. I clung to him, sobbing. He placed a hand on my head and blessed me, then did the same to Celia.

"Farewell, Uncle Henry," she murmured, "I will pray for you."

ও

Captain Miller personally escorted Sir Henry to his bed chamber. Opening the door, he made a quick survey of the candlelit room. He hesitated.

"I respect your bravery, Sir, but I fear if you will not bend to the will of Parliament then you will be broken in the Tower. I advise you to spend the period of our journey in reflection on what continued resistance will cost you."

"I will use the time then for reflection," Sir Henry said calmly.

The two men faced each other. Captain Miller bit his lip.

"If you will give me your parole not to attempt an escape on the road to London, Sir Henry, I will permit you to be in command of your own horse. I would be sorry if your household's last view of you was bound with rope or chains."

"Thank you, Captain. Then I give my word I will not attempt to escape you between this place and London. Now I wish to be alone. I pray you leave me sufficient candles. I will spend the night in reading and prayer." He indicated a prayer book lying on the table.

Captain Miller nodded. He hesitated again and then bowed to his prisoner before leaving the chamber and turning the key in the lock.

Sir Henry listened until the retreating footsteps could no longer be heard. He forced himself to wait a few more minutes, seating himself at the table and turning the pages of the prayer book somewhat at random. Having assured himself that Captain Miller had no intention of returning, he sprung to his feet and took up a candle. He closed the casement. It was raining and blowing hard outside. He hoped the wind would drown out any noise he made. He opened the closet. Working stealthily during the day while a guard stood outside his door, he had succeeded in clearing the shelves, placing their contents on the floor of the closet and in his own chests. With the shelves cleared, the creases were plainer. With the aid of judiciously placed candles, Sir Henry had been able to see that the door was covered with a thin layering of stucco. Some crumbling representations of fruit indicated that the wall had at an earlier period been intended as a decorative feature and it was then that the door had been plastered over. Like his dear wife, his grandmother had died in middle age. His grandfather had not remarried and it was possible that he had covered the door in an attempt to forget what once had been.

Well, no more of that. What mattered now was how speedily he could reveal the door.

He began to scrape at the stucco with his hands. Alas, it was harder than he had hoped and his fingers made but small impression on the plaster. He had hoped to be able to use a knife but the soldiers had assiduously removed the small blade he used for meat. He took up the candlestick once more and with increasing urgency surveyed the contents of the room. His eyes lit upon the empty fireplace. He picked up the heavy iron poker with relief and opened the doors to the closet once more. As silently as possible, he began probing with the poker into the creases, chipping away. He must work quickly if he was to be ready in time. There was a splintering noise and the poker penetrated through to the other side. The noise resounded. He hastily moved to the window and eased it open again. Below he could see the trooper on duty, huddled in his cloak, standing beneath the overhang of a ledge a few paces away. He had not moved. Reassured, Sir Henry redoubled his efforts. After some time, maybe an hour, he had cleared the creases so that on the one side he could see hinges. There was no handle, but a further depression showed where one had been. Pressing against the other edge of the door, he pushed with all his might and the door gave way with a crack. Not daring to take his candle, Sir Henry edged through into his wife's chamber and felt his way towards the door. As he had hoped, it was unlocked. Returning to his own chamber he ascertained that the trooper was still beneath his window. Now he had only to wait in patience for the signal.

ᔕ

I went to my chamber but could not bring myself either to undress or to lie down. The skies had clouded before sunset and I heard the increasing patter of rain on the window. The wind blew hard. I strained my ears. Surely it was taking too long. It must have been well past midnight when I heard shouts from behind the house. Ignoring the drops of rain which blew into my face, I flung open the casement and peered out into the blackness. In the distance to my left I saw a flicker of light. It was some way from the house, and it grew as I stared. The cries swelled to a crescendo. I heard the tramp of boots as the soldiers on patrol ran towards the source of the commotion.

"The tithe barn!"

Peggy slunk up behind me, making me start.

"I think it will serve, Miss Bess, despite the rain. There is a fine wind blowing."

ᔕ

I was rudely woken from my uneasy sleep. In the half light which preceded dawn, I heard the clamour of angry voices, this time within the house, and renewed pounding of booted feet. I could discern nothing from my window except a distant mass of smoke, spangled with red sparks like fire flies, the smouldering ruins of our beautiful tithe barn. Withdrawing once more behind my bed curtains, I feigned sleep. No more than a few minutes later, my door was flung open and Captain Miller strode unceremoniously into my chamber, a drawn sword in his hand. I sat up and screamed. Peggy came running as the agitated officer tore back my bed curtains.

"Mistress Lucie, your father has disappeared from his chamber. There is no trace of him within the house."

"Dear me, Captain," I smiled triumphantly "Is that so?"

He raised the sword convulsively and for a moment I feared for my life. His face was white, his eyes staring. At the last moment he recollected himself.

"I see all too clearly from your countenance, Mistress that you were complicit in your father's fleeing lawful custody."

He turned on his heel and stamped out of the room. Celia and I met at the usual breakfast hour, attempting a semblance of normality. I had seen nothing of Captain Miller since his unceremonious dawn visit, but now he entered the family dining room without preamble.

"Lady Ridgeley, I assume you were unaware that your uncle was planning to escape?" Celia looked suitably grave.

"Truly Captain, if my uncle is not to be found I have no more idea as to his whereabouts than you do."

When Celia had reassured him of her ignorance, he withdrew once more and I breathed a sigh of relief. For the remainder of that day, Celia and I were left undisturbed while searches of the house and grounds continued. It was a strange day, Celia and I in the eye of the storm which had broken with daylight. Four troopers mounted and rode away, presumably seeking Father beyond the environs of the estate. I hoped he had made good his escape on horseback. The next morning, Celia and I were sitting sewing in the sitting room when Captain Miller entered, bowing to Celia and scowling at me.

"Mistress Lucie, I sent word to my commanding officer, Major Balfour, of what occurred here yesterday. He has ordered me to place you under house arrest, pending an investigation of your role in Sir Henry Lucie's escape. You are sadly mistaken if you believe your sex alone will protect you from the consequences of ill considered actions. You will remain within the precincts of the house at all times and will be locked within your chamber at night. The Committee for Sequestration has almost completed its work at Chadshunt and a prospective tenant wishes to consult with them. Since he is a senior officer, and will arrive within the next day or two, it is he who will determine how you will be dealt with, not I. His name is Major Chatterton, presently Governor of Warwick Castle."

With that he bowed stiffly to Celia and left the room. I collapsed onto a chair, shaking. Celia smiled at me encouragingly.

"Courage, Bess. Major Chatterton is a friend of my father and I have met him a number of times. Have you not met him also, at my father's house? This may turn to our advantage. He will soon win your release."

I put my head in my hands. There was nothing for it but to explain to her the full story of the events at Warwick Castle. Her eyes grew wide with horror.

"And this man is a friend of my father. But my father cannot be aware.. well no matter," she finished hastily. "We must remove you before he arrives. As to the Hall itself, I will tell Major Chatterton and the gentlemen of the committee that I am entrusted to look after the estate and it will have no tenant but me. I will write to Sir John and my father and make it so."

And with that my sweet, childish cousin drew herself up to her full, somewhat insignificant height, radiating a resolve I had not guessed she possessed.

❧

I was shocked at being placed under arrest myself. Father had not foreseen that as a possible consequence of his flight. I had little doubt that if I remained, Major Chatterton would have no scruple in finishing what Will had interrupted the previous December.

Celia wrote her letters immediately. I sat by, the palms of my hands sticky with sweat. I rubbed them with a handkerchief and then twisted it between my fingers as I tried in vain to devise my own escape plan. Once a servant had collected them, she turned and smiled reassuringly.

"Well, Bess, what ingenious scheme have you devised?" She folded her small hands in her lap, looking expectant. I shook my head.

"My thoughts are all muddled, Celia, I can think of no scheme." She jumped to her feet.

"It is a sunny day," she said, "Let us see how closely you are guarded. Surely Captain Miller will allow you to stroll in the gardens."

"Are you suggesting I saunter straight past the guards?"

The idea was breathtaking in its simplicity. I hoped Captain Miller would not expect such a bold attempt. I ran up the stairs to my chamber and looked quickly around. I pulled on my straw hat. It would be suspicious if I was carrying anything, even a cloak, on such a warm day. I extracted my largest pocket from a drawer and stuffed it with all the money I possessed, a pearl necklace my mother had given to me, the handkerchief stained with Rafe's blood and Gabriel's music. Tied around my waist beneath my petticoats, the pocket could not be seen. Arm in arm, Celia and I approached the back door to the house. It was unlocked. We opened it and strolled through.

"Halt," one of the troopers was standing a few feet away.

"My Lady, you may continue on your way. You, Mistress" he jerked his head at me, "Back inside."

ᔕ

"I am sorry, Bess, I was foolish to suggest that."

We had retired to my chamber for greater privacy.

"No matter, Celia, it was worth the attempt. Since you are at liberty, perhaps a stroll to find out the numbers and placement of the guards?"

Celia returned to inform me of the soldiers' positions. Front and back entrances were both guarded, as were the main entrance to the stables and the door from the chapel at the end of the west wing. A ramble as far as the gatehouse had discovered that Jacob was performing his duties under scrutiny from a further trooper.

"The servants' entrance was unguarded, Bess. We might make a further attempt from there."

"No. Thank you, cousin. If we are stopped again, it will become clear that you are aiding me. I must go alone." I bent and embraced her.

I glanced out of the window at the sky. The sun was past its zenith, it must be mid afternoon. If I succeeded this time it might be some hours before I was missed by Captain Miller. I removed my soft slippers and replaced them with a pair of boots suitable for walking. The pocket was still in place beneath my skirts. If I could but make my way safely to Kineton I might be able to hire a horse. I had no illusions that I could travel as far as Oxford on foot without detection. On horseback I might fare better. Making my way down the stairs I slipped into the service passage. Past buttery, pantry, kitchens and brewhouse I paced. The servants were accustomed to my forays into their quarters and were not surprised to see me passing through. This time, I paused before stepping outside. Opening the door from the servants' quarters gingerly, I peeped out. Celia had been correct, there was no one in sight. Gathering my skirts in both hands, I made a dash for the cover of the rose garden. Its leafy hedges and the many bushes with their opening blooms provided welcome shelter and I stopped to catch my breath. The strips of grass between the beds stretched ahead, thankfully empty. I hurried through the garden, heading towards the herb garden and the more distant orchard. The heady fragrance of the blossoms filled my senses. As I passed by the arbour, it was a moment before I realised that the delicate scent of the roses was mingled with a more pungent odour.

"Good day to you, Mistress."

Captain Miller had risen from his hidden seat, clay pipe in hand. Despite the mild greeting, his voice was exasperated. He knocked out the pipe and gripped me firmly by the arm. We marched back towards the house.

"Mistress Lucie, please accept that I will not permit you to abscond. If you wish to win your freedom however, there may be the means." He looked at me speculatively. "I should imagine you have some idea where your father might be, should you wish to send him a message?" I was unwilling to admit this might be true.

"What message?" I temporized.

"That if he will return to Chadshunt and surrender himself in your stead, I will free you and permit you to leave for Oxford or where you will. You may give him my word on that."

We had arrived at the back entrance.

"Corporal, escort Mistress Lucie to her bedchamber and lock her in until tomorrow. Place a guard outside her door. Mistress, think well on what I have said. If you wish to send a message to your father, you have only to knock on your door and speak to the guard."

He bowed politely, but I felt his eyes boring into my back as I climbed the stairs with the corporal.

ഗ

I was lying on my bed in a stupor when I heard a brisk altercation outside my locked door. Peggy was arguing with the guard. I brightened. Peggy, just returned from visiting her sister, was unaware of my changed circumstances. Hopes for Peggy's speedy entrance were dashed, but as night fell I heard her voice once more and the door was unlocked.

"No more than a half hour, woman. More than sufficient time to prepare your mistress for the night."

"Oh Peggy, what am I to do?"

Peggy was thoughtful as I reached the end of the tale of Captain Miller's threats and my two unsuccessful attempts to flee.

"You would not send such a message to the Master? It would surely win you liberty."

"How could I ask my father to do that? No, there must be another way. If only Celia and I resembled each other, I might escape from here with ease, for she may come and go as she wishes." My tiny flaxen haired cousin reached no higher than my shoulder.

Peggy chuckled reluctantly.

"You pass for Lady Ridgeley, Miss Bess, with your height? You would pass more easily as a youth." We looked at each other.

ℭ

"I am pleased to hear you that you have seen reason, Mistress Lucie."

Captain Miller was seated behind the desk the next morning in what remained of Father's study, I standing before him as a supplicant. His eyes were watchful.

"If I am permitted to write to him, Sir, I will beg him to come here so that I may be released. I feel sure he would gladly exchange places with me," I finished. I lowered my eyes demurely, concerned that the intelligent pale blue eyes might read deceit in mine.

Captain Miller promptly cleared a table for me and provided me with writing materials. He stood by, observing me closely as I wrote.

"Allow me, Mistress." He stretched out his hand as I reached for the sealing wax. He took the two sheets and scrutinized them carefully, his face puzzled.

"Two letters, Mistress? They are identical, both to your father."

"Forgive me, Sir," I lowered my eyelashes again. "I am unclear as to his direction. If I may be permitted to send the message to two different places."

"As you wish, give me the direction."

He sealed the letters and wrote upon them. Both were addressed to Sir Henry Lucie, one at a fictitious address in Oxford, which lay to our south, the second was addressed care of Lieutenant William Lucie at the garrison in Worcester, many miles to our west.

"If I might be permitted to send two different men, Sir," I said meekly, "The response will arrive the sooner. Two of our grooms would be the speediest messengers."

"Very well."

ℭ

Would I ever enter my bedchamber at Chadshunt again, I wondered, as I attired myself in the doublet, shirt, breeches, cloak and shoes belonging to Joe's dark haired brother Ben. Like Joe, Ben was short for a man and we were much of a height. I looked at myself in the glass. Celia and I giggled. It was just as it had been-was it truly less than two years earlier when we had helped each other dress on Christmas Eve. I packed a cloak bag with a few of my more hardwearing clothes. The contents of my pocket I emptied into a leather purse, tying it securely to Ben's leather belt.

"Here, Miss Bess. Let me comb out your hair. I will tie it back in a tail as Ben wears his." Peggy broke off with a quiet sob.

I embraced Celia and Peggy.

"Look after Hector for me." Taking care that I was not observed leaving my bed chamber in man's attire, Peggy preceded me to the kitchens where I met Joe. This time there would be no return for our head groom. Unhesitatingly, he had pledged to see me safe to Oxford and there enlist in the King's forces. Each clutching one of the letters addressed to my father, Joe and I entered the stables. I kept Ben's hat pulled low over my face and my head down. The guard on duty was expecting us and gave a perfunctory nod as Joe explained our mission. I tied my bag to the saddle and mounted the stolid bay gelding usually ridden by Ben while Joe mounted Fairy. Side by side, Joe on my right hand screening me from the house and its attendant guards, we trotted unhurriedly under the archway and across the court yard.

"Stop!" One of the troopers had emerged from the main entrance of the house and was hurtling down the steps. The guard at the bottom, immediately on the alert, unslung his carbine from its clip. I glanced frantically at Joe. Shortening the reins, I prepared to dig my heels into the horse's flanks. Joe flung out his gloved left hand towards me. Gesturing urgently at me to halt, he drew rein. Now I saw that the trooper held something in his hand.

"Messenger," he shouted at Joe, "The Captain bade me give you these. They are safe conduct passes should you encounter any of our forces."

He handed two small pieces of parchment to Joe, who grunted his thanks and passed one to me. We passed the gatehouse without hindrance. Once on the high road, we both turned south, heading for Oxford. I had timed our departure for shortly after dinner. I calculated that if all went well it would be four or five hours before my non arrival for supper raised the alarm. We trotted through Kineton, keeping a wary eye for signs of pursuit. Avoiding Banbury and the larger towns in case of discovery or pursuit, we made our way before nightfall as far as the village of Hook Norton and spent the night in the taproom of an alehouse, with me still in my character as Ben.

"It's little ale I have left," the tapster grumbled. "Colonel Croker's horse were billeted here last night and they were all for free quarter. I secreted two barrels away or there would have been none for you, lad," he grinned at me, displaying his four crooked remaining teeth. I grunted sympathetically and spat on the greasy rush floor.

The following day we pursued our way towards Woodstock and onwards towards Oxford. Unluckily, Fairy cast a shoe at Woodstock and we wasted time finding a farrier. By the time we made our way through Yarnton on the approach to Oxford, night was falling. We made only slow progress in the dim light, the road being unknown to us and increasingly rutted from the passage of wheels the closer we drew to the city. We did not wish to risk one of the horses putting a hoof in a pothole and breaking a leg.

I realised at this point that there were some difficulties attending our arrival. I was uncertain as to where I might find either my father or my brothers. Approaching from the north, we passed first through the ruins of what appeared to have been the outer suburbs of Oxford. Several red sashed cavalry patrols had thundered past us since we had reached Woodstock, but we had not seen the movement of civilians upon the road since it had become dark. I realised with dismay that Oxford was no doubt under a night time curfew and we might be unable to enter the city. Thinking only of fleeing the rebel troops at my home and reaching the sanctuary of the Royalist capital, I was unprepared for hostility at the point when I had supposedly reached safety. Looming ahead of us were the dark shapes of massive earthworks, some of them topped with cannon.

"Joe, stop," I gasped, "What if they will not permit us to enter the city after dark?"

"Stand fast in the name of the King!" The challenge had come from the fortifications directly ahead. A musketeer approached us, raising his weapon. I heard an ominous click.

13

Oxford, May 1643

"DISMOUNT AND state your business."

The lighted length of match in his hand glowed in the dark. Belatedly, I noticed a barrier across the road. Why had I not considered the possibility of a hostile reception? Joe was looking at me for instructions. I dismounted as slowly as possible, trying to think.

"Just say you're Father's groom and you are riding to meet him," I whispered. "I had better remain as Ben for the present."

"I come to meet my master, Sir Henry Lucie," said Joe hesitantly. "My name is Joseph Port and this is my younger brother Ben."

"Approach slowly," was the reply and we found a blazing torch being held before our faces to illuminate them. "What is your master's direction?" continued the man. "And why do you arrive at this late hour? Where's your safe conduct pass?"

Joe looked at me helplessly, "Sir Henry is unaware that we arrive tonight, Sir. We do not know where he lodges and had expected to arrive before dark to seek him out."

"Wait here. Lieutenant, a word, please, Sir." A tall red sashed officer no older than Harry emerged from the darkness a moment later, frowning at the soldier.

"What's to do?"

The soldier turned his back and dropped his voice.

The Lieutenant sighed wearily and clapped his hand on the hilt of his sword. I realised he was loosening it in the scabbard. My heart gave a further bump.

"Come closer, fellows. Let me look at you. Uncover your heads and make no sudden movements."

Two more soldiers appeared with muskets levelled, lighted match glowing in their hands. Joe removed his hat while I sidled into the shadows. Impatiently the Lieutenant tugged my hat off my head and pulled me into the light. He looked at my face and started. My disguise as a boy was not good enough to stand up to close inspection. He unfastened the clasp on my cloak, pulling it off my shoulders. He ran his eyes up and down me, holding the torch close and whistled. He cupped my chin.

"Well, well, a maid in disguise as a man. This bears looking into. Sir!" he said, turning to Joe, "Hand over your weapons." His words frightened me further. "And you, Mistress, are you armed?"

Dumbly I shook my head while he continued scrutinising me in the light of the torch. A moment later his hand dived to my waist. He backed away, holding aloft the small dagger from my belt. Intended for meat, it had not occurred to me it might be seen as a weapon. His eyes rested on me thoughtfully as he thrust the dagger through his own belt.

"Search them, Corporal. Let us see what they may be concealing. Raise your hands."

The last words, I realised, were for Joe and me. The officer's voice remained quiet, matter of fact. Trembling all over, I raised my gloved hands to shoulder height. Gently, the Corporal ran his hands down me, while one of the other men did the same to Joe. There was a crackle of paper from my shirt. The Corporal tugged at the string tying the neck of my shirt and thrust his hand inside it.

"The bearer is a messenger for the Parliament. Please allow him to pass without let or hindrance and afford him what assistance you may. Signed Captain Asher Miller, Sir James Ramsey's Regiment." The lieutenant finished reading the safe conduct pass aloud.

"Corporal, take three men with you to escort our visitors to the Captain at the north gate."

I did not like either his tone or the strange emphasis he laid on the word "visitors". I opened my mouth, but Joe gave a tiny shake of his head. I shut it again and prepared to mount my horse. I was stopped by a hand on the bridle.

"I think not, Mistress," he said sternly. "The horses remain here. You are both under arrest. I would counsel more truthful answers when you are questioned by the Captain. I have heard he has little patience with spies.

Keep a close eye on them, Corporal. No sudden disappearances down alleyways."

With two soldiers gripping each of us firmly by the arms, Joe and I were marched towards the town. My heart was banging against my ribs and I was having difficulty in breathing. I was exhausted. Ben's shoes did not fit properly and rubbed my heels as I shuffled along. I almost wished I had remained at home to take my chance with Major Chatterton. At least I would have been in familiar surroundings. As I came to this dismal conclusion, the soldiers stopped at a house close by the city walls. The corporal spoke briefly to the sentry on guard outside while I pondered desperately how to persuade the officer that, despite appearances, we were neither messengers nor spies for the rebels. Joe and I were dragged into a candlelit hallway. The Corporal knocked and opened the door to a small parlour, the air thick with lamp smoke and the fug of tobacco. I glimpsed an empty fireplace, a desk covered in papers and several wooden chairs pushed back against the walls. A semi circle of men, backs turned to us, were bending over a table covered with what appeared to be a large map. The Corporal cleared his throat.

"Captain, we have apprehended two rebel messengers attempting to enter the city. One is a wench disguised as a man. They were carrying these."

He held out our passes. One of the officers straightened and swung round to face us. Dressed like his fellows in buff coat and red sash, a sword on his hip and spurs gleaming in the candlelight, he wore a large hat pushed back on his head. Long dark wavy hair fell thickly across his brow, and his slightly slanting eyes were widening in surprise. My heart nearly stopped beating. It was Gabriel.

ꟹ

My relief at it being Gabriel was succeeded in short order by a series of embarrassments. On seeing Joe and me Gabriel recovered his composure very quickly.

"Thank you," he said to the corporal, "Report to Lieutenant Jones and tell him I said all was well. This lady is the daughter of Sir Henry Lucie, who is here with the King."

"Gentlemen," he said to the officers around the table, "Please forgive me, we will resume in the morning." They filed silently from the room, casting me curious glances. He regarded me seriously and said,

"Joe, would you please wait outside while I speak to your mistress."

When we were alone he remained quiet, examining the safe conduct passes in the light of the lamp. A frown creased his brow. Finally, he dropped the papers on the table and looked up at me.

"Bess," he said calmly, "While it makes me happy to see you again, the circumstances are to say the least, unfortunate. Your method of your arrival, your dress2." Here he waved a hand which took in my male attire.

After two days on the road, the jacket and breeches clung damply to me, emphasising my form in a most unmaidenly manner. I blushed and looked down at my feet. I grew nervous again. I hoped he would say no more. He perched on the edge of the table and continued gently,

"Bess, please look at me. While I have no right to rebuke you, it would be better if you mark what I say. This exploit, fleeing your home garbed as a man with no protection but your groom, was foolish and dangerous. It is purely by chance that tonight I was commanding the sentries who stopped you. They are not even my men. You are carrying a piece of paper which declares you to be a Parliamentary messenger. No, let me not mince my words, which says you spy for the rebels. Another officer would have consigned you both to the castle prison. You were brought before me to be interrogated as a spy. Have you any idea how we question those we suspect of spying for Parliament?"

I shook my head miserably. The familiar voice had hardened into the clipped tones of the aristocratic officer. He stood up and moved towards me, his green eyes fixed on me sternly.

"I fear that your father and brothers, being responsible for you, will take a harsher view. I can only give you advice as the comrade of your brothers and one who wishes nothing but good towards you and your family. I understood from Harry that you were to remain in the company of your cousin until she delivered you safely to the care of your aunt. But I have to ask you," he said vehemently, "What possible justification could you have for endangering yourself and your servant in this manner?"

I shook my head in misery, my account of the reason for my desperate journey still born on my lips. A half sob escaped me. The next moment I felt him take my hand in a reassuring grasp.

"Well, I have said enough. I should take you to your father without delay. I will discover his direction." He paused delicately, "Do you have any more suitable apparel in which to meet him?" His voice relapsed into its soft Welsh lilt. I sighed with relief.

"In my cloak bag," I hiccuped, "The soldiers made us leave the horses behind."

He opened the door and handed Joe a freshly scribbled note with a safe conduct pass. "Joe, bring the horses here and find, as well, your mistress's maid's garments."

No longer comfortable in my man's attire, I watched as Gabriel wrote another note. When it was complete, he handed it to one of the men waiting at the door. I perched self-consciously on the edge of a chair, my cloak shrouding me to the best of my ability.

Now alone in the room, I changed into the modest gown Joe had retrieved from my saddle bag. When I emerged, Joe had already departed with instructions as to where to stable the horses and find lodging for himself.

Gabriel was grave as he escorted me towards the centre of the city but did not rebuke me further. After a short walk, we were in the High Street, surrounded by the University's buildings. Gabriel climbed the steps and knocked at the door of a solid looking house of three storeys. He explained to the servant that Sir Henry's daughter was arrived unexpectedly and enquired if my father was within.

A few moments later we were taken to an upper floor and ushered into the presence of my father. Gabriel swept his hat from his head and bowed.

"Sir Henry, forgive this late intrusion. The sentries intercepted your daughter and your groom near the north gate as they arrived in Oxford tonight. I have brought her straight here as I thought that would be your desire as well as hers. I will wish you a very goodnight, Sir, as I must now return to my post. Mistress Lucie, good night."

He touched my hand to his lips, bowed again and left the room, leaving me with my astounded father. I was aware of the fact that I would appear, to my family at least, very much in the wrong. I hoped that time and a full explanation might bring my father to understand my point of view. For the moment, however, discretion seemed in order. I knelt at his feet and said,

"Forgive me, Father, for disobeying your orders. Gabriel, Captain Vaughan, has already pointed out that my behaviour was foolish and dangerous. I believed my peril to be greater if I remained there than if I left."

I felt explanations about impending visits from Major Chatterton were better postponed, especially as Father was still unaware of my other ill-advised exploit, my visit to Warwick. I waited, head bowed. Finally my father raised me to my feet. In a tightly controlled voice simmering with rage he said,

"My daughter, thank God you have arrived here unharmed. Captain Vaughan, also deserves heartfelt thanks. You may sleep on the truckle bed in the closet for tonight. Good night, Bess."

ɞ

I slept the sleep of exhaustion, but in the morning I woke to fresh guilt and anxiety. While I still felt justified in my flight, Gabriel's words had awakened me to the added dangers I had placed both myself and Joe in. What I was to say to my father was a puzzle. I could not fully justify my flight without revealing to him my previous foolishness. I resolved to make a clean breast of it. I would have to strive, as I had done before with Will, to exonerate poor Joe from blame. There was no advantage in delaying the encounter. As soon as I heard Father moving around the room I timidly stepped from the low bed and opened the door from my small closet, emerging in my night gown. He was seated in a chair waiting for me.

"Good morning, Father," I began respectfully, curtseying.

"Be seated, Bess," he growled.

I sat on the edge of a stool, hands folded, the model of a demure daughter.

"I do not expect my commands to be set aside by any of my family, least of all by an unwed daughter, and for that you must be punished. As for Joe, I will have him whipped and dismissed from my service for endangering you."

"Father, no, please don't." I begged miserably. "Joe was trying to protect me. Please do not punish him as well as me. The fault is all mine."

I looked into Father's angry face while my heart thumped loudly. I twisted the skirts of my nightgown in my hands. His gaze was pure steel and I knew he had come to a decision.

"Very well," he said quietly, "Let it be so. The punishment will be yours alone then. And I mean it to be most unpleasant, so that you will understand never to go against my orders again." He unbuckled his sword belt.

"Bend over!"

I clenched my teeth and resolved not to make any sound. Father knew his business, however, and within a few seconds I was weeping and crying out in pain. I did not beg for mercy because I knew it would be to no avail. By the time he stopped wielding the belt I was feeling very chastened. I straightened up with difficulty. Father did not even look at me but seized his sword and left. I went to lie down again on my bed, my flesh smarting as if it was on fire. There was yet a further embarrassment in store for me. Shortly after my father left there was a knock at the door. Groaning I pulled myself upright and called, "Enter." A maid servant entered the room, bobbing a curtsey.

"Begging your pardon, Mistress," she said, "But my mistress, Mistress Adams that is, thought you might like this."

She handed me a small blue and white jar and left. When I opened the jar I discovered it was a herbal salve. I detected arnica, camomile and witch hazel, overlaid by the stronger scent of lavender. My face burned with shame. The house was sufficiently small that my cries had been audible on the floor below. The whole household must know not only of my arrival, but of its outcome. Feeling mortification as well as pain, I began smearing the salve on the reddened welts on my skin.

ᔓ

A little while later I heard the clink of spurs and Harry's quick step on the stair. He knocked briefly then strode in. He placed his helmet and gloves on a chair. I was fully dressed and standing a little tremulously in the middle of the room.

"Bess, you foolish girl," he said embracing me. "How pleased I am to see you. But," he added sternly, "You know, you should not have come."

"Harry, please say no more," I begged. "Father was so angry and even Gabriel rebuked me." My lip trembled. He looked me up and down then nodded.

"I suppose Father whipped you. You must have expected it."

I turned away, reddening. "I had to come, Harry."

Quickly I explained about how Father's flight had placed me under suspicion, about Major Chatterton's impending visit and how I had succeeded in escaping.

"Father gave me no opportunity to explain, but it may be as well he does not know about Major Chatterton."

Harry thought briefly.

"I believe we should enlighten Father about Captain Miller placing you under arrest and about Major Chatterton's treatment of you and me at Warwick. He has the right to know, but there is no reason to inflame his passions with you further by telling him you have been riding about the country in doublet and breeches. And masquerading as a rebel spy to boot."

He chuckled. "I saw Gabriel earlier and he told me in confidence of your unconventional appearance. I would give all the money I possess, not a great deal at present, to have seen Gabriel's countenance. I understand you were at least able to change into female clothing before meeting Father."

"It was thoughtful of him," I sighed, "For he clearly wanted to be rid of me as soon as he might. I had never seen Gabriel so stern."

"Do not take it to heart, Bess," Harry smiled. "He is still the Welsh linnet beneath the grave looks. You must understand his position. Oxford is now where the court and the King reside. Gabriel is presently one of the officers of the garrison, charged with the safety of the city and the King himself. The cavalry patrol the surrounding countryside, but the whole garrison take their turn in standing guard over the defences. Last night Gabriel had charge of a party of musketeers defending the northern approach to Oxford. It is the most vulnerable side of the city. Your thoughtlessness took his attention from his dduties and could have endangered the city had the rebels decided to mmount an attack last night," his stammer re-emerging with his emotions.

He paused, his grey eyes softening as he saw my evident dismay.

"We will say no more, Bess. Fortunately there was no attack. Gabriel will forgive you. You will be guided I know by Father, Will and I from now on. Father will forget in time. Now I too must leave you. I have my own duties. I am taking a patrol out this morning beyond Islip."

I was starting to feel a little better, emotionally if not physically, so I relinquished his hand reluctantly.

"I hope to be able to bring Will to see you this evening. He often rides in from Abingdon." were his parting words.

My next visitor was the mistress of the house. She was a woman of around thirty, dressed in plain but good quality clothes. She had a round, pretty face and large brown eyes which were regarding me kindly. She curtseyed to me.

"I am Emily Adams," she smiled, "Wife to Samuel Adams. I bid you welcome to this house, Mistress Lucie on behalf of my husband and myself."

I attempted to return the curtsey and winced. She dimpled and said,

"Forgive my impertinence, Mistress Lucie. I hope the salve was of some use. The best of fathers can sometimes be a little harsh."

I felt my cheeks burning but could take no offence at her well-meant remarks.

"Mistress Adams, it is I who should be apologising for my unwelcome intrusion into your household. I came unannounced and uninvited, even by my father. I fear that my arrival causes inconvenience to you. I am unsure as to my father's plans for my accommodation and whether I will be permitted to remain in Oxford. I am Elisabeth Lucie, known by my family as Bess."

Mistress Adams smiled again.

"I fear this is not what you are accustomed to at your home, Mistress. But if it pleases your father for you to remain here, please accept the hospitality of our house for as long as you wish. I will see what can be done to make you more comfortable in your father's rooms. In the meantime, you must be hungry. Sir Henry takes his meals either in his rooms or with my family downstairs when he is not busy at the court. You may do likewise. But if you will forgive the informality, while the men are away during the day, I often take my meals in the kitchen. If you would care to come with me now I will ask my servants to give you something to break your fast."

Minutes later, I was by the kitchen fire while a shy kitchen maid put a platter of bread and meat on the table before me with a cup of ale. Mistress Adams tactfully made no comment on my remaining on my feet while I ate. She pottered about the kitchen until I finished my meal and then asked me if there was anything she could do for me. I realised that I had little knowledge of where I was, or who my kind hosts were beyond their name.

"Forgive my ignorance, Mistress, but I would like to hear a little of your husband, his business, and of how things go on in Oxford. Clearly the town is under much strain with the court and so many people staying here."

"My husband Samuel is a lawyer. He is assisting the court with their legal affairs while it remains in this city. I understand your father is also performing some services for the King and it was thus decided that he should lodge with us."

"He is acting as Assistant Secretary to the Council of War. Where do the King and Queen lodge? Are they close by? Has the King brought all his courtiers with him?"

The King is residing at Christ Church. The court has taken over many of the colleges but the Queen is still in the north."

"Why is she there?"

Mistress Adams folded her arms comfortably. "The Queen was raising arms and money for the King in Holland. Poor lady, on her way back from Holland to the north of England she was nearly ship wrecked and was pursued by Parliament's ships. When she landed, the rebels fired upon the quayside where she rested."

"They tried to kill the Queen?"

"They were disappointed in their murderous attempts but now my husband says they have impeached her as they did Strafford. They wish to have her tried for treason."

"How can they do this? How can they even think such a thing?"

"Well, Mistress Lucie, you know the Queen has always been hated as a papist. I've little enough time for papists myself, all plotters and schemers, but threatening the Queen is quite another matter. The rebels are angry because she has succeeded in bringing arms into England. Parliament had control of most of the country's arsenals. I only wish the Queen had arrived a little earlier. I had to give all my copper kitchenware to be melted down for making cannon. Now she is on her way here."

"And do all the townsfolk support the King?"

"Well," she replied, "Not all the town is a friend to the King, but Parliament has not made too many friends here either. Most of the townsfolk seek only peace. Go to the market and you will hear grumbling on every side. Complaints of taxes, complaints of the soldiers who are billeted in their houses, complaints that with so many extra people in the city the scavengers do not remove the filth from the streets as well as they ought, even though their wages have been raised. But," she finished with a resigned smile," the King is the King when all is said and done, and rebels are rebels, however pious they may look and however many prayers they may say. And I don't thank men who wish to come and tell me the way I and my father and grandfather prayed is not good enough for them. I will continue going to St Mary the Virgin's as I have always done, even if there is a statue of the Virgin in the porch. As for the rest, well the army is constructing a new camp at Culham, near Abingdon, I hope it will mean less crowding in the city."

I spent much of the afternoon standing at my window, spellbound by the busy scene below. Oxford was clearly very crowded. Soldiers, richly dressed courtiers, townspeople, servants, beggars, all thronged the street. I noticed quite a few women, gaily dressed. Their painted faces and the way they hung on soldiers' arms made me suspect them to be whores. Accustomed to the gentle sounds of Chadshunt Hall I found the constant noise of street cries, carts and horses' hooves deafening. Troops of cavalry trotted along the wide High Street and I craned my neck to see if I could see my brothers or Gabriel. Overflowing, stinking gutters ran down the middle of the street and pungent street smells wafted through the window. I wondered if I would become accustomed to the stench. It mingled with the familiar odours of horses and massed humanity. Women with large baskets of flowers wove their way through the throng. I determined to bring a breath of the country to our small rooms at the first opportunity.

When I tired of watching, I picked up a lute. I was dreamily playing one of Gabriel's pieces when I heard voices on the stair. It was Father with both my brothers. "Will," I shrieked. He swept me off my feet and whirled me around as he had done when I was a child, laughing. Father remained stern faced, but nothing more was said of my disobedience.

We made a noisy family party that evening, although Father reminded us we were in another family's home. My brothers shared wild tales of army life, of the more outrageous characters they knew, especially Prince Rupert and his exploits. These covered the amorous as well as the heroic and Will cautioned me to keep away from him if I wished to preserve my virtue. We ended the evening with music. Harry picked up the lute. Shyly I produced from my bag the two halves of the piece of music, "Oh, silver is the moon," that Gabriel had written. Harry and I put our heads together over it and sang it through for our small audience.

"We should perform it for Gabriel," said Harry eagerly. I said nothing, feeling lingering embarrassment after my last encounter with Gabriel.

ଡ଼

The next morning, the maidservant informed me that Captain Vaughan was below enquiring after me. Gabriel was standing in the entrance hall. His doublet and breeches were of fine blue linen, with red silk showing through the slashes in the sleeves and matching red ribbons on his breeches. No longer wearing his buffcoat and red sash he was presumably off duty, but the cut of the fashionable suit was unmistakably military and he still wore riding boots, spurs and sword.

"Mistress Lucie, good morning."

He bowed, sweeping off his hat.

"Captain Vaughan," I said awkwardly, "How kind of you to call." I curtseyed.

"I wonder," we chorused. We both hesitated in mild surprise. As our eyes met we burst out laughing. Gabriel began again, "I was wondering, Mistress if you would like me to show you the sights of Oxford, if you have not yet had the opportunity."

"Thank you, Captain," I said formally, "That would be kind indeed." I said, turning to the servant, "Pray tell Mistress Adams that I have walked out with Captain Vaughan."

"The streets are crowded. Mistress Lucie, I beg you take my arm." I did so somewhat self consciously.

We threaded our way down the busy street in silence. My gait was awkward as I remaining in much discomfort from the beating. Gabriel glanced at me curiously once or twice. At the corner of Catte Street he stopped, guiding me into the garden of St Mary the Virgin where there was space to pause without being run down by a cart or the press of the people.

"Mistress Lucie," he began.

"Oh, Gabriel," I interrupted, "Have I so forfeited your good opinion that you will no longer call me Bess?"

He looked embarrassed.

"Well no, Bess, but I feared that after my reception of you on your arrival you might have no very warm feelings towards me. I was undecided whether to call upon you today."

"Oh, Gabriel, it is I who should be apologising. Harry explained how I could have endangered Oxford by taking you away from your duties."

He chuckled, "Harry greatly exaggerates my importance as an officer, although in fairness it would have been better if I could have stayed at my post."

"Harry said the northern side of the city is vulnerable, Gabriel."

I spoke selfconsciously, for I remembered my efforts to impress Rafe with intelligent questions about the impending war. Now I was genuinely interested to hear what Gabriel had to tell me. He sauntered onwards, I shuffling painfully alongside him, but feeling more at ease.

"Sadly the whole city is vulnerable, Bess. The city walls are old and crumbling, and the city in any case has long outgrown them. We try to remedy that, with repairs to the walls, bulwarks of earth, with palisades and with what ordnance we have. Many houses outside the walls have been pulled down as an added defensive measure, and to make room for the new bulwarks. The King has commanded that the townspeople assist with the works. Men and women both take turns with digging with shovels. But I confess that I would rather face an enemy charge than command one of these work parties. The people are reluctant to do their work and are often absent. The defences make but slow progress, despite the efforts of the Dutch engineer in charge. The north side has no rivers to protect it, so that is why it is vulnerable. At Wadham College, the enemy would have very easy entrance, despite the two pieces of ordnance we have there."

Seeing my fresh qualms, he hastened to reassure me,

"But as long as we have a ring of friendly garrisons around the city, at Abingdon, Woodstock, Banbury, the city's protection does not rely on old walls or new, and the works continue day by day. God willing, if Essex or Waller come knocking at the gates, we will be ready for them. Now tell me, Bess, what would you like to see of Oxford?"

"Will you show me where the court is?" I asked breathlessly. He smiled.

"You may have ample opportunity to see His Majesty if that is your desire, Bess. He may be seen at prayer in the cathedral, and I have seen him myself when he has dined in the Great Hall and the people have been admitted. This way then."

Christ Church was a grand and beautiful building. Through one of the gates I saw cattle and sheep grazing in the quadrangle and across flooded water meadows were guns mounted before Merton College. I thought if the King could not reside in one of his palaces, this must provide a worthy substitute. I hoped another day I might see the King himself walking there, or perhaps one of his sons, the Prince of Wales or the Duke of York.

Most of the buildings and trades in Oxford had been pressed into military service in one way or another. The music and astronomy schools were now home to seamstresses who were making uniforms. Brasenose College was guarded, due to the arms and ammunition stored there.

I was puzzled. "If all the colleges are being used by the court and the army, what has happened to the scholars? Are they all gone away?"

"Not all, but some have joined the army themselves. The scholars think war is a big adventure. I heard of one man who found his older son drilling with the soldiers and his younger son, who is no more than 12, trying on the armour. He is not the only father who has had to remove his sons from the martial temptations of this city to keep them safe. The King may be grateful for every soldier recruited, but in conscience as an officer I do not wish to see boys younger than 16 standing in the line of battle."

Sadness flickered across his face. I remembered Father's words that war was not a game and felt shamed that in the past I too had seen war as an adventure. We retraced our steps, going past Merton and on to the Physic Garden by the River Cherwell. Even the Physic Garden it appeared was not immune to the war. While within its walls it was a haven of tranquillity, adjoining it was an earth bank topped with cannon.

"It runs to Magdalen Bridge, protecting the river crossing and the London Road," Gabriel explained.

I was growing weary and my feet were dragging. Gabriel proposed resting. He spread his cloak for me on the grass between the well-tended beds and leaned against a tree. When I continued to stand, he looked puzzled.

"Bess, is there something wrong?"

"No, er, it's just I would rather stand."

I buried my face in a lavender bush to hide my reddening embarrassment.

"Bess," he said quietly, "Forgive me for asking. Did your father beat you for disobedience?"

"He had never been so angry with me before." I mumbled.

"I'm so sorry, Bess. I should have realised that was likely to be his response."

I attempted to force my mouth into the semblance of a smile.

"He has always been a strict father. He brooks no disobedience from his children, although I know he loves us. He had a right to be angry for I had gone against his command. He was inclined at first to lay much of the blame on Joe for bringing me. He swore he would have him whipped and dismissed. I could not allow that to happen to poor Joe."

My lip trembled and I feared I was about to disgrace myself further by weeping. Gabriel was mute. When I looked up at him, the green eyes were fastened on me intently, but I thought their expression had softened. I decided a change of subject was in order.

"What made you decide to leave your home to join the army? Your father has not raised a troop?"

He shook his head.

"My father prefers to live quietly on his estates. His sympathies are with the King and he gave me his blessing. He did extract a promise I tried not to get myself killed or captured. I honoured his first request."

ഗ

For weeks he has been pacing the grounds of his family estate Allt yr Esgair, known as The Allt. He climbs the round tower of its disused castle. He takes solitary rides. He visits the small manor where he lived with Catherine and Michael, where they were happy. The manor is empty now but for a few servants. If any of them approach him he turns his horse's head away. At other times he leaves the reins loose and lets the horse take him where he wills. When the sky begins to darken at the end of the long summer day he rouses himself and returns home, trotting down the valley and towards the gatehouse in the long, low wall.

He makes regular pilgrimage to the parish church near the River Usk, where his wife and child lie together in an unmarked grave. He knows the spot, he knows every blade of grass. He kneels in prayer listening for their voices. But the silence in the churchyard is unbroken save for bird song and the rain which is falling unheeded upon his bare head. They have gone on. He is alone and may not join them, for the Church forbids self-murder.

There may be another way. His father is reading in his study when Gabriel enters. Gabriel speaks without preamble.

"Father, war approaches. I wish to join the King's army and fight."

His father betrays no signs of surprise although the lines on his face deepen, his only sign of emotion. He places a quill between the pages to mark his place and lays the book down carefully on the table beside him.

"Would you have me write to my kinsman Richard Vaughan, Earl of Carberry, Gabriel? I hear he has authority from the King to raise troops in south west Wales. I have no doubt he would offer you a commission when his force is recruited."

"Thank you, Father but no, I do not seek advancement. And I do not want to delay. With your blessing I will ride north presently and join the King where he gathers his forces about him at York."

His expression is bleak as he meets his father's gaze.

"Father, would you put matters in train so that I may make my will before I leave here."

His father picks the book up again automatically and replaces it once more on the table. His hands are shaking. He clears his throat.

"I will do so, Gabriel. That would be a wise step."

"There is the thousand pounds my grandfather left to me."

"Which I still hold for you, yes." His father's voice fades away.

"And the thousand pounds he bequeathed to my brother?" Gabriel pursues relentlessly, although his voice is gentle.

"That now also falls to you. It is for you to decide its disposal."

His father springs to his feet, pacing restlessly to the window and back.

"And is this for love of the King?"

Gabriel grimaces. "Love, Father, no. But I fear our life under a Puritan Parliament would hardly improve. He is no more than the lesser of two evils. Maybe I will find a reason to live."

"Then be a soldier, Gabriel if you must. Take Ieuan or another of the man servants with you. I pray that in your search you indeed find a reason to live. Promise me you will not seek a reason to die."

ᔕ

"In July I joined Sir John Byron's regiment of horse as a gentleman volunteer. His was the first cavalry regiment in being. Within days I was offered a commission as Lieutenant. As to why I decided to fight, it was not for love of the King, lawful sovereign though he is. In truth it was that I needed to get away for a time. The deaths of Catherine and Michael, and – some other events…" His tone was sombre and he broke off abruptly. I met his eyes, green pools of anguish.

After a long pause he said only, "Well it is a good way back and you are already weary." He bowed and kissed my hand. Relieved that we were once more on good terms, I took his arm again and we walked back again in harmony.

14

Oxford, May 1643

THOSE FIRST DAYS in Oxford are all confusion. After the spacious peace of my home, the bustle and constant noise in the streets made my head whirl. I missed Chadshunt's familiar comforts, my large bed chamber, our Great Hall and our gardens. I missed Peggy, Celia and Hector. Yet I was filled with excitement rather than home sickness. My remaining family was together again as it had not been in many months. I was oddly content in my strange surroundings, despite our cramped rooms.

From that day, Gabriel was nearly as frequent a visitor as were my brothers. In Gabriel, I had a friend who I increasingly respected and admired. I hinted to him that I hoped to hear his sweet singing voice in church. I let him know that my family attended St Mary the Virgin. But all my hints were in vain.

"Why Gabriel?" We were threading our way through the throngs towards Christchurch College and its beautiful cathedral in miniature.

"Why what, Bess? Why do we go to hear Master Lawes performing in the cathedral?"

I laughed, "No Gabriel, for surely that will be a great pleasure to hear such an eminent court musician. I know you have said he is thought to be the greatest English musician alive. Does he now spend all his time with the court in Oxford?"

"When the King is here. But I fear he has little time for compositions, Bess. He has joined His Majesty's Lifeguard and is a soldier. I met him by chance with the army, he discovered my love of music, and that is why we are invited to hear him play."

"And he really fights? But he might be killed!" I exclaimed. Gabriel stopped where he was in the street and looked down at me, smiling a little ruefully. "As might you," I whispered.

He pressed my hand and led me onwards, drawing it through his arm again.

"But what was it you wanted to ask of me?"

We had reached the college walls and were loitering with many others to be granted entry by the guards.

"I meant to ask, why you have the name Gabriel. Forgive me, but I might expect your family to be Puritan. Clearly they are not."

The notion amused him.

"Indeed, we are not."

Seeing that I sought an answer he thought for a moment.

"A French ancestor, on my mother's side."

"Ah," that made sense. "Huguenot, no doubt."

His lips twitched.

"Some day, Bess, I will tell you more of my family."

ര

Oxford, June 1643

"Bess, this is not a favourable day to venture out."

I regarded Harry with surprise. It was a warm day and I was sitting, my cloak folded over my arm, waiting for Gabriel to arrive so that we might take one of our regular rambles.

"But I am expecting Gabriel," I protested.

"Gabriel is somewhat engaged, Bess and bade me send you his apologies. He will make you amends another day."

I looked longingly at the all too rare rays of sunshine beaming down on High Street.

"Then why do you deny me the pleasure of a stroll with you?" I complained. "The streets will not be as dirty today. At least I will not be mired to the ankles in mud, although I confess the unpleasant odours are more pungent in warm weather."

Harry glanced uneasily towards the window. I became aware of a growing hubbub from below. Rising above the commonplace daily street commotion was an increasing roar. Curious, I approached the window. Harry blocked my path.

"Harry," I protested, "What is it you do not wish me to witness?" My voice rose in alarm.

"Oh, very well," Harry reluctantly stood aside, "But it is not a pleasant sight for the eyes of a maid."

I knelt on the padded window seat and peered through the open casement. The head of a procession was nearing the house. Two lines of blue coated musketeers were marching down High Street.

"The new City Regiment," Harry commented. "That is their colonel, Sir Nicholas Selwyn riding at the head."

There were several officers on horseback and I was surprised to spot Gabriel among them, mounted on his roan gelding. As he rode beneath my windows, he glanced upwards and I waved my hand. His face was stony and he gave no sign of acknowledgement.

"Where are they going to? Oh."

I had glimpsed the three men, previously hidden in the midst of the marching soldiers. Hands bound, garments torn and muddied, they were stumbling along, their feet bare. The crowd was jeering and pelting them with offal, mud and stones. A badly aimed rock hit the rump of one of the officers' horses and the startled animal lashed out with a hind leg. The head of the procession threatened to disintegrate as the officer fought to control his horse, unsettling the other beasts. The musketeers scrambled to a halt, and one of the prisoners, a scrawny youth no more than 16, took advantage of the confusion to duck beneath the muskets in a short lived and hopeless bid for freedom. His attempted flight was doomed before it started. One of the musketeers promptly reversed his musket and used the butt to deal the unfortunate prisoner a hard blow on the shoulder. He crashed to the ground and I turned away, but not before I had seen him disappear under a hail of missiles.

I buried my face in Harry's doublet.

"I tried to warn you, Bess, it was not a sight for you. Gabriel will be displeased I allowed you to behold these events."

"What have those poor men done?" I mumbled into the comforting softness of Harry's blue silk doublet. He gently pushed me away until I was forced to look at him.

"Those poor men as you call them, Bess, are rebel spies, condemned to hang. They have been brought from the Castle. They will perish on the scaffold in Catte Street, against the wall of St Mary the Virgin. Their public execution is intended as a warning to those who may seek to emulate their treachery."

"Why is Gabriel there?" I whispered.

"It was his men who arrested one of the spies and thus he must be present at his death."

The tramp of the marching feet and the jeers of the crowd were mercifully fading into the distance. They must be nearing the church and the journey's end. Despite the warm day, I closed the casement. I had no desire to see or hear anything further of the executions.

With awful clarity, I recalled Gabriel's words, "You are carrying a piece of paper which avows you spy for the rebels," and a shudder ran through me.

ꟹ

Mistress Adams and I became friends. We roamed the streets or visited the market together. I often regaled her with stories about my old life. She was an only child and envied me my close relationship with Will and Harry.

"Have you always enjoyed your brothers' favour?" she asked one day. "Unlike your respected father, I have never seen them give you a cross word."

We were rambling in the physic garden marvelling at its intricately carved hedges.

"If that were only true, Emily. Alas I have been a sad trial to them at times, Will in particular," I reflected. The events of the previous year in Warwick were still too raw and intimate. But a childhood memory which had not come to my mind in many years surfaced unbidden. She looked at me enquiringly as I giggled.

"When I was 12 I ran away from home dressed as a boy in search of adventure. I had pilfered Harry's clothes."

Her eyes widened.

"What happened?"

"Will pursued me on his horse. I had gone no more than a mile when he found me. Mother told me I would never get a husband with such behaviour, and Father whipped me. Now, I believe I would prefer a little less adventure in my life."

Mistress Adams grinned at me, "So your foray to Oxford dressed as a man was your second such venture."

"Times have changed, Emily. I was a child then. Both my father and Will have made themselves plain in recent months that their place is to command and mine is to obey them until their place is taken by a husband. I would not risk losing for ever my father's favour by further foolish escapades. Since the war began and my mother died he has withdrawn into himself and often I fear to approach him."

I fell silent and my good friend changed the subject.

"I am visiting the market on the morrow, Bess. Do you have any commissions for me?"

I thought for a moment. "I will accompany you, Emily. I should visit the apothecary for some herbs for Harry's cough."

The next day Emily and I elbowed our way through the throngs of men and women crying their wares from their carts. Flowers, fruits and vegetables, poultry and bacon, cloaks, leather straps and pins, all were for sale. I found a long and delicate piece of lace to trim my sleeves and some cloth buttons to replace those missing on one of Harry's doublets. I searched unsuccessfully for some new linen stockings for Will. The farmer's wife carefully wrapped cheese in dock leaves for Emily.

"Will you go with me to the apothecary, Emily?"

We waited patiently in the crowded apothecary shop while other customers, gentlemen and servants, were served or leaned on the wooden counter whiling away the time gossiping. A moth eaten stuffed bear stood in a corner, snarling at the customers. The air was heavy with the scent of herbs, spices and more pungent, unknown substances. The shelves were lined with jars and bottles, many filled with strange looking substances whose use I could only guess at. Bunches of dried herbs hung from the rafters and rows of wooden drawers held other unknown treasures. At Chadshunt we had relied solely on our own herb garden, assisted when necessary by the services of the physician.

"A summer disorder, Mistress," was the apothecary's response to my description of Harry's cough. "I have a syrup which should mend it directly." The apothecary's apprentice climbed a ladder to fetch an earthenware jar on an upper shelf. The apothecary measured some of the thick and golden liquid into a bottle and stoppered it firmly. I sniffed, detecting the scent of honey and the stronger aroma of garlic.

"I would also venture to recommend the making of thyme tea. It is wonderfully soothing to the throat. You may steep the dried leaves in hot water or use fresh if you have some." He paused, his hand on a jar of the dried herb.

"Thank you, Master Rew," Emily intervened, "We have ample thyme in our own garden."

As we approached the house, I observed Father watching us from the window of his room. I went straight away to greet him. He said nothing at first, but as I opened the door again, intending to go to the kitchen to request fresh thyme and hot water, he detained me.

"Bess, you grow too intimate with Mistress Adams."

"What mean you, Father?" His words took me by surprise.

"To speak plainly then, you treat her as a friend, an equal. I am aware you were wont to treat Peggy so. But she is a devoted servant and will never presume to forget that. Master Adams' work at the court means that he associates with gentlemen. But never forget he is not himself a gentleman. Mistress Adams is compensated well for meeting our needs. As our kind hostess who does what she can to make us comfortable, she deserves courtesy and consideration. But no more than that, Bess. You forget your station when you address Mistress Adams as Emily. The distinctions of rank must be preserved."

"And pray, Father, what distinction of rank is suitable for a Baronet who has lost his estates and lives in hired rooms?" I retorted.

He took two steps towards me and struck me hard. I staggered backwards as his signet ring caught me across the cheek bone. For several days after I that I kept our rooms, unwilling to show my bruised face to the world. Harry came to visit us the next evening, but when I heard him bounding up the stairs I fled to my closet and pretended I slept. The next afternoon someone knocked at the front door. I opened the door to our rooms a crack.

"Is Mistress Lucie within?" It was Gabriel.

"Yes, Captain Vaughan," Hannah's voice responded.

"Please ask her if she would like to spend an hour with me walking in the physic garden?"

There was a pause.

"I believe Mistress Lucie is indisposed, Captain. Sir Henry said she would not receive visitors."

"I am sorry to hear that." Gabriel sounded concerned. "Pray convey my wishes for her better health. I will call again."

In the evening Harry came again. This time Father was out and when I again shut myself away, Harry knocked at my door and then entered.

"Bess, why do you keep yourself apart? Are you not well?"

At his urging I emerged shame faced into the light of the candles in the larger chamber. He looked at me and his eyes widened.

"This is Father's work."

"I crossed him again, Harry. I spoke badly out of turn."

Harry's grey eyes clouded with fury.

"Harry, please say nothing. The fault was mine. I hurt Father's pride. I taunted him with our straitened circumstances."

He put his hands on my shoulders and looked earnestly into my bruised face.

"Bess, I would not have you suffer so. Shall I seek to find you another lodging? Perhaps Mistress Adams could assist?"

"No! She of all people cannot help. I must remain here, Harry. I must recollect my duty to Father and all will be well. He was a truly loving father before this war and losing Mother." My voice fell to a whisper, remembering the pain of her death.

"Was he so?" Harry muttered. Putting his arm around me, he drew me close.

Emily became Mistress Adams to me once more as I withdrew, to her mute puzzlement.

ᔓ

For my brothers the army life provided excitement they had not yet tired of. Will appeared one fine morning carrying a large cheese which he presented to me with a grin.

"A present from Prince Rupert. We heard yesterday of a convoy of wagons making its way to the army of Lord Essex. We rode out last night in great numbers, fell upon them at Pangbourne and returned in triumph. The army has the wagons, while Oxford is now supplied both with corn and," bowing, "what seems to be exceedingly good cheese."

I dreamed I was at Chadshunt, walking through the home farm where a flock of our sheep surrounded me, bleating. I woke to find it was early morning and the bleating was not a dream. I pressed my nose to my tiny window. A flock of sheep was being driven down the street by a group of laughing cavalry. A little later Will arrived in high good humour, stinking of the farmyard. I ran to meet him.

"Will, I saw cavalry driving sheep down the street. Why did this happen?"

"Oxford needs meat, Bess. Prince Rupert believes we must seek it out and take it where we find it. There are many farms around Oxford who support the rebels. They will find their sheep and cattle's views turned to a more loyal purpose. Now I must return to Abingdon."

That evening was one of many when Harry and Gabriel visited the house and we made music. I had acquired my own lute and we sang my favourite songs from John Dowland, a court musician in the previous century, Nicholas Lanier, now Master of the King's Music, and one or two of Gabriel's own compositions. When Harry and I performed one of the songs he had written, he listened gravely and then one of his sweetest smiles spread over his face. Over supper I mentioned the incident of the sheep. To my surprise Gabriel became serious.

"Supplying the army is a constant struggle, Bess. Soldiers must eat. But I fear that the King will lose the battle for the hearts of his subjects if we continue in this way. Promises to pay those who billet our men are rarely kept. Any man who refuses to provide what we demand is branded a rebel. We must take care that those who only seek to protect what is their own do not end up taking up arms themselves when they see their wives and children going hungry."

ഗ

A week later, the weather became foul. Mighty gales buffeted Oxford, damaging the steeple of Christchurch Cathedral.

"The servants fear the tempest is an omen, Harry," I confided as I shivered over an unseasonable fire in Father's rooms. "Is it true the rebel army is advancing on Oxford?"

"Oxford will not be allowed to fall, Bess, never fear, it is the King's capital now. We will fight to the last man before that happens. The rain falls and the winds blow on the rebels as well as on those loyal to the King."

Harry's words were reassuring, but the next day he admitted that Essex's army was advanced as far as Thame.

"I would not deceive you, Bess. Essex's forces are advancing on Oxford, but our forces are strong. They will have to overcome the ring of outposts before they trouble us."

Sick with worry, I decided to distract myself by visiting the market, buying flowers to brighten our rooms.

"Might I have a little money to visit the market today, Father?"

He grunted but produced a handful of small coins.

"You will take a servant with you if neither of your brothers visit you this morning."

I waited until past nine o'clock. Neither Harry nor Will making an appearance, I set out with Hannah, the slight maid servant, in accordance with Father's orders.

The day was dreary. I had not advanced many paces along High Street before my cloak was saturated and my shoes caked with mud. I hoisted my petticoats above my ankles in a vain attempt to prevent them becoming splattered with mud and filth. My attention on the dirty streets and the worsening rain, it was only when Hannah and I gained the market I belatedly perceived that the streets were more jammed than was customary. The press of people was uncomfortably tight as they flocked around the stalls and carts. The carts were fewer than I had seen, their contents disappearing as if by magic as I passed by. Hannah was struggling to keep up with me, her slight stature making it more difficult to push her way through what was uncomfortably close to a mob. The throng was at its worst at Carfax, the very centre of the city. A woman with a basket of flowers stood unheeded in the porch of St Martin's Church, sheltering from the downpour. With the greatest difficulty, my cloak almost torn off my back by the proximity of the crowd, I squeezed my way towards her, deciding to buy a bunch of roses to remind me of home. Flowers safely in Hannah's basket, I resolved to go no further.

"Strange, Hannah, there are fewer carts here today, and the people clamouring to buy. It is the inclement weather, I suppose, which keeps the farmers away." I had to raise my voice to be heard above the din of voices and the hiss of the rain.

"Have you not heard, Mistress?" Hannah squeaked, eyes wide as saucers. "The enemy approaches close. There is to be a siege and every goodwife strives to fill her larder."

I stared at her, a shiver that had nothing to do with the downpour coursing down my spine. Harry had said nothing of a siege. Was he withholding the truth? I glanced nervously about me at the crowds, viewing them with fresh eyes. As I watched, a fight erupted between two stout women over the last smoked ham on a cart. Each was tugging at one side of the ham, the owner of the merchandise remonstrating vainly. At last, the prize fell in the morass, as the two women tugged at each other's caps. A ragged boy seized it and took off through the crowds with a surprising turn of speed.

Skirting my way cautiously past the two struggling women, my attention was drawn to a heavily laden cart, propelled by two sweating men, coming to a halt at the end of the row of stalls. As the men whipped the sacking cover off the late arrival, revealing a mound of cheeses, the mob surged forward and the cart tipped over, raining cheeses. With a roar of excitement, the jostling mass, men and women alike, dived on its contents and fists began to fly. I edged away from the cart. Behind me, Hannah screamed and I tried to turn. I might as well have sought to fly. The dense crowd squeezed the breath from my body and I lost my footing on the slippery cobbles, falling face down with a gasp in the filth and mire. I flailed desperately like a landed fish, but now another and another and another had fallen upon my prone body. My face was pressed inexorably into the mud. In my panic, I endeavoured to scream. My mouth promptly filled with the oozing sludge. I was suffocating in mud, crushed beneath the weight of bodies, all oblivious to my plight. With the last of my strength, I wrenched my face sideways and sucked air into my burning lungs. I freed my head from the pile of trapped humanity but as I struggled to free an arm, something struck me hard on the temple.

☙

Gabriel was leading a small patrol of a dozen men through the centre of Oxford. In a bid to keep the rain off, he wore a long riding cloak over a cassack, yet he could feel water trickling off his helmet and down his neck. Progress through the city was ever at a snail's pace, but the vantage point from horseback made it easier to observe the market day crowds, apprehending spies, pickpockets or others bent on mischief. He was wary. The throngs were more tightly packed today and the mood ugly. Rumours abounded among the citizens of an impending siege. Penned within the city, there was a real threat they might turn on those who sought to protect them, and he was on the look out for visible signs of unrest.

As the patrol approached Carfax, Gabriel saw a laden cart, mobbed by the crowd, overturn. Goods spilled into the road and a hundred hands reached for the spoils. Within seconds, a brawl had erupted. Women were being trampled under foot. Shouts of fury and screams of terror arose from the struggling mass. Hands plucked at cobblestones and the air began to fill with flying missiles. Gabriel reined in, aghast at the sight unfolding before him. With no more than 12 men, could he prevent the brawl becoming a full-scale riot? There was no option but to act. He raised his voice above the hubbub.

"Baker, back to the garrison. Beg the Major to send a company of musketeers with all speed. Go. Marsh, blow the advance. Blow to wake the dead. The rest of you, form a single rank to my right. Close order. Draw swords. March."

The trumpeter unslung his instrument from his back and filled his lungs. The call of the trumpet rang out across the street. At a steady march the meagre line of cavalry plunged into the human soup, knee to knee. At first progress was slow, their mounts forcing their way with difficulty, riders driving them on with legs and voice. The trumpeter sounded the advance again, prolonging the notes. Those on the edge of the fray, recognising the military sounds and catching sight of the advancing line of armed horsemen backed away, tugging at their companions' garments. The struggling, clamorous mass thinned and began to melt away, wary of the naked swords and of being trampled under the hooves of the horses. Gabriel's eyes were fixed on the overturned cart. He was drawing closer but at an agonisingly slow pace. Many of the mob were too intent on pillaging to mark the threat from the cavalry. Prostrate bodies littered the ground, some pinned beneath the cart.

"Pistols. Make ready to fire in the air on my command."

There was a flurry of movement as the men drew the pistols from their left-hand holsters. Gabriel cocked his own pistol and pointed it at the lowering sky.

"Give fire."

At his bellowed command, eleven pistols exploded in a small salvo. The crowd swirled away, fleeing the market with their spoils. A space rapidly opened around the overturned cart and the heap of bodies. Gabriel leapt down off his horse. Leaving two of the men to hold their mounts, the remainder of his men followed suit, wading into the tangle of women, felled like ninepins. An elderly woman in homespun was the first Gabriel dragged to her feet. Weeping, she was bewailing her vanished basket and holding her elbow. Gabriel glanced at her quickly and delved for the next prone body. A young woman, clutching protectively at her swollen belly, rose dazedly to her feet, holding on to Gabriel's arm with her free hand."

"Go to your home and rest, Mistress." He urged her gently away and threw himself on his knees in the mire.

"Charles, Jonathan, here."

A stout matron of middle years, her muddied attire that of a prosperous tradesman's wife, was lying pinned beneath a wheel of the cart, her neck at an unnatural angle. With horror Gabriel realised her neck was broken. There was nothing to be done for her. He gestured to his men to cover her face with her cloak.

"Bear her into St Martin's," he snapped at the two owners of the overturned cart, standing helpless and frozen to the spot. There was but one still, form remaining motionless on the ground, face hidden by the cart. He became aware of the shrieks from behind him of a slight woman, who was trying to elbow her way past him. "Mistress Lucie!" It was the maidservant Hannah. With a sinking heart, he gazed at the dark hair, tumbling in strands from a coif, a woman tall and slender, stretched on her side in the mire. He rolled her onto her back, smoothing the matted hair from her brow. Her face was so caked in filth she should have been unrecognisable, but even thus and with her eyes closed, he recognised the finely arched brows, the curves of the full mouth and the contour of her cheek.

"Bess. No."

Gabriel searched frantically for signs of life. At first, he could see no injury, only filth and mud. With shaking hands, he wiped mud from her face. Nose and mouth were filled with oozing filth. He tugged his sash off and began to clean the sludge from them. No good, the dirt was clogged too thick. Surely she had suffocated. As he continued to rub he caught sight of a wound on her temple. She had been struck by one of the flying stones. Could it be that she was just concussed? Hardly daring to hope, he looked more carefully at the neck of her mud stained gown and was rewarded by the sight of her breast rising and falling. She was breathing, but barely. Dim memories of his little son choking on soggy pap abruptly arose. Tearing off his gloves he plunged his fingers inside her mouth, probing for any further obstruction. His questing fingers came upon a viscous lump of mud blocking the entrance to her throat. In triumph, he brought it forth and waited. Eyes still closed, Bess took a shuddering breath and went into a paroxysm of coughing. Gabriel's lips moved in silent prayer. With infinite care, he lifted her in his arms and summoned the distressed maid servant.

ထ

"I have to thank you a second time, Captain Vaughan for restoring my daughter to me."

Sir Henry's voice had an unaccustomed warmth as he surveyed the bedraggled and muddied form of the young cavalry captain. Bess had opened her eyes as Gabriel bore her up the stairs. The women were now tending her.

"It was God's will, Sir that my patrol happened upon the mishap as it occurred. I pray Mistress Lucie will soon be recovered. I will call again on the morrow to see that she is well." He bowed and tramped wearily down the stairs of the house.

ထ

On the morrow I was stiff and sore from many bruises and there was a lump on my brow. My throat too felt bruised and I continued to cough up lumps of mud. I saw nothing of Harry, Gabriel nor Will that day or the next. I was confined to my bed to rest. Hannah waited upon me as I recovered and fed me tidbits of gossip, "The rebels have advanced to Wheatley. Our horse have engaged with them there."

When Will visited the next evening I charged him to tell me the truth and he reluctantly confirmed it. "The enemy is come to Wheatley, Bess. Our cavalry are harassing them to hinder their advance. Gabriel's troop has been in action, but you must not be alarmed that they fight. It is their duty. Not all the horse are engaged. I am here as you see, to bear you company and play at chess with you."

The next day I insisted on rising from my bed. When the rain eased, I flung my cloak around my shoulders and ran the short distance to St Mary's, where I prayed that Harry, Gabriel and the other men would return safely, that Oxford would not be attacked.

ထ

Threatened from without by the enemy, Oxford was increasingly threatened from within by sickness. From the time of my arrival in Oxford, I had heard of camp fever. It started with the regiment of foot, but soon extended its reach beyond the soldiery. Now it was advancing through Oxford, an invisible foe. By early June, as many as 40 a week were dying. Rumours abounded as to the cause. Some of the townspeople claimed that the food stored in the town hall had spoiled.

"Dirt and filth," my father snorted, "Men living cheek by jowl, nothing more."

When Harry broke the news that Joe had the sickness, I determined that I would do something. I was determined that Joe would not die. In desperation I sought my father's permission. "Bess, it's too dangerous."

"Father, it is my duty to do what I can to help Joe. If it had not been for me he would still be safely at Chadshunt Hall."

He heard me silently. "You are neither apothecary nor physician Bess. Yet in these dangerous times he has risked his life for you and Harry too. It is indeed by your folly that Joe resides here in Oxford. If you consider it your duty to make amends by risking your own, I will not forbid it. I will pray that God protects you."

"May I ask Mistress Adams for advice or assistance?"

He frowned but nodded curtly. I hastened to ask Mistress Adams if she had heard of any remedy for camp fever.

"A local physician, Master Willis, attributes its spread to nastiness and filth. I would counsel removing him to his own room and ensure all is clean. The apothecary will brew you a cordial for him. Try to keep his fever down and give him to drink clean water, as much as he will take. There is little else that can be done, but prayer. If he is young and strong he may recover."

Harry moved into Gabriel's cramped lodgings so that Joe could be moved to Harry's quarters. I scrubbed the room thoroughly, then turned my attention to Joe who shivered and moaned as I scrubbed him clean. Harry saw to it that Joe's clothes were burned. He would need nothing but a shirt until, God willing, he recovered. I told Harry firmly it was not the time to be concerned over modesty with a naked man.

ᔓ

Oxford, 17 June 1643

For the following week, I spent day and night with Joe. Harry took his turn when he was able so that I might snatch some sleep. At every opportunity, I washed myself and changed my linen and my apron. I brushed my clothes often and bade Harry do the same. The bushes behind the Adams's tall house were festooned with drying linens.

"Bess! Did you see the bonfires?"

I regarded Harry dully. "Do we have cause to celebrate?" Preoccupied with Joe, I had paid little heed to the blazing pyres dotted around the city.

"The western army has won a great victory at a place called Stratton in Cornwall."

"That is good news, I suppose. But Harry, today Joe thought he was back at Chadshunt Hall and tried to rise from his bed, saying he must take Fairy to the farrier. On occasion he does not know me, and calls me Mother."

Harry folded me in his arms. "You are doing all that you can, Bess. Kneel with me. We will pray that Joe recovers."

By the time Joe was on the road to recovery, the danger to the city was also past. Prince Rupert had defeated the rebels at a place called Chalgrove, ten miles from Oxford. John Hampden, one of the rebel commanders and one of the leading men in Parliament, had been mortally wounded in the battle.

Two weeks after he sickened, Joe's fever dropped and the spots began to fade. On the day when he took some broth and asked for more, I was satisfied he would live. In truth, I had been able to do little for him except dose him with cordial, nurse him and give him willow bark tea for his headaches. It was by God's mercy that he was recovering. I was contemplating a stroll in the fresher air by the river, when after a hasty knock, Gabriel entered Harry's quarters. He sketched a bow and began pacing the room.

"Gabriel, what is amiss?" His face showed signs of strain.

"Lieutenant Stanley has taken the sickness, Bess and does very ill. I have only just heard of his illness. I fear he may be dying."

"Has the physician visited him?"

"He has, and says little more can be done. But your nursing is restoring Joe to health. Would you be willing to pay him a visit?"

I straightened my back wearily. I had been looking forward to a half hour of peace, but I was saddened to hear that the melancholy Matthew was sick. How could I refuse to aid Gabriel, who had in all probability saved my life? I forced a smile. "Of course, I will come at once." As I stood up I staggered. He put a steadying arm around me, looking worried.

"Bess, you are not ill yourself?"

"Merely a little fatigued. I can rest tonight. Harry will be here." I hastily gathered a few supplies and followed him.

Stanley's small and gloomy room stank of sickness. A soldier was bending helplessly over the sick man. I would not have recognised Matthew as the same man who had spent a week at Chadshunt only months before.

His eyes were immense in his face with the fever. There were tell-tale purple spots on his chest and arms. He felt very hot to the touch.

"Gabriel, he is very sick as you say. He is burning with fever. We must strip him. Have someone bring quantities of clean water for sponging him as well as for him to drink. And if we may have a jug of hot water, I will make some willow bark tea. May we have a little light in here?"

Gabriel shook his head. "He cannot bear the light." This was one of the symptoms of the truly sick.

"Matthew," he said in his soft Welsh accent, "Here is Mistress Lucie come to take care of you."

Matthew moaned and looked towards the sound of the voice. Whether he comprehended Gabriel's words or recognised me I did not know. I did what I could, but the purple spots had spread over much of Matthew's body and he was very weak.

As it began to grow dark, Gabriel returned and the sick man spoke his first coherent words.

"Nicholas, don't die. Hold on, I'm here." A shadow crossed Gabriel's face. He bent low over the palliasse.

"Matthew, be at peace, Nicholas is safe now." Matthew shuddered and closed his eyes again.

"Who is Nicholas?" I enquired, as we squeezed through the crowded streets, Gabriel escorting me home.

"The friend who was killed at Edgehill," he muttered. "I don't believe Matthew has ever gotten over his death. They were like brothers."

Gabriel left me with heart-felt thanks, his green eyes warm.

"I'll try to visit Lieutenant Stanley on the morrow," I promised. I said a prayer for Matthew Stanley but feared he might be already beyond my help. My mind easy over Joe, I slept heavily that night. The next morning, I walked by the river Cherwell. Despite the usual refuse being washed down, the air was a little fresher and I sat on the bank for some time enjoying the sun. When I arrived at Joe's quarters, it was clear he would be well enough to report for duty within a day or so, although he was looking uneasy.

"Mistress, Captain Vaughan requests your urgent attendance on Lieutenant Stanley if you can spare the time. He was here an hour or more past. I did not know where he should seek you."

I hurried to Stanley's quarters. Despite my present sad errand, my happiness for Joe lent me a certain lightness of heart, which lasted until I arrived at Stanley's lodgings. Finding the door of his room closed, I eased it open and edged silently inside. I knew immediately that I was too late. The dim light filtering through the shutters revealed Matthew lying straight as an arrow on his palliasse. Attired in a clean shirt, his eyes were closed, his face ghostly white and his hands crossed on his breast.

I turned my eyes sorrowfully away from Stanley's still form to Gabriel, on his knees beside the bed, head bent in prayer. I stared in disbelief at what he held in his hands.

15

GABRIEL ROSE SLOWLY to his feet, the rosary dangling loosely from his hand.

"You're a papist!" I exclaimed, "A recusant." Gabriel's mouth puckered.

"I prefer the term Catholic myself, but yes if you will, papist and recusant I am, as was Matthew Stanley. Yes, I break the law." I dropped my gaze, unable to bear the challenging expression in his green eyes.

"If the Roman rites offend you, Mistress Lucie, you might wish to leave the room before you are tainted." His voice was cold. The silence lengthened between us. Despite chaotic thoughts, I could think of nothing to say. Gabriel's face darkened.

"Mistress Lucie, unless you wish to join me in prayer for Matthew, please leave. This confrontation is not seemly in the presence of his departed soul."

With a sob I ran from the room. As I gained the street, hardly knowing where I went, I collided with Harry, hastening into the house. My eyes were nearly blinded with tears. "Oh Harry."

"What is it, Bess? Is Matthew Stanley..?"

"He is dead, Harry. There was nothing I could do. But it is not only his passing which touches me. I found Gabriel there." I sniffed, groping for my handkerchief. He was..." I sobbed, "...praying."

"Ah." My brother looked thoughtful. "Wait here. I will speak to him."

Harry turned back into the house. He emerged after a few minutes, looking pensive.

"Come, Bess". He tucked my arm through his and we set off in silence for what now passed for my home. Finally, I could bear it no longer.

"Harry, stop, talk to me. I am so upset with Gabriel. Why didn't he tell me?" Harry paused and swung round to face me.

"Tell you what? That he is a pp papist? That I have known for many months? Who exactly are you angry with b Bess? With Gabriel? With me? With yourself?"

"I feel I no longer know him." I retorted. "Now I understand why he never appears at church. Why did you conceal this from me?" I was becoming even more distraught.

"Bess," said Harry patiently, "Gabriel has been a good friend to me, and to you. While we were both held prisoner, it was Gabriel more than any other, his humour, his music, his daily encouragement not to give up hope of release, that kept my spirits up. When I was taken away and tortured he had m made up his mind to seek an audience with the Governor. He cared for my hurts. When he did not join us on Sundays in the castle chapel, at first his broken ankle was ample excuse. Later I guessed he was absenting himself on p purpose. I said nothing, but one day, I chanced upon him unawares and praying – in Latin and with those beads between his fingers. How can you expect him to trust you when he must have feared you would react exactly as you have done? You know the King's laws against Catholics allow heavy fines and imprisonment. That is in time of peace. How do you think Gabriel would fare if he should be captured again by p Parliament and a Puritan commander discovered his religion? They might deny him quarter. The hatred of Catholics in England has never dissipated since the Gun Powder p plot. The Irish rebellion over the last two years has only intensified that hatred."

"And what would happen to him if this became known in the King's army?"

"The King's official p policy is to deny commissions in the army to Catholics, but the King himself has more pressing matters now, and there are many such as Gabriel in our forces. Yet for the sake of his authority as Captain and the loyalty of his troop in the field, Gabriel is wise to keep this hidden. Not all deaths in battle occur at the hands of the enemy, Bess. An easy matter to shoot a captain in the back as he leads his men. If you wish to cause trouble for Gabriel, you have only to make his recusancy known to Father. You know Father considers all good Protestants must hate papists. If Father had known Gabriel was a p papist he would not have made him welcome under our roof. Should you intend to act however I must warn Gabriel. I assured him his s secret is safe with us." His face was grim.

"Harry, please, listen. I will say nothing to Father. I have no desire to harm Gabriel." He nodded.

"I thought to give him comfort by my assurances of secrecy. Yet the only reply he made me was "You must follow your conscience, Harry, as I will follow mine.'"

I went to my bed, but sleep did not come. All I could think of was that Gabriel had deceived me. Our friendship had been warm. We had talked about so many things. He had been open with me to all appearances, entrusting me with memories of his wife and child. Now I knew that behind closed doors he prayed in strange and forbidden ways. He worshipped the Virgin Mary as an idol. As an officer of the King's army I had believed he stood for what was right and best in England's traditions, that he upheld England's law. He was flouting that law repeatedly. How could Harry take his part? Why had I promised I would take no action? Should I not as a good Protestant seek Gabriel's removal from his command?

I sat up and swung my legs over the side of the bed. I would confide in Father, it was the right thing to do. But then I realised there was no light under my door. The candles had been extinguished. Father must be sleeping. I lay down again, undecided. As night drew towards morning, I mused on Gabriel's many kindnesses to Harry, how he had saved me during the near riot, and my resolve weakened. Were these not the acts of a good man? How could I repay them by reporting him? Slowly my sense of justice overcame my indignation, and dawn found me ashamed. Finally, I drifted off to sleep with the memory of Gabriel's hurt and angry eyes as he said "papist and recusant I am".

In the morning my heavy eyes led Father to enquire sharply if I was well. Tremulously I told him I was in need of air. I set out for the command post and enquired for Captain Vaughan. He had ridden out to Woodstock with a patrol, inspecting some of the outer ring defences, and would not be back until night fall.

A visit to Joe improved my spirits. He was sitting fully clothed. I stared at his dress in some surprise.

"Joe, what is this? Lace and ribbons?"

Joe glanced down at his smart new suit of blue with white ribbons.

"Our troop's Music died in a skirmish two weeks past, Mistress. Captain Vaughan has offered me his place as trumpeter now I am recovered. It is an honour." Joe beamed with delight.

"Indeed, it is," I forced myself to smile. Joe would carry messages, might be used for parleys with the enemy and if sent to the rebel camp with a message would be expected to act as spy, making careful observations on enemy strength. It was a position of honour. Gabriel had chosen well.

"Thank you, Mistress, you and Captain Vaughan have both been so kind to me," and hastily left the room with renewed delight for action. I plodded back to the house. My father too had ridden out to Woodstock, the King having taken to spending some time there to avoid the sickness and bad air of Oxford. As evening approached, to my surprise, Will arrived.

"Why Will," I said brightly, "This is pleasant. I did not know you had ridden in to Oxford today." He flopped heavily onto a chair, attempted to rise, and slipped to the floor insensible. My cry for help brought Mistress Adams hurrying in. Smelling salts were brought and Will revived. His first words filled me with horror.

"Bess, my head hurts so, and it is very cold tonight."

It was a warm evening in late June. Will's brow was burning hot.

"Mistress Adams," I heard my voice say calmly, "Pray withdraw from the room and keep your servants away. I fear my brother has camp fever."

With a sense of dreadful familiarity, I persuaded Will to strip his clothes off, sponged him with cool water and examined him for signs of a rash. I opened the window to let in what fresh air there might be in the crowded city, and the odours of sickness and bad humours out. Within minutes there came a gentle tap at the door. It was Mistress Adams. I opened the door an inch or two and we conversed quietly. By now, sadly, I was all too familiar with what was needed.

She sighed, "I will brew some willow bark tea for headache and send to the apothecary for more cordial on the morrow."

"You are very kind. An old shirt for him to wear, if possible, however patched or ragged. I will give you the clothes he wears. Pray have the maids boil them well. They have no lice so there is no need to burn them. If my brother Harry or my father should arrive, keep them away, I beg you."

The last request was predictably more difficult. When Harry came off duty in the evening he made his usual visit to the house. I heard him remonstrating with the servants and turned the key in the lock in a vain attempt to keep him out.

"Harry, go away. Will is sick with camp fever."

He beat upon the door angrily. Will groaned. "Harry," I whispered fiercely, "You make Will's head worse."

"Bess," he hissed back, "Open the door or I swear I will break it down. He is my brother too."

Reluctantly I opened it. He took two quick strides over to Will, lying on the bed.

"Harry," said Will weakly, "You see how I am. You should not have entered. Would you have our family line die out? You must be Sir Henry one day if I die."

Harry looked stricken at these words.

"Don't be ridiculous, Will." I snapped "You are not going to die. But there is no occasion for Harry too to risk becoming sick. He has already helped me nurse Joe."

Harry seized on this.

"And was I not of assistance, Bess? Am I become useless now it is our brother instead of our servant who needs tending?"

"But your duties, Harry?" This was not an idle question. With the sickness spreading, the garrison was overstretched. Should the rebels renew their advance on Oxford, every man would be needed. Harry dismissed this with a wave of his hand.

"I can still perform my duties, Bess. I will care for Will in my time off." I sighed, that would mean no rest for him at all.

"I will lie down for an hour, "I said firmly, "But you must take some rest."

I hugged him tightly and he kissed me gently on the forehead. And so, between Harry and me, we coped. I was very grateful for the able assistance of Mistress Adams and her maids. I slept when I could, but was determined that Harry also took his rest. By degrees we both became increasingly exhausted. After a few days the expected rash appeared on Will's chest. But it progressed little, with his arms and other parts of his body remaining clear. His fever remained high and one night he thoroughly frightened me by moaning,

"Mother, where are you? Why don't you come?"

But when I said tremulously, "Will, it's Bess," he opened his eyes, stared at me wildly and then sighed.

"I remember now. Mother died."

"Of fever," I thought.

What little time I was able to spare from worrying about Will, I devoted to tormenting myself about Gabriel. Why had I reacted so strongly at the revelation he was a papist? Was I truly so filled with hatred for Catholics that I could not bear to retain the friendship of one who had already proved his worth in so many ways? My rage had long cooled. The void had been readily filled with embarrassment. How would we treat each other when next we met? It would be nigh impossible to behave as if our previous meeting had not taken place. Fortunately, or so I told myself, there was presently no need to fear the embarrassment of a chance encounter with Gabriel. On his return from Woodstock, Gabriel had left the next day for Worcester with some of his men, escorting an arms convoy on the last leg of its journey to Oxford from Shrewsbury.

ᔕ

July 1643

A week after Will sickened, the maid tapped at my door.

"Mistress, Captain Vaughan is below and begs a word."

I hesitated. My hair was lank and unkempt, straying from under my coif. I wore a stained and crumpled gown. Well it mattered not. "Ask him to wait below," I said finally. My gaunt, tired features stared back at me from the bowl of water. I glanced at Will, in an uneasy doze. I threw some water on my face, washed my hands and went downstairs. Gabriel too was looking weary, his clothes travel stained and his thick, dark hair rumpled as if he had been running his hands through it since removing his hat. He bowed stiffly.

"Mistress Lucie," he began formally. "I arrived back in Oxford to hear that your brother Will had taken the sickness. I came to offer my assistance, if you are still disposed to receive aid from such as I." The melodious voice was dull and flat.

I began an equally formal reply, "Captain Vaughan, it was most kind of you to come." I dropped a curtsey, but as I did, I swayed with weariness. Two firm hands on my shoulders steadied me.

"You need rest, Mistress Lucie, I will sit with your brother tonight."

"But Harry is helping," I protested.

"Harry is one of my officers, and I know he is on duty. I, on the other hand, am at leisure. Come," and he took my arm, leading me back up the stairs. I was torn between relief and shame, but could say nothing. Gabriel took stock of the situation rapidly. Quietly, he removed his cloak and buff coat and placed them with his sash, doublet, hat and sword over a chair. Once dressed only in shirt and breeches, he turned to me.

"You should rest now, Mistress."

"Gabriel," I said forlornly, "Have I forfeited your good opinion so irrevocably that you can no longer call me Bess?"

He turned back, green eyes wary. "I came here tonight to help your brother because he is sick; and because of my affection for Harry, for both your brothers. They have been companions and friends as well as brother officers. To you I fear," he said in a low voice, "I will for evermore be first and foremost a papist. Am I wrong in thinking that?"

He stopped, his eyes searching my face. My eyes filled with tears.

"Oh Gabriel, forgive me." I groped blindly for his hand. He took mine in his and raised it to his lips, still gazing at me.

"I wish you goodnight then, Bess. Rest, Will is safe with me."

Two days later Father returned. He was aghast to find his eldest son and heir fevered and weak. I was feeding Will broth from a spoon. Will was not yet strong enough to feed himself and anything more than broth made him vomit. Father's first action was to send for a physician, who insisted on bleeding Will. I sat by the bed holding the basin, my head averted. I did not like the remedy a bit. It had not helped Mother. After the physician departed, Father asked Mistress Adams to engage a respectable woman to assist in caring for Will during the remainder of his recovery, so that I might rest. When Gabriel arrived the next morning early to assist with Will's care, it was Father who met him. I was still dressing when I heard Gabriel enter the room.

"Good morning, Sir Henry, I am glad to see you returned."

"Captain Vaughan, this is an early visit, Sir. May I be of service?" Father sounded surprised.

"Gabriel has been assisting Bess and Harry care for me," came Will's weak voice.

"Indeed." Father sounded a little shocked. "We are most grateful to you, Captain Vaughan, but I have now made arrangements for my son's care. I thank you for your kind services and wish you Good Day."

I emerged from the room in time to see Father bow ceremoniously and Gabriel taking his leave again. Catching sight of me, he gave a slight bow, but did not linger.

"Father," I said cautiously, "Was that not a little ungrateful to Captain Vaughan to send him away so abruptly?"

Father scowled. "Indeed not. And if he has laid out any money I will make sure his purse is filled. Do not look so surly, Bess. You should not be encouraging a soldier, Captain or not, to be calling so early in the morning. It has a most familiar look and might harm your reputation. It is well that I was at home."

One day, I woke from an uneasy doze to find Will sleeping peacefully. His forehead felt cool for the first time. Gently so as not wake him I pulled back the covers. The rash on his chest was fading. I fell to my knees, saying a quiet prayer of thanksgiving. Tears dripped down onto my bedraggled, crumpled gown. I stayed only to wash my hands and face and drag a comb through my neglected and tangled hair. How Peggy would have sighed over it. I asked Mistress Adams to send a message to Father at the audit house, where the Council of War met. Then I sped to find Gabriel and Harry and tell them the good news. Heading first for Gabriel's command post, I dashed up to the sentry on the door, gave my name and breathlessly enquired if Captain Vaughan or Lieutenant Lucie were within. The sentry eyed my dishevelled and disreputable appearance and suggested I wait. I followed him into the small entrance. The door to a room was flung open and Gabriel strode out.

"What is it, Bess?" he asked quickly. I burst into tears to his disquiet.

"Will is going to live," I sobbed, "The fever's gone".

Gabriel beamed at me with relief and placed his hands on my shoulders. What he might have done next I do not know, for I threw my arms around his neck and kissed him full on the lips. He tensed in surprise, but before I could pull away he enveloped me in his own arms and kissed me hard. The door had been left ajar. Now it creaked and swung wide open. The officers around the table in the room beyond were staring in astonishment. One of them was Harry.

Harry waylaid me later that day and hissed,

"Where are you going to, Bess? Is this some secret assignation with Gabriel?" He caught me by the hand. I was leaving the house to go to the apothecary.

"Indeed not, Harry. I am fetching more cordial for Will. Why should you accuse me of such a thing? I would not do anything underhand and you insult Gabriel to suggest he would do so."

"Well, you must acknowledge Bess," he continued defiantly, "That having seen you in a most unseemly embrace with him, I could be forgiven for drawing such a conclusion. From having been incensed with him beyond measure, you are now behaving quite shamelessly. What am I or anyone else to make of such a transformation? And of such unmaidenly conduct too? Bess, even in wartime there are rules which may not be broken and boundaries which are crossed at your peril. Have a care what you do. Gabriel is a friend who I respect and esteem highly, as should you. But to bestow your affections on an unrepentant recusant who you can never hope to wed is foolish, dangerous. And behaving like a kitchen maid is not what I expect from my sister."

"I think Harry you have said enough." I glared at him. "You are becoming just like Will. My affections are my own affair. Do you mean to talk to Father of this?"

"Indeed, I do not, Bess. Father's temper is uncertain these days and I do not wish to see you beaten again. But show more caution, my sister. Tongues will surely wag if you behave as you did today for all the world to see. Have a care how you spend time alone with Gabriel. I know him for an honourable man, but still he is human. You should not offer him such inducements to forget himself."

Despite Harry's words, during the next few days I was very happy. Will, although still weak, was visibly recovering. His face was losing the unearthly look he had had while fevered. His blue eyes were still overlarge in his face, but he was drinking broth and beginning to demand meat. Since my impetuous dash, I had only seen Gabriel once. He had called at the house one evening, smartly turned out. I, no longer engaged in such frenzied nursing, was a little more presentable. With my father present, Gabriel could do no more than press my hands firmly to his lips accompanied by a long and searching look from the green eyes which made my heart skip a beat. My father thanked Gabriel again formally for his kindness to Will in his sickness. After a little general conversation, Gabriel rose to go.

"Sir, it grows late. Will, I rejoice to see you recovering so well."

"Father," I said, colouring. "Is there not time for a little music before Captain Vaughan takes his leave?"

"Bess," my father rebuked me, "You must not detain Captain Vaughan from his duties." Gabriel saw my disappointed look and smiled.

"I would be happy to stay for a short time if it does not tire Will. What shall this music be?"

"A new song Harry and I were making a study of," I said demurely. "It is for two voices I saw you Walking By. Will you accompany me?"

I seized my lute and retrieved Gabriel's newest hand written song. Gabriel's voice joined with mine, strong and true, although I noticed a tremor at the words, "Wilt thou be forever mine?"

"Beautifully sung, my dear. And you too, Captain Vaughan. I have remarked before, Sir, you have a fine voice."

"Harry calls him the Welsh linnet," came Will's sleepy voice from the bed. Gabriel chuckled and turned once more to go.

"Let me see you to the door," I said hastily and followed him downstairs before any objection could be made. At the street door, we stopped and looked at each other. His arms went around me. We were interrupted by the opening of the kitchen door.

"I wish you goodnight, Mistress Lucie," said Gabriel clearly and with a deep bow he was gone.

ᔕ

11 July 1643

It was mid-afternoon. I was about to leave the house to visit the apothecary when I was startled by the loud and insistent blaring of trumpets. I ran into the main room to find Will struggling to rise. "Bess, bring me my clothes," he demanded.

"Wait, Will," I begged. "I will ask Mistress Adams if she has intelligence of what has happened."

I paused, craning my head from the open window. High Street was all confusion. Soldiers were tumbling from taverns and lodgings fastening their uniforms as they went. However some of them were then returning. The shops in the street were also in turmoil. A number of apprentices were hastily shutting up their masters' shops, while others were continuing to trade. There was much clattering of wooden shutters. To my relief, I saw Father hastening across the street towards the house. I hurtled down the stairs to meet him.

"Father, is the city under attack?"

"Bess, be calm, it is not. Lord Wilmot's horse left yesterday to support Sir Ralph Hopton in Devizes. Now most of the remaining cavalry is being drawn from Oxford and the surrounding garrisons to ride to the assistance of the western army. The foot remains here to protect the city."

At his words, Will repeated, "My clothes, Bess," with greater urgency. I began to protest but my father sighed,

"Let him be. He is foolish. Let him see how far he can walk."

I opened my mouth but shut it again at the glint in Father's eye. We watched Will struggle into his clothes. They hung sadly loose on him after his illness. Pulling on his riding boots made him break out in a sweat. Tight lipped, I helped him with them.

"And you Father?" I asked anxiously, "My place remains in Oxford," he replied, "But Harry will be making ready to leave."

"I will go to him, Father," I ran out of the door, followed more slowly by Will, who I could hear stumbling down the staircase behind me.

Harry was fastening on his spurs. His eyes were sparkling with excitement. "Harry, you must take care," I pleaded.

"Bess, with God's blessing I will return to you unharmed. But I have done little these months other than routine patrols and a little skirmishing. Now is my chance to redeem myself in the field. I must," he broke off, his eyes lighting on his brother standing in the doorway, weary and pale, clutching it for support. "Will, what madness is this?"

"He would not listen to Father, Harry. He will pay no heed to you."

Harry opened his mouth again to argue, but a further blast from a trumpet down below stopped him. "I must make haste." He glared at Will.

"Very well!" Will said crossly. "I will remain here, Bess. At least let me wish Harry Godspeed, Gabriel also."

Harry jammed his helmet on his head, picked up pistols, armour and cloak bag and clattered down the stairs. Will and I followed slowly as Harry made his way towards the lines of tethered horses.

There was frantic activity in the cavalry lines. A pack of horse boys were saddling the horses. Messengers ran to and fro, but I could see some semblance of order was taking shape. Gabriel was forming up his troop of around 60 men. He was consulting a sheet of parchment and shouting orders. The troop's quartermaster was standing beside him looking worried.

It was the responsibility of every captain to ensure his men had victuals.

"Sir, it will take some time to fetch supplies."

"I will not have the men go hungry," Gabriel said patiently, "As so many did at Edgehill for want of forethought. Take two men and pledge the King's credit. Bread, cheese and ale, enough for three days. Make haste."

ᔕ

Gabriel recalls the bitter cold and his hunger after the battle of Edgehill. It has grown dark. Wounded Royalist officers, now prisoners, are waiting to be removed from the battle field as they are unable to ride.

They have been sitting for hours on the ground at the edge of a hedgerow, in falling temperatures, enduring the pain of their injuries. None of them appear to be seriously wounded. This is not surprising, as the rebels will not trouble themselves with transporting men who are unlikely to survive the journey.

The stench of smoke has faded, replaced with that of sweat, fear, blood. The cold and damp of the muddy ground is soaking into his breeches and chilling him to the bone. He is beginning to believe he will freeze to death before being moved. Gabriel can do nothing but huddle in his cloak and hope that one way or another it will soon be over. He wonders if his servant Ieuan, waiting with the Royalist baggage train, will discover his fate and succeed in carrying the news to his home.

He regrets the promise his father wrung from him that he would not seek death. Lying helpless on the ground at the moment he was taken, Gabriel stared up into the muzzles of two levelled muskets. A bullet in the head at point blank range and he would suffer neither the continued pain of loss nor imprisonment. He opened his mouth to say, "Shoot then." Was it his promise? In place of those words of honour he uttered a weary, "Take my purse and let me live."

The sounds of firing have long since ceased, although the groans and screams from wounded men and horses have not. In the night air, the sounds carry all too clearly, and are the more awful when abruptly cut short. Gabriel tries not to think about dying men who are being slaughtered as they lie so that they can be robbed and stripped more conveniently.

A voice speaks quietly beside him. "I only have a wound to my shoulder. I am going to run."

"God speed."

The dark shape next to Gabriel moves stealthily away. Gabriel holds his breath. A few seconds later he hears a sharp challenge, the crack of a musket and a cry followed by a thud.

"Leave him, Corporal. If he is not dead now a short time will remedy it.

Take two of your men, fetch torches. Bind the hands and feet of the remaining prisoners. The Major will be angry if we lose any more prisoners of quality."

They tie Gabriel's hands with a belt. Their attempts to bind his ankles make him groan. "Sweet Jesu, must you do that? My ankle is broken."

"So you say," the man grunts, knotting Gabriel's fringed silk sash tightly about his ankles. Gabriel had not even seen the face of the unknown murdered officer. Will his family ever learn that he has been shot dead while trying to escape? Better maybe that they believe he has died in the battle. It is unlikely to console them that he survived it lightly wounded, only to die trying to rejoin his own side. The endless night wears on and at last the sky begins to lighten. He has long since lost any feeling in his hands and his left foot too is numb. Only his right ankle, painfully throbbing, reminds him he still has extremities.

He hears the creak of a cart behind him.

"Most of the baggage train was lost to the enemy. We'll have to transport the wounded prisoners in this farm cart. Get one of the women to give them some victuals."

"Our own men haven't been fed yet, Sir," protests the voice.

"Ale then, Corporal. These fine gentlemen must be delivered to Warwick Castle more alive than dead or they will be no use to us as prisoners. See to it!"

One by one Gabriel and his companions have their ankles freed. In the growing light of pre-dawn they are prodded into the cart at sword point. Gabriel, unable to stand, has to be lifted in by two grumbling soldiers.

"Can't we shoot 'im? I thought we was only taking ones who didn't need the surgeon's care."

"Shut up and just 'elp. Try not to drop 'im too 'ard. Praise God that's the last of 'em."

A woman runs up breathlessly, thrusting a couple of leather flasks at the corporal. He takes a long draught before wiping his mouth on the back of his hand and passing the flasks sullenly to the closely packed prisoners. As the cart lurches into motion, Gabriel clutches a flask in his bound hands and drinks gratefully. He passes it to the next man. Like the rest of the army he has not eaten since just after dawn the previous day, but the ale is comforting to his belly. He leans back against the side of the cart, attempting to ease the pain in his ankle and the stiffness in the rest of his frozen body. Squeezed between two men he feels warmer at last and sleeps.

ᔕ

"Lieutenant Lucie, Prince Maurice has arrived from Devizes. The town is under siege from Waller. Hopton's Western Army is trapped inside. Byron's horse are summoned urgently to assist Lord Wilmot with their relief. I want the troop ready to march as soon as I give the word."

Gabriel's eye fell on Will and me. "I am glad to see you so much recovered, Will," he said cheerfully. "Look after your sister. Guard her well, for yourself and for Harry, and for me." The last words were spoken in an undertone, but I heard them clearly. Will glanced sharply at Gabriel, and then at me. He nodded slowly while I blushed in confusion. Gabriel turned to me. "Mistress Lucie," he swept me a deep bow. Then he grinned and jerked his head towards the shed behind the tethered horses. Once inside, his arms went around me. "Gabriel, stop!" I said, "Please promise you will take good care of Harry, and of yourself. I could not bear for anything to happen again to either of you."

He smiled, "I promise to keep an eye on that hothead brother of yours. No heroics. As for me, I'll strive to return to you with body and soul still united." He kissed me hungrily. I returned his kisses, breathing in the scents of leather, horse and ink.

"You smell of ink."

He chuckled. "It takes more than men and horses to fight a war. Even in an emergency there are orders to be written, and my clerk is sick."

He looked at me seriously. "Bess, I had not realised what you meant to me until I found you lying upon the ground during the riot. I feared that you had suffocated and in that moment I knew you had made me live anew. I could not bear for that to be snatched away."

I placed my fingers on his lips. "No more, Gabriel. Not now when you may be going into battle. I feel for you too." He stopped, surprised, but then kissed my fingers and nodded.

"No more then, Bess, if that is your wish. My respects to your father. Tell Will to gain strength. We will return and the King will still be in need of him. Now I must go."

He turned away, fastening the hooks on his buff coat. I followed behind, observing closely everything he did. I wanted to remember. The ease and familiarity with which he strapped on his sword belt, settling the sword on his hip. The slight frown of concentration as he loaded his carbine, taking powder from his flask and a bullet from a small pouch. The quick, neat movements as he slung the strap across his shoulder and checked the clip which held the carbine to the strap. Lastly, he unrolled the tops of his riding boots, pulling them up over his thighs. Carrying his helmet he strode energetically away, that slight hesitation in his gait, calling orders.

"Corporal Fletcher, keep an eye on that man there. I don't want mishaps with men holstering their pistols."

A few minutes later, after a brief hug from Harry, I watched my brother swing easily into the saddle, taking his place at the rear of the troop. Gabriel was already mounted at its head, walking his horse in circles as he observed his men taking up their positions for the march. I had a lump in my throat. The afternoon sun glinted off helmets, swords and harness, and off Joe's trumpet as he raised it to his lips and blew the command to march.

"Come, Bess," said Will stiffly. We strolled back towards the house. "Bess," he said after a minute or two, "Do you and Gabriel have an understanding?" He stopped and regarded me intently.

"An understanding?" I faltered. "No, but I do care for him, and he for me."

There fell an uncomfortable silence. Will began again.

"Bess, are you aware that Gabriel is a papist recusant? Harry confided in me some time ago. We agreed that it would remain our secret. We thought it best not to tell you, women being unsuited to keeping confidences. But now I must make this known to you, for Father would not countenance such an alliance."

"Well in that case it is fortunate we are not betrothed!" I snapped and pounded onwards. He caught me up with some difficulty, breathing unevenly.

"And what of Rafe?" he said accusingly "Is he forgotten?"

My eyes filled with tears.

"Forgotten him? Never Will, he was my first love. But Rafe lies in Radway church yard. Gabriel lives and so do I."

16

Marlborough, 12 July 1643

THE RELIEF FORCE of cavalry hastened towards Devizes, more than fifty miles to the south west of Oxford. Avoiding towns, they followed tracks across hills and valleys, clattering through villages, scattering children and poultry before them. As they approached each village they rode closer together, each man unslinging his carbine from his shoulder and resting it on his thigh. When they reached the village of Letcombe Regis, nearly twenty miles from Oxford, Sir John Byron called a halt for the night. Gabriel briefed his officers. Stretching their backs and thankful to be out of the saddle, the officers stood in a circle, passing flasks of ale from hand to hand.

"Gentlemen, I apologise that the speed of our departure did not allow for a full explanation. Waller has trapped the Western Army of Sir Ralph Hopton and Prince Maurice in Devizes. His guns are bombarding the town. Last night, Prince Maurice and the Marquis of Hertford managed to break out from Devizes with a few hundred horse. Most of them remain at Marlborough but the Prince and the Marquis rode hard all night with only a small group of officers to bring the news to Oxford. They were hoping to obtain reinforcements from Prince Rupert, not being aware he is now escorting the Queen and her arms convoy on the last leg of her march south. His Majesty determined therefore to send our Oxford horse to relieve our army in Devizes. The town's defences are weak, and ammunition is low. Our forces had no more than two barrels of powder last night, but we pray they will be able to hold out by some means until we arrive. Hopton is an experienced commander."

"How will they survive if their ammunition is low, Captain?"

Corporal Fletcher's scarred face, a line across his cheek twisting his mouth sideways in a perpetual grimace, looked worried. He gulped reflectively at the ale.

"They are making bullets from the lead on the church roofs and match from the sashcords of the town's inhabitants. Tomorrow we will rendezvous with Lord Wilmot's cavalry in Marlborough. Our ordnance follows and we will await it there. We camp here for the night. Be on your guard tomorrow as we enter Marlborough. The townsfolk have put up strong resistance before and may do so again."

Rolling themselves in their blankets, the troops camped that night in the fields around the small village. The next morning they rode onwards towards Marlborough. Making their way through the Chilterns, the Royalists crossed the River Kennet at Hungerford. Harry glanced about him curiously as they rode into the half ruined town of Marlborough. There was a fine Guildhall and several churches, some of them with broken windows and holes from musket balls in the stone work. Heaps of rubble and charred timber marked where a number of thatched houses had stood. A pile of bricks and a solitary chimney stack pointing forlornly towards the sky was a monument to a more substantial dwelling. Most inhabitants of the town, wary of the return of the King's troops, shuttered their windows and remained indoors that evening. Two or three small boys ran after the horses, calling insults. A handful of dung hit Harry's shoulder. The boys scattered, laughing.

After posting a strong guard in case of trouble from the inhabitants, the commanders took over rooms at the Antelope Inn in the High Street. The inns were still open for business although much of the town had been burned and looted when the Royalists had stormed it the previous December.

The cavalry were quartered outside the town in barns and outhouses, but many men were wakeful in the short summer night with the prospect of battle ahead. Instead of going to their billets, they tethered their horses in the market square and rested, talking quietly while puffing on clay pipes.

Harry and other junior officers refreshed themselves in the taproom of the Bear, a coaching inn a little further down the wide, once handsome High Street. Leaving the inn, Harry collided with an officer who was swaying and appeared drunk. The man was focussing on Harry with apparent difficulty.

"Forgive me, Sir."

"Willingly, Sir," Harry smiled, "But perhaps you have drunk enough strong beer for tonight."

The other man snorted. "It is not beer which makes me appear so. I rode with Prince Maurice from Devizes to Oxford. I was in the saddle for 14 hours and have slept but little in two, or maybe three, nights. I must sleep now or I will not have the strength to mount my horse on the morrow, nor the power to wield a sword." In the light from the inn Harry realised that the officer was dusty from head to toe, his face streaked with dirt. There was no odour of beer on his breath. Embarrassed at his error, Harry stepped back and bowed.

Harry listened eagerly to the other men, many of whom he now knew from riding patrols around Oxford. They were passing the time with tales of past campaigns. Only when talk turned to Edgehill was he able to contribute his own story.

Sitting lost in thought, Harry jumped when a hand clapped him on the shoulder. He started; it was Gabriel.

"Fear not. You will see action enough on the morrow to satisfy those martial instincts." He said it with a smile. Harry smiled ruefully.

"You think me foolish I daresay."

"Harry," said Gabriel, his voice slipping into a lilt as it softened. "How can I of all people think you foolish? A captivity nigh on six months is enough to give the most idle of men a thirst for action. One skirmish since then is little enough. But take care tomorrow," he cautioned. "No heroics. I promised your sister. I am going to the Antelope now to hear the commanders' plans for the morrow." His voice dropped lower. "And if I fall, tell Bess – well no matter."

ഗ

Devizes, 13 July 1643

The combined forces of the cavalry under the command of Lord Wilmot advanced on Devizes. The relief force had been joined during the night by the convoy of carts from Oxford bearing much needed ammunition and two of the field guns known as sakers. There was no need for concealment as a surprise attack was not possible. Waller's scouts would give him warning of their approach.

They halted on high ground to the north east of the town. One of the guns was fired to alert Hopton to their arrival. An echoing bang was heard from Devizes. Hopton had understood. After some time a messenger came galloping up calling for Captain Vaughan. Gabriel raised his hand and the messenger pulled his horse to a stop.

"Captain, My Lord Wilmot wishes you to attend him."

Astonished, Gabriel leapt back on his horse and cantered towards the commanders. He recognised Lord Wilmot, a handsome man with a mass of curly hair and a long straight nose under well marked brows. A few years older than Gabriel, he was an experienced soldier, a popular and charming commander. Gabriel swung himself off his horse, removed his helmet and bowed.

"Captain Vaughan, Sir John Byron has recommended your name for an urgent task. Our scouts report that Waller's army has withdrawn from before Devizes. They are being formed up on high ground known as Roundway Down. In doing so they have blocked our road to Devizes. It is clear they wish to engage us in battle. We expected General Hopton to march out of the town to join us. With his 3000 foot and our 1800 horse we would be a match for the rebels."

"Yes, My Lord." Gabriel stood rigidly, trying to school his face not to betray his mingled excitement and nervousness.

"Sir Ralph perhaps does not comprehend the urgency of the situation for unhappily his troops have not stirred. You will ride with all despatch into Devizes with a letter requesting he marches to join us. Take a trumpeter, but no other man or you are likely to attract attention. Return to me with his answer as soon as possible. Do not allow the letter to fall into the hands of Waller's men. It contains our plan of battle. Should you be captured, destroy it."

Gabriel bowed again, heart pounding. An aide handed him a letter with Lord Wilmot's seal, together with a pass signed by Lord Wilmot to get him through the Royalist lines into Devizes. Gabriel retained enough presence of mind for some hasty enquiries of Prince Maurice's officers on the best approach to the town in the current state of defences. It would avail him nothing if he were mistakenly shot on his approach to the town by Hopton's men or captured by Waller's army which was now dividing the two Royalist forces. He thrust the letter and pass into his coat and returned to his troop, summoning Joe.

"You will accompany me into Devizes. If we are not to fall foul of Waller's scouts we must take every care. The sun's rays will reflect off everything metal. Remove your helmet and put on your riding cloak. Use it to cover your arms and your trumpet."

"Yes, Sir." Joe was already jogging towards where Fairy was tethered.

"Lieutenant Lucie,"

"Captain?" Harry's voice was hopeful.

"Take command until my return. And don't look so downcast, Harry." Gabriel added quietly. "If I do not return from Devizes you may find yourself leading the troop into battle." Pulling on his broad brimmed hat, he gave a wry smile. Harry looked embarrassed.

Gabriel and Joe set off for Devizes, keeping well to the south of Waller's army. The town lay far below them and it was only when they had descended the steep southern slopes from the Marlborough Road and reached the dusty lanes below that they could spur their horses into a gallop. Despite their caution, they suspected they had been spotted by an enemy patrol. The group of horsemen was high above them, motionless on the crest of a hill, but as they watched, the group began to move as one in their direction. Perhaps realising that they were too far away for a successful pursuit, the group of scouts, if indeed they were, tracked them for a short distance and then turned back.

As the two Royalists drew near the town they were challenged by musketeers hidden in the hedgerows. Gabriel produced his safe conduct and asked to be taken to Sir Ralph Hopton. He fretted at the delay as he was taken from one officer to another. Finally an officer with sufficient authority escorted them through the town. The way was frequently barred by chains, tree trunks and carts. They were forced to dismount, leading their horses around the obstructions in the streets. The Cornish officer led them to a large and imposing stone house. Leaving Joe with the horses, Gabriel followed the officer inside, heart beating fast.

The officer knocked on a door and admitted Gabriel to a well proportioned room with a lofty ceiling where a dozen officers were seated at a long table of polished walnut.

"Sir," said the officer, "This is Captain Vaughan. He bears a message from Lord Wilmot."

"Approach, Captain," barked a man. Gabriel found himself facing an older man, whose eyes were covered by a bandage. Gabriel removed his hat and bowed.

"Sir, I am charged to deliver this letter from Lord Wilmot. I am to bear your reply back to him."

"Thank you, Captain," said Hopton. "We will give you our answer shortly. Rest and refresh yourself."

An aide took the letter, showed Gabriel into a small adjoining room and closed the door. Left to wait, Gabriel paced nervously. A servant entered with a tray of ale, bread and cheese. Gabriel paid it little heed. The room overlooked the street where soldiers were manoeuvring a large farm cart onto its side as a further barricade. The cart in place to their satisfaction, they led away the horses. They were pursued by an elderly, plainly dressed man, shouting and waving his arms at the soldiers. One of the men, losing patience, brandished his musket at the cart's former owner. The man stopped in his tracks, tearing his woollen cap off his head and hurling it to the ground in a gesture of despair or defiance. Gabriel became gradually aware that the hum of conversation from the adjoining room was no longer muted. Voices were raised in apparently heated argument. That did not bode well. Footsteps announced the aide had returned. Hopton and his officers were grim faced.

"Captain Vaughan," said Hopton. "We have considered Lord Wilmot's request. However, he is newly arrived here. Waller is a wily foe, I know him of old. It is our view that his apparent withdrawal from the town is but a ruse to tempt us out so he may fall upon us. We thank our brother commanders for coming to our assistance. But at present we feel it most wise to remain within the town, where our artillery protects us, and our foot are well concealed. We will of course be mindful of changes in circumstance which may occur. My clerk will give you a letter presently. Please convey it to the Lord Wilmot and His Highness Prince Maurice with our compliments."

The colour drained from Gabriel's face.

"But Sir," he protested, "How can this be a ruse? The whole of Waller's army is even now advanced high onto the down. They are three miles outside the town. With your worthy help we may match them. Without, our horse must give them battle alone and unprotected. They will wipe us out."

"Captain," said one of the officers with an edge to his voice, "You have heard our decision. It is not for an officer of your rank to question your superiors. Your orders are to take our answer back without delay. Must we make ourselves any plainer?"

"No, Sir." Gabriel bowed and numbly allowed the aide to usher him out.

∽

"Captain, the two horsemen are returning." The fresh faced dragoon from Colonel Popham's Regiment was fairly bursting with excitement as he made his report.

"Are you certain it is the same two men?"

"I believe so, Sir. One of them is riding a very fine chestnut with a flaxen mane, the other a roan."

"I will lift up mine eyes to the hills. It appears that the enemy fail to do this, or they would not ride this way again. It is time to discover what these intrepid horsemen have been doing. What makes two men so bold as to run the gauntlet of our forces twice? We will intercept them." The 22 year old Captain Harrington gave his usual boyish grin and rumpled his short hair until it looked like a brush. He replaced his helmet and vaulted back into the saddle.

"Sergeant Matthews, remain here on guard with half a dozen of our men. Send word immediately to General Waller if Hopton's army leaves Devizes. I will personally ride with the remaining men and head these two gentlemen off before they can reach safety. I have a feeling that if we can take them, we may learn something of interest."

ശ

Gabriel was dwelling uncomfortably on the unwelcome news he must impart to the commanders that the expected reinforcements were not forthcoming. It was a steep climb once beyond the town. The horses were blown and sweating hard by the time Gabriel and Joe were half way up. Reluctantly they slowed their pace once more.

"Captain, I believe that is the same patrol we saw earlier." Joe pointed up the hill. With a pang of guilt Gabriel forced his attention to Joe's words. Looking above him he saw that the enemy patrol was closer than it had been when they had seen them earlier. This time there could be no mistaking their intention. As he watched, the group divided, with most of the horses setting off in their direction.

Gabriel swore under his breath in Welsh. He had almost forgotten the patrol and their implicit threat. He reined in briefly, casting his eye over the now diminishing distance between them. As he watched, one of the men raised his gun and fired.

"Musket shot, Joe. Still well out of range. They are trying to cut us off before we can rejoin our forces. They are dragoons. Their horses will not be as fast, but theirs are fresh and ours are tired. I fear we will not outrun them."

Gabriel glanced quickly over his shoulder behind them, but Devizes was now a distant huddle of buildings down below. The enemy would catch them long before they could return to its safety, and their message would be lost. Could they escape them if they swung further south, and make their way back from the Marlborough direction?

"Come on." Gabriel spurred his tired horse once more into a gallop, now heading around the base of the four hills on which Roundway Down sat. It was a vain hope and after a few minutes he realised the patrol was continuing to gain on them. He saw the glint as the leading rider drew his sword.

"Captain!" Joe yelled over the sound of the horses' pounding hooves. "Do you wish to turn and fight?"

"They outnumber us too heavily!" Gabriel called back. "Ride for that wood. I think I have an idea."

ശ

Captain Harrington sheathed his sword and held up his hand. The patrol jolted untidily to a halt behind him. One of the horses snorted, backed and kicked out. The beast next to it reared indignantly and a few moments of disorder ensued.

Harrington glared at the offending riders. “Fane and Webb, if you are unable to keep your mounts under control, I will arrange for your swift return to a regiment of foot. Is that understood?”

The two shamefaced men mumbled assent.

“Now those men have ridden into that grove. It is no great size and they will be disappointed if they think to disappear so easily. Fane and Webb you will ride around the wood with as little noise as possible and see they do not make a break for it. The rest of us will advance from this direction. That way..”

He broke off sharply as the notes of a trumpet blasted shrilly through the air.

“Sir!”

“I am not deaf, Corporal. That was the sound of the advance and it did not come from our own ranks. There is an enemy troop approaching the wood. We must withdraw with all speed.” Within seconds the patrol was cantering back up the hill.

ᔕ

Joe lowered the trumpet from his lips. Gabriel grinned at him.

“Sometimes, Joe the simplest ruses are the most effective. Let us be on our way before they begin to wonder how a troop of cavalry approached so close without a sound and realise their mistake.”

He lowered his carbine and they continued on their way towards the hill where the Royalist cavalry waited. Standing before Lord Wilmot again he held out the letter.

“My Lord I bear bad news, Sir Ralph Hopton remains in Devizes. He believes Waller’s leaving the town to be a ruse. I failed to persuade him otherwise.”

There was silence for a moment and then Lord Wilmot took the letter himself with a sigh. “You are not responsible for their decision, Captain Vaughan. Thank you for discharging your commission. You may return to your company.”

Gabriel tried to banish the inner voice which suggested that another man, more eloquent than he, might have been more persuasive. Such thoughts were useless. It was incumbent on him to lead his men to the best of his ability, however poor the prospects now were of success that day. By the time he arrived back at his troop he had himself outwardly under command.

ℰ

"Walk with me, Harry."

Harry heard the quiet voice behind him and scrambled to his feet. Gabriel's face was pale but his expression was determined. He led the way towards the edge of the lines where their conversation would not be overheard. He halted, removing his hat and running both his hands through his hair as if thinking. Harry looked at him enquiringly. Finally Gabriel spoke.

"Harry, it seems we are all to be the forlorn hope today."

"I do not understand you. Is our troop to be given the honour of seizing a dangerous position?"

"I carried a request from Lord Wilmot to Sir Ralph Hopton that he would march out of the town with his foot to join us. He refused. He believes it a ruse by Waller. We know it is not. And so our three thousand Cornish foot remains within the town. They are like to witness the total destruction of Prince Maurice's relief force if Lord Wilmot chooses to fight. I do not think any of us will see Oxford again. We must pray for courage, Harry and maybe a miracle. Our task remains to command our troop. We must convince them we lead them to victory, not certain death. Are you ready?"

Harry nodded. Shoulder to shoulder they marched back to the troop.

ℰ

"Gentlemen," Lord Wilmot began. "The enemy offer battle and we cannot refuse. They are blocking our road to Devizes so we could not retire there for safety even if we would. If we chose to withdraw, it is probable we would only face them at another place of their choosing. We will not shrink from the engagement, but we will have warm work. Sir Ralph Hopton has refused our request to lead his force to join us, believing the enemy have abandoned the siege as a ruse. Our horse face Waller's forces alone. They have more than two thousand foot, we have none. It is possible that Hopton will have a change of heart and march to our aid. In the meantime we must cut our cloth according to our means. Our horse are superior to that of the rebels. We have shown that again and again since Powick Bridge. But we must show discipline as well as courage today. If we are to overcome them we must not repeat the mistakes of Edgehill. Discipline gentlemen."

Wilmot was standing in the shade of a tree at the south east edge of the vast expanse of open pastureland. Beside him were Gabriel's commander Sir John Byron, the Earl of Crawford and the youthful Prince Maurice. On the opposite hill, less than two miles away, could be seen the ensigns of the enemy. There was little breeze and the colours hung limply. His gaze sweeping over the assembled captains of horse, Wilmot smacked his commander's baton against his gauntleted left hand for emphasis.

"You will be divided into three brigades, drawn up in three ranks. Sir John will be in command on the left wing with the assistance of Prince Maurice, I will personally command the right wing. The Earl of Crawford's brigade will be held in reserve. We have had a long march and the men and their horses are already weary. We cannot afford the luxury of a lengthy engagement. If we are to overcome them our best, indeed our only, hope is to speedily break their horse with our charge as we have done before. Once among them we will be safe from their musketeers, ordnance too, as they will not fire for fear of hitting their own men. If we succeed in putting their horse to flight, we may have leisure to turn our attention to their infantry. Should we reach that happy point it requires every available troop to remain on the battle field, however tempting the sight of fleeing rebels may be. Is that clearly understood? Then return to your units."

ℰ

"Lieutenant Lucie," Gabriel roared, "Make ready, we are to fight!" To his astonishment a ragged cheer went up from his troop.

Seeing that he had their attention, Gabriel continued loudly enough to be heard.

"It is not the job of a humble captain to make stirring speeches. I leave that to the commanders. Today we face the rebel army of General Waller. For some of you this is your first time in battle. So a few things to remember. Look well after your horse and he will look after you, if you do not wish to join the foot." This brought a few chuckles. "Guard the back and the side of your companions, for they will do as much for you. And try to keep your heads. Every shot must count. If we should break their horse, do not go galloping after them back to London. Save your galloping for visiting your sweethearts when you return to Oxford. If you become separated from this company, listen for the trumpet and look for our colours. Remember, you are men of Sir John Byron's regiment of horse, not a rabble of London 'prentices. That is all."

Gabriel nodded, satisfied. There was a low buzz of conversation, but the tired men seemed cheerful enough. Cornet Robert Nugent was whistling as he unfurled the blue standard of Byron's regiment with the three white stars which designated Gabriel's unit. Beside him Joe was frowning with concentration as he rubbed down the sweating Fairy. Gabriel walked away to his own horse. Standing beside him, as if adjusting the straps on the saddle he hid his face and prayed for strength and courage.

Without Hopton's foot, the odds against them were overwhelming. Gabriel had enlisted in the army in despair, seeking an honourable grave. He realised with a jolt that he no longer sought it, and desired to live. Well, whether or not he sought death, today he was like to find it. He could only hope that death for him, for Harry and for all Byron's men would be swift, and that they would receive Christian burial. He shuddered at the thought his corpse might be left upon the Down to rot, feasted on by crows until nothing remained of him but bones bleaching among the poppies. Tales abounded of the unquiet ghosts who refought the battle in the fields below Edgehill. Would Byron's men haunt the Down in years to come, a restless and wild eyed horde charging into the guns of Waller's army for evermore? Gabriel took a deep breath. Reaching inside his shirt, he pulled out the crucifix which hung around his neck, kissed it and tucked it away again out of sight. Then he straightened his back and returned to Harry, to await the command to march.

ɞ

Harry pulled off his gloves and retied his red silk sash more securely around his waist. His hands were sweaty and he knew it was due more to nervous excitement than to the warm July day. He took deep breaths to calm himself. He glanced at Gabriel, adjusting his gorget while speaking calmly to one of the other men. Gabriel smiled and clapped the soldier on the back. The man laughed. Harry envied Gabriel's air of quiet authority, the outward calm which he knew was masking Gabriel's own uncertainties.

His thoughts were interrupted by Gabriel.

"Harry, remember to remain in position at the rear of our troop. That way you will be able to take command if I fall." He gave Harry a parting smile, then he hastened away, fastening his helmet.

Following Lord Wilmot's regiment, the long column of cavalry snaked its way slowly onto the open Down. The wide expanse of grass was speckled with poppies. Harry recoiled at the sight, the bright red seemed to foreshadow the spilling of blood. Gabriel held up his hand and the troop halted.

Across the Down, on the opposite hill, Harry could see the glint of the armour of the rebel horse. Further away, in the centre of the rebel battle line, he could see stands of pikes, the squat shapes of artillery ranged in front of them. He pulled his attention back to the troop. The leading companies of Byron's regiment were already manoeuvring into position.

"From the right, first division into battlefield formation. Form three ranks. Open order."

Following Gabriel's orders the corporals swiftly moved their divisions into three ranks. The cornet moved forward to take his place close behind Gabriel. As the men caught sight of the motionless ranks of the enemy facing them an excited murmur broke out. "Silence there," snapped one of the corporals.

Harry reflected that the months of training had paid off. The troop was acting as a single body. Harry kept his eye on the young corporal as he guided the last division into their position, taking up his position to the left of the troop. Nesbitt was newly promoted, having taken the place of a man recently dead of camp fever. Harry remembered his feelings waiting to go into battle at Edgehill. Was it really only nine months ago? Then he had been eager for glory. Now his excitement was almost overcome by nervousness. He tugged at his helmet. He was sweating under his armour and buffcoat. He hoped the order to advance would not be long in coming. He took in deep breaths of summer air. Perfumed with crushed grass, mingling with the scents of leather, horse and sweat. Would this be the last time he ever smelled them? He tried not to think about the probability that in a few minutes he and the entire troop might be lying dead, blown apart by artillery or peppered by musket balls of the enemy infantry, victims of overwhelming forces and Hopton's scepticism.

Next to Harry, Corporal Nesbitt had turned green in the face.

"Corporal," Harry whispered, "You look warm. Take this and dismount for a moment." He thrust a flask of ale at him. "Take a few slow breaths."

Nesbitt drank and a little colour returned to his face.

There was a brief hush except for the jingle of harness, the creak of leather as a man shifted in his saddle, a horse stamping a hoof or snorting. A horse fly landed on the neck of Harry's mount. Harry slapped at it urgently with his gloved hand before it could bite the horse, provoking the horse to kick or buck. Remembering the artillery barrage which had opened the battle at Edgehill Harry was waiting for the guns ahead to open fire. Instead a distant group of enemy horse broke ranks and charged towards the Royalists. He gripped his sword hilt tightly. A trumpet blared from Wilmot's brigade and a troop of horse dashed forward towards the enemy. Harry realised both armies had sent forward their forlorn hope. It was nothing but a preliminary skirmish. He must continue to wait. As he watched, Wilmot's troop of horse disappeared from view. Harry shielded his eyes. From his distant viewpoint the enemy's left flank seemed already in some disarray. The next moment there was a further blast from a trumpet and Wilmot's entire brigade charged.

Harry's excitement was unsettling his horse. A messenger cantered up to Gabriel. He spoke briefly and Gabriel nodded before the messenger moved on to the next troop.

Gabriel was turning to face his men. "Hold your fire until we engage closely with the enemy. They must be allowed to fire first." He took his place in the centre of the front rank. The troop was drawn up in open order. On each side of Gabriel's troop were more of Byron's men. From the rear came the soft thud of hooves on grass and the jingle of bits and spurs as Crawford's reserve horse moved into position.

Gabriel's voice rang out again.

"Draw swords. On my command, engage the enemy's right flank."

Harry drew his sword. He was annoyed to discover both hands were trembling. From the other side of the Down, nearly two miles away, he could hear the regular banging of pistols and carbines. Wilmot's brigade, now wreathed in clouds of black smoke from the firearms, was engaging the left flank of the enemy fiercely. Through the smoke, Harry caught a glimpse of a mass of enemy horse fleeing the far side of the battlefield. He thought they might be Sir Arthur Hazelrigg's regiment, known as "Lobsters" because of their full suits of armour. The stands of enemy pike and musket remained motionless, their outlines shimmering in the heat.

There was a bang from one of the sakers behind them. It was the signal. Trumpets sounded and Gabriel raised his sword. Byron's brigade moved slowly forward. As they did so, a new sound arose from the opposite side of the field, the brisk tattoo of enemy drums. Flanked by tight packed ranks of cavalry, Waller's infantry were on the march. The Ensigns of the enemy foot were swirling the colours from side to side in a fervent display as their drums beat the steady, insistent rhythm of the advance. Byron's horse would have no protection against musket or pike, but there was no turning back now. The trumpets blared again and Gabriel's sword swept down.

"Charles and the Cause!"

17

Roundway Down, Devizes, 13 July 1643

GABRIEL'S CRY WAS taken up by every voice. Harry's horse leapt forward in its effort not to be left behind. Harry nearly lost a stirrup and cursed himself for his inattention. Now he was cantering up hill, with Nesbitt beside him. The enemy were advancing but slowly at a walk march, descending from their position on the hill. The gap between the two armies was closing fast, but not fast enough. There was a loud crash. Byron's horse were within range of Waller's artillery. The guns had opened fire. An iron ball tore through a file of men in the next troop and three men fell in a bloody tangle of limbs and screaming horses. Harry gulped, concentrating all his attention on the red speckled strip of pasture between his horse's pricked ears.

Ahead of him in three orderly ranks, helmets gleaming in the sunlight, thundered Gabriel's sixty troopers. Harry's sword was in his right hand. He dared not touch either carbine or pistol for fear of firing prematurely. He snatched a glance at the ashen faced corporal at his side. Nesbitt was gripping his sword firmly as he stared fixedly ahead. Two hundred paces, one hundred. Now a deafening volley of shot from Waller's musketeers. Most of the balls passed harmlessly overhead or fell short, but a number found their mark. To Harry's right were two riderless horses, while two more carried men who had received their death wound but were being carried forward inexorably with the rest of the wave.

A brief glimpse of enemy colours – indistinct words, a broken crown and sceptre. The enemy officers were screaming commands. Byron's men were silent. They knew their task. Directly ahead, a controlled flurry of movement. Resisting the urge to flatten himself against his horse's neck, Harry watched as the enemy horse halted and the front rank fired their carbines in a cloud of smoke. Byron's men charged headlong into the hail of lead. Men were falling. Yet the Royalists were going too fast and the carbines too inaccurate to do much execution in their ranks. A pause and the banging of long arms was rapidly replaced by the sharper crack of hundreds of pistols. Two shots pinged off Harry's helmet in quick succession and he flinched. One of the shots hit the man ahead and Harry wrenched his horse aside to continue.

Harry's eye was on Gabriel now, outstretched sword in hand. A moment later the sword dropped. Gabriel swung his carbine round and fired. Firing as they went, the front rank smashed headlong into the closely packed ranks of enemy horse. There was terror on the faces of the enemy troopers as they saw they were about to be fired upon at point blank range. Some tried desperately to turn their horses away, others simply reined in. They were fast becoming entangled with their back ranks, continuing to advance.

Byron's looser ranks were carving their way through Waller's men, shooting and slashing. Harry was facing a trooper, staring at him wildly, smoking pistol in hand. Harry's carbine was in his hand and he emptied it. The shot made a neat hole in the man's breastplate and he tumbled backwards with a horrible grimace that parodied a laugh. The man's horse snorted in terror. Harry urged his own beast past, and searched for his next target. He could no longer see Gabriel in the confusion and gun smoke, but he realised with relief that the sounds of enemy gunfire had ceased, apart from sporadic pistol fire. Locked together with the enemy horse, Byron's men were safe from artillery and musketeer alike. The enemy were struggling to hold their line against the furious impact of Byron's men. Harry levelled his pistol at the breast of another enemy trooper. The ball flew upward and struck the man. Harry saw him claw at his neck. Hastily he drew his second pistol. A loud crack and a smell of gunpowder close at hand, part of the left sleeve of his buff coat torn away. An enemy trooper straight ahead, holding a smoking pistol. He stared stupidly as Harry rode up right beside him and fired. Half his face blown away, the man crashed to the ground. His panicked mount shied into Harry's and he smacked it on the rump with the flat of his sword to make it veer away. Harry felt the shock of a blow on his own helmet and the force nearly knocked him off his horse. He snatched at his sword and wheeled his horse, swinging the blade at the trooper who had struck him. As the man raised his sword for a second blow, Harry struck hard. The sword glanced off the man's gorget into the soft flesh of his neck. Tearing his blood stained sword free with difficulty, Harry urged his horse forward again. For a moment there was no one beside him and he was briefly aware of the noise of pistols and carbines all around. A voice was bellowing and he realised it was his own.

ග

The ranks of Byron's horse mingled as they steadily forced Waller's troops back up the slope. At Gabriel's shoulder the colours swayed, two or three neat holes punched through the blue silk. His men were fighting well, better than he had dared hope. He risked a glance behind him. Out of the corner of his eye he saw the orange sashed trooper riding at him swinging his sword. Gabriel fired his pistol but the ball went wide.

"Captain, look out." Harry swept past, slashing at a trooper as he was taking aim at Gabriel. The pistol fired but Harry had deflected his aim. Gabriel caught his breath. Harry had just saved his life. He pushed the thought away. He must keep a clear head.

"Forward, men, one more push!"

Gripping his bloody sword, Harry beside him, Gabriel spurred his horse forward but was confronted by the rebels ahead wheeling their horses away. He stared incredulously. To left and right the same sight met him. No longer massed in their tight six ranks, Waller's horse had broken. Before him, hundreds of orange sashed horsemen were fleeing the battlefield, galloping westwards into the setting sun.

"Follow me."

There was a pounding in Gabriel's ears. Not waiting to see if his troop were with him, he galloped furiously after the retreating enemy. His blood was up and they must not escape. Towards the western edge of the battlefield Gabriel raced, followed by his men. A few of his troop still had loaded pistols and one or two lucky shots found a target as they neared the men at the back of the fleeing horde. A small group of the enemy, realising they were being overtaken, turned and attempted a desperate struggle but were quickly overcome and cut down. It was carnage. Gabriel tugged his sword free with difficulty from the throat of a dying man. As he spurred his horse forward once more, he caught sight of a red sashed horseman galloping back towards them. He was shouting something, waving his arm. With difficulty, Gabriel reined in, held up his hand and yelled at his surrounding troop to halt. He shaded his eyes against the blinding sun.

The horseman was screaming the same words repeatedly. As he drew near, Gabriel realised they were "Beware precipice."

The man was at his side now, breathless.

"There is an escarpment, too steep for horses. Many of the rebels have fallen to their deaths. We came upon it suddenly, the sun is blinding. Turn back."

Gabriel nodded and wheeled his horse. His own orders to his men not to pursue the enemy in an undisciplined chase flooded back to him. With horror he realised that had it not been for the warning he might have led his troop straight to their deaths. "Withdraw," he yelled, heart hammering. He pointed back towards the battle field with his sword.

The fight was not yet over. Behind them, on the flat pasture land of the Down, were the rebel foot. Abandoned by their cavalry they were standing at bay in hollow squares, kneeling pikemen with their 16 feet poles of ash, sharp spikes at their tips, pointing out to repel the horsemen and protect the musketeers and officers in their midst. Wilmot's cavalry were charging the squares repeatedly but the foot were standing firm. As Gabriel approached, Wilmot's force charged again. A volley of shot rang out from the musketeers, and several men fell from their horses.

"Third company, form up. Men we have work remaining to us." Gabriel's voice was hoarse as he attempted to make himself heard over the yells and the crack of muskets and carbines. He coughed as he breathed in a lungful of smoke.

"Captain Vaughan!"

His commander was hailing him.

"Seize those falconets, and turn them around." He indicated two of the light field guns known as falconets, abandoned by their gun crews in the confusion, on the western side of the battle field. Byron turned and cantered with his remaining force to Wilmot's aid.

"Lieutenant Lucie, capture those guns. I believe we can put them to better use. And this time." Gabriel grinned, remembering how Harry had been captured at Edgehill,

"Don't ride into Essex's men. Corporal Fletcher, take ten men and fetch our gunners from the rear. Tell them we require their urgent assistance with our new ordnance."

As Gabriel's men swooped on the guns, turning them, dragging them into position, he heard the sound of drums beating an advance. The steady sound of the drums was coming from the opposite direction, from the south. Had Waller turned back? Had reinforcements arrived to support him? He shaded his eyes, straining them desperately. The drums were coming closer, and now he perceived the swirling standards of red and white were Sir Ralph Hopton's. Hopton's blue coats were finally on the march. Their change of heart was not before time. Gabriel had little time to watch their approach, for Waller's infantry were hastily reforming in marching order. Shepherded by agitated officers, they were preparing to retreat.

Gabriel cantered over to Harry's group with the falconets. "Gentlemen, hasten your efforts to turn the guns around. We may prevent Waller's men leaving the field once our gunners arrive."

Impatiently he leapt down off his horse and joined his sweating men as they heaved on the ropes until the guns were pointing westwards at the files of retreating infantry. Gabriel paced fretfully until the sight of double loaded horses trotting up heralded the arrival of the gunners and their crews. There was little time to explain why they were needed.

"Load with case shot and fire upon the enemy as soon as you are ready." Twice the guns blazed, causing panic in the retreating infantry, their orderly retreat disintegrating as they broke ranks and fled.

"Cease fire, Corporal. Protect the guns until my return. Lieutenant," Gabriel turned to Harry, "Come with me. We will pursue them."

Gabriel and Harry reloaded their weapons and threw themselves back on their horses. Gabriel's men streamed untidily after the running infantry. Other troops were doing likewise. The fleeing men on foot presented easy targets for the swords of the speeding cavalry. Like scythes through a cornfield, the blades rose and fell, cutting easily through the Montero caps, cleaving deep cuts in the backs of their heads and necks.

Cantering ahead of the slaughter, Gabriel and his troop overtook a scampering group of infantry. A number of officers on foot were trying unsuccessfully to rally their panicked men. They were swiftly surrounded by the horsemen. Gabriel's gaze rapidly swept the circle of rebel officers. One or two stared back defiant, but most appeared dispirited, resigned to their fate, whatever that might be. His blood lust ebbed away in an instant. There would be no honour in putting these men to the sword. They had stood bravely in their hopeless attempt to thwart their men's headlong flight, and he respected that. His men raised their weapons and he heard the clicks as they cocked them ready to fire.

"Enough. If you wish for quarter, gentlemen, disarm."

The group of officers eyed the ring of horsemen aiming their carbines and pistols. One tall officer, hatless, his tawny sash dragging in the dust, raised his sword and hurled himself with a snarl at Gabriel. Harry shot him dead. There was a tense moment, then the remaining officers hastily dropped their weapons on the ground. Gabriel nodded at Corporal Nesbitt who dismounted and gathered up the pistols, swords and halberds.

"Fetch an empty ammunition cart," Gabriel murmured to Harry. "We will transport the officers we have taken in that. In the meantime, bind them and place them under guard." In a louder voice he continued,

"Captain Gabriel Vaughan of Sir John Byron's Regiment at your service, gentlemen. I must ask you to remain here until we may convey you back to Devizes."

ꕥ

Waller and his senior officers had escaped by horse, but the defeat had been total. Hundreds of Waller's army had been captured and hundreds more killed, many by galloping into the unseen abyss on the western edge of the down. In addition to the guns which Gabriel had personally seized, the remainder of the artillery and the baggage train had been left behind in the headlong flight. Wilmot's victorious force camped outside Devizes that night. Gabriel made himself comfortable in his tent. He was engaged in the sad task of listing the names of his men who had been killed or injured in the battle when he was interrupted by Corporal Fletcher, looking harassed.

"Well, Corporal?"

"The rebel baggage train, Sir, there are wenches, camp followers."

"What of them? They are the commanders' responsibility thankfully, not mine, but I imagine they will be sent on their way."

Fletcher cleared his throat. "Some of them seek to turn their coats Captain, or rather I should say, their petticoats."

Gabriel laid down his quill with a sigh and a yawn.

"What do you wish of me, Fletcher?"

"May I admit them, Sir? Some of the men are anxious to make the acquaintance of the women."

"Oh very well, Fletcher, but no rutting like beasts in the open, and willing women only. If I find any of my men has taken a woman by force, I'll have him flogged. I want the troop ready to march in the morning with clear heads, and the women gone. Now fetch Kenyon. You may both go through the enemy baggage and remedy any deficiencies in our arms and armour before My Lord Wilmot's men loot everything of value," he finished with a rueful grin.

Gabriel returned his attention to his writing but before long he heard footsteps behind him.

"What now?"

It was Harry, grinning from ear to ear. He was carrying a spy glass and a lute.

"With the compliments of the rebel baggage train." He bowed with a flourish. "Maybe a new song on the stirring exploits of the Battle of Roundway Down?"

Gabriel smiled, the lines of strain on his face relaxing. To most men, the spy glass was more useful, but Harry knew it was the lute which Gabriel would value the more of the two unexpected gifts.

ও

Gabriel finished his report and sanded it with a sigh of relief. He hoped he would not have to go on campaign without his clerk again. There was a discreet cough from the tent flap. It was Corporal Fletcher returned.

"Well, Corporal, is all well with the men? And the women?"

"The men are content, Sir." He paused. "What about yerself, Captain?"

Gabriel looked quizzical. "Turned brothel keeper, Fletcher? Thank you, but no." He stretched out his hand for the lute. "This is all the companionship I require."

Fletcher shook his head. Giggles and grunts floated towards him on all sides as the men took their pleasure with the whores from the baggage train. But from one tent floated only the sounds of muted humming and the sweet notes of a lute as Captain Vaughan explored new harmonies.

ഗ

Devizes, 14 July 1643

Fletcher followed Gabriel's orders, and by morning there was no sign of any women in the vicinity of the troop. The cavalry remained encamped outside Devizes; and Gabriel began to feel that the holiday atmosphere was not good for discipline. With no orders to march, many of the officers allowed their men to visit the town. Gabriel was wary of allowing too many men to visit the town at a time. He rode in alone. It was early, but the streets were already crowded with soldiers. The taproom of the Bear Inn in the marketplace was crammed with red sashed cavalry, but as Gabriel raised his tankard to his lips, a band of Hopton's blue coats entered.

One of the cavalry, a man with a scar down one cheek, and matted brown curls, noticing their arrival bawled,

"Ah, the gentlemen of the foot arrive. Their arrival is late, but more timely than when they march to battle." He belched and swayed. Those nearest to him fell silent. Then one of the blue coats, a middle aged man whose ruddy complexion and disarranged dress suggested that he too had already been drinking replied,

"I do not take your meaning Zur. If thou would'st speak, speak plainly."

"To speak plainly then," slurred the man, "We fought both foot and horse yesterday, while you remained cosy in your quarters. Some might think Cornishmen fear to try their arm in the heat of battle." He turned away and spat deliberately on the floor.

The Cornishman sprang at him and punched him in the face. Companions of both men dropped their tankards and prepared to join the fight.

Gabriel heard the ominous sound of swords being unsheathed and set down his own tankard with a thump. “Cachu hwch,” he swore. Loosening his own blade in the scabbard, he stepped forward with determination.

“Gentlemen,” he commanded, “Put away your swords and cease this disturbance forthwith. “

His voice carried sufficient authority that there was a slight pause in the fighting. Gabriel drew his sword and advanced between the two main combatants. He fixed his gaze on the cavalry trooper and continued loudly,

“You are insubordinate, Sir. Return to the camp or I will have you arrested.” He swung round to face the foot soldier and said,

“You too, Sir”. The man opened his mouth to protest, but either the resolute expression on Gabriel’s face or the restraining hand of one of his comrades made him shut it again.

Gabriel held his breath. There was a long pause during which the two men eyed both each other and the angry officer. Then the Cornishman stamped out of the inn, followed by his companions. The cavalry trooper looked as if he meant to follow but Gabriel put his hand on his shoulder and the man stood still. Gabriel faced the crowded inn.

“Gentlemen, I suggest you all return to your units. There are men enough who fight for the rebels and are anxious to spill our blood. We should not assist them in their task by spilling each other’s.”

He sauntered with deliberate slowness out of the inn, almost colliding with Joe and Corporal Nesbitt. They were both holding a pistol.

“What are you doing?” asked Gabriel puzzled as he began walking down the street to collect his horse. They looked a little abashed.

Joe coughed self-consciously. “Well Sir, we came into the inn as the fight was starting. You might have been in danger intervening single handed. We thought to even the score a little if necessary.”

Back at the camp, Gabriel reported the incident to his commander. Byron listened to Gabriel’s brief account and nodded soberly.

“The Devil finds work for idle hands, and there is little enough love lost between the Oxford Army and the Western Army. We will find them occupation, Captain Vaughan. A great many men and horses broke their necks in that ravine yesterday. Some of our own men are among them. They are as yet unburied. Whether friend or foe it is not seemly that they remain rotting in the open, food for dogs and crows. Take as many men as you need and have them bury the men with their horses in mass graves. And put the rebel prisoners to work too.”

For hours the men were occupied in the ghastly task. Prisoners from Waller's army did the bulk of the work. Royalists and prisoners alike were subdued by the nature and the scale of what they did. Carrying shovels, they scrambled slowly and carefully to the bottom of the steep escarpment at the western side of the Down. Men and horses lay, mainly with broken necks, where they had fallen the previous afternoon. Nearby chalk pits were easily transformed into burial sites. The Royalists interred the smaller number of their own dead in a separate grave. The steep descent, or the distance from Devizes, had deterred the usual looters. Thus it was possible to distinguish friend from foe by their uniforms. It was a small enough consolation. The bodies were stripped of their arms and armour before burial, the horses of their tack. Clouds of flies were gathering in the warm summer's day. Kites and other birds of prey hovered avidly in the sky above, while crows pecked at the corpses, driven away repeatedly by the burial party. Gabriel was standing with a kerchief tied tightly over his nose and mouth against the stench, praying he would never be put in charge of such a task again, when a messenger came slithering down the slope asking for him. He handed a note to Gabriel,

"To Captain Gabriel Vaughan, Sir, the Western army leaves on the morrow, marching towards Bath. Our task here being done, Sir John Byron's regiment returns for the present to support the Oxford garrison. The regiment leaves within the hour. We quarter tonight at Lambourn. Your troop is to follow with all speed when the burials are complete." It was signed by a clerk on behalf of Byron.

When the hasty interment was complete, the prisoners were marched off once more under guard. An ashen faced chaplain led the grimy working party in prayer. Despite the heat, Gabriel shivered. The stench from overseeing the burials clung to him and had permeated his clothes. He would not care to spend any more time there.

ഗ

The afternoon was already far advanced by the time Gabriel found Harry playing cards with officers from the Earl of Crawford's regiment. Gabriel had thrown water over himself and changed his linen.

"Lieutenant, it is time to leave. We follow the rest of the regiment back to Oxford."

Harry lay down his cards and scrambled to his feet.

"Lucie, your losses." reminded one of the players.

Harry returned his gaze to the state of play, grinned and pulled some coins from his purse and hastened after Gabriel.

"Does the the army then return to Oxford?" Gabriel ran his hand through his wet hair.

"The Western army is to pursue Waller. To Bath perhaps. Oxford 's garrison is depleted and we return there for the present. I am not sorry to leave this place, and," he added quietly, "I long to see your sister."

As they rode out, Gabriel slung his buff coat across his saddle, hoping the passage of time and the fresher air would remove the clinging odours of death.

ᘓ

Ramsbury, Wiltshire, 14 July 1643

The sun was dipping towards the horizon as Gabriel led his troop wearily into the village of Ramsbury. They had been in the saddle for several hours. Lambourn was still some miles away and he decided not to attempt to catch up with the rest of Byron's horse that night. Loathe to spend a further night billeted in the unwelcome surroundings of Marlborough he had pushed on, crossing the Kennet at Axford. Ramsbury appeared large enough to quarter his troop. Numbers of thatched cottages, some timber framed, others brick, were clustered thickly along the road. A stream, a tributary of the nearby River Kennet, ran across the expanse of common land. Smoke rose lazily into the air from cooking fires, the cottage doors standing open in the muggy heat.

The street rapidly emptied before them as they rode through the village. Gabriel automatically looked about him for signs of danger.

A woman with a small child clinging to her skirts was talking to another carrying a pail. Two farm labourers were leaning against a fence, pitchforks over their shoulders. At the sound of hooves and the jangle of harnesses they slunk away. A well-dressed man in the act of handing over his horse to a servant, hurried up the stairs to the handsome brick mansion, the door slamming behind him. A young maid with a smaller child at her heels, ran towards the common, kilting up her skirts and driving the dozen geese on the grass before her. It was an all too familiar sight to Gabriel. A troop of 60 cavalry arriving meant forced billeting, at least for a night. Precious livestock would meet an untimely end on soldiers' campfires if not protected.

Gabriel held up his hand to halt as he reined up outside what appeared to be the sole alehouse in the village. Its door remained invitingly open, the only one in the street to do so. A pervasive smell of ale hung in the sir, mixed with those of tobacco and the aromas of cooking meat and onions. Gabriel dismounted and beckoned to his Quartermaster.

"We will rest here tonight. Offer the usual warrants to the villagers. We require lodging for one night, and for men and horses to be fed, the horses to have grain."

Simon Kenyon the Quartermaster tugged at his beard thoughtfully. His spare frame and hollow cheeks belied his calling. "Do you expect resistance here, Captain?"

"No more than is common in these parts. But we are close enough to Marlborough that the people may be fearful. Have a care, Simon, and be patient if you can. Broken doors win His Majesty no friends."

"And for yourself and the other officers, Sir?"

"That looks a likely house." Gabriel pointed with a gloved hand to the large brick house.

Kenyon nodded and strode purposefully away towards the nearest cottage, its door firmly closed. He rapped hard on the door and it was answered by a scowling woman, volubly protesting. Gabriel handed Harry his new spy glass.

"Take four men and ride to the end of the village and a little beyond to see no enemy approaches. If all is secure, post two men on watch and report back. God willing we will have an untroubled night and a speedy return on the morrow to Oxford."

"And Bess," Harry muttered as he turned his horse's head. A few moments later he was trotting on down the street, four riders behind him. The tapster emerged warily from the alehouse, doffing his cap.

"What is your will, Sir?"

Gabriel produced a handful of small coins.

"Ale for the men, but first we will water our horses." He took a long pull at the leather tankard a serving wench was offering, and set it down again. It was a humid, sticky day. Even without his heavy buff coat Gabriel felt over warm in his pale blue suit of light woollen cloth, prickles of sweat trickling down inside his shirt. He tugged uncomfortably at his lace collar, which was sticking to his neck, and rolled down the tops of his boots as far as his knees. The remainder of the troop were leading their horses towards the stream. Most of them stripped off their buff coats and splashed themselves liberally while the horses drank from the clear water. Some unfastened their helmets from their saddles and used them as pails, upending them over their heads.

After watering his own horse, Gabriel ran a hand down the gelding's right foreleg and called to the troop farrier.

"Adam, I fear my horse may have a slight strain. He favours this leg. It feels a little warm."

Adam Wheatley, a farmer's son and now farrier to Gabriel's troop, shrugged his broad shoulders and stooped from his considerable height to look. In his early twenties, he had already a lifetime's experience with horses and the animals trusted him.

"Stand my lad," he said in his soothing voice to the horse. He ran gentle fingers down the leg in question. He scratched his already thinning red gold hair while he continued scrutinising the leg. "I would rub bacon fat in to his foreleg, Captain. But since we have none to hand, I will bandage it without."

ᔓᔕ

Harry and his scouts trotted unhurriedly to the end of the village street, where the cottages thinned and a lane led sharply to the left. The lane was only wide enough for a horse and cart. The way climbed gradually towards the top of a hill. It ran between high hedges, thick with the darkening green of summer growth and dotted with yellow celandines.

Above them the road ran along the crest of the hill, bare but for a few scattered trees. As Harry ran his eyes carefully over the hill top, he caught a glint. He reined up. There it was again. As he looked, the glint was followed by others. It was the setting sun, glancing off helmets. Harry passed the perspective glass to the corporal.

"Corporal Nesbitt, your eyes are keen. I believe there are enemy troops approaching. Take note of their strength. I will return and warn Captain Vaughan. Follow us as soon as possible." He wheeled his horse and spurred back towards the village.

ᔓᔕ

"Have a care with that foreleg, Captain. But I think he will carry you back to Oxford without going lame." Gabriel was standing beside his horse as Wheatley completed bandaging the foreleg.

"Captain, the enemy approaches." Harry reined up breathlessly by the alehouse. "A troop of horse heading this way, orange sashes."

"How far do they have to travel?" Gabriel's voice remained calm.

"A mile or so, Captain, no more."

"Thankyou, Harry. I suspect it may be a roving troop of cavalry from the Gloucester garrison. I hear they patrol far and wide. No matter, we will be ready for them."

"The lane leads sharply off the High Street, Captain, and there are high hedges. They will not see us until they enter the village if we remain out of sight of the road out."

"Then see they do not. Time to play at dragoons.

Corporal Nesbitt," he continued as they were joined by Harry's men, "collect 20 men. Place ten men behind the hedges on either side of the lane. Remove your red sashes or they may show through the hedges. Wait until the tail of the troop draws level and then give them a sudden volley. Leave the horses close at hand with two of the men to hold them so that you may remount presently. Make haste."

"Sir!"

The Corporal grinned and cantered off towards the stream and the rest of the troop. "Lieutenant, to arms with all speed. Form the men up in three ranks at the street's end without sound of trumpet. Open order. Every man to load his pistols and carbine. Since we have the element of surprise, it is important we maintain that."

"At once, Sir." Harry reached for his armour.

"No time for that today, Harry. We will trust in God, and in our greater prowess." Grinning almost light heartedly up at Harry, Gabriel raised his arm and the two men clasped hands.

Gabriel grabbed his carbine and sword belt, rammed his helmet on his head and threw himself onto his horse. He hurled his buff coat onto an upturned barrel outside the alehouse and hastily knotted his red sash diagonally across his chest.

"Captain, your coat," Harry protested.

"I am weary of being basted alive by the sun today, Harry. And besides, it stinks of the dead. I prefer not to fight encased in a shroud." Glancing downwards at his horse's bandaged leg, Gabriel eased him into a gentle canter, throwing up a cloud of dust in his wake. Wheatley reached for his own weapons, leapt onto his horse, and trotted after Gabriel. Harry hastily gathered the stragglers from the stream.

In the fading evening light, the troop took up their positions before the sharp corner at the end of the street. As quietly as possible, the officers beckoned the men in their divisions into the three wide ranks, blocking the road from side to side. Cornet Nugent, his face glowing with excitement, sat his horse behind Gabriel. He grasped firmly the blue colour with its three white stars, drooping limply in the still air. The dust settled as the horses stood, occasionally stamping a hoof, or twitching an ear to shake off a fly. Helmets were strapped firmly to chins, but the troop were otherwise without their armour and one or two had followed Gabriel's example and were recklessly preparing to go into action with their weapons their only protection.

Gabriel reached beneath his shirt for the comforting presence of his crucifix and breathed a quick prayer, but strangely he felt no nervousness. Whether the fierce fight at Roundway Down made a skirmish seem insignificant he did not know. His tiredness had vanished. He felt full of energy and very alive. His excitement transmitted itself to his horse, which began to fidget. Gabriel soothed it with a few quiet words of Welsh, leaning forward and pulling its ears.

Now the sound of hoof beats, the creaking of leather and the jingling of bits and spurs, a troop approaching at a trot. Gabriel raised a cautionary hand. The hoof beats were closer, voices could be heard, a laugh as a man made a jest. Gabriel drew his sword, holding it above his head. The sword swept down. "God and King Charles," Gabriel cried and the troop echoed his words. In a tight line they broke into a gallop just as the double file of orange sashed troopers trotted into sight around the bend.

Byron's men smashed headlong into the surprised rebel troop. The rebel front line was quickly overwhelmed. Pushing forwards, Gabriel's front rank had fired their carbines before the enemy could react. Saddles were emptied and those remaining in the front ranks tried to wheel their horses away from Gabriel's men, the second rank now moving through the gaps and firing in turn. The tail of the rebel column turned and attempted to flee. One or two spurred away, but the remainder were stopped in their tracks by a volley of lead from the unseen men in the hedges on either side of the road. Uncertain which way to turn, the rebel troopers milled around, grabbing for carbines and pistols. A handful managed to make a break around the flank and fled down the High Street. Harry, in position at the back, galloped after the retreating horsemen, followed by Cornet Nugent and his younger brother Jack. One of the retreating troopers stopped and fired his carbine. The shot grazed Harry's cheek. Dropping the reins onto his horse's neck, Harry caught the man, grabbing at the horse's bridle with his gauntleted left hand and swinging his sword at the rebel's head. The man parried, but his attention was divided between sword and freeing his horse. Harry's blade caught him a glancing blow on the helmet, knocking him off balance. He tried again to wheel away but Harry, sword raised high, struck at the man's neck. The sharp sided broad sword did its work and the man collapsed with blood spurting from the wound.

Harry wrenched his sword free and looked around for another victim. His blood was pounding in his ears. Two men were making good their escape at a gallop. A horse ran loose with a broken rein, its rider dying on the ground, while Jack Nugent lowered his empty pistol and replaced it in its holster. Harry reined in, attempting to master his useless blood lust. The main skirmish was continuing at the end of the street, but the remaining rebels were losing the short and fierce struggle against Gabriel's troop. Nesbitt's men had remounted and were charging the hapless troops from the rear. A few men had already been taken prisoner and were sitting on the ground under guard. In the fading light, a pale blue coat lined with white silk was visible as Gabriel wielded his sword. Harry raised his sword above his head. "Back," he yelled to the two brothers and they cantered together up the High Street. The two redheaded men were swinging their swords almost in unison above their heads as they charged two older rebels, who had broken through the ranks of Gabriel's troop. For a moment Harry wondered inconsequently if they had drilled so at their home in Derby before joining the King. Cornet Nugent yelled something and Jack laughed, turning his face towards his brother as he closed with the enemy horseman. He had not seen the pistol emerging from its holster and turned back a moment too late. The high pitched crack seemed loud to Harry above the shouting, the clash of swords and the occasional banging of carbines. A long moment, a look of bemusement on Jack's face and he was toppling to the ground, a hole in his chest.

Harry was close behind, and it was the work of a moment to knock Jack's killer off balance with his sword hilt and send him flying off his horse to the ground. The soldier scrambled to his feet and reached for his sword but it was Harry who now held a pistol in his hand. The man threw down his sword, "Quarter."

Harry nodded sombrely and pointed with his pistol towards the nearby knot of prisoners. He did not see the frantic Cornet until Nugent leapt straight off his horse and landed on the man's chest. He was weeping. The startled captive attempted to struggle into a sitting position.

"Kneel," the word was hissed.

"Cornet," Harry cried. The desperate Nugent drew a pistol and pointed it at the man's head.

"Cornet," Harry shouted again, "I have given him quarter, you may not murder him."

Nugent turned wild eyes on Harry. "He killed my brother."

"And he will answer for it," Harry reassured him, "But this is not the place and you are not the executioner."

Slowly Nugent lowered his pistol. Harry reached behind him and pulled his folded blanket from his saddle. "Cover your brother's face and follow me."

Leaving the relieved prisoner under guard with the others, Harry and the cornet regained the end of the street. The battered remnants of the enemy troop were making a last stand under one of their officers, a tall man with a ginger moustache. The back ranks were engaged in reloading.

"Byron's withdraw." Gabriel was holding his sword above his head. The troop broke away as the enemy carbines discharged. Shot rattled off helmets and a horse screamed as it was hit.

"One more charge men, and the day is ours." Following Gabriel's pale form in the dusk, the panting, heaving mass of horses wheeled tightly and reformed their ranks. As he again urged his horse into the front rank and pointed with his sword, there was a bang from a carbine, followed closely by a second. The first shot dented Gabriel's helmet and the second grazed his left shoulder. He swore loudly as a small patch of blood, dark against the gloom, appeared on the pale cloth.

"Captain, they are shooting at you," Corporal Fletcher exclaimed.

"I wish them better aim another day. Follow me."

Gabriel spurred his horse and as the troop dashed forward the ranks of rebel horse broke for the last time. The ginger moustached officer was leading his remaining troopers away at a gallop.

"Sir, shall we pursue them?"

Gabriel shook his head.

"Enough for tonight, Fletcher. Lock the prisoners in the church. They will accompany us to Oxford on the morrow. Place guards outside the church and a patrol at each end of the village, but I do not believe we will be troubled further."

He winced and clutched his shoulder. Corporal Fletcher's face creased in a frown. "Captain, you are wounded."

"More of a graze, Corporal but it stings like hell's fire. I will have the goodwife bandage it. Officers quarter in the large house across the street."

Having checked with the Quartermaster that the billets were allocated, Gabriel led his horse towards the big house, Harry close behind him. Gabriel looked back. The prisoners shuffling towards the square towered church chivvied by swords and pistols were little more than indistinct shapes in the fading light.

Shadowy figures darted furtively as the villagers emerged from their houses to loot anything of value from the dead rebel soldiers. Gabriel turned away from the distasteful sight. His own men would not be far behind in looking for purses, or a better sword than their army issued tuck. His troop had been mostly lucky with one or two minor wounds like his own although they'd lost Jack Nugent, killed in the skirmish. "I must speak with our Cornet."

"Tomorrow, Sir, will be soon enough," Fletcher assured him. "Kenyon comforts him, he has been like a father to those two young men."

A sullen servant led their horses away to the stable. Tired and grimy, Gabriel and Harry gratefully climbed the steps to the front door of the brick house. An elderly housekeeper bustled forward. When she saw Gabriel holding his shoulder she clucked her tongue and her stern expression softened.

"Here, Sir, come to the kitchen do before you bleed on the mats." Turning to Harry she opened a door, "You may wait in here."

By the light of many wax candles he could see it was a handsome oak panelled room. Harry looked around and whistled softly. Mullioned windows overlooked the darkened street. One stood open to catch the evening breeze, but the air was still and the flame of the candles rose straight in the air, a few insects circling the light. Comfortable high backed chairs suggested the room was intended for entertaining. There was a finely carved mantel over the fireplace. A side table held a large bible. If this was the home of a Puritan merchant, he had done well for himself.

Harry pulled off his gloves, sticky with sweat. He then, with relief, removed his blood splattered buffcoat and sword belt, tossing them on a chair with his helmet.

Harry sat down on a chair and stretched his long legs, wondering to whom the fine house belonged. He heard a firm step approaching and looked round to see the well dressed man again. His handsome dark red doublet with silk lining showing through the slashed sleeves and his expensive boots confirmed he was a man of substance. Under his hat his grey hair was cut short and his thick grey brows were drawn together in a scowl.

"This is outrageous, Sir. I will not countenance malignant troops under my roof."

Harry jumped to his feet, clapping his hand instinctively to his side but then remembered he was no longer wearing his sword. Besides, the man was not wearing a weapon in his own home. Harry bowed stiffly.

"We will inconvenience you as little as possible, Sir. As our Quartermaster will have informed you, we remain only the one night, but remain we must. We ride on His Majesty's business. Now we require rest and refreshment."

The owner of the house snorted, muttered something which on a charitable interpretation might have been "Very well," and stalked from the room. Harry seated himself again, wondering whether to pursue refreshment in the kitchen.

ᘓ

The elderly housekeeper turned her head away modestly as Gabriel removed his coat and shirt. He hastily slid the crucifix on its silver chain over his head and concealed it in his breeches pocket. The day had been a long one. It was only now that he realised how the events of the day, the brawl in the Devizes inn, the burying of the dead, the long march and the skirmish, had taken their toll. He would sleep, on a palliasse if not a bed, and on the morrow he would wake refreshed.

Half asleep, Gabriel heard little of the woman's words as she chattered.

"The Master doesn't hold with Cavalier troops in the house, but I suppose you're God's creatures too, even if you are malignants. But as to what the Master's brother the Major will say, being as he's staying here at present." Her voice droned on.

The housekeeper finished bandaging Gabriel's shoulder. Yawning, he was pulling his shirt over his head when he heard a cry of rage. It sounded like Harry. Instantly awake, Gabriel snatched up his sword belt.

ꕤ

"Well I do believe it is Lieutenant L L L Lucie. I wondered which malignant troop was disturbing my night. And how's your pretty sister? Keeping the Oxford garrison warm at nights I'll stake my life."

"Don't you dare insult my ss sister," yelled Harry as he hurled himself bodily at the hated Major Chatterton.

Laughing, Chatterton stepped aside, avoiding Harry's headlong rush. With a rasp, he drew his sword from the scabbard, casting the belt down with a clatter. Harry backed away, eyes searching wildly for his own weapon. Chatterton stepped between Harry and the chair where his sword lay and laughed.

"Unarmed, Lucie? I believe I might run you through before you could touch me."

He lunged at Harry, who grabbed the back of a chair, keeping it between them.

"A poor defence Lieutenant, for see the length of my sword will suffice." He jabbed at Harry. The broad sword was razor sharp. Before Harry could react, a rent from right shoulder to wrist appeared in his doublet and shirt. Blood welled from the cut, dripping from Harry's wrist to the floor, and he gasped in pain.

Chatterton stood back smiling, his reddened sword point resting on the floor.

"Naught but a scratch. But we should perhaps continue our discourse outside, before we cause some harm to my brother's house."

"Leave him to me, Harry. Major, we renew our old acquaintance. Pray cross swords with me while Lieutenant Lucie recovers."

Chatterton's glance flickered sideways in amusement as Gabriel entered the room, his sword drawn.

"And Lieutenant Vaughan. Well my Welsh firebrand, I will be delighted to oblige you. Maybe Mistress Lucie warms your bed as well as that of other men. I shall seek her out when our army takes Oxford. She will entertain me well."

Harry had now reached his sword. His face was fixed and determined and he gave no sign of having heard Gabriel's words. He advanced, blade raised high, his right arm held stiffly as blood continued to trickle from sleeve to floor.

"Harry," said Gabriel again quietly, "leave him to me. That is an order."

Harry looked up, Gabriel's words finally penetrating his ears. He opened his mouth to protest, then said "Sir," and stepped back, dropping his blade to his side.

"Ah, is it Captain Vaughan now? My congratulations." Chatterton bowed mockingly and gestured ceremoniously towards the door.

One eye on Chatterton, Gabriel backed carefully from the room and quickly ran down the steps. He opened the gate and stood waiting in the darkened street, now lit by a rising moon. His whole body was complaining of fatigue as the muscles tightened in anticipation of renewed combat. He wiped his right hand on his breeches and gripped the basket hilt of his sword more firmly, taking deep breaths.

Chatterton strolled casually into the street, his sword held out before him in readiness. Wearing only a forest green doublet and breeches it was clear that he had been relaxing, not expecting to play a part in the evening's fighting. Harry stood behind him in the doorway, blood running unheeded down his arm, his hand still clenching his sword hilt.

"A gibbous moon, Captain Vaughan," Chatterton said conversationally, "Fortunate for us. It gives us ample light to do our work by. I am pleased to see you mean to fight in your shirt. It makes it easier to see you." He raised his sword and the two men began to circle each other slowly, never taking their eyes from the other's face.

Gabriel replied in kind, determined to match his enemy's confidence.

"I offer you a choice, Major. If you care to surrender to me now, you may join the other prisoners in the church overnight and repair with us to Oxford on the morrow. If not the church, you may rest rather longer-in the churchyard." As Gabriel finished he struck suddenly at Chatterton. The man saw the move and smashed Gabriel's blade out of the way. He stepped back.

"Bold words, Vaughan," he continued as they resumed circling each other. "I do not care however to see the inside of Oxford Castle. Neither do I believe you will succeed in laying me to rest in the churchyard of Holy Cross, charming though it may be."

He sprang forward suddenly at Gabriel, lunging left and then sweeping his sword high to the right. Gabriel sidestepped the first blow and swung his sword quickly up to parry the second. His heart was pounding. He knew that Chatterton was intent on killing him.

Stepping back out of range, Chatterton smiled. "I believe I prefer a third choice. Skewer you like a pig on a spit and then make good my escape. Once I have disposed of you I dare say I can deal with Master Lucie. You fine gentlemen of the cavalry have not made a study of the art of sword fighting. Galloping and slashing is all you know. Now I will show you how to truly use a sword. A pity you will not live long enough to profit from it."

"No more words, Major. Save your breath for fighting. You are of middle years and will tire before I. Let it not be said I defeated you only because you are nearer to the age of infirmity than I."

Finally goaded into a response by Gabriel's suggestion that he was past his prime, Chatterton made his first mistake, rushing at the younger man fiercely. Gabriel danced sideways to his right, and the descending blade met only thin air. Whirling, Gabriel swung downwards at Chatterton's left shoulder. He struck it little more than a glancing blow, but the sharp edge of the blade sliced through the doublet into the muscles of Chatterton's upper arm. A darker patch appeared on the sleeve of Chatterton's doublet. He swore and his blade dropped while he glanced instinctively at his bleeding shoulder. He reacted too slowly to a fresh attack and this time Gabriel's blade sliced though the tendon. The injured arm hung useless and bleeding profusely at Chatterton's side.

"Quarter, Major?" Gabriel enquired mildly, standing back to catch his breath.

"I'll see you damned first."

The speed and ferocity of his charge took Gabriel by surprise. As he jumped back out of range his opponent stopped and laughed. Gabriel was the younger by twenty years and lighter on his feet, but Chatterton was the more experienced swordsman. Taller and heavier he forced the attack, striving to push Gabriel back. His useless left arm must be paining him considerably, but he was showing no signs of weakness.

Now an overhead thrust, parried by Gabriel again and the two locked sword hilts. The two men grappled together. Chatterton pushed hard, grunting with the effort, sending Gabriel flying backwards onto the ground.

With a triumphant cry, Chatterton smashed his blade downwards. Gabriel threw himself clear and was on his feet before Chatterton could raise his sword again.

Gabriel knew that the other man, wounded as he was, could not continue much longer with the fight. He was tiring rapidly himself. His broadsword's familiar grasp was a lead weight in his hand. A short time must end it. Neither would yield, so one of them must fall. He raised his left arm, pushing his hair back from his dripping face. Seeing the movement as a possible opening, Chatterton lunged at Gabriel, who leapt aside. It left Chatterton's chest unprotected for a precious moment. Gabriel raised his arm high and swung the blade downwards, flinging himself forward.

As Gabriel threw all his weight onto his right foot, the weak ankle gave way and he stumbled. His sword blade dropped and instead of slicing into Chatterton's chest, slashed hard across his thigh. The Major cried out, collapsing to the ground. Blood was pouring from the deep wound. Gabriel stood over him panting hard, sword raised. Chatterton glared at him and then threw his sword down beside him with a clatter.

"Take quarter then," Gabriel's tone was contemptuous. He wiped his sword blade clean on Chatterton's doublet and reached for his own scabbard before turning his attention to Chatterton's discarded sword. He caught sight of Harry, standing just behind him in the street, heedless of the blood dripping from his arm. Gabriel frowned and straightened up. "You should see to that wound while I put this man…"

"Gabriel, turn!"

At Harry's desperate warning he whirled. Sword in hand, the scowling Chatterton was somehow on his feet. Gabriel looked on with surprise as the blade slashed hard through his shirt and cut deep into his right side, passing between the ribs. Blood was welling out but he felt no pain. Why were his legs no longer holding him up? Behind him Chatterton collapsed once more on the ground. Gabriel felt nothing as he fell, but for a few moments saw above him an anxious face with grey eyes bending over him. "Bess?" he said faintly and lapsed into blessed unconsciousness.

Carrying the bleeding major, two fearful servants scurried into his brother's house and fastened the door firmly behind them. Kneeling in the dust, Harry looked desperately around. He was relieved to see that he was no longer alone. Attracted by the fight, or simply heading towards their billet in the house, the officers of Gabriel's troop were standing in a semicircle a few paces away. His eyes lighted thankfully on Joe. With a supreme effort Harry took command.

"Captain Vaughan is seriously wounded. Joe, make haste to Lambourn and return with the regiment's surgeon."

"Sir, what of the Captain's adversary?" Corporal Nesbitt's voice was tentative. "Was he not sorely hurt himself?"

"Sadly his wound may not be mortal," Harry snapped. "He will have to take his chances as to whether he has his turn under the surgeon's knife."

ꟹ

The minister for Holy Cross Church, Ramsbury, was engaged in writing an angry letter to Sir John Byron about the ungodly use to which his church had been put. Strongly Puritan in his sympathies, he had been more happily engaged in composing a sermon on the evils of popery, when he had been roused some time earlier by a rude clamour of voices and tramping of boots. To his horror, the disturbance was malignant troops forcing a number of orange sashed prisoners at sword point into his church.

His protests had been ignored, one of the officers telling him he was taking his orders from a Captain Vaughan of Sir John Byron's regiment of horse.

His wife Jane's voice raised in argument with an unknown man broke off abruptly. He heard her footsteps approaching his door. Tossing aside the half written letter and rubbing ink stained hands on his breeches, he flung the door open.

"I'm sorry, Samuel," her pale face was unusually flushed above her white collar and drab grey gown.

"What now woman?" He pushed past her to see two malignant soldiers, red sashed and covered with grime from powder stains, setting down a make shift stretcher on the floor of his parlour. On it lay an unconscious man, presumably an officer, ashen faced. His white shirt and pale blue breeches were soaked in blood.

A young officer was bending over the stretcher. Under its coating of dirt his handsome face was furrowed with concern. His doublet was torn and his right arm dripped blood onto the rush mat. It was evidently he who had been the source of the altercation with the minister's wife.

Seeing the minister he gave a stiff nod.

"Sir, I require you to allow our Captain to be tended here. He is gravely wounded. Our regiment's surgeon will be here in no more than an hour. I understand you are the minister for this village and I have judged your house the most proper place to bring Captain Vaughan."

The minister looked with increasing fury at the intruders, papists all no doubt, and at the blood dripping onto his floor from the two men's wounds. There was a bloody hand print upon the door and a smear on the whitewashed wall. The slender minister drew himself up to his rather insignificant full height and glared at the tall officer.

"I do not give house room to malignants, Sir. Least of all those responsible for turning my church into a gaol. Remove this man immediately. Begone I say. Do not waste my time and that of my servants with capricious demands. He is beyond the help of man. Take him to some other place where he may breathe his last before the Devil claims him."

Accustomed to being heeded, the minister stamped towards the door. He was arrested by the sound of a click. Turning his head he was astounded to see the officer was pointing a pistol at him, his grey eyes cold as steel. "You will have your servants take care of our captain now or I will blow a hole in you.

Corporal Fletcher!"

he bellowed at one of the stretcher bearers.

"Place strong guard on the house where the Major lies wounded. See to it that he is not removed during the night. Strengthen the guard on the church."

The minister was open mouthed. He realised that the officer was addressing him again,

"Pray that my Captain survives the night. If he dies under your roof, I will burn down your church, and the rebel prisoners with it."

18

Ramsbury, Wiltshire, July 1643

TOWARDS MIDNIGHT, THE regimental surgeon strode briskly into the room. He had been roused from his bed by an urgent summons. Sword wound in the side, a bad business. He liked Captain Vaughan, a good officer, and he had followed the trumpeter back with all speed.

Harry greeted him with relief. "Master Rutherford, I rejoice to see you. What do you think? Can Captain Vaughan live?"

"Gently Lieutenant, let me do my work." The auburn haired surgeon, a man around thirty years of age, had removed his riding cloak and was already busy buttoning on a clean white apron over his suit of brown wool. He knelt by the unconscious man.

"Captain Vaughan, Gabriel, do you hear me?"

"He has lost much blood," Harry interjected anxiously. Servants had attempted to stem the flow of blood with rags. These were now blood soaked and adhering to the wound. Rutherford frowned as he considered the options.

"Well I must take a look. I cannot tend him lying on the ground. Lift him into that chair. Handsomely now, have a care. And more light-as many candles or lanterns as you can lay your hands on."

Gabriel groaned as he was lifted onto the chair and his eyelids fluttered briefly.

"Bring water for my hands, also wine, claret if you have it, and a bowl." The surgeon opened his bag and produced a small, sharp knife and a roll of clean linen bandages. He used the knife to cut through Gabriel's blood soaked shirt, folding it back to expose his torso. When a servant appeared with the water and wine, he washed his hands. To Harry's surprise he then poured some of the wine into a bowl.

"Now the pain will worsen while I treat him. Give to him as much wine as he will take, but have a care he does not choke. You two, stand by to hold him fast."

The surgeon's long, slender fingers delved deep into the wound. He probed thoroughly, carefully removing some small reddened fragments of Gabriel's shirt which had been carried in by the sword. Gabriel groaned and muttered, trying to move. Rutherford smoothed out the tiny fragments of shirt and held them carefully against the hole in the shirt where the sword had penetrated.

"I believe I have them all. That is well. The wound will fester if any remains within it."

Taking a small length of bandage, the surgeon rolled it tightly and immersed it in the wine until it was sodden. Finally he looked up at Harry.

"Now to place a tent in the wound. For this he must not stir."

The two soldiers gripped Gabriel's shoulders tightly. As the small linen tent was pressed firmly into his wound he screamed and then went limp. Rutherford straightened up and nodded.

"I think he may do well now. The wound needs to be left open for a few days. When it begins to resemble well hung flesh, then the tent may be removed and the wound sutured, not before. The evil humours must be allowed to leave. The blade passed between two ribs and clipped the liver. That is why there is exsanguination. Does he remain here, or will you have him transported back to Oxford?"

"I have thought Master Rutherford to take him to his father's house. It is a three or four days journey but he will receive better care there, saving your presence than he may happily receive in Oxford. He may not remain here."

Rutherford stroked his auburn beard and sighed.

"Oxford is as you say. It is crowded and the morbus campestris still holds sway there. Well I pray that he may survive the journey. He is a gallant gentleman. I will write you directions for his care. Now before I return to the regiment, let me look to your arm."

ᔕ

Ramsbury, July 1643

The next morning, a somewhat calmer Harry sought a hasty interview with a stony faced Master Chatterton. Harry nodded to him stiffly.

"Sir, is your brother expected to recover from his wounds?"

The man glared at him.

"That I cannot say. Forgive me if I do not thank you for your enquiry."

"I leave him in your care then, on one condition."

"Say it," the man spat between clenched teeth.

"He is my prisoner, and a prisoner of His Majesty. Do I have your word as a gentleman, and his, that if he recovers enough to ride, he will present himself at Oxford Castle as a captive? Should he break his word, I will hold you personally accountable."

The grey haired Chatterton turned so scarlet with rage that for a moment Harry wondered if he would have an apoplexy.

"Damn you yes, you have my word."

ꟹ

Oxford, July 1643

The days after the army's departure were tense times for me once again. Then the news came back that our army had defeated Waller's at Devizes. Prince Rupert had arrived back in Oxford after escorting the Queen and the artillery train on the final leg of their journey from the north and was marching west with a large body of men. The mood in Oxford was jubilant. Messengers came and went from Lord Wilmot's forces at Devizes. I was excited when within a few days a letter sealed with Gabriel's signet ring was delivered to the house. I tore it open. It was dated the 14th day of July.

"Dearest Bess," it began, "I thought it was time I told you how we go on here with the army. What your brother tells you I do not know, but we won a great victory at Devizes and Harry stopped a Roundhead from putting a bullet in me by smacking him with his sword. We were greatly outnumbered but our commanders were cleverer than theirs and our men more valiant. We put them to flight, both horse and foot. My men captured some cannon left behind in their headlong flight and put it to good use so that there are now fewer rebels to make war on us in future. For which action I received commendation from my commander.

Your brother is in high spirits and gains in confidence as an officer. He has put the past behind him. As for me I am much occupied with the care of 60 men. But not so occupied I do not remember your kisses. I have mused upon your lips and eyes and you may expect that your lute will be put to work again before long when I am able to complete my latest song and find means of sending it to you.

I long to see you." It was signed with a linnet. I kissed the letter and folded it away carefully.

A few days later, I was delighted to receive a letter from Celia, accompanied by a letter to my father in an unknown hand.

Celia's letter was dated the 20th of July. She wrote thus:

"My dear Bess, how long it seems since I saw you. I daresay you have had many exciting times in Oxford, although I hear that many men have been sick with fever. I am quite frightened by this and pray that you, my uncle and your brothers are all well. Peggy comforts my worries and tells me you are strong and too healthy to sicken. I hope this may be true. Peggy and I are become great friends. I forgot to say what I should have begun with that I am as you will guess still resident as Tenant at Chadshunt Hall. The Parliament has given my Husband a paper which says he may reside here as Tenant and I am allowed to remain here on his behalf.

Major Chatterton arrived a few days after you left. He is a Horrid Man and I cannot think why my Father would be his friend. As Lady Ridgeley I was accorded all due respect by him, but I cannot like him. He questioned Peggy and the servants about your family and seemed most displeased that you in particular were absent. He talked of his wish to be better acquainted with you. His countenance when he said that was twisted into a most unpleasant smile. I could not bear him near me and was at considerable pains to prevent him from kissing my hands.

Happily he did not remain above a day or two. He brought some men who made disturbance with renewed searches for Plate and I know not what. My presence prevented them from causing damage and I am content I was of use in this. When Major Chatterton went away I thought he would return to Warwick but I have since heard he has leave of absence to visit his family. My husband has been here and stayed some little while to be assured of my safety and to make himself acquainted with the estate. Since there are no longer any "malignants" – how I detest that term, there are now only a handful of soldiers here as a guard for my protection. I wish I could see you dear coz but suppose this is not possible in these times.

Peggy sends her affectionate duty. She misses you and so I believe does Hector, who is near full grown.

My husband tells me there are important matters that touch upon the tenancy and I enclose a letter from him for your father. I hope these letters will find you. I pray that this war does not last long and that we may be together again when it draws to a close. Your loving cousin, Celia Ridgeley."

When I finished reading Celia's letter I turned my attention to my father who sat his chin propped in his hand, still clutching the letter from Sir John Ridgeley.

"What is it, Father?" I asked with some concern.

He looked up at me,

"Sir John Ridgeley is now official tenant of the Hall on behalf of

Parliament." I nodded,

"Yes, Celia remains there. Is this not a good thing Father, she protects the estate and our people from annoyance."

Father frowned impatiently, "That is so, but there is more. As the Committee for Sequestration has declared our estate forfeit, Sir John will be collecting our revenues on behalf of Parliament. We must pray that the King's cause prevails or we are like to lose our home in perpetuity."

I stared at him in horror. Somehow I had failed to truly understand what Parliament had ordained. We were effectively banished from our home until the war was over, however much Celia might wish to mitigate their sanctions.

"Well, "Father continued, "We have set our feet on this road and must continue. I must acquaint your brother. As heir to Chadshunt Hall, this touches Will more closely than all. But there is a crumb of comfort. If we should dare to venture back we may at least carry away the few possessions we have secreted in our hiding place."

Will was sufficiently recovered that he was taking daily exercise and talking of reporting for duty in a few days. He returned from his walk a little later and my father acquainted him with the grave situation and for his thoughts of making a sortie to rescue what valuables we could. By the start of August their secret preparations were ready. The evening after their departure I heard hurried steps on the stairs and Harry strode into the room. He was dusty from the road and looked as if he had ridden hard.

"Harry," I cried, "You are safe! I had no idea the army was returned." I noticed that his right sleeve was hanging loose and the arm was bandaged. "But what is wrong with your arm?"

"It is nothing Bess, already mending." I was relieved.

"Did Gabriel return with you?"

"Bess," he began, his face grave.

"No!" I cried, "No, I will not hear it," and in my fear I clapped my hands to my ears as if I could blot out bad tidings.

"Bess," he cried, "He is not dd dead. But he is ww wounded. He was wounded in a fight with Major Chatterton. He fought him to ss save me."

I dropped to the floor on my knees, speechless. Harry helped me to a chair. When I had command of my voice again I looked up at Harry pleadingly and asked,

"How badly is he wounded?"

"He has a great slash from Chatterton's sword in his side. But the surgeon stopped the bleeding. Joe and I conveyed Gabriel to his home in Wales. We feared to make his wound bleed afresh so we spent five days and nights upon the road. We stayed but one night at his home and then returned here. Bess, he was alive when we left him. I came as soon as p possible to bring you the news, unwelcome as it is. I have asked his family to send word of his recovery to me here."

He did not add "or of his death" but I silently filled in the blank.

"I must go to him." The words were out of my mouth without conscious thought and I jumped to my feet. I knew I could not remain in ignorance and fear at Oxford. Harry looked at me with pity and then turned away.

"Harry, speak. If you will not help me I will ask Joe."

"Bess, I see that matters have progressed between you even further than I feared. I had hoped it was not so, but as he lay on the ground wounded, Gabriel spoke your name, nothing more.

Would you expose Joe once more to Father's wrath? That must not be. If you are determined to go to Gabriel it is I who must accompany you." He spoke almost fiercely, although he swayed with tiredness.

"My sweet brother," I replied, "Then we will set off at day break. You must rest tonight. I will take Fairy."

Harry hesitated again.

"Bess, I say I will accompany you but in truth I do not know how we may win Father's consent. The very notion is madness. Your safety on the road, the making of a long journey to the side of a man to whom you are not contracted. I will say all I can of how Gabriel saved my life. Our family is truly in his debt. Yet I know the very suggestion of you making such a journey will anger Father. He will deem it as unseemly as it is dangerous, and rightly so. Why do you smile?"

"Father and Will are away, Harry. They are gone secretly to Chadshunt to fetch away some of our hidden treasures. I do not expect their return for some days. I will leave Father a letter. He may not approve but he cannot prevent me. If there be displeasure, I will bear it on our return." Harry bit his lip but, seeing my resolve, made no further attempt to dissuade me.

"At least let the letter be from my hand Bess, not yours. I will take responsibility." My protests at this were met with,

"Consider it if you will the price of my own consent."

He spent some time composing the letter to Father while I acquainted a shocked Mistress Adams of our journey. What Harry wrote I do not know. He stroked his beard and clicked his tongue while he wrote. A final sigh was followed by him signing his name with a flourish, sanding and sealing the letter.

An hour later our preparations were done. Harry obtained a letter of safe transit for me to show to Royalist patrols if necessary. I lay down upon my bed but slept little. Every time I closed my eyes I saw Gabriel's face before me. Not smiling and healthful as I had seen him last, but pale, suffering or, worse, his eyes closed in the sleep of death.

It was only a few days Harry and I were upon the journey, but I feared we would be too late. We took byways and narrow tracks where possible, hoping to avoid rebel patrols. Striking south through Abingdon we then turned westwards. We could not take the more direct road past Gloucester, because it was held by Parliament. Yet the way across the Severn estuary might too be fraught with danger, for Parliament held Bristol. Either way held dangers, but in the interests of haste, Harry decided to try the Severn route. We crossed empty Oxfordshire downlands where the wind blew hard in our faces and tugged at our hats. Riding high along the Ridgeway, the valley floor below us, I asked Harry about the curious white markings cut in the chalk below us.

"The ancient White Horse, Bess, the figure can be seen more plainly from across the valley." Harry's attention returned to the mound known as Uffington Castle which rose above us.

"It was carved by the ancients. They made Uffington Castle too. For what purpose I know not, but it commands a view of more than one county. We must approach with caution. While we can see those who approach, we too can be seen."

No sooner had he said this than we caught sight of two horsemen above us approaching the Castle. The sun caught the glint from their muskets.

"They might be King's men?" I suggested hopefully.

"We are far from any garrison here. They are more like to be deserters, dangerous to any wayfarer."

Harry glanced at them worriedly and then at me. I could see he was desperately thinking what was the best course of action. Harry was travelling dressed as a gentleman not a soldier. He wore a thigh length dark blue embroidered cassack over his doublet in place of his usual buff coat, and a broad brimmed hat. He wore his sword openly but had two pistols concealed in his bags. I was carrying his dagger in my cloak bag, but I had little idea of how to use it.

"Do not show signs of alarm," Harry cautioned, "We will continue slowly and hope they leave us alone."

As we continued on our way at a steady trot, I heard a bellowed challenge from above us. The riders were cantering down the slope towards us. They were close enough for us to see their tattered green coats and dirty Monmouth caps but without scarves or sashes.

"Deserters, Bess, without a doubt. We must hope we can outpace them, that their horses may not be as swift as ours. Go."

Abandoning the pretence we urged our horses into a gallop. We sped down the track, heading for distant woodland where we might hope to lose them. I glanced over my shoulder as often as I dared. The men were not gaining on us but neither had we managed as yet to shake them off. Harry drew level with Fairy. He called to me but the wind whipped his words away.

"Speak more plainly," I cried.

"Dip in the track – ahead. Ride for the woods – to your left. I will draw them off. Make for the village of Bishopstone, north west of the Ridgeway – short distance. Meet me – churchyard after night fall. If I fail you, find – nearest gentleman's house – throw yourself upon his mercy."

Reluctantly I nodded. It was not the time to dispute my brother's authority over me. Our pace slowed as the track descended. We had reached the dip Harry spoke of. Harry had reined in and was delving into his bags. Temporarily hidden from our pursuers, I turned Fairy's head towards the woods, which were now close by. Not daring to look round or hesitate, I urged my mare once more into a gallop. It would be a poor return for Harry's sacrifice if I was overtaken and captured. Behind me I heard a crack from Harry's pistol and an answering deeper note from a musket.

19

Chadshunt Hall, August 1643

"DO YOU SEE the signal yet, Will?" The dark shape that was Will edged back around the broad trunk of the oak tree.

"I thought I saw a glimmer for a moment, Father but I was mistook. No, there it is now." A lantern had flashed three times from an upper window of the Hall. Now all was dark again. Sir Henry was holding the horses and the sumpter pony that they had brought to carry what they could. All three animals had sack cloth tied over their hoofs to lessen their sound.

"John Dale was to give the signal himself. If he deems it safe we may proceed, Will. We must take the horses no closer than the orchard. If we approach too close to the stables the other horses may sense their presence, giving the alarm."

Reaching the orchard they tethered their horses to the apple trees. The summer night was fine. They had chosen this night because the moon was old. A light wind was blowing the thick clouds across the sky. Sir Henry kept an anxious eye on the heavens. They needed the cloud cover to prevent a myriad of stars bringing unwelcome light.

Sword in hand, they moved cautiously towards the herb garden. Each had a pistol wedged in the folded down bucket top of his boot. These were for use as a last resort only as a pistol shot would carry far on the night air. Near the gate to the herb garden, a man emerged from the dark shape of the wall. There was a soft challenge.

"Lucie," Will gave the password and the shape resolved itself into their head game keeper Tobias.

"Master." There was a catch in Tobias's voice and he bowed his head as Sir Henry reached his side. "It is good to see you, Tobias," Sir Henry replied gruffly. "Do you keep watch?"

The man nodded. "My son Richard stands guard outside this wall on the side nearest the house. You will find Ben within the garden. He has a lantern for your use."

"The Roundhead soldiers?"

"Abed, Master Will. There are four patrolling outside the Hall, but they rarely venture this far."

Entering the herb garden, Sir Henry and Will sheathed their blades and greeted Ben softly. "Your brother Joe is become a fine trumpeter, Ben."

"My love and duty to him." He kindled a spark with flint and tinder, lighting the lantern. With Will's assistance Ben rapidly pulled aside the plants and opened the trapdoor. Will took the lantern and slid down the ladder. He glanced quickly around into the shadows.

"Is all well?" his father's whisper floated down from above.

"I believe so Father, there is no sign of disturbance." Sir Henry threw down the sack cloth bags. There was room for only one man at a time below ground. It was too small to be called a room and Will shivered, remembering that Harry had spent an entire day there effectively entombed. Following his father's instructions, Will rapidly filled the bags with plate, jewels and coin.

As they closed up the hiding place, there was a soft call from Tobias. "Someone approaches." Hastily Will extinguished the light. A moment later the gate opened and a woman slipped inside.

"Master Will, one of the soldiers heard something," said maidservant Mary. "He called out and then ran off. I believe he goes to alert the other men."

"Father, there is not time to make good our escape. If there be no more than four Roundheads patrolling, surely we may overpower them." Will was drawing his blade again.

"And what of the others, who are sleeping? They will bring down the wrath of Parliament on this house and on your cousin Celia. They will not believe her innocent," Sir Henry warned. "No Will, I have an idea."

"Halt. Show yourselves."

The glow of the slow burning match pierced the gloom. A woman giggled. The soldier raised his musket and then paused. Moving towards him from the direction of the herb garden were two figures in close embrace.

"Ben, I will go no more abroad with you after dark I swear. Now look, you have brought me shame."

A second soldier approached with a lantern, musket over his shoulder. He raised the lantern and clicked his tongue in disgust.

"One of the trollops from the house and the man who has been swiving her. Cover yourself decently wench, you too fellow." He gestured at the woman, in the act of hurriedly lacing up her bodice, and the man who was fumbling to fasten his breeches.

"It is well after curfew. You were lucky we did not shoot you. Remain within the doors after night in future."

Turning he gestured with his musket. They marched the servants back towards the house.

Bishopstone, Wiltshire, August 1643

Within minutes I was in the comforting embrace of beech trees, growing thickly about me. I knew I was now hidden from pursuit, but continued on my way as fast as my tiring mare and the thickness of the overarching boughs allowed. The summer's day was not yet advanced into evening. It was dim but not dark. Reaching the far side of the wood I saw below me nestled in the down the roofs of the village. I withdrew again into the wood's shadows, not wishing to draw attention to myself, a stranger and a woman alone. I found a small stream, where Fairy and I drank gratefully. I refilled my leather bottle. I loosened the mare's girths. Then with Fairy grazing placidly on grass which grew in thick clumps between the trees, I removed my collar and splashed water on my hot face. Beside the trickling water I listened to finches and sparrows squabbling over worms and a blackbird chirping and trilling in a nearby tree and the sound of Fairy tugging at the grass. Slowly my breathing returned to normal and my body ceased to tremble. It was peaceful.

I turned from contemplating the erratic progress of my latest leaf boat to strain my ears yet again. What was happening to Harry while I took my ease beside the stream? Was he riding unharmed towards the village by some circuitous route? Or was he stretched on the ground, somewhere on the ridge, staring at the sky while his blood mingled with the soil? The gentle murmurs of the trickling rivulet had no answers for me. The sun made its slow descent. "Meet me after nightfall," Harry had said. Surely the sun had never set so slowly, even in summer time. It seemed the day would never end, but then I realised I could see a single star winking at me. It was time to move.

I rode slowly and cautiously towards the village. The village centre was easily found, a cluster of thatched houses and a mill beside a mill pond. I avoided the inn, with its voices and welcoming lamp light. The aroma of roasting meat wafted towards me through an opened shutter and my belly rumbled. Nearby was the tower of the village church. Dismounting again I led Fairy cautiously into the darkened churchyard. The church, surrounded by a low wall, was in darkness. At last there was a creak from the churchyard gate. Peering into the gloom I saw a horse being led slowly in. It was Harry. Abandoning Fairy, I hurtled towards my brother.

"Harry you're safe. You are not hurt?"

"Safe enough Bess, just weary. I had to lead them around and about a good while. I could not risk bringing them straight here." I hugged him, breathing in the familiar mix of horse, sweat and tobacco.

"Shall we go to the inn for the night?"

He hesitated. "I think not, Bess. Those men may return. We had better not be seen here. We will rest outside the village."

And so it was that my mother's worst fears were realised. Some way beyond the village Harry and I found a sheltered hollow in the downs. We hobbled the horses and left them to graze. Supper was hard biscuit and cheese with a few handfuls of early blackberries I had picked in the woods. Then we rolled ourselves in our cloaks with a blanket apiece, the slopes above us dotted with sheep, moving like wraiths as they cropped the grass.

When the sun rose the next morning I woke to find Harry sitting beside me vigilant, pistol in hand. "Harry, you have not slept?"

"I am rested Bess, do not fear. I have stood watch many a night, one more is no hardship to me. But we should be on our way."

"I'm sorry, Harry."

"How so?"

"I nearly got you killed yesterday through my insistence on travelling to Wales."

"Whereas I myself might only achieve the same end through riding into battle." As he laughed, I realised it was some time since I had heard my brother laugh.

We rode on. There were occasions when we heard the beat of many hooves and turned aside into hedgerow or wood. If it had been left to me alone I would have ridden like Prince Maurice had from Devizes to Oxford, stopping for neither sleep nor food. Harry insisted we must rest, stopping at alehouses for a few hours snatched sleep, breaking our fast and resting the horses.

Reaching the Severn estuary we rode along the bank until we reached the ferry at Pilning. Harry swept an anxious eye over the wide brown waters. The water appeared reasonably calm, but it was not only the state of the wind and tide which worried him.

"Currents be strong, Sir. Taking you and the lady over the water now, hazardous mind. Might be rebels around too." He was eying Harry and me.

Harry dug in his purse. The ferryman pursed his lips over the silver and grudgingly nodded.

"That will do. A fine day for it Sir, now the King holds Bristol."

He chuckled at the look of shock on Harry's face.

"Fell to the King three, four days ago. You're safe enough, Cavalier."

Fairy rolled her eyes at the sight of the ferry boat. She snorted and backed. It took all my powers of persuasion and I finally had to blind fold her before she would walk on to the ferry boat. There were storm clouds above as we crossed the wide river. A sudden squall of rain ahead whipped the water into white peaks. Further north the sun streaked sudden fingers of gold across the meadows, pointing towards Gabriel's country of Breconshire. I hoped it augured well. Once in South Wales Harry was more relaxed. The country was strongly Royalist and the only cavalry patrols we saw wore red sashes. Now our path took us through flooded meadows and roads made slippery with mud.

The next day, riding through the small town of Crickhowell, we came to Gabriel's valley. Harry pointed, "Yonder is Allt yr Esgair." My weariness promptly vanished and I urged the tired Fairy into a canter down the hill.

"Steady, Bess," called Harry. "The road is wet from the constant rain."

I fought back both smile and sob, remembering Gabriel's jests about Welsh rain. We had been riding through a downpour for an hour and more, but I had taken little note of it, knowing that our destination drew near.

Approaching the estate, we rode unchallenged through an archway in a high wall onto a private road. On the side of the hill stood a castle with an imposing round tower. A fallen section of wall suggested that the castle was no longer lived in. To our left was a long barn and stable block, to our right were low ramparts. We reined in. A groom with a sack covering his shoulders braved the rain. I dismounted hastily, throwing Fairy's reins at him. The man gaped at me. He was clearly not accustomed to unknown females arriving like a whirl wind. I broke into a run, Harry pounding after me. Catching up, he marched me briskly across the lane to the imposing gatehouse where a liveried porter, evidently recognising Harry, admitted us without question.

Through the stone arch of the gatehouse and on the far side of the cobbled courtyard, surrounded on all four sides by the house, I could see the double doors to the house. These were the only things I could focus on. All else was a misty haze at the fringe of my vision. This might have been my dream of arriving at Rafe's house, so unreal did everything seem. In place of the golden afternoon and the blurred group of waiting figures of my dream were wet cobbles, grey in the falling rain, and the closed doors ahead. During our long ride I had forced myself not to dwell constantly on the probability that fever and inflammation had robbed Gabriel of his life. Now my fears flared like a bonfire on Gunpowder Treason Night. I could barely mount the steps. Harry pounded on the doors. A man servant opened them. I tried to guess from his demeanour if the house was in mourning for the heir.

"I am Elisabeth Lucie," I gasped. "Is Master Gabriel? How does he?"

From behind the man a cool female voice with a familiar lilt to it broke in with a few words in Welsh to the servant. She continued in English.

"Lieutenant Lucie, you have returned, this is most kind. And this must be your sister?"

As she came closer I could see a tall, slim and upright lady of late middle age, her hair covered by an embroidered coif. Fixing me with a somewhat quizzical gaze I immediately saw myself through her eyes. I had arrived with no attendant other than my brother. My skirts were stained with grass and mud from the roads. Rain dripped from my hat and cloak onto the floor and my boots had muddied the rush mats beneath them. I dropped the most perfunctory of curtsies.

"Mistress Vaughan," I began.

"Lady Vaughan," hissed Harry in my ear. "Lady Vaughan," I resumed hastily, "Does Gabriel live?"

She could not have missed the strain in my voice. Her eyes softened.

"He does, Mistress. And if you are the Bess whose name he has been repeating, I hope your coming will comfort him. I will take you to him, but I pray you if he sleeps do not disturb his rest."

Harry at my heels, I followed her through fine rooms which I took no heed of, up the stairs and through an open sided long gallery which overlooked the courtyard. She stopped at a panelled door and opened it gently, motioning me to wait. A moment later she slipped out again.

"He sleeps," she whispered. At this I must have looked truly forlorn for she gave me a measuring glance and then said,

"Go gently Mistress, you may look on him. His father attends him."

Leaving Harry in the gallery, I tiptoed into the darkened room. The bed curtains were half drawn. By the light of a single candle I saw Gabriel lying on his back with his eyes closed. A dark haired man who resembled him, knelt in prayer beside the bed, a string of beads in his hands.

The vision of Gabriel kneeling at the deathbed of Matthew Stanley rose before me like a nightmare. Gabriel's father raised his head, his green eyes challenging. I experienced a deep sense of shame remembering how I had recoiled then. If I loved the man, I could no longer hate his faith. There was a groan from the bed. Gabriel's eyelids fluttered open.

"Bess," he murmured, "I knew you'd come, my love," and closed them again.

ᔕ

The Allt, Crickhowell

For the next few hours Harry and I were left to wash off the grime of travel and rest in hastily prepared bed chambers. In the glass, framed by a mass of tangled hair, long descended from the confines of my coif, I saw a grimy, mud spattered, countenance. Exhaustion overcame me and I fell into a sound sleep.

The rain had stopped and the shadows were beginning to deepen on the late summer afternoon. A watery sun was making a fleeting appearance. I drew back the bed curtains and peered cautiously around the room for any indication that this was a papist house. There were no crucifixes or statues and I rebuked myself for continuing to pass judgement.

There was a light knock on the door. Harry entered and perched on the edge of the large bed. "Well, Bess," he smiled, "Are you rested? Are you a little happier now? I thought we would have broken our necks with the speed we travelled at."

I nodded. "Yes Harry. I feel relieved and will hope to see Gabriel again as soon as I am permitted. But I need guidance how to conduct myself in this house."

My brother clicked his tongue in annoyance.

"In what? Do you not know what to say to the man whose side you have dashed headlong to? Or is it his family who you fear?"

I felt the heat rising in my cheeks.

"Well Harry, it's just that you know they are pap– Catholics. Do his family know we are not?" Harry rolled his eyes.

"I spent one night only under their roof before, but I recall nothing shocking. Certainly no priest appeared to forcibly baptise me into their faith." His mouth twitched.

"Oh Harry," I said crossly, "will you not be serious?"

"Will you not be sensible?" he countered. "We are guests and will be treated as such with courtesy, the more as they must realise we are both devoted to the welfare of their son. For the rest, I imagine they will assume us to be Protestants if we do not tell them otherwise. They will be perfectly accustomed to living among us, and will no doubt be easier with you by far than you are with them. Now I believe we should pay our respects to

Gabriel's parents in proper fashion."

He stood up and prepared to leave the room.

"Harry stay," I said desperately. "There is the other matter. What will they think of what lies between their son and me?" He plumped down again on the counterpane.

"Bess, that I cannot answer. What does lie between Gabriel and you? Has he asked to wed you? If so that is a serious matter, for I feel sure he has said nothing to our father. Much as he respects Gabriel, he will never consent to you marrying a Catholic."

The heavy weight, which had lifted a little from my chest, descended again. I answered him hesitatingly as I had Will.

"Harry, Will asked me if we had an understanding. I said no, but in truth I do not know. I love him and I believe he loves me too. You witnessed our embrace in Oxford. He would have spoken I think before your departure for Devizes. I stopped him because I feared if he did he would fall in battle."

"And indeed he was wounded, for all your superstitions. But answer me honestly, Bess. Do you love this man enough to marry him, to take him with all he stands for?"

I was silent, my thoughts in turmoil. After a long pause, Harry nodded as if satisfied,

"I see you are as yet uncertain. Think well, my sister."

Feeling more dejected than I could have foreseen an hour earlier, I followed Harry downstairs. I paused to look at the family coat of arms.

"What does the family motto mean?" I asked Harry.

"Non revurtar inultus. I will not return unavenged. An ancient war cry, I should imagine."

"Indeed you are correct, Lieutenant." Sir Thomas had approached us unobserved. "An ancestor fought at Agincourt. You will see the tale on the tapestry which hangs in the Great Hall. Our family badge is also curious. You may have observed it on the livery of the servants."

He held out his hand and I saw a signet ring on his finger which resembled one Gabriel wore. The carved red stone showed the heads of three men, their necks encircled by a scarf. He gave me a light hearted smile. This reassured me more than all I had been told earlier that Gabriel would truly recover. I had seen the same small carving on Gabriel's signet ring, but the representation was too small for me to see the significance.

"But come, join us for a glass of wine and I will tell you more." In the drawing room, Sir Thomas beckoned one of the liveried servants to approach.

"Aron," he said in English, "Pray permit our visitors to examine the family badge." The man obligingly presented his shoulder.

"Oh." What I had taken for a scarf was a serpent wound around the necks of the men.

Sir Thomas laughed.

"A common reaction, Mistress. Our family claims descent from Moreiddig Warwyn. They say he was born with a serpent wrapped around his neck."

"A delightful legend, my love, but if you continue your tales of your ancestors it will be night before you are done."

Lady Vaughan smiled, her blue eyes sparkling with mischief. Formidable as she appeared on first sight, I decided that Gabriel's mother might have a softer side if I could get to know her. Lady Vaughan treated me with great kindness, although she remained reserved whenever she spoke to me directly. I felt she would not be tempted into unseemly or impulsive outbursts. For the present, a little reticence on both sides was welcome. I had no wish to cause offence or prompt unwelcome questions.

Sir Thomas Vaughan was another matter. His strong physical resemblance to his son unsettled me. His colouring, his eyes, height, even the way he held himself, all was like Gabriel. The searching way he had inspected me when I entered the bedroom too was like Gabriel. His face, when I had leisure to regard him more closely, bore lines which Gabriel's did not. Around his eyes were the crinkles of much laughter, while harsher lines about the mouth spoke of past griefs. Allowing Harry to assume the role of elder brother and chaperone, I kept my eyes demurely downcast while I sipped my wine. Sir Thomas continued to regale us with anecdotes, but I was anxious to return to Gabriel. I put down my wine glass and rose to my feet. Harry launched into a pre prepared speech.

"Sir Thomas, it is kind of you and Lady Vaughan to receive us. Your son has performed many services for our family. Most recently, he saved my life at Ramsbury, receiving his hurt as he did so. I would I may repay him one day. In the meantime I am yours to command in any service I may carry out."

He finished this graceful speech with a bow and I inwardly applauded his diplomatic abilities. I remained dumb and sank into a deep curtsey.

"Lieutenant Lucie," replied Sir Thomas "We are already indebted to you for the pains you took in returning our son to us. Were it not for your care it could have been a fatal journey. Say no more of obligations."

"Sir Thomas," I said hesitatingly, "Might I visit Gabriel again, at least if he is awake now?" I coloured, feeling the eyes of his parents on me. Sir Thomas spoke to a servant briefly in Welsh.

"He is awake, Mistress and would be happy to see you. Maybe you would like a few minutes alone?"

My heart was beating rapidly as I followed the servant back to Gabriel's room. The servant knocked, went inside for a moment and then held the door open for me. Gabriel, propped on pillows, was looking eagerly towards me. I was shocked at his appearance. He was pale beneath the tan he had acquired in the field and his eyes seemed overlarge. As he tried to move he groaned and sweat broke out on his face. I flew to his side and leaned over the bed. He peered at me with desperation in his eyes.

"Bess, it truly is you. I thought I dreamed you earlier. You have been much in my thoughts, waking and sleeping. How came you here?"

"Harry brought me," I replied, "But what of your wound?"

"I will live," he said gently, "But a sword thrust in the side and a damaged liver is not to be recommended. That I am alive is a testament to your brother's care as much as to the surgeon's skill."

"May I see how the wound heals?" I asked trembling. His mouth twisted humorously.

"Truly Bess, I think there should be a better way for a man to persuade a maid to see him unclothed, but if you really wish it."

He reached for his night shirt but I stopped him and pulled it gently up at the side. A large bandage covered him from chest to hip. It appeared fresh and there was no blood seeping through, neither was there a stench of putrefaction. This was all I could tell at present. I gently lowered it again and covered him modestly with the sheet.

"May I kiss you?" I asked softly. He held out his arms in answer. I leaned carefully over the bed and pressed my lips gently to his. "Don't move," I said sternly, and kissed him again. I pulled away reluctantly. "I love you, Gabriel Vaughan," I whispered. I took his hand and he gripped mine with surprising strength.

"I love you too, Bess Lucie," he said. "I wish though that you had not required I nearly meet my death before I was permitted to tell you." I laughed. His green eyes gazed into mine, "Will you be my lady?"

I took a deep breath and answered, "Aye, My Lord."

There was a creak and a discreet cough. I jumped guiltily, snatching my hand from Gabriel's. Sir Thomas was standing in the doorway, a wry smile on his face. He said something softly in Welsh to Gabriel, who replied briefly in the same language, a note of challenge in his voice. His father laughed, strode over to the bed and ruffled his son's hair. He turned to me.

"Mistress Lucie, will you join us for supper?"

"Of course, Sir Thomas."

Heart thumping, I curtseyed and followed him. My head was in a whirl after Gabriel's last words. The lofty Great Hall was oak panelled, but airy and light. High windows admitted as much light as possible from the rain drenched sky of early evening. One wall was almost covered by a large tapestry and a fine carpet hung on another. In spite of the summer day a coal fire was burning in the substantial hearth. The long table was covered with an expensive tablecloth which was laid with silver plates and bowls. My gaze took in the range of hot and cold dishes and I hoped our unexpected arrival had not caused panic in the kitchens. I seated myself on the edge of a padded chair next to my brother.

Nothing alarming transpired in the way of popish rites during supper, Gabriel's father saying the blessing in English before eating. I was far too excited to eat much. We talked of Gabriel's progress. Once we had assurances that the physician was confident of a good recovery, the conversation turned to our journey and ultimately to the war.

Harry's previous visit had been too brief, and Gabriel's parents too much alarmed, to acquaint them with all events. When Harry concluded with a description of his own unsuccessful fight with Major Chatterton which led to Gabriel being wounded, Sir Thomas frowned, knuckles turning white as he clutched his knife and spoon. "And does the man still live?" he asked, fixing his eyes on Harry, "For you say he has caused much injury to your family as well as to my son."

"I am uncertain, Sir. Your son wounded him in both arm and leg and I saw him fall. He had surrendered to Gabriel before dishonourably attacking him again. It is probable that he did not die, unless through fever, but he may well be our prisoner. His brother gave his word the Major would present himself at Oxford Castle if he recovers."

Sir Thomas nodded harshly. "I would know more of this man. I will be happy to hear he is no longer a threat to both our families."

The following day I was permitted to sit with Gabriel when he was awake. My care for him was limited to discourse and such tasks as assisting him to drink, his mother clearly feeling more intimate nursing unsuitable for a maid. A servant was always close by, and we had few opportunities for more embraces. Gabriel said no more of his love and, as if by common consent, nor did I. That did not prevent me being in a state of constant almost feverish excitement whenever I was with him. When Gabriel slept, I roamed the grounds of the estate by myself or with Harry.

When we met at mealtimes, Sir Thomas engaged me in easy conversation, talking of music, dogs and horses. Lady Vaughan remained polite but distant. I remembered Gabriel's telling me that his wife had felt uneasy with her mother in law. However, I also feared that Sir Thomas had overheard or seen his son's somewhat unorthodox proposal of marriage. It would be small wonder if he had acquainted his wife with it. I decided it was time I shared the news with Harry.

We were walking by a narrow stream which ran through the grounds.

"And so," I finished, "I now consider myself betrothed." Harry scrambled down the bank and began throwing pebbles into the water. He threw them savagely and a pair of water fowl flapped away in protest. I put my hand upon his arm.

"Harry," I pleaded, "Please do not say that you are angry with me. You are the one person in my family who I hoped would not oppose our union." He turned on me a look of exasperation and then, relenting, smiled at my despondent face.

"No, Bess I am not angry, but I am amazed that within hours of letting me believe you were uncertain of your feelings you accepted him. Besides, there is no contract and the objections which I mentioned before still hold. Father would not stand for it. And what does his own father say?"

ɞ

When I next visited Gabriel, he was struggling into a sitting position. The effort made him break out in a sweat. With considerable annoyance I bade him lie down and reached for the jug of buttermilk.

"Thirsty?"

"Not for that, but my mother insists it is the best drink for invalids, that and small beer. I would prefer mead. At least she has heeded the advice of our regimental surgeon to ply me with eggs and flesh to build up my strength. It is well Harry carried Master Rutherford's orders, or she would be feeding me naught but broth."

He pulled a face as he drank, then looked at me enquiringly. I was twisting the ends of my collar nervously.

"Gabriel, did your father overhear your proposal of marriage?"

He grinned ruefully,

"Enough to know how the land lies, Bess. What he has told my mother I know not. But she has eyes in her head. I believe they will not discuss our union until I am stronger. They would not risk me bursting the wound open again by fighting my father."

I laughed but cast an anxious look at his side. The physician no longer made a daily visit but there was still the risk of inflammation. He saw my glance and smiled reassuringly, taking my hand and kissing it.

"I will be well soon, I promise."

Within a few days, Gabriel's improving health was marked by the opening of his shutters to let in air and light. Dark rings shadowed his eyes and his skin was stretched tightly over his cheek bones. Realising I was staring, I forced myself to turn away and study the room. It would have been a handsome chamber, were it not for the traces of sickness. Bandages, salves and empty draughts stood by. A small table near the bed held writing materials and a book. I picked it up. "The Imitation of Christ?" I read the title out loud and looked at him for an answer.

"An old companion," Gabriel smiled, "Although it has made little enough impression on my life I fear."

I nodded and continued my survey. My attention was caught by a miniature hanging beside the fireplace. It was a boy, twelve or thirteen years old, with soft brown hair, fair skin and blue eyes. He reminded me a little of Lady Vaughan.

"My twin brother, Michael." Gabriel had noticed my gaze. His tone told me that his brother no longer lived.

"Not a very fortunate name in our family," he reflected.

"Was he killed?" I hesitated.

"Killed at Edgehill?" Gabriel finished for me. "No, he was not." Gabriel's brow wrinkled as he spoke.

"That would have been a terrible day for my parents if they had lost us both that day. `The likeness of me, from the same period, hangs in Father's study. In happier times they hung, one above the other, in Mother's chamber. After Michael died, Mother could not bear the daily reminder. So I to Father and Michael came here. He bears me company. The loss has softened a little by the passage of time. Although I do not think the death of a child ever truly leaves you."

I was silent, remembering that Gabriel too had lost a son.

"Michael was older than I by a half hour, and thus my father's heir. God and nature had surely intended him to fill that place. As you see, we did not closely resemble each other, neither in countenance nor in nature. He was tall and fair, favoured our mother. Do you recall the day in Oxford when you asked me of my name and I promised to tell you more one day? Michael and I were born on September 29th. It is the feast day of the Archangels Michael and Gabriel, Michaelmas. And thus we were so named. We were always together. Our favourite game was to play at knights of King Arthur in the old castle. As we grew older he loved to ride, hawk, hunt. Our father taught both of us to use a rapier. He was quicker on his feet than I. Always laughing. But no ear for music," he chuckled suddenly.

"What happened?" I whispered.

"It was a fine day in autumn. The sun was shining. You already know how rare those days can be here in Wales," he smiled. "We were fourteen years old, both at our books, I at my Greek, Michael at his Latin. He begged Mother to let him have a half day holiday. She could never deny him anything. I remained at my books with my tutor while Michael rode away on his pony. An hour later it came back without him, in distress. Father and a groom rode out immediately. My brother had tried to leap a tall bank with a hedge on the top. Michael's neck was broken.

I was the quiet, studious second son. I had thought to enter a French monastery. Now I was heir to my father's estates and was expected to marry. And I missed my brother. This house was so quiet somehow. I could not fill it with his voice or with his laughter, so I turned to my music to fill that void."

"And the monastery in France?"

He smiled suddenly and pulled my hand to his lips. "I do not think I was destined to be a monk."

20

I COULD NOT prevent the Lord's Day arriving to cause further disturbance to my peace of mind. Harry and I joined the Vaughans to break our fast. Lady Vaughan said casually to me,

"Mistress Bess, one of the servants will escort you and your brother to St Edmund's parish church. The vicar is a most pleasant man. As I understand you are musical, you should enjoy the organ and choir which I am told are very good." I was pleased that I had progressed to being Mistress Bess but I was uncomfortable at being reminded of the difference in our beliefs, and made no reply. Harry glared at me.

"Thank you, Lady Vaughan."

As Harry and I later crossed the courtyard towards the gatehouse with a servant, I cast a longing look upwards at the long gallery, and Gabriel's chamber. Lady Vaughan accompanied us out of the house. Her expression was calm, her posture erect as she watched our departure. I wished, not for the first time, that I could read the thoughts swirling beneath the imperturbable fine-boned countenance.

The music was as good and the vicar as pleasant as we had been promised. But I confess I spent the communion service distracted by thoughts of Gabriel and wondering idly what popish prayer might be going forward in our absence. Most of the prayers were in Welsh and it was only when the sermon began in English that I dragged my attention back to what was going forward around me.

We returned to dine with Gabriel's parents and to talk as usual of everything but of how they viewed my relations with their sole surviving son. After dinner I escaped once more to Gabriel's room.

"I think our days of private conference in this room are numbered, Bess," he said at once." My mother talks of me progressing to sitting in a chair within a few days. Once I gain strength she will become concerned for your reputation." This naturally distracted me from the questions I longed to ask. When my protests had died down a little, and I was sitting beside the bed while he held my hand, Gabriel said, "But Bess, you came bursting in. What is it love?"

I blushed, "I could not but wonder while Harry and I were at church if you also prayed and in what manner." He dropped my hand and quietly regarded me.

"My parents came to my room and we prayed together. But if you ask in what manner we prayed only to satisfy curiosity and to wonder at the strangeness, you will forgive my lack of a further reply," he said softly. "We had no priest visit today and so we were limited in which popish ceremonies we could engage in."

His words were cool and I regretted my questions and the frank inquisitiveness which had prompted them. We said no more. I longed to find a way back from this misstep, but in our conversations in the following days I could find no way to raise the matter and make amends. Although still affectionate, I feared Gabriel had withdrawn from me.

We had been at The Allt nearly a week, when Harry suggested during dinner that we go for an afternoon ride. I thought I saw a fleeting look of relief in Sir Thomas's eyes. He nodded courteously, saying he would have his head groom Twm point out the best rides to us. We set off down a lane through the wooded valley, the Brecon Beacons looming above us. Fox gloves, yellow buttercups and loosestrife grew in profusion under the trees. I picked a posy for Gabriel's room. It was quiet in the lane with only the sound of birdsong, blackbirds and thrushes. A more distant tapping suggested a woodpecker and sounds of quiet chewing came from the horses as they grazed the rich summer grass.

We started up a hill, in the hope of gaining a better view of the curious, flat topped mountain Crug Hywel, sometimes known as Table Mountain, when a Welsh shower made its sudden appearance. It was the work of a moment. Like the lowering of a curtain, the mountain tops were blotted out by mist. As I raised my hand to point this out to Harry, the mist descended upon us as heavy rain. We turned our horses' heads back to The Allt. Cantering through a steady downpour, the road beneath their hooves churned to mud as rivulets ran down the banks, becoming streams across our path.

We left our steaming horses with a surprised Twm and his stable lad. "Come, Harry before we become even wetter. This is our shortest way."

I pulled my hood well down over my head. I pushed through the small door near the gatehouse and dashed for the closest door in the north wing of the main house. To my surprise the door, which usually stood open, was bolted. The next door was also shut fast. Harry and I scurried across the slippery courtyard to the main entrance. The increasingly heavy rain had soaked through the hood of my riding cloak and was dripping down my neck. The door was shut. I knocked but no one came to answer it. Harry pounded impatiently with his fist on the wooden panels.

At length, we heard footsteps approaching. I heard bolts being drawn back before the door was opened slowly by a man servant. The steward stood behind him, his face pale and apprehensive. It cleared as he recognised us. "Ah Mistress Lucie, Lieutenant, you have returned. Forgive me, we did not expect you so soon." He bowed and turned abruptly away.

"Rhedwch! Dwedwch wrth yr offeiriad ei bod yn ddiogel i ddod allan!" he snapped to the man servant who I heard break into a run towards the kitchens and buttery. Somewhat perplexed, Harry and I hastened to our separate chambers to remove our wet clothing.

"Harry, was that servant concealing a weapon?" I muttered as we climbed the staircase.

"It looked like a pistol, Bess. Perhaps we were both mistaken. The servants here do not normally walk about the house carrying arms. Why would they?"

I went to Gabriel's room a little later with the posy in a vase. I found him seated in a padded chair beside the bed, albeit still propped against pillows. He saw the flowers and smiled. "I fear you had a wet ride, Bess."

"We were drenched. Gabriel, I was puzzled to find the doors bolted when we returned. The servants seemed upset by our early arrival, I might almost say frightened." He did not answer but reached for the despised buttermilk. I seized the jug and poured him a cup. He drank slowly. Gabriel took my hand in his.

"A Catholic priest visited this afternoon, Bess. He brought me Communion because I am sick. And he was here when you returned prematurely. That is why the doors were locked." I remained silent. Gabriel looked uncomfortable and I wondered if he was already regretting the dangerous disclosure. I kissed his hand lightly and left the room. For the first time, I realised how little I knew about the secret life of the recusant Catholics. If I wed Gabriel did it mean that I too would enter a world of locked doors and clandestine prayer?

☙

Within a few more days Gabriel was well enough to take short walks, at first within the house, later around the grounds. We roamed the old castle with its round tower, one or two gaps showing in its walls.

"Are these the scars of long ago battles?" I asked curiously. Gabriel chuckled.

"Nothing so dramatic, Bess. My ancestors cultivated a taste for a more comfortable style of living and built The Allt more than three hundred years ago. As the castle became disused, it has fallen somewhat into decay. We no longer have a use for it, although it could be made habitable again if necessary. Some of its stones were used in building the present house. My Grandfather added the hall, and my father has made modest additions to the kitchens and other offices. My family was prominent in Wales once, but our fortunes took a turn for the worst. We championed the losing side in the struggle between the houses of Lancaster and York. My ancestor was sent to kill Jasper Tudor, uncle to Henry Tudor, but was captured by him instead and beheaded. Since then, the Vaughans have been content with a quiet life, keeping apart from battles and the struggles of kings."

"Until now," I countered.

He took my hand, his green eyes gazing into mine. "This war will not last for ever Bess. I pray that when it ends the King will be secure on his throne, a wiser ruler than before."

"And what will that end be for you and me?"

"We must hope that your family and mine will be left to enjoy our former way of life in peace and prosperity."

He smiled reassuringly and strolled slowly on, having neatly side stepped the question closest to my heart, for much as I cared for our families, I had been thinking only of ourselves.

ഗ

Harry was restless and eager to return to the army. "Bess," he said one evening as we climbed the stairs with our candlesticks, "We should remain here no longer. Gabriel recovers well, but will not return to duty for several weeks. I on the other hand have overstayed what would be considered reasonable length of absence from duty. I must escort you home to Oxford without delay. No doubt Father and Will are back there and will be awaiting our return."

Two days later found me bidding Gabriel a reluctant farewell. Despite my misgivings as to the future, I shared a passionate embrace with him in the privacy of the walled garden. It left me with flushed cheeks and a burning desire for greater intimacy. Sadly, this was for the time being the stuff of my dreams, and his. Reality was a warm farewell from Sir Thomas and a friendly whilst still reserved one from Lady Vaughan.

"I thank you, Mistress Bess for your kind visit and for your care of my son. He is fortunate to have such devoted friends as you and your brother.

I wish you both Godspeed."

ᔕ

Gabriel stood watching in front of the gatehouse, his father beside him, as the little cavalcade trotted down the lane and under the archway leading to the high road to Crickhowell. Once, Bess turned in her saddle and Gabriel raised a hand in farewell. As they turned back towards the house, Sir Thomas put an arm about Gabriel's shoulders.

"My son," he said softly, "I would see you happy again, but think well on what you do. That is all I ask."

"Father, I will," promised Gabriel. He returned to his chamber to read and think. A little later he was approaching his father's study as his mother stood in the doorway.

"Our son recovers well." His father's voice was cheerful. "I think the cure began with Mistress Lucie's arrival."

"She has assisted for certain, but I think our physician must also take credit." His mother's words were sharp. Catching sight of her son she said no more.

Gabriel was no longer willing to stay abed in the mornings. Each day he woke feeling his energy returning. Stretching his limbs he revelled in his returning strength. His sword hung in its scabbard on a hook, undisturbed since he had sheathed it after the near fatal fight with Major Chatterton. He hefted it experimentally. It felt heavy in his hand. The close connection forged in many months of drill and battle had been broken. He resolved to practice as soon as possible.

It was easier to deal with matters of returning his body to the health and strength a soldier required than it was to resolve his feelings about Bess. His mind turned continually to her and to all the events of the past months. It brought him as much disquiet as joy.

His parents had questioned him little during his long period of recovery. Now he grew strong enough for modest exercise they began to enquire about his experiences, although not about Bess.

"I would follow Prince Rupert anywhere," he said, "He is a truly inspiring commander, but he does not place enough importance on discipline," he went on with exasperation. "And Prince Rupert is not the only commander who pays little heed to discipline. When we were in Devizes the men were left to while away the time with drink. For that I blame the commanders, all the commanders. The horse and foot were at each others' throats after an ale or two. I stopped a bloody nose or worse myself when I came upon their wrangling. It happens often enough in Oxford."

Of the sickness in Oxford he said only that one of his comrades had died and that he had helped to nurse another back to health. Of course, at this his mother had protested, "Gabriel did you not do enough as a Captain that you should also expose yourself to sickness unnecessarily."

"Alice, my dear," said his father, "We must trust in God to protect him. Our son must do what seems right to him, even where it takes him into danger."

Gabriel talked of occasions when his men had picked up people acting suspiciously. "There was one notable occasion when a maid essayed to enter the city at night," he chuckled. "She posed as her groom's younger brother. My men detected her disguise immediately and thought her a spy. However when they brought her to me it was none other than Mistress Lucie, taking desperate measures to join her family."

Lady Vaughan looked shocked and clicked her tongue in disapproval. "But how came she there in such a manner? Could not her father or brothers have arranged a more suitable mode of travel?"

"There was no time to seek her father's approval. Her decision to travel garbed as a man was I believe entirely her own notion." His mouth twitched as he recollected with appreciation how the male garments had clung damply to Bess's form.

Sir Thomas smiled, "I'll warrant that gave her father a fine surprise when she arrived in boots and breeches."

"My dear," said his wife, "Such unseemly behaviour in a maid. I would not like any daughter of mine to behave thus."

"No more did Sir Henry," said Gabriel ruefully. "She smarted for it the next day."

"A valiant lass," chuckled Sir Thomas.

But Gabriel was no longer listening. The laughter had left his face as he reflected uncomfortably on the harsh beating Bess had received for her disobedience. If her father had reacted thus at her fleeing to Oxford to join her own family, what would he have to say to her sojourn in Wales at the home of another man? He could only hope that Harry would be able to protect her.

ꟹ

Oxford, August 1643

Our return to Oxford was in a more leisurely fashion than we had left it. As need for haste was past, I did not quibble at Harry's detours around rebel held Gloucester or his choice of byways and lanes to lessen our chances of further meetings with enemy patrols. We spent most nights in village alehouses. On approaching a likely village each evening, Harry would bid me remain in a wood or copse beyond the boundaries of the village until he had checked for the presence of enemy soldiers and found a respectable looking alehouse.

My spirits however were nearly as low as when I had left Oxford many days earlier. While relieved about Gabriel's recovery, I was less optimistic as to how we could be together. His parents, his home, the differences of faith between us had taken on a visible form, threatening to blot out the happy memory of his declaration of love.

I was at least relieved of one remaining cause of agitation when we returned. As we approached the Adams house, Will emerged. He was safely returned from Chadshunt.

"Will," Harry hailed. Will glanced round. His face filled with joy but by the time he was at our side he was looking sour. He embraced us both and then stepped back, focussing his attention on Harry. "You had better pay your respects to Father without delay. How he will receive you I cannot say, but I would hear him out in silence, remembering your duty to him." He paused.

"And Captain Vaughan, does he recover well?" His words were abrupt and formal. It was Harry who answered,

"Gabriel was severely wounded but he hopes to return to his duties before many more weeks have passed."

"I am pleased to hear it," Will's voice remained cool. "It would be best Harry if you see Father alone. I will take Bess to rest elsewhere while you converse."

Harry nodded stiffly and climbed the steps to the house. Will pulled my hand through his arm and bore me as rapidly down the street as the crowds would permit. He said nothing until we turned from the Corn Market into the bustling courtyard of the Golden Cross Inn, a large coaching inn much frequented by courtiers and officers.

"Now, Bess, I imagine you are in need of refreshment." He summoned one of the scurrying inn servants and engaged a private room. Within a few minutes I was seated in a comfortable chair at a table in an upstairs chamber while servants brought water for me to wash and steaming plates of roast lamb, cabbage and fresh bread. It was close to evening. I was tempted to lie down upon the curtained bed, but feared if I did I would sleep until morning. Harry and I had been riding all day once again with little respite and

I had not eaten for many hours. I fell upon the food with my usual hearty and unladylike appetite. Will ate little but sat back in his chair and swirled the wine around his goblet.

At last, my hunger abated, I wiped my mouth and sighed,

"Well, what is it Will? I imagine Father was enraged when he discovered our absence. Is that why you are uncommunicative and why Gabriel has become Captain Vaughan to you?"

Will chewed a finger nail and frowned.

"Father was indeed most vexed at your journey. He is naturally grateful to Captain Vaughan for saving Harry however. I did not seek to mar that gratitude by any unwise disclosure concerning your relations with him, much less his recusancy. All his rage is now directed at Harry, who took upon himself the entire responsibility for your reckless journey. It was gallant of our brother, for I imagine the idea originated with you. Did it not?"

"It did, Will. I could not remain here in uncertainty. Harry saw that and it took little persuasion."

"In other words you were determined to have your way as always. Good Christ, Bess, when will you understand you are subject to Father's commands until you are wed? I have told you before I would rescue you no more from your rashness and disobedience. Now you embroil Harry in your foolishness."

"Father will not whip him will he?" my voice trembled. Will snorted in amusement.

"I imagine not, Bess. Harry is a grown man, not a servant or a wife to be beaten at Father's pleasure. He will feel the lash of Father's tongue, no more."

At nightfall, I accompanied Will once more to the house. Father received me stiffly as I curtseyed to him but only said, "I am glad you are returned safely, Bess." Harry was not to be seen and I realised he had already left the house.

After two days when Harry did not cross our threshold, I persuaded Will to take me to Harry's lodgings and leave me alone with our brother. Harry was polishing his armour without much enthusiasm.

"Harry," I hugged him. He sighed and patted my shoulder, returning to his polishing.

"I am sorry, Harry, it is my fault Father is angry with you." He smiled reluctantly.

"I am not a child, Bess. I could have refused to take you to Gabriel. The decision was mine. I follow my own path now. It may not always be that of Father." His hand clenched the rag he held.

"Harry, he has not disinherited you?"

He looked surprised. "I think not, Bess. But indeed if he were to do so it matters not at present. For what inheritance can Will or I claim? What dowry for you?"

At mention of a dowry his face clouded further and an awkward silence fell. I kissed Harry and left him to his thoughts.

ও

The Allt, September 1643

A week after Bess's departure, Gabriel attempted a short ride around the estate. His wound had knitted together well, but as he climbed gingerly into the saddle, pain shot through his side. Gritting his teeth, he urged the horse into a gentle canter. He rode for less than an hour but by the time he returned he was white faced and sweating. His mother met him anxiously,

"My son, you undertake too much too soon. You need more rest."

Sir Thomas looked at Gabriel and shook his head but said nothing. Gabriel withdrew to his room and winced as he lay down. The day after Gabriel's overambitious attempt, his mother said, "The Hendersons are to dine with us on the morrow. And they will be content to see you mending, Gabriel," she said, stroking his hair affectionately. "They have not seen you for a year and more. I believe you have not seen them since," she broke off.

"Since the deaths of Catherine and Michael," Gabriel finished for her sombrely, "But I will be glad to see them again. How does my old friend Elspeth? Was she not to wed last year?"

"She was," said his mother, "But unhappily the match did not take place, for the young man died of an ague." There was a pause. "And now," she continued, "She is 21 or maybe 22 summers old and she lives still with her parents. I hope you will wear your new doublet, Gabriel. The army may not mind its officers wearing old and faded clothes but they have no place at table in our hall when we have guests." And with that pronouncement she swept out of the Great Hall.

ও

The next day Gabriel, wearing a new green velvet doublet in deference to the visitors and his mother's wishes, watched as their carriage drew up outside the gatehouse. Elspeth jumped down as soon as the step was let down, followed more slowly by her parents. She wore a large blue hat over her coif, which she removed now, brushing impatiently at a blonde curl which had escaped. She skipped towards Gabriel, smiling widely.

"Gabe."

He laughed, "It's a long time since anyone called me that. How do you, Elspeth?"

"And what do your soldiers call you?" she said dimpling.

"Sir," he smiled, "Or Captain."

"Captain! I was not aware. "

"Well, it matters little now," he sighed, "Whether I retain that rank remains to be seen."

"Hmm," she surveyed him critically. "You look a little older, and I think I see a grey hair. You hold yourself more stiffly than in the past, but I feel sure that is due to your wound and may pass." She made a circle of him, tapping her chin in thought.

"You are thinner and paler than I like to see, and your hair is sadly neglected. Is this how a veteran of the war should look?"

"Elspeth," interrupted her father, a handsome man of modest height who was dressed in deep red velvet. "Your tongue runs on sadly, child. Have you quite forgotten your manners? Pay your respects to Sir Thomas and Lady Vaughan." Elspeth laughed and curtsied prettily to them.

"It is so many months since I saw Gabe I forget myself. Would you forgive me if I take him for a walk in the gardens before we go in? It is a beautiful September day and I should like to see how the hedges grow in the circular garden."

Gabriel smiled at her. "Then come, do not stand on ceremony."

As they sauntered slowly towards the garden, Elspeth looked at him more seriously. "I am so sorry you were wounded, Gabe. Are you in much pain still?"

"I hope to be able to fight again before many more weeks are past," he said. "The pain is no longer bad, although I cannot yet comfortably sit a horse. I will return to Oxford and the army before September draws to a close."

They had passed into the circular garden and she found a sheltered bench to sit on. Gabriel seated himself beside her. "You wish to ask me something further?" he said, regarding her intently. Elspeth hesitated, running the brim of her hat through her fingers.

"Gabriel, you have suffered much the last year and more. I do wonder if the King has not required too much of you. Would you not prefer a little peace? Could you not now leave it to others to take up the sword? My dear friend, I would have you preserve your life and liberty."

Gabriel got to his feet. He offered Elspeth his arm and they strolled out of the garden and across the brook in the direction of the castle. After a long silence he said, "You speak nothing but the truth Elspeth. My life has not been easy in recent times.

I truly long for peace, but if the King should lose the war, there will I fear be little peace for those who have supported him, and for Catholics like your family and mine there may be worse times ahead. At least our houses are no longer searched at dawn by armed men hunting our priests. If the Puritans were in power this would change for the worse. Do not forget that when the King recalled Parliament in 1640 one of the first things they demanded was the rigorous application of the existing penal laws against Catholics. As we know to our personal cost."

They turned their steps towards the house. Elspeth was quiet and finally Gabriel turned to her once more. "I fear to offend you Elspeth by asking, but to what end do you visit today? I think there is something in the wind."

She stooped to brush a leaf from her petticoats, and then made a slight adjustment to her boot. Gabriel continued to regard her, waiting for her to speak.

"Why, for me a visit to an old friend surely, to see how he fares. But I fear for your mother and mine there is more. I think they begin once more to plot an alliance between our families. You know that the man I was to marry…"

"Yes," he pressed her hand.

"And you being a widower now," she hedged.

Gabriel gave an exclamation of impatience. "I am sorry if my plain words offend you, Gabe."

He frowned and sighed. "Not you Elspeth. You are as dear as a sister to me and have been these many years. But my mother …. You should know Elspeth that I am in love. We are not yet formally betrothed but I love her as she does me. Although why anyone should acquiesce to tie their fortunes to mine is a mystery."

She regarded him with a puzzled frown, "Lady Vaughan is not content? Who is the lady?"

He looked at her with a rueful smile. "Her name is Bess Lucie, daughter of Sir Henry Lucie. Her brother Harry fought at Edgehill and we were imprisoned together. He has been Lieutenant in my troop since May."

"What is your mother's objection?"

"Her family is Protestant," Gabriel replied gloomily.

As the Hendersons' coach clattered away down the lane, Lady Vaughan turned fondly to her son. "Gabriel, did you not think dear Elspeth looked very well today?"

"She did," agreed Gabriel quietly.

"I have been thinking," she continued, as they strolled back towards the house, her hand on his arm, "if your father and I might not prevail upon you to quit the army and settle down. Dear as poor Catherine remains in your memory, you should think again about an heir to the Vaughan name."

Gabriel stopped where he was and his colour rose. "Madam," he said formally, "No one holds the future of this family and our estates in greater importance than do I. But this war is not yet at an end. Mother, I must continue to fight. The Parliament would suppress our faith for all time. With this king I do not say we have hope of redress against the laws, or freedom of worship, but his heart is not in persecution. He loves his Catholic Queen too well. If you wish for your grandchildren to be brought up Catholic, pray that the King wins this war and not the Puritans who control the Parliament. As soon as I am whole, I leave again for Oxford. And Mother," he finished softly, "I pray you make me no matches. I love dear Elspeth as a sister. But there is only one Elisabeth who I wish to marry. And her name is Bess."

He raised his mother's hand to his lips and marched away, but not before he heard his father saying, "There Alice, I counselled you that meddling with our son's affections would come to naught." He did not hear his mother's reply.

ഗ

By mid September, Gabriel was feeling sufficiently strong that he could no longer justify in his own mind remaining in Wales. Sir Thomas was watching as he returned from a canter around the estate. "Well my boy, how does that feel?" he asked as Gabriel slid to the ground, still a little stiffly.

"I will do well now, Sir," Gabriel smiled reassuringly. "My wound rarely pains me now and I can ride with no discomfort. It is time I return to the army."

"Ah," said his father, "well then, return you must. You have nothing to detain you here." He said the last word with a delicate inflexion which made it a question.

Gabriel shook his head firmly. "Nothing, Father."

Gabriel strolled through the stables with the head groom. "I need a steady horse, Twm," he said. "And," he added ruefully, "One with smooth enough paces that will not jar me unnecessarily these next few weeks." The groom pointed to a well muscled bay gelding at the end of the row, placidly munching hay.

"I would take Blackbird, Master Gabriel. Steady as anything, he is." Gabriel eyed his broad back and strong hind quarters.

"I will try his paces. Is he fit enough to go all day?"

"Aye, Master Gabriel," the man said confidently.

Gabriel rode Blackbird around the yard and then out for a short ride around the park. He was satisfied. He reflected with a sigh that the war was depleting his father's stables of his best horses. He had lost his first horse at Edgehill and his second had been left behind at Ramsbury in the aftermath of his wound. He thought of Bess's attachment to Fairy, then dragged his mind away from her with an effort.

"We will need to ready him for battle, Twm."

The next day they commenced with the groom discharging a pistol at a distance, while Blackbird munched on a bucket of oats. The horse tossed his head but showed no alarm. They spent some time discharging the pistol progressively closer.

"Fetch Huw," Gabriel said," We need more sound of fire."

The gamekeeper arrived grinning and carrying two long fowling pieces. He was followed by Sir Thomas.

"I suppose you will be requiring the huntsman's attendance shortly," Sir Thomas said drily.

"I will, thankyou Father,"

Gabriel's tone was preoccupied. He cantered slowly in circles in the park while the men loaded the guns with powder charges and fired them repeatedly. Finally, Gabriel loaded his own pistols with powder, and discharged them at a gallop. He turned the horse and trotted back to the men grinning.

"Faster than I am like to ride him while giving fire. If I attempt firing a pistol at speed I am more in danger of hitting the horse beside me or one of my own men than I am the enemy."

For the next week, horse and rider trained intensively. Gabriel was intent on restoring his own fitness for combat while he accustomed Blackbird in the limited time available to the manoeuvres demanded of a cavalry horse.

Strolling into the park towards the end of the week, Sir Thomas watched a little wistfully at the returning vigour in the movements of his son as Gabriel swung himself into the saddle once again. A row of lifesized straw figures swung in the breeze. Gabriel trotted away from the figures until he was a hundred paces or more from them. He reined in, then spurred the horse into a canter. As horse and rider sped across the grass, Gabriel drew his sword in a fluid movement. He charged the swinging figures without slowing. Sir Thomas saw a blur of movement and one of the figures had lost a straw limb. Using only his legs, Gabriel wheeled the horse and the blade flashed out again. A second straw manikin collapsed to the ground, straw torso parted from the head, bouncing on the rope which still tethered it to the branch.

As Gabriel climbed the steps into the house later, whistling, his father met him in the entry.

"I thought to have raised a scholar and a monk in you, my son. But I perceive I was wrong. I seem to have raised a warrior. Non revurtar inultus."

Gabriel glanced at his father in surprise. Sir Thomas was smiling, but Gabriel saw the lingering sadness in his eyes.

ထ

On the eve of his departure, Gabriel rode around the estate with his father visiting the tenants. Many he had not yet had a chance to visit and there were clucks of disappointment from the women folk when they learned he was again about to leave for the war.

"Why can't you stay home and take another wife, Master Gabriel?" said one elderly farmer's wife. She had known him since he was in smocks.

"Plenty of girls would have a handsome man like you with that flowing dark hair and those green eyes like a cat." Gabriel laughed,

"Nay, Goodwife Morgan, the lasses will be looking for younger men than I, who am now twenty six summers old."

"Goodwife Morgan, is it now, young master?" she replied, "Megan you called me when you were no taller than my knee. Remember when you climbed that apple tree yonder and fell from a branch upon your head? You gave such a bellow I thought it was a demon come from hell."

Gabriel laughed and bowed ceremoniously. They went on their way through fields now bare following the harvest which had been gathered in while Gabriel was recovering.

"And the harvest was a good one, Father?"

"Aye Gabriel, I wish you might stay another week and join us for the harvest supper, but I know you feel you may not linger. Thanks be to God the barley, wheat and oats all did well. And our flocks on the hill farms all thrive. Your mother will give you a good fleece to take with you. And no trouble as yet from the Committee for Sequestration in these parts looking to confiscate our flocks or rents for our support of the King and add to our woes. Parliament has few supporters in most of Wales."

Gabriel nodded. "We must be grateful for that. With God's help the King will win the war. But Father, an enemy army when it loots or even on the march is not something to be encountered lightly. What will you do if a rebel army should come to The Allt?"

"That is not very likely, Gabriel. Besides the house is strong enough," Sir Thomas protested. "Our ancestors built it as a fortified manor, to withstand an army."

"Our ancestors built the house to impress exalted visitors Father, not to repel a hostile force. There are arrow slits and ramparts to be sure, but they were designed for show, nothing more. Besides, an army these days has muskets, not arrows, ordnance too. A culverin or saker, even a smaller gun like a falconet, would soon make a breach in the house walls. The wall around the park is low. Truly Father, the house cannot be defended."

Months of reviewing and building the defences at Oxford had given him hard won insights the peace loving Sir Thomas had never had to gain. Sir Thomas looked gloomy. Gabriel was disquieted as it had been no part of his intentions to add to his father's worries.

"What counsel then do you offer me, my son?" Gabriel and his father locked eyes, both aware with a shock that this was probably the first time the father had asked the son for advice on a matter of note.

Gabriel answered readily enough, for he had had much time for reflection while confined to his bed. "I would fortify the old castle, Father. Begin now, the gaps in the walls are not so many they cannot be mended. The harvest gathered in, the men will have time on their hands before the winter sets in, the women too. In Oxford both men and women labour to build the defences. If the rebels ride down the valley you may then withdraw for refuge into the castle. Do not remain within the house itself. A sacked house in flames is a terrible sight. I saw too many houses burn like torches in Birmingham. In fact I fired houses myself," he admitted. There was a heavy silence.

"Then may God forgive you, Gabriel," said Sir Thomas, "For you would not have done such a thing lightly."

"I pray He will, Father," said Gabriel soberly, "I have slain men in battle who would else have slain me, but the deaths of the women and children of Birmingham rest heavy on my conscience."

That evening Gabriel strove to cheer his parents by playing sweet tunes on his lute and singing in his clear tenor voice. He finished with "Oh silver is the moon" and "When maids go a wooing".

"My own compositions," he smiled, "But they are better with two voices."

"Excellently played," his father applauded, "Did you not say you wrote these songs for Master Lucie and his sister?"

A shadow crossed Gabriel's face. "Yes, indeed," he said quickly, "Well I must go to bed. I have a long ride tomorrow."

Gabriel went to his bedchamber, but instead of undressing, he pulled out a letter from a drawer and stared at it.

"My dear Bess," it began, "I have thought much of you and your sweet face since you left with Harry to return to Oxford. My love for you is strong, and my body burns to be united with you. But I cannot forget the expression on your face when you first saw me at prayer. Nor that Sunday at The Allt when you asked in what manner I had prayed with something between detachment and avid curiosity. You must have realised that it opened a gulf between us. In these intervening weeks I have been unable to fill it, even while the memory of your parting kisses lingers on my lips.

If you truly wanted to know more of my faith you had only to ask me, but you have not shown any inclination to do so. My father has asked me to think on what I do. I must honour that."

The letter was unfinished. He had neither had the heart to finish nor despatch it to her. Yet it reflected his thoughts and fears. He left his room and paced up and down the gallery to calm himself. The moon shone through the wide gaps in the side which lay open to the elements. He stared at the moon, cold and remote. It would shine on, whatever happened in his affairs or the affairs of men. He stopped and tried to pray for guidance, but the words would not come. He must make his own decision. To continue in the present state of uncertainty and with a half commitment was dishonourable to him and unfair to Bess.

Slowly, Gabriel reentered his chamber and picked up the letter. He reached for ink, for a pen. He brought the candle closer and he began to write.

21

GABRIEL'S CLOAK BAGS were packed and there was little else remaining to do the next morning but break his fast and take leave of his parents. His sword hung by his side, but he wore neither buff coat nor anything else which would identify him as an army officer. This was partly due to the sad state of those garments which had been blood stained, lousy and torn by the time of his arrival home, partly for safety. A private gentleman riding alone would attract less attention if he should encounter a troop of enemy soldiers. His father had wanted to send his servant Ieuan with him again but this time he refused.

"If I cannot make shift to defend myself by now Father, it would be unfair to expect Ieuan to perform that office for me. And in Oxford I may hire a servant, as I have done before. Now I must take my leave."

Gabriel knelt before his father for his blessing. Sir Thomas felt there were matters troubling his son. He looked at Gabriel searchingly but no further words passed between them. A few minutes later Gabriel had mounted Blackbird and The Allt was left behind him.

∽

Oxford, September 1643

Though I no longer feared for his life, Gabriel provided ready sources of agitation once my mind was easy over Father and Will. Try as I might to blot out the memory by dwelling on his kisses, I was haunted by the expression on Gabriel's face as he said, "We were limited in which popish ceremonies we could engage in".

I had been brought up to dislike, mistrust and even fear papists. My old nurse had frightened me when small with stories of Bloody Mary and the Gunpowder Plot. Now I came to question for the first time why Catholics were still to be feared and hated. The pope remained a shadowy and distant figure. But Gabriel and his family were flesh and blood.

I did not dare share these thoughts with my father or Will. To Harry then I hesitatingly revealed the change in my views. "Harry," I ventured one evening as he strummed his lute. "Why are there still English laws against Catholics who are otherwise loyal and law abiding? It is becoming a mystery to me."

Harry stopped his strumming and regarded me with pain in his eyes. "And does Gabriel now teach you to question our Church and our laws?"

"Harry," I snapped, "He has done no such thing. But how can I continue to acquiesce in such treatment of the family of the man I love, a man who you may remember has spilled his own blood to keep the lawful king upon the throne? And," I added a little reproachfully, "Who is even now sick with a wound he received defending you."

"Bess," Harry said thoughtfully, "You let your love for Gabriel blind you. Have you forgotten the past and Bloody Mary? Have you forgotten the Gunpowder Plot? I have told you it is a serious matter, your feelings for Gabriel. I will always be grateful to him and count him as a friend. How could I not? I owe him my life. But I do not see a path for you and Gabriel through this maze of difficulties. We can only hope that his services to our family may in time reconcile our father to your love."

He laid down the lute and wished me goodnight, leaving me despondent. Harry spoke only truth. Since King Charles had married his Catholic Queen, the prejudice against Catholics in the realm had intensified, the flames fanned both by the hated presence at court of Catholics and priests, and by the King's reluctance to enforce England's laws against them with any consistency.

I slept little that night, meditating on Harry's words. My love for Gabriel had indeed blinded me to one reality. As things stood in England between our two churches I did not think we would be permitted to marry, whatever the views of our parents. It was a long and painful wait over the next few weeks for Gabriel to return. I jumped guiltily whenever he was mentioned until Will said to me, "Whatever is the matter with you, Bess? You grow paler day by day and your spirits seem very low. I believe the air of Oxford no longer agrees with you, since your return from Wales."

"I am well, brother," I answered shortly and picked up my sewing, affecting an air of nonchalance. In private I kept picking up my prayer book, hoping it might provide a solution and then putting it down again discouraged. Finally, I asked Mistress Adams if she had a bible I might borrow. I carried it away and opened it eagerly, turning from place to place. Finally I found the signpost I sought.

ꕥ

Oxford, 26 September 1643

Gabriel arrived in Oxford on a cool September morning. Autumn had set in with a sudden chilly blast. Most of the cavalry regiments including his own had just returned to Oxford after a great battle at Newbury, where the fighting had been intense and losses heavy. Sir John Byron welcomed him warmly, relieved to have an experienced captain return. The regiment had been at the centre of the fierce fighting and had lost many men, including the King's Secretary of State, Viscount Falkland, who had been fighting as a volunteer with them that day.

As Gabriel had expected, his former billet was occupied by another officer. After some thought, he settled on a small cottage not far outside the north gate. It would be a short ride only and would repay his efforts with greater space. And privacy he added to himself.

Within an hour, Gabriel entered a nearby tavern in search of refreshment. He was settled into his new lodgings. He had engaged a maid servant from nearby for household tasks and found a man to look after Blackbird.

"Gabriel!" It was Harry. "Sir, I mean," he corrected himself. "You are returned. May I take you to my sister? Or will I tell her of your return?"

Gabriel hesitated. With constraint he said,

"No, thank you, Lieutenant. I have much to do today. Would you be kind enough to deliver this letter to her?" He retrieved a letter from his purse and held it out. As Harry accepted the letter, Gabriel avoided meeting his eye.

"Let us share a jug of ale while you tell me more of the fight at Newbury. I am thankful you are returned unharmed, Harry." Gabriel said with forced cheerfulness.

"We suffered losses, and we could not win the field. We withdrew, as did the enemy," Harry buried his face morosely in his tankard and seemed disinclined to say more. They sat in silence amidst the hubbub of the taproom, Gabriel's unwillingness to visit Bess an unspoken hindrance to further conversation. Ill at ease, Gabriel rose to leave after draining his own tankard. As he bade Harry farewell, a thought struck him.

"What of Chatterton? Did he keep faith by rendering himself a prisoner?"

"He did not. I made enquiry at the castle some days past. Nothing has been heard of him. If he be not dead from his wound, then he has broken his parole."

"I feared as much," Gabriel muttered, "But you had scant choice in leaving him behind."

ᘛ

When Harry visited the house in High Street that evening, he was looking perplexed.

"Is something wrong, Harry?" Glancing up from the hemming of his new shirt, I took my scissors and cut the thread. Harry glanced sideways at Father, reading and puffing on his clay pipe.

"Captain Vaughan is back in Oxford." Father raised his eyes from his book and frowned but said nothing.

"Is he, is he well?" I felt absurdly self-conscious.

"Well enough." There was definitely something strange in Harry's manner. "How is the progress on my shirt, Bess?" Harry approached to inspect my sewing.

"Is Gabriel below?" I mouthed at him. Harry gave a tiny shake of his head and surreptitiously handed me a letter. I slipped it into my sleeve and ran downstairs to the garden. It was growing dark and the first drops of rain were falling as I broke the Vaughan seal and strained my eyes to make out the words.

"...If you truly wanted to know more of my faith you had only to ask me, but you have not shown any inclination to do so. My father has asked me to think on what I do. I must honour that. I believe it would be best for both of us if we agree to meet no more. My love for you will only grow stronger and it will make the parting more painful, for part we must. We cannot marry, Bess and I was very wrong to ask you to wed me. You are of a different faith, while mine is outlawed and I will not abandon it. The law forbids us to wed and your Father would be of the same mind, did he realise our feelings for each other.

"Farewell, My Lady. I will always love you, but I pray that you at least will find happiness in the future. Forgive me.

"Your faithful and obedient servant, Gabriel Vaughan.

"Post script please keep my music, I hope the time will come again when you will be able to enjoy it and remember me without pain."

It was worse, far worse than I had feared. I had to speak to Gabriel. Harry took one look at my wan face and must have realised what the letter contained.

"Where is he?" I whispered. Harry shrugged his shoulders, regarding me apprehensively.

"It is too late tonight to go forth," he muttered. I went to my closet to think and to face a night of lying sleepless upon my bed.

ᔕ

Gabriel returned hastily to his new lodgings to prepare before he returned to duty. The servant had prepared him a simple meal. He ate a little, then threw himself on the bed and tried to rest, but Bess's face rose before him. "Forgive me, Bess," he murmured and then fell to his knees and tried to pray. For once there was no comfort there. He was angry with himself for not having the courage to see Bess face to face. The prospects for a happy outcome to their love had never been promising, given the obstacles. He should not have told her how he felt about her. Now he had made her doubly wretched by offering her marriage and then abandoning her. Why had he come back to Oxford at all he asked himself? Once he had delivered that letter to Harry, there was no longer any future for him in the city.

The night was wet. Gabriel, huddled in his cloak, forced himself to do one round after another of the defences. The rain fell heavily, soaking him to the skin, but for once he made no attempt to shelter from its relentless downpour.

When morning came, Gabriel returned to his small cottage and looked about him bleakly. During the night he had come to a decision as he rode through the rain. He could remain no longer in Oxford where, even should he not encounter Bess, Harry would be a constant reminder to him. Yet he could not return to Wales. He had vowed to himself to fight for the King as long as it was necessary. Gabriel resolved to apply to be released from Byron's regiment so that he might join the Earl of Newcastle's northern forces who were besieging Hull. He would fight once more. And if he died in battle so much the better, for he would no longer have to endure the reproaches of his conscience and the renewed pain of loss.

Gabriel went to the command post in search of Sir John Byron to request release from the Oxford garrison. Being told his Colonel was expected back later that morning, Gabriel turned his steps into the High Street. He had not gone very far when he heard, "Gabriel, wait." It was Bess, her face wan and pale from lack of sleep. He looked at her wretchedly.

"Gabriel, I was seeking you. Harry gave me your letter."

"Then you have surely read it. What more is there to say?"

he said hoarsely. They turned their steps towards the busy corn market. It was a market day and they were forced to make their way through crowds of servants and townswomen loudly bargaining for cheeses, poultry or pots and pans. Bess clung to Gabriel's arm and eventually they found a quieter corner in an alley way. "Speak then," said Gabriel sadly. He gently removed her hand from his arm, turning his head away from her.

Bess took a deep breath,

"It is I who should ask you for forgiveness. I have been blind and ignorant, small wonder that you felt a gulf between us. You are right that being of different faiths we cannot wed."

He nodded sadly, "Then sobeit. Farewell."

"Gabriel," Bess's voice rose in exasperation, "You must listen to me. I too have been tormented while you were away but I had come to a decision I would tell you of." A little shyly she took hold of his hands and looked up at him. Puzzled, he reluctantly returned her gaze.

"Don't urge me to leave you or to turn back from you. Where you go I will go, and where you stay I will stay. Your people will be my people and your God my God. Where you die I will die, and there I will be buried."

Gabriel stared at Bess in silence, open mouthed. She turned a rosy pink and said uncertainly, "Are you not acquainted with the story of Ruth from the Bible?" He nodded. She looked relieved.

"Bess," he said, "You propose to turn papist on my account. You cannot be serious." She laughed shakily.

They turned to walk on, Bess now clinging tightly to Gabriel's arm. Gabriel's thoughts were in a joyful tangle. "My love, think well on what you promise. You will be joining a faith which is illegal in this country, and which most of the population abhors. Our priests are subject to imprisonment and death if they are taken within the realm. I do not even know for certain when I can find one to marry us. You should also realise that my family estates, should Parliament win the war, could be considered doubly forfeit, as the estates of a family which is both Royalist and papist. We may be left with nothing."

She shook her head. "Remember my own father is like to lose his own estates through the sequestration. We may yet be paupers together."

His only answer was to pull her swiftly into an alleyway and kiss her fervently. Her hood fell back from her face. Bess returned the kiss enthusiastically. Two fighting cats, a group of ragged children and a beggar woman of indeterminate age stopped to watch with interest. "A silver penny for my children, kind Sir. Health and fortune to you and your fair lady."

Gabriel laughed and flicked a penny at the woman. She caught it neatly and bit it as they turned back into the street, dodging the circling urchins who were now attempting to reach Gabriel's purse. "Off with you now." He aimed a kick at a scrawny backside and the boy skipped smartly away.

Gabriel reached to pull her hand through his arm once more, but Bess hesitated. "I must return before I am missed from the house. Gabriel, are you on duty tomorrow night?"

"Tonight yes," he said, "Not the next."

"Then pray visit me," she whispered, "for my father rides to Woodstock and will not be back. I will expect you for supper."

He kissed her hand.

"In the meantime I will speak to my colonel, for I fear I must again take my leave and briefly return to my home. I would obtain my father's consent to our marriage. I feel sure he will not withhold it."

"Now, you mean," she replied drily.

ও

The palms of my hands were damp with sweat as I twisted them together waiting for Gabriel to arrive the following evening. I had made my decision. I was to marry the man I loved in spite of his faith. Yet I feared that the war might yet part us, before we were wed. I had therefore determined that if I could not influence the war and could not be sure of when and how we would wed yet I would be his. I needed to prove to him how deeply I loved and trusted him, and I wanted it to be now.

I knew what a risk I would be taking and what a risk I would be asking him to take. My impulsive invitation to him was to be the scene for my attempted seduction of him. Why had I come to such a decision? My motives were not clear even to myself. I only knew I longed to be united with him in body. I would be his wife then in spirit.

Was I wrong? I knew that in the eyes of both our churches we would commit sin. In the eyes of my family I would have disgraced myself beyond redemption. Could I do it? But then I reasoned that by becoming a Catholic my family would no doubt consider me lost to them even if Gabriel and I were wed. I thought of my father's angry face as he had told me never to disobey him again. I recalled Will's angry words to Rafe, "My sister's virtue is as dear to me as my life, or hers."

What would Will say when he heard we were wed? Well that was for the future. For the present I had taken what steps I might against discovery of my rash proposed actions. I had chosen a night when not only my father was away but also Master and Mistress Adams, who were visiting his sister, recently delivered of her first child. Three of the servants had accompanied their master out of Oxford and the remaining servants I had told I would need nothing after supper. We should be safe from discovery.

I paced the floor of our small rooms, waiting impatiently for the sky to darken and Gabriel to arrive.

ᔕ

When Gabriel arrived at the street door, his heart felt lighter than it had in many months. Bess had threaded her hair with new ribbons. He was touched that she had clearly gone to some trouble for what appeared to be a special occasion. A simple supper of pasties, bread, cheese, nuts and apples with a jug of wine was already laid out on the small table in the room. The house was quiet and the servants left them to themselves. When they had eaten, Bess asked Gabriel to play her lute. He smiled and obliged, singing a few of her favourite songs. Finally she asked him to sing her favourite folk tune, "Let no man steal your thyme." As he sang, she joined in and then came to sit on the floor at his feet, resting her head against his knees. When he finished, he played with her long dark hair, pulling it loose and twisting it round his fingers. Then he stood up reluctantly. "My love it grows late, I should leave you to your rest."

She took his hand. To his amazement she whispered, "I pray you, My Lord, stay with me tonight." Gabriel's heart began to beat as fast as if he were going into battle. He carefully laid down the lute. "What are you saying, Bess?" he said, "Do you wish me to bed you before we are wed? This is a step from which there is no return for you. It is too great a gift, too great a sacrifice."

She nodded firmly. "Gabriel, you have said it may be many months until we are able to wed. I already consider myself your wife. I would have you lie with me tonight." She pulled him down towards her and kissed him lingeringly on the lips.

Gabriel tried again, his rational mind in increasing disagreement with his body. "Bess, my love, this is madness as well as sin. Why would you not wait? Consider your father's ire at bringing dishonour to the family."

"My father's ire," she interrupted a little sharply, "will I fear be as great however we proceed. My brothers have both warned me he will never consent to our marriage. If he were aware you are a papist, you would not have been welcome in his house. No, Gabriel, if these were times of peace then yes, I would consent to wait. But my love, we are in the midst of a war. You are a soldier and if God looks kindly upon us, I may be carrying your child when next you ride away to fight." She finished this speech with flashing eyes and uplifted face which did Gabriel's resolution no good at all.

He was not at all sure that the possibility of leaving Bess with child was an argument for proceeding further. But looking at her determined expression, and feeling by now that his body was strongly in favour of this rash proposal, he could no longer deny her. He shook his head and chuckled.

"Does the idea of my being with child by you amuse you?" she asked in confusion.

"No, my love, but surely it is oft that a maid refuses the arguments of a man who longs to bed her. That I should be striving to preserve your virtue, even while my whole being protests at my refusal, is what gives me cause for mirth. But if you are resolved, I will say no more."

After a long pause he removed his doublet and boots, placing them next to his coat and his sword belt. He breathed a brief prayer for forgiveness for what he was about to do, chiding himself the while for hypocrisy. He must ride to see his father now without delay. Then he gently took her hand, picked up the branched candlestick and led her through into her small closet.

❧

In the course of the burdensome weeks and months that lay ahead, Gabriel was to turn often to memories of that single night for comfort. Yet in truth they were fleeting, impressions rather, speaking more of warmth and joy than of any sequence of events.

He recalled hesitation and impatience, the texture of Bess's skin, pale in the flickering candle light, the little wriggle Bess gave freeing her soft, warm breasts from the shift when he loosed the tie at her neck, her erect nipples, her delicious tremor when he took a nipple in his mouth and nipped it gently, the tangle of bed linens and how they nearly caught alight on the candles as they tumbled from the trundle bed; his own shadow looming over her on the whitewashed wall, tousled hair standing out like a medusa.

The entrancing perfume of the bushy mass of springy hair between her legs, how he teased her over its tight curls, the contrast to the long straight locks curtaining her bare shoulders; the hammering of his heart as he covered her with his body. Her small cry, whether of pain or pleasure when he penetrated her for the first time – he had not paused to enquire, the small patch of blood on the linen sheet, glistening in the candle light when he withdrew, brown and smudged by morning, the stickiness of her thighs, still wet with his seed when he took her a second time and the trusting way she had parted her thighs, comprehending now what was expected of her, how she had thrown her arms around his neck and kissed him deeply as he was entering her.

Bess running her hand over the puckered long, red scar down his naked side, her dark hair falling in tendrils across her pale breasts, his increasing urgency, cupping her rounded buttocks so that he might thrust deeper as the grey light of dawn began to infiltrate the room and he knew that their night was almost at an end.

Above all his own feeling of joy, transcending pleasure, which pervaded his whole body, the sweet release as he spilled his seed and knew that she was truly his, now and for all time. He had not thought to have such joy again in his life. As to the aftermath, there was the consciousness, and with it misgiving, that he had taken her maidenhead and with it her honour, that a price might be extracted from him, and ultimately from her, for what they had done.

ᔕ

Gabriel stretched himself and pulled his shirt over his head. He bent his head and kissed me. "I must leave you, my love."

"I know," I sighed dramatically. "Oxford is only safe when you are personally on duty." He grinned and threw a pillow at me, then picked up his breeches and strolled into the other room, fastening them while humming "Let no man steal your thyme". I picked up my discarded shift and pulled it on, giggling.

A moment later I heard the door into the passage click open. I froze.

"Father?" Will was standing on the threshold. He stared at me in my crumpled shift then at Gabriel with his half buttoned breeches. For a moment there was complete silence, then Will advanced on Gabriel, drawing his sword.

22

"WILL, WHAT ARE you doing?" I squeaked in terror. Will ignored me.

"Have you lain with my sister this night, Vaughan?" he asked in a dangerously quiet voice.

"That I have," replied Gabriel equally quietly, "With her consent."

"By her desire!" I broke in hotly. Will continued to ignore me. His face was white with rage.

"I'll not see my sister dishonoured," he said. "Draw your sword." He grabbed Gabriel's sword which lay where he had left it and held it out to him.

Gabriel edged slowly towards him, arms extended, palms up.

"Will, be patient. I have no wish to fight you."

"Coward," spat Will and he deliberately slashed through Gabriel's left sleeve. A thin line of blood shone through the tear in the sleeve. I ran between them then screaming, "Will, stop!" A heart beat later I heard Harry's quick step on the stair. Time seemed to stop. Harry took in our little tableau – the furious Will, sword raised, eyes flashing, Gabriel standing with arms outstretched in a placating gesture, and me, dressed only in my shift, trembling between the two men, while attempting to shield my unarmed lover from my brother's fury.

Harry moved swiftly, putting his hand on Will's sword arm.

"Will, s stop. Think on what you d do. Would you kill the man our sister loves?" There was a long pause. Will did not move. "Go, Will," urged Harry, "I will not leave him unpunished."

Will dropped his arm and nodded curtly at Harry.

"I will wait below then. When you are done with him, bid the papist leave and take his trollop with him." He sheathed his sword and stamped from the room. I gasped in shock at his words. Numbly, I returned to my closet and started to dress. Tears fell from my eyes, blinding me to what I did. Gabriel was talking quietly to Harry in the other room. I could hear little of what they said, but the constraint between them was evident from the tone of their voices and in the long silences.

When Gabriel returned to me a few minutes later, I was sitting on the bed weeping, my few possessions piled beside me. Gabriel put his arm around me tightly.

"Dry your tears, Bess. I trust this estrangement with your brother will not be of long duration. But you cannot remain here. Harry and I have agreed you are to move into my cottage, with him for protection and to preserve your reputation. I will journey to my parents to seek their consent to our marriage. What your brother Will is likely to say to your Father I cannot say. But I think for the honour of the family it is unlikely he will spread the tale of this night abroad in Oxford."

Sniffing, I made my way into the other chamber. I sat anxiously on the edge of a settle. Gabriel placed himself next to me and took my hand. Harry was sitting silently, chin resting on his hand. He glanced at me reproachfully but said nothing. To Gabriel he said sternly,

"I will counsel Will to t take no action, and to say nothing to our father. If you are able to leave today that would be best. I acknowledge that you love my sister well, but you have dishonoured both her and our family this night. I would not have believed it of you, Gabriel."

Harry's voice dropped low but his final whispered words blasted my unwilling ears like cannon shot.

"I might have been wiser to have left you lying in your blood."

Gabriel flushed darkly and bowed his head, but said nothing in his defence. I felt his shame and wept again, knowing this was my doing. Finally, Gabriel looked up and regarded Harry with pain in his eyes.

"You are right, Harry. I ask your pardon. I have taken advantage of your sister's love for me. I love her well, beyond reason. What would you have of me?"

Harry was mute. His mouth was set in a harsh line I had never seen before. For a long moment, I thought he was not going to reply, but then he clenched his fists.

"Goddamn it, Gabriel," he said hoarsely, "As if there were not already b barriers and to spare to your marriage." He stood abruptly and motioned to Gabriel to do the same. Gabriel dropped my hand, rose slowly to his feet and faced Harry. I looked from one to the other, perplexed. Harry was looking angry, Gabriel oddly resigned.

"Bess, please go into your room and close the door." Gabriel's voice was calm but firm. I opened my mouth to ask him why but shut it again as the green eyes regarded me steadily. He was standing stiffly, his hands clasped behind his back. Irritated and puzzled, I did as he had bidden me. The moment I had closed my door I heard the sound of a blow, followed by a gasp. It was followed by the sounds of several further blows in quick succession. Then there was silence except for panting and gasps of pain.

After waiting a few more moments, I cautiously opened my door. Gabriel had collapsed on the floor, holding what I suspected were bruised ribs. Harry was standing over him breathing heavily and sucking grazed knuckles. He held out his other hand and helped Gabriel to rise. For a moment they gazed at each other, then Harry dropped Gabriel's hand and stepped back a pace. To my amazement he bowed to Gabriel, a twisted grin on his face. Gabriel inclined his head. "Come Bess," he said, sounding much more cheerful, "We have much to do, my love." I stared from him to my brother and back again. I would never understand men.

We descended the stairs slowly. Harry went first, on the lookout for the furious Will. I followed, clinging to Gabriel's arm. We gained the street in safety and I looked back at the house, wondering if I would ever enter it again, at least while my father was under its roof. To my relief, there was no sign of Will. We did not linger, but threaded our way through the noisy streets, busy with the start of another day in wartime Oxford, the clattering of carts entering the city, barrows and horses' hooves, interspersed with bawls from above of "Gardy loo" as chamber pots were emptied from windows. I felt sick with dismay. Gabriel went ahead of us to make what preparations he could, while I followed more slowly with Harry, carrying my small bundles of possessions.

With difficulty did I keep my tears in check. That such a night of happiness could turn to such a morning of misery made me feel weak and ill with shock. If it had not been for Harry's steadying arm I would have slipped and fallen a dozen times into the filth of the gutters, overflowing with overnight slops.

Harry glanced at me every few minutes. Finally, reaching a quieter spot as we left the city behind us, he halted and looked hard at me, his grey eyes regarding me coldly.

"Bess, what can I say to you? I know how deeply you love Gabriel, but how could you be so foolish? How so wanton as to consent to lie with him before you are wed?" He paused, evidently anticipating an answer.

Timidly I replied, "But Harry, it was not like that at all."

"How not?" he snapped, "Are you telling me he took you against your will? If that be the case, I have a further score to settle with him."

"No, Harry, but you are wrong, very wrong to think that he urged or cajoled me to lie with him. It was Gabriel who reluctantly agreed to lie with me, after I pleaded with him."

Before I could say more, Harry dealt me a stinging slap across the face.

"How could you do such a thing? Have you quite lost your w wits? Had it not been for everything he has done for me these last twelve months I would not have prevented Will forcing him to fight. I would even have drawn my own sword to avenge your honour."

More quietly he went on, "If what you say is true then it is you who should have been punished. Why did you keep silence? Why did he not defend himself instead of allowing me to b beat him like a dog?"

"Do you believe he saw any other choice?" I said hotly. "Do you think he would have sought to turn away your rage by tarnishing me further in your eyes? Or sought to inflame matters more by returning blow for blow? If you can ask that, then you do not yet know Gabriel."

A few minutes later we arrived at Gabriel's cottage. If he noticed the strained silence between my brother and I he said nothing. I could see from the faraway look in his eyes that he was planning his approaches to both his commanding officer and to his father.

"Bess, I must leave you shortly. As soon as I am permitted, I will ride to The Allt. I travel light and hope to return with my father's answer and more certainty around our future before many days have passed."

By noon, Gabriel was ready to leave once more for his home. He kissed me goodbye under the watchful eye of Harry and promised once more to make what haste he could. "Look after her, Harry," he said awkwardly and trotted away.

ও

The Allt, 3 October 1643

Once outside Oxford, Gabriel increased his speed. Although less than two weeks had passed since he had left his home, his body had grown stronger and he was able to keep moving until Blackbird showed signs of tiring. He reflected ruefully that he would be more comfortable if he was not suffering freshly bruised ribs. During the hours of daylight he concentrated on following the road and keeping a wary eye for Parliamentary troops or patrols. He avoided Gloucester. Even so he had to turn off the road several times, hiding in a copse or behind a hedge until rebel soldiers had passed. But as a single horseman he managed to avoid too much attention. He spent three nights on the road, staying in alehouses. He used the time, beside snatching a few hours of sleep, in considering how best to approach his parents.

On the fourth afternoon, he rode down the familiar valley. As usual it was raining and he was well wrapped in his cloak. The groom ran out to greet him.

"Master Gabriel, we did not expect you, Sir."

"Good day, Twm. As you see I am bringing Blackbird back unharmed. Is my father at home?"

The groom nodded and Gabriel strode off into the house, too nervous to wait. As he removed his wet cloak and hat, shaking the rain off them, he was met by his mother who swept into the hall, her tall figure erect, having heard his arrival.

"My son," she cried, "What brings you back to us so soon? Are you well?"

"I am well, Mother," he replied, kissing her. "I am only returned because I have urgent business to discuss with my father." She regarded him uneasily then clapped her hands, summoning the servants to bring warm water for Gabriel to wash his hands, food and drink to refresh him.

Gabriel's father smiled to see him, then looked at him searchingly. Gabriel embraced him.

"Father, I am well, but am returned to see you on urgent business. The matter cannot wait."

His father's brow furrowed but he led the way to his study and closed the door behind them.

"Sir, I am come to beg forgiveness. Rwyf wedi dod â gwarth ar y teulu.

I have brought dishonour to the family."

Startled, Sir Thomas glowered at his son's bent head.

"Kindly look at me, Gabriel," he said tartly. "I do not wish to converse with the top of your head. What mean you by dishonour?"

"Father, you know I love Bess Lucie," he began, "And wish to make her my wife."

"Yes, yes but what of this?"

"These four nights past I bedded her," Gabriel said baldly.

His father had been seated, but now he leapt up, glaring at Gabriel.

"Is this how you repay the kindness of her brother in saving your life and restoring you to us? By seducing his sister?" Sir Thomas's tone was anguished beyond measure. "As well you did not become a monk, Gabriel. You would have mocked your vow of chastity."

He shot a look of disgust at his son and turned his back to him, resting his hands on the window ledge. The wind was rising and the rain lashed heavily against the window panes. Gabriel rose tiredly to his feet.

"Would you have me leave here then, Sir? I bade you farewell once before, thinking myself unlikely to return. Now I am tethered to life by my love for Bess and may not abandon her. She is cast out by her family and I will make her my wife by whatever means I may. If I am no longer welcome at The Allt, we will live upon my Captain's pay. I pray you, do not forsake her should I die."

His father saying nothing, Gabriel reached for his damp cloak resignedly and turned to go. He pressed his brow briefly against the wooden panelling and then pushed the door open with resolution. At the creak from the hinges, Sir Thomas spun round.

"Gabriel, eisteddwch. Sit down," he snapped, "I have not given you leave to depart. You are my only living son and I would not be estranged from you, much as I abhor what you have done."

Gabriel dropped his cloak on the table and sank once more into the chair, regarding his father warily.

"Now," Sir Thomas continued in a calmer tone, "As to what occurred, I command you to speak plainly and do not add to your sin by any deception. Answer then, did you take Mistress Lucie by force or contrive to place her in a situation where she had no alternative but to submit to you?"

"Dim, Tad, gyda'i chaniatâd cariadus. No, Father, with her loving consent. She lay in my embrace all night. But when morning came we were surprised by her brothers. Will drew on me and wished to fight, but Harry loves me well and forbade his brother to kill me. He made Will leave, but then showed his own displeasure by beating me soundly with his fists. Harry has taken Bess to my lodgings. He remains with her there until I return. I am now bound to her by honour as well as love. I had hoped to receive your blessing on our marriage."

Gabriel took a gulp of ale, relieved that his father now knew all. Sir Thomas folded his arms. Finally he said drily,

"And so the dishonour to our family is from bedding her or from the fact of its discovery by her brothers? I would wish to be clear on the matter." Gabriel's cheeks were crimson.

"Indeed, Father you are right. I believe I would have felt comparatively little guilt had it remained a secret. You might say that Harry beat me into a sense of shame. I was too filled with joy until the moment I saw the anger and disbelief in his face. Sir, although Bess and I have sinned, I hope you will not forbid our marriage, for Bess is willing to embrace our faith."

Sir Thomas nodded slowly. "Then we may hope to make things right, and what has gone before may be forgotten once she is your wife. What of her own family? Do you expect them to be reconciled to the match?"

"I fear not. Sir Henry Lucie hates papists. If he learns we lay together he may not be satisfied with casting Bess out. He may desire to be revenged upon me."

"I pray he will do no such thing, Gabriel. To seek revenge on an officer of His Majesty's forces at such a time would be preposterous. Well, I counsel caution. We will hope that wiser heads will prevail once you and Mistress Lucie are wed. Now, as to how best to arrange your marriage…"

"I hope we may arrange this speedily," Gabriel interrupted eagerly.

His father's green eyes regarded him steadily, "Well yes, I imagine speed is necessary, now she may be with child by you." Gabriel bit his lip but said nothing.

"Remain here while I acquaint your mother." Gabriel sighed and turned his attention to his untouched plate.

Minutes later, the door opened again. This time it was his mother. She paused on the threshold, regarding him with a frown. Then she swept in. He stood and faced her.

"Your father has acquainted me with your recent doings with Mistress Bess. Gabriel I despair, I thought you a man of greater principle and certainly greater sense. What were you thinking of? You are twenty six years old and have been married before. Why would you behave like a youth of 18? Did she bewitch you?"

Gabriel's face darkened with rage.

"Madam, I pray you do not talk of Mistress Lucie lightly. She gave herself to me in proof of trust and love, and fearing that it might be long until we could wed. It is neither her fault nor mine that with the unsettled state of the country and the perilous position of our priests we cannot be sure when that may be." Lady Vaughan sighed.

"Well, she is a foolish child, but a brave one I know, and your father tells me she is willing to join our faith. She must truly love you, my son." Her eyes softened as she looked at his stiff, defensive stance. "Be easy now, we will of course consent to your marriage and will do all we can to arrange it. We must turn I think to the Jesuits for assistance.

I thought at first of their mission house at Cwm. It is no more than a day's ride from here, on the border between Monmouthshire and Herefordshire. The difficulty is that Mistress Bess will require schooling in our faith for at least several weeks before you may wed and they could not accommodate her there. It would be too dangerous for her. The county sheriffs continually search for the place, they know it exists. There could be a raid upon Cwm at any time. To be sure we could request that one of their number makes a stay with us. But as known recusants it might not be safe for a priest to stay here. I would never forgive myself if a priest was taken by the sheriff's men under our roof. Besides, there are so few Jesuits to cover Wales."

"Then what, Mother do you propose?" Gabriel interrupted restlessly.

"My cousin Frances has some connections presently staying at Basing House in Hampshire, the seat of the Marquis of Winchester. I have never visited it and neither I believe has Frances, but the Marquis is well known to be both a strong supporter of the King and hospitable to Catholics, being one himself. His house is now one of the largest fortresses for the King in England. His Majesty quite depends on the Marquis and many Catholics have taken refuge there in these hard times. Bess would be quite safe there. One of the Jesuit priests in residence might school her and then wed the two of you. I will send a messenger to Frances today entreating her assistance."

To this hopeful news, Gabriel responded with a wordless embrace.

"Well, well," Lady Vaughan said indulgently, "It is time you wed again my son, and I think she may make you a proper wife. She has plenty of spirit and bravery which, sadly, is like to be more use in these times than how she manages her servants and her dairy. In return for my pains, I pray your lady will present you with a large and flourishing family who may live here when your father and I are dust."

ᔕ

Oxford, 3 October 1643

Sir Henry wearily climbed the stairs to his High Street rooms on his return from Woodstock. The hour was late and he was surprised to find his eldest son there. Will was sitting in a chair by the light of a single candle, evidently engaged in no occupation but deep thought. There were deep shadows under his eyes and harsh lines creasing Will's handsome countenance suggested the thoughts had produced no happy conclusions. His shirt was crumpled, his doublet unbuttoned, the pearl buttons gleaming softly in the candle light and his stockinged feet thrust out in front of him.

"You keep watch late, my son," Sir Henry began mildly enough. He removed his hat, pulled off his gloves and unbuttoned his cassack as he spoke. "Is something amiss that you are waiting for me? You look as if you have not slept in many hours."

Will looked bleakly up at his father. He appeared to be struggling for words and Sir Henry's alarm increased.

"Speak, Will. What ails you?"

"It is Bess, Father. I would not alarm you unduly. She is well, but perhaps it were better she were dead," he finished bitterly.

"What mean you Will? You speak in riddles. What of Bess? Is she not here, asleep in her bed?" Sir Henry's voice rose in agitation. He glanced towards the closet where Bess normally lay. Its door was shut and he supposed her to be asleep.

Will leapt up and grabbed his father's hand in both his own.

"She is no longer here, Father. She is gone, gone away with Vaughan. He seduced her, debauched her in these very rooms four nights since. Harry and I surprised them together, both half naked. He had but just risen from her bed. Now she has fled with him, I must believe against her will as much as against her duty. He has abducted her. What more can be expected of such a man? He is a papist."

Sir Henry turned white with shock and his whole body stiffened. Will pressed him firmly into a chair and leapt down the stairs two at a time in search of a restorative. A glass of wine brought a little colour back to Sir Henry's cheeks, but for many minutes he continued speechless while Will prowled about the room. Finally Sir Henry spoke, in a dull thread of his usual deep tones.

"And what of Harry in this matter? Tell me he is not complicit."

"Harry is innocent. Yet his friendship with Vaughan runs deep. He was as shocked as I, but he stayed my hand when I would have stuck Vaughan with my sword. He promised to punish the villain and I hope he has been as good as his word. I have spent the last nights here, awaiting your return."

"And yet the man still lives?" his father mused. "Well I will remedy that. Where may they be found?"

"I believe he is gone from Oxford, Sir. For the present you have no redress, unless you approach the King to send out patrols seeking him."

"His Majesty has greater use for his patrols than the capture of one rogue captain of horse," Sir Henry snapped. "No, we will wait for him to come to us. As to Bess, speak no more of her. She is no longer of our family. But I will wait, and I will deal with Vaughan. He need not believe he has escaped justice. Though it take me a year, ten years, he will pay for this stain on our family honour."

He brooded silently until his eye fell again absently on Will's drawn, haggard face.

"Go and rest, Will," his tone was gentle. "Sleep in there, it is empty now," he added caustically, pointing to the door of Bess's little room.

Will shook his head. He removed his doublet and lay down on the ground, folding it under his head for a pillow. He pulled his cloak over him, for the nights were growing chill.

"I prefer the floor, Sir. It has no taint of sin. I would not lay my head upon the bed where my sister played the whore."

When Will woke in the morning it was his father who was sitting upright and motionless in a chair, as if he had not slept. His features might have been carved from granite. When the maid servant brought bread and small beer for their breakfast, Sir Henry detained her.

"Hannah, will you beg Mistress Adams if I may borrow her bible."

"At once, Sir." She bobbed a curtsey.

Will was puzzled. Hannah returned carrying the leather bound bible. Sir Henry took the heavy book and placed it on a table.

"Approach, Will. I would have you witness my vow."

Will took his place hesitantly beside Sir Henry as he placed his hand on the book and closed his eyes.

"I, Henry Lucie, do swear that to avenge the honour of my family, I will not rest until Gabriel Vaughan is dead by my hand or at my behest."

Will had turned pale. His father's eyes bored into his.

"If I fail in this task, I would have you undertake it in my stead. Do you so swear? Place your hand on the bible."

Will shook his head violently. "I need no vow, Father. I will follow your wishes." He stopped, hesitating.

"What if Bess should be with child by him? If you kill him, what would become of her and the child?"

"She will starve then, she and her bastard spawn. Or she may turn to whoring. She already has the taste for it."

ᔓ

Oxford, 4 October 1643

For the first day or two after Gabriel left, I started at every sound. Harry had counselled me to keep the door locked while he was away, against possible visits from an angry Will. All remained quiet however. After a few days I could stand the confinement no longer and cautiously sallied forth, keeping a wary eye open. On my return from my walk, Harry's horse was tethered outside. Harry was pacing in the small yard behind the cottage, among the handful of scratching hens. He silently handed me an unsealed letter. It bore neither signature nor salutation, but I recognised Will's handwriting. Heart thumping, I began to read.

"When I rescued you from your foolish escapade at Warwick Castle, I warned you that there must be no more such occasions. For I would no longer extricate you from situations in which your recklessness had placed you. Alas, you heeded me not. You have been foolish and wilful again and again, coming to Oxford against the express commands of Father, most recently travelling to Wales knowing full well that he would not have given his consent. This time, you have put yourself in a position from which there can be no return. I trust that when you bear the name of Vaughan you will treat it with more regard than you have shown for the name of Lucie.

You may warn Captain Vaughan that it were well if our paths do not cross in the future. Mine takes me away to join Prince Rupert once more. I have acquainted Father with your shame. He knows now that you are to go away with the papist, setting aside our family and any hope of his consent. Captain Vaughan has made himself an enemy. Father will neither forgive nor forget.

That you have chosen such a path is beyond my understanding. For the love I have borne you, I hope it may not bring you lasting sorrow."

A moan made its way unbidden from my throat. Harry regarded me with pity. "Have you read it?" I asked.

"I have not, but observed Will's countenance while he wrote. I had asked him if he would write to you, hoping it might be a letter of reconciliation. I see clearly that is not the case. May I see it?"

I watched Harry apathetically as he perused it, absentmindedly tugging at his beard. When he was done, he crumpled the letter angrily between his gloved hands. He raised his arm to throw the letter on the fire which burnt in the hearth. Something made me snatch it from him. "Harry, no." He looked at me in surprise.

"I wish to keep it. Bitter though it is, this may be the last letter I will ever receive from my brother."

The Allt, 4 October 1643

Gabriel stayed but two nights at The Allt. On the second evening, he waited until it was dark. There was one more conversation he needed to hold. Taking a shaded lantern, he left The Allt on foot and made his way quietly to the parish church of St Edmund. Both church and churchyard were deserted and silent, as they had been on the night when Gabriel had secretly buried his wife and son in the hallowed ground forbidden to Catholics. Holding the lantern close, he made his way to the well-remembered spot near the low stone wall where they lay. Uncovering his head, he knelt on the damp grass. Only the sound of the river Usk beyond the walls broke the stillness.

"Catherine, cariad," he began in Welsh, "I am come to visit you one more time and bid you farewell. Know that I have learned to love again. I did not think that would ever be, but it is so. I am to wed and it is time to let you go. I have worn your ring from the day we married until today. Now I return it to you. It will lie in the earth with you and our son. Maybe I will join it here one day. In the meantime, I pray you release me. I would not have sad memories of your love cast a shadow over my wedding night." He slid the ring from his right hand and kissed it. Taking a small roll of silk from his purse he carefully wrapped the gold band with its dragon carving in the miniature shroud. Plucking his dagger from his belt, he plunged it into the grass, scooping out a cavity. He placed the tiny parcel in the ground and covered it over. Then he bowed his head and pressed his lips to the ground.

23

Basing House, Hampshire, October 1643

Gabriel and Bess arrived at Basing House on a wet and windy October afternoon. Perched on top of a hill beside the River Loddon, a massive circular Iron Age earth work at its base, Bess had never seen such an imposing house. Despite the rain lashing down, they halted to take in the sight of the imposing buildings in the distance. Gabriel whistled softly.

"Gabriel, are all these buildings part of Basing House?" Bess sounded shocked. "It looks like a palace. And what is that behind it? Surely a castle?'

"It is often called Basing Castle Bess, although it is also known as the Old House. The building with the high towers must be the New House. Queen Elizabeth stayed here with all her court. The tale is that she remained so long and brought so many courtiers that the Paulet family were near ruined.

Now the place is a stronghold for the King. It would take an army, and a strong army at that, to make an assault on it. And so it is become a refuge. It is known by all that the Marquis is Catholic and so there are many Catholics here already. That wins the place no friends. But let us make haste, the rain falls ever heavier and we should seek shelter within its walls.'

As they drew nearer they could see that while the Castle was protected by defensive walls, the New House had not been built as a fortress. Linked to the Castle by a bridge and gateway, the magnificence of the New House was more than a little threadbare. Bess could see it was crumbling in places. Many of the windows were boarded up and there were gaps in the stonework of the parapets.

Work on improving the original ancient defences was underway. A new line of earthworks outside the walls, and ramparts topped with cannon, showed that the Marquis was taking no chances.

"Surely noone would try to attack such a colossal place?" Bess was staring at the soaking blue coated men, plastered with mud to the knees, as they wielded their picks and spades.

One of the soldiers was engaged in heated argument with an officer. Work on hammering stakes into the sides of a massive ditch tailed off as men paused to listen to the dispute and take sides.

"… Not a task for soldiers. We were promised more men from the town." There was a murmur of agreement from other men.

"We may have more men from the town on the morrow. For the present, exchange your musket for a shovel. You grow soft, Wheeler. If you spent less time flirting with the maids in the kitchens and sneaking into the brew-house, you might find the act of wielding a spade less fatiguing."

The fair-haired officer was flushed with annoyance. Belatedly aware of the two riders, he broke off abruptly. Gabriel reined in beside him and swept off his hat. Water cascaded from the brim.

"Good day to you, Sir. My name is Gabriel Vaughan, Captain of Horse in the Oxford Army. This is Mistress Elisabeth Lucie. Would you direct me to the Governor?'

The harassed officer looked relieved at the interruption.

"I am John Cleere, Lieutenant of Colonel Rawdon's regiment." He turned to the discontented soldier. "Wheeler, since you do nothing useful here, you may accompany Captain Vaughan and the lady. Take them to Colonel Rawdon."

The scowling Wheeler brightened. A stout man of middle age, his ruddy nose and the way his coat strained at the buttons, suggested that he did indeed spend more time drinking than fighting. He swung himself up behind Gabriel with practiced ease.

Before they reached the gate, they passed a number of farm buildings within a separate walled area. Crossing a lane which ran between the farm and the main house, they stopped at a heavy door set into a high arched brick gateway in the curtain wall. A sentry admitted them and they continued towards the nearby stables under the north wing of the New House.

Dismounting stiffly, they looked around in awe at the size of the courtyard and the labyrinth of buildings. A groom appeared and led the horses away.

A housekeeper welcomed Bess to Basing House and bade her follow inside the New House where she would find her a lodging. Wheeler escorted Gabriel to the military Governor of the garrison. They passed through a bewildering range of buildings and courts, all part of the New House, crossing a bridge and the bailey until finally they reached a gatehouse, four storeys high with a tower at each corner. Gabriel whistled again.

"This is known as the Great Gatehouse, Sir," Wheeler said helpfully.

"Queen Elizabeth stayed in one of its chambers, so they say."

They passed under the archway of the Great Gatehouse and through into the Old House. At the door of the Governor's quarters, Wheeler paused.

"Visitor from the Oxford Army, Sir. Lieutenant Cleere bade me bring him to you."

Looking up from a desk covered with documents, the elderly Governor, Colonel Rawdon, took in Gabriel and Wheeler standing on the threshold. A clerk sorting a large pile of papers at the same desk gestured at them to enter.

"Sir," Gabriel bowed, removing his dripping hat once more, "My name is Gabriel Vaughan, Captain of Horse, serving with the Oxford garrison. I am come to present myself on temporary attachment."

Rubbing his back, the elderly Governor rose slowly and broke the seal of the proffered letter.

"Well, Captain Vaughan, so you are come here with your betrothed in the hope of being married. Your Colonel commends you to me and offers me your services while you remain here." A brief smile flitted across the stern face.

"You are welcome. Another experienced officer is a useful addition. We have two troops of horse. You may take command of the second troop, under Lieutenant Colonel Peake. Have you any experience commanding musketeers?'

"A little, Colonel, in the garrison at Oxford, but none in action."

"You will need to gain more experience here, for our horse may be of limited use in a siege and our garrison is small. My Lieutenant Colonel, Thomas Johnson, will give you duties with the musketeers so that you gain greater ease."

Rawdon turned to the clerk. "Adam, ask Lieutenant Cuffaud to find quarters for Captain Vaughan with the other officers."

Within a short time, Gabriel was established in a compact, simply furnished room. He was to report for duty at dawn the next day.

"It is not time for you to rest, Captain," grinned Lieutenant Francis Cuffaud. "We work harder here than no doubt you gentlemen of the Oxford garrison are accustomed to."

Cuffaud was tall and straight shouldered. His handsome face was marred by a recently healed deep scar across one cheek. He continued with a smile.

"And if we find you are absent when you should be performing your duties, we will seek you in the company of your lady love." Placing his hand on his heart, he gave a mock bow.

"Captain Vaughan?" A servant interrupted. "Lady Jane Grenfall wishes to see you." Gabriel followed the man down endless passages and flights of stairs. The servant finally knocked on a door and ushered him in. It was a comfortable room, furnished with several padded chairs. A tapestry with a hunting scene hung above a fire blazing in a grate. A fashionably dressed, bearded man with his back to the hearth broke off in midsentence.

A woman of around his mother's years was seated regally on a padded chair. Gabriel instantly noticed her long pearl necklace which ended with a crucifix contrasting with the black of her garments. She rose and returned his bow with an inclination of her head.

"So, Master Vaughan, you must resemble your father's family as you do not have the look of your mother's. Are they well?"

"They are, Lady Grenfall."

"I am aware of your purpose. Your mother wrote to me." Her voice softened. "Your mistress must be an unusual young lady to be undertaking this venture." Her face relaxed into what Gabriel took to be intended as a friendly smile. He found her formidable.

"I have no doubt you will be of use to the garrison," she continued. "With respect to your wishes regarding your lady, this is Father John Allen, to whom you must make your case. I will leave you to talk with him."

With that, she swept from the room. Gabriel was lost for words and stared at the man with surprise. He recovered himself,

"Please excuse me, I did not realise who you were, Father."

The priest smiled broadly.

"I am a Jesuit, Master Vaughan. We are taught to be masters of disguise for our safety and it becomes a habit. England is not a healthy place in these times for Catholic priests as you will be aware. Being Welsh can I assume you have had occasion to meet the brethren from Cwm?" Gabriel nodded. "But tell me why you require my services." Now leaning against the fire mantle, Father Allen gestured that Gabriel be seated.

"Father," Gabriel began hesitatingly, "I am come here with my betrothed, Elisabeth Lucie, daughter of Sir Henry Lucie of Chadshunt Hall in Warwickshire. We wish very much to be wed. Bess's family is Protestant but she is willing to be received into the Church. My family welcomes her, but we wed without her father's consent."

The priest nodded thoughtfully. "I see, and is the lady aware what she undertakes?"

"I have given her no instruction Father, but it was her own suggestion that she should embrace our faith. I did point out there are certain drawbacks to being a papist."

The priest chuckled.

"Indeed you may say so. I should speak to the lady herself without delay."

Gabriel hesitated. "Father, I will fetch her to you. But first, will you hear my confession?"

"Of course, Master Vaughan. You are a soldier; and like many who have been in battle no doubt find the deaths of those you have killed lying heavy on your conscience. You must remember the Church does not call these regrettable deaths murder."

He looked searchingly into Gabriel's impassive face. "We will go to the Marquis's private chapel."

The chapel was on an upper floor of the Great Gatehouse, looking south over the inner courtyard. A supply of wax candles stood next to the altar, and prie-dieux with well-thumbed prayer books, showed that It was in daily use.

Even with grey rain clouds outside, the chapel's long windows decorated with the Paulet motto Aimez Loyaute, Love Loyalty, let in much natural light. A window to the south showed biblical scenes with iridescent greens, blues and reds. A smiling Christ child with a gold halo, sat on his mother's knee, half wrapped in her blue mantle. Saint Joseph's crimson cloak was more suited to a knight than a humble carpenter. The ceiling was deep celestial blue with silver stars and touches of gold leaf. The chapel showed signs of a century or more of use. The gold leaf was tarnished and a few stained glass panes were cracked or even missing.

Gabriel was awestruck. In all his life, he had never entered a Catholic chapel. He knew only the cramped and hidden rooms where his own and other recusant families were accustomed to pray. This small chapel was as wonderful to him as a cathedral. It was utterly beautiful.

With a sensation of unreality he followed the priest's example, dipping his fingers into the holy water stoup protruding from a wall, and genuflecting. Gabriel breathed in deeply.

"That scent…'

"Have you have not smelled incense before?"

Gabriel shook his head. "It would be a brave or a foolish man who would have such filling the air of his house."

"And yet you are come from Oxford, where Her Majesty is.'

Gabriel smiled wryly. "Until Her Majesty invites me to join her private devotions, I must pray as do other Catholics, in secret.'

The priest stood patiently near the altar. His mouth suddenly dry, Gabriel hastened towards him.

"Be calm Gabriel, prepare yourself with prayer. I will wait." Draping a stole around his neck, Father Allen knelt in prayer.

Gabriel knelt and tried to compose his thoughts and pray. A jumble of painful memories laced with shame shot through him. Try as he might, he could not bring them into a semblance of order. He nodded to the priest that he was ready to begin.

Briefly, he told of his night of delight and shameful sin with Bess and its aftermath the following morning. "And you wished me to know this before I meet her?" the priest asked.

"Yes, Father," said Gabriel, "For it is possible she is already with child by me. But there is more, much more, that I must confess."

"Continue, Gabriel."

"I am attached to the Oxford garrison as captain of cavalry. Most of the time it is routine patrols, supervising the continuing work on the fortifications, trying to stop fights breaking out between the soldiers and townspeople. The town is overfull, and there is a constant need for vigilance against spies from Parliament. There are frequent arrests of suspected spies. And sometimes it is to me they are brought for questioning."

Bound to a chair, the terrified man with bruised face and bleeding lips spits out broken teeth in a bloody foam. After another blow to his cheekbone, the chair tips and crashes to the floor. Gabriel glances away, sickened by the sight and by his task. He notices the fresh spatters of blood on his leather glove, then he heaves the chair with its burden upright.

"I tell you, Your Honour, I am just a poor man, nothing more."

"While you were pissing on the wall outside a house in Magpie Lane you were seen. You pushed a letter through the window. We have that letter."

Gabriel's voice is harsh. He grabs the bundle of match, the brazier ready at hand to light it and reaches for a knife. He pauses deliberately so that the spy may absorb the sight. The man stares in horror at the unlit match, beads of sweat breaking out on his forehead.

"Enough," the man whispers. "No more, Sir. I beg you. Please. Do not put lighted match between my fingers. I will tell you what you want to know. Only let me live."

"Sir, I entreat you, do you have my John?" The woman is dirty, bedraggled, bare headed. Her lank, dish clout hair frames her careworn face.

"Your man's name, Mistress?"

"John. John Beecher, Your Honour."

Gabriel shakes his head. "I have never heard that name, Mistress." Her thin shoulders sag.

Now off duty, Gabriel was about to return to his quarters. Filled with pity, he hesitates. "Describe his appearance, his garb."

"He has a bad limp, Your Honour, a sword wound caused it, he can no longer work at his trade. He has a brown jacket with two buttons missing, grey shirt, grey breeches, brown cap, no collar or stockings.

Gabriel looks reflexively at his leather glove. His heart sinks. Now he recognises the man, although not by that name.

He forces himself to speak brusquely to her. "He confessed to spying for the rebels, Mistress. I sent him to the Castle. They hanged him today."

The woman stands quite still. Her over large eyes search his face. Then with an air of resignation she turns away.

"Wait." Plunging his hand into his pocket, he pulls out a few silver crowns. "Take these."

He places three crowns in her hand. She stares at the coins. These 15 shillings could buy her food and lodging for some days.

"I do not want your money, Sir, I want my John back." Now the tears come.

She drops the silver at his feet. In the empty room, the sound of spinning coins on the wood floor reverberates like the roll of drums.

∽

"I have myself faced interrogation. I can imagine only too easily the methods you have employed." The priest's voice was grave. "Yet it was a kind gesture to offer the woman your own money in charity.'

Gabriel shrugs, "My Captain's stipend is eight shillings a day, at least when I receive it. I can afford to lose a day or two's pay. And besides, I am heir to my father's estates." He rubs his face as if to wipe away the memories and looks up bleakly at Father Allen.

"Though it was a vain attempt. Instead of easing her loss, I belittled her dignity."

He is mute for a few moments. "Does anything else trouble your conscience?" the priest prompts.

"There is worse, Father." Gabriel continued hurriedly. If he stopped he feared he would not be able to go on.

"Last April I marched with Prince Rupert and his troops to secure the Midlands for the King. We had to make them safe before the Queen could continue her journey south from York with her convoy of arms and ammunition. Our first task was to relieve Lichfield, which had been taken by the rebels. Birmingham was on our road to Lichfield, a small town but an annoyance to the King, as a maker of swords for the rebels."

ထ

Prince Rupert's troops are relaxed as they approach the unfortified town of Birmingham. The Prince is already planning how he will make his attack on the rebels holding Lichfield's fortified cathedral close. He sends his quartermaster ahead to arrange billets for his men for the night.

"Surely that cannot be earthworks ahead, can it Will?"

Gabriel is riding at the back of his troop in the Lieutenant's position. Will Lucie has trotted up from his own troop of Digby's horse and the two men are debating the rival merits of cards and dice for the evening's entertainment.

Gabriel has no sooner spoken than he hears a challenge from the modest breastwork at Camp Hill, followed by the unmistakeable sound of a volley of musket fire. A cloud of smoke blows towards them. They stare at each other in disbelief.

"I must return to my troop," Will gasps and canters off.

A few minutes of confusion ensue. The drums of the foot begin beating the commands to form into battle order. The file leaders of the musketeers hastily light the match of their companions so that their muskets can be made ready to fire. Gabriel unties his helmet from the saddle and rams it on his head, but there is no time to put on his armour. He grabs powder flask and bullets, loading the pair of pistols he carries in holsters on his saddle.

The Prince orders the horse to form up in three ranks and attack the rudimentary earthworks. Gabriel's troop charges. As they draw closer, Gabriel sees there is only a small garrison of musketeers behind the earth works. The Royalists fire their carbines one rank at a time, but cannot approach closely enough to use swords or pistols against the small, impudent force. On the second charge, Gabriel's captain, leading his men, is hit by a musket ball and falls. As the troop retires unsuccessful for the second time, a shocked Gabriel takes command. "Cornet Clarkson, you will act as Lieutenant. Pass the colours to Corporal Dodds.'

The foot have also been unsuccessful. The ground is scattered with dead and wounded Royalists. Behind him Gabriel hears the drums beating for the foot to fall back and reform. He gallops up to Prince Rupert and his commanders with a proposition.

A few minutes later, Gabriel's troop, with Will's troop close behind, have stealthily retreated and are making their way around the flank of the defenders into the fields behind Birmingham. A short ride brings them to the rear of the garrison. The Royalist musketeers are continuing to fire volleys from a safe distance. Gabriel's and Will's troops approach without sound of trumpet. They halt and line up, the unsuspecting rebels behind the earthworks ahead continuing to face forward, firing at the Royalist musketeers who are facing them.

A single trumpet sounds and the troops of Royalist horse charge. Assaulted from front and rear, the garrison defending Birmingham flee into the town, pursued by the Royalist horse, who are increasingly angry at the persistent, if futile, resistance.

Gabriel's troop and Will's canter together down the narrow street. Sporadic firing breaks out from the houses. The street is emptying of civilians, but Gabriel catches sight of aprons and coifs fleeing indoors. Children are being dragged by the hand. A wooden rattle and a hobby horse lie discarded on the cobbles. He reins up hastily, holding up his hand.

"Do they not see their cause is lost? They only make matters worse for themselves," he yells to Will in frustration.

"Throw down your arms and surrender," he calls. The only answer is a further burst of musket fire from inside the houses. A messenger canters up.

"Sir, the Prince commands our troops to fire those houses where the rebels take refuge."

"Dismount and leave the horses," Gabriel shouts to his men. "Corporal Barlowe, one man to hold every 10 horses. You know the drill." He swings down off his horse and ducks as another musket ball flies past his ear.

More musket fire. The man next to Gabriel gives a cry and drops to the ground.

"Jesu," Gabriel cries, "Will these people not abandon their attempts? Mr Clarkson! We burn the houses. Begin with those who are giving fire."

"Sir?" the newly acting Lieutenant Clarkson is looking puzzled. "How may we burn the houses? We have no torches."

"With powder, match. Pull the coals from the kitchen fires. Cast them into hay or straw. These houses are mainly wood, and wood will burn."

Gabriel leads a few men into the nearest house at a run. A musket poking from the upstairs window fires as they burst through the door. A bubbling pot sits forgotten, suspended from its hook. Grasping the fire irons, Gabriel pulls burning coals onto the greasy rushes strewn around the floor. They readily begin to smoulder. One of the men grabs tallow candles and adds them to the pile, while Gabriel sprinkles a small amount of powder from his flask. With a bang, the floor erupts into flame. The woman of the house is being held back, screaming for help and clawing at the soldier who grasps her by the waist.

Attracted by the woman's cries, a wild-eyed man hurls himself down the stairs, raising his musket. Gabriel is waiting, with loaded pistols. He fires. The man falls into the burning rushes where his shirt catches alight. The woman is screaming and cursing as Gabriel and his men leave for the next house.

Darkness has come early on this day. The sky is black with smoke from the muskets of the rebels, the pistols and carbines of the Royalist cavalry. Gabriel is hoarse with yelling, his lungs are filled with grit.

Will the rebels never give up? Gabriel has lost 4 or 5 men from his troop, as well as his Captain. He is angry at such futile waste of life in a skirmish which can only have one end for the people of Birmingham. A man runs from a burning house, his clothes alight, the flames already licking at his hair. He throws down his musket. Above the crackling of the inferno he screams "Quarter." Gabriel does not hesitate. He shoots him in the heart.

The flames rise higher as the Royalist troops advance through the narrow streets. In the smoke and confusion it is difficult to maintain order, more difficult to distinguish friend from foe. Gabriel takes in another lungful of smoke, coughs and tries to clear his head and throat. It is time for his men to regroup. They have done their work. Birmingham is burning and they should return to the horses. The musketeers will patrol the streets in their stead. Mingling with the smell of smoke is the aroma of roasting pork. He gags at the realisation that it is burning human flesh.

Gabriel pauses. It was cool in the chapel, but his forehead is beaded with sweat. He forced himself to continue.

By the livid light of the flames, Gabriel sees a woman facedown and motionless on the ground. The back of her head has been smashed by a ball. Blood and matter cake her hair. He stumbles on something. Irritated at the obstruction he kicks out, trying to free his foot from whatever has snagged it. His spur has caught on the apron of a little girl. She was no more than three or four years. His boot flies back causing the body to shudder. The child's hand is grasped in death by the woman. Her apron and little blue smock are soaked in her blood. She has been shot in the chest.

For a moment, Gabriel is rooted to the spot, then he bows his head to the dead child. The sorrowful gesture is an empty one. It is he who has killed her, he or his men. He has taken command of the troop of fifty men and so the responsibility is his.

Back with the horses, Clarkson asks, "Sir, what orders?"

Gabriel straightens his shoulders, "We pursue the rebels. Now they flee the town we will follow them where they run. There can be no escape for them."

"No quarter, Sir?" Clarkson asks hesitantly.

"No quarter." He responds flatly. Wearily, he lifts himself back into the saddle and raises his hand. The trumpeter blows the command to march and his troop marches out of Birmingham five abreast. The small rebel garrison of musketeers has melted away into the night. The people of Birmingham are all too visible beneath the moon and the stars, bolting into the fields before Prince Rupert's vengeful cavalry.

ᔓ

Gabriel buried his face in his hands. "It was a night of blood, Father and for this I was promoted to the rank of Captain. The soldiers of the garrison escaped. In their stead we cut down the people of Birmingham, slashing and shooting from our horses as they tried to hide in the hedges. As for the women, I saw a half dozen being dragged by their hair and stripped. They had run into the fields together, seeking safety I suppose in company with other women. It did not serve. They were thrown to the ground in the hedgerows and raped. They screamed for mercy while I rode on, leaving the men to their sport. When morning came, the sun's rays showed me my sword blade stained red from tip to hilt, my coat and breeches stiff with the blood of those I had killed. And the guilt I feel for the deaths of those I slew in battle is but a feather weight when placed against the deaths of men, women and children who did not themselves bear arms against the King.

For many months I sought to forget. At first I told myself that this was war and such things happen. Later, I sought the excuse that I but followed the orders of Prince Rupert. But as the months have gone by I see only too clearly that these do not excuse my actions. A part of me feels compelled to go back there to make amends, even while the war continues." He fell silent, his hair screening his face from view.

The priest regarded him for a few moments.

"Gabriel, you are right to think that neither war nor the chain of command removes your guilt for these crimes. These were indeed grievous sins. But this is not the time for restitution. One day this war will end. If you are alive and free, go you to Birmingham and see what amends you may then make. To go there now would be to put yourself in danger unnecessarily."

Gabriel looked at him in surprise.

"Do you say that, Father?"

"I do. I suppose you think Jesuits in England court danger. If I were not concerned about my safety, I would not be creeping around the realm in disguise. There is a difference between being prepared for the worst and actively seeking it. When you ride to battle you accept you may meet your death, but seek to avoid it. If you return to Birmingham as a soldier while the war continues, it would be to knowingly seek your own death. That is forbidden by the Church. But I will give you a heavy penance for your sins, one you may start at once."

Gabriel bowed his head.

"As for Mistress Lucie," the priest continued,"She will discover she too has a penalty to pay." Gabriel's eyes widened in alarm.

"Oh do not fear, nothing too arduous," the priest grinned, "But she may find she has scant time with you, and it will lessen the chances of temptation."

ᔓ

Gabriel was subdued and thoughtful when he came to find me. "Father Allen wishes to meet you without delay. Don't be nervous, Bess."

"Will he ask me many questions?"

Gabriel smiled at me reassuringly. "He knows our situation and he is friendly as well as courteous."

My heart thumped uncomfortably as Gabriel pushed me forward and closed the door leaving me in a richly decorated room with a blazing fire in the grate. Sitting before the fire was a man reading. I assumed the priest must have gone elsewhere and considered leaving.

"Mistress Lucie? Please come in." I curtseyed nervously.

The man approached me, smiling. "I am Father John Allen of the Society of Jesus, Mistress Lucie." He led me to a comfortable chair near to his. "Since we are to be spending quite some time together, I think we might be more comfortable if we addressed each other informally. You may call me John if you wish. Might I call you Bess?"

I realised that I was staring. I had been imagining a severe and grey bearded man in clerical black, or gaudy vestments. This man was not as ancient as my imagination. His long brown curls fell to his shoulders and he wore a red velvet doublet. I had never seen a man of a cloth like this.

"I can see that like your betrothed you are a little startled at my appearance. Gabriel at least has the advantage of having met other Jesuits where you do not. We use different identities and other means of attempting to preserve our lives and liberties. Allen is not my real name, but it is the name I now go by." Father Allen smiled. "Please be seated and allow me to pour you some wine. Tell me a little of your family and your life."

Haltingly, I told him of my home, my parents and my brothers. Then of Rafe, of Harry's imprisonment, of my mother's death and of how I had come to meet Gabriel. How my brother, father and I had been forced to flee our home for the comparative safety of Oxford. He listened, occasionally interrupting with a question. Finally, I told him of how I had developed feelings for Gabriel.

I hesitated, embarrassed. "John," I said, using his Christian name hesitantly, "I began falling in love with him before I knew he was a Catholic. I only found out when I came upon him praying beside a dying man. He was using a rosary and I realised what that meant." There was a short silence.

"And how did you feel?" the priest asked gently.

"I was shocked," I replied honestly." I had never known any pap– Catholics before. My family are Protestant and I was brought up to hate and fear Catholics. My nurse used to scare me with tales of how the wicked papists had sought to blow up the Parliament. My understanding and my change of heart began when I recovered from the shock of the first time I saw him praying. For once I realised that it was a Catholic who I love, my prejudices gradually began to fade. If Gabriel was Catholic, they could not be as I had been told. I know him to be a good, brave man as well as the man I now love. He has been a true friend to both my brothers, comforting and helping Harry during their shared imprisonment and caring for my brother Will when he had camp fever. He was seriously wounded when he interceded for Harry in a sword fight. And yet now Will has tried to kill him." A tear trickled down my cheek.

I felt a comforting hand on my head. "Life can be very hard, Bess and even those we love can be unfair. Gabriel has made full disclosure to me of your relations so I am aware of why your brother Will was angry with him. Tell me, why do you wish to become Catholic?"

"So that I may wed Gabriel. My love for him is deep, and I hope that with your assistance I will come gradually to an acceptance of his beliefs. I acknowledge I must undertake this if we are to wed. I do not expect to experience the Road to Damascus like Saint Paul," I finished with a weak smile.

The priest's face creased in a grin. "A good and honest answer, Bess. A practical one too. We cannot all expect to encounter visions to help us on our way. You will attend the daily Mass in the chapel. That will familiarise you with our most important rite. Gabriel will accompany you when his duties permit. Come and see me afterwards. We will begin your lessons tomorrow." His expression and voice softened.

"But before we proceed further, I must warn you of the dangers in what you are doing."

"I know there are laws against Catholics," I mumbled, realising I knew very little of what those laws were.

"And Gabriel is accustomed to living with them, Bess, with running the risks in breaking them. You are not." His tone chilled me.

"Non-attendance at services of the established church, recusancy, may lead to repeated fines, fines intended to cripple rich and poor. Gabriel's family could lose two thirds of their estates. Recusancy can even lead to imprisonment. Your marriage will be valid in the eyes of God, but in English law it will be a crime. If it comes to the attention of the authorities, you may be arrested. If your children are not baptised as Protestants in the parish church, you may be arrested again. Should the rebels win this war, matters might worsen. Lastly, when you die…"

"Then Gabriel and I will be laid to rest side by side!" I interrupted passionately. The priest slowly shook his head, his sad eyes meeting mine.

"When you die, Bess, your children will creep to the churchyard at night and bury you there in secret, so that you lie in hallowed ground. You will have neither headstone nor foot stone, for the law says that the mortal remains of Catholics are to be left at the crossways for wild beasts."

The words struck me like a physical blow. Was this truly the law of England, my own country? For several minutes, I remained motionless, contemplating the flickering flames of the fire as if I could see into my own future there. Finally, Father Allen rose to his feet.

"Perhaps you wish to reconsider your decision?" he enquired gently.

I stared at him, but no words came.

"We will speak again in the coming days, Bess. It is a hard road before you."

I had wandered down the passage a few paces when I was met by Gabriel. He had clearly been waiting, and his face lit up at the sight of me. When he saw my downcast looks, his expression changed.

"Gabriel," I whispered, "I love you more than I can say, but I am no longer sure that I can do this. Please leave me to myself. I must think."

He regarded me forlornly, bowed and strode away. As his footsteps receded, I listened for that slight hesitation in his step, the memory of a limp, now no more than an echo, that would be for me forever Gabriel.

24

Basing House, October 1643

I BLUNDERED MY way back to my chamber. I sought solitude, but my new bed mate, Mary Frost, was already there and I hurriedly withdrew. I fled down the long corridor, trying the handles of doors until I found one that opened into a silent and empty room. As I crossed the threshold, my foot went through a half-rotted floor board. Well, it was sufficient for my present needs. I sank upon a chair riddled with tiny holes from wood worm. In the damp and musty room, I sat and pondered.

I had known so little of the law. Would it have stopped me making my rash offer to convert if I had known the full extent of the penalties? I had not thought properly, I truly had not, about the possible legal consequences that might follow marrying Gabriel. I had thought only of my father's anger. Gabriel's explanations about locked doors on that day at The Allt had puzzled me, but too much had happened since then. I had paid little attention to his warnings when I had told him what I was prepared to do for him.

The gloomy sky outside the window darkened into night while I wrestled with my new fears. I felt despondent and apprehensive. Yet did the law of England truly matter now, I wondered, for war had come, and fresh, untold dangers with it. Gabriel might be killed at any time by a bullet or a sword thrust. Time enough, I reasoned with myself, to worry about peace time dangers when England was once more under the rule of law. I would not delay in becoming his wife, for only God knew how long we would have together.

∽

The next morning, I had just finished dressing when there was a tentative knock on my chamber door. Gabriel was attired once more as a soldier.

"Good morning Bess, I am going to Mass. Will you go with me?" his voice betrayed his uncertainty.

"I will go with you, Gabriel," I replied solemnly.

The green eyes widened in delight.

"Then you have thought,"

I nodded, "And I have recovered my courage. Forgive me, Gabriel. Father Allen talked much of danger and it frightened me."

He drew me to him, my head against his shoulder. "I will do what I can to protect you, Bess. Come." He bore me on his arm through the labyrinth of passages and rain drenched courts until we arrived at the Great Gatehouse. We went through a door and ascended a spiral staircase. We entered a chapel of colour and light, flickering candles, paintings and statues. Men and women were already there, silently praying. Gabriel uncovered his head, dipped his fingers in a small bowl of water and crossed himself. Hesitatingly, I did likewise. He ushered me towards a prie dieu and knelt. Father Allen, recognisable as a priest in his vestments, appeared.

I knelt beside Gabriel for the first time in a Catholic chapel feeling a little dazed at the chain of events which had led me to this place. It was barely nine months since we had met. I gazed at this passionate, spiritual man beside me, his head bowed in prayer. His good humour and outward calm hid a complex nature. It was with difficulty I stopped myself reaching for his hand. The unfamiliar Latin prayers went on around me. I lifted my eyes to take in my surroundings. Damp patches on the painted ceiling and walls showed the chapel had suffered some decline. Rain, coming from one broken pane, was trickling down the wall. The gold crucifix and tall gold candlesticks on the altar were an indication of past glories. The cushions on which we knelt were of richly embroidered velvets in faded reds and blues. As Gabriel and others of the congregation filed to the front of the chapel to receive Communion, Father Allen glanced my way and gave me a brief smile.

After the service, Gabriel escorted me to Father Allen's room in the Old House.

"Gabriel, do you have a chapel like that at The Allt?"

Gabriel burst out laughing. "Bess, the Marquis is a very wealthy and powerful man. My own family are considerably less exalted. I believe The Allt's old castle had a chapel several hundred years ago. But since Queen Elizabeth's time we have not dared have a visible chapel. When you go there again, I will show you the hidden upper room where we have Mass when we are able. Everything is stored there. But no stained glass or beautiful carvings, alas. Maybe in our children's day, or their children's, it will be so," he finished wistfully.

As Gabriel turned to leave me at Father Allen's room, I asked him, "Will you meet me at dinner?"

Gabriel looked to the priest who shook his head slightly and Gabriel shook his own.

"Not today, Bess."

ᔓ

Those first few days at Basing were as confusing as my first days in Oxford. Finding my way around was a puzzle, but Mary Frost was often at hand to help me. She was a Catholic of about my own age whose husband's estates had been seized by Parliament while he was away fighting for the King. Within a few days, I could find my way without too many false starts to the Great Hall where we dined, to the chapel, and to Father Allen's room where we continued our lessons. Gabriel's own lodgings were unknown to me. I only knew he slept in the Old House with the other officers.

I did not know what had passed between Gabriel and Father Allen at their first meeting, but I had a strong feeling that Father Allen, friendly and informal as he was to me, had laid down strict rules for Gabriel. Gabriel had said little, but I noticed that he was careful to confine his physical contact with me to the touch of our hands and the occasional chaste kiss. After our night of intimacy in Oxford I found this hard, as no doubt did he.

The next day, Thursday, my first opportunity to see Gabriel was in the evening when he escorted me to supper. His had spent the day with the garrison strengthening the Basing House defences. Colonel Rawdon's men had been brought in to assist Basing House's small garrison, following a minor attack on the house in July.

"The size of these earthworks puts those at Oxford to shame, Bess,"

he said, taking a piece of fowl and starting to eat hungrily. I pulled a dish of leeks towards me and reached for a jug of ale.

"Did you see the stakes with iron spikes on the tips, the storm poles? They will be a fearsome obstacle for cavalry to overcome should this place come under attack again."

Friday morning, Gabriel again accompanied me to Mass. After three days and two lessons with Father Allen, the service was no longer quite so strange, although the intoning of the Latin prayers tended to send me into a trance. I still had very little idea what anything meant. Afterwards, he escorted me to the priest's study. When I asked if we would meet at dinner, he shook his head.

Entering the Great Hall for supper that evening, I stopped on the threshold and scanned its vast expanse. The lofty painted ceiling with its arched beams, colours dimmed by many decades of wood smoke, soared above a tiled floor of blue and white. The floor showed signs of a century of use, with those tiles in the centre of the floor chipped or discoloured. A long tapestry, with faded colours of blues, greens and reds, depicted Queen Elizabeth entering the Great Gatehouse with her retinue during a visit to the House in happier days. I was searching for Gabriel. Other officers were seated at the other end of the long table, but he was not among them. I debated asking if they knew why Gabriel was absent. There was something he was not telling me. Fearing to appear foolish however, I said nothing.

I seated myself next to Mary, who was talking to Catherine, another Catholic who had taken refuge at Basing House, awaiting eventual escort back to her father's estate after being ambushed on the road by rebels. Mary and Catherine were aware of how matters stood between me and Gabriel and thought my impending conversion rather romantic.

"And how is our little heretic this evening?" Catherine gibed with a broad grin. I felt myself blushing.

"Is everyone but me at Basing a Catholic then?"

Catherine only laughed at my question, but Mary stared at me,

"Bless you, Bess, no. Colonel Rawdon and most of his men are Protestant. Behind closed doors, there have been quarrels between Colonel Rawdon and the Marquis's own officers. Colonel Rawdon is the military Governor, but he now commands the Catholic officers of this house. I do not think they are overfond of being commanded by a Protestant. One too, who began the war on the side of Parliament."

This news shocked me. "But how did he then come to fight for the King? Can the Marquis trust him?"

"He was Lieutenant Colonel of the Red Regiment of the London Trained Bands since before the war began. But earlier this year he left to join the King. His loyalty is not now in question. The Marquis must trust him to have placed the safety of Basing House in his hands."

I wondered whether a fortress sewn with these seeds of mistrust was as safe a harbour as Gabriel had believed.

The next day, I came upon Gabriel supervising a party of men working on the defences. They were digging deep entrenchments, and packing the excavated earth into newly erected walls. Despite the cool damp weather, he had stripped to his shirt and breeches. He was striding energetically around the earthworks, occasionally scrambling down to the bottom of a steep ditch to inspect it. He waved cheerfully at me and wiped his brow, leaving a streak of mud across it. I grinned.

"Shall I see you tonight at supper?"

He bowed with as much of a flourish as could be managed by a man liberally streaked with mud and hatless.

When the expected knock on the door arrived, I was ready for him. Before he could pull away, I wrapped my arms around his neck and kissed him firmly on the lips. For a few moments his arms came around me, but then I felt him check and pull back.

"Gabriel, why do you reject my embraces?" I asked hurt. "Do you no longer desire me?"

"Oh, my love, you cannot believe that?"

"Then why?"

He looked somewhat embarrassed. "Father Allen cautions restraint until we are wed. He has warned me therefore against being too much with you, at least alone."

"Is that why you do not come to table to eat?" I snapped. "On Wednesday and again yesterday I hardly saw you. What kept you from me?" He took my hand and started to pace slowly along the passage.

"I am fasting twice a week, on Wednesdays and Fridays. I may not join the company at table, for on those days I am to eat nothing but a little bread."

"But why?" I asked confused and annoyed, "To what purpose and by whose orders?" He looked at me, ran his hand through his hair. I continued to stare at him and finally he sighed and stopped where he was.

"On Father Allen's orders. As to why-do you remember when Will and I spent a night at your father's house in April?"

Puzzled, I nodded.

"I told you something of how we had taken Birmingham. I did not tell you all. I made full confession to Father Allen. In the heat of battle I slaughtered innocent men, women and children. I am no better than a murderer."

"Gabriel, no," I cried in disbelief.

"Let me finish," he said sadly, "And so now I am to fast and pray, for as long as the war continues. And when there is peace, I have told him I will return to Birmingham to see if I can make amends."

He took my trembling hand again, and we wandered onwards, our hands closely entwined.

For my next lesson, I went in a mood of defiance. We had been starting to work our way through a catechism, but when Father Allen told me to open the book, I did not move. He narrowed his eyes. I opened and shut my mouth. The priest was still waiting quietly.

"Gabriel says you bade him fast twice a week and it is because he killed people in Birmingham." The words tumbled out in a rush.

Father Allen pressed his hands together thoughtfully and rubbed them against his brow.

"Bess, what do you know of the sacrament of Penance? Little I imagine." Confused I nodded silently. "I think perhaps we will make that the subject of today's lesson. Know that there is a difference between killing and murder. Gabriel understands that distinction. Do not try to come between him and his conscience.

And," in a steely voice he continued, "Never seek to discuss with me again what he has told me under the seal of confession."

I said nothing more to either about fasting, or Birmingham.

ઙ

When my courses arrived on time I had a small pang of regret. I knew that I was not with child from our stolen night in Oxford.

"Some private words with you," I whispered to Gabriel. He took my arm and marched rapidly to one of the rooms at the end of the hall.

"Speak then," he urged, with something of disquiet in his tone.

I tried to smile reassuringly, though my lip trembled, "I am not with child, Gabriel."

"Ah," it was more of a sigh than spoken word. He stared at the blue and white tiled floor for a few moments. Looking up at me again, he must have seen my disappointment. He took both my hands in his and pressed them firmly.

"We should first ask God to sanctify our marriage, Bess. It is then He will bless us with children. Now was not the time." He smiled at me, the green eyes pools of longing. Raising my hand to his lips, he kissed it.

Except on Gabriel's days of fasting we would meet for dinner or supper depending on his duties. Gabriel had a further distraction. The Marquis had his own musicians and so I would sometimes happen upon Gabriel trying out a new song or harmony, sitting side by side with a lutenist, their brows furrowed in concentration.

I roamed the Old House and the New, making acquaintances among the many residents. There were many servants and I had no domestic responsibilities. I frequently made my way to the defences to see the continuing progress when I knew Gabriel was to be found there. Two Dutch engineers were in overall charge, and were engaged in damming the River Loddon to flood the marshland to the north of Basing House. I visited Fairy in the New House stables and sometimes rode out on her, accompanied by Gabriel or one of the servants if he was unavailable. Time hung heavy on my hands and he understood that. Caution was necessary however in case of Parliamentary patrols in the area. Colonel Norton's men, who had attacked Basing House in July, were a constant threat, and Waller was believed to be building a new army.

As I had predicted, I experienced no blinding, sudden spiritual revelations. In wishing to marry the man I loved, I gradually accepted his beliefs. By the end of October, Father Allen had agreed that we might set a date for our marriage for late November. This would enable messengers to be sent to Gabriel's parents and to Harry, inviting their attendance.

I began to consider wedding clothes. I obtained suitable materials from the housekeeper. With the assistance of one of the maids, I began sewing my bridal gown. Catherine had recently embarked on a romance with a Lieutenant of the garrison, Edward Watson. She watched me dreamily as I stitched.

I had promised Gabriel that his people would be my people. The Vaughans would soon be my own family. Despite Father Allen's warnings, and my fears, I was still unsure as to what the law might mean for them.

"Have your family been punished for their beliefs?" I asked abruptly. Gabriel and I were trotting side by side through the woods on Cowdray's Down, not far from Basing.

He drew rein, swinging down off his horse and leaving him to graze. I did likewise, tethering Fairy. Gabriel took my hand, looking thoughtful and began to lead me slowly along the Down. He stopped, gazing down towards the tiny figures of the men plodding back and forth with buckets of earth and stones towards the Loddon's growing dam. When he turned towards me, his green eyes were wary.

"Bess, I should have spoken more to you of this earlier. I told you that the family fortunes declined after my ancestor Roger Vaughan was beheaded by a Tudor. Through the reigns of the Tudor kings and queens, King James too, we led a quiet, discreet existence. What accommodations were made since the reign of Queen Elizabeth to protect our family and estates I do not know. There are many other Catholics in Wales. During the reign of King Charles we have been aided by this, by employing mainly Catholic servants and by the half-hearted application of the penal laws at the King's behest. He has no power to abolish those laws. Only Parliament could do that, which they will never do. They are more like to craft harsher ones."

"And what has that meant for the Vaughans?"

"We have been careful, Bess. Occasional attempts to report our family as popish recusants have been quietly dropped after pressure from our family, or the complainants bribed. The parish records must show our constant non-attendance at the local church, but until recently we were fortunate.

Only convicted recusants are fined, and we had never been charged.

When a priest visits The Allt, we spread the word quietly to those families we know and trust. We bolt the doors while Mass is said and our gamekeepers patrol the grounds. Since Parliament's decree of '41, we take extra pains to protect the priest. It is treason now for any priest to be in the realm. Yet our priest's hole was home only to dust and spiders, a storage place for all we need to celebrate the Mass. We have never had to hide a priest, from the far-off days of Queen Elizabeth until that day you and Harry returned early from your ride." He paused, smiling.

Suddenly the events of that day at The Allt became clear. "You thought we were men searching for the priest?"

"Yes, we feared you were the sheriff's men, and we opened up the priest's hole. But there is more, Bess. When the King was forced to recall Parliament in 1640, they insisted that the full force of the law be applied against Catholics. This time, he could not resist their demands. An example was made of hundreds of families. Our own luck had run out. Bribes were offered to informers and a parish constable, attracted by the prospect of more money than he could earn in a year, betrayed us. Father and I were arrested and indicted for recusancy at the Brecon Quarter Sessions in February last year.

I would prefer to forget that day. First there were the hostile bystanders, townspeople, outside the Guildhall. A company of militia was on duty to keep order. As we were marched inside to answer the charges, the crowd broke into a chant, 'Hang the papists.'

Trust me, Bess. Those words are as ugly in Welsh as they are in English. I had never thought to hear such words in my own country of South Wales. We reached the doors unscathed, our cloaks splattered with mud and offal. It was little enough compared to what I have since faced in battle; and yet in some way the personal animosity was worse. It will no doubt sound strange to you that I, a Catholic all my life, did not fully comprehend what persecution meant until that day.

I had been inside the Guildhall with Father many times before, on property and other legal matters. It is a fine modern room, the Great Hall, oak panelling, portraits of gentlemen in ruffs hanging on the walls, black and white floor tiles. There is a chimney and a fireplace at either end, lamps around the walls. A comfortable room where gentlemen do business.

That day was different. When we entered the hall, the first thing I saw, prominent in the middle of the table before the justices, the brass bindings gleaming in the firelight, was a bible. Instead of sitting at the long table, we stood before it with guards on either side. We were required to take our oaths upon it, but it was a Protestant one. Once we had refused, the rest of the proceedings were mere formality. The questioning by the justices, the witnesses' sworn statements and the studied unpleasantness."

He stopped, his voice thick with emotion.

"You were found guilty?'

"That was never in doubt. Duly convicted of recusancy, we were released. The clerk offered to show us the back way out so that we might leave the building discreetly. Father refused.

"We will leave the way we entered. Come Gabriel, we have nothing to be ashamed of." The chanting from the street was louder than it had been earlier. The clerk, a quiet middle aged man, was tugging at Father's sleeve.

"Sir Thomas, I beg you, do not go out into the High Street, let me escort you through a back way. I would not have your death, and that of your son, on my conscience.'

And so we slunk out, like the criminals we were, in secret. It was full dark by the time we reached The Allt. My mother and my wife were both waiting fearfully. I can still see their faces in the cold moonlight, my mother pale and silent, Catherine in tears, running to meet me.

We presented ourselves again at the May Sessions for sentencing. It was no more than weeks after the deaths of Catherine and Michael. I cared not what became of me and took little note of the proceedings. Heavy fines for my father and I were recorded. For months, we expected a visit from the Sheriff to collect monies or to round up our cattle. Since then a year and more has passed. They have not yet come, and I have heard that we are not alone in this. The sheriff's men have other concerns. It seems at present, we must be grateful for the coming of war.

Bess, I tell you this not to alarm you, love. But as it is a fact of my past, so it is a part of our future, yours as well as mine." His expression was desolate.

I pushed the rebellious lock of hair back from his brow and kissed him deeply. "Gabriel, I belong to you and you to me. What King or Parliament may do to us I do not know. Little do I care so long as they do not part us."

∽

5 November, 1643

"Captain Vaughan, it is time you exercised your troop." Lieutenant Colonel Peake, the Deputy Governor, smiled at Gabriel.

"Our scouts tell of Waller gathering a much larger force at Farnham Castle. His intentions are not clear. It may be that he plans a decisive battle with Lord Hopton. But I like not the building of a force so close to Basing.

Take twenty men, ride toward Farnham and observe his strength.

"If we are to get close to Farnham, Sir, is it best we pose as rebel forces?" Gabriel suggested.

"A worthy notion, Captain, but take care your patrol is not captured as spies."

Accordingly, when Gabriel left Basing the next day, he and his men were wearing the orange tawny scarves of Parliament about their waists. They rode south towards Alton at first, intending to pose as a patrol returning from Portsmouth. The weather was worsening, with rain and mist. As they descended the high ground from Bentworth towards Alton, they heard the unmistakeable sounds of an army on the march, the steady beat of the drums, the jingle of harness and armour, the rumble of artillery carts. They halted on a hill above the town, watching the army streaming out, evidently heading towards Winchester.

Gabriel caught his breath at the sight of the force. Though the view was partially obscured by mist, with the aid of the spyglass he counted the colours of at least 15 troops of horse and twice that number of companies of foot. The horses in the artillery train were pulling ten heavy cannon.

"Waller's Field Army," he shouted through the rain to Captain Robert Amery, passing over the glass for confirmation.

Amery nodded, rain dripping off his red curls, "But much grown. This is not just Waller's own men, he has been reinforced."

"From London, I think," Gabriel said grimly. "It is a worthy force to take on Hopton's army. They will meet at Winchester without doubt."

"Should we ride ahead and warn Lord Hopton?"

"He will have his own scouts, Robert. Our task is to bring intelligence to the Marquis. We will report on the mighty force which has passed by. Thankfully, it is not our concern at present."

Gabriel and his men turned northwards once more towards Basing House without approaching nearer to Waller's forces. By the time they had reported the size of the new army and the direction of its march to Rawdon and Peake, darkness had fallen and the weather had worsened. The night was cold and rain beat upon the walls of Basing House.

6 November, 1643

I woke early. I was restless. It was several days since I had left the House, and I was impatient to take Fairy for a canter before shutting myself away again to study. Gabriel had cautioned me that I should not go beyond the precincts of the House without consulting him, for fear of rebel patrols. Searching for him, I encountered Catherine's lover, Lieutenant Watson.

"Have you seen Captain Vaughan, Lieutenant?"

"I believe he was out on patrol yesterday, Mistress and returned very late. Do you wish me to rouse him?"

"Please don't do so on my account, Lieutenant. I am going out for a ride and had thought he might accompany me. No matter, I will go alone, I will not go far."

The Lieutenant looked uneasy. "I fear that may be unwise, Mistress. I do not think Captain Vaughan would wish it. We believe General Waller's army now lies near Winchester. Colonel Rawdon sent out patrols to the south west an hour ago to track them. If you await their return I will make enquiry as to whether it is safe to go forth."

I had heard only of a small garrison at Farnham Castle. Set on my own childish, obstinate desires, I was reluctant to abandon my outing on a rare morning which promised to remain dry at least for an hour or so.

"Winchester is some distance from Basing, Lieutenant, but if you fear the rebels march in that direction I will head south. Thank you for your kind concern."

I hastily turned on my heel before he could say more. To my annoyance he fell into step with me.

"Then if you are determined to go forth, permit me to accompany you." With some reluctance I agreed.

Lieutenant Watson and I arrived at the New House stables. A number of empty stalls showed where the horses had been taken for their early morning patrols, but the air was thick with the warm and fetid odour of beasts munching hay, while sleepy eyed stable hands shovelled the night time harvest of manure into the drain. I ignored the Lieutenant's marked silence when instead of waiting for a groom to saddle Fairy, I did so myself. I compounded matters by leaving the lady's side saddle on the rack and reaching for one of the saddles intended for the men of the garrison. I only rode side saddle when forced to, a form of independence which Gabriel was already inured to.

I consented to put my foot in the Lieutenant's hand to mount and then led the way from the New House at a brisk trot across the court to Garrison Gate. I waited impatiently while a guard opened it for us. Beyond the Grange, the flooded marshland gleamed, as the dammed River Loddon spread its clammy tentacles between the high ground to the north, and Basing House. It was a cold, damp day. Within a short time, the sun struggling to make its presence felt was obliterated by a thick descending fog. Skirting the new entrenchments, I re-entered the park and turned south. We had gone no more than a mile however, when the Lieutenant's horse pulled up lame. He dismounted and discovered a stone in the gelding's shoe.

"If you wish to walk him back slowly," I said, "I will ride a little further and explore the nearby woods. I know my way."

The earnest Lieutenant looked perturbed. His long jawed, rather homely face, creased into an anxious frown as he stood looking up at me. "I do not believe Captain Vaughan would wish you to continue alone, Mistress. I would counsel you to return to the House."

I was irritated by this, not least by being expected to defer to the hypothetical disapproval of an absent Gabriel.

"Nonsense, Lieutenant," I responded brightly. "There is no cause for concern either by you or Captain Vaughan. I will return within the hour." I turned Fairy's head and trotted away before he could say more. After the constant bustle of Basing House, it was a comfort to be alone. I slowed my pace. Once inside the woods, it was eerily quiet. I heard nothing but the sound of Fairy's hooves and the songs of a bird or two.

The trees were almost bare of leaves, but bushes of hazel and blackthorn grew thickly on either hand. The path wove sharply between banks and hummocks, so that despite the stark outlines of the tree trunks, the way was not plain to me.

Reaching a clearing in the woods, I reined in. I was no longer certain of my bearings and feared I had strayed too far westwards. The sun was no longer my visible guide. To my astonishment, I heard voices.

Peering through the dimness I saw two dismounted troopers, partly obscured by their grazing horses. One was drinking from a leather flask while the other was engaged in emptying his bladder. So close to Basing House, surely they must be two of our scouts? Yet the men were unknown to me. Basing had no more than two troops of horse, Lieutenant Cuffaud's troop and that of Lieutenant Colonel Peake, now commanded by Gabriel. I knew most of them. One of the grazing horses moved, revealing the sashes around the waists of the two men. They were the orange tawny of the rebels.

Every nerve in my body tensed in fear. They must be enemy scouts. Should I run or should I try to discover their purpose? If the House was threatened it was my duty to find out. I dismounted as silently as possible. Holding my petticoats above my ankles, I crept towards the men, skirting the clearing and keeping a screen of dark green holly bushes between us.

"Approaching in this fog will give the army enough cover."

"As long as it does not clear," said the other. "We will report we have seen no patrols abroad from Basing House in this direction. They do not realise we have turned back towards them. If the General approaches from the south with all speed, he may take the papists by surprise."

I had heard enough. I reached Fairy unobserved, but as I untied her reins, one of the horses raised its head. Sensing Fairy, it whinnied. The men glanced round sharply. Peering through the fog, they spotted me as I hitched up my skirts and flung myself desperately into the saddle.

"Stop her!"

I dug my heels into Fairy's sides and gave the mare her head. "Go, Fairy, go'.

"Stand or I fire!"

I flattened myself against Fairy's neck and urged her into a gallop, praying I could lose them in the fog. I heard the crack of the carbine and a shot whistled by my ear, immediately followed by a crack from the second man's carbine. I was too far ahead for them to attempt a pistol shot. They must not close that gap.

I galloped back in what I hoped was the direction of Basing, branches whipping at my clothes and clods of earth flying up from Fairy's hooves. My world had shrunk to the muddy strip of path I could see between the mare's ears as she pounded steadily towards safety. The only sounds I could hear in the eerie silence were her hooves, the creaking of leather and the horses of my now silent pursuers. Rising above them was the thumping of my heart, louder in my ears than any drum beat.

She was sweating heavily, but her pace did not falter. How much further did we have to go? I lifted my face from Fairy's mane for a hasty glance ahead. Looming out of the fog were the ramparts of the Old House, the dim outlines of the turrets of the New House beyond it. Behind me I could hear the muffled hoof beats of the two horses. Were they gaining on me? I could not tell.

25

Basing House, 6 November 1643

GABRIEL, STANDING ON the roof of the Great Gate House, was peering out. A thick fog had descended, making it difficult to see very far beyond the precincts of the house. He told himself there was no cause for concern about Bess. She was an accomplished rider. Yet he could not help fearing she might have encountered the enemy. With Waller's army on the march towards Winchester, there were likely to be flanking patrols over a wide area. Early morning patrols from Basing House were not yet returned. If she had only asked his advice, he would have told her not to go out. But he had been sleeping, exhausted from the previous day's sortie, and he had been brought the news by a shame faced Lieutenant Watson. There was a shout from a sentry near him on the roof.

"Sir, a horseman approaches at a gallop from the south west." Gabriel turned and then heard, "It looks like a lady." After a pause the sentry continued, "There are two others behind. They appear to be pursuing her."

Gabriel snatched a perspective glass from the sentry and trained it in the direction he was pointing. It was Bess on Fairy. She was hatless, lying flat against the mare's neck, her cloak streaming out behind her as she galloped past the walled garden towards the Grange. Just emerged from the fog bank were two orange sashed troopers. They were trying to intercept her before she reached the only unblocked entry, Garrison Gate.

Gabriel leant over the edge of the roof and cupped his hands. "Corporal Hare," he shouted desperately to an officer in the court below, beside his horse.

"Yes, Captain?"

"Get on your horse and ride for Garrison Gate. Fast as you can. Have the sentry unbar it for Mistress Lucie. Rebels approaching. Tell the musketeers on the ramparts to hold their fire. They might hit her. Go!" For a long moment the man paused, then he leapt onto his horse's back.

Gabriel was frantic. He could see that Fairy was tiring. Her pace was slowing as she neared the Grange. The leading trooper was gaining on her fast. Gabriel watched helplessly, clutching at the brick wall under his hands. The distant figure pulled a pistol from its holster and took aim. There was a puff of smoke. "No," he whispered. Too far away to hear the shot, Gabriel held his breath while an invisible ball flew through the air. Fairy did not check and Bess still clutched her round the neck. Gabriel could bear to watch no more. As the man drew his second pistol, Gabriel launched himself down the spiral stairs. At the bottom of the Great Gate House he turned and sped towards the bridge. Across the bailey. Towards the Barbican.

As he hurtled towards the inside arch of the barbican, he heard slowing hoofbeats. Corporal Hare was smiling.

"Rebels turned tail, Sir."

He was followed by Fairy, her chestnut sides dark with sweat and heaving with the effort. The mare clattered over the bridge and came to an abrupt stop in front of Gabriel. Bess was clinging to her mane, gasping and crying. Gabriel caught her as she half fell.

She turned wild eyes on him. "General Waller's army is advancing on Basing under cover of the fog."

Gabriel turned to the corporal. "Corporal Hare, send for Colonel Rawdon immediately." Within a few minutes the Colonel approached.

Bess briefly explained what she had heard.

Colonel Rawdon frowned, "So their march towards Winchester yesterday was intended only to deceive us. They have lost the element of surprise now and will be aware of that. Nevertheless, I think we can assume an attack will still occur today. Lieutenant Cuffaud," he called. "Take a patrol out immediately to see how far away Waller's main force is."

Gabriel bent and kissed Bess softly. "My love, I think you may have saved Basing House." He looked at her with concern. She was trembling all over. "Go and rest, Bess. I will visit you as soon as I am able." She nodded and walked shakily away.

Drums began to beat and the sound of booted feet rang through Basing House as those of the garrison not already on duty ran to their quarters to fetch arms and armour.

ᔕ

Gabriel had returned to the roof of the Great Gatehouse. He was scanning the swirling fog through his glass. A hand clapped him on the shoulder.

"Gabriel," it was the captain of foot, Robert Amery. "The waiting is always the hard part, is it not?" Gabriel smiled and nodded. Amery fastened his helmet, his blue eyes regarding Gabriel thoughtfully.

"I understand we have to thank Mistress Lucie for raising the alarm. A brave lady."

Gabriel sighed, "Indeed she is, Robert." His tone was one of desolation and Amery looked at him again, hesitating.

"I think you are somewhat downcast, Gabriel. Forgive me for saying so, but you appear more nervous than I would have expected from a seasoned officer like yourself."

Gabriel stiffened and frowned. He swung round, but then, seeing the concern in Amery's eyes, relaxed his posture. "For one moment, I thought you were accusing me of cowardice, Robert. Indeed, I am feeling a heightened sense of nervousness. I am not accustomed to being under siege, but I believe the chief reason is Mistress Lucie's presence here. She is now in danger and it is because I brought her here."

"Indeed, you did," smiled Amery, his mouth curving into a characteristic grin. "I observed that she arrived here trussed across your saddle, struggling and screaming."

Gabriel smiled unwillingly, "A fine jest, Robert, but if it were not for me, she would yet be safely at Oxford, with her father and brothers to protect her."

"Gabriel," Amery smiled. "I have only had the honour of knowing your lady a few weeks. But from what I have observed, not least today, she will face those dangers with courage as long as she knows she can be by your side."

The two men were silent, straining their ears as well as their eyes. Muffled by the fog the sound of the rumble of carts and the beating of drums was audible. They listened for a minute or two. "Quite a number of drums, I think," said Gabriel softly. "We counted ten heavy guns too. After our capture of Waller's artillery at Roundway Down, I am surprised that Parliament entrusts him with such a force." He forced a laugh.

Amery nodded. "If your lady heard correctly it is Waller's field army which approaches. It appears they turned back from Winchester. It was a mighty force we saw yesterday."

"Coming with such strength means a serious offensive."

"Do not fear, Gabriel," Amery said confidently, "This is the largest stronghold for the King in all England, stronger since the work we have done on the defences these last months. We may have but 500 soldiers, but It is not easily taken, and the King will not allow its destruction. It is not known as Loyalty House for nothing. Your Bess will be safe. And thanks to her, we are ready for Waller."

The garrison had not been idle during the few hours Bess had gained for them. Muskets, carbines and pistols were cleaned and loaded. Pikes and musket rests were brought out ready for use. The three small drakes were loaded. Precious supplies of ammunition, gunpowder, shot and match stood ready. The entire garrison was in arms, Rawdon's foot manning the Old House, the Marquis's own companies under Peake positioned in the courts and on the towers of the New House, while the two troops of horse were to be held in reserve to carry out sorties or to act as a forlorn hope.

Inside the House, the Marquis's physician, pressed into service as surgeon to the garrison, was supervising the neat piles of bandages and dressings, standing ready for the expected influx of wounded men. Lieutenant Colonel Thomas Johnson was reviewing supplies of ointments and salves. They had been made from the herbs he had cultivated in the walled garden.

The livestock from the Grange were hastily herded through Garrison Gate and corralled on the bailey. Gabriel watched the milling herds of cattle, the pigs and poultry as the servants ran back and forth, shooing them into pens.

"Is it wise to have the cattle so near the guns, Robert?'

"The New House stables are already full with horses and none of the courtyards are as spacious as the bailey. And we could not leave them at the Grange, Gabriel, or they would be roasting atop the enemy campfires by tonight."

ᔕ

Waller's army slowly emerged from the fog. The sounds of drums and trumpets were joined by the growing rumble of artillery carts, the sounds of hooves, and marching feet until the ground shook. Glimpses of a multitude of regimental and company flags swirled by invisible hands pierced the gloom. First came the cavalry, riding in files of five. When the infantry regiments appeared, the line of men appeared endless. Gabriel watched glumly as several thousand foot marched into position and heavy artillery pieces were hauled by horses onto Cowdray Down overlooking the House.

"Gentlemen," Colonel Rawdon approached the group of officers on the roof of the Great Gatehouse, "A drum has come from Waller. He has summoned the House to surrender. The Marquis is composing his letter of refusal. In the meantime, we have a little respite. You may stand your men down for an hour and send them to eat. I daresay," he smiled thinly at Gabriel, "You will wish to take the opportunity to see how your lady fares after the adventures of the morning."

Gabriel made his way hastily to the New House in search of Bess.

ർ

I had gone to my room, but it was all I could do to peel off my sweat-soaked bodice and mud splattered skirts, and throw myself on the bed. I lay there shivering in my shift, reliving my desperate ride. The crack of the carbines reverberated in my head. My thoughts were making me more rather than less agitated. What would happen now? I had paid little attention to the accounts of sieges, Reading, Gloucester and others. During the brief siege of Warwick Castle last year I had still been at home, with my mind on my own concerns, Rafe being uppermost. The fortifications of Basing House had been strengthened over the past weeks. They seemed formidable. But what if the rebels overcame them? What if the Marquis surrendered? I had a hazy notion that ladies might be safe. But what of Gabriel as an officer of the garrison? Might they shoot him?

There was a quiet tap at the door. I hastily picked up my cloak, wrapping it about me. Cautiously, I opened the door. Gabriel stood there, smiling down at me reassuringly. "Oh, Gabriel, I am so pleased to see you."

I pulled him into the room and held him close. My cloak fell to the floor and he tore himself away. "Bess, much as it delights me to see you in this state of undress...."

I sighed. "Wait outside then." I scrambled into dry clothes, fumbling with the laces as I attempted to make haste. Gabriel was waiting. He kissed me passionately and then reluctantly broke away again.

"Come, Bess." He tucked my hand in his arm.

"Where are we going?"

"To eat. Rule one for a soldier and a soldier's lady is to eat when the opportunity presents itself. We may be too busy later. Waller has sent a messenger with a demand for surrender. It will be refused, but in the mean time we may eat and make ready."

Many of the garrison were snatching a hasty meal and the Great Hall was crowded. Catherine was sitting beside Lieutenant Watson and laughing at something he said. Servants were scurrying in and out with platters of pies, dishes of meat, onions and baskets of bread. We sat at one end of a table where we could talk more privately. Gabriel ate sparingly himself but observed me carefully as I forced myself to eat some mutton. He poured me some ale and I drank thirstily. My normal hearty appetite had deserted me.

"Try this," he passed me a dish of apples. "Now Bess, your cheeks are still pale. You know I will do all I can to protect you my love. What fearful imaginings fill your head?" He smiled at me gently.

"I was so frightened, Gabriel when those men chased me. They both fired at me. I heard them. I thought they would shoot me, or Fairy. To you who have been in battle it must sound ridiculous. You see, no one has ever tried to kill me before." I toyed with my apple.

"My poor love, it is no wonder you were scared. But you rode bravely and you escaped them to raise the alarm. The garrison honour your courage. You are safe now."

"But even if I am safe you are not. For you will fight them. And what will happen to you if the House falls?"

"You paint too gloomy a picture, Bess. And you forget I am a soldier, accustomed to fight. I am only sorry I am unable to send you to safety first."

"I am not afraid as long as I am with you."

"Captain Vaughan," a breathless servant stopped beside us. "Colonel Peake requires your urgent attendance."

"Go then, Gabriel." He kissed my hand and left the hall at a run.

ᔕ

Peake was waiting for Gabriel by the New House stables. The former bookseller's tall, round shouldered figure and characteristic sweeping gestures disguised the man of action he had become. His long thin nose was almost quivering with excitement. Francis Cuffaud was already there.

"Gentlemen, the enemy have sent an advance guard of horse through the park ahead of the main force. I believe we should bid them welcome by riding out to meet them.'

"Both troops, then Colonel?"

"Yes, Captain, our entire cavalry force of 100. I believe we will make an impression if we respond swiftly. And I think we may spring a small surprise.'

Grinning, Cuffaud called for his troop's trumpeter, who blew the command to form up. Grooms ran to saddle the horses and within minutes the two troops were mounted and clattering out of Garrison Gate behind Gabriel and Cuffaud.

"Diversionary only, Francis," Gabriel cautioned. "We are to show that we are not cowed by their numbers and do not intend to shelter behind the walls. There are too few of us to take undue risks at this stage.'

Cuffaud grinned, 'But I think we may have some sport, Captain." The troops cantered forward towards the park and Waller's army.

ꕥ

I knew I would be underfoot as the cavalry prepared for action, but could not prevent my feet taking me towards the New House Stables. I arrived to find them empty of horses, the grooms folding away blankets and returning with full buckets from the water tower in preparation for the return of the two troops. The sight of the routine preparations calmed me. Colonel Peake emerged from one of the stables and I studied him, wondering if he could tell me any news. He smiled down at me sympathetically.

"If you will accompany me to the top of one of the New House towers, Mistress, you will have a bird's eye view of Captain Vaughan as he rides into action.'

I scrambled hastily after him, through the New House until we reached the spiral stairs of the most southerly of the towers, which rose high above the newly dug retrenchments. Beyond lay the park, rapidly filling with marching enemy troops. It would have been a magnificent sight if it had not been so terrifying. Company after company of marching men in coats of yellow, red, green. The huge swirling standards of the infantry, all accompanied by the insistent, thrilling beat of the drums.

"Do not be overawed by their numbers, Mistress. These are not seasoned troops for the most part. I believe Captain Vaughan helped destroy Waller's last army. These are new levies, just raised. Most are the trained bands from London. I recognise their colours. They will not be happy camping in the fields and fighting in winter so far from home. I know Londoners. I had a print shop there with my brother before the war broke out.

"And now our play begins." He pointed ahead. One of our troops was cantering into the park. I was peering from the tower window but the angle of the tower was blocking my view and I hurried out onto the ramparts. Peake followed me, pulling out a leather-bound spy glass.

"Lieutenant Cuffaud's troop." He handed me the spy glass. I accepted the unfamiliar instrument with caution. Through it I could see plainly the long fair hair of Lieutenant Cuffaud at the head of the troop. As I watched, they reformed in ranks of ten. Cuffaud was holding his sword over his head. The trumpeter beside him raised the trumpet to his lips and the troop charged. The oncoming troop of rebel horse halted, hastily reforming their own lines. After a moment, I heard a volley of cracks as the enemy discharged their carbines. I clutched the brick beneath my hand and a chunk fell away, landing unseen far below. Peake clicked his tongue in annoyance.

"These walls are in poor repair. I fear they will not withstand cannon shot for long," he muttered. Watching the cavalry, I paid little attention to his words.

"Why do our troops not give fire?'

"We have little shot to spare, Mistress and besides, we do but seek to give the enemy a bloody nose.'

As the two sides clashed, Cuffaud's troop divided, wheeling neatly to left and right. Swords glinted as the tiny figures circled each other.

"Surely our troop is outnumbered, Colonel?" I saw Cuffaud smacking one of the enemy's horses on the rump with his sword as it came too close. A blow from a sword nearly sent him falling from his horse. Two men, both enemy I thought, were down, their panicked horses running free. As I watched, the sword of an orange sashed trooper sliced sickeningly into the shoulder of one of our own men like a knife into a side of beef. I was not able to see who it was, but I saw him clutch at the wound and reel in his saddle. The spy glass trembled and I returned it to Colonel Peake as if it burnt my hands. The clear view, which made me feel as if I stood at the elbow of the skirmishing men, unnerved me. It was one thing to know that they were in combat, quite another to see their blood being spilled a drop at a time.

"Where is Gabriel's troop?" I had seen no sign of them and I was not sure if that made me more or less uneasy.

His smile broadened. "You were looking at them.'

ℰ𝒪

"Another troop of horse is most welcome, Captain Vaughan." Gabriel bent his head politely to Waller's Lieutenant Colonel, a splendidly attired man in his thirties, astride a black stallion.

"Colonel Norton wished to play his part, Sir. We will ride under your colours today.'

"Very well, follow us across the park. We will give the papists a small foretaste of what is to come, while our forlorn hope musketeers deploy in that lane. Your troop will form the second line.'

Waller's skirmishers trotted forward as an impudent troop of horse emerged from Basing House and cantered towards them. The leading troop engaged with the horse from the House. Gabriel watched critically, as Cuffaud charged across the wet park, wheeled the troop, withdrew and regrouped. It was time for Gabriel's troop to engage. He nodded to his trumpeter beside him. The man blew two blasts.

"For God and the King!" Gabriel roared. As one, the troop tore off their orange sashes and followed him as he spurred forward, crashing into the back of the rebel troop. The rebel horse were caught between the troops from the House on both sides, the press so tight they could scarcely wield a sword. Waller's Lieutenant Colonel swore loudly as he realised Gabriel had tricked him.

"I'll see you damned, Sir for this. Expect no quarter when we next meet," he snarled as he tried unsuccessfully to fight his way towards to the impostor. "Withdraw," he yelled, swiping viciously with his sword at the nearest man in Gabriel's troop. Ducking hastily, the trooper narrowly avoided decapitation. Moments later, the black stallion was leading the troop back towards the safety of Waller's main force.

Leading two captured horses, and leaving five enemy troopers dead or dying on the ground, the Basing cavalry withdrew in triumph. Gabriel patted Blackbird and dismounted in the courtyard by the stables, handing his reins to a groom. "He's done well. Give him plenty of oats." He grinned at the groom, a lad no more than 13 years old, his head capped by short spiky fair hair that reminded Gabriel of stubble in a corn field.

"Good boy, Blackbird," the boy breathed, rubbing the horse between the ears.

"I am glad to see you recovered from your fever, Watt."

"But men may take me for a rebel now, Captain." The boy tugged at the short tufts and frowned.

"It will grow anew," Gabriel reassured him, ruffling the spiky hair.

Peake emerged from one of the towers, closely followed by Bess. From the direction of the Old House came the sharp tattoo of drums.

"A forlorn hope of musketeers has been seen marching up the lane. Our foot will oppose them. Not you, Captain Vaughan, nor you Lieutenant Cuffaud. Rest your men. I fear they will be needed again on the morrow.'

❧

I felt calmer, knowing that Gabriel was unlikely to fight again that day. I realised with shame that there was at least one person at Basing in greater danger than I, and I had not given him a moment's thought. I found Father Allen in his room immersed in a book.

"Father," I said urgently, "Should you not hide? If the House should fall, you do not wish to be taken." He closed the book and smiled at me.

"Bess, as I told Gabriel some weeks ago, as a Jesuit I have to be prepared for the worst, although I do not seek it. I will not be taken cowering under a table or behind a screen."

I continued to stand on the threshold, hesitating.

"Bess, I find that activity is of great assistance at times of trial. It distracts the mind. Fetch your catechism. I think now would be an excellent time for a lesson. And, if we are overcome by our fears, we have always prayer to fall back on," he finished teasingly.

It was a strange afternoon. In the comfortable light and warmth of the Jesuit's room, sitting beside a crackling fire of fragrant logs, we calmly discussed the importance of the sacraments. I could feel my heart beat slow as we talked. My mind strove to concentrate on his words, even while my ears strained for every sound. Orders were bellowed and there was the regular tramp of boots as the garrison moved around. There were sporadic bursts of distant musket fire as musketeers from the house skirmished with Waller's forlorn hope. After an hour or more, Father Allen closed the book and smiled.

"I think that will do for today, Bess. Are you feeling better now?" I nodded. "Then we will resume on the morrow unless we are prevented by General Waller."

On my way to the New House, as I crossed the bridge, there was a loud crash of cannon fire. I jumped out of my skin, not knowing which way to run for safety. Instinctively, I fled back towards the Old House, where I was most likely to find Gabriel. I joined scurrying women and servants, all crossing the court, making for the Great Hall. Beneath the gaze of portraits of Paulet ancestors, servants hastily pushed the polished furniture of oak and walnut back against the walls to create more space. Pails full of water were lined up in corners and beneath tables as a precaution against fire.

"Bess, are we going to die?"

Mary's face was pale and she grabbed my hands tightly, the gold rings on her fingers cutting into me. I wriggled my hands free.

"Not today," I answered with more conviction than I felt. "This is not called the Castle for nothing, Mary. Gabriel's men have already driven off a troop of horse. Waller's army will soon be on its way back to London, tails between their legs."

The hall was crowded with women, one or two elderly men and a score of children, mostly clinging to their mothers and wailing with fear.

"Mother, will General Waller kill us all?" a little girl of eight or nine was gazing wide eyed at her mother. There was a further crash from far overhead. It sounded as if a chimney stack had been hit. The glass in the windows shook. Some of the panes were decorated with the family motto Aimez Loyaute. The Paulets were paying for that loyalty.

Observing the sobbing children, my own fear was swallowed up in a surge of wrath against Parliament and Waller. I had an idea. My small cousin Meg had always enjoyed my stories when she visited Chadshunt. "Tell me another, Bess," she would beg, settling at my feet, her doll in her lap.

I skipped towards the children and clapped my hands. "Who would like to hear a tale of daring deeds? And the day General Waller ran away?"

I pulled a cushion off the bench, spread my skirts and sat on the floor near the marble fireplace. Within a few moments, I had a semicircle of children around me, the smaller ones sitting on their mothers' laps. The fire crackled and popped as I began.

"It was a warm night last summer when Prince Maurice and his brave companions escaped from Devizes at midnight. General Waller and his army had surrounded the town, but now his soldiers were all asleep and their horses were snoring in the fields."

A little boy giggled. There was another boom from a gun, followed by a crash as masonry splintered. I continued with my tale.

ꕤ

"And so," I concluded, "Prince Maurice and Captain Vaughan and the rest of our cavalry chased the Roundheads over a steep cliff and all of the bad men and their horses died. Then General Waller and his foot soldiers ran away as fast as their legs would carry them. The townspeople in Devizes cheered our brave soldiers and rang the church bells. And that is the end of the story of Roundway Down."

"Is Prince Maurice here?" one little boy enquired hopefully.

"No, but Captain Vaughan is here with the garrison. And Colonel Rawdon and all our other brave soldiers."

One of the boys leapt to his feet, waving a wooden sword. "When I am a man I will kill General Waller."

"I will kill him too," shrieked his brother, not to be outdone.

"You do well to keep up our spirits, Mistress.'

The Marchioness, her children and Lady Grenfall had entered. I glanced up and scrambled to my feet, shaking my skirts into some semblance of order. Lady Grenfall's austere face relaxed in an indulgent smile as she looked at the two small boys waving their wooden swords.

I curtsied to Lady Honoria. Her face showed signs of strain but her voice was firm as she continued, "I trust Sir William's stay will not be of long duration. While we remain dry inside the House, his soldiers suffer all the hardship of a wet and stormy camp. Colonel Rawdon and my husband are both of the opinion we will not have to endure this bombardment overlong. A drum has arrived, requesting a parley and offering ladies fair quarter. I thank God I am not yet in a condition to accept fair quarter at Sir William

Waller's hands."

I realised that there had been no sounds of cannon fire for some minutes. I collapsed thankfully onto a bench near the fireplace. My relief increased when a grinning Gabriel entered the room and sat down next to me. He stretched his boots towards the glowing logs.

"Gabriel, does a drummer requesting a parley mean General Waller is already seeking terms?"

"No, Bess he merely seeks to 'avoid the effusion of Christian blood'. A fine way of saying he hopes that having endured an hour or two of his ordnance we will be prepared to prematurely surrender the House 'for the use of the King and Parliament' as he describes it. Ignoring the fact that without the King, there can be no Parliament. No doubt Waller wishes to retire to Farnham before too many of his raw recruits desert. But I came to hear your tales of my wondrous exploits at Roundway Down. It seems I am too late."

I laughed, but a few moments later two loud bangs sent Gabriel to his feet.

"Remain here Bess, I will return. There should be no fighting at present, not during a parley."

Some minutes later he reappeared.

"Waller has apologised. Two guns exploded by accident. No damage has been done." More seriously he continued, "Waller is offering women and children free passage out of the House. Bess, if you wish to seek safety, the opportunity is there. Take it and none will think the worse of you, my love. Shall I see you safe out of the House?" Standing so still he might have been holding his breath, the green eyes were fixed on me intently.

"Gabriel, can you really ask me that? Would I leave you while other women stay? I do not deny that I am frightened. But, if I abandoned you here, I would leave my heart behind."

Gabriel hugged me. "When last I saw my mother, she said you would make me a proper wife, for you have plenty of spirit and bravery. I know that to be true. Stay then, Bess. I love you."

The parley over, and Waller's terms refused, we braced ourselves once more as the bombardment of the House was renewed. The boom of the guns, followed by crashes as they found their mark, continued until late in the evening. When night fell, instead of going to our chamber in the New House, the housekeeper found Mary and me an empty bedchamber on an upper floor of the Old House. It was chilly and smelled musty from disuse, but Gabriel had advised me that the Old House was safer, being stronger.

"They but seek to cause us fright and to disturb our rest, Mary. We should sleep."

I forced myself to lie down upon the bed, blowing out the candle. After some time, the bangs ceased. Waller's gun crews also needed their rest.

ᔕ

7 November 1643

It was raining. Gabriel drew his cloak tightly about him. He wore both sword and pistol, his carbine slung over his shoulder. From a tower of the Great Gatehouse Gabriel strained his eyes in the half light, watching distant, shadowy figures creeping towards the cottages which lay between Garrison Gate and the church.

A flicker of light appeared from one side of a cottage underneath its thatch. Moments later, it was echoed on the other side, and then a whole row of flickering lights took hold. The handful of empty timbered cottages flared. The families were already within the relative safety of the walls of the House. Gabriel smiled grimly. War destroyed homes and livelihoods. The levelling of dwellings beyond city gates or the curtain walls of great homes such as Basing House was a necessary evil, a desperate measure to keep the enemy from the gates. The cottages could not be left to provide cover for the enemy. Captain Payne's troop from the Marquis's regiment had done their work well.

As dawn broke, Waller's heavy guns opened fire. Robert Amery strolled over as Gabriel peered through his glass to see the fall of the shot.

"Warm work for the enemy, Gabriel, but I fear they will tire themselves for little result."

"Their fire appears to be directed at the Gatehouse, Robert. Can we do nothing to counter it?"

"I believe we may attempt something, gentlemen." Colonel Rawdon approached, Lieutenant Colonel Johnson at his side. "Captain Amery, I believe we may be able to bring one of our guns to bear on the enemy if we mount it on the roof yonder. Take as many men as necessary and act with all despatch."

Lieutenant Watson ran up, sliding to a halt on the wet ramparts.

"Colonel, we have sighted a body of musketeers wading across the Loddon. The first men are making towards the Grange."

The north side of the House was under attack. "Do we defend the Grange, Sir?" Johnson enquired eagerly.

"I fear it may not be defensible, Johnson. It has no fortifications. The boundary wall is solid enough, but it was intended to keep cattle within, not armed men without. You may take a company of men to the Grange and we will test Waller's skill and resolution. After the freezing waters of the Loddon, his men may already lose heart. Captain Vaughan, go with him. Cut your teeth as a captain of foot."

"Sir, if we are to show them we mean business, would not a larger force be better? Once lost, the Grange may be hard to recover and so close to the House as it is, our walls would be within pistol shot."

Rawdon glared at Gabriel. "Captain, I am aware of how close the Grange is to our walls. But I have only 500 men with which to defend the entire House and I cannot afford to employ too many defending Basing's farm." He stalked away with an energy which belied his sixty years.

ᔓ

"Don't you worry, Cap'n Vaughan, we'll look after yer. Won't we lads?"

Corporal Hodson grinned ferociously, displaying a wide gap in his front teeth. Chuckles followed his words as the musketeers checked their arms. Each man was wearing a bandolier with 12 small chargers of powder along with a pouch full of bullets. They carried matchlock muskets but the heavy rests had been abandoned as they were cumbersome to carry.

"Jus make sure you keeps yer powder dry and yer match alight if you don't want some rebel shooting you up the arse." It was not yet raining, but the skies were grey and the reminder was timely.

The 40 men marched briskly out through Garrison Gate and into the Grange. The wall of the Grange seemed high enough and thick enough to be defensible, whatever Rawdon feared, but with only a handful of men, the Governor was probably correct. Gabriel heard the heavy bar crash down as Garrison Gate closed behind them. Once they were inside the gate of the Grange, Hodson began thrusting pieces of timber into place wedging its gate shut. Gabriel stopped him.

"I would not waste too much time with that, Corporal. If the enemy scale the wall, the gate will only delay us when we need to flee. We must ensure we can withdraw without unnecessary losses."

Johnson ordered his small force to spread out along the perimeter wall, the bulk of them facing towards the approaching force of enemy musketeers. Gabriel paced along the line, hands behind his back, observing the men. They were busy with scouring sticks, powder, wadding and bullets as they cleaned and loaded their muskets. Not trusting himself with a musket, Gabriel was carrying his familiar carbine on a strap and had a pair of loaded pistols thrust through his belt. He strove for his habitual appearance of calm. If the men realised their officers were as apprehensive as they were, they would be likely to panic and run. He reached surreptitiously for the crucifix inside his shirt and then smiled humourlessly, remembering that at Basing there was no need for concealment. With an odd feeling of relief, he crossed himself openly and muttered a brief prayer. Peering through one of the musket loops he saw the front ranks of the enemy break into a jog. The range was closing rapidly.

"Make ready!" he shouted. One of the muskets exploded prematurely.

"Dickson, yer pillicock," one of the corporals snapped.

"First rank, present!"

Muskets were raised to chest height and thrust through the loops.

"Fire!"

"Well done, men!" Johnson yelled as the volley created a few gaps in the line and the advance wavered.

"Second rank, present!" Gabriel shouted as the remainder of the company took their places at the loops. The first rank hastily reached for scouring sticks, powder and bullets once more.

The second rank also felled several of the enemy, but by now they were at the wall and beginning to climb.

"Company, withdraw ten paces." Gabriel had one eye on the men reloading, the other on the top of the wall. The first heads appeared over the coping. Enemy musketeers were scrambling up the wall with assistance from their comrades.

"First rank, make ready to fire."

"There are far too many of them, Captain. We must withdraw," Johnson muttered to Gabriel.

Gabriel nodded, his eyes still on the wall. "First rank, present."

"Second rank, provide covering fire as we withdraw."

"Fire!"

"When I say run, make for the Great Barn," Johnson shouted.

"Second rank, make ready."

"Present," Gabriel continued, forcing himself to keep his voice calm.

"Run!" Johnson shouted. Gabriel fired his carbine at the enemy soldiers astride the wall. There was a ragged last volley of musket fire as the company ran for the Great Barn. As the last musketeer ran in, the solid doors banged shut on their swing bars.

Gabriel noted that the Great Barn was easily four times the length and twice the height of a normal barn. It was stacked almost to the rafters with goods, from barrels of beer to bedding. It contained everything needed to ensure the House a comfortable winter.

"Corporal, wedge the doors shut. But ensure one of the doors nearest the road can be opened quickly. We do not wish to be caught like rats in a trap."

Casting lingering looks at the barrels of beer and cases of smoked hams, the men took up positions in the clear space around the walls at the musket loops.

"Stand to yer arms," Hodson commanded. "If I sees one of yer so much as look at them casks of beer, I'll 'ave the skin off yer backs. Don't think I won't."

The enemy were charging the barn in a frontal assault. At their head, brandishing a gleaming sword, was an officer in a fine suit of green, slashed with blue. Johnson was clapping his hands in his enthusiasm.

"Now, Captain Vaughan, we may take a crack at them. They are sitting ducks while they are out there and we in here."

"Shoot the officer, Colonel?"

"Young popinjay," Johnson snorted. "No, we will take him prisoner if the opportunity presents itself."

The forty muskets maintained a steady fire, but it could not be continuous. With every volley, enemy musketeers fell, but still more came over the wall.

Gabriel reloaded his carbine again sombrely.

"What are your orders, Colonel? The men have but two shots each remaining. It will take the enemy some minutes to break their way in here, but then we will have to resort to hand to hand fighting with swords and the butt end of muskets."

"No, Captain Vaughan," Johnson said regretfully. "We will retreat to the House. We must abandon the Grange."

"Corporal Pollen," Gabriel shouted, "Take half a dozen men. Back to the gate, now! Open it and prepare to cover our retreat."

"One more volley, men. Make every shot count." Johnson ordered.

The muskets of the remaining men cracked once more.

"Pick up yer pieces and make fer the doors!" Hodson shouted.

The men streamed out of the open barn doors towards Garrison Gate and safety. Gabriel and Johnson brought up the rear, keeping a wary eye behind them. The first few enemy soldiers rounded the corner of one of the barns. Seeing the retreating Basing men, they halted and raised their muskets. Gabriel fired his carbine and Johnson, his pistol. The volley of enemy fire followed. A Basing man fell to his knees with a groan. Two men hesitated.

"Leave him," Hodson snapped. Pollen was standing at the gate and a minute or two later the small force was entering the sanctuary of Garrison Gate. They left behind them a score or more of dead and wounded enemy musketeers, and one of their own. Colonel Rawdon pronounced it a satisfactory result. Yet there was no escaping the unwelcome fact that, despite their efforts, the Grange had fallen to the enemy.

Gabriel and Johnson retired together to the Great Hall. Gabriel looked at the platters heaped with loaves and meat and wondered how many days the food would last, now that the farm was in the hands of the enemy. Johnson ran his hands through his black curly hair and the scent of camomile wafted towards Gabriel. Johnson's friendly, still boyish face bore the signs of strain. Like Gabriel, his cheeks and brow were smudged with powder stains.

"We did our utmost, Captain Vaughan." He sounded uncertain. As Gabriel cast about for words of reassurance, Colonel Peake dropped himself wearily onto the bench next to Johnson.

"Gentlemen, Colonel Rawdon and I have apprised the Marquis that the Grange is lost. We are grateful for your worthy efforts."

Johnson shrugged his shoulders, dispirited. "Yet the Grange is now in enemy hands, Robert, and they are doubtless enjoying our provisions."

"They are indeed," Peake confirmed. "The sentries on the ramparts opposite the Grange report men staggering from the Great Barn as if drunk. Colonel Rawdon has decided our best course is to fire the Grange. That way we destroy the provisions before the enemy attempt to remove them. Even if the buildings were empty, we should destroy them, so the enemy may not use them for cover."

"I suppose we must, then, no help for it." Johnson cracked his knuckles. "Did the Marquis consent to the loss of a year's provisions? The House will no longer have the capacity to survive a long siege with all those mouths to feed and most of the stores gone."

"Rawdon persuaded him of the necessity, Thomas. And we should act without delay. It will be perilous, far more so than this morning. The enemy may now fire at us from under cover and it is we who must attack from the open. They will not stand calmly by while we burn the buildings about their ears, and their numbers are many times ours."

"We killed a score or more I believe, Sir," Gabriel interjected, "but there must have been close on two hundred came over the wall."

"And there are plenty more since come, Captain. They have spread out along the north side of the House, along the road towards the church. Our only hope is to surprise them. They may not expect a sortie under their noses." Peake paused. He dropped his voice, his gaze sweeping between Gabriel and Johnson.

"I seek only volunteers to carry out this task. No more than 25 men, for the garrison can afford to sacrifice no more." He paused for his words to sink in.

"Then I will lead this small band," Johnson answered firmly.

"You and I together, Thomas. We few, we happy few, we band of brothers," Peake, the former bookseller quoted, grinning.

"With respect, Colonel," Gabriel interrupted. "It is senseless for both of you to take part in such a risky venture. If I might have the honour of again supporting Colonel Johnson, I am more than willing to do so."

Peake looked as if he was about to argue but then shook his head resignedly.

"You are in the right of it, Captain Vaughan. I dissuaded Colonel Rawdon from leading the sortie himself, using the same argument. Very well. Now as to the best plan of attack." Johnson cleared his throat loudly. Gabriel glanced up and saw Bess approaching the table.

"Oh, Gabriel I am relieved to see you." She dropped a curtsey to the two colonels and continued,

"I heard that you had gone outside the walls."

"Only to the Grange, Bess." He lowered his eyes, hoping she would not ask too many questions. He could see that she wanted to sit with him. He longed to do so, to eat, drink and talk with her and pretend for a few precious minutes that he would see her again that evening. But there was not the time and he feared if he lingered in her company he would lose the will to carry out the desperate task he had volunteered for.

"Gather your men then, Thomas. Captain Vaughan will follow your orders. If you are ready, Captain." Peake said meaningfully, rising to his feet.

"I am, Colonel. We are setting fire to a few barns, Bess. I must leave you for the present, love." Gabriel kissed her hand, holding on to it a moment too long.

"Take care then not to singe your beard. I care for every hair of your head," she said lightly and strolled away. Gabriel began to follow Peake and Johnson from the hall but could not resist turning for a last sight of Bess and as he did so their eyes met. He feared that, after all, she had not been deceived.

ᔓ

Johnson had followed Peake's orders to the letter. Twenty three musketeers, all volunteers, waited tensely inside Garrison Gate. Many had taken part in the morning's foray. Each man had been issued with a helmet in place of the normal musketeer's woollen cap, and a red sash. Gabriel and Johnson were dressed similarly. They were wearing buff coats, but not armour, as it would impede their ability to move. In addition to muskets and swords, the men were carrying torches, thick pieces of wood, wrapped in tallow soaked rags, ready to light. Two tall, burly men were also carrying axes.

Gabriel eyed the sky doubtfully. The wind was increasing and the clouds threatened a downpour. If it rained, there was a danger all their fire-making efforts would be in vain. The wind, on the other hand, might serve to cover the noise of their approach.

Johnson was issuing final orders.

"Remember, our task is to fire the barns. Hodson and Pollen's torches will already be alight. Only use your muskets if you must. Reloading wastes valuable time, which we do not have. The enemy are too many for us to make much of a fight of it, so only engage with them to defend yourselves. Do not waste time attacking them. As soon as every building is afire, we retreat. Our hope is to surprise them, so the faster we go, the easier our task, and the better our chances of withdrawing without heavy losses.

We will divide into two parties. I will command the assault on the Great Barn with Corporal Pollen's assistance. Captain Vaughan will lead the assault on the lesser barns and outhouses, with Corporal Hodson. Do not attempt to go to the aid of any man who is wounded or captured. It will slow us down and endanger others.

Captain Rowlett has taken one of guns loaded with case shot into the lane which leads towards Basingstoke. When it fires, that is the signal to make our sally. It should provide a diversion while we break through the gate into the Grange. If it is guarded too heavily, we will need to climb over the wall.

Are there any questions?"

There was silence.

"Then may God be with us."

ശ

Basing House, earlier that day

The Marquis's physician was supervising the care of wounded soldiers in the cellars of the Old House. Rather than remaining idle, and letting my fears grow unchecked, I made myself useful. I and other women from the household were soon occupied with carrying water, mopping up blood and vomit and offering reassurance to those suffering. Waller's guns continued to be an unnerving accompaniment to our activities. The blast was followed by a loud crash whenever they hit part of the outer walls or demolished another chimney.

Despite the neat piles of salves and other herbal remedies made by Lieutenant Johnson, the air was close and stank with blood, sickness and the stench from opened bowels. I could not help remembering how both Mother and Harry had tried to spare me from unpleasant sights. Theirs was a foolish hope in the midst of Civil War. And it would not be right to spare myself if I could. The men were fighting and dying. The women must care for them as they bled.

Lady Honoria herself came to the cellars to encourage our efforts and to remind us to take turns at resting and refreshing ourselves. She smiled at me.

"Are you not to wed Captain Vaughan, Mistress Lucie?" I nodded, surprised that she knew my name.

"A brave soldier, Mistress. I pray that he returns safely from the Grange." She smiled and moved on. I felt the blood draining from my face. I climbed the steps from the cellar mechanically and entered the Great Hall.

To my intense relief, Gabriel was there, seated at a table with Colonels Peake and Johnson. He spoke to me briefly of being about to fire some barns, before following the Colonels from the hall.

I was too sick with nervousness to eat much, but I drank some ale and crumbled some bread. It was hard to appear calm when all I could hear was cannon and musket fire. Firing barns did not sound particularly perilous, but as I returned to the cellars and the wounded men, I was counting the hours until I might hope to see Gabriel again. He would reek of smoke, and I would tease him about his blackened face and singed lace collar.

Thinking of smoke, I became gradually aware that I could smell it more strongly than usual. That and mingled odours of roasting grain and meat. I realised that I must be smelling the burning barns. Well, that was good, I reasoned. If they were well alight, his task would soon be done, yet my heart was banging against my ribs.

"Water," the wounded man muttered. I jumped up to fetch some and nearly collided with Catherine who was descending the steps. Her face was pale.

"Bess, have you heard from Captain Vaughan?"

"I saw him at dinner, Catherine. He had just returned safely from the Grange. Now he is setting fire to some barns."

She stared at me. "But, Bess, do you not know? The barns are part of the Grange, and it fell to the enemy this morning. Edward told me that a handful of our men have returned there in an attempt to burn them down. They are all volunteers. It is doubtful that any will return alive."

ꟹ

The Grange

"Starting to rain, Cap'n. That'll send the whoresons packing I reckon," Hodson chuckled. It was mid afternoon and Gabriel's party had torched all but two of the smaller buildings. Their efforts had been at a cost. They had come under heavy fire as soon as they entered the Grange. Setting fire to thatch, wood and straw as they went, they had embarked on a deadly game of hide and seek with the enemy among the scattered buildings. Of the 11 men who Gabriel had taken with him, only five were yet alive. The others lay in the mud, or their bodies were fuelling the leaping flames. Leaving Hodson and two men on guard outside, Gabriel pulled open the heavy double doors of another barn. Smoke stung his eyes and throat. He and his two musketeers entered the dim interior.

"Far enough, I think. Throw down your weapons. Your sword, please, Sir. I feel sure General Waller would like to make your acquaintance." There was the click of muskets being cocked. A score of enemy musketeers were standing in two ranks facing the doors.

And so, for him it was over. Gabriel felt almost relieved. He had done as much as could be hoped for with such a small force. Now he had only to decide whether to surrender or to die fighting. Waller had a reputation as a gentleman, but Gabriel had no wish to face interrogation on the size of the garrison and their defensive plans. It made the choice easier.

"Hodson!" he yelled.

"Cap'n!" came an answering shout from outside the barn.

"Barricade the doors and fire the barn. Shoot any who try to escape."

An answering thud confirmed that the doors had been barred. Smoke began to creep underneath them.

"A valiant decision, Captain, but I believe my men and I will have time to break out after dispatching you and your men."

It was possible that he was correct, but Gabriel hoped to persuade him otherwise. As his eyes became accustomed to the gloom, he took stock of the enemy officer facing him. The man was tall, wearing a green coat with gold lace and a broad brimmed hat. The coat was travel stained and dark with rain, but the absence of blood stains suggested he had not been engaged in close combat. He might be inexperienced. There might yet be a chance for

Gabriel and his men.

"If you will agree to let my men out unharmed, Sir, and that your men will take no further part in today's fighting, I will have the doors unbarred, and I will fight you in single combat. The victor goes free."

Nobody moved, but there was the sound of crackling flames, and a tongue of fire shot up the wall. The enemy officer glanced at the rapidly spreading flames and scowled.

"Very well. You have my word."

"Hodson!" Gabriel yelled again, "Unbar the doors. Men coming out. Don't shoot."

A welcome gush of cool, wet air blew in as the doors opened, in spite of the flames building around the doorway. Gabriel and the enemy officer regarded each other. In silence, they prepared to fight. Gabriel removed his heavy helmet along with his carbine and pistols. The fight would be with swords alone and other weapons would act as an encumbrance. Gabriel scuffed his boot experimentally across the trodden earth floor, testing its surface. It appeared firm, but space to wield a sword was limited by the heaped provisions. At one end of the barn, bales of straw were piled almost to the roof, and flames were already spreading up one wall. Gabriel drew his sword and added his baldric and scabbard to the pile of discarded weapons.

"Are you ready, Sir?" Gabriel bowed his head in acquiescence. The other officer was bouncing on the soles of his feet. No more than 20 or 21, he was impatient to fight. As Gabriel stood quietly waiting, the man made a sudden rush at him. Gabriel stepped aside, raising his sword. The fight began in earnest. Despite the open doors, the air was filling with choking smoke. The barn was burning and it could not be a long encounter if either was to survive it.

Gabriel fought defensively, looking for a weak spot. His opponent was attacking fiercely, but although he had some skill, he was relying more on power and energy than finesse. Time slowed for Gabriel as it often did in battle. His sword arm was reacting automatically while his brain devised a plan. With each reply to the other's blade, he began to turn him imperceptibly until his back was to the wall with the bales of straw. Slowly he began to up the pace, with each clash of steel he was forcing the officer a little closer to the bales which were now beginning to flicker with flame.

Three paces from the wall, Gabriel's opponent realised his intentions. Laughing, he spun half round on his heel, his momentum taking him back towards Gabriel again. He lunged. Gabriel reacted too slowly and the blade slashed through his breeches. It struck him no more than a glancing blow, but the edge of the sharp blade cut into the outside of his right thigh. Gabriel gasped in pain, flinging himself desperately sideways as the triumphant officer lunged again. The man followed him across the barn, and now his back was at the smouldering bales. Gabriel had him where he had planned, but at a price. Blood was seeping from the wound and burning pain was shooting through his thigh.

The officer glanced over his shoulder as the straw burst into flames. Without dropping his guard, or taking his eyes off Gabriel, he sidestepped neatly away from it. Behind the blazing straw, the brick wall appeared solid enough, but the flames had climbed hungrily into the old, dry timbers of the arched roof. Neglected through the many years of the estate's impoverishment, the timbers were rotted almost through in places, and now they were well alight. Above the two duelling men, a massive beam threatened to fall, but both were oblivious to the danger.

Panting for breath, Gabriel choked on a lungful of smoke. A bright orange flare belatedly drew his attention to the half-rotted beam, blazing fiercely above his head. The enemy officer, noting only that his opponent was distracted, charged at Gabriel in what was clearly intended as a final onslaught. Gabriel brought up his sword to parry but out of the corner of his eye he saw the orange blur descending from the roof. He twisted sideways and lost his footing. His sword flew from his hand and he landed on the wounded thigh with a cry amid a shower of sparks. For a moment, he could do nothing but lie there groaning. With difficulty, he raised himself, bracing the good leg to haul himself to his feet. Looking about him wildly for his adversary, he retrieved his sword from the ground and began beating with gloved hands at the sparks which had landed on his sash and breeches.

There was a scream. Less fortunate than Gabriel, the enemy officer was pinned helplessly beneath the heavy beam, the smouldering wood glowing. Through the crackle of the flames, Gabriel caught the words "Help me!" He hesitated before grabbing one corner of the beam in his gloved hands and heaving. The beam was too heavy, and he relinquished it hurriedly as the flames threatened to burn through his leather gloves.

"For pity's sake," the officer whispered. The flames were licking at his face and his hair was alight. Gabriel understood. He limped to his abandoned carbine, cocked it and discharged it at the officer's head. Then he staggered from the building.

It was raining heavily now. Hodson and his men were standing outside the door. Hodson regarded him in relief.

"You're alive, Cap'n! I heard a shot."

"The officer is dead, Hodson. And I may be of little use at present," Gabriel groaned.

"Let me have a look at that, Sir. Doesn't look too deep, but we should tie it up." He hastily ripped a strip of cloth from his red sash and bound it around Gabriel's thigh.

"There, Cap'n. No doubt now which side you're on!" he grinned.

Gabriel grimaced at the feeble joke.

"Any sighting of Colonel Johnson's men?"

"Heavy firing coming from the Great Barn, Cap'n."

"Then we must go to them. We have yet men remaining and we have not expended all our ammunition."

Hodson regarded Gabriel doubtfully but nodded and the six men trudged onwards through the downpour towards the sounds of firing.

There was a distant roll of drums, many drums, coming from Waller's command post on Cowdray's Down. The weary group of men paused to listen.

"Retreat, Cap'n. That's the retreat them drums are beating. Buggers 'ave 'ad enough!"

Sure enough, men could be seen retreating towards the boundary wall. Some were staggering, drunk rather than wounded. They were firing their muskets haphazardly as they went. Most were simply running.

Smoke was pouring from the interior of the Great Barn as winter stores were consumed by flames, but the massive brick structure itself appeared unscathed. "Take more than a few torches to destroy that," grunted Hodson.

"We have done enough for today, Hodson. That smoke spells the end of Basing's winter stores. We have fulfilled our purpose."

The yard of the Great Barn bore witness to a fierce struggle. The ground was littered with bodies. In the midst of the yard, Johnson's last four men were engaged in hand to hand fighting with those few of the enemy who were ignoring the continuing command of their drums to withdraw.

Hodson glanced at Gabriel.

"Support our men, Corporal. I will do what I can to assist."

With a yell, Hodson and the others threw themselves into the fray, wielding the butt end of their muskets. Gabriel reloaded his carbine and pistols. He would be little enough use at present with his sword. He scanned the yard, peering through the billowing smoke. In the corner of the yard, a furious sword fight was in progress. It was Johnson engaged with an officer in green coat and tawny sash. Unobserved, Gabriel drew closer to the fighting pair. He was uneasy. Johnson was much the older, and a valiant soldier, but the life of a herbalist and botanist did not offer combat opportunities. Gabriel could see that Johnson was tiring, while the young Roundhead was not. As Gabriel watched, the green suited officer spun, delivering a lightning fast backhand blow which sent Johnson's sword flying out of his hand. The man stood back, grinning, waiting for Johnson to surrender. Instead, the furious Colonel drew his dagger and threw himself towards the Roundhead. Gabriel reacted without thought, firing the carbine. The officer fell backwards, shot through the jaw.

"That was ungentlemanly, Captain Vaughan," Johnson protested, panting for breath.

"My apologies, Sir, but I do not believe Basing can afford to lose you."

The death of their officer was enough to send the remaining handful of enemy in headlong flight towards the boundary wall. As darkness fell, the bedraggled survivors of Colonel Johnson's group made their way back through Garrison Gate. More than half their fellows lay dead. They could not retrieve their bodies and give them burial until it was safe to do so. The enemy had abandoned their attempt on the outer defences and withdrawn. How far remained to be seen when daylight came.

Gabriel limped painfully towards the cellars of the Old House. Not wishing Bess to see his hurt, he was relieved that she was not there. A woman cleaned his wound. The Marquis's physician was moving wearily from one wounded man to the next. His white apron was stained crimson. He glanced briefly at Gabriel's thigh and motioned him to sit. Gabriel collapsed thankfully onto a stool.

"Not deep," he confirmed. "I will suture it for you presently."

Gabriel's clothes were soaked through and he was shivering. The cellars had been chosen for safety, not warmth.

"Gabriel!"

It was Bess. Realising he must present a sorry sight, Gabriel forced himself to his feet and smiled at her. He was muddied from coat to boots. Rain was dripping off the end of his long hair. His gloves, coat, breeches and sash were blood stained, holed and singed from sparks and embers. She threw her arms around his neck.

"Thank goodness you are safe. I heard you were returned. I was looking for you. Did you bring a wounded man down here?" He shook his head, embarrassed.

"Captain Vaughan, pray sit down and I will attend to your wound."

Gabriel sighed. This was not the best way for Bess to discover he was injured.

"It's nothing, Bess," he said hurriedly, for her face had blanched.

"I will be the judge of that, Captain Vaughan," the physician said briskly. "Mistress Lucie. Bring Captain Vaughan some wine. It will dull the edge of the pain while I mend this slash."

The wine did little enough, but Gabriel got through the stitching of his flesh as best he could.

"Gabriel, if you are going to do something truly dangerous, promise me you will trust me enough to tell me in future," Bess whispered as Gabriel limped up the steps from the cellar.

"I promise. Truly, I am more weary than anything for it was a hard fight today. Go to your bed now, Bess. We will see what the morrow brings. Tonight the rebels have been defeated by our fire and the rain."

"Then, is Waller truly gone?"

Gabriel hesitated. He knew she desperately sought reassurance, but did not want to give her false hope when that hope might be speedily dashed.

"For the moment, Bess he is gone, but I fear he will be back. He did not bring that huge force upon us to give up so easily. I fear there may be worse to come."

Gabriel shuddered inwardly. Bess's safety lay in him guarding the House with his life, not his death. He hoped he would be up to the challenge.

He watched her walk away, turning frequently to look at him, as if fearing he might vanish.

ഗ

8 November 1643

An uneasy calm settled on Basing House.

Rowlett's action in the lane with the saker had been intended chiefly as a diversion while Colonel Johnson's party attacked the Grange. It had achieved more than that, however. Rowlett had trapped a troop of Waller's own regiment. Prisoners had been taken and Waller's own Captain Lieutenant, a man named Clinson, had been killed. Scouts brought intelligence that Waller's army had withdrawn but not far, only to the nearby town of Basingstoke and its surrounding villages.

We waited for Waller to attack again.

The morning was spent in the sad task of retrieving the bodies of those who had fallen beyond the walls. Servants from the House dug a row of graves in the orchard and prayers were said for Protestant and Catholic alike.

I returned to the cellars. There was little to do. Only two or three men remained. Those most seriously wounded had not survived the night, while the others had returned to their own quarters. Gabriel too, on Colonel Johnson's orders, was resting to allow his wound some time to heal.

My lesson with Father Allen provided welcome occupation. The priest greeted me eagerly.

"Bess, I think this will be our final meeting. I believe you are ready. Providing the rebels do not return, I propose we receive you into the Church on the morrow."

"So soon?"

"Events have come upon us swiftly, Bess. A little longer might have been better, but these times are perilous. Now let us make the most of this hour to ensure you are properly prepared. You may tell Gabriel if he wishes to be present he should be here at dawn." His eyes held mine. "You are looking anxious, Bess."

I took a couple of deep breaths. My hands felt clammy. "Nothing Father. It's just..."

"Just real and no longer playacting at being a papist?" I nodded, embarrassed.

"It is natural to feel some apprehension at this step you are taking, now that the day has come. Talk to Gabriel today. I will expect you at the chapel an hour before dawn so that we may pray together and I may give you absolution for your sins."

26

THE DOOR BURST open. Father Allen looked up, disturbed from his writing. An agitated Gabriel limped into the room.

"Father, I must speak with you without delay."

"You appear overwrought. Is your leg paining you?"

"I did not come here to talk of my wound!" Gabriel snapped.

The Jesuit regarded him coolly. "Might I assume you came to talk of Mistress Lucie?"

"I did, Father." Gabriel shifted uncomfortably, aware that this was a priest he was sparring with.

"Bess has just informed me you propose receiving her into the Church tomorrow."

"I thought it were better not to delay. I have the holy chrism so that she may be confirmed."

"This is madness, Father. You must realise that Waller and his army may return at any time."

"That is what has led to my proposal," the priest continued strongly. "... Which Bess has accepted."

Gabriel pressed a hand to his forehead.

"Gabriel, I was under the impression you wished Bess to become a Catholic. I do not understand your anger."

"My concern is for her safety, Father. When I brought her to Basing, I believed I was bringing her to a place of safety. Two days ago we were being pounded by the rebels' siege guns. Under the rules of war, if a siege ends after a garrison has refused terms, as Basing has, and the defenders are later forced to surrender, quarter may be refused. And Catholics are less likely to receive mercy if Basing surrenders. It is possible that they may be put to the sword, both men and women."

"Sadly Gabriel, yes I am aware of that. To be blunt then, you fear that by becoming a Catholic Bess places herself in danger."

"In greater danger," Gabriel corrected.

"That may indeed be so," the priest said calmly, "But my concern is for her soul."

Gabriel glared at Father Allen. "Well Father, I love Bess, and I would rather she remained a live Protestant."

"Than a dead Catholic," the priest finished for him. He steepled his fingers in thought, then glanced at the desperate man.

"Gabriel, some weeks ago I received a rather similar visit from Bess on another matter. I advised her then not to try to come between you and your conscience. I give you now the same counsel. The decision should remain with Bess. Does she waver in her resolve?"

Gabriel regarded him bleakly, "She does not."

"Then heed my advice. We will expect you at the chapel around dawn."

ഗ

Gabriel's words before he bedded me were that there was no going back. Now I was preparing to take another irrevocable step. This was one for which I had been preparing, a necessary one if Gabriel and I were to be truly man and wife. I was no longer in any doubt as to the risks in being a papist. He was resigned and chastened after his abrupt visit to the priest.

"You are resolved then, Bess to do this?"

"You know I am." I kissed him softly on the lips.

I tossed and turned in bed. Mary sighed and shifted beside me. I took long, slow breaths. Was I having second thoughts? I knew that was not the case. I had made the decision many weeks ago, before I had even arrived at Basing. From Gabriel's first kiss I had been lost and had unconsciously set my feet upon this path. Whatever happened now, I reminded myself that we would remain together.

The hour before dawn found me nervously approaching the Great Gatehouse by candle light. To my surprise, Gabriel emerged from the shadows. He kissed my hand. It was accompanied by a look which, by the flickering light of the candle, made me go weak at the knees. He pressed into my hand a small silver crucifix on a delicate silver chain. "Shall I place it around your neck?"

I nodded. His hands were shaking. His breath was warm on my neck as he gently fastened the chain. I shivered at the touch of his hands.

"I love you," I whispered.

"I will return later." He pressed my hand and disappeared once more into the shadows.

I climbed the spiral stairs, in darkness but for the meagre light from my candle, and edged into the chapel, already illuminated by the glow of the tall candles on the altar. Their comforting light calmed me. The air was scented with burning wax and the lingering traces of incense. I dipped my fingers into the stoup of water and made the sign of the cross. In the space of a month, what was once strange was now a calming ritual.

Father Allen, in his vestments, was kneeling before the altar. He rose. His smile at me intensified as he noticed the chain about my neck. "From Gabriel?"

I nodded.

"Welcome, Bess. You are come to be reconciled to the Church. Gabriel will join us as you make the Profession of Faith. Then joining with the rest of us from this House you will celebrate your first Mass as a Catholic. It is then that you will be confirmed and receive Communion. But before that you must first confess your sins so that I may give you absolution.

Prepare yourself. When the hour candle burns near to the next ring, come forward and kneel. God and I will listen."

I was eighteen years old. What did I have to confess except my previous adherence to the Established Church of England, and my one great sin that I had lain with Gabriel? Was I not a dutiful daughter and a loving sister? Was I then quite perfect? I knew I was not. I saw my father's angry face as he prepared to beat me.

Was I sorry that I had lain with Gabriel? I still grew warm with happiness as I remembered the joy and pleasure of that one night. But then I was forced to remember the next morning – I saw Will's face, white with rage as he advanced on Gabriel, his sword drawn. I saw Gabriel's flush of shame at Harry's words, "you have brought dishonour to our family". It was I who had brought dishonour to my family. And I had permitted Gabriel to take the blame. I had caused a rift in my family, had caused Gabriel to bring shame to his own family. That night had all been part of my dream of independence. I had given no thought to the future consequences for my family and Gabriel. My heart was heavy as I acknowledged to myself that I had confused wilful disobedience for independence.

Well there was nought to be done to mend matters. I could only make my peace with God.

"Come, Bess." Father Allen was standing beside me. The hour candle was nearly burnt down to the next ring. I rose and followed him.

ℴ

Gabriel looked down at Bess as they descended the gatehouse stairs together after Mass. He grimaced, hoping she would not have cause to regret what she had just done. His anxiety of the previous day had not left him. His heart had been thumping so loudly he had scarcely heard Bess's words as she quietly recited the Profession of Faith, which marked her change of allegiance to the church of Rome.

"Gabriel," Bess's voice interrupted his thoughts. "I feel different somehow. I had not thought I would. It is very odd..." Her voice trailed off as she touched the silver crucifix around her neck and stared at it. Her brow creased into a small frown. He could see that something troubled her.

"What is it, Bess?" He stared at her. "Would you prefer to set it aside for a time until you become accustomed to being a papist?"

"It is not that which concerns me." She reached for his right hand, caressing his ring finger. A pale band showed where Catherine's ring had sat.

"I have nothing to give you in return, as Catherine did." There was a catch in her voice. "I have no money, Gabriel, no dowry."

Relief and compassion fought for control of his emotions before both were overtaken by exasperation.

"Never say you have nothing to give me, Bess. You have given up everything for me and I can ask no more. I have not even thanked you for the sacrifice you make." He took her hand and pressed his lips to it.

"Come now, let us break our fast."

ಌ

12 November 1643

On Sunday, Waller returned. Despite urgent messages from the Marquis, nothing had been heard from Hopton and the hoped for relief for Basing House.

It was mid-morning when scouts brought word that Waller approached. Beating drums and the sounds of tramping feet, hooves and rumbling carts swelled until it seemed that they were within the very walls of Basing House.

The sky was grey and lowering. The garrison doggedly prepared themselves, with a sense that the day would be one of reckoning. Officers were tense, snapping reminders to keep muskets covered and powder dry.

Father Allen threaded his way unobtrusively through the men of the garrison, a stole about his neck, hearing confessions and giving absolution. Gabriel was one of those who knelt before him. He had killed men enough in the last few days to feel the need for a fresh shriving of his soul. He was only sorry he had no more sins of the flesh to confess. When the drums of the garrison began to beat the alarm there was only time for a last kiss.

ᔕ

I joined the other women and children in the Great Hall, casting about for the most useful task. The Marchioness called for our attention. Lady Honoria had a sparkle in her eyes. I realised that she was as much a force to be reckoned with as her husband the Marquis. "Ladies, if you are not caring for children, please come with me. We must strip the lead from the roof for bullets. The servants are waiting in the kitchens to melt it down. Fetch your cloaks and your gloves."

With a bang, Waller's guns opened fire. We heard the replying higher note from a small gun mounted on the roof.

After a moment of stunned silence, at least forty women got to their feet including Catherine, Mary and me. As we walked in solemn procession towards the turrets of the New House, I closed my eyes for a moment to pray that Gabriel would be safe.

ᔕ

"Where's Hopton then? Got lost on the road from Winchester? How about Prince Robber? His dog's got more balls than him."

Gabriel had taken twenty of his troop out on the fastest of Basing's horses to see how the enemy were approaching, but they were barely beyond Garrison Gate when they encountered a large body of horse cantering towards them. The enemy horse halted and then divided. Some rode off towards the south side of the House and the park, others remaining in view not far from Garrison Gate. A further troop peeled off towards the New House. It was the group nearest Garrison Gate who were shouting insults.

"Shall we make a charge, Captain? See if we can scatter them?"

Cornet Hide drew his sword eagerly. Gabriel eyed the enemy cavalry.

"No, Francis," Gabriel slowly motioned a cautionary gesture towards the Cornet. "We should withdraw before they cut us off from the House." Still watching the enemy, Gabriel continued, "They will charge us in a few moments. When I lower my sword, make for Garrison Gate."

Never taking his eyes from the enemy, Gabriel drew his sword, and held it above his head as if about to lead a charge. The enemy officer in the front rank mirrored his action. Gabriel's sword swept down and his small band abruptly wheeled their horses, galloping towards the safety of Garrison Gate.

Cursing the soreness from the slash in his thigh, Gabriel hurried towards the officers standing on the roof of the Great Gatehouse.

"The House is surrounded by cavalry. We had scarce left the gate when they were upon us."

"A break out by our horse is not likely to succeed then," Peake reflected thoughtfully. "I had thought they might reach Hopton."

Colonel Rawdon lowered the spyglass. "We have too few horse to hazard them in such a venture. No, Robert, our two troops of horse must fight on foot today. Every man will be needed here. Waller means business this time. We will make no more sorties from Garrison Gate. Captain Vaughan, return there and have the men barricade it heavily. Use wood, earth, everything you can find. That gate must stand."

Gabriel gave a short bow and made his way back to the gate.

Waller's artillery was already making its presence felt. No longer on Cowdray's Down, they were drawn up in the small wood to the north east of the House, considerably closer than before. The officers watched the fall of the shot. Most of the balls were either hitting, or falling short of, the New House.

"They are concentrating their fire power on the New House," Peake went on thoughtfully. "They have realised it is the weakest point. We will load the gun on the roof of the New House with case shot. If we can hit a few of their gunners it may cool their ardour."

"The Marquis and I are agreed we must prepare in case we need to fall back to the Old House. If it comes to it, we will make our last stand there." Rawdon's voice was sombre.

"Lieutenant Watson, fetch every servant, man and woman who can wield a spade, except those employed in casting bullets. Barricade each window and door to the Old House. Leave only this Gate House unbarred."

"What about the bridge from the New House, Colonel?" Johnson asked.

"That we will leave for the present, Thomas. If we need to abandon the New House, we will deal with it then. Let us hope the situation does not become that desperate."

"I will do what I can to prevent the encirclement becoming complete," Johnson promised. "I will take a sally party out to the half moon at the south west corner. I believe we may give a good account of ourselves."

"Then do so, Johnson. You might use the lane beneath it to surprise them," Rawdon added. "Lieutenant Cuffaud, move one of the drakes onto the bailey. The Great Barn still stands. Fire the piece at it. See if you can demolish it so the enemy may not use it in their attack. They have already taken the church for that purpose. Well, what is it, Cuffaud?"

"Sir, the cattle are on the bailey, what of them?"

"Do not talk to me of cows, Cuffaud. Your family may have land and cattle, but I have lived in London these many years. Move them!"

"Colonel!" Captain Rowlett had been missing from the group. Now he arrived looking gloomy.

"Well, Captain?"

"Corporal Martin is not to be found. He must have deserted over the wall last night."

"He will be able to tell them of our strength," Peake muttered.

"True enough, but not how we dispose our forces today. He may be of little use to them." Rawdon countered.

The officers dispersed swiftly to their tasks, with Johnson taking his party to one of the new defensive earthworks known as half moons from their shape.

ග

A soldier waving his arms and gesturing was trying to coax a herd of cattle away from the bailey. Cuffaud was commanding a team of men and horses as they dragged a gun into the middle of the bailey. Half a dozen cattle stampeded towards the ditch.

Gabriel's soldiers were shovelling mounds of earth to fortify the Garrison Gate.

"That should hold them for a while, men." Gabriel brushed muddy gloved hands against his breeches, making them muddier. His riding boots had sunk into the mire as he added his own efforts to the hasty reinforcement, and he tugged them free with difficulty.

"I hope that will withstand cannon shot, Captain Vaughan." Peake was making the rounds of the tiny garrison, spread pitifully thin around the mile of defensive walls and earthworks. He peered closely through his short sighted eyes at the mound of packed earth, strengthened with stones and wooden bars, which was buttressing Garrison Gate. "I trust we may give a good account of the House now. Colonel Johnson has been holding them off to the southwest. He ambushed a company in the lane below the half moon."

"I fear they play with us, Colonel. They have not yet attempted to press home an attack. Do they mean to but sit before the House and skirmish with us the whole day through?"

"Colonel Peake!" a cavalry trooper arrived at a gallop from the Old House. "A message from Colonel Rawdon. A large body of foot is in sight. They are approaching through the wood with scaling ladders."

"They are coming, then," Gabriel muttered. He crossed himself, and

Peake followed his example.

"Defend Garrison Gate, Captain Vaughan. Man the ramparts. Use the musket loops in the wall. I will return to Colonel Rawdon and ask if he can spare you any more men. How is the leg?" he asked abruptly.

"I can wield a sword well enough or fire a gun, Sir."

Peake's eyes softened and he clapped Gabriel on the shoulder.

"Hold them off as long as you are able, Gabriel."

ꕥ

"They mean to storm," Rawdon declared. "They used the wood for cover. We could not see them until now. From the number of colours there must be at least two thousand of them. And they are dragging two drakes."

Peake trained his own spy glass on the wood. Sure enough, he could see two labouring teams of five horses heaving two of the small field guns towards the house.

"Wet underfoot, that may slow them down." he muttered. It was raining again and the wood would be slippery with mud and fallen leaves. "Do you recognise any of the colours, Colonel?"

Rawdon trained his glass on the infantry approaching from the north.

"Fructus Virtutis, that is Waller's own regiment. And with him is the Red Regiment, the red ensigns with the silver palm leaves. That is my own old regiment. Good troops. I trained them myself." He lowered the spy glass, drumming his fingers against it.

"I think we can take it that if Waller throws his most seasoned troops against the north side of the House, that will be the focus of his main attack. We had better place sharpshooters on the north facing towers of the New House. If they can pick off a few of the enemy advance guard it may blunt their enthusiasm."

"And what of Garrison Gate? Can I send more men to support Captain Vaughan?"

Rawdon tugged at his moustache. "How many does he have?"

"Just the 80 musketeers, Sir."

"Very well, you may send him his own troop of horse. That will add another 50 men to hold the north side of the house. They are not accustomed to fighting on foot, but they know Captain Vaughan. Send that young whippersnapper Hide with these orders for Captain Vaughan. He must hold out as long as practicable. If the fight goes against them and the enemy succeed in scaling the walls, he should save as many men as possible and pull back into the Old House."

Peake clattered down the spiral stairs towards the court. Rawdon reflected that thus far they had been lucky. Johnson and Vaughan had made a valiant effort at the Grange, but the real victor had been the weather. Was it an unreasonable hope that their small garrison would hold out against a determined onslaught from the large force? Was it possible Hopton might yet arrive in time to save them from defeat and surrender?

ᔓ

While my hands engaged in the task of stripping lead from the roof, my mind had leisure for what Gabriel had termed my fearful imaginings. My thoughts described two separate and never ending loops of what might be. In both, I saw the future. They began alike, with scenes of Gabriel's parents in Wales making ready for the journey to attend our wedding; and Harry setting out cheerfully from Oxford on the same mission. Then they sharply diverged. In one, Gabriel and I, surrounded by family and friends from Basing, knelt before the altar after our hands had been joined in marriage. Feasting, dancing, singing, then Gabriel bedding me once more. Gazing into his eyes and knowing I would never be parted from him. In the second imaginary future, Gabriel's parents and Harry arrived at the smoking ruin of Basing House to find me kneeling on the cold ground of Basing's orchard beside Gabriel's grave.

An hour or more passed while I continued to move mechanically about the roof of the southernmost tower of the New House, where a dozen of Lady Honoria's female army was busily engaged. The rain fell upon us and the wind snatched at the hood of my cloak. My only conversation with the other women was shouted questions of where to move to next, what parts of the roof would most easily yield the coveted lead to our unskilled quest. Our voices were shrill, battling the sounds of wind, rain, and over all the deep boom of Waller's guns.

There was a sudden silence. The guns had stopped. I paused to peer down from the roof. Distant cries were coming from behind the House. Like air escaping from a ruptured pig's bladder, my thoughts freed themselves in a rush from the twin loops of my best and worst hopes. I skidded across the wet lead, peering northwards. Across the vast central court of the New House, the northern tower was bustling with tiny figures. A group of our soldiers was loading the field gun placed on the roof. Others were running towards the edge of the roof, carrying muskets. They knelt and the distant crack of shots floated towards me, followed by the deeper note of the drake.

"Bess, are the enemy advancing?" Mary stared at me, her eyes like saucers.

The wind had torn the hood of her velvet cloak from her head. Water was dripping off the end of her snub nose and trickling off her curls unheeded. Mary was proud of her luxuriant curls. Part of my brain wondered how long it would take to restore them to their accustomed state, while common sense interjected that if Mary were killed or taken prisoner her curls would be of little moment.

We were probably in no danger so far above the fighting, but should we break off our work of lead gathering? We had all abandoned what we were doing, pails cast aside. More shouts from the northern tower. Our musketeers were traversing its roof towards its southern edge. A fair haired officer directed their movements as they spread out and reloaded their muskets, not Gabriel then. I stood irresolutely, Mary now clinging to my arm. Moments later, a multitude of enemy soldiers came into view. Marching rapidly along the side of the New House to the brisk tattoo of drums, they were heading in our direction. Some carried tall ladders between them, others muskets or pikes. Tawny sashed officers on horseback cantered ahead of them.

There was a clatter of boots from the stairs. Captain Rowlett burst onto the roof, a score of musketeers with him. He stopped abruptly at the sight of the frightened women huddled together like sheep, and muttered something then cleared his throat.

"Ladies, please withdraw, the enemy are below and you will be safer within the House." He gestured toward the staircase, his gaze already directed towards the enemy. Hundreds of green coats and yellow coats were flooding towards the half-moon at the south east corner of the New House. I leant over the roof, slightly dizzied at the drop beneath me. There was firing from the half moon. A company of our blue coated men was there, shooting at the enemy in a bid to halt their advance. They were so few and the enemy so many. I marked the fall of enemy soldiers, but still they came on, one of them brandishing an ensign of green and yellow.

"Ladies, please!" there was increasing urgency in Captain Rowlett's tones as he marshalled his small force of musketeers. "Covering fire," he snapped.

The men were kneeling, sheltering their weapons as best they could from the wind and rain as they rammed scouring sticks down the muzzles of their muskets, and poured powder from the small wooden chargers. Our small force below fired a ragged last volley and fled. It was Colonel Johnson leading them. One of the bluecoats pitched forward on his face, flinging out his arms. Colonel Johnson hesitated briefly before running on, shepherding his men towards the House. The unfortunate blue coat disappeared beneath the oncoming rush of enemy feet and I closed my eyes in horror, but not before I saw the descending poleaxe. I stumbled. Nursing a bruised shin,

I wiped the tears from my eyes. The unseen obstacle was a sizable pile of bricks and other building rubble. I turned back towards the inert mass of what I abruptly recognised were possible deadly missiles.

"Captain Rowlett!" The officer paid me no heed, his attention focussed on his musketeers.

"Ram down your wadding, hard now, or the bullets will fall from the muzzle when you point your muskets downwards."

I peered gingerly over the edge. The rebels had formed up in ranks and the closest men were almost directly underneath. I was looking down upon the tops of their heads, protected only by knitted Monmouth caps. Green and yellow clad shoulders jostled below, a forest of pikes, the long ash staves tipped with sharp steel points pointing skywards. I picked up my skirts and crossed purposefully towards the pile of rubble.

"Bess, what are you doing?" Catherine stared at me. I hefted a heavy brick in each hand and marched towards the southeast edge of the roof. My hands were shaking, but I only knew I must act. I could not bear to retire below and hear the shots followed by the screams of dying men. Neither could I stand here only to watch more men die before my eyes.

"Catherine, Mary," I panted. I placed the heavy bricks on the leads a few paces from a kneeling musketeer. "Let us see how many heads we can break? Did you never learn to lob a ball when you played with your brothers?"

Grasping a brick with both of my gloved hands, I lifted it above my head. It was many times heavier than anything I had thrown in games with Will and Harry. I aimed as best I might, hurling it savagely at the pikemen and musketeers far below me.

ക

"Captain Vaughan, we are running low on ammunition." Gabriel was kneeling beside one of the musket loops in the curtain wall. He paused to fire his carbine and then turned his attention to Corporal Fletcher.

"Send Cooper to the Old House cellars. Tell him to take a horse. If Colonel Rawdon can spare it, he should bring a loaded cart."

To preserve their dwindling supply, Gabriel ordered every third man to hold his fire. There was little enough ammunition on the bed of the small farm cart clattering towards them but Gabriel was grateful for it. Driving the cart with Cooper was Watt, the groom.

The boy wore one of the army issued tucks, dangling from a tattered sword belt. He was dressed as usual in the grooms' uniform of brown tunic and breeches, the Paulet crest on the shoulder, but a battered pot helmet sat awkwardly atop his small head.

"Turned soldier now, Watt?"

The groom set his jaw. "I want to fight, Sir. I took the sword from one of the rebel prisoners."

Gabriel studied the boy who reached only to his shoulder. He recalled his own words to Bess,

"I do not wish to see boys younger than 16 standing in the line of battle." Watt's hazel eyes in his freckled face gazed pleadingly.

"Captain," it was Fletcher at his elbow. "Where should we store the ammunition?" He waved his hand at the scanty number of boxes and the solitary barrel being unloaded by two of the men.

"Far enough away from Garrison Gate in case they try to blow it, under the overhang. Cover them with oiled cloth before the rain soaks them.

Oh, very well, Watt, return the cart to the stables and then report to Corporal Fletcher. But you are neither musketeer nor trained swordsman. You will act as a messenger. Bring a horse." The boy opened his mouth to protest.

"Those are your orders, messenger," Gabriel held his gaze.

"Aye, Sir." Watt leapt onto the cart and flicked the reins hard. The draught horse broke into a lumbering trot. Gabriel relaxed his severe expression and permitted himself a wry grin.

"Captain Vaughan!" The shout came from the small tower in a corner of the curtain wall. "The enemy is massing outside Garrison Gate."

Gabriel ran awkwardly to the tower and launched himself up the short flight of steps.

"In what force?" he gasped.

The sentry pointed wordlessly. A musket ball flew past Gabriel's ear as he peered over the edge. There were a hundred or more of the enemy close to the gate. What were they intending? There were pikemen and musketeers enough to storm the gate, but how did they intend to force it? They were not carrying the scaling ladders so were presumably intending to go through, not over. Gabriel hoped they had done enough to protect the gate, but if the enemy applied one of the small bell shaped bombs known as a petard to it, he was fearful of the result.

"You have not seen a petardier there?"

"No, Captain."

The cluster of enemy soldiers parted sufficiently for Gabriel to see a huge, heavily bearded man wielding an axe. Clad in the armour of a pikeman, he was more than six foot tall.

"Concentrate your fire on that man." The sentry fired his musket. The ball bounced off the giant's back plate before he was once more hidden from view. The sound of crashing blows joined the sounds of musket fire as Gabriel descended from the tower.

"Corporal Fletcher, withdraw half the men from the defence of the curtain wall. Form them up in ranks of five with loaded muskets, facing the gate. And have your best shots at the musket loops nearest the gate. See how many of the enemy they can account for."

Hearing the clatter of hooves behind him, he paused. It was Watt, mounted on one of the cavalry horses from the New House. Now Gabriel could get word to Rawdon and Peake of the new threat.

Within minutes Watt was back, followed by Peake. The deputy Governor swung down off his horse.

"The enemy are offering sharp entertainment then."

Peake's short-sighted eyes scanned the row of musketeers kneeling at the musket loops and the half company drawn up in ranks a few paces from Garrison Gate.

"How many have you lost?"

"No more than seven, Sir, mainly lucky shots through the musket loops."

"They have not employed their scaling ladders?"

"Not as yet, Colonel."

"And the enemy at the gate, what progress do they make?"

The steady thud of the axe could still be heard while Gabriel led Peake towards a stretch of wall where Fletcher was overseeing several men stealthily loosening bricks from three small sections.

"Ready, Captain, when you give the word," Fletcher muttered. Each hole was wide enough for two kneeling men to fire point blank at the enemy while two more fired over their shoulders.

Gabriel crouched beside the stretch of wall. He nodded at the loosened bricks. Quietly the men slid the loosened bricks from the wall. The first twelve musketeers took up their positions.

"Now!" the muskets exploded in a volley. The thud of the axe abruptly ceased. Shouts of alarm issued from the enemy side of the wall. Fletcher was martialling the next twelve musketeers into position. Hardly daring to breathe, Gabriel peered through one of the gaps. The giant was being dragged away, blood pouring from his head. At least half a dozen enemy were strewn across the ground. Fletcher's men fired a second volley and the group before the gate scattered in disarray. A crimson suited officer commanded in vain for his men to stand firm. Gabriel tapped a kneeling musketeer on the shoulder and indicated the officer. The musketeer fired and the officer staggered, clawing at his bleeding leg.

"Shall we capture him, Colonel?"

"Yes, fetch him in, Gabriel."

Watt slid down from his horse.

"Let me get him, Sir."

He ran towards the wall and slithered nimbly through one of the new holes in the wall, his small body squeezing through the narrow aperture.

"We had better stop those up again," Peake jested, "Before an army of boys takes the House."

Two musketeers were clambering up a ladder against the wall, hauling a second ladder for the drop on the enemy side. There was the high pitched crack of a pistol and a cry. Gabriel whirled back towards the gap in the wall. In his small brown tunic, a scarlet patch spreading across his chest, was Watt. Gabriel gave a howl of rage and drew his sword.

"Captain Vaughan!" Peake grabbed his sword arm. "The battle is not yet won. Private vengeance must wait."

The crimson suited officer dropped his smoking pistol. The musketeers had reached him now. One drew his sword and the other dragged the officer roughly to his feet. Half carrying him they pushed him up the ladder and down the other into Basing House.

Gabriel glared at the captive officer. A white, wretched face stared back at him defiantly. He was no more than 18. Gabriel lowered his blade.

"We will bring in the lad's body at nightfall, Gabriel," Peake murmured. "We will not leave him lying there. He was a valiant and loyal soldier. Unlike his coward of a brother, the deserter."

Gabriel forced himself to concentrate. Now the enemy were gone from the gate, the loosened bricks must be replaced, the men redeployed along the wall, and they must ready themselves for the next onslaught.

"Watt Martin was a brave lad, Sir." Fletcher's lined face creased into deeper folds as he spoke.

Gabriel swore. Fletcher looked at him in surprise.

"Fletcher, are you saying Watt was Corporal Martin's brother? Has Corporal Martin deserted?"

Fletcher nodded slowly.

"Find Cornet Hide. Have him take charge here. Corporal Martin was in the working party last week when we discovered the weak section of wall. If he leads them to it, the enemy will storm the New House with ease. I must go to Colonel Rawdon at once."

ꕥ

"Damnation!" For once, the elderly Governor seemed at a loss. "You are certain Martin was of your party?"

"I am, Colonel Rawdon," Gabriel confirmed glumly. "He even jested of how the enemy would rejoice if they knew of it."

"A sorry jest now, Captain. The enemy will pay him well for such intelligence," Peake sighed. "Well we can do naught but post a stronger guard at that stretch of wall."

Rawdon snorted. "A stronger guard, Robert? You might as well say fresh troops, for there are none to be had." He lowered himself tiredly onto a stool, suddenly resembling the elderly man he was.

As if mocking them, a musketeer running towards them called out, "Sir! Captain Rowlett says fresh troops are advancing towards the New House. Towards the south east corner, Colonel, near the lower half moon."

"Then tell Captain Rowlett I will come at once."

The three officers looked at each other grimly.

"The south east corner, Colonel, that is…"

"Yes, Captain Vaughan, I am sensible of the fact that the weak section of wall is on that side of the New House."

Rawdon pushed himself to his feet and with renewed energy ran down the stairs of the Great Gatehouse, Peake at his heels. Gabriel hastened after them to where Rowlett was waiting.

They watched in silence as the new companies of foot advanced towards them. The front rank of the enemy was closer now. Through the grey curtain of rain Gabriel could see clearly the sticks of the drummers as they rose and fell, and pick out the number of stars denoting the company numbers on the colours as they dipped and swirled in the hands of the ensigns.

"London Trained bands, the auxiliaries I think," Rawdon muttered, "They will be raw. At least that is in our favour."

"Colonel, is it not likely they will have Martin with them? They will need his services to point out the section of wall." Gabriel asked thoughtfully.

"And they may well not trust him out of their sight," Rawdon snorted, "In case he seeks to trick them. They will hide him among them surely, in a coat of green or yellow, lest we discover him. Yet it is our best hope. Fetch Somers, if anyone can pick him off, it will be the head gamekeeper."

The group in the tower watched tensely as the troops came closer. A company peeled off, heading away from their fellows, parallel to the wall.

"Oh Jesu, is that not a petard they are carrying?" Gabriel passed his spyglass to Rawdon.

"Captain Rowlett," Peake ordered, "Bring all the men down from the New House towers at once, and place them behind that section of wall. If they make a breach, it is our only hope. Send the women and children to the Old House for their safety."

"Sir, I see him, Martin," Gabriel was exultant. Fortune favoured them. Whether through lack of forethought, or the want of a spare uniform, Martin was still clad in his blue uniform coat.

"You are certain it is him?" Peake peered short sightedly at the man in the blue coat.

"It is, Sir. Sandy hair, jug ears. I can see his features plainly, he is not so far away."

"Somers!" Rawdon barked at the gamekeeper. "The man in the blue coat is a deserter and a traitor. Shoot him. Shoot to kill."

The gamekeeper lifted the musket and took careful aim at the man in the blue coat. As he fired, Martin belatedly realised his danger and attempted to conceal himself behind another man. It was too late for him. The bullet hit him between the eyes and he toppled backwards.

"Got him, Sir!" the gamekeeper said with satisfaction. There was consternation among the group carrying the heavy bell shaped petard. For a few moments, they stood stock still. A further shot from one of the garrison accounted for another rebel, and the clustered men scuttled forward once more, edging as close as they could to the wall. They were hidden now by the wall and protected from all but the luckiest of shots from the garrison.

There was nothing to be gained by contemplating the catastrophe bearing down upon them. Gabriel joined the men mustering hurriedly behind the weakened section of wall in time to see Bess with a dozen other women running down the stairs from one of the towers.

"Gabriel!" she threw her arms around him. Her fur lined cloak was drenched, her skirts were soaking and grimy, her face was streaked with dirt and her hair trailed from her coif in untidy strands over her shoulders. She had never appeared more beautiful to him.

"Go, my love, be safe." She gave a wan smile and then was gone with the other women, chivvied by two of Rowlett's men towards the comparative safety of the Old House. Gabriel took several deep breaths to prepare himself. He took both the pistols from his belt and loaded them, wrapping them once more in oiled cloth against the rain. He tugged his wet riding cloak tight in the hope of protecting them. His carbine was loaded, hanging on its shoulder strap.

The rain was falling heavily and the temptation to hunker down in the shelter of the wall was strong.

"Stand twenty paces back," Rowlett ordered. "Too close and we will be all blown to bloody shreds when they breach the wall."

The dripping men, shivering from cold and apprehension, edged backwards until Rowlett was satisfied. Gabriel took up his place beside him in the front rank. They both drew their swords and waited for the blast. It could not be long in coming now.

ෆ

We were shepherded through the court and across the high bridge to the Old House. Mary was sniffing again and one or two other women had turned pale, but most were beyond feeling fresh alarm and we neither questioned our orders nor engaged in converse. It would not be true to say that we were inured to peril. Rather, we were weary and numb in mind, body, spirit, resigned to whatever was to come. It was no more than mid-afternoon, but the day seemed to have stretched already for many hours.

I had no idea how much time had elapsed while we had hurled stones, bricks and timber. I only knew that the corner at the top of the tower was well-nigh empty of building materials. My arms ached from lugging heavy weights. I thought with savage satisfaction we had broken more than a few heads. More importantly, the enemy had become reluctant to endure the hail of missiles and had withdrawn from beneath the tower, leaving an abandoned colour planted in the ditch below the half moon.

I dawdled, glancing wistfully behind me towards the New House. I would have preferred to remain near Gabriel to encounter the unknown threat.

The lanky and ginger haired soldier snarled,

"Mistress Lucie." He had that underfed look about him. He clearly longed to be rid of us so he could return to the New House.

We shuffled under the archway and crossed the court into the Great Hall. There was a distant boom from behind us. It came from the New House. Although I had never heard one, instinctively I knew it for the explosion of a petard. Now I knew why Gabriel had stood where he did. Our soldier escorts hurtled through the double doors and back across the court. I picked up my skirts and made to follow them.

A firm hand grabbed me by the wrist. Thinking it to be Mary or Catherine, I tried desperately to shake myself free.

"Mistress Lucie." It was Lady Honoria. Her stately demeanour was undiminished, despite her grimy and stained velvet skirts and the water dripping from her cloak onto the tiled floor. Lines of strain showed on her face, but there was steel in her voice.

"Do not attempt to follow them. We are all in God's hands. If Captain

Vaughan is unharmed then you should not distract him from his urgent duties. If he is dead, there will be time enough to mourn him."

ꩧ

"Pray God it does not bring down one of the towers upon us," Rowlett muttered to Gabriel.

"Amen to that, Isaac."

Gabriel planted his legs firmly apart and winced as his wounded thigh gave a sharp twinge. Well it was likely to be of little consequence in a few moments. There were no more than sixty men standing ready to defend the impending breach. The enemy would pour through in their hundreds when the petard exploded. They would be overwhelmed.

There was a flash, followed by a deafening roar. Gabriel staggered as the ground shuddered and the pile of stone and brick for repairs to the New House shook. A few bricks rolled to the ground. The air was heavy with thick, black smoke. Men were picking themselves up from the ground. Then there was silence. Gabriel regarded the intact wall with disbelief.

"Holy Mother of God. They exploded their bomb, Gabriel and the wall still stands." Rowlett spoke in disbelief.

The two men embraced and laughed. Their informer dead, the enemy had mistakenly chosen the strongest part of the wall to explode their petard.

Gabriel climbed to the top of the New House's south east tower shortly after the failed attempt with the petard. Peake was there, a spyglass to his eye. He grunted in evident satisfaction and passed the instrument to Gabriel. The heavy rain was impeding the besiegers more than the besieged.

"It seems the weather has bested our valiant foes, Sir."

"I think we may stand the men down shortly, Captain Vaughan."

Gabriel pushed his dripping hair from his eyes, and summoned a corporal to dismiss his men. He peered into the darkening, rain soaked landscape. Green, white and yellow coats of the three London regiments, their colours fading in the gloom, were withdrawing towards the shelter of the woods once more. They were pursued by a final discharge of case shot from Amery's gun on the roof of the New House. The small pieces of metal cut a swathe through the retreating troops and those at the tail broke into a run.

The short winter day was coming to an end and night was descending on the scene of bloody devastation in a stifling shroud.

"Gabriel," it was Cuffaud, the scar on his face standing out lividly against the murky, green-tinged sky, "If you seek Mistress Lucie, you will find her in the walled garden."

Gabriel frowned. The garden was quite some distance from the citadel of the Old House and was hardly safe. Bess was hurrying along a path from one of the small corner towers. She dashed towards him, sliding on the churned gravel, muddied skirts clutched in her hands.

"Gabriel, you're alive!"

He folded her in his arms. For a moment they clung to each other as the relentless downpour pelted them with freezing drops of rain. It was fast turning to sleet.

"What is it, love?" he asked anxiously. Her beautiful face was stained with tears.

"That terrible explosion…"

"Did no damage. Let us return to the Great Hall before we drown."

"I cannot. Edward Watson is dead, Catherine is sitting by his body and will not leave him. I was coming to find you, Gabriel. He was hit in the head by a musket ball."

"Ah, then indeed I am very sorry." The conventional words seemed inadequate.

Gabriel tucked Bess's arm in his and tramped wearily up the stairs of the small tower to where the Lieutenant's body lay. Catherine was sitting on the wet stone, his head cradled in her lap. The right side of his face was powder stained but otherwise unmarked, his long jaw intact, a single brown eye staring sightlessly at the leaden sky, but the left side was a mass of bloody pulp and splintered bone.

"Mistress Catherine," Gabriel began softly.

She showed no sign of having heard. Bess put her arm gently round Catherine's shoulder.

"Catherine, listen, Gabriel has come. You cannot remain here." The only answer was a sob.

Gabriel tried again.

"Mistress Catherine, Lieutenant Watson has died bravely. He has given his life that others may live and be safe. It is not fitting that his body remains lying in the rain and the wind. Let him be carried to the chapel. We will pray for his soul and on the morrow all will give him honour as he is laid to rest."

Catherine regarded Gabriel blankly for a moment but then nodded reluctantly. Gabriel covered the body with his own cloak. Two of Watson's men had been standing awkwardly nearby for some minutes, holding a makeshift stretcher of coats and muskets. At a sign from Gabriel, they lifted the Lieutenant onto the stretcher.

There was little rejoicing that night by the garrison, despite their unexpected deliverance from Waller's force. No one knew clearly as yet how many men had died defending Basing House. Men and women alike were exhausted and shocked. Most were too tired even to eat the hastily prepared potage from the kitchens.

Outside the walls, from Basing Park to Garrison Gate, the bodies of the fallen of both armies stiffened in the freezing slush, the blood from their wounds turning from red to black as the final light leached from the sky.

The next day the inhabitants of Basing were once more in the orchard, bidding a sad farewell at a second row of graves, scooped with difficulty from the half frozen soil.

Catherine was calmer now, although her white face was stark with the sorrow of a sleepless night. Bess and Mary at her side, she stood beside the grave of Edward Watson.

Colonel Rawdon's voice was hoarse. He had to stop several times as he read the roll of those who had died. When he was finished, musketeers fired a volley in salute. Gabriel was standing next to one of the graves with his head bowed. As the silent mourners trooped out of the orchard in search of warmth, Bess went to him.

"Who lies in that grave, Gabriel?" she whispered.

Gabriel raised his head. "Just a boy, Bess. Yet he would have made a fine man."

ꟷ

16 November 1643

We woke to the sounds of approaching drums and trumpets. Mary sat bolt upright beside me. She clutched the coverlet tightly to her chin, as if that might offer protection against armed men. Her delicate finger nails had been gnawed to the quick in recent days.

"Help me with my laces. Stay here, I will go and find out what I can," I said with an attempt at calm. With Mary's help, I struggled hastily into my clothes, pulling on a cloak, but had not gone very far from the chamber door when I met Gabriel, hurrying to find me.

"Rest easy Bess, it is Hopton's army. We are safe."

At his words I sagged at the knees with relief and clung to him. He stroked my cheek lovingly and I turned up my face for a kiss.

"Wait," I remembered, "I must tell Mary."

After reassuring her, and seeing the lifting of one burden from her, I rejoined Gabriel. We climbed to the roof of the Great Gatehouse to watch

Hopton's forces marching into the grounds regiment by regiment. The officers took over some of the more habitable rooms in the New House, while the men made themselves as comfortable as possible in the ruins of the Grange and the surrounding fields. Scouts reported that Waller had withdrawn to Farnham. The London troops were melting away by the day, back towards their homes.

Hopton's army marched away a week later, leaving us secure for the present. Catherine accompanied them. One of the captains was her cousin. He was to escort her home at last. Gabriel and I watched the army's departure, standing on the roof of the Great Gatehouse once more. I leant against him, huddled under his cloak, our mingled breath crystallizing in the chilly air. He held me tightly. It had snowed the night before and Hopton was anxious to leave before the roads became impassable.

"If only the army had arrived from Winchester a few days earlier," I sighed. Gabriel shifted from one booted foot to the other but said nothing.

"What is it?" I was suspicious of his silence and twisted round to look at him. His shoulders stiffened and he took a half step back.

"Hopton remained at Winchester waiting for additional forces to arrive," he muttered. "He delayed marching to relieve Basing House. The General believed we could hold out for a week or so without assistance."

"Then he could have arrived earlier?" I felt an angry flush warming my cheeks.

"Bess, Hopton was correct, we held them off." Gabriel was looking apologetic.

I was silent in my turn as I thought of the rows of freshly dug graves. I drew a shuddering breath and smiled at him tremulously. We were alive, we were together, but I wondered how many more men would die futilely like Edward Watson in this bitter and hopeless struggle, this war without an enemy.

27

26 November 1643

WALLER'S FINE FORCE had proved to be nothing but a motley collection of men, a sham army.

Basing's garrison was stronger, united in the common Royalist cause. Yet religious tensions were insidiously chipping away at the fabric of the garrison. I had thought little of Mary's comment about disagreements between Catholic and Protestant and it was brought unwillingly to my notice by one of the maids.

A chill breeze wafted through a crack in the window pane. I edged closer to the blazing logs. I had resumed the wedding preparations which had been interrupted by the siege. A maid was embroidering a fleur de lys on my bodice. We were seated between a bright fire and one of the high windows in the New House to catch the best light on this dull November afternoon as we stitched.

"Have you been at Basing many months, Dot?"

"Come with his Lordship from London, Miss Bess last year. The city folk are not overfond of papists and matters were worsening. So back he came to Basing and I come too." The maid looked as if she would have said more. She pressed her lips tight and then resumed sewing, the tip of her small pink tongue protruding as she concentrated on the fleur de lys.

"And now it is become your home, Dot?" I enquired.

"She shook her head. "I's not sure as I will remain many more weeks, Miss Bess." She glanced nervously over her shoulder. "Rob and I want to wed. He's a loyal man, Miss Bess, loyal to His Majesty. Fought like a fiend last week by all accounts, but he says he'll be damned if he'll die to keep a papist in his house."

I stared at her.

"No offence to Captain Vaughan, Miss Bess. I'm sure he's a good man, brave too. But there's plenty of others thinks like my Rob and it's my belief they'll not remain here much longer."

ఌ

Gabriel's parents arrived for our wedding, accompanied by several armed manservants. While I knew that they had given their consent to Gabriel's marriage, I remained in some doubt as to the warmth of that acceptance. They had been kind to me on my visit to The Allt, but the kindness had been touched with a formality. It kept me at arms' length and reminded me that I was an outsider, an Englishwoman and a Protestant. How would they view me now, as a trollop who had wantonly seduced their son? Or would they accept me as a fellow Catholic?

I was summoned to one of the ground floor chambers in the New House, and obeyed with trepidation. I hesitated on the threshold. The servant bustled past me with a jug of water and a towel, which he placed on a small table. A second servant trundled in, bearing a tray laden with wine, glasses, cold meats and nuts. Gabriel was talking earnestly to his parents. He was wearing his bad weather cassack with his carbine over his shoulder. He had clearly been on duty when they arrived. Lady Vaughan was seated on a padded chair, looking weary, but when she caught sight of me, she stood and drew herself very erect. Then she smiled as I had rarely seen her smile before and I realised that Gabriel had inherited something of her looks after all. I sank into a deep curtsey. Gabriel reached out to take my hand, but Lady Vaughan forestalled him by holding out her arms to me.

"Come here, my brave child. Gabriel has been telling us of your valour, riding to warn the garrison." I blushed.

"It was little I did, Madam, but to gallop away as fast as I might. I was beside myself with fear."

Despite her long journey on horseback, she smelt of clean linen and lavender. She hugged me tightly and then stepped back, regarding me approvingly.

"Let me embrace you too, Bess." The man who I would soon call Father swept me into his own arms. I gazed into Sir Thomas's green eyes and knew I would come to love him well for his son's sake and for his own also.

ఌ

28 November 1643

"Mistress Lucie, I am bid tell you that your brother is arrived and you may find him at the New House stables." Snatching up my cloak, I ran through the house, out through a side door into one of the courtyards, and on until

I reached the stables. The wind whipped at my cloak.

"Harry, Joe," I cried.

I was relieved to see them arrived safely. Scouts returned daily with tales of minor skirmishes in the area between groups of cavalry from the armies of Hopton and Waller, but no further approach had been made towards Basing. I had also worried that Harry might have been unable to obtain leave, or might have left Oxford for Lancashire or Yorkshire. I had heard talk before we left Oxford that Lord Byron, as he now was, and his regiment, were to join the northern army.

"Bess," Harry folded me in his arms and then held me away from him, scrutinising me. "Well, becoming a papist has not spoiled your beauty. You look unchanged-except for this." He frowned, pointing at the crucifix which hung around my neck. I regarded him uneasily. "Take no heed of me, Bess," he sighed, "But what is this I hear of a siege?"

"Over now, Harry," came Gabriel's voice from behind me. "We sent Waller back to Farnham with his tail between his legs." The two men faced each other. Lingering awkwardness from the circumstances of their parting hung heavy between them. Gabriel held out his hand to Harry. Harry embraced him warmly and I saw Gabriel visibly relax.

"Is Basing safe from further attack?" Harry continued.

"For the present," Gabriel reassured him. "The weather was a friend to us, being exceeding bad. It will soon be Christmas and Waller will not risk another engagement here in mid winter. A few skirmishes between patrols, nothing more. Basing is safe for the time being."

"And who is to be groomsman?" Harry enquired, steering the conversation in a more light hearted direction.

Gabriel's brow furrowed in thought. "I had thought to ask Rob Amery, a captain in the garrison.

Now Bess, has Harry told you of the surprise he brought? I see he has not, come with me."

Gabriel took my arm and steered me towards the central gatehouse of the New House. "I will see you at dinner, Bess." Gabriel kissed my hand. "I must speak to Rob Amery without further ado."

I strolled into the gatehouse. Standing inside the porter's lodge out of the wind, her familiar round face beamed at the sight of me.

"Peggy!"

I had not seen her since the spring. Now a few grey hairs were sprinkled among the brown and there was a line between her brows I did not remember. She kissed me, then like Harry she stood back, surveying me critically. She was, I thought, a little rounder.

"You are more beautiful than ever, Miss Bess. I wish your poor mother could see you. Although maybe as well she does not," she finished, lifting my crucifix disdainfully and dropping it as if it's touch might burn her fingers.

"I never thought I would see the day a Lucie would turn papist. But if ever there was cause to do so, it is Master Gabriel," she finished with a smile.

"But Peggy, in spite of your misgivings you are come to see my wedding, papist or no. For I do not think you have journeyed all this way to bid me change my mind."

"No indeed, but I nearly forgot," she produced a letter. "This is from Lady Ridgeley. She bid me wish you joy. Joe came in secret and escorted me to Banbury where we met Master Harry. Never have I been so far from Warwickshire. What adventures we had on the road. But tell me, is it true that papists…"

"Peggy," I interrupted, "Very little that is said about papists is true. Let me find you a place to rest and refresh yourself." A servant led her away. Eagerly, I broke the seal on my cousin's letter.

"My dear coz, I understand that I am to wish you joy. I wish that circumstances were kinder and permitted me to attend your nuptials. Indeed, I wish I had had the opportunity to meet your intended. I understand he was a regular visitor to Chadshunt before you left. Peggy sings his praises, telling of his kindness to your brothers and his feats of daring in battle. More importantly, she tells me of his handsome looks, his long dark hair, and mesmerising green eyes. Not tall she says, but carries himself well, always straight backed and quietly dignified. And can make his presence felt without raising his voice. I believe she is half in love with him herself.

I was shocked to hear that Captain Vaughan is a papist, more so that you become one yourself to wed him. But what of that? These are serious matters which in truth I do not understand. It is enough that you love him. Now for my own news. After Major Chatterton rode away in the summer, my husband visited me. He made a stay of quite some weeks. Dear Bess, I am now with child and expect to be confined by Easter tide. Sir John is delighted with me. He hopes for an heir. For myself, I hope for an easy confinement and a healthy infant. I am uncertain as to your future plans, but will find means to send you word. I may return to Sir John's estates for my confinement.

I am sorry to hear that Uncle Henry and my cousin Will are not yet reconciled to your choice. I hope that they will accept it in time. If they love you, they will surely do so. I wish you every happiness in your love match. I might almost say that I envy you. But the life of the wife of a papist, and one who is a soldier in the King's army, is perhaps not one that I would seek. When all is said and done I enjoy my comforts too much. I remain dear Bess, your loving cousin, Celia Ridgeley."

ɷ

"You honour me." Amery hesitated, frowning. He laid down the rag he was using to clean his scabbard, staring at the scrap of woollen cloth.

"Then I will expect you outside the chapel in the Great Gatehouse at the appointed hour two days hence. I thank you, Rob. I can think of no other man I would prefer to have as my groomsman." Gabriel was already turning away, but Amery grabbed him by the sleeve.

"Gabriel, I said you honour me, but I fear I cannot accept."

"Cannot?" Gabriel repeated slowly.

Amery reddened and his blue eyes clouded. Toying with a loose button on his doublet, he avoided Gabriel's gaze.

"I am a sworn officer of His Majesty," he muttered.

"As am I," Gabriel interrupted indignantly.

"And I must uphold His Majesty's laws, the laws of England." Amery raised his eyes reluctantly to meet Gabriel's. "I wish you and Mistress Bess all happiness, Gabriel, but I also hold the King's commission. I cannot be an active party to the contracting of an illegal marriage, conducted by a priest whose very presence here is treasonous," he finished vehemently.

"I comprehend your position, Robert. I had hoped you might overcome your Protestant scruples." Gabriel's voice remained calm, but he had coloured. "No matter, I will approach Francis Cuffaud. He is Catholic. I have no wish to place you in an invidious position." He offered Amery a slight bow and turned on his heel.

Gabriel hastened to the New House stables. A groom approached him for orders. After the man had saddled Blackbird, Gabriel trotted through the court, across the bailey and out of Garrison Gate. Once past the Grange, he spurred his horse into a gallop across the wintry landscape. The wind stung his cheeks and tore at his hair and his cloak streamed out behind him. Amery's words had cut deep. Gabriel rode furiously in an attempt to purge the bitterness those words had aroused in him.

At the top of Cowdray's Down, he drew rein and dismounted. The remains of Waller's breastworks and gun emplacements scarred the terrain and lead shot was scattered on the ground. Gabriel glanced at the debris through unseeing eyes and gritted his teeth. He had no quarrel with Rob Amery but that of their different faiths. They had fought side by side, he and

Amery, did that mean nothing? They might be forced to do so once more and he must not allow his crushed pride to endanger the relationship of two fellow officers. A quarrel would serve no useful purpose. It might damage the fragile accord within the garrison of Basing House. He must forget the incident and be content. Slowly, he remounted Blackbird and trotted back towards the fortress house which the King depended on and which must be safeguarded at all costs.

ඌ

30 November 1643

Gabriel woke just after dawn. It was their wedding day. He would be a married man again. This morning Bess would be moving into a grander chamber suitable for a bridal. Tonight he would join here there as her husband and no man could then deny him the right to share her bed. His heart quickened its beat at the thought.

Although excused from duty that day, he threw on a thick cloak against the chill and made his way out of habit up to the ramparts. Looking out towards the crumbling sections of wall he noted that, impressive though it looked, Basing House was sorely in need of yet more repairs and strengthening, lest it be forced to endure a second siege. Patching the damage caused by Waller's guns had been in progress for the last two weeks, but it would be difficult to withstand a further assault. The enemy had found the chinks in the walls, the potentially fatal weakness of the New House. Should they return, they would waste no time in concentrating their efforts where they would be most effective.

He crossed the bailey and strolled onwards towards the walled garden. Lieutenant Colonel Johnson was there. He was sighing over the trampled remains of the oiled linen frames which had protected his more delicate plants from the elements.

"Gabriel, I did not expect to see you here this morning. Have you not better things to do, preparing for your marriage?" Johnson stooped to pick up the crushed stem of a small lemon tree, shaking his head.

Gabriel smiled, "I could not sleep, Colonel. But you are right, I should make ready. Did nothing remain of your endeavours after the fighting?"

"Sadly no, Gabriel, but I am beginning anew. My herbs endured better, those anyway that are hardy enough to survive the cold. I wish I could have brought some of my specimens from my London shop. Now there was a fine array! I once had a rare fruit from the colonies, called a banana. I hung a bunch of the fruit to ripen in my window and people came from miles around to see it."

He stooped once more to his beloved herbs, oblivious to Gabriel's continued presence.

Returning restlessly to his quarters, Gabriel took the empty water jug and set off for the kitchens in search of hot water. His stomach rumbled at the aromas of cooking already wafting from pots and cauldrons. The clockwork jacks furnished a soft and rhythmic click as sides of venison and beef rotated slowly beside the fires. He would have liked one of the fresh baked loaves that were emerging from the ovens, but he would be fasting until after the wedding Mass. He watched hungrily as a tray of pies took its place in a warm bread oven.

Harry had been sharing the small room with him since his arrival. He entered the room as Gabriel was clumsily attempting to shave. Gabriel preferred his beard to be closely trimmed. "Give me the razor, Gabriel," Harry grinned, "Your hand is shaking. I've seen you calmer before riding into battle. Bess will not want a bridegroom who has died from accidentally cutting his own throat." He reached for the horn handle. Obediently, Gabriel perched on a stool while Harry finished shaving him and surveyed him critically. "Would you have me trim your hair as well as your beard? And I will send a servant for more hot water and towels – I believe this is one day when Bess may prefer that you do not reek of the stables."

ഗ

I had woken early. Now I was waiting in what was to be my bridal chamber for Peggy to help me make ready. A shame I had woken so early, I reflected. The day would seem overlong now until darkness fell, bringing Gabriel to my bed.

I was content that Peggy was with me. A small voice whispered that if only Mother were there I would bear more easily, my estrangement from Will and my father. To Will I was now the papist's trollop. To Father? A daughter lost, I supposed. Once started, the conversation in my head continued. "What would she think of you marrying a papist? Is it any more likely that she would countenance the match than Father?" I knew the answer to that was not one I cared to hear, so I bade the voices stop their argument and took a turn around the spacious bed chamber.

Gabriel and I had been honoured by having it assigned for our use. It was grand and well appointed. Unlike many in the New House this chamber was in a good state of repair. The carved wall panelling was intact. The windows had tightly fitting casements with leaded glass. Beyond the curtains, was a fine view of the frosty park. A woollen tapestry of a cheerfully coloured hunting scene adorned a wall.

I inspected the imposing bed. There were heavy velvet curtains, one continuous outer valance and four tie backs edged with braids and tassels. Neatly folded on top of the richly embroidered counterpane was my silk nightgown, brought by Peggy as a wedding gift. There was even a woven carpet on the floor, stretching from bed to hearth. I tiptoed around it, not daring to tread upon such a costly piece of art. I had never before seen a carpet placed upon the floor.

Arriving at the looking glass in the corner of the room, I stared at my reflection, willing Mother's image to appear behind me. Naturally, she did not come. I sat down on a padded chair feeling almost melancholy, regarding my hands. They were long fingered musician's hands like those of Mother and those of my brothers.

ᔓ

A warm summer day at Chadshunt, I about 4 years of age. A more youthful Peggy and I are near the fish ponds. Harry is nearby climbing a tree. Peggy sits on the grass with me, mopping her perspiring face. Suddenly she cries, "Master Harry, come down at once. You will tear your breeches." She picks up her skirts and sets off towards him at a run. The carp flashes beneath the surface, it's scales catching the sunlight. I seize the opportunity to take a better look at it. I reach forward to touch it…

The water is oh so cold as it closes over my head. My layers of silk skirts and linen drift over my head and fill with water, shutting out the light. I open my mouth to scream and water rushes in.

Firm hands are lifting me from the water. I see the hands first as I emerge choking and crying. I think it is Peggy, but it is the slim, cool hands of my mother, her jewelled rings dazzling in the sunlight. The wide sleeves of her gown are soaked to the elbows. She clasps the soggy mass which is me to her bosom. "I thought I'd lost you," she murmurs into my wet hair.

ᔓ

A tear trickled down my cheek as I recalled Mother's words. I knelt by the bed, pressing my face into the feather mattress. "Dear Mother," I whispered, "Forgive me for forsaking the faith of my family for the love I bear to Gabriel. He is a good man, kind and brave. He loves me and I know that he will protect me for as long as he lives. How I wish you were here with me today."

For a long moment, I paused. I felt her hands upon my shoulders. I could almost smell the rosewater which would drift towards me from her skirts.

The door opened and Peggy bustled in at the head of a small procession of servants. She was almost submerged in the folds of my wedding gown. Behind her came two men lugging a wooden bath lined with sheets. The spell was broken. Two maid servants bore pails of steaming water. Panting, they put them down, dumping the water in the wooden bath. A third maid carried towels and a basket. She scattered dried rose petals, camomile and sage into the warm water. The bath was luxury such as I had rarely known, even at Chadshunt. I picked up the cake of scented soap she had placed on the towels and inhaled deeply. In Oxford I had used what soaps came to hand, and such as I could buy at the market. This was a costly soap, delicately scented with rose, made from olive oil rather than animal fats.

As I prepared to step into the warm water, I remembered I was still wearing Gabriel's crucifix. I carefully unfastened the silver chain and put it on a side table. It was the first time that I had removed it since he had placed it about my neck three weeks earlier. For Gabriel it was a reminder of what I had done for him, and his face would glow every time his eyes rested on it. The crucifix acted as a constant reminder to myself that I was no longer the person I had been before, and served the same purpose for others in the house.

An hour or so later, I was arrayed in my wedding finery. Peggy dropped pins and muttered under her breath as she wrestled with the familiar task of coaxing my straight and wayward hair. It was to be a fashionable style, pinned high on my head with tendrils drooping in hopeful waves to either side of my face.

"What ornaments will you wear?" was Peggy's final question. I hesitated, looking from Gabriel's crucifix to Mother's string of pearls. I decided to wear them both. The crucifix on its delicate silver chain I hung about my neck once more while Peggy threaded Mother's pearls through my hair. It brought Mother closer to me.

There was a tap at the door. Peggy opened it a crack. I recognised Francis Cuffaud's voice. "For Mistress Lucie from Captain Vaughan." Peggy returned, clutching a velvet covered box in her hand. I opened it to find a scroll of paper and a folded scrap of silk, which proved to contain a beautiful pair of tear drop shaped pearl earrings. She immediately seized the earrings and placed them in my ears. I untied the little scroll, fastened with ribbon, to read Gabriel's message.

"Go crystal tears, like to the morning show'rs

And sweetly weep into thy lady's breast.

May these tear drops of pearl be the only tears I see about your face on this our wedding day. This is the very last time I will address a letter to you as Mistress Lucie.

Your loving and devoted servant, Gabriel Vaughan"

It was followed by the usual miniature drawing of a linnet. I began to sniff.

"Mistress Bess," Peggy was alarmed, "You will have red eyes and nose if you carry on so. What has Master Gabriel said that upsets you pray?"

"Nothing," I hiccuped," he is so thoughtful."

I carefully rolled Gabriel's message, the ink only slightly smudged by my tears, and returned it to the velvet box.

ɷ

Gabriel was fidgeting until finally Harry passed him as fit for his wedding. His thick hair hung neatly just below his shoulders. He wore a fine white cambric shirt with lace cuffs, a deep embroidered collar under a blue doublet slashed with white silk, a rich blue velvet coat and matching breeches with white ribbons. A deep lace trim showed over the folded down bucket tops of his highly polished pair of boots. He had spent quite some time the previous day polishing the boots. His sword belt was new, its buckle adorned with the Vaughan family crest. His wide brimmed hat was decked with a blue feather and he carried soft calfskin gloves. Harry was less gorgeously dressed, but was also wearing his best coat and breeches, deep red in his case, with a new shirt which he had brought with him from Oxford. His wide brimmed hat had a feather which had been dyed red to match his coat.

There was a knock on the door. Francis Cuffaud bowed low to Gabriel, sweeping off his hat with a flourish.

"It is time I fetch my sister," Harry grinned. He clapped Gabriel on the shoulder and hurried out.

Gabriel and Cuffaud descended the stairs and crossed the court towards the Great Gatehouse. Gabriel's parents were standing with the priest outside the gatehouse. His mother hugged him while his father ran his eye critically over his son and nodded. Father Allen smiled encouragingly. "Your singers are ready, Gabriel." The wait seemed interminable.

"Do you have the ring safely, Francis and the silver and gold?" Gabriel asked Cuffaud for the second or third time. Gabriel's parents had brought with them a wedding ring of rose coloured Welsh gold. Finally, at the cheerful sound of the Queen Elizabeth's Galliard, Gabriel relaxed and released his tight hold on his gloves. Musicians, two playing viols and one a lute, crossed the court towards the Great Gatehouse. They were followed by Peggy and a noisy cluster of well wishers.

Gabriel turned.

Bess, hanging on Harry's arm, was advancing slowly towards him. The bodice of her pale blue gown was embroidered with gold fleur de lys with the deep lace collar also embroidered in gold. Her hair piled high on her head was falling down in waves around her face on to her shoulders. She had pale blue ribbons in her hair entwined with a string of pearls. She was wearing the pearl earrings and pale gold gloves, another of his wedding gifts to her.

She stopped beside him and looked up at him trustingly. His eyes held hers for a moment. She was so lovely. His heart turned over.

Father Allen cleared his throat. "Behold, brethren, we have come here in the sight of God, the angels, and all his saints in the presence of the church, to join together two bodies, of this man and of this woman."

The familiar words drifted over Gabriel's head.

"Gabriel, do you wish to have this woman as a wife, and to esteem her, to honour, hold, and protect her, healthy and sick, just as a husband ought to do for a wife, and to forsake all other women, and to cling to her so long as your life and hers will endure?"

"Elisabeth, do you wish to have this man as a husband, and to obey him, to serve, esteem, honour, and guard him healthy and sick, just as a wife ought to do for a husband, and to forsake all other men, and to cling to him so long as your life and his will endure?"

Nothing seemed very real except Bess standing beside him. Now Harry was removing Bess's glove and placing her hand in Gabriel's.

"I, Gabriel Thomas Francis Vaughan take thee, Elisabeth Jane Lucie...."

A few minutes later the rose gold ring was on Bess's finger. Father Allen pronounced the blessing making them man and wife. He led them up the gatehouse stairs into the chapel, where they knelt before the small altar. The spectators crowded in behind them. The Mass began, and the choir of four, who Gabriel had secretly trained, took up their places at the back. Moments later they broke into the haunting music of William Byrd's "Kyrie". Bess's mouth formed a perfect "O" of amazement. Gabriel smiled. It had been worth sacrificing those precious hours of rest.

Gabriel and Bess descended the stairs from the chapel to the sound of a bellowed command, followed by the clash of swords. Lieutenant Cuffaud had drawn up the men of Gabriel's cavalry troop outside the Great Gatehouse in a double line, making an arch of swords. They passed underneath and then onto the Great Hall wedding breakfast.

The table was laid with the fine silver plate of the House, decorated with the crest of the Marquis and the motto Aymez Loyaulté. Besides the roasted haunches of venison and beef and platters of partridge and pheasant, there was an array of boiled puddings and baked pies, adorned with pictures of fish or fowl to signal their contents. The centrepieces were a peacock, arrayed in all its feathers, and a pastry representation of Basing House, complete with miniature figures of men and horses, the towers flying tiny flags of marchpane.

Gabriel and Bess sat at the high table flanked by Gabriel's parents, Harry, Francis Cuffaud and Thomas Johnson. Below them the long tables were crowded with chattering members of the garrison and the other Basing House residents. Gabriel was hardly aware if he ate or drank. He only noticed when he brushed his lips against the crystal goblet he shared with Bess. He inhaled the delicate scent of rose petals and herbs which was wafting towards him from her hair. They spoke little, but constantly interrupted their eating to touch hands.

The tables were now spread with custards, syllabubs, coloured marchpanes and candied fruits. Flagons of mead were placed on the tables beside those of wine. Gabriel caught his father's eye and Sir Thomas rose to his feet.

"Ladies, gentlemen, officers of Basing House."

"Sir Thomas, I would take it as a personal favour if I might say a few words." Heads turned. Sir Thomas bowed and resumed his seat. Noone had noticed the Paulets enter. The Marquis inclined his head gracefully.

"I wish Captain Vaughan and his gallant lady every happiness. It is not many weeks since they arrived here, but Captain Vaughan has fought with courage and valour in defence of this place and we are indebted to him. Scarcely less are we indebted to Mistress Elisabeth Vaughan who warned us of the approaching rebel army at some considerable peril to herself.

Yet it is only because of her wish to join the true faith that Mistress Vaughan is here with us. A pity more do not do so. It would be a fine thing indeed if all those within our walls were Catholic."

A servant was at the marquis's elbow with a glass of wine. Paulet raised it with a flourish,

"To the health and happiness of Captain Vaughan, and Mistress Vaughan."

"And to the victory of His Majesty." Johnson was on his feet, raising his own glass.

The Paulets withdrew and the company, having drained their glasses, seated themselves once more. The buzz of conversation resumed, but there were some discontented murmurs.

"He should not have said that," Johnson muttered to Gabriel. "With more than half the garrison Protestant, the Marquis chose his words ill. Basing House depends upon the goodwill of all of those within its walls."

ɞ

Father Allen led the blessing after eating, then the tables were pushed back against the walls, to make room for dancing. The immediate danger past, the long windows had been uncovered in the Great Hall. This frosty morning had brought sunshine, but now the shadows were lengthening as the light already began to fade. Most of the guests remained, men from the garrison among them, but Thomas Johnson took his leave, grasping Gabriel's shoulder and speaking to him in an undertone. He turned to me with his most boyish grin.

"Mistress Vaughan, I bid you joy. We must learn to do without your husband for the space of a few days, as we did before he joined our company. Health and happiness to you." He bowed deeply and strode towards the doors.

As Johnson pushed them open, Rob Amery entered. I had been puzzled by his absence. I had thought he was to be Gabriel's groomsman. Instead, Francis Cuffaud had filled that office. Amery had laid aside his buffcoat and arms, but the fact he wore the rusty red coat and doublet he wore most days suggested he was just come off duty. His air was uneasy, and as Gabriel noted Amery's approach, his face took on the expression of carefully controlled calm that I had seen before at moments of crisis.

The hall was wide, and the seconds lengthened as Amery threaded his way between the boisterous wedding guests across the tiled floor. Amery was standing before us now. He bowed to me.

"Mistress Vaughan, I wish you every happiness." Amery glanced towards Gabriel. "And you too, Captain Vaughan." I noted a tension between them that I did not comprehend.

"Thank you, Captain Amery," I wondered at Gabriel's formality.

"I am sorry that your duties prevented you from joining us earlier, Robert," I smiled. "I had thought you were to be groomsman."

"Forgive my," Amery broke off, bowing his head.

"Pray do not apologise for your lateness, Robert. Gabriel and I would both have regretted your continued absence, is that not so, husband?" I laid the faintest stress on the last word and Gabriel responded, as I thought he might, with a smile of pure joy at the realisation.

"Indeed we would, Bess." His face became serious once more. "You are welcome Robert, even now. I hope we will not be divided thus in future."

The words were curiously phrased, but both men bowed. The musicians struck up the music for a galliard.

Gabriel led me to the dance floor as Amery walked away. I had rarely danced with Gabriel. He was in constant demand as a musician and I belatedly recognised this masked some reluctance on his part. That slight hesitation in his step would never leave him and he was wary of stumbling or making a false step. It gave me a momentary sadness to think I would never see him as he had once been, before Edgehill. Harry, on the other hand, was dancing with more than his usual level of exuberance, kicking his long legs wide and making Mary laugh as he capered and spun.

As the sky began to darken, servants brought trays of savouries, slices of the traditional rich fruit Banbury cake with jugs of mulled wine. Gabriel and I had retired to our seats. I had pleaded fatigue as an excuse as Gabriel's limp became increasingly obvious. The musicians laid down their instruments. The breathless dancers sank gratefully onto chairs and benches. As Gabriel rose, the company fell silent.

"My friends," he said, "I am not a man for grand speeches. I offer you grateful thanks on behalf of my bride and myself and for your support today. I prefer to express my thoughts through music, so I crave your indulgence for a few minutes."

He reached for his lute. Harry sank into his place beside me as Gabriel began to play. All were silenced by the gentle and haunting melodies. When he started to sing in Welsh his mother wiped away a tear.

"And now a song for my wife," he grinned. The atmosphere in the Great Hall was transformed as he began with the opening bars of "Seven Months Married." He finished to raucous applause and laughter. After a slight pause, Gabriel invited Harry to join him. Rising shyly to his feet, Harry provided harmonies as they sang Gabriel's composition, "Oh, silver is the moon".

"I will sing just the one more; for those who are bashful with their sweethearts and fear to make their feelings known. I give them this song, 'When Maids go a wooing'."

There was general laughter. "Harry, would you sing with me again?" He shot me an impudent grin. With the memories that I had, I flushed to the roots of my hair.

When the song ended, there was an expectant pause. I felt the eyes of more than one hundred guests upon me. I rose. Self-consciously, I whispered to Gabriel and then to Peggy. The crowd parted before me as I slowly walked through the tiled hall followed by Peggy, Lady Vaughan and Mary. The musicians took up their lutes and accompanied our procession to the door of the bridal chamber. Maid servants strewed the bed with armfuls of sweet herbs and then left closing the door behind them.

Peggy hurried forward. I hesitated awkwardly and felt my cheeks burn as she and my new mother in law, unlaced the back of my bodice and helped me out of the layered petticoats. It all seemed very public. Lady Vaughan was looking quite frankly at my body as I undressed. And I thought it was with approval. At last in my night gown, I was ready and climbed into the bed.

Peggy opened the door, admitting Gabriel, Harry, Francis and my new father in law, Sir Thomas. Father Allen followed. He blessed the bridal bed, sprinkling it with holy water. This was the signal for everyone to leave us. Harry leaned over the bed and gave me a final hug.

Harry turned to his brother in law. Holding Gabriel's gaze he said seriously, "Look after her well, she is yours now."

"Harry, you know I will guard her with my life," replied Gabriel. The two men grasped hands.

Harry closed the door behind him with a firm click. Gabriel locked it and then leant against it, gazing at me. His arms were folded and he was very still. I knew Gabriel's moods of stillness by now. This time he was waiting, taut as a bow string. I could see the tension in his shoulders.

"Well My Lord?" I stared into the green eyes, their expression so intent I was beginning to feel quite uneasy. I was sitting in the middle of the bed, hugging my knees under the embroidered covers. I patted the bed tentatively.

"Bess," Gabriel's voice was husky, "This is our wedding night. I should be loving and gentle with you. But I have been holding my passions in check for so many weeks I fear I cannot do that. I need to take and possess you. I need you to submit to my demands. Will you do so?"

My heart pounded loudly. I nodded, blushing. Never taking his eyes from me, Gabriel rapidly stripped off his clothes. Tossing them aside was quite unlike his habitual careful orderliness. By the flickering light of the many wax candles, I ran my eyes over his body. I had only seen it before so briefly, the dark line in his side where the sword had scarred him, the half healed tear in his thigh from the more recent wound, patches of shadow at chest and groin where he was lightly furred. Like a cat preparing to pounce, he stood motionless, regarding me with a hint of challenge in the green eyes. Then he moved purposefully towards me, throwing back the covers and jerking the bed curtains closed behind him.

We were cocooned by the heavy drapes. The candles glowed, casting flickering shadows. Gabriel reached for the silk ribbons at the neck of my nightgown, tugging impatiently. Kneeling before him and with trembling fingers, I untied them. He motioned for me to remove my nightgown. As I pulled it over my head he cupped my breasts with his hands.

Still looking at me intently, he parted my thighs roughly with his knee. He threw himself upon me then, thrusting urgently inside me. I tried to put my arms around him but he held them down with his own, pressing me hard against the bed. He would not have me move. This was possessing me, the right of conquest. Despite the physical onslaught of his body, I felt my own responding to his demands. His eyes continued to bore into mine but he remained silent. I felt as if my soul was drowning in his, that I no longer had a separate existence. I was truly his and we were one. I cried out at the relentless pounding but he only thrust harder and stopped my cries with his mouth. Finally I felt his body convulse and the warm rush as he spilled his seed inside me. He collapsed on me with a sigh, his body now radiating relaxation.

"Gabriel," I whispered with difficulty, "You are suffocating me." He rolled off me. A few minutes later, with a satisfied smile, he settled himself against the pillows.

"Well, Mistress Vaughan, I believe we may now say we have consummated the marriage," his expression was serious but his eyes sparkled, "And I have therefore done my duty to you as a husband." He smacked me lightly on the posterior.

"Oh," I said with feigned innocence, "Foolishly I believed you to be taking your pleasure with me. Now I see you were only concerned to perform your duty."

"Indeed I was," he agreed gravely.

He slipped on a bed gown and padded over to a table by the fire where stood a jug of wine with a tray of sweetmeats. He poured two glasses and climbed back into bed with a handful of sweetmeats. "Crumbs," I said reprovingly, covers pulled up to my chin. He laughed and proceeded to feed me with the sweetmeats.

"I know you enjoy your food, my love. I need you to keep up your strength."

"Why?" I enquired with my mouth full of sugar plums.

"Drink your wine and I will tell you." Obediently, I sipped the wine and handed him back the empty goblet. I looked at him enquiringly. "Because now we have done our duty it is time we took our pleasure." He removed the bed gown and I saw that he was indeed planning on further marital activities, imminently.

"Gabriel," I said a while later, "Say something romantic to me in Welsh. Whenever you sing in Welsh you never translate. You could be singing about your horse for all I know."

"Mm," he mumbled, "When I am less occupied, wife." I smacked his own bare posterior and carefully removed my nipple from between his lips. "Very well," he sighed, "You drive a hard bargain, but so do I. Wait until I am done." I winced as he eased himself inside me.

When we next surfaced for air, I reminded him about the Welsh songs. He thought for a minute, running his hand through his tousled hair. I pushed it out of his eyes, laughing. He picked up a lute and strummed gently, making adjustments to the tuning. "Shall I sing and then translate?" he asked obediently. I nodded. "Very well, this is Dacw Nghariad." I listened while he sang, accompanying himself on the lute. The image of him sitting up in bed, the bed gown draped loosely about his bare shoulders, was one of the enduring memories of our wedding night, a peaceful harbour in the midst of past and future dangers. The English went like this,

"There is my sweetheart down in the orchard,
Oh how I wish I were there myself,
There is the house and there is the barn;
There is the door of the cow house open.
There is the gallant, branching oak,
A vision, lovingly crowned.
I will wait in her shade
Until my love comes to meet me.
There is the harp, there are her strings;
What better am I, without anyone to play her for?
There's the delicate fair one, exquisite and full of life;
What nearer am I, without having her attention?"

Leaning against him, I drifted off to sleep, lulled by the sweet sounds of the lute and Gabriel's voice. "No horse then, after all," I mumbled.

"Just cows."

28

1 December 1643

THE NEXT MORNING I woke to the blissful feel of Gabriel's warm and naked body against mine. We had slept close, curled up beneath thick covers over the large feather mattress. But as he roused from sleep I felt him becoming roused in other ways. He kissed the tip of my nose. "Good morning, wife." He plucked the bed covers off me. I shivered in the chill of the room, the fire having died away to a faint glow during the night. He smiled, "I wanted to see you properly in daylight. For the first time." His eyes travelled over me from my tangled hair to my bare toes. They lingered at various points in between. He touched my hardening nipples lightly and then leaned forward kissing them in turn. "Now turn over." I regarded him in surprise.

"There is more than one way for a man and a maid to lie together."

"Not a maid any longer," I reminded him.

"Wanton," he chuckled. "Do as I say and roll on your belly. Did you not vow to obey me only yesterday?" I rolled obediently and a warm hand felt between my thighs, stroking.

"Ooh," I said.

He stopped. "You are not too bruised?" he asked apprehensively, drawing back. I reached for his hand and replaced it in answer.

"Bess?" I turned back to look at his enquiring face. "Did your mother tell you much of what a woman should expect in her duties as a wife?"

A little shyly I replied, "Enough for me to know that when a man lies with a woman there may be consequences nine months later."

"Consequences?" he laughed, his lilt accenting the word.

"And what does the church say about this?" I asked artlessly, gazing at him.

Gabriel's grin widened. "It says be fruitful and multiply as well you know. So obey its commands and mine. Back on your belly so I may fill it with my seed. I want an heir. And I want you."

For four days we took delight in exploring each other's bodies. When our chamber door was shut, we were not disturbed. On the day after our marriage we reluctantly dressed, made ourselves presentable and went to the Great Hall for dinner. Gabriel's parents were waiting for us so it was well that Gabriel had taken the time to shave. He bowed formally to them and I curtseyed with modestly downcast eyes. Glancing up, I caught Sir Thomas looking his son over carefully and then doing the same to me. I felt my cheeks turn rosy under his scrutiny.

"Gan eich wynebau gwenu, cymeraf yn ganiataol nad oedd eich clwyfau ddim yn eich poeni neithiwr," Sir Thomas said with a grin.

Gabriel burst out laughing and Lady Vaughan shook her head at her husband.

"What did your father say?" I whispered as we took our seats.

Gabriel cleared his throat. "He noted our apparent sense of wellbeing and contentment after our wedding night."

"Hmm." I decided it was time I started learning Welsh. And then the delicious aroma from sturgeon stuffed with turnips wafted towards me. Having eaten very little since the wedding breakfast I realised that I was ravenous.

The weather was cold and sunny. After dinner, Gabriel and I decided to go for a short ride. I took delight in the way in which Gabriel stood beside me as I prepared to mount Fairy, quietly instructing the groom to stand aside so that I could place my foot in my husband's hand. As I settled myself in the saddle our eyes met and my heart turned over at his look of joyous serenity. We clattered out of Garrison Gate and past the burnt-out Grange. The ground was soft but not too muddy for a gallop. Fairy, confined too many days in the stable, flicked her ears and lengthened her pace as Gabriel led the way on Blackbird. My cloak floated out behind me and the cold air rushed past my ears. When we reached the woods where I had encountered the Roundhead patrol only weeks earlier, Gabriel checked. I pulled Fairy up beside him.

He sensed my discomfort, "There is no need to fear Bess. The way is clear. I spoke to our scouts before leaving the House. I would not see you endangered unnecessarily a second time, my love." Remembering his words to Harry that he would guard me with his life, I smiled at him painfully but said nothing. He looked puzzled. We rode back quietly, our horses blowing and snorting, side by side.

On our return there was a fresh tray of food and wine in our chamber. The fire was blazing anew and the bed had been made. Our bed gowns had been retrieved from where they had landed and hung tidily over two chairs, warming before the fire. I was a little discomforted by these intimate attentions from the invisible servants.

In the middle of the night, I was woken by a kiss on my bare shoulder. Yawning, I reached a tentative hand downwards in confirmation. I laughed, "Do you never tire, my love?"

"Indeed, I do Bess, but not of you. Open your legs," he finished huskily. I did as I was bid, reflecting that if I were not already with child it was not for want of Gabriel's efforts, or mine.

The next day I bade a reluctant farewell to both Joe and Peggy. Joe was obliged to return to his duties in Oxford and had promised to escort Peggy back to Banbury. Peggy crushed me to her bosom, "It does me good to see you looking so happy, Mistress Bess." Her eyes crinkled into a smile. I told her I would send for her when I could and gave her a letter for Celia.

Joe and Peggy had departed under clear skies, but within a few hours, the weather returned to its sullen December downpour. It was cosy in our chamber before the fire. Our privileged status as newly weds apparently brought such privileges as unlimited supplies of food from the kitchen, wine and thick logs of oak and ash to burn in the grate. Although these were supplied on the orders of the housekeeper, I suspected that the Marchioness was keeping an indulgent eye on us. I was nibbling on a dish of nuts which had appeared while we were out of our room at dinner. Gabriel was dividing his attentions between me and a new song which he was composing in my honour.

"Gabriel," I said suddenly. He added a couple more notes to the sheet of music and then laid down the quill.

"Mistress Vaughan?" he replied teasingly.

Leaning against his knee I stared into the fire. "I was just thinking about your brother."

"Ah?" the slight question strengthened the upward inflexion in his lilting voice.

I pressed on. "I was thinking he sounds a little like Rafe."

"How so?" I had his full attention now.

"Always laughing and joking, a bit too reckless." He frowned, his green eyes searching my face. How could I explain? I thought of how Rafe had died in a headlong dash after the enemy. I knew somehow that Gabriel would not, indeed had not, done so. But perhaps his brother might have.

"Gabriel, I think there is more than one type of courage. Rafe possessed plenty and from what you say your brother was his like. Had Michael lived I fear he too might have died at Edgehill like Rafe, galloping after the enemy, heedless of his safety. You are not so reckless."

"Am I not?" he smiled. "I recall the day I first kissed you. And the night

I threw caution to the winds, spending it with you."

"In that case I hope our own children will be possessed of calmer heads and much good sense."

"Let us hope there will be many of them for us to make studies of their characters." He smiled again but this time there was longing in his face.

I kissed him softly. "Gabriel Vaughan, I hope to bear you many children." I took his hand and led him once more towards the bed.

On the fourth evening I noticed that Gabriel was making love to me with increased urgency. As he rolled off me, temporarily exhausted, I raised myself on one elbow and stroked his long hair, the curls now in somewhat of a tangle. "What is it, Gabriel? Something troubles you I think."

He was mute for a moment. "I must return to my duties in two days Bess, as must Harry. Our holiday time is nearly over. My parents leave for The Allt tomorrow. And I fear I must leave you shortly to journey to Oxford. There are messages to carry to the garrison there and I believe I may conveniently combine that with some other business. I would not leave you, but should be gone no longer than four or five days. Harry and I will travel there together."

"May I not go with you?" I protested immediately.

"My love," Gabriel sighed, "In these troubled times, travel is to be undertaken only when necessary. We should also discover what welcome you will receive there from your family. With Harry's assistance I mean to make enquiries. It is safer for you to remain here. Waller has left to lick his wounds in Farnham, and with Lord Hopton's forces in Winchester, Waller is unlikely to make another attempt on Basing House."

"Please take care, Gabriel," I said nervously. "If Will should still be in Oxford…"

"Never fear Bess, I am no more inclined now than before to fight your brother. Besides, Harry has assured us that Will has left Oxford to ride with Prince Rupert's forces. I have no reason to think I will encounter him unawares. Harry may perhaps remain in Oxford some time. Byron's horse have ridden north, but the time of year and the weather are not conducive to a solitary ride thus far. He will keep me informed." With that I had to be content.

ᔕ

7 December 1643

Three days later I woke as it was getting light to see Gabriel beginning to climb from the bed. "Must you leave so early?" There was a tremor in my voice.

Gabriel leaned over and kissed me. He padded over to where his shirt was lying, pulled it on and then climbed back upon the bed carrying his lute.

"A suitable farewell then, My Lady, until we meet again". He grinned, although his eyes were serious.

Sweet stay a while, why will you rise?
The light you see comes from your eyes:
The day breakes not, it is my heart,
To thinke that you and I must part.
O stay, or else my joyes must dye,
And perish in their infancie.

Deare let me dye in this faire breast,
Farre sweeter then the Phoenix nest.
Love raise desire by his sweete charmes
Within this circle of thine armes:
And let thy blissefull kisses cherish
Mine infant joyes, that else must perish

"Must you choose something sad?" I reproached him as his sweet tenor voice fell silent.

"Then I will work on a merrier one of my own while I am away from you. But I should be back in a few days so I fear there may be insufficient time to finish it."

I smiled reluctantly, "That is very like what you said when I rebuked you for having taught Harry no more than two or three songs while you were both prisoners."

"Well I am a free man now my love, so I will hasten back to you whether my song is finished or no."

∽

Oxford, 8 December 1643

Gabriel and Harry were smoking a last pipe before retiring for the night. Gabriel was tense but hopeful. He had returned to Oxford with Harry early that morning.

"Will you take me to your father so I may make my case for reconciliation?" he pressed Harry. Now they were wed Gabriel was certain that Bess' father would forgive and welcome her, them, back to the family.

After a thoughtful silence his brother in law said,

"It would be better to make the first approach by letter. I will make ready to speak with him and hope to bring him to an acceptance. As you are already wed, he cannot seek further to prevent your marriage. I hope he will see the sense of accepting it, both for the honour of the family and for the love of Bess."

Gabriel sharpened a quill, threw it aside and took another. Finally dipping it into the ink he began to write with resolution. Sprinkling sand over the letter he folded it, sealed it with his signet ring and handed it to Harry.

"I will see it delivered immediately. I will visit my father on the morrow to seek to arrange a meeting between you."

It was still early so Gabriel visited a barber's shop, had his beard trimmed, and brushed his clothes in the hope that he would make a visit to his new father in law on the morrow.

Byron's regiment of horse had ridden north and he was therefore no longer part of the garrison. He would either rejoin Byron's in the north, taking Bess with him, or remain in Oxford with the remainder of the garrison, and the Oxford Army. The decision hinged in part on how matters resolved themselves with Sir Henry. If all went well, he could bring Bess back from Basing House in a day or two.

Harry and Gabriel heard marching feet, followed by a heavy rap at the cottage door.

"Who can it be at this hour?" Harry asked looking at Gabriel. Harry unlatched the door. Two flaring torches illuminated a red sashed corporal and four soldiers from a regiment of foot.

"Captain Gabriel Vaughan?" the corporal enquired looking back and forth at the two men.

For a long moment, Gabriel surveyed the armed men. He knocked the ashes from the bowl of his clay pipe into the hearth. Then he rose slowly to his feet, slipped the signet ring off his hand and placed it on a shelf.

"At your service," he replied, his face expressionless.

"Captain, you are under arrest and are to be taken to Oxford Castle. Guards, seize him."

Gabriel stood rigid as two of the men grabbed his arms and bound them tightly behind him.

Harry sprang forward. "Stay, gentlemen, there must be some mistake. I am Lieutenant Henry Lucie, also of the garrison. Captain Vaughan is a valiant soldier who has been an officer of the garrison for some months."

The corporal laughed. "Lieutenant Henry Lucie? Well, this should be no surprise to you then, Sir. Captain Vaughan is arrested on the orders of Sir Henry Lucie. He is charged with rape and abduction."

"Guards, take the prisoner and march on."

Gabriel had been silent, but now he burst out with, "Harry, protect Bess and tell her to do nothing foolish."

"Be resolute. I will do all I can to win your release," cried Harry, but Gabriel and his guards were gone.

ᘓ

Before Gabriel and his escort had marched very far it began to rain heavily. Without a cloak, his velvet doublet was soon soaked through. The night was cold and he was shivering. The rain fell on his bare head and trickled down his face. He shook his dripping hair out of his eyes as he could not reach it with his hands and concentrated on not missing his footing in the ill lit streets. He was angry with himself for misjudging Sir Henry's reaction so badly. He could only hope that Harry might be able to act on his behalf and that Bess would not decide to proceed alone. It was the fear of this which had prompted his final words to Harry.

The lateness of the hour and the wet weather meant that the streets were fairly quiet. But there were sufficient numbers of people loitering that Gabriel's face burned with shame. Being taken prisoner in battle was at least honourable, arrest as a felon was not. When they reached the castle, he was marched from the gate house to St George's Tower. He shuddered at the thought of becoming an inmate. He was all too familiar with the brutal treatment of its prisoners. The corporal brought his party to a halt.

"Prisoner for you, Sir. Captain Gabriel Vaughan. Here is the arrest warrant." He handed the document to the officer on duty.

"He is to be kept in chains."

Caleb Brown was Captain Smith's Lieutenant. Gabriel knew him for a brutal man. His stomach clenched at the thought of what he must endure. There would be no rescue that night.

"It will be my pleasure, Corporal," Brown laughed.

Alone in the gate house, Brown turned to Gabriel. He was a stout man with a ruddy face which hinted at a good humour he did not possess.

"Captain Vaughan, your servant," his eyes gleamed with delight. "I did not expect to have the pleasure of entertaining you. Now we must not spoil that fine velvet doublet and those boots. Pray consign them to my care."

He nodded to one of his men, who cut the ropes binding Gabriel's wrists. With numb fingers, Gabriel unbuttoned the embroidered doublet and tugged off his leather riding boots. He had no doubt they would be sold in Oxford's market on the morrow.

Brown himself searched Gabriel thoroughly, chuckling with satisfaction as he found a handful of loose coin. Then he whistled in surprise.

"Well looky here, we have us a papist." He pulled the rosary out of Gabriel's pocket and dangled it before his eyes, laughing.

"Maybe the Queen would like it as a gift." He weighed the silver crucifix and the string of amber beads appraisingly, then stuffed it into a pouch on his belt along with the coins.

"Come along, Captain, we must show you to your bed chamber." Humming tunelessly, he shoved Gabriel out of the door.

29

Oxford, 9 December 1643

HARRY ROSE BEFORE dawn, splashed icy water on his face and left the cottage, swirling his cloak over his shoulders against the chill in the air and chewing on a piece of yesterday's bread. He hastened to the house in High Street, arriving as the sky began to lighten. A maid servant was already sweeping the front steps. "Is my father at home, Hannah?" he enquired.

"He is, Lieutenant," she said. Harry bounded up the stairs. At the top, he met his father leaving his rooms. Seeing his son he scowled, but opened the door and retraced his steps.

"What is it, Harry?" he asked. "As you see, I am about to depart. My business is pressing."

"It can be no more pressing than mine," retorted Harry hotly. Reflecting that this was not the best way to commence, he took a breath. "Gabriel was arrested last n night and taken to Oxford Castle."

"I am pleased to hear it," Sir Henry replied tersely. "I would have been disappointed if my orders had not been carried out."

Harry bit his lip. This was not a promising beginning. He went down on one knee to his father. "Sir I b beg you, have him released. He is the beloved husband of your daughter and my friend." He searched his father's face for signs of compassion.

"Must I remind you, Sir of how he saved my life or his care for Will when he lay sick. " Sir Henry looked on impassively as Harry continued,

"Have you no compassion or gratitude? Have you f forgotten how you have enjoyed his company under our roof? If none of this has weight with you, would you deprive His Majesty of a loyal and experienced soldier and officer?" Still kneeling, he paused for an answer.

Sir Henry glared at his son. "Do not rebuke me, Harry that I have punished this villainous and insolent young man. That he was our guest is no recommendation to me now. It only serves to remind me that he took those opportunities at Chadshunt of worming his way into Bess's good graces as well as ours. He bewitched her with his music and his tales of his deeds in the field."

The baronet's face flushed with anger.

"Will tells me that he made bold approaches to her from the first and flaunted his affections openly before leaving for Devizes."

"But, Father," Harry interrupted desperately, "Gabriel is accused of rape and abduction. Surely you do not believe this? Bess went with him willingly. She wished to marry him."

Sir Henry stared into the distance out of the window, his back straight and stiff. Turning back, he locked eyes with Harry,

"Fortunately, your brother has retained a proper notion of what is due to this family," he snapped. "It was he who informed me that Vaughan had lain with her, taking advantage of my absence. Will told me how he surprised him in the very act of rising from your sister's bed. The coward refused to fight honourably when Will challenged him. And finally that he abducted Bess, forcing her to flee with him and consent to marry him to cover her shame.

As to this plea from Vaughan for reconciliation," Sir Henry snatched a letter from a table and brandished it at Harry,

" I would have thrown it on the fire. I stayed my hand because in it his own testimony proves him guilty. I have kept it, therefore, as evidence for his trial. He will die for violating my daughter and for the lasting dishonour he has brought on our family. I had hoped you would have set more store by family honour than to plead for one who has sought to destroy it. I have no more to say. I bid you good day, Harry."

ഗ

Standing in the street, Harry twisted his hat in his hands, uncertain how to proceed. He must send word to Bess without delay. She could not be left unawares of her husband's situation. He would task Joe with taking the letter to her. Harry himself had to report for duty that night. Failure to report for duty was insubordination and he would be no use to Gabriel if he was detained himself on a disciplinary charge.

Back at the cottage, Harry seized parchment and wrote hastily," My dearest Bess, I write with distressing news. I know this will alarm you, but Gabriel has been arrested on Father's orders. He is held in Oxford Castle on charges of rape and abduction. I pleaded with Father to have him released but in vain. I will go to Gabriel and seek to bring him comforts. He must be aware that I seek his release. The castle prison is a harsh place, but I will do everything I can to prevent him suffering deliberate ill treatment. He commanded me to protect you and you to do nothing foolish. I will write again when I have more news. Your affectionate brother, Harry."

The prison held Parliamentary soldiers captured in battle, together with spies and common criminals. Harry had been inside the prison escorting prisoners and knew the conditions. The cells were overcrowded, with no sanitation and bad food. The brutality was calculated and jail fever was rampant.

Gabriel had been wearing only doublet and breeches when he was arrested. Harry quickly surveyed the cottage trying to decide what Gabriel would need. He filled his purse with coins. Some of the money was Gabriel's own. Harry would need it for bribes. If offered sufficient inducements, the guards would provide better lodging and allow a prisoner to keep the food brought by their friends. He gathered up a blanket, a thick cloak and a pair of gloves. What else might he take? He dropped all the food he could find into a bag. At the last minute he pressed quill, paper and a small quantity of ink into the bag.

ᔓ

In the guard room, a stout officer with lank hair, a jolly face and grease stains on his buff coat, was sitting on a stool toasting his hands at a brazier. Harry noted the man's size and hoped he would be receptive to bribes. "I wish to meet with one of the prisoners, Captain Gabriel vVaughan," he began. The man grinned with delight,

"That could be arranged. I am Lieutenant Caleb Brown, Sir, assistant to Captain Smith. You might consider me deputy Governor of the castle prison."

Nodding toward a cane lying on a shelf he continued darkly,

"If you need help questioning him we are always at your service."

"That will not be necessary." Harry wanted to wipe the grin off the man's face but it would not help Gabriel.

"He is a friend and I merely seek an interview and to see to his w welfare." He opened his purse and carefully placed a few small coins on the table.

"The man's eyes gleamed and he sat up straight. "And who wishes to see him?"

"Lieutenant Henry Lucie," said Harry curtly.

"It's a weary way to the top of the tower, Sir," Brown complained.

"The officers and gentlemen are not lodged there. Why is he in the tower?"

"I thought a papist might not be welcome among the officers of the Parliament, but if you so wish it."

Harry blushed and placed one more on top of the little pile of coins. "I expect to be able to leave him some comforts," The two men locked eyes. "And that he gets to keep them."

Still smiling, Brown called over his shoulder.

"Ethan! Here!"

A tall corporal in an equally dirty red uniform coat shambled in, scratching his crutch. "Bring the prisoner Captain Vaughan down here. Top of the tower. Came in yesterday."

Waiting together in the guard room the two men eyed each other. In an effort to appear calm, Harry clenched and unclenched his fists until he heard Ethan's heavy footfalls and a second set of footsteps, stumbling and uncertain.

Harry raised his hand to Brown,

"I will see Captain Vaughan alone."

Brown looked mildly surprised at Harry's steely expression,

"Will you now? Well you'll forgive me if I ask you to surrender your sword first. I'll have to check you for weapons. You'd be surprised, Sir, what people try to smuggle in."

Reluctantly Harry handed over his sword. The man's foul breath assailed him as he searched Harry quickly. "In here, Ethan," he called.

"Very well, then we'll leave you with the good captain for a few minutes."

Gabriel stumbled through the doorway. The door was locked behind him. Harry was not overly surprised to see that his brother-in-law was in chains and already filthy. He noted that Gabriel's doublet and leather boots were gone. But he was not prepared for the black eye and the swollen lip. One side of his face was covered with bruises. Worst of all, Gabriel was clearly in considerable pain and breathing unevenly.

"Who has done this to you?" Harry asked, surprising himself at the calmness in his voice. Gabriel gasped as a fresh spasm went through him.

"A welcome to the jail, you might say. The cell was already crowded. It was my misfortune that one of them was a spy I had arrested myself. In the daylight he knew me for the source of his present misery. Others were happy to assist him in my beating. It was fortunate the corporal came for me when he did to bring me to you. I imagine the prisoners will finish what the corporal and your visit interrupted. At least I will not suffer the disgrace of a trial."

Gabriel's green eyes blazed in his white face. Harry could see that talking was paining him. He continued although his breathing was becomingly increasingly ragged,

"Harry, I fear I must bid you farewell. And I ask you to escort Bess to my parents. They will offer her protection. Tell her not to waste her life in useless regrets, for I have none." He fell silent. The room was not warm despite the fire, but Gabriel's face dripped sweat.

"Gabriel, do not talk of farewells," Harry urged. "This man is happy to take bribes. I will persuade him to close confine you for your safety. I will tell him that if you d die through neglect or mistreatment I will see him punished and removed from his p post. Then I will redouble my efforts to have you freed. I will think of something. I swear I will not allow you to be harmed f further." Gabriel bowed his head in thanks.

Harry knocked on the door. When it opened, he said tersely,

"A word in private with you. Captain Vaughan is to remain close by until we have spoken." Brown jerked his head at the corporal named Ethan, who tugged Gabriel out into the dark and narrow passage. Harry drew himself up and spoke slowly and carefully, determined to control both his temper and his stutter.

"Lieutenant, the prisoners are in your care. Captain Vaughan has suffered considerable mistreatment since his arrival. He tells me that his fellow prisoners having recognised him were beating him. They are like to beat him to death."

Brown sneered at Harry. "Prisons are not healthy places, Sir. Many men die of jail fever and the like."

"That may be so, but it will not be the fate of Captain Vaughan, or I will do all I can to have you dismissed from your post. On the other hand I am prepared to reward you handsomely if you will keep him close confined and allow me to supply his wants."

The officer stroked his chin, "And just how handsomely might that be, Lieutenant Lucie?" Harry weighed the man up. Then he removed the purse from his belt and tossed it on the table. Brown opened it ravenously and counted the coins. He pursed his lips, looking Harry up and down, clearly assessing the quality of his cloak, doublet and boots.

"That might be sufficient to move him to the room where the officers and gentlemen of the Parliament are lodged. But then he may not be welcome among them as a Royalist and a papist. And he might be recognised again." Brown paused to give weight to his threat.

"I will have him close confined for tonight and," gesturing with his chin to the bag Harry had brought, "You may leave that for him. If you wish him to have a private chamber, you will need to do better than this," he said with a mock bow.

Handing Harry back his sword Brown concluded, "Present yourself by midday with fifty crowns or I will return him to the common soldiers in the tower."

Gabriel was leaning painfully against the stone wall in the dark passage with Ethan firmly gripping his arm. Harry thrust the blanket and bag at Gabriel who clasped them awkwardly in his manacled hands.

"Can you not remove the irons?" snapped Harry.

"Now that I may not do, Sir. I have my orders," smiled Brown. "But we will take him now to the private chamber which you bespoke. Until the morrow, Lieutenant."

"Harry, be easy," Gabriel murmured. "I thank you for your love and kindness."

He smiled at Harry through his swollen lips. Harry watched as Brown jerked on the chain between Gabriel's wrists and dragged him down the dark passage.

Harry pondered how he might get fifty crowns by the next morning. It was already past noon and he must report for duty at sunset. Should he approach his father again? Harry could not bear to believe his father's words that he sought Gabriel's death. Would he relent if he knew how much he had already suffered? It was too great a risk to rely on his father having a change of heart, but saving Gabriel was all that mattered at present. It would take too many days to send to Gabriel's own family for help. There was only one course of action left to him.

Hannah answered the door to the house in High Street. "Is my f father at h home?" Harry stuttered.

"He is not, Sir. I believe he will not be back until dark."

"Thank you, Hannah, I will leave him a letter then." The maid stood aside and Harry climbed the stairs, heart beating fast. He shut the door firmly and went straight to the chest where his father and Will had stored the money and other Chadshunt Hall valuables. Hidden under linen and blankets at the bottom of the chest was the silver. He counted out fifty crowns. There was no surety Brown would not demand more. Biting his lip, Harry depleted the precious hoard as heavily as he dared. Later he must explain to his angry father. With luck, it would be some weeks before Sir Henry might miss the money. He poured the stream of silver into a purse, closed the chest and quietly left the house.

Basing House, 10 December 1643

Mary and I were eating supper in the Great Hall when a servant approached me.

"Mistress Vaughan, a messenger has arrived. He is at the New House stables."

Hoping it might be good news from Gabriel, I ran across the court and through the New House. To my surprise, it was a grave faced Joe. Silently, he held out a letter. By the light of the flaring torches, I recognised the Lucie seal and ripped it open with foreboding. When I finished reading it, my legs turned to water. Joe caught me.

"Joe, I must go to Gabriel. I must make my father see reason. How can he be so cruel?"

"Mistress Bess, you are not to put yourself in danger again."

Joe spoke with the authority of one who had not only suffered enough of my escapades but who had seen battle. I heard a light foot step. It was Mary. I burst into tears and thrust Harry's letter blindly at her. She read it quickly and then looked at me, her face full of concern.

"Bess, your husband commands you to do nothing foolish. Place your trust in your brother."

I continued to sob. Joe was looking at me for instruction.

"What is it, Joe?" I sniffed.

"Would you write a letter to your brother or your husband, Mistress? If you do so, I will return to Oxford without delay." His face was pale and weary beneath his weathered brown complexion and he was unconsciously rubbing his back and stretching his feet. "Oh Joe, you must rest tonight. I will not let you ride through the night. It is more than forty miles. I will write letters and you may take them back to Oxford in the morning. I need time for reflection."

A servant led him away to snatch some much-needed sleep. I trudged back to my solitary bed chamber, Mary beside me. She consoled me in a low and soothing voice, but I heard little. I was making plans. I would do my best to honour Gabriel's command to do nothing foolish. That did not mean I was prepared to remain tamely at Basing. I read again Harry's words, soon to be burned into my mind, "He is held in Oxford Castle on charges of rape and abduction. I pleaded with our father in vain. ... The castle prison as you may have heard is a harsh place..."

It would be a long night. Seating myself at a table, I reached for a quill and made sure there was plenty of paper and ink. I commenced with the easiest letter, a reply to Harry.

"My dearest brother, I commend your efforts for Gabriel and thank you for sending word to me. You may imagine my distress, my rage with our father. I will heed your warnings and my husband's command to do nothing foolish. But neither can I remain idle while my love endures I know not what in Oxford Castle. I enclose a letter to Gabriel in the hope that you may find the means of placing it in his hands. Lest you both fear for me, I solemnly promise to take all possible care for my safety. I pray you continue your attempts to care for and free Gabriel. I will apply myself to our father, although I fear that if he will not heed your pleas he is unlikely to heed my own, however desperate. Your loving and grateful sister, Elisabeth Vaughan."

Writing to Gabriel I ruined one sheet of paper when my tears fell upon the page and made the ink run in streams. I did not want him to see I had been weeping so began again.

"Dearest of husbands, it is useless for me to feign calm at the news Harry sent. I feel rent in two, by what you must be suffering and by the fact it is my own father who has put you in that terrible place. I have promised Harry that I will abide by your command. But while I live I cannot remain at Basing in ignorance, doing nothing to aid you. Faithful Joe carries this letter and I will also entrust him with one to my father in which I will beg him to rescind the order for your arrest. What else may be attempted at present I know not. I will take further counsel of Harry if my father does not relent. My thoughts, my prayers and all the love in my breaking heart are with you. Your obedient and loving wife, Elisabeth Vaughan."

I kissed the letter and clutched it to me. With luck it would be in Gabriel's own hands the next day.

I was ignorant of the law and the penalties which it might exact from Gabriel were he found guilty. Whether he were in peril of his life, I did not know. But I had heard enough during my time in Oxford to be aware that many died in the jail at Oxford Castle before they could be brought to trial. To wait upon the outcome of a trial at an unknown date would be to subject Gabriel to certain suffering and possible death from any number of causes in the intervening months. He must be freed, whatever the cost.

I turned to the most difficult letter of all, the one to he who was the cause of my distress. The one I had called Father for all of my life. For hours I sat, pen in hand, the empty sheet of paper before me, until I knew that dawn could be not too far away. Sighing I dipped pen in ink.

"Honoured and respected Father," I began, with a strong sense that in truth I no longer owed either of these to my father. "It grieves me more than I can say to hear that my beloved husband is imprisoned in Oxford Castle and that it is so by your command. Dear Father, how came you to do this to him, and to me? How accuse him of rape when I joyfully married him? That we married without your consent was cause of grief to both Gabriel and me. I feared that your dislike of Catholics would prejudice you against all Gabriel's other qualities and the happy history of how he has brought comfort to our family, to both my brothers in the past year.

We hoped that time would mend the breach. In his eagerness to make amends, Gabriel approached you, seeking your early forgiveness and reconciliation. If you had brushed aside his advances, I would have been saddened and hoped that you would soften with time. But, instead of being content with rejecting his approach, I fear you now seek his death.

Dear Sir, I beg you, for the love between us, for the love which was between my mother and you, do not cause us this anguish. You know how bad conditions in the jail are, better than I. If my husband now suffers pain, hunger, cold or sickness as well as loss of liberty, it is by your will. I pray you, have pity on him and me. You deprive the King of a brave soldier, as well as me of a husband. Once more I ask you, forgive Gabriel his love for me and I my love for him. Your sorrowing daughter, Bess."

I lay down upon the bed which Gabriel and I had shared for those few days, until dawn broke. I slept little, but buried my face in his pillow, drinking in his scent. Then I rose, gave the letters to Joe and wished him Godspeed. I began my preparations. After a little persuasion, Mary agreed to help me. With as much calm as I could muster, I told Father Allen of my father's revenge on Gabriel.

"My dear Bess, I will pray for his safety and early release. But since God sometimes needs our assistance, let me think a while how we may do so. What are your plans?"

"To ride today to Oxford," I declared with determination, " Go to Harry and see what else I may do. I may visit my father if he has been unmoved by my letter."

"Then make ready, Bess. But first break your fast, wash the tears from your face and return to me."

Obediently I did as he had bidden me. By the time I had breakfasted, Mary had returned with the things I had asked her to obtain. I dressed once more as a boy in the plain shirt, breeches and coat of a servant, with a soft felt hat which I intended to pull low on my brow. I would have no Joe to accompany me and must find my own way from Basing to Oxford. I would carry a pistol in the holster on my saddle. I had no knowledge of swordsmanship but Gabriel had shown me how to load and give fire before we left Oxford.

When I returned to Father Allen, he frowned at my appearance but then nodded. "You are determined then to ride today alone. Kneel down, and we will see if we can offer you a little protection." Kneeling at his feet, his hand on my head, I closed my eyes and listened to his calm, reassuring voice as he blessed me. Then he made the sign of the cross over me.

"And now, Bess, here is a letter. Lady Grenfall is presently at Oxford. I believe she is with the Queen and may be able to assist you. If your pleas to your father fail, approach her with this letter. I will hope to see both you and your brave husband here again. Go with God."

My wedding ring I removed and hung on a chain around my neck. In a purse on my belt was the crucifix and chain Gabriel had given me, together with all the money I possessed. As I was making ready to leave, Mary came running after me.

"Bess, you should talk to Sam, one of the grooms, whose clothes you wear. He often makes the journey to Oxford and will tell you the best and safest road." It was sound advice. Sam grinned at the sight of me in his clothes. He advised me of which roads to take, where I might find a respectable but quiet inn if I needed rest.

"Do you have a safe conduct pass to take you into Oxford?"

There was a further delay to my journey's start. I could not believe that I had forgotten something so important to my plan. I hurriedly approached Captain Amery.

"Be wise, Mistress Vaughan. Take great care upon the road and be guided by your brother when you arrive. I pray that Captain Vaughan may soon be free once more."

Pass in my purse, I saddled Fairy. I strapped the holster with its pistol and a cloak bag containing clothes and other provisions to the saddle. It was full daylight by the time I headed out of Garrison Gate. Fairy lengthened her stride into a canter and I began to pray. Under my breath, I chanted my own version of the Kyrie.

"Lord keep him safe

Christ keep him safe."

To the rhythmic accompaniment of the mare's hooves, I sped onward towards Oxford.

30

Oxford, 12 December 1643

DESPITE MY ANXIETY to reach Oxford, the heavy rain and bitter cold winds, coupled with the need for caution, forced me to turn into the quieter, less travelled roads. Approaching Newbury, I spied a patrol of Roundhead troops and turned aside to spend the night in Didcot.

The ostler led my weary mare away to the stable. The innkeeper's wife looked sharply at me when I requested lodging and food in as deep a voice as I could manage. But in time of war any traveller might have secrets. She said nothing. My money was as good as the next man's. The inn was quiet. I drank some ale and ate a pie, resolving to keep up my strength for what might lie ahead of me. If the bed had fleas at least I knew I had better lodging than my poor husband was likely to have.

I arrived in Oxford before noon and went straight to Gabriel's cottage. Harry was not there, but the servant who cleaned and cooked said she thought he would be back for dinner. After rubbing down Fairy and seeing she had food and water, I retrieved my gown from my pack and changed thankfully out of my man's attire into that suitable for a married woman. From the chain around my neck I took Gabriel's ring and replaced it on my left hand. The soft rose coloured Welsh gold glowed in the light from the fire and I felt a little comforted. I took the crucifix from my purse. I hesitated and then hung it around my neck. Whether it was a wise thing to do in Oxford I did not know. But, I reasoned, it was a poor beginning if I was afraid to acknowledge my new faith.

I sat down to warm myself. Before long I heard Harry's brisk step. He stood stock still when he saw me, seated before the fire on a stool.

"Bess," he clasped me in his arms. "I feared you would come. Can you never obey commands? Gabriel told you to do nothing f foolish." His cloak was soaked but I clung to him nevertheless.

"I am sorry Harry but I had to come. I took very great care upon the road. Have you seen him? How does he?"

Harry busied himself removing his wet cloak and hat and turned away from me. “Harry, what is it?” I was frightened that he did not speak.

He forced a smile. “Be calm. I have seen Gabriel now s several times. Bess,” he continued hesitantly, “Are you aware that the prison in the castle is known for habitually mistreating its p prisoners? “

I felt the blood drain from my face and sat down with a thump on the stool. “What have they done to him, Harry?” I whispered.

Harry crouched down next to me and took hold of my hands, the grey eyes full of concern. “I did not mean to frighten you, my dear sister. He is kept in chains and has been beaten by other prisoners. I think they cracked several ribs. I have b bribed the officers to keep him close confined so that he is safe from further assault. He has food now and some basic necessities. He will recover from his injuries in time.”

I leapt to my feet, “I must go to him.”

“No!” He took me by the shoulders and forced me back down onto the stool. “Bess no, it is not fitting. I know Gabriel would not wish you to go there.” Harry’s voice was filled with alarm.

I looked at him forlornly.

“He has already received comfort from the loving letter which you wrote him. I was able to see him yesterday and gave it to him. I d delivered your letter to our father also but have not yet heard from him.

I am visiting Gabriel again later today. I try to see him daily, both to bring him food and to satisfy myself of his welfare. If you would c comfort him, write him a letter. Then rest yourself, for you have had a long, cold journey from Basing.”

I was impatient to see Gabriel, but Harry was obstinate, refusing to take me with him unless Gabriel gave his consent. With this I had to be satisfied. I therefore contented myself with writing Gabriel a hastily penned letter. Harry warned me that the letter was likely to be opened and read before he gave it to Gabriel, so I was careful not to say too much, nor to write anything which might be construed as a plot.

"My love, forgive me that I was unable to stay away. I await your commands as to whether I may see you but earnestly entreat you to allow me to do so. Harry has told me how you fare. I know he is doing all he can. We have no word yet from our father. I have faith in your courage and fortitude as I do in your love. Bess.”

I folded the letter. To my surprise, I spotted Gabriel’s signet ring lying on a shelf. He rarely removed it from his hand. I pressed the ring with the Vaughan coat of arms firmly against the wax. Then I put it carefully into my own purse for safety.

Harry took the letter from me and put it into a bag along with food from the servant, bread from the bakers and a small earthenware pot, which he attempted to conceal. "What is in the pot?" I enquired sharply.

Harry sighed. "A salve from an apothecary for Gabriel's b bruises."

I turned my back so Harry could not see the tears. "Then go," I said in a muffled voice, "I would not detain you from him."

ꕤ

Oxford Castle, 12 December 1643

Gabriel was sitting on a stool in his cell, rubbing his fettered ankle when he heard the key turn in the lock. He got defensively to his feet, gasping in pain from the cracked ribs.

"Visitor for you, papist," said Ethan, standing aside. To Gabriel's relief it was Harry. Ethan went out again, locking the door behind him. Harry embraced Gabriel warmly.

"I did not expect you to come to my cell," said Gabriel, puzzled.

"To ensure they provide what I have paid for and they have promised, I wanted to see for myself where they have lodged you," said Harry.

"Well indeed, we should put small trust in them," Gabriel replied softly. "I am afraid I have but little accommodation for visitors. Would you care to have my seat?" He smiled wryly at Harry who was momentarily choked for words and could only shake his head, pushing his brother in law gently back onto the stool.

"I paid for you to have a fire. I see you have none."

It was a cold December day and even colder in the cell. Gabriel was wrapped in the cloak Harry had brought him with a blanket around his shoulders. There was a small, battered table and a mattress on the rush covered floor but the brazier was unlit and only a little light came in through a small barred window high in the wall. A tallow candle flickering feebly on the table contributed no more than a glimmer of light.

"How are your ribs?"

"The pain only comes when I breathe now, the problem being that I need to breathe quite frequently," replied Gabriel. Harry smiled reluctantly at the jest. "A fire would be welcome. More candles too. They help to keep the rats away, at least I can see them coming."

Harry handed the bag of food to Gabriel and then pulled a letter from his coat. The seal was broken, but Gabriel recognised it immediately for his own and started.

"From Bess," said Harry quickly, "She is arrived from Basing." Gabriel raised a hand to run it through his hair in his habitual gesture. The heavy chain pulled against it and he dropped the hand, regarding it blankly.

He stared at Harry. "Bess is here?" He unfolded the short letter and read it, looking dazed.

"She wishes above all things to visit you. Will you permit it?"

The colour drained from Gabriel's face.

"Harry no, you are not to bring her here. I forbid it. This is no place for a lady and I would not have her see me like this." He lifted his manacled hands and indicated his filthy clothes and unkempt hair. Chained to the wall by his ankle, he was unable to move more than the length of the chain permitted.

Tactfully, Harry said nothing for a few minutes, pouring some ale for Gabriel. Gabriel accepted the beaker and drank.

"Harry, I believe it would still be best if you would escort Bess to my parents in Wales. I do not know when if ever I will be able to care for her again. And she is my responsibility. God forgive me, I married her and have brought all this trouble upon her, myself and you too."

"I thought this might be what you would s say. But Gabriel, you take too gloomy a view. Bess and I seek your release. I had hoped to approach Lord Byron on your behalf, but he has left with the army for North Wales. If things go badly, I will s send a messenger to him. And if you come to trial…"

"When, Harry, not if. I fear that is not in doubt." Gabriel's voice was calm but firm. "I will be tried for my life at the Lent Assizes. Rape is a felony and a capital offence. Sir Henry knows the law, he chose well in framing his accusation. He wishes to be rid of me."

"But there is every hope you will be found not guilty of these ridiculous charges. Do not talk of taking her to your parents yet. Here," said Harry, pushing the food towards Gabriel. "Fill your belly. Regain your strength. Bess needs you."

Gabriel obediently pulled a pie from the bag. Harry stood watching him eating while trying but failing to think of words to cheer him.

Gabriel asked suddenly, "Did the Marquis send a servant with her?"

"She travelled by herself in man's attire, riding Fairy. My sister does not lack courage."

A moment later the key turned in the lock. Ethan looked in briefly. "You must leave in two minutes, Lieutenant."

"Very well," Harry replied reluctantly. Gabriel hastily folded Bess's letter.

"Harry, there is a loose brick at the bottom of the wall," he pointed."

Pull it out for me and you may hide the letter behind it with the other you brought. I would keep it by me. Tell her it was a comfort. If you have left me paper I will write her a letter."

The door opened again. Harry embraced Gabriel once more and left quickly, fearing he would betray himself with the emotion he felt. He passed the man a coin and said,

"Give him a fire. I will return on the morrow." The corporal pocketed the coin and nodded.

Gabriel listened to the receding footsteps. The sight of Bess's words had cheered him, even while knowledge of her nearness had turned him cold with fear. As he finished the piece of pie, he was surprised to hear footsteps returning. The key turned once more and Ethan stood in the door, grinning unpleasantly. Gabriel regarded him warily.

"Why are you returned?"

"Not for the enjoyment of your stinking papist company. I am come to light the fire in accordance with his lordship's wishes."

Gabriel's face brightened at the prospect of warmth. The brazier lit, Ethan grinned unpleasantly.

"And I am to search the cell of any who entertain visitors. Stand aside."

He shoved Gabriel against the wall and began tossing his few possessions carelessly around. He helped himself to a loaf. He regarded the stock of writing materials thoughtfully but then shrugged and left them. Finally, he rummaged through Gabriel's bedding.

"I fear you have made no interesting discoveries because I have nothing to hide."

Ethan glared. "I may also search your person if I am suspicious." He pulled the blanket from Gabriel's shoulders, cast it to the floor and then tugged at the clasp fastening his cloak. It followed the blanket to the floor. Pushing Gabriel away from the wall again, he shuffled behind him and tore his shirt deliberately down the middle. He made a show of looking under the ripped shirt. Finally, he reached for the buttons on Gabriel's breeches. Gabriel tensed. Ethan licked his lips. With elaborate slowness, he unfastened the breeches and pulled them down.

"A fine discovery at the last. A papist's pecker looks like any other." He reached out his hand and squeezed hard.

Gabriel hit him. The heavy manacles caught Ethan in the nose and Gabriel heard the crunch of breaking bone. Ethan staggered away from him, his nose bleeding heavily,

"You will regret that." Leaving a trail of blood from his nose, which Gabriel knew the rats would find later, the corporal left the cell, slamming the door loudly and locking it. Gabriel sighed and collected his scattered clothes, attempting to restore some semblance of decency to his dress. Then he waited for the inevitable retribution.

An hour or more elapsed before the key turned in the lock again. Caleb Brown entered the cell slowly, closing the door and leaning against it. He smiled at Gabriel with his usual appearance of geniality, his eyes cold. "So, Captain," he said brightly, "You have been naughty. You would have me set aside the special arrangements the good Lieutenant was at such pains to make for you. They did not include provision for assaulting your guards. As I daresay you are aware, the punishment for that is flogging." Still smiling, he folded his arms and stared at Gabriel.

Gabriel struggled to keep his voice calm, "You will do what you will. When is it to be carried out?"

The lieutenant pursed his lips. "I am still considering how many lashes you have earned. You broke his nose and if it were left to him I have no doubt he would flog you to death." He paused, head on one side, watching his prisoner. Gabriel realised that the man was playing with him. His only defence was not to let Brown see the fear and anger which was churning inside him. He would rather by far face the enemy on the battlefield where he had a fighting chance. He looked away, fearing these thoughts would be evident in his expression. The silence lengthened. Gabriel's heart beat loudly in the quiet cell.

"I think, given the seriousness of the assault, a total of four score lashes. Shall we say three o'clock tomorrow? Lieutenant Lucie is usually here around that time. I am sure he would wish to be present. Do you have anything more to say?" Gabriel regarded him steadily but remained silent. "Then I will wish you a good night's rest, Captain and we will meet at three." The key turned in the lock. Gabriel crossed himself and buried his face in his hands.

ೞ

Two days had elapsed since Joe had delivered my letter to my father. I was not hopeful. At the same time I hoped that my tears might melt my father's heart if my letter had not. And my fears for Gabriel had proved true. I would recount his sufferings to my father and hope that they would have a softening effect. I determined to wait no longer for a reply from my father. I asked Harry to escort me to the house before it grew too dark. Harry hesitated, looking at the sky.

"Very well, Bess, but we must make haste. The streets of Oxford are no place for a lady after dark, as you well know."

The streets were still crowded with those returning home before dark. We rode past the castle. I stared hard at its forbidding walls. Tears blurred my vision as I wondered in what part of it Gabriel lay.

When we reached the house in the High Street, I alone dismounted. Harry remained with the horses. Hannah answered the door. I nervously enquired if my father was home.

"I believe so, Mistress," she said with unaccustomed caution in her voice. "I will tell him that you are here."

I was about to say that I would go up unannounced, but something in her voice and manner stopped me. I nodded uncertainly and followed her into the hall. From there, my heart hammering, I watched her climb the stairs and heard her tentative knock at my father's door. I held my breath.

"Sir Henry, Mistress Vaughan is below and asks to see you."

After a slight pause, he replied with a cold and unfamiliar voice,

"Thank you, Hannah. I know no Mistress Vaughan. No one of the name of Vaughan is welcome here and should not receive admittance. Inform the other servants of my wishes."

The door was closed firmly. As Hannah made her way down the stairs I tried to climb them myself crying,

"Father, no." She gently stopped me. Shaking her head, she beckoned to me silently and I followed her into the kitchen.

"I am very sorry, Mistress Vaughan. I believe it will do no good trying to see your father again. He was in a very great passion when he heard from Master Will what had happened. He could be heard throughout the household. Neither would he take heed of Master Harry's pleas. Mistress Adams approached him herself, when she heard he was imprisoned, but to no avail. She is of the opinion that nothing will satisfy him but your husband's death."

My countenance as I left the house told Harry all he needed to know. He slid off his horse and embraced me tenderly.

"Come Bess, I will take you home. All is not lost. We will make fresh plans on the morrow."

After Harry left for his night patrol, I paced the small rooms, touching those things which belonged to Gabriel, observing the neat way he arranged his possessions in the limited space. His razor and combs were folded tidily in a piece of linen beside the bed. His long leather buff coat, helmet and sash were all as he had left them. In the closet, carefully put away, were a pair of black leather gloves I had given him as a wedding gift no more than two weeks earlier. I realised afresh how he had been taken without even being able to dress appropriately for the weather. Despite the cold evening, I worked myself into a lather as I paced the rooms. Gabriel's sword hung on a hook in its scabbard and I took it down, rubbing the shiny basket hilt with my thumb and wondering wildly if I would rather plunge the blade into my father's bosom or my own. When Polly the servant came with supper, I had no appetite. She saw me cradling the sword in my lap and must have seen the look in my eyes. She took it from me gently.

"Now you give me that, Mistress Vaughan. Not dead yet, is 'e?"

I relinquished it reluctantly. I reflected that I still had the letter from Lady Grenfall. I would ask Harry to discuss it with Gabriel on the morrow. I would act no more without his approval.

I woke to another grey morning. Harry was stirring the glowing embers of the fire. After Harry had slept we dined together. He seemed as resolved as I to put the previous evening's setback behind us. I told him of my resolution to approach Lady Grenfall and he agreed to obtain Gabriel's consent that afternoon.

ᔕ

Oxford Castle, 13 December 1643

It was a little before three o'clock when Ethan ushered Harry into the cell. Gabriel was on his knees, praying. The corporal was rubbing his hands repeatedly up and down his grimy coat in excitement.

"We will return shortly, papist," he said. Harry passed Gabriel the bag of food but Gabriel shook his head.

"I fear I have little appetite today, Harry. You will have noticed that man's face?"

"It looks as if he has been in a brawl and had his nose broken."

"He provoked me beyond bearing. It was I who broke his nose and now I am to be flogged."

The brazier was out and the room chill, but Harry marked the sweat on his Gabriel's brow and hastily passed him a bottle of ale,

"Drink."

Gabriel tilted the bottle into his mouth, watching as Harry's expression changed to angry determination.

"Harry," he urged, "There is nothing you can do to prevent this. I must accept the punishment. Men are flogged regularly in the army and in prisons. You know that as well as I. You have seen it happen. It is painful, bloody and humiliating. I should survive, but it is hardly a prospect I relish.

As Julius Caesar said, "It is easier to find men who will volunteer to die, than to find those who are willing to endure pain with patience."

Harry smiled reluctantly.

"I was brave enough to break that man's nose." Gabriel continued, "Now I have to find the courage to suffer the consequences. All you can do is support me by being in attendance. See that they do not exceed their authority."

Moments later the door opened again. Lieutenant Brown stood there expectantly. Gabriel got to his feet and laid aside his cloak, striving to appear calm. Brown smirked at Harry,

"Delighted to see you, Lieutenant. If you are ready, Captain." He bent and undid the chain on Gabriel's ankle.

"Lieutenant," Harry pleaded, "He is still not recovered from his p previous injuries, will you not d delay another day or two to make him stronger?"

"Harry," Gabriel interrupted urgently, "Do not concern yourself. I would rather it were over as soon as possible."

"Spoken like a sensible man, Captain,"

said Brown with glee. He followed Gabriel and Harry along the passage, and then down the winding stairs from the officers' cells. Gabriel knew exactly where he was going. Official punishments including floggings and executions were carried out below in the vast courtyard. Gabriel had seen Colonel Fielding led out to the block there for surrendering Reading to the rebels. He had received a last minute reprieve.

Strange as it was, he felt some relief. He had spoken truth to Harry. He wished the punishment to be over as soon as possible and hoped his body would be strong enough to bear the whole punishment. If not, he would be forced to undergo a second beating.

It was a raw and wet afternoon with the rain increasing to a downpour. Gabriel shivered in his ragged shirt. He set his jaw. He would not give the man added satisfaction by struggling or showing fear. He marched steadily across the courtyard, looking neither to left nor right.

31

THE WEATHER HAD not deterred a small crowd of idlers. Both men and women were gathering to watch the entertaining sight of another human being suffer. Ethan, grinning with delight, held the whip with its knotted thongs. A uniformed drummer completed the spectacle. Brown produced a key and unlocked the chain between Gabriel's wrists.

Harry watched helplessly. Gabriel's torn shirt was removed and he was bound to the whipping post with his hands above his head. Gabriel gasped with pain as the strain increased on the cracked ribs. A leather gag was thrust into his mouth. The rain was plastering Gabriel's hair to his bared shoulders. He shook his head in a vain attempt to flick it from his eyes.

Brown grabbed Gabriel's long hair and twisted it in a knot so it would not obstruct the whip. Harry's stomach lurched. He turned away, only to catch sight of the avid crowd of onlookers, sacks or cloaks held over their heads, shelling nuts and drinking ale as if at the play.

For the benefit of the crowd, Brown declaimed, "Gabriel Vaughan, you are sentenced to four score lashes for a serious assault upon a prison officer. Corporal, do your duty."

Gabriel was standing motionless, his brow pressed against the post. Harry had seen that stillness before. He knew Gabriel was gathering his inner strength.

Ethan licked his lips as he raised the whip. Brown stood back, arms comfortably folded, oblivious of the drenching rain. To the accompanying tattoo of the single drum, he began counting aloud. Gabriel flinched as the whip landed on his back for the first time but made no other movement. His back was quickly covered in angry red weals. A minute or so later a rivulet of blood was trickling down the centre, mingling with the rain. There was an "ah" of satisfaction from the crowd and they pressed forward. Drops of blood sprayed Harry's cheek and he vomited on the ground. The man nearest to him, craning his neck for a better view, gave him a curious look. Harry could no longer watch. He kept his back turned, hearing the crack of the whip, the beat of the drum and Brown counting. There was a long pause after "thirty six". Harry forced himself to look around. Gabriel had fainted and was hanging limply by his wrists. Brown picked up a bucket standing in readiness and threw water over his head to revive him. After a pause, Gabriel lifted his head and struggled to regain his footing. Brown adjusted the ropes binding Gabriel's arms, pulling them higher above his head. Ethan was bent over, panting with exertion. Brown took the whip from him, running the strands matter of factly through his fingers, clearing them of the clotting blood. Harry's stomach was empty, but he dry retched.

The regular crack of the whip resumed. At "fifty one" there was another pause. Taking slow, deep breaths, Harry turned back to see that Gabriel had fainted again. Harry stared in dismay at Gabriel's back, at his legs running with blood and the puddles of rain stained red. Brown approached Gabriel once more and slapped his face hard. Gabriel tried to raise his head but failed. Lieutenant Brown, his face and coat liberally splattered with blood, paused for breath. His eye met Harry's.

"Can't flog him in his sleep, can we, Lieutenant?" he jibed. He raised his gloved hand and slapped the semi-conscious Gabriel across the face a second time.

Without thought, Harry flung himself forward, snatching the whip from Brown's hand and hurling it away.

"Do you want to kill him?" he gasped. "No more."

Brown glared at Harry briefly, but then his usual mask of good humour dropped into place and he nodded.

"As you wish, Lieutenant. The remaining thirty strokes then on another day, as soon as he is able. A fine half hour's entertainment. I hope it was as much to your taste as it was to mine."

Harry strode forward to catch Gabriel as he was untied, and laid him gently down. He mastered the impulse to strike Brown.

"Have the goodness to carry him carefully back to his cell. I wish to stay awhile and tend to him," Harry said as he extracted some coins from his purse.

"Always a pleasure to be of service, Lieutenant. Ethan, have one of the guards help you carry the prisoner back to his cell. Have a care of him, mind."

He reached to replace the chain on Gabriel's wrists.

Harry grabbed his arm,

"Leave that until the morrow. He is in sufficient agony and in no position to escape or cause other annoyance."

Brown looked hard at him but, apparently reading nothing sinister in the request, shrugged his shoulders.

"As you wish."

The crowd of onlookers dispersed in high good humour, leaving a covering of nut shells and orange peel on the wet ground. One among them left hurriedly. He had watched from a corner of the courtyard, solitary and silent.

Back in the cell, Gabriel was laid on the mattress and his ankle chained again to the wall. Brown followed Harry in to the cell.

"No more than one hour, Lieutenant." He left, locking the door behind him.

"How many?"

Gabriel's voice was a thin thread. Harry stared at him, but Gabriel said no more. Harry shuddered as he understood.

"50, 51 maybe."

"Ah."

There was a wealth of meaning in that single syllable. The four score lashes were not complete, there was more to be borne.

"Bess," it was no more than a whisper.

"She is safe," Harry reassured him, "Lie still while I staunch the bleeding."

Despite his caution, Harry's attempts caused Gabriel to faint again. Harry surveyed dejectedly the unconscious form of the man who he had followed into battle and who he loved as a brother. His back had been torn methodically from shoulder to waist. His breeches were soaked in blood, his legs and feet stained a dark red. Harry covered him carefully with the cloak and blanket.

"I swear to you, Gabriel," Harry said softly, "By all I hold holy, I will win your release. You will suffer no more flogging."

He banged on the cell door.

ↄ∽

I approached the house in High Street somewhat cautiously although I knew my father was not in. Mistress Adams drew me instantly into the kitchen where we could speak freely. We had not seen each other since my flight to Basing. Although not a great lover of papists, she was fond of me and wished me and Gabriel every happiness on our marriage.

"My dear friend," she said, "I must seem untimely with my good wishes when your poor husband is confined in the castle jail. What news do you have of him?"

I sighed. "I may not go there, but my kind brother visits him daily and has made arrangements for what comforts he is permitted to bring him.

Though it is little enough he can do. Even with Harry's help, Gabriel is kept in the harshest of conditions." There was another pause.

She went on awkwardly,

"I was sorry to hear that your father refused to see you last night."

"I must thank you for speaking to him yourself. Hannah told me you tried to bring him to reason."

She dismissed my thanks with a shake of her head.

"I fear I did more harm than good. Although he remained courteous to me I could see that my plain speaking vexed him. My husband forbade me to interfere again, telling me to mind my house and not the affairs of other families. Bess, I do not think Sir Henry will change his mind. He has become a different man these last weeks since you left Oxford. His temper is disturbed and there is a harshness in his manner which now appears in his dealings with all."

I sighed. "I fear this is but the latest change to his character. He was always a strict father, but loving too. You will recall how he reacted to my arrival in Oxford when I had contravened his orders. I believe the events of the last year, my poor mother's death, my father's estrangement from his brother and Harry's protracted imprisonment, have all changed him. The sequestration of the family estates is a constant source of anxiety as you may imagine. Maybe if this war will end I may recover the father I once loved. But it will not be in time to help my poor husband. I should leave. Harry will return soon and I would have news of Gabriel."

We bade each other a warm farewell. I rode away from my visit to Mistress Adams, Emily with my heart a little lighter. The friendship, which my father forbade me continue, was now restored.

I had only been back at the cottage a short time when Harry arrived pale and anguished. A lump of ice settled in my heart.

"Harry, what is it?" He regarded me tenderly.

"Bess, be assured that Gabriel lives. But yesterday, shortly after I left him, Gabriel attacked a guard. Harry took a breath, "For this offence they sentenced him to four score lashes. He was flogged today. By his wish, I witnessed the carrying out of the punishment. He bore it most bravely."

Harry's voice seemed to be coming from a long way away. He paused and seemed to shudder.

"But Gabriel fainted. They will wait until he is a little recovered before they complete his sentence."

"Harry, they will kill him! We must rescue him or he will die. They have flogged him because he is in their power and because they are cruel and inhuman. We must get him out of there now."

Harry shook his head and sighed, "And how do you propose we rescue him?"

"Can you not bribe the guard?" I said wildly.

"Bess I have already bribed the officer. When I proposed Gabriel was unchained, the man stuck fast. And he will certainly not agree to let him escape. If Gabriel were some pickpocket detained in the marketplace, his disappearance might be overlooked. But Gabriel is a captain of the garrison, detained on written orders from our own father. The jailer will not risk his own position."

"Then might we rescue him by force?"

"Bess, that is foolish. Am I to scale the tower wall like some crusader of old while trusty Joe waits below? And then make my way past gatehouse, drawbridge and garrison unobserved? You are dreaming. For Gabriel to be released, the charges must be dropped, or he must be acquitted at his trial, or the orders for his detention must be rescinded. You and I know the charges are false, but he is lawfully detained. We will not resolve this in the present hour. Now let me rest awhile as I am on duty tonight."

He stretched himself out on the bed. I looked at my beloved brother as he slept. There were lines between his brows. They had not been there when the war began. He was barely twenty years old, but he was no longer the carefree brother who had danced with me and fenced with Will at our home. I recalled his excitement when Father had announced his intention to raise a troop for the King. Now he was forced to find ways to frustrate Father's wishes.

When Harry awoke, I renewed my entreaties. It was all he could do that day to prevent me from riding to the castle and demanding Gabriel's release. My fears brought on a feverish headache and in desperation, Harry sent Polly to Mistress Adams. Emily arrived in some haste. She coaxed me to drink a potion of valerian and honey. By degrees I became calmer and slept.

I opened my eyes the next day to another grey, overcast morning and to Harry sitting by the fire with his head in his hands. As full consciousness dawned, the memory of the previous day returned in all its misery.

"Harry," I murmured.

"How is it with you this morning Bess? I think we must approach Lady Grenfall for her assistance."

"Then let us visit Lady Grenfall without delay." I struggled to my feet.

"Stay a while. Are you sure you are well enough to go today?" I glared at him.

"Harry, do not prevent me. No more delays. Harry, I cannot live without him." Seeing my renewed agitation, Harry hastened to soothe me.

"Bess I do not seek to prevent you. But you must prepare properly. Break your fast, wash yourself and dress in your smartest gown if you are to visit the court. If you go there like a mad woman they will turn you away for sure."

Reluctantly, I saw the sense in his words. I breakfasted on a warm loaf from a baker's shop, Harry watching me like a hawk the while. Polly heated water so I could bathe then she ministered to me, washing and combing my hair. There was no looking glass in the cottage, but I stared at my reflection in the steaming bowl of water and saw a wan and fearful face with dark shadows around the eyes. My best clothing was at Basing, but I found a clean gown which remained from my earlier sojourn. I fastened Gabriel's crucifix around my neck and knelt by the bed to pray for him and the success of my venture.

Harry and I set off for Merton College. The Queen was lodged in the Warden's House, I had been told, and I hoped to find Lady Grenfall there. I carried the letter to her in my hand. When we arrived at the gatehouse we were stopped by soldiers from the Queen's Lifeguard who demanded our business.

Anticipating such questions, Harry was wearing his red sash and buff coat. I explained that I had business with one of the Queen's ladies, a friend, and they let us pass. A smartly dressed servant took us to the warden's lodgings. We climbed the stairs to the small and crowded suite of apartments. Among the throng of courtiers and officers, Lady Grenfall was nowhere to be seen. Disappointed, I approached another of the servants and asked him if he was aware of Lady Grenfall's whereabouts. He returned. Lady Grenfall was with the Queen but begged us to wait. After a short time, she approached us.

"Mistress Vaughan, I understand that you require to see me urgently. I was not aware you were in Oxford."

"Indeed Lady Grenfall. I am come here with my brother in much distress." I began to cry. Harry briefly explained Gabriel's predicament.

She looked grave. "I am grieved to hear this news, Mistress. How do you believe I may be of assistance?"

"You are a friend to the Queen," I burst out, "Could you not ask her to sign a release order?"

She sighed and shook her head.

"The Queen is not well. She is with child again. Further, she is reluctant to sign such orders unless she believes they will meet with the King's approval. Mistress Vaughan, what is your father's position here?"

When I explained my father's work with the Council of War her face fell.

"I fear your father is too much in favour with the King. The release order were best come from your father himself. Have you tried speaking to him?"

"He will not even see me," I said dully. "He has given orders I am not to be admitted to his presence."

"Then it may be the best we can do is ensure Captain Vaughan receives a fair trial," she murmured.

"But that may be weeks or months away. And they are to flog him again within days."

"And if they do, then your husband will bear it as he did the last. You must be strong and brave for him, as he is himself. Take heart, Mistress. Bring me word if you have news of the date of his trial. If I can assist you in any way I will. I will pray for his release."

She smiled sadly and pressed my hand.

ᔕ

Harry was quiet as we made our dejected return to the cottage. My hopes were in tatters. The final throw of the dice had rested on Lady Grenfall. I knew it would be fruitless to visit my father again. We entered the cottage and Harry prodded the smouldering logs into a glow while I watched, indifferent as to whether I were warm or cold. He set me on a stool and crouched beside me, holding my hand tenderly.

"Bess, I believe it may be best to honour Gabriel's wishes and take you to his parents. I could be there and back in little more than a week. While I am away, Joe could visit Gabriel in my stead."

He gazed at me, gauging my reaction.

"I see you are wearing your obstinate face, sister. I will speak to Gabriel of this today. Let him be the judge, Bess. It may strengthen him in this time of trouble to know that you are safe and cared for."

I opened my mouth to protest. Harry shook his head and repeated,

"Let Gabriel be the judge."

ᔕ+

Oxford Castle, 14 December 1643

When Harry arrived at the castle that afternoon, he found an unknown officer in the lieutenant's lair. He had to explain himself at some length. The man protested that Caleb Brown was sick of an ague while Ethan was not on duty. However, he responded readily to the glint of silver in Harry's purse, and took Harry to Gabriel's cell.

When Harry entered, Gabriel woke from an uneasy doze and feebly tried to sit up.

Harry attempted to raise him by slipping an arm under his flayed shoulders. Gabriel groaned in pain as Harry placed him carefully on his belly and produced bandages, further salves. "I thought I had given up the need for a nursemaid when I grew a beard," Gabriel whispered hoarsely.

"Gabriel," Harry looked away awkwardly. "I have counselled Bess to remove to your parents. All our efforts to free you thus far have failed. Would you have me take her to The Allt? I could ride on to see Lord Byron and ask him to intercede at your trial."

Harry poured broth into a beaker and held it to Gabriel's lips. Gabriel said nothing but took the beaker from Harry and, holding it shakily, succeeded in sipping from it unaided, although as much went onto the mattress as into his mouth. He handed it back and looked at Harry desolately.

"If you can obtain leave to go."

"If I can persuade Bess, you mean."

Gabriel's eyes widened in dismay.

"Harry, tell her it is my wish. Writing materials?"

Harry hastened to find paper, quill and ink. Lying all the while on his belly, Gabriel propped himself painfully on one elbow and laboriously wrote.

"Would you have me write to your dictation?" Harry asked, observing the slow progress.

"No, Harry, allow me this small personal effort."

Harry could see the effort was not a small one, but he waited while the quill scratched, raggedly and with frequent pauses, across the paper. Harry folded it carefully away.

"I will leave you now, Gabriel. If all goes to plan you will see Joe here in the afternoon in my stead."

He embraced Gabriel quickly and banged on the door. Riding back toward the cottage, he wondered how difficult it might prove persuading Bess to honour her husband's wishes.

∽

Harry left the cottage again that night after a difficult conversation with Bess. He was on his way to to seek leave of absence. A voice called to him in the darkness and a ragged urchin approached.

"Lieutenant Lucie? A gent wishes to speak with you at the Golden Cross."

"On what matter?"

"e'll tell you 'imself."

"How will I know him?"

"You'll find 'im in a private room."

Harry went swiftly to the prosperous inn. The courtyard was thronged with soldiers, ostlers and women. He passed into the taproom. When he gave his name he was taken up a narrow flight of stairs at the back of the inn to an upper chamber. More than a little suspicious and with caution, Harry wrapped his cloak around his left arm as a defence and loosened his sword in its scabbard before entering the room.

ᔕ

I waited apathetically for Harry to return from his unwelcome errand. Not knowing how long he might be, I passed the time by reviewing each painfully written word in Gabriel's letter to me, thus successfully increasing my distress. I could barely recognise it as his hand and pictured all too well the effort it had cost him.

"My beloved wife, I would have you go with Harry to The Allt. Do not delay. There you will be safe and my mind will be easy. My body will mend in time and we will be together again. Have faith. I love you. Gabriel."

He had tried to draw a linnet, but the strokes had faltered after a few lines and he had abandoned the attempt. The sight of the half drawn bird made the hot tears fall. They splashed onto the precious words and I dashed them away angrily. I knew that for once I must do as I was bid. I would abandon him, seeking my own safety and hopefully procuring him peace of mind if I could do nothing else for him. Harry and I would leave for Wales on the morrow.

32

Golden Cross Inn, Oxford 14 December 1643

"COME IN, HARRY," the familiar voice called from within the room. It was his brother. "Will!" Harry clapped his hand on the hilt of his sword as he stepped through the doorway. Will leapt to his feet and moved slowly towards him, arms outstretched.

"I am here unarmed," pausing for Harry to confirm what he said.

"Harry, I owe you an apology. I know what has happened while I have been away with Prince Rupert."

"Do you, Will?" Harry's voice had a dangerous edge. "You keep our f father very well informed it seems. He knows of the night that apparently saw our sister raped. And of her f forced marriage. I attended that marriage, Will. I saw our sister's joy and that of her husband. I do not ask if you know of what has happened to Gabriel. For you have sat in j judgement on him with our father. You have condemned him. No doubt you rejoice at his sufferings. I bid you goodnight, brother. I do not wish to breathe the same air as you. If Gabriel is condemned at his trial, I will seek you out and I will fight you."

"Harry wait, I beg you. It is not true."

"In what particular? Do you deny he is imprisoned or that he suffers? Yesterday I saw him flogged. He stood in the rain while his blood ran down his legs and stained red the puddles on the ground."

"As did I." Will's words were muffled. Harry stared at him. Then he flung his cloak on a chair but remained standing, folding his arms. He glared into Will's imploring blue eyes.

"Explain yourself, then," he snapped, "But make haste. I have to arrange leave to escort Bess to her husband's parents. Gabriel wishes to be assured she has their protection since he is no longer in a position to protect her himself."

Will turned to the fire and kicked at a log. He broke his silence with a shaking voice.

"Harry, I said I owe you an apology. More than that, I seek pardon and forgiveness from you and from Bess. I would beg Gabriel that he forgive me, but after all that he has suffered due to me, I know he will not."

Will went on, desperation in his voice, "That morning, when you and I discovered Bess and Gabriel together, I was angry, very angry."

"I too was angry," interrupted Harry, "But I did not seek to make a false report. I counselled you to say nothing to f Father. Or at least to use discretion in what you told him."

"Your warnings came too late. I was waiting for him on his return to Oxford the next day. I apprised him of Bess's disgrace. He made a solemn vow that Gabriel would not live. When I left Oxford, I charged Joe to keep me informed of where Bess was and what doings there were with Gabriel. By then, my temper had cooled. I sought only to know what went forward. I hoped to have an opportunity to make amends."

"Do you mean to tell me that Joe has been spying on us?" Harry was becoming even angrier.

"Spying Harry, no. But his loyalty is to the Lucies, not to the Vaughans. You must realise that. When I heard that Bess and Gabriel were wed, I realised their love was real. That our sister had wed a papist filled me with sadness. But she was wed to a man she loved. This was a man who I respected and could not find it in my heart to hate. Harry, I wish I had found the courage to attend their marriage myself. My pride would not allow it. With Father it was not so. His ire festered like a sore. He sought only revenge, and Gabriel's end. When Gabriel's letter confirmed he was returned to Oxford, it was the opportunity Father had waited for and he acted immediately.

Acquit me of planning Gabriel's arrest, I pray you. Father kept me in ignorance. I argued enough with Father for him to realise my change of heart. I think he suspected I would forewarn Gabriel. When I returned to Oxford yesterday, Father announced that Gabriel was in chains awaiting trial. We did not part on cordial terms. Father left for Abingdon and I went directly to the castle. I hoped to find a way to aid my sister's husband. I was in time to see him most brutally flogged. I seek to make amends, Harry, in any way possible."

"Say you so?" Harry regarded him fiercely.

Will shrugged, "I do."

"Then I think there may be a chance. Gabriel was arrested on written orders from our father. And he could be released on a similar warrant."

"That would be so but what of it? Father is in Abingdon, but even if he were in Oxford it would be of no help. He will never relent."

"Does Father have his seal with him?"

"His signet ring?" Will asked. "The family seal is with his papers in the chest."

"Will, could you counterfeit Father's hand and s signature?"

"Harry, you are asking me to commit forgery. That is a very serious matter."

"Is it more serious than the miscarriage of justice, for which you are in part responsible?" Harry was livid. "Do you wish to truly make amends, brother, or do you prefer to watch Gabriel receive a further lashing in a few days' time? Do you wish to attend his trial at the Assizes? Do you wish to see him hang when you could have saved him? The choice, I think, is yours."

Harry stared at his brother, waiting for his reply.

"But what of the officers at the castle prison? Would they allow him to be released while still under sentence of flogging?"

Inwardly Harry breathed with relief. "That is why we need to act with the utmost despatch. Lieutenant Brown, who sentenced Gabriel to the flogging, was sick of an ague today. We can only hope it continues a day or two longer."

ᔕ

Oxford Castle, 15 December 1643

Gabriel was perching uncomfortably on the stool in his cell, his head in his hands. The light filtering through the small window told him it was mid afternoon. He wondered how far Harry and Bess might have travelled on their road to Wales. Joe would be able to tell him how many hours they had been gone. He should arrive shortly.

Gabriel heard footsteps and looked up expectantly as the door was unlocked. The guard who had been on duty the previous day stood in the doorway. Next to him stood not Joe but Will Lucie. He was in his uniform of buff coat and red sash. His sword hung at his side. Gabriel stared in disbelief and horror. Something must have gone badly awry. Will had betrayed him to Sir Henry. What had become of the plans Gabriel and Harry had made? Will spoke quietly to the guard then entered the cell. The door closed but was not locked behind him. The sound of the guard's steps receded. As Will crossed the floor of the cell towards him, Gabriel struggled painfully to his feet, murder in his eyes. Desperation lent him strength. He grabbed the astonished Will and flung him back against the wall, attempting to throttle him with the chain which held his wrists together. Will gasped in surprise and then fear as the chain tightened against his throat.

"What has happened to Bess?"

Gabriel released the pressure for a moment to allow Will to speak.

"Nothing," Will gasped. "She is safe, here in Oxford."

"You lie, she should have left Oxford. If she is still here you have done something to her. Tell me the truth. Understand I have nothing now to lose."

He tightened the chain again around Will's throat.

"Gabriel," gasped Will, "I bear an order for your release. Bess remains here in Oxford. With you a free man there is no cause for her to leave."

"If this be truth why is not Harry here himself?"

"They know Harry as your friend. We thought it best for me, an officer of the army, to bring the order myself as it bears my father's seal. I stole it. Gabriel I beg you, believe me. I am here to free you. We must make haste."

"Show me the order. No sudden moves, Will. If you lie, I swear I will kill you."

Will fumbled blindly in his purse for a piece of parchment with a large seal attached. He unfolded it and held it up so Gabriel could see it. Still holding Will pinned against the back wall, Gabriel scanned the order quickly. It was as Will had claimed, and was signed Henry Lucie. Shaking his head in disbelief, Gabriel released Will. They regarded each other warily.

"I will tell you more later," Will said cautiously. "Are you able to walk?"

"If my ankle is unchained I can make the attempt."

"We must make haste," Will repeated, peering nervously over his shoulder. Moving slowly and painfully, Gabriel gathered up his cloak and few possessions including Bess's letters to him. The effort of restraining Will had sapped his strength and he could only stand unsteadily, supporting himself against the wall. Will summoned the guard to unlock Gabriel's chains. With Will supporting him, Gabriel crept down the stairs, across the courtyard and past the guard house. Their progress was agonisingly slow. At the gatehouse, there was a sharp challenge.

"Sir, what authority have you for removing this prisoner?"

There was a tense moment as Will handed over the release order.

"Your name?"

"Lieutenant William Lucie," Will answered reluctantly.

The guards peered at the seal, nodded and indicated they would be keeping the order.

Gabriel and Will passed under the gateway and across the drawbridge. "Written proof of my perfidy for my father," Will sighed. "I fear I too will be absenting myself from this city for some time to come."

Oxford, 15 December 1643

Harry and I were waiting near the castle with a covered cart drawn by two horses. My breath came fast as if I had been in a race. I was holding Fairy. We were dressed as a yeoman and his wife as we did not wish to excite suspicion as we left the city.

"Bess, please try to appear calm," Harry said for the tenth time. "You are unsettling Fairy and anyone looking at you will suspect you of something untoward. You are supposed to be a goodwife about to return to your home after delivering a load of hay."

"Oh Harry," I whispered "Supposing something goes wrong. What if Lieutenant Brown is back on duty? What if Father's signature is suspected as a forgery?"

"Then Will is likely to be arrested himself. But do not alarm yourself, Bess, for I see them approach."

I followed Harry's pointing hand. I saw two men working their way towards us through the crowds. One was staggering, supported by the other. I clutched Harry's sleeve. It was indeed Gabriel and Will.

"Bess! Compose yourself." Harry cautioned. "And don't move."

I was anything but composed, but somehow I kept my feet from running towards them. I watched the painfully halting progress of my husband. It was dogged determination and the good offices of Will that kept him upright and moving. One or two people glanced curiously at their crabwise gait, but Oxford in wartime had many strange sights. To my relief, they were still unchallenged as they threaded their way through horsemen and carts across the street to us.

"Gabriel," it came out as a sob.

"Bess." The word was no more than a whisper and Gabriel swayed as he spoke it.

"Into the cart with him quickly," Harry urged.

Gabriel was half lifted into the back of the cart by my two brothers while I looked up and down the street nervously.

"Bess!" Harry hissed at me. "Climb in and cover him up with the sacks. We must go!"

Harry climbed onto the driving seat and clicked his tongue to the horses. Will mounted Fairy and took up position close behind us. I scrambled into the covered cart. With what felt like unbearable sluggishness, we plodded forward. In company with a stream of carts, carriages and horsemen, we headed for Oxford's south gate.

Once outside the city, Harry drew the cart off the road. Will climbed into the covered cart and transformed himself from cavalry officer into farm servant. Then we continued, as simple farm folk, down the Oxford Road towards Abingdon.

ᔕ

East Ilsley, Berkshire, 15 December 1643

It was a slow, nerve wracking journey back to Basing. Every minute felt like an hour. We dared not push the horses beyond the speed of a trot. Any faster would have aroused suspicion, besides jarring Gabriel unbearably as we rattled over the rutted road. He lay quietly under the sacks but the bumps, ruts and holes in the road jolted him. Several times I heard a groan, broken off short.

We passed through Abingdon with as much despatch as possible. This was where we believed Father to be. The cold weather was its own excuse for us concealing our faces in our hoods. On the road several times I was alarmed by the thunder of horses. Royalist cavalry patrols passed by with a jingle of harness, mud spattering from their flying hooves. Each time Harry eased our cart towards the hedge. Once the patrols had passed us by, I breathed a sigh of relief.

We had only been a few short hours upon our journey when the winter day ended. It was threatening rain again and we sought shelter at an inn at East Ilsley which Harry had marked out beforehand. We were far enough away now from both Oxford and Abingdon that the likelihood of pursuit was lower. But we could not yet relax.

The taproom was quiet. The coins Harry passed the man chinked loudly enough to suggest that the landlord would not be inclined to ask questions. When a ragged and injured man stumbled through the door, our host turned away. He busied himself with his back to us as Gabriel was whisked upstairs to the one room available to travellers. I endured a tense, uncomfortable night wrapped in my cloak, dozing on a settle in the tap room with Harry, in our character as yeomen farmers. Every sound alarmed me. A branch tapping at the window was a Royalist patrol seeking Gabriel. The hoot of an owl was men creeping up in ambush.

Will passed the night with two loaded pistols beside him in the upstairs room with Gabriel. Gabriel was in no condition to bear arms, but I had brought his sword with me among several of his possessions from the cottage. I saw him settled on a lumpy and far from clean straw mattress. He promised to sleep but only after he insisted on having his sword beside him. I opened my mouth to protest but Harry's words of the previous May, "I'll not let them take me alive again," came back to me.

I woke soon after first light. The rain had held off and Harry was keen to set off as soon as possible. I tiptoed upstairs into Gabriel's room. Will beckoned to me to follow him out again.

"Gabriel slept badly," he whispered. "He is in much pain. I would not wake him yet. He has been sleeping heavily this hour." Will was looking decidedly sleepy himself. We hurriedly conferred with Harry downstairs. Reluctantly, Harry agreed to postpone our departure by an hour. Will would snatch some sleep and Harry would have the horses ready.

A servant was stirring the banked fire in the chilly taproom. Requests for a bowl and jug to wash were met with a bovine stare so I asked for ale and bread instead and wandered outside into the yard to find a pail to wash in. After splashing icy water on my face I felt more wakeful. When I re-entered the inn, a stale loaf and some ale was brought to me by a servant. But after one or two bites the bread stuck in my throat and the smell of the ale turned my stomach. The servant had disappeared. I abandoned the attempt to eat.

A footstep made me start, but it was only Will descending. Gabriel was stirring and we should be on our way. Standing on tiptoe, I kissed him on the cheek.

"Thankyou, Will," I said.

He reddened with embarrassment. "Do not thank me, Bess. I am greatly to blame. If I had not lost my temper and spoken to Father this would not have happened."

"Will, we will not haggle over blame. It is true that you kindled Father's rage. But I do not think that he would have been easily reconciled to my marriage and the end might have been the same." He continued to regard me sombrely.

"I do not see how Gabriel can ever forgive my treachery."

"Your actions that you have taken to free him plead for you eloquently. He is a fair man and I think you will find he says little more. Even if the Vaughan motto is 'I will not return unavenged'," I smiled at him.

Will laughed, his face creasing into the more light hearted lines of the brother I had grown up with. "If I had known that were his family motto I would hardly have dared face him yesterday. As it was, he tried to throttle me." Shocked, I opened my mouth but he shook his head.

"There will be time for questions later, Bess. I will help Harry with the horses. Be ready." He left through the door to the stable yard.

I waited on the settle with my cloak draped around my shoulders in the still chilly tap room. The street door behind me clicked open. Two soldiers, cavalry from their dress, stood on the threshold. They were wearing orange sashes. My confused thoughts tried to decide whether they were a greater or a lesser threat to us than if they had been a Royalist patrol. The situation was absurd, but I could see no humour in it.

The two soldiers sauntered towards me.

"A fair maid," said one, a tall thickset man. "The day has hardly begun and already it promises well. An hour would be well spent in her company."

He removed his helmet, placing it under his arm. He tilted my chin. I edged away from him, deciding it was better not to make a commotion. Gabriel was upstairs and I could not risk him attempting to intervene. Had my brothers seen the men arrive? Where were they? The man promptly sat down, wedging me into a corner of the settle, an arm draped around me. His other hand flicked the cloak off my shoulders. He trailed a grimy fingernail thoughtfully down my throat, onwards towards the laces of my bodice.

The other had also removed his helmet. A younger man, lithe with a shock of red hair, he smirked as he surveyed me,

"Nay, John. Not a maid. She is already plucked. Do you not see she wears a wedding ring upon her hand. Where is your husband, my sweet wench? Did he abandon you here?"

"He did not."

Gabriel was at the foot of the stairs, his sword drawn. The redhead paused and groped wildly for his own sword. Then he took in Gabriel's condition. Gabriel was barefoot, standing unsteadily, sweat breaking out on his face. And he was having difficulty holding the wide blade steady.

"Brave Sir, I fear you attempt too much." The redhead laughed, removing his hand from his sword hilt.

"We mean your lady no harm. If she will share a few kisses with us while we take our rest, we will be on our way. You would not begrudge a little pleasure to soldiers of the Parliament?"

Gabriel advanced, holding his sword level.

"Gabriel, no," I whispered. Seeing my husband was not about to back down, the red haired man scowled and drew the sword from its scabbard.

"Benjamin, have a care," the older man cried in alarm. While our attention was on Gabriel, Will had approached stealthily with a levelled pistol in his hand.

"Leave my sister alone." The last time he had come to my rescue it was with the self-same words. Will caught my gaze. I felt the man shift. Will's attention had strayed for a moment too long. There was a sharp crack beside me. My attacker was holding a smoking pistol and I saw blood spreading over the left wrist of Will's white shirt. Will gasped and fired. The man dropped to one knee, clutching his thigh.

The other lowered his sword, staring at his companion trying to stem the flow of blood. My husband was very weak but found strength enough to raise his sword once and slash downwards. The man fell, blood spurting from his neck.

I began laughing hysterically. Harry, appearing at this moment from the stables, took in the bloody scene and swiftly took control. He pushed us urgently from the room. Servants were running, drawn by the sound of the shots. They would find the two men on the floor, one dying, the other bleeding, in pain and groaning. Gabriel was barely able to stand. Will was bleeding heavily from the wrist and was white with shock. Somehow, we got Gabriel back to his former hiding place in the cart. Harry and I placed Will between us on the driving seat and tethered Fairy to the back of the cart. None from the inn were brave enough to pursue my armed and determined brothers.

We set off once more for Basing, as fast as we dared. My heart was thumping loudly. Will was holding a pistol in his good hand and I had another concealed beneath my cloak. Gabriel had wiped his bloody sword and lay with it beside him, together with a loaded carbine. Every shadow in a hedgerow now concealed a marksman to my fearful imagination and as we clattered through each village I looked nervously around for soldiers. We were lucky that the cold weather and the time of year meant that there were few soldiers on the road. We encountered only one cavalry patrol that day. Heading towards us at a canter the group glanced at us only briefly and passed by without slowing. We pressed on with little rest. We were no more than a mile or two from Basing, and it was growing dark, when we received our first challenge from a patrol. Harry stopped the cart, looking wary. I clutched my pistol more tightly. Behind me I felt Gabriel stir. The patrol came along side the cart. "Francis," I cried with relief. It was Francis Cuffaud.

"Mistress Vaughan," he said, "I did not expect your return in this manner."

"Lieutenant Cuffaud," broke in Harry, "We must reach the House without delay. We had some trouble with a rebel patrol this morning. My brother here is wounded and Captain Vaughan is also injured."

Francis glanced from Harry's anxious face to Will's white one and nodded abruptly. He was clearly bursting with questions but they would have to wait.

"Thomas, ride ahead and warn the guards at Garrison Gate of our approach."

"Aye, Sir." The man turned his horse's head and cantered off. The towers of Basing House were visible ahead. We were safe for the present.

Epilogue

Basing House, December 1643

GABRIEL'S ROAD TO recovery was long and hard. The Marquis's physician was waiting for us. Francis Cuffaud had sent an urgent summons to him to treat both Gabriel and Will. The physician assured Will he should regain most of the use of his arm. The bullet had ploughed a painful furrow through his left forearm, glancing off one of the wrist bones. This meant an enforced stay at Basing of some weeks as Will's arm was in a sling, so riding was not advisable.

The physician confirmed that Gabriel had two cracked ribs which would take weeks to heal. Breathing would still be painful. During our flight from Oxford Gabriel's tattered shirt had stuck to the welts on his back. They had partially scabbed over so removing his shirt made them bleed afresh.

It was night by the time the physician had finished dressing Gabriel's back. I climbed into the bed, our marriage bed, beside Gabriel. His back too tender to bear the touch of clothing against it, he could only lie on his belly. I kissed him desperately. I took his hands and pressed my lips to his bruised wrists. He lifted a trembling hand to stroke my hair, but that was too great an effort. He let it fall again.

After another restless night, I realised that he needed freedom to move around without the danger of me brushing against his back. Reluctantly therefore, and despite his protests, I slept on a trundlebed. It was as it had been before we wed, our intimacy unwillingly restricted to exchanging looks, the touch of our hands and kisses more chaste than either of us desired.

Gabriel did not quit our room for the first week. During the day, he slept for hours at a time. I spent many of those hours with my brothers. Will was more affectionate with me than he had been for many years, yet he avoided Gabriel.

"William," I chided on the fourth day after our arrival. "Why do you not visit Gabriel?"

Assiduously evading my gaze, Will adjusted the sling carefully.

"I am plagued with regrets, Bess. For my treatment of him, for my betrayal of him."

I shook my head at him. "Don't be foolish, Will. In Gabriel's deliverance, you have cut yourself off from Father. Not only that, you were wounded defending him and me. Gabriel has forgiven you."

Will had learned at last that he was not always right. Confident, yet self-controlled, Will was not accustomed to being put to rights, or accepting advice from others, least of all his younger sister. Thus, when he eventually entered our chamber on that evening, I recognised the struggle it must have cost him. He greeted Gabriel with some constraint, but Gabriel smiled at him readily enough. I was stitching at a new shirt for Gabriel by the combined light of fire and candles.

"Would you leave us, Bess?" Gabriel requested softly. "I believe Will and I need some private conversation together." I never knew what passed between Gabriel and Will, but thereafter, Will became as frequent a visitor to our room as Harry.

Gabriel was quieter than usual, but talking pained him, and if he was silent for long periods, I hoped he would recover his cheerfulness once his pain eased. He said little of his experiences in Oxford Castle. I had heard more than enough from Harry to have little appetite for further details. The mass of welts which covered Gabriel's entire back, the abrasions to his wrists and ankle, all spoke of his suffering.

There was no treatment for the ribs but rest and time. The bruising was beginning to fade. After a few days, the physician removed the dressings from Gabriel's back and gave me a pot of greasy salve redolent of Colonel Johnson's herbs. The first time I smeared it on his skin, I felt Gabriel relaxing at my touch, some of the tension leaving his knotted muscles. I worked my way gently up until I had nearly reached his shoulders. Seeking to avoid clogging his hair with the greasy substance, I lifted the long thick locks in my hand and twisted it into a knot so that it would be out of the way. Gabriel gasped and flinched away from me, his whole body contorting.

"What is it, my love?" I cried in fright.

There was a lengthy pause. In a dull, flat voice Gabriel eventually replied, "There is nothing amiss. Leave my hair, let it be." I dropped his hair and nothing more was said.

When Gabriel had fallen asleep, I hurried to find Harry. His face darkened as I described Gabriel's strange reaction.

"What is it, Harry?" I probed. "That meant something to you did it not?"

Sadness filled his grey eyes. Harry granted me a small, harrowing window into that day in the castle courtyard. Until now, despite the sight of those awful weals which covered Gabriel's back from shoulder to waist, I had somehow managed to shield myself from picturing the man I loved bound to the whipping post. Now I could not.

Wrapped in a thick, fur lined cloak, I paced the grounds of Basing House. The view from the top of the Great Gatehouse was one of leafless trees beneath a milky white sky which threatened more snow. Beyond, stretched the dull gleam of the Loddon and the flooded marshes. The peaceful scene could not diminish the horror within me. In search of comfort, I descended the stairs to the chapel.

"What is it Bess? Is Gabriel well?"

Father Allen had entered the chapel noiselessly, and heard my muffled sobs.

Haltingly, I explained.

"His spirit is bruised as well as his body, Bess. But, with God's help, they will both recover and he will be well again. You are his wife. Give him the comfort of your body. Remind him that his own body can be a joy to him and not just a burden."

That night, when Gabriel and I made ready to sleep, I did not go to my trundle bed. Instead, I stripped off my shift, put the candlestick on a table near the bed and climbed under the blankets with Gabriel.

"I am your wife," I whispered. "Come back to me, Gabriel Vaughan." I put my arms carefully around his damaged ribs and rested my head on his shoulder.

He reached out a trembling hand and cupped my breast. I kissed him hard on the lips and reached for the hem of his loose bed gown. He laughed suddenly.

"Seduction, wife?" There was a lightness in the lilting voice I had not heard in weeks.

"It is, My Lord."

ೞ

Winter blanketed Basing. Ice rimmed the puddles remaining from the November storms. The sentries on the ramparts huddled in their cloaks and stamped their feet to try to warm them. On Christmas Eve it snowed. Inside Basing House fires roared, the yule log blazed and servants brought mulled wine and platters of food. It might almost have been any other Christmas and the country not in the grip of civil war. As for me, I cared not for the present, for the war, or for anything else save Gabriel.

At the start of January, my brothers rode away in search of the young Earl of Northampton's regiment of horse.

"I will take Harry with me, Bess," Will said. "James Compton, the new Earl, knows me well, and our welcome at Oxford is uncertain at present. Unless Harry wishes to remain here as part of the garrison?"

But Harry did not feel his place was at Basing, where nothing awaited the garrison but the prospect of possible future sieges.

"Will you not stay for the 12th night celebrations?" I urged in vain. The weather was growing colder and they were anxious to be on their way before they might be prevented by snow drifts.

On 12th night, Gabriel sat beside me in the Great Hall, tuning a lute for the first time since our return. I recognised the melodic strains of Dacw Ngharíad. His cheeks had colour in them and if it was partly due to the nearby flames, I felt confident that it was also from returning health.

The morning after, I woke beside Gabriel and stretched. He was lying on his side, propped on his elbow and looking at me pensively. I was more absorbed in observing how comfortably he lay. His ribs were healing fast.

"Soon the new year will arrive Bess, 1644. I wonder what it will bring for us and our country?"

I smiled at him.

"For the country, I pray we will have peace." I paused. "For us, I pray a healthy child."

The green eyes widened. He folded back the bed covers and ran his eyes carefully over my breasts, already beginning to swell.

"I have missed my courses, Gabriel. I believe I may bear you a child at harvest time."

Gabriel swung his legs over the side of the bed and reached for his clothes. I stared in astonishment and some alarm at the speed of his movements. His head emerged from his shirt and he reached for his stockings. He bent and kissed me briefly.

"Basing may be under siege again at any time. It is no place for a pregnant woman. It is time to go, Bess. I am taking you home to Wales."

Glossary

Cassack – 17th century equivalent of a poncho, buttoned down the front.
Coif – linen cap, worn alone or under a hat
Country – used as an alternative word for "county".
Curtain wall – a defensive wall around a castle, fortress or town.
Dragoon – mounted infantryman, who dismounted before a battle and fought on foot.
Drum – not just the object. A drummer carrying a message was also referred to as "a drum".
Forlorn hope – a small spearhead force, often used at the start of a battle with a particularly dangerous move. Due to high casualty rate were often volunteers.
Gibbous – any moon that appears more than half lighted but less than full.
Harquebusier – term for standard cavalryman during the Civil War. Lightly armoured they wore a leather buff coat and/or back and breast plates plus a metal helmet. When fully armed they carried a carbine (shorter than a musket), two pistols and a sword.
Matchlock – one of the most common types of muzzle loading muskets. The disadvantage was that to ignite the powder charge in the priming pan, the musketeer had to carry a large supply of burning slow match. They were also a hazard near ammunition carts.
Marchpane – marzipan
Music – term for a trumpeter
Palliasse – straw mattress
Petard – primitive bomb, attached to a gate or wall to blow a hole
Prie dieu – a piece of furniture for use during prayer, consisting of a kneeling surface and a narrow upright front with a rest for the elbows or for books
Quarter – agreement not to kill a defeated combatant
Saker – one of several types of ordnance. Medium size cannon. Shot typically weighed 4–7 pounds.
Sumpter (horse etc) – packhorse or mule.

Historical Note

This is a work of fiction. While the major events and battles described did take place, I have taken liberties here and there, and all mistakes are my own. Apologies to the 3rd Earl of Lindsey who I sent at least a day early to captivity in Warwick Castle and then removed unceremoniously from his room in Guy's Tower into a room in Caesar's Tower. (He was getting under the feet of my main characters.) And to the inhabitants of Birmingham, whose treatment by Prince Rupert's forces was worsened, courtesy of 17th century propaganda newsheets and my imagination.

The families and other characters

All members of the Vaughan and Lucie families in this book are fictitious. However –

The Vaughans (including the Earl of Carberry) were very active in the Civil War, raising more than one regiment for the King. A branch of the Vaughan family lived near Crickhowell, at Tretower Court, the model for Allt yr Esgair. Henry Vaughan the Silurist is Gabriel's alter ego. Henry and his twin fought as Royalists, although not in any of the battles mentioned in this book. The family were Protestants, not Catholics! Somewhat strangely, Henry was married twice, to Catherine and then Elisabeth. I only discovered this after I had decided to give Gabriel two wives – Catherine and then Elisabeth....

The Lucie family were also participants in the Civil War. One of them was captured at Hopton Heath.

Of the other characters, Sir John Byron was an ancestor of the poet Lord Byron. All regiments mentioned existed, as did the generals and colonels listed. Names of members of the garrison of Basing House are mostly drawn from a 1644 list of its officers.

Catholics and the Civil War

The Civil War was a religious as well as a political conflict. Those fighting for Parliament included Puritans and other non conformists. The King's army were more likely to be "High Church" Anglicans. The situation was complex however, so that is a generalisation. Those Catholics quietly participating in the conflict fought for the King.

Catholics were still subject to the numerous laws against them enacted during the reigns of both Queen Elizabeth I and King James I. If convicted, they were liable to heavy fines and imprisonment, were not supposed to travel more than five miles from their home and were not allowed to inherit. Following the Gunpowder Plot of 1605 there was an upsurge of anti Catholic sentiment. In 1625 Charles I married a French Catholic princess, Henrietta Maria. Part of the marriage agreement is thought to have been a secret promise to give Catholics freedom of worship. Charles had no power to repeal the legislation against Catholics, but its enforcement became sporadic during the years prior to the Civil War. Parliament protested repeatedly to the King. From 1640-42 the conviction and fining of recusants (those who refused to attend the compulsory Anglican church services) increased dramatically in the lead up to the Civil War. The position of Catholic priests (including Jesuits) was dangerous as since a new decree of 1641 they were automatically charged with treason if captured.

Rules of warfare

The treatment of prisoners of war at that time was hit and miss. If "quarter" was given, i.e., the defeated were not killed on the spot when they attempted to surrender, officers were mostly well treated, often being ransomed or exchanged. "Common soldiers", ie the rank and file, were more likely to change sides or be allowed to go home. Many were conscripts. If imprisoned, common soldiers were sometimes treated very badly-some being held in Warwick Castle's dungeon for example. Later in the war, there were more instances of the defeated being put to the sword. Surrender terms were not always adhered to by the victors, particularly in the cases of lengthy sieges. Warwick Castle was the first place to hold POWs – this being the Royalists captured at Edgehill in 1642. These included Lord Lindsey who allowed himself to be captured so that he might be with his dying father. I am not aware of deliberate ill treatment or executions of Royalist POW officers at Warwick Castle by Major John Bridges, the Governor.

Oxford Castle was notorious as a prison. Under the control of the Royalists for most of the Civil War, it treated all POWs, suspected spies, criminals awaiting trial at the Assizes, with uniform brutality and many prisoners died there from ill treatment and neglect. Soldiers fighting for Parliament were advised to fight to the death rather than allow themselves to be taken there as prisoners. While the events described are fictitious they are probably representative of what went on. Flogging continued in British prisons until the 20th century.

Deliberate destruction of hostile towns by the other side occurred on various occasions. The Battle of Camp Hill in Birmingham on Easter Monday 1643, for example, was one of Prince Rupert's less glorious exploits. Rupert used tactics he had learned as a mercenary in the European wars by torching much of the town. The Royalists used similar tactics at other places including Marlborough, Cirencester and, most notoriously, at Bolton.

The "rules" for the conduct of sieges are pretty shocking to those used to the Geneva Conventions. The besieging army would start off by "summoning" the besieged commander to surrender and offering what they considered generous terms. These depended on the relationship between both sides (eg were they kinsmen, neighbours or already on bad terms), the strategic importance and the character of the besieging commander. Minimum terms offered at the start of a siege seem to have been sparing the lives of women and children (but not necessarily allowing them to go free.)

At best, the besieged might be promised they would be allowed to march away "drums beating and colours flying" with arms and possessions, or for the owners to remain in the house or castle providing they ceded control to the other side and accepted the installation of a garrison.

As the siege progressed, the besieging army would send fresh offers of terms, generally less generous as time went on. During the siege, both sides would typically fire at each other with muskets or cannon and the besieged would often have "sorties" where they would send out a group to surprise the enemy, take prisoners and steal their supplies. When the besiegers lost patience and/or decided they were now in a strong enough position, they would "storm". At this stage it was no holds barred, and if the besieging army made it inside the castle or town they tended to kill people! Followed by protracted pillaging of anything and everything – furniture, bedding, plate, even panelling and other building fabric. Rape was not unknown but seems to have been infrequent, however sexual assault was common and women as well as men were likely to be summarily stripped of most of their clothes. (Clothing was an expensive commodity, which is why battlefield dead were usually naked by the time they went into the grave.)

17th century concepts of honour

Officers and gentlemen (but not "common soldiers") were expected to keep their word, whatever the personal cost. Harry's condition that Major Chatterton should turn himself in at Royalist Oxford once recovered was not an unusual request. This happened with wounded officers, and the people affected mostly honoured their promises. It was a practical solution which was much easier than trying to transport and care for wounded prisoners who might not survive the journey. Whether Harry was wise to take the word of this particular gentleman remains to be seen…

Locations in the book

For those who like to know if locations are real, Warwick Castle, Oxford Castle and Basing House all "appear as themselves".

The small village of Chadshunt, close by Edgehill, has a Chadshunt House, built in 1631 (not open to the public). Chadshunt Hall, however is based on Loseley House in Surrey, as it was in the 17th century when the west wing still stood. The family motto can be seen above the front entrance doors.

Tretower Court and Castle near Crickhowell, ancestral home of a part of the Vaughan family, bears a close resemblance to The Allt.

Brecon has a modern-day Guildhall. Its 17th century predecessor has disappeared without trace, so the design is my own.

The locations in Oxford all exist, as do the various churches mentioned in the book. The Beauchamp Chapel in the Collegiate Church of St Mary, Warwick is well worth a visit.

The wide plain high above Devizes, where the Battle of Roundway Down took place, is still covered in poppies.

In the case of Basing House, distressingly little remains of either Old House or New House and the internal layout is uncertain. The Great Barn stands, however, undamaged except by a dent from a cannon ball, and you can still walk through Garrison Gate. It was the largest private house in England at the time. The resident ladies at the time of the first siege of November 1643 took an active part in the defence from loading muskets to hurling missiles from the battlements. The tale of Basing House is not yet done…

The music

In the course of researching this book, I became addicted to the works of various Renaissance composers. The songs of John Dowland and others are quoted in the story. William Lawes was contemporary with the civil war. His career as court musician to King Charles I was cut short by the civil war and his untimely death in battle. William Byrd's "Mass for 4 voices", which Gabriel arranges to be performed at the wedding, is designed for a curiously small number of singers. Performing this work would have been solely in secret, during the illegal Catholic Mass, held in gentlemen's houses. Designing choral works to be performed by larger numbers would have been useless.

Dacw 'Ngharīad is a traditional Welsh love song. As usual with folk songs, the date of its composition is uncertain.

Thanks to

Rachel Miller Johnson, my wonderful and endlessly patient editor, without whom this book would never have seen the light of day.

Alan Turton, historian and former curator Basing House and his wife Nicola, "Lord and Lady Basing" for advice on the Basing House section, ongoing support and assistance over the last year, including a hand drawn map of where the petard attack happened.

David Allen, archaeologist Hampshire Cultural Trust for archaeological findings and his time on a wet June day at Basing House.

Dr Stephen Rutherford, Cardiff University for insights into 17th century battle field surgery (and allowing me to name a regimental surgeon after him).

Rev. Prof Austin Cooper, AM, Catholic Theological College, Melbourne for assistance with 17th century Catholic conversion procedures and the treatment of English recusants.

Michael Arnold, author of the Stryker Chronicles

Cadw, particularly the staff of Tretower Court and Castle

BCW Project

Warwick Castle archivist and "behind the scenes" staff

Oxford Castle Unlocked

Wiltshire Museum, Devizes for information on the Battle of Roundway Down

Loseley House for information, and for allowing me to use it as the model for Chadshunt Hall

Battle of Worcester Society

Sue Port for advice on the Lucie family

And the following friends and family: Elana Solomonidis, Naomi Black and Dr Ros Black for comments on the manuscript, "Captain Asher" Miller for consenting to become a Roundhead captain in the book, and for geological advice, Richard Slade for consenting to become a Puritan minister, Veronica Corlett for showing me the real Crickhowell, Dunstan and his creative writing group in Worcester for comments on the "silver buttons" scene, Clare for correcting my Welsh, and my extended family for advice, argument and frequent comment on extracts. Last but not least, my long suffering husband, children and dog, who have had to endure Early Modern music constantly playing in the background, my glazed looks over the dinner table and the fact I have been living in the 17th century "24/7".

Printed in Great Britain
by Amazon